P9-DGY-715

RICHMOND HILL
PUBLIC LIBRARY
OCT 0 7 2014
CENTRAL LIBRARY

DO OR DIE

Also by Suzanne Brockmann and available from Center Point Large Print:

Infamous

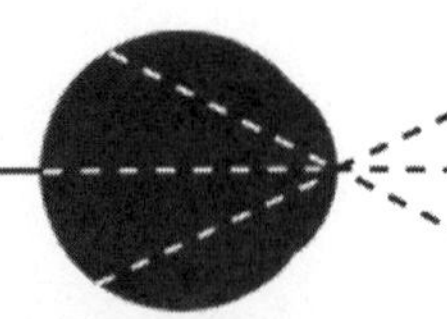

This Large Print Book carries the Seal of Approval of N.A.V.H.

SUZANNE BROCKMANN

CENTER POINT LARGE PRINT
THORNDIKE, MAINE

This Center Point Large Print edition is
published in the year 2014 by arrangement with
Ballantine Books, an imprint of The Random House
Publishing Group, a division of Random House LLC.

Do or Die is a work of fiction.
Names, characters, places, and incidents are the
products of the author's imagination or are used
fictitiously. Any resemblance to actual events, locales,
or persons, living or dead, is entirely coincidental.

The text of this Large Print edition is unabridged.
In other aspects, this book may vary
from the original edition.
Printed in the United States of America
on permanent paper.
Set in Times New Roman type.

ISBN: 978-1-62899-025-6

Library of Congress Cataloging-in-Publication Data

Brockmann, Suzanne.
Do or die : reluctant heroes / Suzanne Brockmann.
pages cm
ISBN 978-1-62899-025-6 (library binding : alk. paper)
1. Private investigators—Fiction. 2. Kidnapping—Fiction.
3. Embassy buildings—South America—Fiction.
4. Romantic suspense fiction. 5. Large type books. I. Title.
PS3552.R61455D6 2014b
813′.54—dc23

2013046239

To my mother and father, Lee and Fred Brockmann, who taught me that love is the most powerful force in the world, that only with love can we build and grow and learn, and that in the ongoing epic fight against injustice, ignorance, and fear, love *always* triumphs.

ACKNOWLEDGMENTS

Thank you to everyone who participated in the creation of this book.

Thank you to my early draft readers, Lee Brockmann, Ed Gaffney, Deede Bergeron, and Patricia McMahon.

Thank you to my agent, Steve Axelrod, and to Lori Antonson.

Thank you to my editor, Shauna Summers, and to the rest of the team at Ballantine and Random House, including Crystal Velasquez and Gina Wachtel. Big thanks to the art department for the terrific cover, too!

But thank you most of all to my extremely patient family: my zen-master husband Ed; my shining son, Jason, and his wonderful boyfriend, Matt; my amazing daughter, Melanie; my brilliant grandson, Aidan; my fiercely supportive parents, Lee and Fred (or Mom and Dad, as I like to call them!); my constant-as-the-North-Star friends Bill, Jodie, and Elizabeth; and my schnauzer-powered unconditional-love delivery vehicles CK Dexter-Haven and Little Joe.

Last but certainly not least, I want to thank *you,* my readers, who trust me enough to follow wherever I take you, and who continue to give me permission to write the stories of my heart.

As always, any mistakes I've made or liberties I've taken are completely my own.

DO OR DIE

PROLOGUE

August 29th

Several years ago . . .
Istanbul, Turkey

Ian Dunn's job for this assignment was a simple one.

Charm and distract.

And make sure Prince Stefan stayed here, at the Kazbekistani embassy in Istanbul, while Ian's former SEAL chief and right-hand man, John Murray, used his SpecOps training to break into the prince's hotel room and download the contents of the man's laptop onto a flashdrive.

Someone, somewhere—probably sitting at a desk in some windowless room in the basement of the Pentagon—believed that the jet-setting prince had information about a person of interest wanted in connection to a missing stash of sarin nerve gas. And, because Prince Stefan's laptop computer was too low-tech to properly hack, that unnamed someone had reached out to Ian in order to gain the information the old-fashioned, hands-on, up-close-and-personal way.

And that brought Ian and his motley crew all the way to Turkey, where tonight he'd donned a tuxedo for what was hopefully his final tiresome, up-close-

and-personal evening with the prince, so that Johnny could take the hands-on approach with that laptop.

In the past few days, ever since Ian had become inseparable besties with Prince Stefan, he'd discovered that not only was the title purchased, but also that the prince was as mean and soulless as he was petty and stupid.

His family was of Eastern European descent, with some real royalty thrown in via a connection to Vlad the Impaler—who hung from a branch that Ian would've kept secret, had the family tree been growing in *his* yard. But the prince found the connection boast-worthy, along with the fact that his grandfather and father had taken most of the family fortune and fled to South America when it became clear that the Second World War was going to, quote, *end badly for them,* end quote.

And yes. Over the past few days, Ian had confirmed the fact that the "family fortune" was, in fact, ill-gotten gains from Grandpa's collaboration with the Nazis. Some of the loot had been left behind, hidden on the farm where Gramps and Daddy had lived in Poland—not far from Auschwitz.

About a week ago, Prince Stefan had followed one of his grandfather's treasure maps and he'd found nearly three million dollars in antique jewelry beneath the straw-covered dirt floor of a dilapidated barn. Just as Grampy had promised.

A more patient man might've extracted the gems

and melted down the precious metals, getting more for the items overall, but Prince Steve was in need of some immediate cash. Which meant he was looking for a buyer who didn't care from whence his shameful treasure had come.

Enter Ian, with his hard-won reputation for knowing exactly how to fence stolen jewelry.

It didn't take much digging to discover that the K-stani ambassador was a potential buyer. Not only did the extremely wealthy man have a thriving side business, buying and selling precious metals and gems—his diplomatic status gave him access to move stolen goods easily throughout the region—but he himself was also something called a "Holocaust collector." And yes, that was as hideously awful as it sounded. The man had a fascination for everything from anti-Semitic propaganda to SS uniforms and weaponry to lamp-shades made with human skin. Jewelry stolen from people who'd been rounded up and exterminated was right up his ugly-ass alley.

Ian didn't know the diplomat personally, but he knew a guy who knew a guy. And so he held his nose and made a few phone calls.

Which led them to tonight's show-and-tell with the prince and his plunder, followed by what was promising to be a teeth-grindingly awful embassy dinner with several dozen other guests who shared the ambassador's and prince's narrow worldview.

But the dinner meant that Prince Stefan would be out of his hotel room for long enough to allow

Johnny M. to wrestle with his laptop and download its contents.

Ian didn't have to like it—he just had to do it.

But when the prince was lovingly laying out his collection of stolen necklaces, brooches, rings, and bracelets on several yards of plush maroon velvet, Ian knew that, for him, dinner was out. Not gonna happen, and not just because he had to clasp his hands behind his back to keep himself from punching the prince in the face when the idiot held up a particularly dazzling diamond necklace and jovially said, "Heil Hitler, am I right, or am I right?"

No, dinner was not going to happen because luck had delayed the ambassador, and Ian and the prince were still waiting here, still all alone in this embassy sitting room, when Ian's Bluetooth-disguised headset clicked on.

"Download complete." Johnny M.'s salty voice came through Ian's earpiece, loud and clear.

Suddenly, Ian had options. He had choices. And he knew—instantly—what he was now going to do.

He was over near the door, and he opened it to peek out at the still-empty corridor. Luck *was* on his side—this *could* work. He shut the door again.

The prince had crossed the room and was now pouring himself a glass of something from a bar setup, droning on again about how special it was for him to see—in person—the farm where his father and grandfather had spent the bulk of the war.

"The barn was just as they'd described it," he said as Ian approached him. He turned to make a disparaging face. “I’m afraid there’s no hard liquor here—only this ridiculously sweet wine.”

“It’s traditional. It’s what they serve in Kazbekistan,” Ian said as John’s voice clicked on again.

“I’m out of the hotel, and clear,” Johnny said. “Repeat, I am free and clear.”

Those were the words Ian had been waiting for, and he threw all of his outrage and disgust into a very solid uppercut to the prince’s chin.

Boom.

Punching the idiot in the face felt as good as he’d imagined it would.

His Majesty didn’t have time to register his royal surprise. He probably didn’t even recognize that Ian had hit him. He just shut down. His eyes rolled back in his head as he crumpled onto a red-satin-covered chaise lounge—which proved to be far less of a stupid-ass piece of furniture to have in an embassy sitting room than Ian had originally thought when they’d first been shown in.

As he fell, Prince Stefan’s wineglass went flying, but it landed on the carpet and didn’t break. Ian took care of that, crunching it into pieces with the heel of one of his shiny black rented shoes. Shoes he was now going to have to run in—which was going to suck.

So be it.

He toppled several chairs as he moved swiftly to the fourth-floor window that overlooked the glimmering lights of the ancient city. The K-stani embassy was housed in a building that dated back to the relatively recent nineteenth century, which meant ledges and stone ornamentation abounded. Climbing down to the ground would be difficult but not impossible.

Ian unlocked and opened the window wide as he activated his headset microphone and spoke to his team. "Slight change of plans, gang."

Three of his four teammates spoke almost at once, groaning and moaning, as the curtains moved in the warm night breeze. This was one of the major differences between leading a SEAL team and leading a group made up of friends and family. SEALs didn't bitch and moan when their commanding officer gave an order. At least not to the CO's face.

"Are you fucking kidding me?" Ian's brother Aaron's voice went up an octave.

Shelly, who was back in the States with Aaron, running support from thousands of miles away, put it more diplomatically. "Is that really necessary, sir?"

"Define *slight,*" Aaron demanded.

Francine's grim voice cut through. "I'm in the limo, right out in front of the embassy. Since John has the flashdrive, the job's over, we're done. Ian, walk out the door and get into this car."

"Pull onto the street on the west side of the building, France," Ian ordered the woman who was both the best driver he'd ever worked with and his sister-in-law, as he headed over to the table that held the jewelry. "Point the car so it's heading north. I'll be running, probably full sprint, when I reach you. Be ready to evade and escape after I'm in the car."

"Ah, shit, really?" his brother's voice said, even as Francine muttered her own expletive-laced affirmative.

"Evade and escape who?" Francine asked.

"I'm not sure just yet," Ian admitted. "It depends on how the next few minutes play out. Be ready for anything."

Even Johnny, usually taciturn, couldn't keep himself from chiming in. "Sir, we got what we came for. Francie's right for once. I know this guy's an asshole, but just take a deep breath and walk away."

"Can't do that," Ian said as he swiftly rolled the jewelry into two large but easily pocketed packets. He secured them inside his tuxedo shirt, then buttoned his jacket over it.

Shelly was the only one who offered assistance. "I still have you on the fourth floor of the embassy, in the northeast corner of the building. Infrared SAT images show only one other source of body heat with you, currently motionless. But there are six, repeat, six assumed unfriendlies getting off the elevator on your floor. Whatever you're up to, ready or not, here they come. You've got maybe twenty seconds, tops . . ."

Ian wasn't quite ready, so he moved fast.

The room didn't have a mirror, so he had to use the glass of a framed picture—moonrise over the harsh Kazabek landscape—to get a glimpse of his reflection as he messed up his hair. That wasn't enough to make him look as if he'd been in a down-and-dirty fight with a cat burglar—no, make that *two* cat burglars. It would have to be two, if anyone was going to believe that they'd overpowered a former Navy SEAL.

He'd felt something tear in the right sleeve of his jacket when he'd punched ol' Steve, and he reached up, found the give in the shoulder seam, dug his fingers in, and gave it a tug . . . and fabric ripped.

But it still wasn't enough.

Blood.

Blood always did the trick.

Ian quickly went back to the wineglass he'd broken and picked up a shard. Head wounds bled like crazy—he wouldn't have to do more than scrape himself, but over his ear, so the flow wouldn't obscure his vision and . . .

"Shit," he said, because it hurt like hell.

Meanwhile, Shelly started a countdown—presumably *one* would be when the ambassador and five guards came through that door. "Ten . . . nine . . . eight . . ."

"Johnny, get to the extraction point," Ian quietly ordered his former chief as he wiped off and then tossed the piece of glass before smearing blood across his face. In the process, he got it all over his hands, which added nicely to the effect.

"Already on my way," the man reported.

"Seven . . . six . . ."

"Car's in position." Francine sounded annoyed.

But then again, her usual emotional state was one of being permanently pissed off.

There was only one more thing Ian had to do after giving himself a quick visual check in that picture's framed glass. He scrunched up his face and hunched his shoulders, staggering slightly as if he were still dazed from being hit over the head by a blunt object.

Yup, the blood sold it.

"Five . . . four . . ."

Ian kept his stagger going as he propelled himself across the room and over to the fire alarm. He hit the wall with his shoulder on Shelly's *three,* and slapped a hand up, reaching for the pull-down alarm. He left a nasty streak of blood on the wall before his fingers found the lever on *two*.

The alarm—a combination of old-fashioned bells and a more modern electronic shrieking—went off on *one* as the door opened, also right on cue.

"There were two of them," Ian shouted as he continued to use the wall to hold himself up. "They took the prince's jewelry and went out the window!" He pointed with that bloody, Oscar-worthy hand.

The ambassador stepped back, letting his muscle move swiftly into the room. Two of the guards went to the window; the others came toward Ian and the prince.

"I'm fine—I'll be okay. But the prince is hurt. Help him," Ian said, not wanting any of the guards to feel the packets beneath his shirt. He straightened up, pretending to shake himself off before he pushed past the ambassador, who was still in the doorway. "The thieves left just moments ago—maybe we can stop them before they get down to the street!"

He heard the order being given for the guards at the embassy door to hold all traffic, both into and out of the building, but he ran toward the stairs anyway. Down the hall, to his left . . .

As Ian threw open the door to the stairwell, he was aware that several of the guards were on his heels—including one man that he recognized as the embassy's head of security.

That was not good. Or . . . maybe it was. If this guy was with Ian, the security staff at the door weren't likely to stop him.

He hoped.

The HOS raised his voice to be heard over the ringing alarms and the clatter of their shoes on the slippery marble stairs. "Can you describe your assailants?" His English was impressive, which for some might've been a bad thing. But not for Ian.

Ian's ability to communicate had always been one of his biggest strengths.

"They were dressed in black." As they went down the stairs that wound down and around—a half flight, then a landing, another half flight, another landing—Ian described what he himself would've worn, if he were attempting an early evening burglary in Istanbul. "Masks on their faces—nylon. But thick nylon—so thick, I can't even tell you their skin color. One of 'em had dark hair, I do know that.

The other might've had a shaved head, but that's just a guess. He might've been blond with a crew cut. I honestly couldn't tell."

The HOS had a face that was unreadable—or maybe it was just the shitty lighting in the stairwell that made him seem impassive.

Either way, Ian needed to give the man more. He held up his right hand. His knuckles were battered and already starting to bruise from punching Prince Steve. "Another educated guess is that they're wearing body armor. I fought back, but it was like hitting a brick wall. And then they hit me, took the jewels, and went out the window."

His head was still bleeding, and he transferred some of it onto the banister as punctuation.

But there was still nothing on the HOS's face—no reaction, no sense that the man either mistrusted Ian or that he believed him.

So Ian pushed it, saying, "If we don't stop these guys, the prince is going to crucify me. I told him your embassy was safe."

That got him a flash of the HOS's dark eyes. "It is. We have an extensive state-of-the-art surveillance system—cameras, both inside and out. There *will* be footage of what transpired."

Uh-oh.

But Ian had left his mic hot, and his support team had heard that. Aaron's voice clicked on, over his headset. "Shelly's already hacked into the embassy computers and . . ."

"Whoopsie," Shel's voice said. "Looks like

today's footage from the security cams, both interior *and* exterior, has been mysteriously erased. Don't you hate when that happens?"

"Thank you," Ian said as he jumped down the last half-flight of stairs. Of course now HOS was looking at him sideways, so he added, "For letting me know that we'll catch these guys—that whoever they are, we've got them on tape."

He pushed open the door to the first-floor lobby where, thanks to the fire alarm he'd pulled, it was chaos central.

Fire trucks had already arrived, and the guards at the entry had failed to keep out both the firefighters and local police, who were already working to evacuate the building.

This would be a really good time for Ian to go in one direction and the HOS and his men to go in another.

But the HOS stayed on Ian's heels as he went out into the warmth of the night.

So Ian slowed. "Which way?" he shouted to the HOS.

"Over here!" The man pointed around to the east side of the building, just as Ian expected him to—the sitting room had been in the northeast corner, the window that was the alleged burglars' escape route faced east.

The two guards immediately took off in that direction.

"I'll go 'round the other way," Ian volunteered. "We'll meet in the middle."

He didn't wait for permission; he just took off, heading for the west side of the building—where Francine was waiting behind the wheel of the limo they'd rented to drive Prince Stefan to the embassy.

Unfortunately, the HOS followed Ian.

The sidewalks in this part of town were cobblestone, and slippery as all hell. Ian used that as an excuse to shift onto the street as he turned the corner and . . . Yup, there was Francine, by the car.

She'd left it idling, in getaway mode, taillights lit, but she'd gotten out and was standing beside it—because theirs was not the only car waiting at the side of the road, and she wanted to make sure Ian saw her.

The narrow, normally lightly trafficked street wasn't empty as he'd hoped.

The other guests for the embassy dinner, arriving in their limos and Rolls-Royces, had been pushed here, out of the way of the fire trucks and police vehicles. Some had gotten out of their rides and were cluttering up the sidewalks in their tuxes and sequined gowns—blocking access.

And okay. It was not what he'd been anticipating, but Ian could work with this.

The HOS, as expected, was not pleased. "Clear this area," he shouted in a variety of languages.

"Maybe they can help us," Ian suggested to the man, skidding to a stop beside Francine, to ask, "Excuse me, sir"—with a hat pulled down over her hair and face, she could've been a height-challenged young man—"have you seen two men, dressed all in black . . . ?" He, too, repeated the question in German and his terrible French.

Francine shook her head as she climbed back in behind the wheel.

And this was where HOS should've continued swiftly down the line, asking the same question of the potential witnesses, before telling them, again, to clear the area.

But from the corner of his eye, Ian could see the HOS reaching into his jacket, where there was probably a handgun of some kind.

Apparently Ian's communication skills had failed him.

So he gave the HOS the same message that he'd given Prince Steve back in the embassy. Boom. A knockout punch to the face.

The HOS went down and Ian relieved him of his weapon before jumping into the car.

"Go," he said, but Francine was already on it, driving away.

She covered her headset mic to say, "You're bleeding."

"I'm fine," Ian said. "Self-inflicted." He saw out the back windshield that some of the tux-and-sequin-wearers had seen him throw that punch. Several rushed to the HOS's side, shouting for the police—who couldn't follow them, thanks to the snarl of limos and Lamborghinis.

Still, as Ian watched for pursuers, Francine drove like the pro that she was, moving them quickly into the labyrinth of streets, taking them far from the action at the embassy.

No one chased, no one followed, and Ian finally felt secure enough to focus on applying pressure to the cut at his hairline.

"We're clear," Francine announced over her headset. "Heading for the extraction point."

They were leaving the country via private jet from a small airport outside of the city. The client had arranged the flight, which meant they'd board the plane without even so much as a conversation with customs, which was nice.

"Johnny, tell the pilot to be ready to go wheels up as soon as we arrive," Ian ordered.

"Aye, aye, sir."

Francine covered her mic again and asked, "Did you do what I think you did?"

"Yup," Ian said.

He pulled out the packet that he'd tucked into the left side of his shirt and opened it, wanting a closer look at one of the pieces—a silver locket.

Its delicate chain had become entangled with a diamond necklace and an emerald bracelet. He gently pulled it free.

The locket had caught his eye back at the embassy, in part because of its lovely simplicity, in part because he'd wondered if it opened and . . .

Yes. The inside held miniature photos—one on each side. On the left were a young man and woman on their wedding day, circa the late 1930s. On the right was a photo of a little girl, maybe four years old, with her mother's sparkling dark eyes and joyful smile.

And Ian knew that he'd made the right choice.

Because maybe—just maybe—that girl had survived.

She'd be around eighty now. And for her, this locket would be priceless. As would every other piece that someone else's mother or grandmother had worn against their skin.

Francine glanced at him as he wrapped it all back up. "Three mill's a pretty good haul for one night's work," she commented as she pulled the limo onto the runway, not far from the waiting plane.

Ian tucked the packet back into his shirt. "Yeah."

They got out of the car and were halfway up the stairs to the plane when Francine said, "So now you're a jewel thief."

He couldn't argue with that.

Johnny was waiting for them in the cabin, and he handed Ian the flashdrive that held the contents of Prince Stefan's computer, then helped the co-pilot secure the door.

Ian strapped himself in, his two teammates on either side of him—both already settling in for a trans-Atlantic nap—as the jet screamed down the runway and lifted them safely away and into the night.

PART ONE

TEAM HERO

CHAPTER ONE

Monday

Ian Dunn was not what she'd expected from reading his file.

Phoebe glanced at Martell Griffin, who was sitting beside her at the interview table. Even though he nodded very slightly to acknowledge her silent surprise, his eyes never left Ian and the guard who was escorting him into the little room. It was a reminder that this man—the prisoner—was dangerous.

On paper, Dunn had come across as the unscrupulous love child of Captain America and James Bond, capable of damn near anything. He was a former Navy SEAL turned international jewel thief—*alleged* international jewel thief, because he'd never been charged for that particular crime.

Still, after skimming the file that she'd been handed just this morning, Phoebe had imagined someone who looked more like Cary Grant. Someone slender and light on his feet. Someone capable of becoming invisible when wearing cat burglar black.

But this man in prison garb was built like a boxer. He was Mack truck huge. Piano mover massive.

His only hope at achieving invisibility would be if he tried disguising himself as a small planet or maybe a large moon. Provided it was a very dark night and everyone looking for him was drunk.

He was bigger than Martell, which was saying something, since the African American former-cop-turned-lawyer was tall enough to tower over Phoebe—remarkable since she'd been Amazonian herself since fifth grade.

But Ian Dunn made Martell look nearly undernourished, and Phoebe feel practically petite.

Along with being huge, Dunn was also sweaty. His prison-issue T-shirt was soaked around his collar, down his chest and beneath his arms, too, and it clung to his powerful upper body. The array of tattoos on his massive biceps gleamed as they stretched the edges of the fraying and faded orange sleeves.

His too-long dark brown hair was dripping onto his face, and as Phoebe watched he used the bottom hem of his shirt in an attempt to mop himself dry. As he did so, he displayed an impressive, glistening set of hard-cut abs along with the waistband of a pair of dull orange athletic shorts that he wore dangerously, precariously low on his hips.

And great, he'd lowered his shirt to find her staring at his crotch—her gaze had inadvertently traveled south, following the arrowlike trail of dark hair that pointed the way down from his near-perfect belly button as if it were a flashing neon sign.

Phoebe pushed her glasses up her nose, aimed her eyes at his face, and forced what she hoped was a polite, professional smile, even as he grinned down at her. His blue eyes were twinkling in a face that was broad and cheerful and big-boned with a nose that was too large and a brow that should have been much too heavy for him to be called *handsome*.

Should have been, but wasn't.

Still, despite the fact that his winsome smile had the power to make the hearts of half the population flutter, Ian Dunn looked more like a man who threw oxen at the local county fair.

More, that is, than the criminal mastermind he allegedly was.

Except that wasn't just a mix of good humor and wry appreciation gleaming now in his eyes as he continued to aim his amusement at her. As he pulled out the chair and flopped down into it, his entire manner was easygoing and relaxed, as if they were meeting at the picnic area of the local softball field where he was taking a break from the game—instead of in an interview room in a Florida state prison where he was halfway through an eighteen-month sentence.

But there was sharp intelligence in Dunn's eyes, too.

Phoebe watched while he turned and nodded reassuringly at the guard, whose movements were almost apologetic as he used a short plastic restraint to lock the band around Dunn's left ankle to a metal anchor in the floor.

The prisoner's hands were cuffed, too, Phoebe realized, but he rested them on the table as if he barely noticed or maybe just didn't give a damn.

"Nice to meet you in person, finally," Dunn said in an evenly modulated, accent-free voice. His words were odd, because neither Phoebe nor Martell had so much as sent him a letter, let alone spoken to him on the phone. There hadn't been time. She herself hadn't known she was coming here until a short, chaotic hour ago. "But you *know,* if you'd called ahead, I would've showered and dressed for the occasion."

He smiled as he turned slightly to glance over his broad shoulder at the door that closed behind the guard with a solid-sounding *thunk.*

It was then that his face almost imperceptibly hardened as he looked from Martell to Phoebe and then back to Martell as if he'd used his criminal mastermind to detect that, yes, Martell was in charge of this little meeting. His smile was still securely in place, though, as he leaned in and lowered his voice and asked, "Are you a friend of Conrad's?"

Phoebe glanced at Martell, who narrowed his dark brown eyes slightly at Dunn as he asked, "Who's Conrad?"

The intensity—if that was, in fact, what it was, and not merely her overactive imagination—vanished from Dunn's eyes and face as quickly as it had appeared.

"Apparently not," he said with a shrug as he sat back in his chair. "No big, just an acquaintance I thought might be mutual." He folded his hands across his stomach, his movement limited by those cuffs. "So. What are you here to sell me? Although it's probably best if you start with your names, so I can stop thinking of you as Diverse Lawyer One and"—he looked at Phoebe with another of those sunny smiles—"Diverse Lawyer Two."

"I'm Martell Griffin," Martell said. "And yes, Ms. Kruger and I are lawyers, but only she is here as *your* lawyer. She works for Bryant, Hill, and Stoneham."

"Whoa, wait, really?" Dunn laughed but then frowned slightly as he asked Phoebe, "Is that . . . ? That's not . . ." He stopped himself and started over. "Where's Uncle Jerry?"

Uncle who . . . ? The question was as cryptic as the one about Conrad. Phoebe quickly glanced at Martell, but he shook his head in a silent *I don't know*.

"J. Quincy Bryant. The B in B, H, and S," Dunn explained, even though her silence hadn't dragged on for *that* long. As easygoing as he pretended to be, this was not a patient man. "The J is for Jerry, at least for those of us whose granddads knew him before he was a total soulless douchebag." His warm smile softened the potential edge of his words.

In fact, this man could announce *I'm here to rob your house,* and if he accompanied his words with one of those smiles, most people's first reaction would be *Oh, how nice. Do come in.*

Phoebe looked down at her file in dismay,

wondering how she'd failed to make note of the fact that one of the senior partners was this man's uncle, although *that* certainly explained the reason the elite firm represented him. She wished someone had told her that she was going to have to deliver some very bad news to a family member.

"He's not a real uncle, we're not actually blood relations." Dunn saw her face and again was quick with the explanation. "Don't worry, you didn't miss it, it's not in there."

Okay, that was good, except *now* what was she supposed to tell him? Anything? Or nothing?

"The relationship was more of a my-grandfather-died-saving-his-life-in-Vietnam thing," Dunn continued almost cheerfully. "Uncle Jerry felt indebted. Although it would've been nice if the support had been more proactive. Grocery deliveries and rent assistance while I was still a kid instead of criminal defense after I'd crossed the line, you know what I mean? But hey. Better late than never, right?"

Phoebe knew, from a brief family history, that Dunn's grandfather, John, had been KIA in Vietnam when Ian's father, George, was just a boy. George, who had died from hepatitis four years ago, had been a lifer in prison in Concord, Massachusetts, locked up for his part in a robbery in which a security guard had been killed, albeit accidentally. And although it had never been proven, it was believed that Ian had learned at least some of his mad breaking-and-entering and burglary skills at an early age, from Dunn Senior, who'd learned it in turn from an uncle. A real one. *That* info was in her file, along with a long list of other *allegedlies.* Some of them pretty impressively crazy.

But the present-and-living Dunn had asked her a question. *Where's Uncle Jerry?* She cleared her throat and decided it was best to be vague. "Mr. Bryant is currently unavailable."

"No offense," Dunn said easily, "and I'm sure you're equally douche-tastic as a lawyer—and I mean that in a good way. But whatever you're here for, Ms. Kruger, I'd prefer to wait until Unca Jer gets back from his vaca. Or you can ask the firm to send over his son-in-law, Bob-the-incompetent—if it really can't wait."

And now they were both looking at her.

Martell Griffin, too, had been surprised when Phoebe had been waiting for him outside the prison's gates this morning. He clearly hadn't expected Dunn to have representation present at this meeting—or maybe his surprise was that she wasn't Mr. Bryant or his son-in-law, Bob Middleworth. Especially considering the magnitude of his offer.

And so Phoebe changed her mind. Both men needed an explanation, and outside the prison walls, the news had probably gone public anyway. "Mr. Bryant and Mr. Middleworth were injured in a car accident last night, and I'm so sorry to have to tell you, but Maureen Middleworth—Mr. Bryant's daughter—was killed in the crash."

"Oh, shit," Dunn said.

"The firm's experiencing some chaos," Phoebe

continued. "As I'm sure you can imagine."

"I'm sorry," Dunn said, with regret in his eyes. "Poor Jerry. He must be devastated. Bobby, too." He shook his head, took a deep breath, and blew it out. "Wow. I appreciate your stepping up and filling in, Ms. Kruger, but . . . I can certainly wait a few weeks—months even if it takes that long—for Jerry to get back."

Martell spoke up. "*I'm* sorry, but this situation, however, can't wait."

"It's gonna have to," Dunn said as he turned his gaze to Martell. He obviously and visibly appraised the lawyer's well-fitting suit, his crisp white shirt, his brightly colored tie, as well as the hard planes and angles of a stern face that screamed serious business, accompanied by a gleaming and carefully shaved head. He appraised, but then immediately dismissed. Dunn's body language was as clear as if he'd flicked away a used tissue. "Isn't it." He made his words a statement, not a question, and the testosterone levels in the room rose substantially as Martell bristled, appraising him back.

Lowlife, convict, prisoner scum was the silent message Martell sent in response to Dunn's dismissal, but the prisoner's response was only the smallest of mournful smiles. Which served to piss off the lawyer more thoroughly.

"Mr. Dunn, I realize this isn't the best time, considering the circumstances, but aren't you even the slightest bit curious?" Phoebe asked, because having the two men sit there in silence, staring each other down, wasn't helping to move this meeting forward. And she had other things to do today.

Dunn again looked over at her, and she could practically see the wheels turning in his gigantic head as he tried to figure out the best way to push *her* buttons. And wasn't that interesting? He really didn't care why they were there. This meeting was little more than a game to him.

As Phoebe watched, he went for the obvious, with an insulting term of endearment. "Honey, I'm intensely curious—but only about things that *really* matter." And yes, he put the cherry on top by proceeding to undress her with his eyes.

"I prefer to be called *Ms. Kruger,*" she corrected him, forcing herself to remain as expressionless as humanly possible. Still, she couldn't stop herself from swallowing—damnit—because yikes, when he set his animal magnetism on *kill* like that, the man was a true force of nature.

And naturally, in turn, he made note of her almost microscopic gulp. His smile broadened.

Fine. Let him think he had the power to turn her knees into Jell-O. She, however, knew better.

"And this does matter," she informed him crisply. "The reason Mr. Griffin requested this meeting—the reason your Uncle Jerry's firm sent me here, with him, to talk to you. Matters. Immensely. Lives are at stake—starting but not ending with two innocent children."

He laughed his surprise. "And only I have the secret code. Or something like that, right?"

"Or something like that," she agreed, turning to Martell. She herself knew only the basics of the situation. But one thing she did know, with certainty, was that the deal the other lawyer was offering was a gift from on high. "Mr. Griffin, I believe that's your cue."

But Dunn was already shaking his head as he told Martell, "Whatever you think I know, you're mistaken."

"Whatever you tell us," Phoebe interjected, despite having passed the invisible talking baton to Martell, "whatever you say, regardless of its legality, will not be used against you, now or in the future. You will receive immunity. Completely. I've made *very* sure of that."

Martell chimed in: "Play your cards right, Mr. Dunn, and you *will* walk out of here, with us, today. A free man."

Dunn laughed again, but his laughter faded as he looked from Martell to Phoebe. "Whoa, wait. He's shitting me, right?"

She shook her head.

Dunn got very still as he gazed at Martell. "Who *are* you?"

"I'm here on behalf of, well, the government, is what it comes down to," Martell told him, "even though I don't work for them directly and I can't be specific about the organization in charge of this mission. What you need to know is that I'm here to offer you your freedom, effective immediately, in exchange for your cooperation in—"

"No," Dunn interrupted him, turning his chair as far as he could with his tether in place. "No way. No deal. No thanks. Not interested." He raised his voice and called toward the door, "Hey, Roger, we're done in here!"

This time it was Martell who was so surprised that he laughed. "Are you kidding?" He looked at Phoebe as if she could help. "Is he kidding? He wants to *stay* in *prison?*"

She shook her head. She, too, was clueless.

Which was proving to be a not-unusual state for her in this, her first week of employment at the prestigious law firm. Upon her arrival, she'd been thrown into the deep end of the pool, assigned to assume the caseloads of three lawyers who'd recently been jettisoned. She'd spent most of the past week paddling desperately just to keep her head above water.

And then today had happened, creating even more chaos. Since she was one of the few lawyers who'd never met the boss's poor deceased daughter, she'd been hurriedly handed Ian Dunn's file, which was marked *Top Priority.* And the waves she'd thought were formidable turned out to be mere swells as this latest tsunami washed over her. It was part of her new normal.

And *that* was a total change of reality for her, since she prided herself on her ability to always—*always*—be one of the few people with a clue in any given room.

But now that she'd met him, it was clear that Ian

Dunn's file was incomplete. Phoebe was going to have to dig deeper to figure out what made him tick. Which she would do as soon as she found both a little time and some Internet access.

"Roger!" Dunn called again. "Where the hell are you?"

But Martell stood up and knocked on the table in front of the man. "He won't come back in until *I* tell him we're done. And we're not done until you listen to what I have to offer, and then walk out of here with me, because that's what sane people do when they're handed a Get Out of Jail Free card."

Dunn looked from Martell to Phoebe, and his eyes were no longer warm. In fact they were positively steely. "I've been locked up for nearly a year, so maybe things have changed out beyond these walls. Is that really legal now?" he asked her. "Forcing me to do something I'm unwilling to do?"

She cleared her throat. "This is an unusual circumstance. Not only are those children's lives at stake, but from what I understand, this is a matter of national security. And Mr. Griffin *is* offering you quite a—"

"I'm not interested in what he's offering. While I wish you luck in finding someone who can help you save the world, it's not gonna be me. Not this time."

Phoebe blinked at him. "As your lawyer, Mr. Dunn, I *highly* recommend that you—"

"You're not my lawyer," Dunn said evenly, almost pleasantly, "and I don't give a shit what you recommend. No deal. Get me out of here. Now."

• • •

Well, wasn't this a goatfuck of a different color?

Ian Dunn didn't know his lawyer, Jerry Bryant, very well, and he'd never actually met the son-in-law, Bob, who was supposed to show up if Jerry couldn't attend a jailhouse meeting—of which there had been decidedly few. The story Ian had told about his grandfather and Vietnam had been just that—a story. It was cover for why Bryant personally represented him.

And not only had Ms. Kruger failed to respond correctly to his coded inquiry about the fictional Conrad, but Ian had been told, again and again, that *only* Jerry or Bob would act as his conduit to his current asshole of an employer. Somehow, in the confusion created by the fatal car accident, one of the firm's junior lawyers had been sent here, probably also by accident.

"We've found the man who can save the world—and those kids," the lawyer named Martell Griffin now told Ian as neither he nor Ms. Kruger moved to call the prison guard. "And it's you."

Ian silently shook his head as he glanced over at the woman who looked as if she'd graduated from law school last Tuesday—she seemed to be that freaking young. But from what he knew of Bryant, Hill, and Stoneham, they didn't hire anyone right out of school, so she had to be older. Late twenties, maybe early thirties. The dewy freshness of her porcelain-perfect complexion was no doubt due to massive hours spent huddled in a windowless law office.

She wore her brown hair pulled up into some kind of bun thing on the top of her head, and with those dark-framed glasses and the square-cut pants suit that didn't succeed at hiding her substantial curves, she gave off quite the hot librarian vibe.

She was pretty, but she didn't give a shit. In fact, she worked hard to hide it—including by covering those eyes with those clunky glasses.

Ian had expected a woman with her pale skin to have blue or maybe green eyes. But hers were the richest, deepest, darkest shade of brown. Meeting her gaze was like falling backward into a warm, moonless night.

And . . . yesssss.

It had been *way* too long since Ian had had the pleasure of female companionship. And it was going to be even longer before he got some, because he wasn't walking out of here with Julie and Linc, no matter what they offered him to become the third member of their ridiculous child-rescuing Mod Squad.

Ian's little brother's life depended on him staying right where he was. And the fact that Aaron was no longer actually little didn't matter. Dead was dead, and Ian was determined to ensure that Aaron lived to a ripe old age. Besides, the kid had his own kid now. Which meant the stakes were even higher.

"I'm going to count to ten, Julie," he now told Ms. Kruger, whose first name probably wasn't Julie, but he could file that fact, too, under *things about which he didn't give a damn.* "If you don't fetch Roger and get me the fuck out of here, I'm going to spend the afternoon writing a letter of complaint about you to the Board of Bar Overseers, which I know won't do much—except submerge you, hipdeep, in bureaucratic bullshit that you'll have to wade through for months to come. You look, to me, like a girl who has better things to do."

She didn't flinch. In fact, his fighting words made her raise her chin. "First of all, I haven't been a girl in years. Second, I can and will argue that it's in your best interest to listen to Mr. Griffin's proposal. And third, it's Phoebe, not Julie, and I *still* prefer Ms. Kruger, thank you very much, Mr. Dunn."

"One," Ian responded as he met her steady gaze and held it. And held it. Phoebe, huh? The name suited her, although she probably wished it was something easily shortened and crisp, like Kate or Jenn or Meg. On the other hand, maybe she liked having a name that matched the softness of her appearance so that her not-a-pushover personality could be used as a secret weapon, to catch her opponents off guard.

"Two," he said, and added the tiniest of smiles to their staring match, just to make her think that he was picturing her naked. Which he now, of course, was, since doing so made this SNAFU slightly less of an ordeal.

On the other end of the table, Martell Griffin heavily exhaled his frustration.

Phoebe took the opportunity to end their stare-down game by looking over at Griffin as the other lawyer said, "Let's talk about the Kazbekistani embassy heist," he started. "In Istanbul, on August the twenty-ninth—"

"Oh, here we go." Ian rolled his eyes. *This* again. Was this *really* what this was about? Jesus Christ, that had gone down years ago, and he'd never been formally charged, thanks to Shelly's quick work with the embassy's security camera files. "Three," he told Phoebe before telling Griffin, "Believe it or not, even *I'm* not crazy enough to scale a four-story building and climb in a window—during an embassy dinner party—for only a three-million-dollar payout. How many times, on record, do I need to say that?"

"As many as you want," Griffin countered, "but we all know that you're lying."

"I don't know that he's lying," Phoebe spoke up. "I mean, I'm not *one hundred* percent convinced that he is. The facts—"

"Put him in Istanbul at the time of the burglary," Griffin finished for her.

"That's circumstantial evidence at best," she argued.

"Look," Ian interrupted her. "Sweetheart, if you really want to help me, go get Roger and—"

"The Kazbekistani consulate, in Miami this time," Phoebe interrupted him, "is where Mr. Griffin's clients believe the children are being held. And they and Mr. Griffin seem to think that makes you uniquely qualified to help them out. They claim you're familiar with the consulate's methods of security."

"Allegedly familiar," he told her, adding, "Four, five, *and* six, for believing their fairytale shite."

"What I believe," she continued, unflinchingly direct, "without a doubt, is that Leo Vaszko, age seven, and Katrina Vaszko, age thirteen, are being held, against their will, in the Miami consulate. If they're not rescued, they'll be spirited out of the country and returned to their father—a notorious and dangerous Kazbekistani warlord. They'll never see their mother again."

Ian narrowed his eyes as he looked back at her. "Since when does the federal government get involved—to this extent—with the rescue of kidnapped children?"

Phoebe glanced at Griffin, because, yes, that *was* a good question, wasn't it? The lawyer cleared his throat and shifted in his seat.

"So who's their mother?" Ian asked, because there was definitely more to this situation than met the eye.

"Dr. Lusa Vaszko," Griffin said.

Ian didn't know the name. "Doctor of what?" he asked.

Another round of throat clearing. "She's, um, a nuclear physicist."

Ah.

"My client," Griffin continued, "wants to ensure that Dr. Vaszko is not forced to return to Kazbekistan, where she could be pressured into heading their budding nuclear program."

Yes. That was more like it. Ian nodded. "So I'm

supposed to, what? Provide you with a detailed report on K-stani embassy and consulate security procedures? Even if I'd had access to that information all those years ago—it *was* all those years ago. Their entire security system has been revamped, and the ambassador's new—the position's turned over at least twice since then. You don't need me. Any team of Navy SEALs worth their billion-dollar training can insert, covertly, into that consulate and save those kids." Even as he said it, he recognized the flaw in that plan.

"For obvious reasons, we can't use Navy SEALs," Griffin confirmed. "Or even former SEALs. At least not any who haven't spent time in prison."

Because a team of SEALs covertly entering a foreign consulate would put the U.S. into a diplomatic shitstorm if something went wrong and they got caught. It might even be misconstrued as an act of war.

"Likewise, we can't use the FBI or CIA—or even the local police," Griffin continued.

But since Ian's résumé now included *convicted felon* and *alleged international jewel thief* along with *former Navy SEAL* . . . He realized exactly where this meeting was going. "You want more than information from me," he said, looking from Phoebe to Griffin and back. "*That's* what this is about. Oh, no. No, no. I can't do this. Besides, you *do* know that if there's proof that the ambassador's committed a crime, you *can* go into a consulate and kick his ass—"

"We believe the ambassador is purposely being kept in the dark," Griffin said. "And our current relationship with Kazbekistan is so fragile, we can't take any risks whatsoever. Kicking down doors isn't an option. The rescue must be done with stealth."

Ian just kept shaking his head. "I can't help you."

"There's more," Griffin said. "The FBI has identified one of the men responsible for the kidnapping as an alleged acquaintance of yours. George Vanderzee. Nicknamed—"

"The Dutchman," Ian finished for him with a laugh. Jee-zus. He knew Vanderzee well. Half K-stani and half Dutch, he looked European, but embraced his Kazak mother's traditions and culture. He also made his money from others' misfortunes. Ian had used him in a gun-running sting back in '09, not long after he'd left the Navy. "Fantastic. He's a fucking lunatic. And FYI, he pronounces *Georg* the German way: Gay-org. It's spelled without the final E."

"Not in my file, it's not," Griffin said.

"Your file is wrong," Ian informed him. "You *do* know that his involvement makes the job harder, not easier?"

"Mr. Griffin's client believes that his involvement makes you the right man for this job," Phoebe pointed out. "You'll win your immediate freedom, as well as your complete and total immunity—"

"I don't want it. I'm not taking this deal,

regardless of what's offered," Ian informed her, adding, "Seven, eight, nine . . ."

Phoebe ignored him, her full attention on Griffin, who'd closed his file and almost violently pushed it back into his briefcase as he stood up.

"This meeting is over," the lawyer said. "I'm done wasting time. I got blood in this game. My dearest friend on this planet is in the hospital, clinging to life as we speak, having nearly died defending those children. Who I am now going to help find. So no more bullshit—I'm going straight to Plan B."

Whatever he was planning, Phoebe clearly wasn't in on it. She stood up, obviously startled as she watched Griffin cross the room while she echoed, "Plan B . . . ?"

Griffin picked up the phone that would connect him with the guards, even as he rapped impatiently on the door. "Hello! We're done here."

Ian moved his chair as far as he could, given his restraints, straining his neck to watch as pretty Phoebe joined Griffin at that door.

"Plan B?" she asked again, lowering her voice. "We didn't discuss any Plan B, Martell."

"I'ma get Dunn the hell out of here despite the lack of any agreement," Griffin said, interrupting himself to speak into the phone. "Yeah, open the door. Now." He hung up and told Phoebe, "We'll make this deal after he's free."

"With what leverage?" Phoebe put voice to Ian's own amazement.

"The threat to put his sorry ass right back here

after he gets a taste of that freedom he says he doesn't want," Griffin said. "Along with a shitload of money. Everybody has a price. Dunn's got his, and with stakes this high, my employer will be willing to pay."

"You're going to just check me out of a maximum security prison," Ian protested, "like it's some kind of spa or resort hotel?" He laughed. "You do that, and there's no one on this planet who won't know that I'm now working for the FBI or the Agency, or whoever the hell you bow to as your evil overlord. Which makes me immediately unusable. Hello."

Martell Griffin smiled, but his eyes were ice. "We know a lot about you, Mr. Dunn. We'll spin it like you made a deal on the local level."

Ian laughed. "That's crazy."

Phoebe obviously thought so, too. She tried to speak quietly, but the room was so small, Ian couldn't help but hear her. "If Dunn was really behind the embassy heist in Istanbul," she told Griffin, "he's got more money in an off-shore account than either of us can imagine."

"I wasn't and I don't," Ian insisted, but neither of them so much as glanced at him.

"Maybe so," Griffin answered Phoebe with an extra-large dose of grim. "But money's not the only thing we have to offer." The door opened. "Everyone has a price," he said again, "including Ian Dunn."

And with that, he stalked out of the room, with Phoebe right behind him.

"Shit," Ian said into the empty room, as the door closed with a thunk. If this clown succeeded at getting him out of here, not only would nine months of hard time be flushed down the crapper, but Aaron would be in imminent danger.

Ian *did* have a price, but Phoebe was right. It had nothing to do with money. In fact, it had to do with only two things: the safety of his brother, Aaron, and the safety of Aaron's family.

Aaron had just gotten Rory down for a nap when the phone rang.

"Motherfuh—" He cut himself off, in case the shrill ringtone had woken up his son. At eleven months old, Rory was starting to make word-sounding noises, and *motherfucker* was not going to be part of his vocabulary. At least not until he went to school and heard it from some other kid with crappier parents.

Getting him to nap today had been a battle for the ages, with Rory sobbing as if his life was ending—which was always jarringly reminiscent of the first painful months of the baby's life. But time had been on Aaron's side. Tired was tired, and with the kid wearing himself out even further with all the drama, it was just a matter of *when* before the eyes started rolling back in that tiny, brilliant, sweet-smelling little head.

Aaron answered the phone with a whispered, "Yeah? What?" which probably wouldn't win him any prizes if the caller were someone from that nursery school Shelly so desperately wanted Rory to attend.

Like one nursery school over another made a shit of a difference in Rory's future as the next president of the United States, or whatever Shel had in mind.

Aaron himself hadn't gone to nursery school or preschool or early childhood development school or whatever the fuck it was called these days.

Which . . . actually argued the case in Shel's favor, since Aaron was now a stay-at-home-dad with a warrant out for his arrest.

And oh yeah, his only living family was his douchebag of a brother, Ian, who had vanished almost a year ago—no doubt gone off to save the world. Son of a bitch.

Ian had sent some lame-ass unsigned card when Rory was born. A card, and a hundred thousand dollars in U.S. savings bonds. His generosity was a thinly veiled reminder that he'd wanted them to move far away—or at least to leave Florida. He'd wanted them all to go—Aaron, Shelly, and Shel's older sister Francine, too. But Ian couldn't support them forever. His funds were not limitless, and Sarasota was where Shelly had a high-paying job and part ownership of a thriving computer software firm. The hope was that in just a few years, the company would go public, and Shelly could cash out, leaving them set for life—and free to vanish for good. Besides, Sarasota was a fairly large city, well over an hour away from Clearwater. As long as they were careful and kept their heads down, they were safe enough. They'd had that argument with Ian—and won it—long before he'd disappeared. Living under assumed names in Florida was safer than using their real names in Alaska—a fact that Ian had finally conceded mere days before he'd left.

Since then, there'd been monthly postcards that all said the same thing in Ian's crappy printing: *Love you. Miss you. Stay safe. Don't be stupid.*

Right now, though, there was silence on the other end of the phone, and Aaron heard himself saying, "Ian?" because he was just *that* stupid. He was loaded with undying hope that would spring to life at the tiniest spark. Like, what he was actually, stupidly thinking right now was maybe—*maybe*—Eee was calling from some spooky overseas job, hence the flaky connection.

Yeah, right.

Whoever was on the other end didn't say a word, and the connection was cut with a very definite *click*.

Aaron looked at his phone and the caller ID, of course, said *private*.

"Fuck you," Aaron whispered to the phone, and to his brother, too, wherever that douchebag was. And he went down the stairs and turned on the baby monitor in the kitchen, and got to work doing the dishes and cleaning the counters so that the granite sparkled and shone. If he was lucky, it would earn him not just a grateful smile but maybe a little something extra when Shelly got home from earning the big bucks that kept their perfect little family afloat.

CHAPTER TWO

Phoebe learned quite a bit in the hours immediately following her prison meeting with Martell Griffin and Ian Dunn.

First, she discovered that processing the release of a prisoner took several hours—which was actually much faster than she'd expected.

Second, she found out that Martell's need to rescue those kidnapped kids was deeply personal and heartfelt.

He'd told her that he was good friends with a man who ran a Sarasota personal security firm called Troubleshooters Incorporated—a man who'd been assigned not to protect those kids, but to analyze and write a recommendation for upgrades to the security team currently being used to protect them. Ironically, he'd been in Miami, doing a ride-along with the Vaszko children and their bodyguards when the kids had been grabbed in a brazen daylight attack that left their two guards dead and Martell's friend Ric seriously wounded.

Shot in the chest, Martell had told Phoebe when they'd first left the prison interview room, as he'd gone through his phone, searching in vain for messages about Ric's status. He'd then told Phoebe that he'd hoped to have a voice mail or text waiting for him from Ric's wife, but there was nothing.

No word.

Which was not good.

Martell had been deep inside of his own head, in his own private unhappy world, so Phoebe had left him pacing in the prison parking lot. She'd spent the bulk of the wait for Dunn's release researching the former SEAL in the air-conditioned comfort of the Northport Coffee Shack.

Where she'd learned quite a few additional interesting things—not the least of which was a wealth of information about Navy SEALs.

Phoebe had heard a lot of buzz about SEALs since the death of Usama bin Laden. She'd assumed the SEALs were merely the Navy's version of the Green Berets or Delta Force. But SEALs weren't your everyday, ordinary commandos, they were *super*-commandos. Apparently, the training that they underwent was *the* most challenging and rigorous in the entire military. In fact, it was so intense that the vast majority of SEAL candidates dropped out. Only the best of the best made it through the program.

And Ian Dunn had, at one time, been one of them.

He'd joined the Navy as an enlisted man, but during his ten years of service, he'd not only gotten his college degree, but he'd also crossed over into officer's territory by attending something called OCS—Officer Candidate School. By the time he'd left, he was a lieutenant and a SEAL team leader.

And that was another thing she'd discovered—that SEALs always, *always* worked in teams.

Which made her wonder: Where was Ian's team? If, after leaving the Navy, he'd indeed become a thief of international renown, surely he hadn't done it by suddenly, uncharacteristically pulling a Rambo, and working alone.

So Phoebe had dug deeper, exploring, searching.

She'd found no mention of Ian's mysterious teammates, but she uncovered what seemed to be quite the urban legend about him on more than one military discussion board.

The rumor, at least in the SpecOp or SEAL community, was that Ian Dunn gave away most of what he stole in his varied and apparently frequent heists. He only kept enough for operating expenses. And supposedly, the vast majority of the jewelry and artwork he quote-unquote *liberated,* was already stolen or otherwise ill-gotten gains. Nazi treasure. Fortunes made from war profiteering, or from the blood and tears of orphaned slaves.

But not everyone on those Internet boards considered Dunn a hero. One anonymous poster claimed that when Dunn had left the SEAL teams, he'd cut ties and hadn't looked back.

That same anonymous person, jackal99, pointed out that the SpecWar community was made *very* uncomfortable whenever a highly trained, highly skilled SEAL went rogue. It happened. Rarely, apparently, but it did happen.

"We all wince and start to sweat a little," this alleged former SEAL wrote, "because we know what Dunn's capable of. So we pretend that he's working for the good guys, and the discomfort caused by his being out there is easier to deal with."

It was fascinating.

But, without a doubt, *the* most interesting thing Phoebe found was a tiny little article that popped up when, on a whim, she did a Google search comprised of the month and year of Dunn's legendary—and alleged—embassy heist, and the words *Nazi treasure*.

According to this article, just a few short days after the burglary at the Kazbekistani embassy in Istanbul, the Los Angeles–based Simon Wiesenthal Center received a mysterious delivery of a package filled with priceless jewelry, believed to have been stolen by the Nazis during the Holocaust. The organization was working to identify the pieces and track their original owners, to see if there were any surviving family members or descendants.

So, yes, *that* had been an informative few hours.

But then Martell had texted, letting her know that Ian Dunn's release was imminent, so she'd packed up her computer and headed back to the prison.

Martell was right where she'd left him, wearing out his shoes, worrying about his friend.

As Phoebe parked her new car in the mostly empty lot, his cell phone was to his ear. She gave him a questioning look as she climbed out into the heat of the day, not wanting to interrupt.

In response, he grimly shook his head, and mouthed the words *Nothing yet*.

There was no way he was going to get news of

his friend's death via anything other than direct communication. So this was a case of no news being extremely bad news.

And, oh God, now, as Phoebe watched, Martell's shoulders slumped and he leaned back against his own car, his hand up over his eyes. His long, elegant fingers massaged his forehead as he murmured something inaudible into his phone.

Phoebe sidled a little closer and . . . *Thank God?*

Yes, that was definitely a *Thank God,* and then, "Give him a big, wet kiss for me, and tell the dickhead that I'm working my ass off to clean up his mess for him." Martell managed to laugh, even as he wiped his eyes and said, "No, seriously, Annie. Tell Ric not to worry. I can't tell you who I'm working with, but we're on our way to finding those kids. Tell him we *will* get them back. He needs to concentrate on healing. Yeah." He ended the conversation with an "Aight," and then a "Yeah, been there, done that. Believe me, I'll be careful. Love you, too."

"Your friend's okay," Phoebe surmised.

"Gonna be," Martell told her as he checked his email and text messages one more time before pocketing his phone. "Gonna be a long road back. But if I could do it, he can, too."

Had she just misheard what he'd said? "You . . . were shot?"

"Just like Ric. Point-blank in the chest." He put a hand against his tie. "A few years ago. It was something of a surprise when it happened."

"Oh my God."

"Usually when you encounter the business end of a handgun, there's some, well, foreplay, if you'll excuse the expression. A conversation, at least. A little *Hello, how are you, and yes, this is a loaded weapon, thanks for noticing*. But this wasn't your everyday, average mugging. I'd interrupted an abduction in progress."

"Were you out of uniform?" Phoebe asked, because, jeez, for someone to just shoot a cop . . .

"I wasn't a uniformed officer," Martell told her. "I was a detective. But this happened after I'd left. In fact, it was after I passed the bar. Most people think it's why I left the force, but it's not."

"I wasn't thinking that," Phoebe said.

"Yeah, you were," he said. "But it's okay. Like I said, everyone does."

What she'd been thinking was that Martell was so . . . healthy. Tall, and handsome, and self-assured. And, yes, unafraid. Phoebe wouldn't've faulted him one bit if, after an assault like that, he'd quit his dangerous job as a police detective and stayed hidden in the safety of the shadows, flinching at every loud noise.

Of course, maybe he was like her and walked around packing heat, and fully trained in self-defense. In fact, the first thing she'd done after leaving the prison earlier this morning was to move her Glock from the lockup in her trunk and back into her shoulder bag, where it usually lived.

Across the pitted, dusty, and barely graveled

parking lot, the barbed-wire-topped inner prison gate began to creak slowly open, and Phoebe shaded her eyes to get a better look. But the outer gate remained tightly shut, which made sense.

The entrances to the prison—even the one for visitors, over on the other side of the complex—were designed like the doors in that ancient TV show *Get Smart*. Before the second door opened, the first shut, guaranteeing that there could never be a direct mass rush for freedom, even in the unlikely case of the prisoners overpowering the guards and gaining control of the security grid.

This gate here was essentially the service entrance. This was where prisoners came to be processed, and after serving their time and repaying their debt to society—assuming that was even possible—they were spit back out, into the harshness, heat, and dusty parking lot of the real world.

"You ready for this?" Martell asked Phoebe. "He's not going to be a happy camper, and it's imperative that we don't lose him."

She glanced at him, startled. "He's not wearing a tracker on his ankle?"

"Nope." Martell gave her a tight smile. "Can't risk it."

"Wow," she said. "You're more of a gambler than I thought."

He laughed, but it was humorless. "Yeah, I kinda went all in."

Phoebe chose her words carefully. "You know,

Dunn may not be willing to do this job. He might decide to just disappear," she pointed out, as the inner gate creaked closed, locking with a bang that made the entire compound seem to shudder. "It's been my experience that alienation, anger, and betrayal aren't usually the start of a beautiful friendship."

"I don't need Dunn to be my friend," Martell said tightly. "In fact, it'll help enormously if he decides to rob the consulate at the same time that he's saving the Vaszko kids. Further proof that the U.S. had nothing to do with the rescue mission."

"I don't think he's really a jewel thief." Phoebe told the other lawyer a bit of what she'd just uncovered. "I mean, most of what I found out is at least part urban legend, true, but I think it would be a good idea if we viewed some of the so-called facts as, well, potential misinformation."

The look Martell gave her would have been funny, if lives weren't at stake. "So what are you saying?" he asked. "That Ian Dunn's, like, what? *Batman?*"

"More like Robin," Phoebe said, adding, "Hood."

Martell was not impressed. His laugh was more of a scoff. "I'm pretty sure Robin Hood'd be on board for saving two little kids."

"Not if whatever he was doing in prison was more important," Phoebe volunteered. "Maybe his current mission will save *more* lives—like, hundreds or thousands."

Now Martell was looking at her as if she were

full-on insane. “His current mission in prison is to pay for the damage done while playing Demolition Derby in a bar parking lot during a drunken temper tantrum.”

Phoebe shook her head. “I’m sorry,” she said. “But this is not a man who has a *drunken temper tantrum*. As far as I can tell, Ian Dunn doesn’t touch alcohol.”

“Because if he does, he gets ’faced and ends up destroying private property,” Martell argued. “Hundreds of thousands of dollars’ worth of it.”

“You’ve met him,” Phoebe said. “Is this really a man who staggers out of a bar, gets into his car, and intentionally crashes into more than a dozen parked vehicles? Because some woman refused to dance with him? I just can’t see him doing that.”

“Alcohol does strange things to some people. He pled guilty.”

“Exactly. I think he was in prison because he wanted to be in prison,” Phoebe told Martell. “And I think you pulling him out like this is a big mistake. I think it’s likely that a lot of people are going to be pissed off, particularly when your government client has an ah-ha moment and its right hand discovers what its left has been doing.”

He narrowed his eyes at her. “You think Dunn is already working for the feds.”

Phoebe nodded. “I think it’s entirely possible.”

Martell remained unconvinced. “Look, I’m just doing what I need to do to get this job done. If Dunn’s such a big hero like you say, then he’ll help us save these kids. And if he isn't . . . Well, he's going to help us whether he wants to or not."

"Okay," Phoebe said. "Assume I'm wrong. Completely. He's a criminal with a single motive—to make himself rich. I still don't understand how you can be so convinced that Dunn is going to go from *No deal* to *Thank you for the beating, my government master. How next may I please you?* in a matter of a few short hours."

Martell laughed at her bad Igor imitation. "He won't want to please me," he told her. "But he'll have to."

Now she looked at him through narrowed eyes. "What haven't you told me? What's not in my copy of Dunn's file, that I also didn't find today on the Internet?"

"Have you ever heard of Manny Dellarosa?"

Phoebe squinted. "That name is . . . not completely unfamiliar."

"The Dellarosas are a local mob family. They run drugs, up out of Clearwater, north of Tampa. They also dabble in prostitution, human trafficking, gambling, and the random chop shop. They own two legit businesses—a trucking company and a series of warehouses scattered across the state—mostly to launder their ill-gotten gains.

"Manny's the boss," Martell continued. "His brother Davio is his second in command; Davio's son Berto is also involved. There's a fourth Dellarosa—Vincent. Manny's son. But he's the family screwup. His job seems to be to spend their money, to get into trouble, and then run to Daddy for help."

"And Ian Dunn is connected to them how?" Phoebe asked.

"A year ago, Dunn tried to frame Vincent for the very crime for which he's serving time. That couldn't have made Daddy Dellarosa happy, and in the end—presumably after pressure was applied—Dunn ended up pleading guilty to all charges."

And *that* was why the name Dellarosa was familiar. Vincent Dellarosa was on the lengthy list of people whose cars were damaged by Dunn, outside of that bar.

"I didn't see a copy of the police report," Phoebe admitted. "As far as I could tell, from the moment our firm was involved, Dunn's goal was to plead guilty, pay retribution, and accept responsibility, all in exchange for a lighter sentence."

"Whatever went down," Martell countered, "it had to create tension between Dunn and the Dellarosas, right? So fast-forward to today, where Vince, the black sheep son, is currently awaiting trial for murder, over in Orlando."

"Seriously?" Phoebe asked.

Martell nodded. "*Trouble* is that young man's middle name. Here's where this works to our advantage: Daddy and Uncle Davio Dellarosa are going to hear about Ian Dunn's early release from prison, and think that he traded information for his freedom." He smiled tightly at Phoebe as an alarm bell finally rang and the outer gate slowly opened.

"Especially when, whoopsie-daisy, we leak information that Dunn's going to be a star witness at Vincent's impending trial."

"But . . . Wait. Doesn't this mean that Dunn's going to be targeted by the Dellarosas?" Phoebe asked.

"In theory," Martell said happily. "I don't know this for sure, but if there is a God, then, yes, the Dellarosas are gonna come for Dunn, guns blazing. And *that,* my dear Ms. Kruger, is the reason he's gonna agree to help us. Because we'll keep him safe, and then we'll keep him hidden until after Vince's trial is over. He refuses to help us, then he's on his own."

This was going to be interesting.

Phoebe liked Martell. She really did. He was intelligent and funny and extremely easy on the eyes, with his broad shoulders, handsome face, and quick smile. But she suspected he'd seriously miscalculated this situation, thinking for even one slice of a second that Ian Dunn would need or want anyone's help; that he wouldn't prefer to be left to himself, to go deep into hiding until the threat from the Dellarosa family—if there even was a threat—was past.

And there he was. The former prisoner, now an official ex-con. Dressed in jeans and a T-shirt, clunky black boots on his feet. He carried a hooded sweatshirt and a plastic grocery sack that probably held the few personal items he'd had with him in his cell.

He stood there, just looking at them, long after the gate had opened wide enough for him to slip through.

But he didn't move.

And he didn't move.

He looked from Phoebe to Martell and back, and shook his head, just very slightly, as if they were unruly children who'd bitterly disappointed him.

And if only half of what Phoebe had discovered over the past few hours was true . . . they'd put him in some serious danger, *and* potentially screwed up whatever mysterious mission he was currently on.

Martell spoke first, turning to unlock his car with a *click* and a whoop of his aging antitheft system. "Come on, Dunn. I'll drive you to a hotel. You'll be safe there. You can take a shower, get something to eat while we talk."

The sound of his voice seemed to unpin Dunn's feet from where they were planted in the dusty ground, and he finally came through the gate, his stride as loose and easy as it had been when he'd walked into the prison interview room. "Yeah, no, I think I'll catch a ride with my cute new lawyer."

Martell laughed and purposely repeated Dunn's words. "Yeah, no, I don't think so."

"You know, maybe that *would* be a good idea," Phoebe told Martell. Not only would this prove to Dunn that she was not afraid of him, but it would give them a chance to talk privately. Not that she'd necessarily be able to share anything she learned with Martell, considering client-attorney privilege.

Still, she might find out exactly what was going on. As in, who was this Conrad that Dunn had asked about, back in the interview room. She didn't believe his *mutual acquaintance* explanation for one hot second.

"Feel free to follow," Dunn told Martell. "After Pheebs and I talk we'll stop and all have lunch."

And *that* was when Phoebe should have realized that something was up. For him to have gone from a cold *No deal,* back in the prison, to a friendly *Feel free to follow, we'll all have lunch* was completely ridiculous.

But the reasonableness and ease with which Dunn spoke those words fooled her, and she turned and opened the driver's side door of her new car.

Phoebe's shiny new car—a gift to herself for nailing the job at BH&S—had a keyless entry that she adored. She no longer had to dig to find her car keys at the bottom of her bag; she just had to touch the handle, and her car door would unlock. Likewise, she just had to toss her bag onto the passenger seat, and the car would sense the presence of the nearby key, and start with a touch of a button.

It was fabulous.

After she unlocked her car, she climbed in behind the wheel. The door hung open as she focused on balancing her bag on the armrest between the two front seats and clearing the wrappings from a quickly grabbed breakfast off the passenger seat to make room for her newest client.

And this meant that she was completely surprised by what Dunn did next.

He moved inside of the open car door, and she sensed more than saw his sweatshirt and plastic sack of God-knows-what whizzing past her head as he threw it into the back, as almost simultaneously he put his left hand beneath her thigh, and his right hand between her lower back and the seat.

"Hey!" Phoebe heard herself say as he seemingly effortlessly lifted her up and tossed her over the armrest. She landed butt-first in the passenger seat, her feet tangling with the steering wheel only briefly, because he was there to help her get them free.

Her surprise was echoed by Martell, who shouted, "Dunn! Stop! What the hell!" from the parking lot.

But Ian Dunn was already behind the wheel, door closed and locked, car started and in motion.

"I'll drive, okay?" he said in that very same reasonable, friendly voice, as he peeled away from Martell, a spray of dust and gravel making the other man turn away to protect his eyes.

"No, it is *not* okay!" Phoebe watched out of the back window as Martell sprinted for his own car, no doubt to give chase.

"Better fasten your seatbelt," Dunn told her calmly as he gunned it out of the lot and onto the equally ill-repaired road.

"This is *exceedingly* not okay," Phoebe said as she belted herself in, reaching to pull her bag up from the floor, where it had fallen when she'd been jettisoned from the driver's seat. "In fact, this fits the definition of felony kidnapping!"

"Not if you tell me it's okay if I drive," Dunn pointed out, glancing at her as he adjusted the seat, pushing it all the way back, as far as it could go. Even then his legs were clearly too long, and he shifted to get as comfortable as he could.

"I am *not* going to tell you it's okay if you drive," she sputtered, even as she reached one hand into her bag, feeling for . . . "It's my car, and I was driving, and you physically accosted me, which makes it—"

"Kidnapping," he finished for her. "I get it. So have me arrested and send me back to prison. Oh, wait. That's exactly what you *don't* want to do."

"Stop this car," she said, aiming her handgun at him, right through the leather of her bag. "Right now, Mr. Dunn, or I will shoot."

She had to admit that it must've looked ridiculous, like she was only pretending she had a weapon and was in fact doing nothing more than pointing her finger at him. But she knew that getting the Glock out of the bag would mean temporarily not aiming it at him—during which time he could easily take it from her. Even while driving. He was, after all, a former Navy SEAL.

Dunn looked from her face to the bag and back into her eyes before he returned his attention to the road, even as he shook his head. "Nah," he said. "You're not going to shoot me. I mean, seriously, Pheeb, if you were really going to do that, you would've pulled the trigger before I got the car up to speed. You do it now, you'll probably die, too, you know, in the fiery crash? But if it makes you feel better—more in control—by all means, keep your *weapon*"—he made quotation marks with his fingers even as he held on to the steering wheel with the palms of his hands—"securely aimed at me."

"What is *wrong* with you?"

Dunn glanced at her again and sighed. "For starters, my mother was sixteen when I was born, my father barely older. He already had a criminal record which made it impossible to find work, so he got in too deep with a gang of total, well, assholes, if you'll pardon my French. There's no other word for them, at least not less offensive. Anyway, *that* nearly killed him, but it didn't quite, so now he was a one-legged ex-con—yeah, *that* sucked—who *really* couldn't find a job, so when I was three, he trained me to gain entry of houses through doggy doors—"

"That's *not* what I meant," Phoebe interrupted, but then interrupted herself. "When you were *three?*"

"Well, three and a half," Dunn said as if that were better.

"God! That's child abuse." She caught herself. He was trying to distract her. "What I meant was . . ." She took a deep breath and rephrased. "There's just no way someone in your alleged position wouldn't be grateful to be released early. Therefore you had a reason to want to stay in, which I really hope you will share with me, so I can work with you, and whichever agency you're working for, to find a solution for this problem with Mr. Griffin."

He'd adjusted the rearview mirror, and was now fixing the ones on the sides as well. He seemed to be a very good driver, except for the fact that he was going much too fast.

"I'm not working for any agency," he said, completely unapologetically. "Good guess, but no. You're wrong about that. I can't tell you anything more. If I did, well, I'd have to kill you."

He spoke the words so casually, as if he were joking, his eyes on the road in front of them. But just the same, Phoebe knew he meant it at least as a partial threat. An intentional reminder that he was a dangerous man, regardless of the fact that she was the one in possession of a weapon.

"No, you wouldn't have to," she told him, choosing not to let his statement go unchallenged. "As your lawyer, you can tell me anything."

He glanced at her again. "You're not my lawyer."

"Yes, I am."

"No, you're not."

This was petty. And childish. "Yes, Mr. Dunn, I am."

"Really?" he asked. "We're going to keep this up? Because you're not my lawyer, Jerry is."

"I don't have anything else to do while being abducted," she pointed out. "Except defend the fact that, yes, while Mr. Bryant is unavailable, I am your attorney. At least slow down so Mr. Griffin can follow us more easily."

"It's not a fact, because I never agreed to it." Dunn didn't slow down.

"Yes, you did," she countered. "You called me your *cute new lawyer* in the parking lot."

"That was bullshit," he said with another glance at her. "Not the cute part, the lawyer part. You're very cute. But bullshit doesn't count." He added, "I *do* have something else to do right now. I need to use your phone."

She hugged her bag more tightly to her chest. "Am I or am I not your lawyer?" she asked, adding, "No bullshit this time."

Dunn actually laughed. "You're freaking kidding me."

"If you're my client, Mr. Dunn, you can use my phone," she told him as matter-of-factly as she could manage. "If you're my kidnapper, you can't."

"This is *not* okay!" Martell shouted at the ass-end of Phoebe's zippy new car as he waddled down the road after them in his ancient and ailing POS.

He'd had the money for a new car, and he'd had the make and model of the shiny all picked out. But then his sister's youngest son had gotten sick. And while the hospital bills were covered—hallelujah—the time that Denise spent at Jamie's bedside during his chemotherapy had resulted in her losing her job. Martell's brother-in-law had been ready to get a second job to keep their mortgage paid, but that would've meant he'd never see his child during what might well be Jamie's last few months on earth. So Martell stepped in. His new car could wait.

He'd been karmically rewarded by the boy's improved health. Even though Jamie wasn't out of the woods, his cancer was shrinking in response to his treatment. Martell thought of him—and prayed for him—whenever he drove his piece-of-shit anywhere. And he drove around a lot. Because he worked for himself, he used his car as a rolling office. He damn near lived in the thing.

But it did what he needed it to do, got him where he needed to go. He was, after all, a lawyer now. Car chases, like this one, were no longer a part of his job description.

At least that's how it should have been.

"*Son* of a *bitch!*"

This was all Ric's fault, and now that his longtime friend was no longer kicking at death's door, Martell could properly put blame where blame was needed.

Although the hard truth was that this situation was his own sorry fault.

"Just say no," he shouted in frustration as Ian Dunn took a sharp left and Phoebe's car vanished from his line of sight. "Why can't I learn to just say no?"

By the time he got down there and made that same left, sure enough, the other car had already disappeared. But this was the way to the interstate—there was no question that that was where Dunn was heading. North or south, though, *that* was the big mystery.

Martell pulled over to the side, his AC wheezing

as it tried to keep the air in the car below eighty degrees. Tried and failed. He unlocked his cell phone and scrolled through his list of contacts. He found Phoebe's cell number and dialed.

It rang once, twice, three times, but she didn't pick up, and she didn't pick up, and it finally went to voice mail.

"This is Martell Griffin. Call me when you get this," he said, just barely managing to squeeze out a "please," before he hung up. This wasn't her fault.

And she *was* the guy's lawyer. He wouldn't hurt her. Martell hoped. He called her home phone—she'd given him that, too, back when she'd surprised him by showing up at the prison this morning. He left the same message, then briefly shut his eyes as he forced himself to breathe and to remember that Ian Dunn hadn't been convicted of a crime in which anyone had been injured. Despite the damage he'd done to the cars parked outside of that bar, he wasn't known for having a temper—in fact the opposite was true. He had a reputation for being ultra-chillaxed and low-key. At least when he wasn't drinking.

Still, the man was a former Navy SEAL, which meant that he knew how to kill quickly and efficiently, in ways that Martell could only imagine.

But hell, *how* he could imagine . . .

Martell had met plenty of SEALs and former SEALs while doing the occasional odd job for Ric, and they were holy-mother-of-*what-the-fuck* crazy—every single one of 'em.

Start with the fact that the training they went through to become a Navy freaking SEAL was just shy of torture—carrying telephone poles up and down the beach and into the freezing surf; running, running, always running, in full combat gear on soft sand; jumping out of airplanes and waiting until they nearly hit the ground before opening their chutes; swimming, miles and miles when they weren't fricking running; exiting submarines via torpedo tubes—yeah, that shit was full-frontal insane. And that's what they did in the morning, before they had lunch.

The training didn't end when they became honest-to-bejesus SEALs and won their freaky little eagle-shaped pin to which they gave the extremely irreverent name of "Budweiser" despite the fact that it meant the world to them. Yeah, that's when it all got even harder. And that's also when they went out into what they called the *real world* and saved people from pirates, and ended the terror-reigns of dickheads like Osama bin Laden.

And *that* was what they called just another Monday.

Part of the job, nothing to see, move it along . . .

Yeah, they did it all without trumpet fanfare, as a matter of course, risking life and limb, working cheerfully together in close-knit teams even if they hated one another's guts, saying shit like *The only easy day was yesterday.*

Which made it impossible, when around them, to complain about things like the meatball sub that was barely lukewarm when it had been delivered for lunch, or that boring legal brief he had to stay up into the wee hours to write because he'd procrastinated as long as he could and it was due in the morning.

Wah, wah, wah. And here he was, again, about to run crying to his evil government overlord, as Dunn had labeled Martell's contact, because another Navy SEAL had figuratively kicked his ass.

Martell fumed, pissed as much at himself as he was at Dunn, as he again scrolled through his list of contacts to the number that the FBI team leader, Jules Cassidy, had given him just a few hours earlier today, when Martell had agreed to take on this assignment.

Which was supposed to have been brief, since this job was, quote, *so freaking easy,* unquote.

Martell had worked with Jules in the past, and he hesitated before pushing the button that would place the call, not sure if being personal friends with his evil government overlord was going to make this easier or harder.

Harder. Definitely.

In fact, he could already hear the disappointment in the FBI agent's voice. *You lost him. Already.* Dude wouldn't even make it a question, and then he'd sigh. Just a small exhale, barely audible. But that would make it worse.

Still, Martell hit *call,* knowing that time was of the essence. The FBI would be able to use their high-tech computers to find the license plate number of Phoebe's car. They'd probably even be able to access satellite pictures to track and intercept it and its occupants.

The line rang once, twice, then beeped quietly—and died.

He dialed again.

Same thing.

That was weird. There was no option for Martell to leave a message—but maybe he didn't need to. Maybe the super-secure line would make a note of his cell number. And Jules or one of his FBI underlings would swiftly call Martell back.

He hoped.

He sat in his car, staring at his phone, willing it to ring.

But it didn't.

And . . . it didn't.

"Shit." So okay. He could just sit here, idling at the side of the road with his thumb up his ass. Or he could head up toward the dog track, to the low-rent motel that was the designated temporary safe house. Martell was supposed to have brought Dunn there, checked into a room, locked the door, and hunkered down to wait for additional contact.

Driving in that direction was as good a plan as any as he waited for a call back from the FBI, while praying that Ian Dunn wasn't in fact a psychotic former Navy SEAL turned serial killer who was intending to cook and eat Phoebe Kruger for lunch.

Martell put his POS back in gear and sputtered his way toward the interstate.

CHAPTER THREE

The state of Florida was huge, but sheer luck had moved Ian down to the East Northport Correctional Facility, just a few short miles from Sarasota, where his brother's family currently lived.

He floored it as he now headed north on the interstate, grateful that he didn't have to make the long drive down from the prison in Stark, and praying, as he swiftly punched Aaron's number into his cute new lawyer's phone, that his luck would hold.

But his brother didn't pick up the landline at the house. Instead, the voice mail clicked on without any kind of personalized greeting, which was good. Maybe Aaron had finally learned *some*thing about how to be invisible. Ian tapped his fingers on the steering wheel as he waited for the beep.

"Two seven zebra foxtrot," he said. "D.A., this is Eee." In addition to the verification code that they'd set up over a year ago, Ian also used their childhood nicknames, so that there would be no question in Aaron's mind who was calling. "If you're screening your calls, this is a code one, repeat *code one*. Proceed to Contact Point Charlie, repeat, CP *Charlie*."

He hung up, and then dialed Shelly's work number, but immediately got an automated message. It came through the speaker at a blaring volume as an additional *fuck you.* "The number you have dialed has been disconnected. . . ."

That wasn't good.

Ian hated surprises of any kind, and this was an unpleasant one. The main reason Aaron's family had stayed in Sarasota, less than two hours south of Clearwater where the Dellarosas were based, was Shel's job. If that had changed, Ian should've been notified during his biweekly phone call with Shelly's kickass sister Francine.

Still, there was no time to fume. He moved on, trying the burner phone number that he'd been given for Francine's next contact call, knowing that she, in turn, could call Aaron and Shel on their cells—numbers Ian didn't have, since they changed them, both regularly and randomly, as a precaution. But that line just rang and rang and rang—no doubt because it hadn't yet been activated. "Fuck."

Ian glanced over to find Phoebe watching him.

"Calling the members of your team?" she asked.

Just because Phoebe Kruger had told him that his lawyer Jerry Bryant was dealing with a personal tragedy didn't make it true.

"I don't have a team." It wasn't a lie. He didn't really—not anymore. Ian dialed Jerry's personal number at the law firm.

Phoebe was undaunted. And perceptive. "Calling the *former* members of your team?"

Ian didn't answer as the line was picked up by a woman with a British-sounding accent. "J. Quincy Bryant's line. This is Susan."

The name was common enough—it shouldn't have surprised him or affected him in any way. But it did. Because whoever this Susan was, she was *not* the Susan he wished he could talk to right now. That Susan, *his* Susan, the closest thing to a mother he'd ever had, had been dead for years. Her accent had also been an inerasable New Jersey.

"Hello?" this Susan said, a tad impatiently, despite the Julie Andrews vowels.

"Yes. Sorry. Mr. Bryant, please."

Ian heard Phoebe sigh as Susan said, "I'm so sorry, he's out of the office due to a death in the family. May I ask what this is regarding?"

"How about Ms. Kruger?" Ian asked, glancing again at Phoebe, who was shaking her head. "Can you connect me with Phoebe Kruger?"

"I'm sorry, who?" Susan asked.

"I'm a new hire," Phoebe interjected, and Ian repeated that info into the phone.

"Ah, yes," Susan said. "There she is. One moment . . ."

There was a click and then a beep and then voice mail kicked in. "This is Phoebe Kruger—"

Ian ended the call as he glanced at her again.

"Well, you are thorough, I'll give you that," she said.

"How new of a hire?" he asked.

"This is my first week."

"And who assigned you my file?"

"The office manager," Phoebe told him. "She was really upset. She said it was urgent, and she didn't know what to do. So I took the file from her. I told her I'd take care of it."

"And that you have," he said. "See what you get for being nice? Next time, head down, scurry for the far corner of the room."

She laughed her disbelief as Ian looked back at the phone.

Next up on his call list was Manny Dellarosa himself. Because maybe if Ian could tell the mob boss everything—and get him to believe it—Manny could stop this disaster before it started. Ian pulled that number, too, from the cobwebby corners of his brain, dialed it, then waited while it rang.

A male voice picked up—far too young to be Manny. "Yeah."

"Is he there?" Ian asked, following the unspoken paranoid rule of never using Dellarosa's name during a phone call or indoor conversation. It could get confusing, but in this case, he'd called Manny's private line.

"Who's this?" It wasn't Manny's asshole of a brother, Davio, either. Davio was ten years younger, but still too old to sound that youthful.

"An old friend," Ian answered. "He'll want to talk to me."

"Maybe so," the man responded, "but he can't. You must not be very close. He's in the hospital. Heart attack." Nor was it Manny's son, Vince-the-fuckup, or even crazy Davio's son Berto.

"Shit," Ian said, and glanced over to find Phoebe watching him closely. "How bad is he?"

"Stable," the man said. "In for observation."

Yeah, what else would he say? That Manny was in his seventies and in shitty shape from years of cigarettes and alcohol?

"Tampa General?" Ian asked.

"No, Sarasota Memorial. He was over on Siesta, having lunch, when he dropped."

Okay, this was not good. It meant Manny Dellarosa's army would be wandering around here in Sarasota, rather than safely committing crimes up in Clearwater.

"They didn't want to move him," the man added.

It was entirely possible that Manny was at death's door. Still, Ian knew enough not to ask who was in charge while Manny was laid up.

The answer to that was a given. Davio, Manny's psycho brother.

"I need to get a message to him," Ian said instead. "In the hospital. I need you to tell him Ian Dunn called. Tell him there's been a mistake, that Mr. Bryant and Mr. Middleworth are both unreachable, but that nothing has changed. Can you get that to him? It's an emergency."

"Lotta people have emergencies. You'll have to wait in line," the voice said, and ended the call.

"Shit."

This time Phoebe's eyebrows rose almost imperceptibly in a question, even as he became aware that the phone he was holding smelled faintly of something nice, something decidedly female. Hand lotion or shampoo or maybe just perfume, although if Phoebe was currently wearing any, it was subtle and not at all overpowering. He glanced over to find her still watching him.

"Is there anything I can do to help?" she asked, adding, "Within the confines of the law?"

"Good thing you qualified that," Ian said, as he used his thumb to dial Johnny M.'s number this time, one eye half on the road and half checking the rearview, scanning for both marked and unmarked police vehicles. Last thing he wanted was to get stopped for speeding. "Or I'd've asked you to rob the convenience store at the next exit. I mean, I could use a little cash, right?"

"There's no need to be dickish," Phoebe said as Johnny's cell phone rang.

And rang.

"Come on, come on, come on," Ian muttered. It was time for his luck to change.

" 'Lo."

At least he thought it was his former SEAL chief's trademark one-syllabification of *hello,* but Phoebe spoke simultaneously, asking, "Who do you *really* work for?"

He shot her a *shhh* look, holding up one finger in warning as he said, "Johnny?" into the phone. "It's Eee. I could use a little help."

There was silence on the other end, and Ian knew John was waiting for verification.

"Nine," Ian said.

"Zed four," Johnny responded, and Ian knew it

was really him. Forget about the fact that he knew the code—only John Murray would say *zed* instead of *zero*.

"Queen alpha four," Ian said.

And Johnny finished the sequence with "Queen bravo eighty-four, but I don't do this spooky shit anymore, sir. Kath died and I got full custody of my kid."

"I heard. I'm sorry," Ian said.

"It sucks, but . . . One day at a time, right?"

"I'm currently working the ten-seconds-at-a-time plan," Ian told him. "And I wasn't calling to talk you in, Chief, as much as I'd like that. I just need some info if you have it."

"I've been out of the loop for almost a year. Same as you, I guess."

"D.A. and Shel." Ian got to it. "Have you heard from them lately?"

"Last contact," Johnny reported with a heavy sigh, "was . . . Christmas? Yeah. I got one of those family holiday newsletters via encrypted email. Fuckin' Shel. Way to work the normal, right?"

No kidding. "Any mention of a new job or, I don't know, an impending move?"

"Nah, it was mostly about the kid. Only thing about the two of 'em was something about some race—a half marathon—that they were planning to do this spring. They bought one of those running stroller things, so they could push the kid, too."

Ian tried on the possibility that his brother's family was safely out of town. But no, that would've been too easy. "Can you send me what Shelly sent you?" he asked.

"Sorry, sir, it had some kind of security code embedded, and it self-deleted from my email account fifteen minutes after I opened it. Fuckin' Shel." He laughed again. "Good thing I read fast."

"Do you remember anything else about the race?" Ian asked. "Was it local or . . . ?"

Johnny sighed. "I don't. To be honest, I'm pretty sure Shel didn't say. I remember the part where the kid got some stomach virus on Thanksgiving and projectile vomited all the way from the dining room onto the living room sofa, like he'd medaled in some Olympic sport. I remember thinking why the fuck do you need to tell *that* to everyone you know? I mean, Merry Christmas, but Jesus Christ."

John Murray was one of the best operatives Ian had ever worked with, both inside and out of the SEAL teams. His memory was still exceptional—Ian didn't doubt that for one second.

"How about Francine?" Ian asked about Shel's sister, even though he knew she and Johnny had never really gotten along. "Have you heard from her?"

"Nope."

"Do you still have a number for Shelly at work?"

"Yup," John said, but then rattled off the same phone number that had triggered the disconnect message.

"Will you do me a huge, and text me whatever email addies you have for all three of them?" Ian asked. "And I hate to impose, but I kinda need that right away, because this is not my phone."

"You got it, sir," Johnny said. "Sorry I can't do more."

"Good luck with the kid," Ian said. "And you might want to keep your head down for a while. There're gonna be people looking for me."

"Fantastic," Johnny deadpanned. "But I'm clean. I'm the inventory manager at a building supply company. Which isn't as bad as it sounds."

"You always were a shitty liar."

"Yeah." He sighed heavily again. "It sucks, but kid's gotta eat, so what are you gonna do? Luck back at ya, LT," he said, and cut the connection.

Phoebe—Ian's cute new lawyer—was still watching him, listening at least to his side of the conversation. She held out her hand for her phone, but he shook his head and tucked it down between his legs, close to his crotch on the seat, so she wouldn't be tempted to take it back before John's text came in.

But she held up a note-sized pad and a pen and said, "I was going to write down the email addresses for you."

His first thought was that she no longer had one hand tucked inside of her giant bag, although it was still on her lap. It was the perfect time to grab it from her and disarm her—assuming that she really did have a weapon in there.

But she had the thing securely tucked between her legs and her arms and her stomach. Ian would've had to elbow her hard in the face to force her to let go, and doing so would've radically changed the semi-friendly dynamic that they'd established.

Besides, even if she had a handgun, there was no way that she was going to shoot him and make a mess in her new car. At least not as long as he didn't threaten her. Or try to elbow her hard in the face.

"Thanks," he said instead, shaking his head no, "but if there's something new that I don't already know, I'll commit it to memory right away."

She figured out why, her awareness easy to read on her expressively pretty face. "You don't want a paper trail. Except hello. Text messages live forever. If this is information you don't want public, then—"

"He'll use code," Ian told her.

"All this cloak and dagger is impressive," Phoebe said, "as you reach out to your former team members. Is it standard for the Agency?"

He glanced at her again. She was so softly sweet-looking, he had to keep reminding himself that she was a lawyer with BH&S, which put her on the same level of the food chain as a saber-toothed tiger. She was gazing back at him with expectancy and confidence in her eyes, waiting for his answer.

"If I admit that I'm Agency, will that make you want to sleep with me?" he asked.

She laughed her surprise, but couldn't hide the rush of color that tinted her cheeks. Wasn't *that* interesting? "No," she said very firmly, making sure that *he* saw that she wasn't thrown enough to break eye contact.

"Then I won't bother lying," Ian replied, with a shrug and a smile. "Sorry, sweetheart, but I work for myself, and I don't have a team."

"Which is what you'd say if you worked for the Agency," Phoebe said. "And excuse *me,* pookie-pooh, but I'm sitting right here, listening to you attempt to make contact with your team."

"See now, I'm thinking *you* probably work for the Agency," he countered. And even though he was only teasing, when the words came out of his mouth he realized that it was entirely possible that she *was* a highly trained operative in charge of monitoring his every move. She *was* remarkably unfazed by her abduction. Plus, to have her show up at the prison, as his lawyer, in place of Jerry Bryant? A brand-new hire . . . ? *That* was a classic Agency move. And sure, she *said* that she took his file from a distraught office manager, but that could've been bullshit, too.

"Where'd you work before BH and S?" Ian asked.

She laughed, because she saw right through his casual question to the interrogation that it was. "Seriously?"

"Hell, yeah. Let's hear your cover story, Agent Kruger."

"How about I just tell you the truth about my work history?"

"You say tomato, I say to-mah-to."

"Watkins Associates," Phoebe said. "A big firm up in Jacksonville. I got the job out of law school—

Boston University. Before that, I attended University of Tampa. You need more?"

"Please."

She made a disparaging noise, but continued. "I grew up in Spring Valley, New York, just north of the Jersey border. Only child, parents divorced. My mother finally remarried three years ago, my dad's out in Seattle, still trying to 'find himself.' Whatever that means. I interned out there summer before law school. All that rain, plus three winters back in Boston was enough to convince me to target the sunshine state after graduation, and take the bar exam down here."

Ian moved from the left lane all the way to the right, timing it perfectly so that he took the exit for Clark Road without using his signal or slowing down. He glanced at Phoebe. "Don't stop there."

"What else is there to tell you?" she asked, as he stopped at the red light at the end of the exit ramp. "Oh, my grandmother's sister, my great-aunt Alice, had a beach condo here in Sarasota, which is what brought me here first. Mom and Grandma and I came down for vacations, starting right after the divorce, which was when I was three. We drove down every February, and came back again for the summer. Stayed two months each year, because Mom was a teacher and had summers off. She'd get a part-time job, and I'd hang with Grandma and Alice. It was pretty great. I loved it here, and I'm glad to be back."

Ian believed her. Of course, if she were with the

Agency, her cover story would sound heartfelt and be believable. “Why,” he asked, “do you carry a handgun?”

Phoebe blinked. “That’s none of your business.”

Ian nodded. That was actually a better answer than her giving him some story about how she’d been burglarized or mugged and now yada yada yada. If she *were* Agency, she was damn good, sitting there, looking steadily into his eyes.

The phone beeped then, and the text came in, and Ian read it, deciphering Johnny’s code. Shit, these were the same email addresses that he already knew.

The traffic light finally turned green as he took out the phone’s battery and pocketed it. He then handed the neutered and GPS-free phone back to Phoebe, taking the opportunity to run his fingers across the palm of her hand and to get as much skin-to-skin contact as he could, even as he pulled out onto Clark Road. He knew it would unsettle her, regardless of who she worked for. And as long as she was with him, it was best to have her unsettled. Besides, she was smart and funny and cute as hell, even given her potential Agency status. If they actually ended up in bed, he would not complain.

“Thanks,” he told her. “FYI, your buddy Martell called a coupla times, left a coupla messages. You’ll have to call him back later. And oh, yeah. You’re fired.”

Phoebe was not surprised when Ian Dunn reneged on his *no bullshit* rule.

He'd agreed that Phoebe was his lawyer only so that she'd let him use her phone to attempt to contact his team of fellow jewel thieves: D.A., Shelly, Francine, Johnny, and some mystery man who was in the hospital—a man who knew the lawyers from her firm, and whom Ian needed to contact urgently. *It's an emergency.*

What was *that* about?

But now, as Dunn fired her yet again, she didn't argue or accuse him of being a liar. She simply nodded and told him, "I'll need that in writing." She gave him her best fake-apologetic smile. "It's the firm's policy. Surely you know that. We do a lot of criminal work, and felonious tempers do tend to flare, creating what we call *termination false positives*. And you know that old lawyers' prayer: *If the crime's misdemeanor, the perp is a weener; first-timers will quite often cry. So give me a felon, the coffers are swellin', but, God, will those bullshitters lie. Get it in writing is better than fighting, espec'ly when they shout 'You're fired!'* "

Dunn was laughing. "That's a prayer?"

"Lawyers commonly pray in nursery rhyme verse," she told him.

"Please tell me you didn't make that up on the spot," he said. "Because if you did, I may have to rethink my plan to release you as my hostage. You could be useful to have around."

"I'm not a hostage. I'm also not an Agency operative. I'm a lawyer. *Your* lawyer," she corrected him. "At least until I get that letter of termination."

"Give me some paper," Dunn said. "You must have some in your bag. It's big enough to hold a full ream. Or maybe even a case."

"Ha ha, you are *so* clever and witty, but no, sorry." Two could play the bullshit game. "It has to be written on *your* letterhead, on twenty-pound paper, linen blend with a watermark preferred. It's the firm's policy. Size twelve font, by the way. Well okay, we're a *little* more flexible about that. We'd accept eleven. Maybe ten *if* it's Times New Roman."

He glanced at her only briefly as he slowed a bit, moving into the left lane on Clark Road, as if he weren't quite certain of the turnoff he was about to make and needed to read the street signs. "I like you. You're funny and you don't take any shit. But just so we're clear, I really don't work for the Agency, or for the CIA or the FBI or even the French Foreign Legion," he said as he squinted against the glare of the afternoon sun. "I know you want to think I do. Unless, of course, your *am I with the Agency* question was only intended to throw me off of the fact that *you're* with the Agency."

"As super whiz-bang cool as that would be," she said. "I'm not the one making phone calls and being all *code one, checkpoint Charlie, queen alpha forty-seven, hike*."

"It's *Contact Point Charlie,*" he corrected her. "And if you really need to know, all of the *cloak and dagger,* as you called it, is because there are some really bad people out there who want to hurt my family."

And . . . cue the violins.

According to the research that Phoebe had done, Ian was unmarried, no children, with parents who were both deceased. His one brother, Aaron, was wanted in connection to an unsolved murder—apparently someone had been killed in his apartment—and had probably long since self-deported to South America or Thailand.

"Your family," she repeated, allowing her skepticism to ring in her voice.

She'd used her computer skills to dig into dark, shadowy corners, but had found no records of marriage or even domestic partnership. She'd found no evidence of any business or financial partnerships, either. No cosigners on Dunn's bank accounts—which were remarkably meager for someone who'd allegedly stolen tens of millions of dollars' worth of precious jewels and artwork. He owned no property, nor did he currently hold a lease on an apartment. There was a storage space in his name—the smallest one available—in a town just north of Gainesville, but it was paid for yearly, via direct transfer from his bank account.

Perhaps most importantly, Phoebe had discovered that no one had visited him, not even once, during the nine months he'd spent in prison. Not even this D.A. and Shelly that he seemed so concerned about. Of course he might've had phone contact with someone—she hadn't been able to check those records yet.

Still, when Dunn glanced at her again and said,

"Yup. My family," she felt a ping of doubt—mostly due to that research she'd done about SEALs and their teams. Ian Dunn may not have had a family according to traditional definitions, but despite his denial, he definitely still had a team.

He'd also just pulled onto a side street and into a quiet little neighborhood of modest single-story houses, all with postage-stamp-sized, neatly kept yards. It was the perfect place for someone's perfect little Brady Bunch family to live.

And, okay. Just because she'd found no public records didn't mean this man didn't have a wife and ten kids, all using fake names.

Dunn took another turn, putting them onto a cul-de-sac called Monteblanc Circle. He then pulled up outside of a lovely little two-level house—the only one with two stories in the neighborhood—that had been painted a rich shade of golden beige which, with the orange-and-pink-streaked barrel-tile roof, made the place look like a tiny Spanish hacienda. Unlike the green-lawned houses that surrounded it, its yard was classic Florida xeriscape—palm trees and just a few flowering plants growing from beds of mulch, surrounded by the gleaming brightness of crushed white shells. The number *24* was displayed in shiny black numerals on the stucco wall next to the front door.

Maybe Ian Dunn didn't have a lot of cash in his bank account, because it was all in the account of his common-law spouse. Francine? Or Shelly. Or even D.A. . . .

As if he'd read her mind, he said, "Family doesn't have to be validated by a marriage license, or a birth certificate, or even related by blood. Although in this case, it is." He sighed as he put her car in park, and then added, "In a perfect world, Pheebs, I would simply get out and let you return to your previously scheduled life. But this is not a perfect world."

"Which is just as good," Phoebe pointed out, "because there's too much at stake here for me to just wave good-bye and drive away."

"You're really not afraid of me, are you?" He seemed bemused.

"I *am* holding my Glock on you, Mr. Dunn."

"What kind of Glock?" he asked.

"A great, big, shiny one," she told him.

"Hah!" he said. "Mistake! Glocks aren't shiny."

He was right. Hers was a dull black so that it wouldn't reflect light.

"I was using the Joss Whedon–approved use of the word *shiny,*" Phoebe told him calmly. "It means *cool* or *sweet* and not necessarily literally shiny. FYI, I've got the girly Glock—the nineteen. It's slightly smaller and lighter, but still a nine millimeter and very effective, particularly at close range."

"My lawyer is pretty, but very bullshitty, the truth is whatever will fly," he said. "And I *did* just make that up."

"Well, that's obvious," she said scornfully. "*Bullshitty* is weak."

"No worse than *weener*. I need you out of the

car, please," he said. "With your bag, and whatever arsenal is in there. Including your magic car keys."

"So you really *don't* want me to drive away," she clarified. "Although you might want to reconsider the fact that I won't shoot you while you're in my new car, for obvious hygienic reasons. But as soon as we're both out on the street . . ." She shrugged expansively as she opened the car door. "All bets are off."

Dunn opened the driver's side door, but waited to put a foot out on the ground until she'd done the same. "Not all of them. I'm going to bet that, as my lawyer, you'll choose *not* to shoot me. In fact, I'm so confident, I'll thank you in advance. Thank you."

"So now I'm your lawyer again," Phoebe said as they got out of the car slowly and carefully, with Ian mirroring each of her movements. She looked at him over the roof. She'd almost forgotten how tall he was. "That's convenient."

"Don't slam the door," he ordered, but then quickly added, "Please. Close it as quietly as you can."

"Who exactly are we sneaking up on?" she asked as she did just that, first pulling the strap of her bag over her head so it crossed her chest, her right hand still inside of it, her finger through the Glock's trigger guard. Not because she was going to use it—she doubted he'd give her reason to—but because if her hand hadn't been in her bag, he probably would've tried to take the weapon from her. And he definitely would have succeeded. "D.A., because Shelly's at work?"

"We're sneaking up on the very angry people who are going to try to kill me," he told her quite matter-of-factly as he led the way up the mottled pink brick pavers of the driveway, and around to the side of the house, past the attached single-car garage, where he stopped at the gate of a tall white fence. "The people who got an agitated phone call the nanosecond the paperwork about my release went into the prison system. They don't live here—you're right. D.A. and Shelly do. But it's entirely possible that the angry people got here first. Of course, maybe they're merely on their way."

"Do they have names, these angry people?" Phoebe asked as she followed. The fence's gate was secured with a combination padlock. It was small and inexpensive—the kind she'd had for her bike when she was in middle school.

"They do," Dunn said as he opened the lock easily—clearly he knew the combination. He turned to glance down at her, and again she was struck by his height.

As a tall woman, she wasn't used to tilting her head up for eye contact during a conversation. It was hard to decide which was more disconcerting—that, or the fact that his eyes were such a bright shade of blue.

He went through the gate first. It was designed to close automatically, with a powerful spring in the hinges, and he looked back to be sure she had her hand against it before he let go, so she wouldn't get smacked in the face.

"Might one of their names be Conrad?" Phoebe asked as she followed him down a path of those same pink pavers. It led around the side of the house, past a pair of pristine trash containers, past the softly purring equipment for the house's central air, and the louder whirring in-ground pool pump. "Or was that question that you asked back in prison just more code? You say *Are you a friend of Conrad's?* And if we answer with *The Hot Pocket is in the microwave,* you know you can trust us to . . . what?"

The same white crushed shells that were in the front yard were on either side of the path, and everything was kept almost ridiculously clean—no spiderwebs or even stray fronds from the palm trees. Whoever lived here—cousin D.A. and his wife Shelly? Lover Shelly and their son D.A.?—was meticulous, if not full-on anal.

Again, Dunn didn't bother to answer her. Instead, he put his finger to his lips, then held his hand out in a gesture that said *wait.*

So they waited. He was clearly listening—for what, Phoebe had no idea. Maybe for sounds of movement from the backyard or the house, maybe to see if they'd triggered some kind of alarm . . .

Whatever the case, they stood there for a long time before Dunn finally moved. He then opened the door to the screened-in pool cage that extended across the entire back of the house, again holding it for her so that she could follow.

He put his fingers to his lips again, and she

complied by making sure the screen door didn't slap shut.

It was pretty back there, with more of those pink brick pavers and a massive kidney-shaped pool with sparkling blue water that was deep enough to allow for a diving board. A double lounge chair with comfortable-looking blue cushions and an outdoor dining setup were beneath two umbrellas in matching shades of blue. It was cool and peaceful—and secluded. The screen of the pool cage was completely enclosed by a high white privacy fence that was nearly hidden in some places by the thick, lush vegetation of a tropical garden.

No one was out there. It was deserted.

The back wall of the house was made up of a series of huge sliding glass doors. Dunn went down the line, tugging on the handles, but all were securely closed and locked.

"Or is the name of the dangerous people who want to kill you perchance Dellarosa?" Phoebe whispered as she watched him.

It was purely a fishing expedition, but before the name had completely left her lips, Dunn had moved. Fast.

One second he was peering into the house through the glass, hands cupped around his face to cut the glare, and the next he had her up against the stucco-covered wall, his body pressed against her, his left hand down in her bag, his fingers around her wrist, tight enough that she inadvertently released her grip on her Glock.

"Who the hell are you?" he asked, his voice a gruff whisper.

And okay. *Now* she was a little bit scared. Not a lot, because he wasn't cutting off her air. He didn't have her by the throat—instead, his forearm was against the upper part of her chest, up around her collarbone, keeping her shoulders securely pressed against the wall. But he was big and powerful, with an intensity that lit his eyes and hardened the planes and angles of his face.

He had two scars, she noticed, since his face was just a few scant inches from hers. One was up near his left eyebrow, the other on his chin. Neither was big nor particularly noticeable, but they made him seem oddly real. They gave him a sense of history; of life lived well—or at least lived with some amount of abandon or gusto.

Which was interesting, considering the whole not-cutting-off-her-airway thing.

This was a man who was always and absolutely in complete control.

Even when she'd riled him, as she'd done with her mention of the Dellarosas.

Which made her realize that maybe Martell was right about using the threat from the mob boss as leverage.

"What do you know about my connection to the Dellarosas?" Dunn asked her. "Can you or someone from your firm contact Manny Dellarosa for me? Or did his brother Davio send you?"

CHAPTER FOUR

Aaron returned from the grocery store to find a strange car parked in front of his house.

It was a nice car. Dark color—not quite black, not quite gray, fuel efficient but capable of getting up to speed when needed. Brand-new model, still had a trace of glue on the back window where the sticker had been.

He didn't slow, didn't falter. He just kept going around the cul-de-sac and went out the way he'd come, into the neighborhood, heading back toward the main road.

The car had been empty, with no one inside to see him and follow. That was good at least.

Aaron had also made note of the fact that whoever had been formerly driving that car wasn't sitting on his front stoop, waiting for him to get home.

No doubt they'd already overridden the security system and let themselves in through the back.

He was calm and thinking clearly, even though the world had gone into high-def around him—a sign that his body was creating large amounts of adrenaline. He glanced in the rearview mirror at Rory, who was fast asleep in his car seat, a goofy smile on his sweet little face as he dreamed about something good. Rice cereal or sweet potatoes. They'd yet to give him ice cream. They were taking their time introducing potential allergens, because

Shelly had been allergic to everything as a little kid. Food allergies ran in the family.

Aaron turned right on Clark, realizing that he'd already figured out where to go, what to do. Drop the little man at Shelly's sister Francine's apartment, then circle back around on foot, to try to get a look at the owner of that mafia-black vehicle.

Of course, if Davio Dellarosa or his thugs had found the house where Aaron and Shelly lived, it was possible they'd also found Francie's apartment, too, so he got out his phone and called her.

It rang once. Twice.

"Come on, come on, come on," he muttered. His sister-in-law currently worked nights—legitimate nights, waiting tables at a twenty-four-hour restaurant right off the interstate—but she'd be awake by now, wouldn't she . . . ?

"Hello?"

"France," he said. "It's Aaron. Are you okay?" As soon as he asked, he realized why Ian had been such a stickler for what had seemed like clandestine bullshit. How exactly was she going to answer that question with her phone on speaker, some asshole's gun against her head? *No, genius, I'm not okay . . . ?*

Knowing Francie, she'd get herself killed, shouting out the truth, or yelling for him to save himself.

He quickly spoke over her with Ian's code, saying, "You still looking to moonlight as a dogsitter, cuz I just met a guy at the gym who's going out of town."

At the exact same time, she was already answering his question with a question, "What's going on?" And then she realized what he was saying, so she cut him off with, "Yes, I'm supposed to say *yes,* right? If I'm alone and I'm safe, it's *yes,* or shit, maybe it's *what kind of dog does he have, because I don't do* . . . I forget. Pit bulls, which is stupid because I like pit bulls. They're misunderstood."

"Close enough," Aaron said. "I'm pulling into your driveway. Get your ass down here. Bring your bug-out bag."

"Fuck!" she said. This was an occasion where Shelly wouldn't bitch about Francine's potty mouth, because the word was entirely appropriate. "No way! Not now! It doesn't make sense, I *just—*" She cut herself off. Started over. "What happened? What's going on?"

Aaron told her about the car parked in front of the house. "Plus I got a phone call hang-up this morning."

"God *damn* it!" She came out of her second-floor apartment, carrying a bag that was barely larger than a school lunchbox, which really shouldn't have been that big of a surprise. It was Shel whose bug-out bag was the size of Texas, even though it was supposed to be necessities only—something you could grab, and go. "We're supposed to be safe."

"Apparently that was just wishful thinking." Aaron got out of the car and cut the phone connection as she came down the stairs and moved into normal conversation range.

She was wearing . . . What the hell was she wearing? Pink boxers and a nearly transparent tank top, beneath which she wasn't wearing a bra. At least she wasn't wearing it in the traditional way. She had one looped around her neck like a doctor's stethoscope. She also had a pair of jeans and a T-shirt hanging over her arm. She'd managed to put on her socks and sneakers, although the laces flopped about, untied.

No doubt about it, with those assets, even with her blond hair in a fuzzy braid and no makeup on her almost ridiculously beautiful face, she could have made a fortune in Hollywood.

Truth was, Shel's sister Francine was the best driver Aaron had ever met—and that included his Navy SEAL brother. She was no slouch when it came to security, either. Rory was safe in her capable hands.

"I haven't even showered yet," she grumbled, as she threw her bag into the back, next to Roar's car seat. "I smell like feet, ass, and onions rings." She realized that he was holding open the driver's side door for her. "Where are *you* going?"

"You remember where the safe house is?" Aaron asked.

"Yeah, but I'm not going to say it out loud," she countered, narrowing her eyes at him. "Especially since we're going there together. Right?"

He shook his head. "I'm going back to take a look." She started to argue, but he cut her off. "Only a look. I'm not stupid."

"That's arguable. But I'm not going to tell you what to do—only what I'd do. What your brother would want us to do. Which is get the fuck out of here. Fast."

"Yeah, well, Ian's not exactly here, is he?"

"It's common sense. We get to safety, then regroup."

"And what happens if, after we regroup and go back to investigate, the car's already gone?" Aaron asked. "Do we just stay away from the house, never go home again, in case it *was* Davio? Maybe someone just parked in front of the wrong house." But as he said those words, he didn't believe it. "I'll go, I'll look, I'll meet you. Soon."

"Suit yourself." Francie shook her head in disgust as she tossed her clothes onto the passenger seat—with the exception of the bra which she now fastened, backward, the clasp around her waist. She twisted it so that the cups were facing forward, and she tried to pull it up underneath her tank top—or maybe she *didn't* try, at least not very hard—to keep it all under cover. With Shel's sister, anything was possible.

But accident or not, she very definitely flashed him a nipple in the process, then laughed at whatever strangled noise had come out of his throat.

"You know, you could've married *me,*" she teased him as she climbed behind the wheel.

Aaron said what he always said when she got obnoxious. "Only in your dreams, Angel-cake." He closed the door, and she rolled her eyes and laughed derisively up at him through the open window, same as she always did.

This time, though, neither her laughter nor her tough-guy attitude hid the cloud of worry in her eyes. "I love you. Be careful."

"I will. Text Shel. Three words: *Code one. Charlie.* Then shut off your phone. Completely. You know the drill, France."

She nodded. "Way better than you, babe."

Aaron looked past her at Rory, who was still sound asleep in his seat, still dreaming about things that made him smile.

"We'll be okay," Francie said, and he nodded and turned to go, but she caught his wrist. "No unnecessary risks. And FYI, that car could be the police. Looking for *you*."

Aaron was well aware of that. He almost got in beside her. Almost. But he had to go and look. He had to know.

"If we need to move on, well, then we'll move on," Francine told him. "A full year is a pretty good run. Especially since we're living practically in the motherfucker's backyard. You know that, right?"

"Yeah," Aaron said. "I do know. Text Shel, then go."

She nodded again, reaching for her phone as Aaron turned and set off at a quick jog back toward his house. As much as he wanted to, he couldn't sprint. Last thing he needed was to get stopped by the cops for being large and running without sneakers on.

He knew all the cut-throughs—the backyards without fences or pool cages—because he made a point to run the route every few weeks. Sometimes he did it under the cover of night, sometimes during the day. He knew all the obstacles and all of the alternatives, and in a short amount of time, he was back behind the very solid white fence that provided him and Shel and Rory with privacy. There was a reason theirs was the only house in the neighborhood with a second level. They could see out, over the fence, from the master bath's window, but none of their neighbors could see in.

He'd drilled a peephole into the tough plastic wall for precisely this reason, although he never went onto the patio without checking to be sure the hole was properly corked.

Because a large man could stand on their neighbor's side of the fence and be completely hidden from view by the shrubbery and tropical plants that grew in their garden.

Exactly where he was standing right now.

Hoping that a spider wasn't on the verge of crawling down his shirt, and that the lush vegetation didn't include poison ivy or one of its tropical cousins, Aaron used his pinkie to push the tiny cork through. He could imagine it falling, near-silently, into the flowering shrubs that lined his side of the barrier, in the yard just outside of the pool cage, to the right of the house. The previous owners had used the contained outdoor area for a dog run, and after Rory got a little bit older, he and Shel had been planning to do the same. Get a dog, or better yet, get two. Butch and Sundance. Shelly already had their names picked out.

Stick around for a few decades.

Grow up and grow older here, together, in their beautiful home.

Christ, this was his *home*. For the first time in his life, Aaron had *had* a home that was really and truly his own.

Francie's words echoed in his head. *If we need to move on, well, then we'll move on.*

A year *was* a pretty good run, considering that he and Shel had been nomads for so long, first in the Marines, and then working for Ian. But Aaron had wanted more. He'd wanted happily-ever-after.

He closed one eye and brought the other to the tiny peephole, expecting to see nothing but an open or broken door, assuming that whoever belonged to that car was already inside his house.

Instead, she was right there, lurking near the slider to the kitchen—a woman. And even though she didn't look like any mob hit man Aaron had ever seen, he could tell, immediately, that she was carrying. Her hand was in her bag and she held herself at ready. Her clothing was dark—the kind of outfit that a businesswoman might wear. The better for getting lost in a crowd after a gangland-style execution.

Her shoes were . . . stupid. Really nice and extremely expensive, but they were not designed for running or even moving swiftly, and it was this that made the hair on the back of Aaron's neck rise even more.

Whoever she was, she was confident that she wouldn't have to run. Not even a little bit, not ever.

She came, she killed, she slowly strolled away.

As he planned his next move—she would hear him if he took her photo with his phone, so he worked to change its settings to silent—she said something. Her voice was too low for Aaron to make out her words, but he put his eye back to the peephole so he could look at her again. And he realized that she wasn't alone, because she wasn't on the phone—she wasn't wearing a Bluetooth or any other kind of headset. And he realized in a flash of horrified dismay that Ian was with her—his brother was here!—and that she must've had him at gunpoint.

Except Ian moved toward her so quickly that she didn't have time to aim her weapon and fire. He pushed her hard against the wall in a full body slam that made Aaron's teeth hurt in sympathy. He knew exactly what that felt like—although he wasn't too sympathetic because his brother had just essentially disarmed his captor.

Ian said, "Who the hell *are* you?" Those words came through clearly. The next part was harder to hear, *what do you* something, then, "Or did his brother Davio send you?"

Words to make Aaron's blood run cold.

"No!" The woman's voice was low but clear.

"God, no! The Dellarosa thing was just a guess. A good one, apparently. I had no idea—"

Aaron was up and over the fence in an instant—he'd practiced that move weekly, too. But he realized, as he was in midair, his boots heading for the crunchy gravel in the dog yard, that his surprise entrance was going to be viewed by his brother as an attack, rather than the appearance of the cavalry reinforcements that it truly was.

Sure enough, Ian heard Aaron before he even hit the gravel, and did one of his Navy SEAL ninja moves, going from up in the mystery woman's face to a left-handed draw with a deadly-looking Glock. Right or left hand didn't matter—Eee could shoot the stinger off a wasp at a hundred feet in the dark. But what surprised Aaron was the fact that his brother didn't pull Dellarosa's hit woman in front of him as a shield. Instead, Eee stepped in front of the bitch, as if he were protecting *her*.

It didn't compute, but Aaron had other things to focus on—such as making sure his own older brother didn't kill his ass. As he headed for the gravel, he had to decide whether to curl down and make himself the smallest target possible, or to go big and make sure Eee recognized him, maybe by shouting out some of that verification code that his brother was so keen on using, if you could overlook all the months that he didn't bother to visit, call, or write more than one of his stupid postcards.

But Aaron didn't get a chance to say more than

“Yo, Eee!” because he didn’t stick the landing. His ankle rolled—*son* of a bitch—the pain hot and sharp. As he went down, hard, he kept his hands spread, out and empty, to show that he wasn’t armed.

The stones in the dog yard were various shades of yellows and browns, most of them round and smooth, but not round enough or smooth enough to keep from tearing the crap out of his elbow as he bounced through them a few times before skidding to a stop.

Ian had moved with him, tracking him with the business end of the sidearm that he didn’t fire and he didn’t fire and . . . The expression on Eee’s face didn’t change. He didn’t blink, didn’t smile, didn’t otherwise move a muscle, he was so in the moment. But Aaron knew that he’d been recognized because his brother lifted the barrel of the weapon and turned his attention back to the woman, who’d taken advantage of the few seconds of chaos to make a break for the door that led out of the pool cage and around to the other side of the house.

Ian stashed the Glock in the back waist of his jeans, his movement deliberate and calm in comparison to the woman’s flurry of panicked flight. Just a few steps and a turn and he caught her by the arm, and he used her own momentum to swing her back around.

Those shoes she was wearing were definitely not made for running. As Aaron watched, pushing himself up and onto his feet—ouch—she tripped or maybe slipped on the pavers that surrounded the pool.

And instead of catching her, steadying her, and keeping her from falling, Ian put his other hand on her real-woman-sized butt and pushed, giving her lift—enough so that she went, pinwheeling and flailing, shoulder bag and all, into the pool.

Splash.

It was only then that Ian turned to Aaron and said, “Hey, D.A. Nice to see you.”

He’d pushed her in.

Ian Dunn had pushed her into the swimming pool.

Phoebe sputtered and coughed as she flailed her way up to the surface. Her wet clothes were heavy and she only managed to get a quick bit of air before the water closed over her head again.

She was in the deep end, and it was pretty freaking deep, and she struggled to get the strap of her bag up and over her head, because it was helping to weigh her down. She wasn’t a particularly strong swimmer to start with, and the cut of her jacket made it hard to move her arms, so she kicked her feet, which did little more than dislodge her shoes. Still she somehow again broke surface, and she tried to see which way she needed to swim to get to the shallow end, but she ended up gulping water instead of air, which was not good.

“Oh, for the love of God,” she heard Dunn say before she went under again.

There was *no way* that she was going to drown in

someone's backyard swimming pool, but now she was gagging and choking, her lungs burning, and the urge to inhale was strong even though she was underwater, and she had to get back to the surface, but she couldn't.

And the consternation and annoyance she was feeling took a solid turn into a flash of full panic—holy God, was she *really* going to drown in someone's backyard swimming pool?—when she suddenly felt Dunn join her in the pool with a rush of force and bubbles.

She felt his arms go around her and he unceremoniously hauled her up out of the water so she could breathe. Air, air, real air! She flailed as she coughed and spat and choked, and the terror wasn't gone because she still couldn't stand and there wasn't much of Dunn to grab onto because he had her from behind in a rough version of a lifeguard hold. She felt him pull her through the water, and even though she couldn't see much of anything through eyes that were both stinging from chlorine and tearing from the coughing that still wracked her, she tried not to fight because she knew he had to be taking her to the side of the pool. And sure enough, he kept one arm around her, looped just under her arms, as he grabbed for the edge to keep them from both going under again.

And still, Phoebe could do little more than cough and wheeze and hack as her lungs burned and she replaced water with air, thank God. She felt Dunn maneuver his leg beneath her, attempting to support her butt with his rather massive thigh, as if she weighed little more than a child.

It served to boost her up a bit more out of the water, which was good, except when he tried to loosen his hold on her, which made her turn toward him in alarm and grab him more tightly.

Before jumping in to rescue her, he'd taken off his shirt and his jeans and probably his boots as well, and her hands slipped against the wet smoothness of his shoulders and back. He was a large man, and there was a lot of smooth skin beneath her fingers, covering a vast expanse of very firm muscles.

"I got you," Dunn said into her ear. "You're good." His voice changed then, and Phoebe knew that he was talking to the man who'd come over the back wall—the one that Dunn had drawn her Glock on before he'd tossed her into the pool. Why on earth had he tossed her into the pool? "Who the hell lives in Florida but doesn't learn to swim?"

"I know how to swim. I just don't do it particularly well," she tried to protest, but her voice was weak and the man who was outside the pool spoke over her.

"Who the hell buys a house in Florida—in cash," he said, with a ton of snark in his tone, "but then doesn't live in it for more than a few days before vanishing off the face of the earth?"

"I'm fine, thanks," Dunn said. "How are *you?*" He didn't wait for the other man to respond. "Help me get her out of here." He spoke into her ear again. "Come on, honey. Loosen your death grip on me, and use those hands of steel to grab onto my brother, Aaron."

His *brother?*

Phoebe looked up, way up, at the man standing at the edge of the pool. Up closer like this, even without her glasses, which were now at the bottom of the pool, she could see that he was younger than Dunn by quite a few years. His hair was shorter and lighter, and his eyes were more green than blue. And even though he was tall, he wasn't quite as super-sized. He was more sculpted, more . . . elegant. More slender and beautiful and less raw-boned. Less Stone Age and more Bronze Age—but still the kind of man who enjoyed living in a cave. He was completely, obviously, *absolutely* Ian Dunn's brother.

"Aaron, Phoebe." Dunn kept the introductions cursory. "Phoebe, Aaron."

With a great deal of unhidden disgust, Aaron held out his hands and Phoebe let go of Dunn and reached for him. He took her by the wrists, and she did the same, and with Dunn pushing from the pool, she was up and out of the water and plopped inelegantly down onto the pink brick pavers, still working to spit the last of the chlorinated water out of her raw and burning lungs as her hair dripped into what was surely her makeup-streaked face.

Former SEAL that he was, Dunn wasn't going to need any assistance getting out of the pool, and Aaron didn't try to help, instead stepping back so as not to get splashed. But Dunn first dove to the bottom to collect her glasses, and then her bag and shoes, which he set beside her—as if they weren't completely ruined and useless. Her phone, her wallet, the files she'd taken for one of the other cases she was supposed to be simultaneously working on . . .

"You pushed me in," Phoebe accused him in a voice that was raspy and raw as she put her glasses on with shaking hands, while he used the edge of the pool to thrust himself up and out, water sheeting off of him.

She expected him to deny or at least make excuses: *It was an accident; I tripped; I didn't mean to . . .* But instead he said, "Yup. Sorry. It had to be done," as he used his hands to squeegee off his face and push back his unruly hair.

From her vantage point, looking up at him through the water-spotted and slightly blurry lenses of her glasses, he was quite literally larger than life. Right at that moment, with his hands up on his head, his muscular chest bare, and his boxer shorts clinging to him in a most revealing way, water matting the hair on his chest and his legs and his eyelashes, he was ridiculously attractive. Even with his more conventionally handsome younger brother standing next to him.

Of course the fact that Aaron was looking down at her with unconcealed dislike in his pretty hazel eyes might've had something to do with it, as if she weren't a person but instead a pile of excrement left on his pool deck by a wart-covered troll with an intestinal ailment.

"Phoebe who?" Aaron was asking Dunn. "Who the hell is she?"

"Phoebe Kruger." Dunn glanced down at her. "She says she's my lawyer."

"I *am* your lawyer," she said, still in that raspy voice, taking the opportunity granted by the eye contact to ask, "It *had* to be *done?*"

But Aaron was even more incredulous than she was. "Your *lawyer* works for *Davio Dellarosa?*"

"No," Dunn said, but then corrected himself. "Well, she might. But it's more likely that she works for Manny. We just met this morning, so . . ."

"I don't," Phoebe said. "Work for Manny. Or Davio. Or any other random Dellarosa." With her ability to breathe mostly back, she started to peel her wet jacket from her shoulders—until she realized that the water had made her white blouse transparent. Neither man noticed, since Aaron had gotten way up in his brother's face.

"What the hell, Eee?" he asked. It was then that Phoebe saw that he was holding her Glock. Dunn must've put it down when he'd shucked off his jeans and boots and shirt, and Aaron had it now. He held it like he knew how to use it, which wasn't comforting at all. "You think she works for the Dellarosas, so you bring her *here* . . . ?"

"It really doesn't matter who she is or who she works for," Dunn said, wringing out his shorts as best he could.

"Damn straight, it doesn't matter," Aaron retorted. "She could be motherfucking Mother Teresa, and you *still* shouldn't've brought her here. The more people who know where we are, the more likely one of them will tell someone who'll tell someone else, who'll pass along the info to that motherfucking maniac who—"

"Probably already knows exactly where you and Shelly live," Dunn calmly finished for him. "Aaron, it doesn't matter who Phoebe is or who owns her. It doesn't matter if she does legal work for Manny Dellarosa or washes his dishes or even sucks his dick. Or does all three simultaneously. Because Manny knows. He knows, because I made a deal with him to keep you safe. He's been keeping Davio in line."

Aaron was silent at that, just staring at Dunn.

Phoebe raised her hand, her need to set the facts straight winning out over her desire not to upset the man who held her handgun. "For the record," she said, "I've never so much as *met* Manny *or* Davio Dellarosa, let alone—"

"Since when?" Aaron interrupted her to ask his brother. The expression on his face was terrible, and Phoebe closed her mouth, focusing instead on becoming as small and invisible as possible. Just as she'd had no desire to drown in someone's backyard swimming pool, she hated the bitter irony of being shot and killed with her own deadly weapon. "This deal you made . . . ?"

"I contacted Manny a year ago," Dunn told his

brother quietly. "When we realized that Pauline was going to die. I knew Davio would find her from her death certificate, if not from her medical records. And if he found her, he'd find you."

Okay, wait, who was Pauline? Dunn had mentioned a *Francine,* during his attempt to get in touch with his former teammates. But as Phoebe looked from Dunn to his brother and back, she decided now was not the time to ask.

Aaron, meanwhile, was staring at Dunn. "Jesus," he breathed. "What did you *do?* Are you actually *working* for Manny Dellarosa?"

"I am," Dunn responded, holding the other man's gaze. "At least I was. Before today's shit hit the fan."

"Jesus, Eee," Aaron said.

"I did what I had to. And it was working. The deal I made. But it all got royally fucked up today."

When Martell Griffin had handed him that so-called Get Out of Jail Free card. But the truth was, nothing was ever entirely free, was it? Especially not if Manny and Davio Dellarosa now believed that Ian had information that could hurt their family.

"Right here, right now, we've gotta go," Dunn continued. "You've gotta call Shel and go pick up your kid. We'll meet at the contact point and regroup. I'll fix this—I will. I *can*. I just need a little time. And a chance to talk to Manny." He glanced over at Phoebe at that, and she shook her head.

Despite what he believed, she did *not* have access

to Manny Dellarosa. Although, maybe her law firm did. And wasn't *that* a creepy thought?

"So everything we did, everything you put in place to keep us safe and hidden was, what?" Aaron was asking his brother. "Just one of your bullshit con jobs to keep us on a tight leash, while you sold your soul to the devil? God, I knew it—all that time. I fucking knew it!"

"No," Dunn said, as he stripped off his wet boxers. He'd apparently decided not to put his dry jeans on over them. And yes, now he was standing there buck naked, and completely unselfconscious about it. "The secrecy you maintained was insurance. Plus, I wanted to be sure that you kept your head down. The Dellarosas aren't the only ones looking for you—I'm sure you remember. And FYI, I didn't sell my soul—I just sold a little bit of my time."

As Phoebe watched through her eyelashes, Dunn pulled on his jeans, commando.

"Go inside, but be careful," he commanded Aaron. "I doubt they made it over here before me, but still . . . Get your go-bags, and while you're at it, grab something for Phoebe to change into, will you?" He threw another glance at her.

She turned her head and quickly put on her best *I absolutely wasn't looking at your naked ass* face, instead watching Aaron as he limped across the patio and over to the slider that had a keyhole.

He grimly unlocked the door, but he turned before he went into the house, and he said, "It was *my* time, too. That you sold to Manny. Or maybe you didn't think I'd notice when you vanished off the fucking face of the fucking earth, you fucking *douchebag*."

He didn't stick around to hear Dunn's rebuttal, which was a quiet but heartfelt and drawn out "Shhhhhhit."

Phoebe cleared her throat, twice, three times. But when she spoke, her voice was still froggy. "I could, um, actually use a restroom," she said. "Before we get back in the car?"

"We don't have time. You should've gone when you were in the pool," Dunn retorted.

She laughed her disbelief. "Oh, is that why you threw me in?"

"No," he said. "I had to make sure that if you were wearing a wire, it shorted out."

A *wire*.

"Unlike you, I don't work for Manny Dellarosa," Phoebe said. "Or his brother Davio or his son Vincent"—she ticked them off on her fingers—"or his nephew what's-his-name—Berto—or any other stray Dellarosas."

"Which is what you'd say if you *did* work for them," he retorted, throwing her own words back at her. Paraphrased, yes, but close enough.

"That's true," she said, which surprised him a little—she could tell. "Your brother said—and okay, tangent! There's a warrant out for Aaron's arrest in connection to an unsolved murder. As your lawyer, I *have* to advise you to convince your brother to surrender to the police—"

"That's not going to happen," Dunn said. "Davio Dellarosa wants him dead. If D.A. goes into the system for any reason at all, the Dellarosas have the connections and manpower to reach him, and I'll be burying him by Friday."

Wait a minute. "Aaron's nickname is D.A.?"

"Double a," he told her as he sat down on the lounge chair to tie up the laces of his boots, "r, o, n?"

She got it. "So Shelly's his . . . ?"

"Spouse," Dunn said, which was kind of a weird word choice, similar to saying *vehicle* for *car*.

"And who's Pauline?"

"One of Shelly's half sisters," he told her.

"And she died?" Phoebe asked.

"Last year," Dunn confirmed.

"So who's Francine?" Phoebe asked.

"Shel's other half sister," Dunn said. "The younger, not dead one."

"Big family," Phoebe said.

"Not really."

"I'm an only child," she reminded him. "So, rewind back to your brother. Aaron. Davio Dellarosa wants him dead because . . . ?"

"It's a long, ugly story," Dunn said, "and we need to get moving. Besides, I took care of that."

"By making a deal, with Manny," Phoebe said. "You went to jail, and Manny made *his* brother, Davio, stay away from *your* brother, Aaron."

"That's how it worked."

"So you became, what?" Phoebe asked. "Manny Dellarosa's Northport prison inside man?"

"No." Dunn was absolute. "I wouldn't do that. I was serving time for Manny's fuckup of a son, Vincent."

Whoa. And suddenly it all made sense. It was Vincent Dellarosa who got drunk and trashed the cars in that bar parking lot. But because Ian Dunn had made a deal to protect Aaron and his family, he'd confessed and then pled guilty to the crime.

But then it *didn't* make sense. "If you were simply doing Vincent's time," Phoebe pointed out, "then you should've been turning cartwheels at the idea of getting out early."

"It's not that simple," Dunn told her.

"Try me," she said.

There was more to this—she could see it in Dunn's eyes. But he shook his head. "Imagine if you were Manny Dellarosa, and you had a deal with me—an illegal deal—"

"I'm highly aware of the illegality," Phoebe said. "And as your lawyer, I have to advise—"

"Shh," Dunn said. "You're Manny. And I'm me. And I don't contact you. I just suddenly walk out of the prison, a free man. Aren't you going to wonder exactly what I know about you and your fuckup of a son, Vincent? What deal went down between me and the authorities? FYI, Vince currently has a homicide trial on his to-do list. I'm betting this time, Manny's not finding any takers to plead guilty for him. The death penalty really gets in the way of that."

"So you think the Dellarosas are going to believe

that you have incriminating information about Vincent," Phoebe said. "And come after you." Just as Martell had predicted. She cleared her throat. "Then the best thing to do is to get your family to safety—"

"Which is exactly what I'm doing."

"I can help," she told him. "I can contact Martell—"

Dunn had already started to laugh. "Deliver my brother to the FBI, who will immediately arrest him and charge him with murder, or even manslaughter? I don't think so."

"Did he do it?" Phoebe asked.

"Kill the guy? Hell, yeah. He protected himself—and Shelly—from a hit man that Davio sent to waste them."

"If it was self-defense," Phoebe started.

"It was."

"Then it should be easy enough to clear up," she countered.

"It should be," he agreed. "But it's not. Because the authorities can't tell their own asses from their elbows, and while they take their sweet time piecing together the facts in the case, Aaron will be sitting in jail where Davio Dellarosa will end him. So, no. I'm not putting him in that kind of danger."

When she opened her mouth to keep arguing, he stopped her.

"Look, it's not going to happen," Dunn said. "I don't trust you, I don't trust Martell. And I sure as hell don't trust the FBI. So I'm going to take care of my brother *my* way. Same way I've done ever since he was two, when our mother ODed. I'm not stopping now."

Sweet Jesus. Phoebe lowered her voice. "Aaron doesn't know you were in prison, does he?" From what Aaron had said, Ian had just mysteriously disappeared.

Dunn glanced toward the house, as if making sure Aaron wasn't within earshot before he sighed heavily. With his elbows on his knees, his hands were up on the back of his neck as if he had a headache. "No."

Apparently Dunn had disappeared right after making contact with Manny. He'd obviously stayed away from his family from that moment on—maybe to keep them from talking sense into him, maybe out of his desire to keep them safe. Phoebe could imagine the months' worth of meetings that his deal with Manny had triggered—and not just with Manny's screwup of a son to get the facts of the crime straight so that Dunn could make a believable confession, but also with the lawyers hired to guide him through the maze that was the Florida legal system. There would have been at least one deposition, a meeting to hammer out the deal in exchange for that guilty plea, a sentencing hearing—all before the start of that eighteen-month sentence.

"Mind taking my Glock away from him before you drop that anvil on his head?" she asked.

Dunn smiled slightly at that. But his smile faded.

"Do me a favor," he said quietly. "And if you're working for them—the Dellarosas—just tell me you are. And then help me get in touch with Manny, so I can clear this shit up."

"I'm not working for the Dellarosas," Phoebe said for what felt like the hundredth time. "Nor am I working for the government agency who hired Martell Griffin to convince you to save those kids. I'm your lawyer."

He was silent, just sitting there, gazing at her. When he finally spoke, he said, "I'm going to be really disappointed when you change your clothes, if there's a wire under there."

"If you think I'm going to *change my clothes,*" she said, "right here on the pool deck, in front of you, you're sadly mistaken."

Dunn shrugged expansively. "Hey, totally up to you. I asked Aaron to get you something dry to wear because I didn't think you'd want to mess up the leather interior of your new car. If you don't care about ruining it . . ."

"I need a bathroom," she reminded him.

"And I need a mango lemonade with a little umbrella in it, while I sit with my feet up on the beach at Coki Point in St. Thomas, looking out at the Caribbean for about three weeks straight."

"I'm serious."

"I am, too," he countered. "I'm not going to let you go into Aaron and Shelly's bathroom and take whatever wire you're wearing and flush it or hide it or eat it or—"

"If I were wearing a wire, edible or otherwise," she countered, "then whoever was monitoring the transmissions lost contact with me—abruptly—when you pushed me into the pool. So where are they? Where's my backup, rushing to my rescue?"

Dunn didn't respond—apparently he didn't have an answer for that. And the silence of the afternoon worked beautifully as her Exhibit A. Moments ago, there'd been birds chirping merrily from a nearby ficus tree, but even they were now still. Nothing moved, nothing stirred.

As Dunn glanced up at the tree, his eyes narrowed slightly.

"I mean, either I'm an asset or I'm not, right?" Phoebe continued. "Or—here it comes, wait for it . . . I'm telling you the truth when I say that I was never wearing any kind of wire in the first place."

It was then that Dunn launched himself forward off the lounge chair and directly at her, on top of her, pushing her with the full force of his XXL body, back into the pool.

Phoebe felt herself shouting with alarm and surprise, but the sound of her voice was drowned out by some kind of roar. And it was only right before the water once again closed over her head that she saw what looked like sprays of dust from the pool deck and from the wall of the house. And she realized instantly what that was.

Someone was shooting at them.

The birds had gone silent because someone was

out there, and Dunn had realized it and saved their lives. That roar was gunfire, the sprays of dust were from bullets digging into the stone and stucco.

She grabbed her glasses off her face and held her breath as best she could as Dunn dragged her with him, across to the far side of the sparkling water, where they'd be sheltered from the bullets by the wall of the pool. He kept her tightly against him as he pulled her up and out of the water just a little bit, just enough so that she could breathe with her head tipped back.

Her jacket was too heavy. It was pulling her down again, and she clawed to get it off while still clutching her glasses in one hand. Dunn helped her, tearing at her shirt as well—taking the opportunity to see for himself that she wasn't wearing a wire, shorted out or otherwise.

Unless, of course, it was hidden in her pants. But he didn't try to get those off of her.

"Aaron!" he was bellowing, "I need cover! At least one shooter in the tree at ten o'clock!" He swept his hair out of his face with the hand that he wasn't using to keep her anchored to him, and drops of water sprayed her as he said far more quietly but no less intensely, "When he lays down fire—big breath and a push. When we get to the other side, I'll help you out of the pool. Then we're heading for the house, for the door Aaron used. Keep moving, even when you get inside—get back, away from the glass, head for the front of the house, stay down, got it?"

Phoebe nodded, slipping her glasses back on. "I want my Glock back."

Dunn smiled at that, just briefly. "Yeah, I want your Glock back, too. *Aaron!*"

"Eee!" came his brother's answering shout from the house. "Go!"

Big breath and a push—but Phoebe did little more than draw in a lungful of air and use one hand to keep her glasses on her nose, before Dunn used his tree-trunk-like legs to push off the pool wall and propel them underwater and back toward the house. She just clung to him, along for the ride.

When they came up to the surface, she could hear Aaron laying down covering fire which meant—please God—that whoever had been shooting at them was now focused on ducking and not being killed, and was thus unable to shoot back.

Or at least she hoped so, because she was about to be a great big target.

Dunn was up and out of the pool first, quickly reaching down to grab her by both arms and pull her up, too. He could have left her there—of that she was well aware—but he didn't. She barely had her feet beneath her before they were running full-speed for the house, with Dunn shielding her as best he could.

That wasn't just her Glock making that racket—Dunn's brother was firing a second weapon, too, from the second-story window of the house. He was probably doing it double-fisted, as befitted his super-macho action-star vibe.

Dunn pushed her through the slider, but her wet feet slipped the moment she stepped onto the tile floor and she lost traction—except she didn't need it because Dunn was pushing her down, diving with her, somehow managing to be both beneath her and on top of her, skidding with her onto the floor as whoever was out there started shooting again.

And this time the bullets took out the glass doors, shattering them with a crash.

But they were still sliding, and then Dunn was pulling her with him again, scrambling farther into the house, past the kitchen island and into the main part of the great room, heading—or so Phoebe believed—for the front door.

He'd somehow managed to scoop her bag from the pool deck, which was good because it held the keys to her car. Although, shit! "The key fob's wet," Phoebe said, and the look Dunn gave her would've been comical under other circumstances, because it was clear he had no idea why she'd told him that.

"My electronic car key," she tried to explain, "went into the pool. I don't know if it's waterproof—if it'll still work to start the car."

That *was* where they were going, right? Out the front door to where her car was waiting?

But Dunn didn't open the front door. Instead he said, "It's okay," as he scrambled up to his knees and opened the door to a closet that was perpendicular to the front entrance. He pushed aside a pair of slickers—one bright yellow and the other fire-engine red.

"Come on," he said, looking right at her, reaching out to grab her hand, as if he wanted her to . . . go *into* that closet . . . ?

It was then that Aaron came thundering down the stairs as, simultaneously, the living room window shattered, shot out by gunmen who were apparently also out front, in the street.

There was no going out the front door—it was clear they were fully surrounded—and Phoebe let herself get pushed by Dunn into the closet, even as Aaron dove the rest of the way down the stairs. Dunn caught his brother and all but tossed him through the closet door, too. Aaron then pushed Phoebe even farther in, and she stumbled over boots and at least two pairs of baseball cleats and part of a fishing pole before she realized that this wasn't just your average, everyday, run-of-the-mill coat closet where they were going to huddle in fear before being executed by the mob.

Instead, there was a door—a small door that she had to duck down to go through—that led into a room.

And yes. This house that Ian Dunn had bought a year ago to keep his brother safe had a panic room.

Chapter Five

Martell became aware of the tail about halfway to the designated safe house-slash-motel.

The car behind him was nondescript—a white four-door sedan with Florida plates.

Whoever was following him was doing a piss-poor job of it, clumsily staying directly on his ass instead of keeping several car lengths between them. They raced to keep up through yellow traffic lights and cut off other cars so that horns blared.

Martell would've had to have been dead not to notice.

He tested his theory, pulling last minute into a left turn lane, and the white car followed.

He drove through a drugstore parking lot, and the white car followed.

He went full around a block: right turn, right turn, right turn, right turn. And the white car followed.

He slowed way down, looking hard into his rearview mirror. Martell couldn't tell if the driver was a man or a woman because a hat was pulled way down, its brim hiding his or her shady face.

Martell again called the number that his FBI contact had given him, but again, it simply stopped ringing and disconnected.

His choices were simple. Work to lose the tail—which he could easily do, considering his/her tailing skill level was zero point zero zero one. Or he could stop in a well-populated public location and get up in the other driver's grill. Literally.

There was a busy Mickey D's on the corner with a police car sitting in the drive-through, so Martell pulled in—and the white car vanished. Just like that, it ghosted and was gone.

Well, okay then.

That was a third option. Scare the guy away.

His stomach rumbled loudly, and he wasn't one to take a sign from God for granted, so he parked in order to go inside and grab a burger. The line at the counter wasn't long, plus it was time to try calling Phoebe's various phones again.

Her cell rang, but it went to voice mail, so he left another message—"Checking in, hope you're okay, call me"—then did the same on her home phone as he got a double cheeseburger and fries to go.

It was all of three and a half minutes by the time he'd paid and was carrying his bag of heart attack out the door. But as he stepped into the sunlit warmth of the afternoon, he'd already gone all *Princess Bride* inside his head. He'd taken a Wally Shawn–inspired path in which he'd started wondering if the driver of the white car only wanted Martell to *think* that said driver's tailing skills were inept. What if, in fact, the driver of the white car had a double-oh-seven level of tailing abilities? Except now Martell would act all free and clear, and unwittingly lead the way to the motel safe house, since the white car obviously wasn't on his ass. Meanwhile the white car's driver had gone all super-stealth, except Martell would never know it, because he'd focus all of his energy on watching for a badly hidden white sedan.

Although . . . what if the driver of the white car wanted Martell to figure all that out, therefore thinking dude *had* mad tailing skills so that Martell then intentionally *stayed away* from the help that he'd receive by going to the motel safe house . . . ?

Or what if—

"Keys to the car. Hand 'em over." The voice was low and gruff, but definitely female.

She had one hand on his shoulder as something hard and cold and metal jabbed into his side. A gun barrel? Yes, that was definitely a weapon of some kind poking him in his ribs.

He glanced over his shoulder, but she was shorter than he was, so he only saw the top of her head. Which had that hat on it.

He also saw skin. Pale skin. Shoulders and boob-tops, complete with cleavage. Whoever she was, she was wearing an outfit that was strapless, black, and skin tight, like she was some kinda comic book villain or maybe a Bond girl.

She took the opportunity to give him a flash of her weapon—a small but deadly little .22 caliber—as she fired off more orders: "Don't turn around again. Don't stop walking. Just hand me your keys and get into your car, behind the wheel."

He looked over at that police cruiser. It was just pulling out of the other side of the fast food restaurant's driveway, and she jabbed him again.

"Nice, but don't even think about it. Keys, Martell. *Now*."

She knew his name. *That* couldn't be good.

He got a glimpse of straight jet-black hair hanging lankly past a smooth, pale chin, a mouth darkened with purple or maybe even black lipstick—gothish—as he handed his keys over. A little weapon like the one she was holding lost a large percentage of its danger value when it wasn't at a supremely close range. So his plan was to run like hell back toward the restaurant after she took it away from his ribs, as she went around the back of the car to climb into the passenger's side.

Martell felt his adrenaline surge as he waited, as he mentally prepped for the coming sprint.

She used the key fob to double-pop the locks, which opened all of the doors, not just the driver's. "Open it," she ordered, so he did.

"Sit."

Son of a bitch. He did that too, slowly, knowing it would be that much harder to break into a sprint from this position, but then she made it yet harder by closing the door for him.

Before he could properly Plan-B it—she had the keys, so hitting the lock button and securing the doors wouldn't help—she opened the back and climbed in directly behind him.

"My weapon is still on you," she announced. "And I know *you* know it's got a small caliber, but at this range, even fired through the seat back, it has the power to sever your spinal cord. So don't do anything stupid. Just drive. Slow and steady." She dropped the keys over his shoulder and into his lap.

Martell fumbled them, finally got them into the ignition and put the car into reverse, his mind whirling as he tried to work out a new plan. Plan C. Get out of the car. He had to get out of the car. As he pulled out of the parking lot, he took a left on the side street, heading away from the busy traffic and higher speeds of Route 41. He caught sight of her car—that white sedan—parked at the far end of the McDonald's lot. He was stupid to have missed seeing it, coming out of the restaurant. But okay. He knew this neighborhood and he *was* going to get away. The residential streets were in a grid, all with intersections that had four-way stops. He would not be able to get up much speed—which would allow him to dive-roll out of the car when he got the chance and . . .

As he slowed toward the first stop sign, he realized that she was no longer holding her weapon on him. She must've put it down because she was using both hands to adjust the control buttons on something she'd gotten out of the leather messenger bag she wore, its wide black leather strap across her black-leather-bustier clad chest.

She was muscular—her arms and shoulders were well defined, but she was lean. Like a long-distance runner or a triathlete—except she must've worked out on a treadmill in a basement gym. Her smooth skin was nearly neon white. Plus, she must've been wearing some kind of extra-padded Wonderbra to have that mega-cleavage, boobs-on-a-plate effect. In fact, she was in serious danger of a nipple pop, because the dominatrix-style strapless top she was wearing was cut so low.

The whole look would've been hot if she hadn't just threatened to sever his spine.

But it was then that something registered. Some faint whisper of recognition even before she looked up at him, meeting his gaze in the mirror, even before she said—in a voice that was now remarkably businesslike and matter-of-fact, "It's okay. We're clear. We can talk. Good job playing along, by the way. But keep driving now. Let's make sure no one's following us."

That thing she'd taken out of her bag? It looked like some kind of bug sweeper—some kind of device that could seek out and find any electronic surveillance devices. What the hell . . . ?

As Martell braked for the stop sign, he looked back at her again. And she must have seen the massive confusion in his eyes, because she said, "It's me. Deb."

Deb? Did he know any Debs? He flipped through his mental file of the women in his life, and he came up Deb-less. No Debbies or Deborahs either.

She took off her hat, as if that might help. But all that did was reveal more of that obviously dyed-black goth-girl hair. Chin length, stringy, and mussed from the heat plus the hat, she had almost ridiculously short bangs that framed her pale, narrow face. It was hard to tell the color of her eyes because she wore so much dark black eyeliner around them.

And okay. It was hard to tell the color of her eyes because his own gaze kept slipping down toward that impending costume malfunction.

He knew her, he knew her—how the hell did he know her . . . ?

"Deb Erlanger," she clarified, adding, "I work with Jules Cassidy?"

Aha. The invisible lightbulb over his head clicked on. Deb Erlanger, FBI Agent. Whom, to be fair, he'd met only a few times. Who worked directly for his evil government overlord.

"Drive," Deb said, but this time it wasn't an order as much as it was a strongly implored request.

He put his foot on the gas, glancing again in the mirror.

The Deb he'd met in the past had been almost invisible. She had light brown hair that she mostly wore pulled back into a ponytail, baseball cap shading her perpetually makeup-free face, sneakers on her feet. Her standard uniform had been jeans and a T-shirt, with a light jacket to cover her shoulder holster. She was tough and efficient and dedicated to her job.

Martell had never, not even once, been tempted to imagine himself doing the hot-and-nasty with her.

Until today.

The whole goth thing usually scared him, but today it was a good kind of scary. Still, he knew that he'd have plenty of time to relive his fear and ponder a few fantasies—later.

Right now, he forklifted his mind out of the gutter. "What's going on?" he asked, admitting, "I seriously didn't recognize you."

"Yeah, the disguise went a little extreme. When I think *disguise,* I think inconspicuous." Exasperation tinged her voice as she climbed over the seat, moving into the front. He forced himself to keep his eyes on the road as the bustier fail he'd been predicting actually happened, times two, and she had to tuck herself back in.

"God, I need a shirt," she muttered. "You don't happen to have . . . ?"

"Sorry." Martell shook his head, trying to sound sincere. "You'd fit right in over at the Ringling School of Design."

"That's what Yashi said." She gestured to her outfit. "This is his doing—Joe Hirabayashi, he works with me. This is his getting back at me for an assignment where he had to wear a kilt. Like it was my fault I'm not a man. I couldn't do it. It wouldn't have worked. Put me in a kilt, I'm a Catholic school-girl."

Martell could picture *that* quite clearly, too, which was *not* okay. "What's going on?" he asked again.

"I should be asking you that," Deb countered. "You're supposed to have Ian Dunn with you. And, apparently, some lawyer named Phoebe Kruger? What happened?"

"They, uh, decided to ride separately," Martell said.

"They ditched you," she correctly interpreted.

"Pretty much."

She sighed—a much larger sigh than her FBI boss would've allowed himself. "Well, that's just great. So what's your plan?"

"Go to the safe house and wait for contact—which I no longer have to do, since you've made contact. Hope Phoebe calls me back soon . . . ?"

She looked at his Mickey D's bag. "Eat a little lunch?"

"That, too. Although after being scared shitless, it's gonna take time before my digestive system kicks back in."

"Sorry." She was about as sorry as he was that he didn't have a spare shirt in the car. "I had to make sure your vehicle wasn't bugged and, well, I was supposed to intercept you before you took Dunn to the motel—because it's not safe anymore. There's been a leak in the department, somewhere—not necessarily having anything to do with this assignment, but there's definitely been a system-wide security breach, so we're being extra cautious with all our covert ops, across the board. The contact number that you were given has been changed. Everything's been changed."

"Including your need to recruit Dunn to rescue those kids?" Martell asked, unable to hide his hope from his voice.

"Not that," she told him, as she stole a few fries from his bag.

"Help yourself," he said.

"Thanks." She took more.

A woman who ate French fries without either an apology or an encyclopedic explanation as to why she really shouldn't be eating French fries. Be still his still-trembling heart.

"Take a left here," she ordered, pointing with one of the fries. "We're heading toward the harbor. Yashi's renting some kind of vacation cottage for our new safe location. As soon as he gets the keys, he's going to text me the address. Meanwhile I'll call HQ and see if they can track Phoebe Kruger's car, see if we can't find Dunn that way. Assuming he hasn't ditched *her* by now, too."

She dug in her bag for her phone and just that small amount of motion created . . .

"Uh, you want a heads-up when you pop?" Martell asked her. "Like, *Hello! Nipple!* Or would you prefer it if I just ignore . . . ?"

"Shit!" She tucked and pulled as she actually blushed beneath her undead-flavored makeup, even as she laughed her dismay. "Sorry! No! Don't ignore! Please. God. Thank you. I'm so sorry. But maybe don't shout *nipple*. Please?"

"Boob?" he suggested.

Deb laughed again. "Yeah, 'cause that's better?"

"We could go with a code word," Martell said. "Xylophone."

She laughed again, still blushing as she focused

on dialing her phone. "As soon as we get to the safe house, I'm changing my clothes, so . . ." She put her phone to her ear, then grimaced before leaving what had to be a message. "It's Deb. Our little glitch with the lawyer just got bigger. Call me ASAP."

Before Martell could comment, she turned back to him with that same briskness. "I know you just met Phoebe Kruger," she continued. "But give me your impression. Do you believe her, trust her . . . ?"

"Believe and trust her about what?" Martell asked.

"To start, is she . . . who she says she is?"

His voice went up an octave. "Are you kidding me?"

Deb sighed again. "Nope," she said. "We're not sure exactly how Bryant, Hill, and Stoneham knew to send her to the prison. We're still looking into that. Was it you, by any chance, who contacted the firm?"

"No, ma'am," Martell said. "In fact, I was intending to bitch about her to your boss. But then I figured you FBI guys arranged it, to expedite whatever deal we struck."

"Nope," she said. "It wasn't us. She just showed up—no clearance, no background check. Although we're running one right now."

Martell stared at her as he rolled to a stop at a red light. "And I wasn't informed about this *before* I let her vanish with Dunn because . . . ?"

She looked steadily back at him as she ate more

of his fries. "You *let* Dunn vanish? You're telling me you honestly could've stopped him?"

Martell didn't answer until the car behind him honked. Light was green. As he looked back at the road and drove, he admitted, "No."

"Mistakes happen," Deb said, not unkindly. "Across the board. What we have to do now is fix this one. Which starts with you telling me whether you think Phoebe Kruger is a potential problem."

Ian Dunn's brother Aaron owned a house with a panic room—which was good, because Phoebe was on the verge of panicking as she was pushed inside.

Aaron slapped on an overhead light, and she looked around.

It was tiny—jail-cell-sized—but high-tech and well supplied. A toilet and miniature sink sat out in the open in the corner on the far end, and shelves lined one full wall, with a bunkbed setup along the other. Near the door was a huge flat-screen monitor that looked to be hooked into some kind of intricate computer surveillance system. That same wall also held a phone and a clock.

Dunn came in last and slammed the heavy steel door shut behind him, and Aaron helped him throw an array of deadbolts and locks.

The sudden silence was jarring, but it didn't last long.

"Who's hurt?" Dunn asked, moving purposefully to the shelves that held supplies—clothing, blankets, bottles of water, and cans and jars of food—as well as a heavy-duty first aid kit.

"Not me," Aaron said, despite the fact that blood from a skinned elbow was dripping down his arm. He was already at the computer, turning on the monitor and flipping down a futuristic-looking keyboard and mouse that had been built into the wall. "But my beautiful home has just been turned to total shit by the fucking Dellarosas."

"I'm okay," Phoebe said, although when Dunn shot her an odd look, she was suddenly acutely aware that she was standing there, still dripping wet, in little more than her pants and bra.

He was soaked, too, but when he took a towel from a pile that sat, neatly folded, on those vast and cluttered shelves, he handed it to her before taking one for himself. "Your leg," he said, and she realized that she was, absolutely, bleeding, too. She'd torn her pants and scraped her knee at some point, but it wasn't that bad. And if that was the worst of it . . .

It occurred to her that Martell had been dead right—that releasing Ian Dunn from prison would send the Dellarosas after him. How had he put it? *Guns blazing.*

"My biggest concern is, What happens now?" Phoebe asked as she dried her face, her glasses, and her hair as best she could, before draping the towel—whoops, now streaked with the remains of her mascara—around her shoulders as a pseudo-shirt. "All over this neighborhood, people are calling nine-one-one, reporting shots fired. What do we do when the police arrive?"

"Mother*fucker!*" The computer screen had flickered to life, and whatever Aaron saw there wasn't good.

Phoebe stepped over to look, and it was obvious, with just once glance, that his security setup was not only high-tech but also extremely well conceived, with feeds coming in from nine different cameras—the big screen partitioned into nine separate high-def rectangles.

Four of the cameras were positioned around the outside of the house. Three covered the home's interior—inside the front door, in the kitchen facing the back sliders, and the last in what looked like an upstairs hallway. The final two screens showed a video feed that had been hijacked—somehow—from two county traffic cameras. One was at Clark and Beneva, the other at an intersection that Phoebe didn't recognize.

But it was the exterior camera that was up on the roof of the house that had caught Aaron's grim attention. It was positioned so that it revealed the street back behind the pool deck of his lovely home.

"God damn it," Dunn said as he, too, moved closer to the monitor. "I thought Shelly was smarter than you."

Most of the shooters were already zooming away from the attack in a variety of vehicles—with that amount of gunfire, the police had to already be on their way. But one car—a large black sedan—had stopped on that street within view of the roof cam.

"No, no, no no no no *no!*" Aaron said as, on the computer monitor, a heavy-set, balding, dark-suited man climbed out of the stopped car.

Phoebe then saw that three men were approaching the heavy-set man. Two of them were oddly golf-ready, wearing plaid shorts and polo shirts—as if they'd been called away from a game—but the third wore khaki pants, a shirt, and a tie, his dark brown hair gleaming in the afternoon sun. Khaki was being tightly held by the two golfers, and even though he struggled, he couldn't get away from them as they dragged him over to Heavy-Set.

"Berto's not going to hurt him. Not badly." Dunn's words were quick and his voice was low, and Phoebe saw that he was holding Aaron tightly, pinning him in place—as if to keep him from leaving the safety of this little room.

What was that about? Was Berto—as in Dellarosa—the name of the heavy-set man? And what did any of this have to do with Shelly? What was Phoebe missing here?

On the video monitor, Heavy-Set opened the trunk of his car. His movements were jerky and even though Phoebe couldn't hear him, she could see that when he spoke, his words were angry.

Khaki, still held by Golfers One and Two, stopped struggling and stood taller as he faced Heavy-Set, defiantly lifting his chin—and it was quite the chin, in a movie-star handsome face.

"He *will* kill you, though. You go out there,

Aaron," Dunn was saying as he continued to hold on to his brother, "you're not only dead, but Shelly will be forced to watch you die. Don't do that to him."

Phoebe looked back at the screen in surprise, and the words left her lips before she could stop herself. "Shelly's a . . . ?" *Man,* she was about to say.

Spouse.

It was beyond obvious that Aaron's spouse, Shelly, was the handsome, khaki-clad man who was now being punched hard in the stomach by Heavy-Set, who really put his substantial heft into the blow.

Aaron made a sound as if he himself had just gotten hit as Shelly doubled over.

"That's Berto, crazy Davio's oldest son," Dunn confirmed as he pointed to the screen, tapping the image of Heavy-Set for Phoebe's benefit, before telling Aaron, "Manny's in the hospital right here in Sarasota. He was in town, having lunch. He had a heart attack."

The fact that mob boss Manny Dellarosa had had a heart attack was news to Phoebe, although Dunn had probably found that out during one of the calls he'd made with her phone. *How bad is he?* His words now made sense.

"I don't know what his condition is," Dunn told his brother. "But it wouldn't surprise me if Davio's moving into place for a power grab. If that's the case, in the fight between his father and his uncle

Manny, I honestly have no idea where Berto's gonna land."

As they watched, Berto reached out and seemed to touch Shelly, almost gently, on the side of the head.

But as Aaron whispered, "I'm going to kill him," Phoebe saw a flash of glare on metal and as Shelly slumped, clearly unconscious, she realized that Berto had hit Shelly in the head with a gun.

As they watched, Golfers One and Two unceremoniously loaded Shelly into the trunk of Berto's car, closing it tightly.

"Yeah, I think this time I just might let you," Dunn told his brother almost matter-of-factly, as Berto Dellarosa and his two plaid-wearing underlings hustled back into the sedan and pulled away. "But not right now. Davio's gunning for you. You leave this room, you'll be killed, and that won't help Shel. You know that, D.A. So instead, we're gonna wait, we're going to find out where they're taking him, and then we're gonna get him back. Berto's not going to kill Shelly. You *know* he's not going to kill him."

On a different camera feed, Phoebe saw a fleet of police cars and a SWAT truck speeding through the intersection of Clark and Beneva. She couldn't hear the bevy of sirens through the solid walls of the panic room, but there was no doubt about it, Sarasota's finest were on their way.

"Berto's not going to kill Shel," Dunn said again.

Phoebe looked at Dunn, and she didn't want to

contradict him or even question him because his steady stream of words were clearly calming Aaron down. Still, she had no idea how he could be so convinced that "crazy" Davio Dellarosa's son Berto wouldn't do some serious damage to Aaron's spouse.

Dunn met her eyes. He clearly knew what she was thinking, because he said, "Aaron met Shel—Sheldon—at school, when they were both kids. It was a private high school. D.A. went there on scholarship while I was in the Navy. After Shelly graduated, he enlisted in the Marines, mostly to follow Aaron, but partly to get away from home, because there was a shit-ton of pressure to join the family business."

"Oh, no," Phoebe said, knowing exactly where he was going.

Dunn nodded and said it anyway. "Oh, yeah. Shel's last name? Dellarosa. Berto is Shel's brother. Davio's their father."

And there it was. The final puzzle piece. It explained the connection between Dunn and the Dellarosas, and was the reason why Ian Dunn had gone to work for Manny—gone to *jail* to work for him—in a deal that had protected Aaron from a murderous father-in-law who wanted him dead, probably for being gay.

I'm going to take care of my brother my *way. Same way I've done ever since he was two, when our mother ODed. . . .*

It was unbelievably romantic and sweet.

"Eee, I gotta get out of here," Aaron said now. "Before the police arrive."

"Yeah, I don't think that's gonna happen," Ian said. "If I were Davio, I'd leave a team behind. Take advantage of the situation to erase the ongoing problem that is you."

"At least that way I'll have a chance," Aaron argued. "There's no way the police aren't going to run our prints—they're all over the freaking house—I mean, I live there, right? And I'm just as dead if I'm arrested and put into jail." He turned to look at Phoebe. "How good of a lawyer are you? Because I'm wanted for murder. I'm not guilty—it was self-defense. Although that's probably what they all say, right?"

It was. Phoebe glanced over at Ian, who'd gone over to the supply shelves and was checking the waist sizes on what looked like a pile of brand new stonewashed jeans.

He glanced back at her as he said to his brother, "I told her about Davio putting a hit on you, and how it'd be easy for him to pay someone to kill you if you're in jail."

"I'm still skeptical about that," Phoebe said. "I find it hard to believe that the authorities wouldn't provide proper protection. But okay. When the police arrive, we'll use your phone to establish contact and negotiate. I'll ask that we're all taken directly to a hospital. What you do after we arrive there is . . . Well, don't tell me. I can't know. And, really, Aaron, if I'm honestly your lawyer, I have to recommend that you turn yourself in. I'll ensure that you're protected, and I'll defend you to the very best of my ability—"

"Yeah, that's not going to happen, either," Ian said, and she turned to find that, once again, he'd stripped out of his wet clothes in order to change into something dry.

She turned abruptly toward the monitor where a Mylar-clad SWAT team was entering the house, weapons drawn.

"Davio's reach is too long," Ian continued. "All it'll take is one mistake, and Aaron's shivved by some lifer with nothing to lose." He exhaled, hard. "No. Get us to the hospital, we'll do the rest."

"There's no guarantee that I can get us there," Phoebe cautioned, looking back at Ian after hearing the sound of his zipper going up. She let herself watch while he pulled a plain white T-shirt over his head, his movements smooth and efficient. "I'm willing to try, but . . . There's only one way I know—absolutely—that you'll both walk away from this as free men."

Ian Dunn was no dummy. She could tell from his face that this time, *he* knew what she was going to say before she said it.

But she said it anyway. "I'll call Martell Griffin."

"Yeah, because he's been *such* a help so far."

"Who's Martell Griffin?" Aaron asked, looking from Ian to Phoebe and back.

"I don't see that you have a choice," Phoebe told Ian. "But you *do* have the opportunity to negotiate with him from a position of power, at least for the next few minutes. That changes, dramatically, after Aaron's in police custody."

Ian was silent and completely still, just standing there gazing back at her.

"Who's Martell Griffin?" Aaron repeated his question, and Ian didn't turn toward his brother, but he did briefly close his eyes.

Phoebe didn't back down. She just calmly stood there, waiting for him to look at her again, even though in truth her heart was pounding in her chest. Almost unbelievably, Martell's plan had worked. "Think of it as a win/win. Especially for those kidnapped children."

Ian made a sound that was roughly laughterlike at that, as behind him, Aaron sat heavily down on the bunkbed with a heartfelt "Jesus H. Christ. Really? You *really* just said the words *kidnapped children?*"

Ian still didn't turn toward his brother as he finally nodded. "All right," he said. "But I think it's more *you win.* Call Martell. But tell him to get a pen and start writing, because the list of what I want is massive."

He took a breath to elaborate, but Phoebe cut him off. "First, here's what *I* want," she said. "A shirt and a dry pair of jeans—whatever's on that shelf'll be big, but they'll do. I want you both to turn around and sing, loudly, while I not only change my clothes but I also pee."

"I'm gay," Aaron pointed out.

She smiled tightly at him. “I really don’t care. And oh, yeah. Last but not least. I want my Glock back. And I want it now.”

Was Phoebe Kruger a potential problem?

Martell would’ve answered FBI Agent Deb Erlanger’s question differently fifteen minutes ago—before his phone rang, and he answered it to find Phoebe herself on the other end.

Gladness and relief quickly morphed into annoyance that she hadn’t called him sooner, since Ian Dunn obviously hadn’t murdered her.

But after he’d put the call on speaker and she’d gotten past her assurances that she was fine—but refused to reveal where she and Dunn were hiding, not that he’d expected her to—she’d started in on some full-scale, nuclear lawyering. Her sentence had started with the phrase *Ian Dunn will help with the rescue of the kidnapped children only if . . .*

And then she hadn’t stopped with her bullet-pontification for a good long time.

The woman was scary good. Martell looked down the list of demands again and, yup. She’d thought of everything, and then some things he himself never would’ve come up with. Access to high-tech equipment and weaponry, funds to hire a team of fellow “security breach specialists” to assist Dunn, access to surveillance information, full autonomy in all stages of the op, and money. Lots and lots of money.

Deb had already passed the lengthy list on to her FBI superiors.

"Other than being a kickass lawyer," Martell now told Deb as they sat in wait mode in the parking lot of a pizza parlor, and ate a real lunch, "I don't think Phoebe's a problem. At least not in the way you mean. I think she's exactly what and who she says she is."

When Martell had first met Phoebe, he'd thought *pushover* and *nepotism-tastic; undergunned* and *in over her head.* He may have even included a misogynistic chuckle and a *poor thing* in there, too.

But then they'd had a conversation during which he'd revised that first impression all the way up to *definitely in possession of smarty-pants, but possibly a little underexperienced and absolutely overwhelmed.*

She'd apparently since handled whatever had been overwhelming her, because this phone call had been from a lawyer-shark hybrid who didn't know the meaning of fear.

No doubt about it, Martell had just gotten chewed up into a million little pieces, at which point Phoebe had ended this first part of their negotiation-slash-extortion by letting him know that Dunn was going to set up his own private safe house location, thank you very much, so they would take a pass on whatever the FBI was already putting into play. However, they were going to need more manpower, so Martell should consider himself necessary, because somebody's sister and baby son were going to need security, so his new job was gonna be to help keep them safe. And that was code for

Regardless of that law school diploma on your wall, homeboy, congratulations, you are going to be doing some babysitting.

And no doubt about it, life was bitchslapping him for his sexist arrogance. He was a better-than-average small-town lawyer whose expertise went a long way toward helping people with minor legal problems. Or even major-but-simple legal problems, like the genius clients who'd "caught a case" by walking into a liquor store with gun in hand, demanding the cashier deliver the contents of the cash register.

The whoopsie-that-was-a-misunderstanding-slash-accident defense *never* worked, but Genius and his vast array of brothers-from-other-mothers had to be talked down off that legal ledge. And that was something Martell excelled in doing. His *Dude, you cannot win this, so let's take their generous deal and get you into a detox and rehab program while we're at it* speech was a thing of true beauty.

He'd also been a better-than-average small-town police detective, too. Yes, Sarasota was a city, but its problems were mostly small-town. And he'd liked that. He may have thought about it a time or two, but he'd never truly aspired to join up with the FBI or the CIA.

Which meant that right about now, *undergunned* and *in over his head* applied rather poetically to Martell's own desperately dog-paddling ass.

Deb, however, was flatly unimpressed by Phoebe's first-class lawyering. "Look at these demands. This is insane. Five million dollars? No one's going to approve that kind of a payment. It's just not going to happen. Some of this other stuff—immunity, plus a major clean-slate sweep, not just for Dunn, but for all these other people whose names he gave you . . . Aaron Dunn—that must be his brother. *That* we can do, assuming he's not a serial killer or a terrorist." She looked over at Martell as she tapped the legal pad with one finger. "This, by the way, is what Ian Dunn *really* wants. The money's just a distraction. Or a negotiating tactic. Something for him to give up." She smiled. "Although, really, it all depends on how dire Dunn's current situation is."

Current situation? Calling from the parking lot of some nice restaurant while he sat beside his attractive lady lawyer, breathing in that new-car smell? "I'm pretty sure he's got the upper hand," Martell pointed out as he gathered up their trash.

"The fact that he initiated the negotiation means that something's going on," Deb countered. "I'd bet it's something major."

"Well, you're the FBI agent," Martell conceded, with plenty of *but I don't believe you* in his tone.

She looked over at him. "Yes. I am," she said, and okay, he'd admit it, when she got quiet and intense like that, she was a tad scary, even with the constant threat of impending nipple pop hanging over her head.

"I'll throw this away," he announced, way too cheerfully, trying his best not to trip as he got out of the car.

When he came back, Deb was chewing on her lip and aiming all of her attitude at her phone. "FBI headquarters just texted me an address," she said. She clicked over to her GPS.

"Just an address?" Martell asked. "Nothing else, like, *This is the self-storage unit where Dunn stashes the bodies of the women he kills, hashtag wait for the SWAT team?*"

"My boss is having something of a crazy day himself," Deb informed him. "This looks to me like a residential area. Twenty-four Monteblanc Circle?"

Martell leaned over to look at the tiny map on her phone. He became immediately aware of three things.

One, she smelled kind of like a man, with a not unpleasant trace of a product—deodorant or maybe hair gel—that Martell had smelled before, used in too-large quantities by some of the guys at the gym. And that probably meant that she had a boyfriend. A manfriend—excuse him—this was not a woman who dated boys. A full-grown, adult male friend—whose products she'd borrowed, most likely after a night of creative, athletic, inspiring lovemaking.

And wasn't *that* disappointing?

Two, his face was now mere inches from that magnificent shelflike presentation of the top hemisphere of her bosom. Keep his eyes on the map, keep his eyes on the map . . .

And three, the address she'd been texted wasn't that far from the intersection of Clark and Beneva, which, in turn, wasn't all that far from where they were right now.

So Martell backed away from Deb, from her exposed boobtops and her regret-inducing man-smell, as well as her GPS map, and he put his POS into gear.

"I'm pretty sure Ian Dunn had Phoebe call to negotiate first and foremost because he wants money," Martell said as he pulled out of the parking lot and headed back south on 41.

"Bet you your shirt you're wrong," Deb said, picking up his cell phone from the cup holder. "What's your passcode?"

He looked at her in disbelief.

She held out the phone to him. "Or do it yourself. I need to use your Internet. I want to Google the address so we don't go in there completely blind if it's like, I don't know, property owned by one of the Dellarosas maybe . . . ?"

Martell keyed in his code. "Why would Dunn seek out the Dellarosas? And what do *I* get if *I'm* right and *I* win the bet?"

"You get to keep your shirt," Deb said, frowning at his phone. "Property is owned by someone named S. Jackson, which sounds like an alias to me. The title changed hands around a year ago. It's a four-bedroom house on a double lot." She glanced up. "Take the next left."

"Is it me," Martell said as he did just that, "or is there suddenly an overabundance of police cars in this 'hood?"

The patrol cars weren't just idling at the sides of the road—they were parked. And yes, the SWAT team was already here.

Uniformed officers were out of their vehicles and were crawling damn near everywhere.

In fact, one of them—much too young to have been on the force back in Martell's day—stepped out into the street and signaled them to stop.

Deb already had her FBI ID out. She started to lean forward, to talk to the officer through Martell's open window, but then stopped, no doubt thinking *xylophone*.

Definitely thinking *xylophone*. She met Martell's eyes and smiled wryly, handing him her ID instead. "Tell him to come around to my side."

"Good plan." Although he would *ask* instead of *tell*.

"I'm gonna win your shirt."

"Not sure I ever agreed to that bet."

"Your silence was implicit agreement."

"I don't believe I was silent. Good afternoon, Officer."

One look at Deb's ID, and the uniformed cop sputtered and quickly moved, not to talk to her, but instead hurrying to find his boss.

Martell meanwhile parked since it was clear that they could drive no farther. All kinds of emergency vehicles were blocking the road.

Deb got out of the car and he followed as the junior policeboy came back with Sarasota's newest lieutenant, who was, happily, an old friend of Martell's.

He leaned in closer to Deb to say, "Lieutenant Lora Newsom. Transplanted here in Florida as a uniformed officer, originally from someplace where they grow a lot of corn. She's the real deal. Earned this job the hard way. Be as honest with her as you can, and she'll be an ally."

Deb nodded.

The blond-haired lieutenant's eyes widened very slightly at her first look at Deb's attire, but other than that, she didn't blink. She just nodded tersely to Martell, as if not at all surprised to see him with an FBI agent. She handed Deb's ID back to her. "Why do I already hate this? That's a rhetorical question, Martell. You don't have to try to answer that."

"Nice to see you, too, Lora."

Deb jumped right in. "Twenty-four Monteblanc?"

Newsom sighed and nodded, leading them back past the rescue vehicles. "That's our crime scene. It was quite the Wild West shootout."

"Anyone dead?" Deb asked.

"Miraculously no," Newsom reported. "But we've currently got something of a standoff. An unknown number of perps have taken shelter in some kind of dedicated safe room on the first floor of the home. We're confident they can see us via camera access. I've got people holding up a handwritten sign with a phone number in front of their video cams, and a negotiator standing by, but so far no contact. Are there hostages? We don't know. The car out front belongs to a lawyer named

Phoebe Kruger. We've found her phone number, but she's not answering our calls." Her blue eyes narrowed. "So what can *you* tell *me?*"

"We're pretty sure this incident is related to an important national security case I'm working on," Deb said. "I'm afraid I can't tell you much more than that. I'm hoping the people inside the safe room are mine. If they are, it's best if they remain anonymous for now."

Clearly unhappy, Newsom nodded as she glanced at Martell again, obviously wondering what kind of SNAFU he'd gotten himself involved with this time.

But then, holy Jesus God on high.

They rounded the last SWAT truck, and 24 Monteblanc Circle came into view.

Martell had thought Lt. Newsom was exaggerating about that *Wild West shootout* thing, but the place was trashed. Nearly all the windows in the house had been shattered, and the walls riddled by bullets that had left behind lines of gray holes—chips and gouges in the painted stucco.

And there was Phoebe's new car. It had gotten the shit shot out of it, too. Windows broken, tires flat. Finish dented and pierced in those same telltale automatic-weapon-fire lines.

Martell could see the security camera positioned near the front door. It seemed intact, so he took out his phone as he approached it. And then he took off his button-down super-lawyer dress shirt and he handed it to Deb.

She was right behind him. She tried to hide her smile but failed. "Thanks," she said, as she put her arms into his sleeves and buttoned the damn thing up to her neck.

Martell held out his phone and pointed to it as he stood there in his white beater and smiled cheerfully up into the camera.

Any second now, his phone was gonna ring.

CHAPTER SIX

"Ah, shit," Ian said on an exhale.

And Phoebe looked up to see Martell Griffin standing—and smiling—in front of the video camera that was positioned right outside the front door.

"We knew this might happen," she told Ian, even as her own heart sank. "I mean, his client *is* the FBI. It actually gives me a sense of renewed hope and security that they, you know, found us." She pumped a fist through the air. "Yay, Team America."

The face he made said, *Are you kidding me?*

Aaron, meanwhile, looked up from where he'd been sitting on the lower bunk, head in his hands. He'd been grimly quiet ever since his brother had told him that Martell Griffin was the liaison to a government agency who wanted Ian to lead a rescue op.

"Kidnapped children," Aaron had said, incredulously repeating what he'd heard Phoebe say just moments earlier. "How many kidnapped children—and please don't say a busload."

"Two," Ian had told him. "Their mother's a nuclear physicist—she's believed to be the real target. Intel puts the kids inside a foreign consulate in Miami. They need someone without any government connections to go in and get them out."

Aaron took that news relatively calmly. "So what happened? You took this meeting with this Griffin guy, and with Manny's heart attack putting him in the hospital, crazy Davio was suddenly in charge, and he immediately thought you were doing some kind of double cross?"

"That's as good a guess as any," Ian had said, obviously intentionally leaving out the part where he'd been approached about this "job" while serving time in prison.

He'd also failed to mention to his brother that he had a connection to the alleged dangerous kidnapper, Georg Vanderzee, AKA the Dutchman. Phoebe had noticed that, too. Was it because Aaron didn't know the man, or because he *did,* and he would've exploded at that news?

Since they were all still trapped in the tiny panic room, where there was no privacy, she hadn't gotten a chance to ask Ian about that.

After making the initial call to Martell, they'd gone into wait mode—both brothers preoccupied with their own dark thoughts.

Phoebe had tried to engage Aaron in a conversation—"So, you and Shelly were high school sweethearts?" But he'd answered monosyllabically, so she hadn't pushed for more information.

Still, there was a story there, and Phoebe suspected it was a good one.

But now Aaron joined them at the monitor, looking over Phoebe's shoulder at Martell Griffin, who was still smiling expectantly into the camera.

"Who's that?" Aaron asked, pointing to a woman with jet-black hair—clearly it was dyed—who stood slightly behind Martell.

"I don't know," Ian said. "But she's . . . certainly interesting."

As they watched, the woman—whoever she was—covered her *interestingness* with Martell's shirt.

"We still hold a powerful hand," Phoebe reminded Ian. "They need your help to save those kids. Now. Not in a week or two. We have plenty of food in here. We can certainly wait—"

"We're not going to wait," Aaron said. "We have to find Shel, fast, and—"

Ian cut his brother off. "I know."

Outside the house, Martell continued to gaze up at the camera, with that expectant half smile on his handsome face.

"Jesus, he's gonna kick my ass, and love every minute of it," Ian finally said. He turned to Phoebe. "Do it. Call him. You know what I need."

She punched Martell's number into the panic room's phone. "Need as opposed to want," she clarified. She nodded. She *did* know. Ian *wanted* the money and the equipment and the high-tech support.

But all that he *needed* was guaranteed safety—witness protection program level—for his brother, and for his brother's family. He needed full amnesty for Aaron, which would give the younger man a clean slate. He also needed the federal authorities to dismiss any potential aiding-and-abetting charges against Sheldon and his sister Francine, who'd helped Aaron hide from the police for all this time.

And Phoebe knew that she had been right in assuming that the three of them, Aaron, Shelly, and Francine, worked with Ian—that they were, indeed, part of his team. Doing God knows what—anything was possible, from contracting out as private-sector spies for the CIA and FBI, to actually being a gang of international jewel thieves. Bottom line, Ian had asked for full immunity for all of them, in connection to the impending rescue mission.

In other words, they would not only be cleared of any past charges, but the authorities also wouldn't arrest them for helping Ian break into the Kazbekistani consulate.

Ian's own immunity, however, was not a need. He'd made that very clear. His own immunity and safety were negotiable.

Ian caught Phoebe's arm before she pushed the button that would connect the call.

"A detail you need to know: We need to walk out of here," he told her, again using that word. "Aaron and me. No questions, no stopping us. Towels over our heads so the legions of cops out there don't see us. Free and clear. We'll need a vehicle, and I want you to be the driver. No one follows, no tracking devices, no surveillance."

"Um." She chose her words carefully. "What if I . . . don't want to be the driver?" she asked.

"Deal's off," he said. He smiled. "I should've said *need,* not *want*. I *need* you to drive, which works out nicely since you, apparently, *need* to help save those poor, unfortunate, helpless, frightened little kids. Win/win."

Phoebe looked at him. "Desperate," she said. "You left *desperate* off your list of adjectives. Forlorn. Vulnerable. Terrified." She'd intended to mock him, but realized that instead she was talking herself into it.

And Ian knew that. "Exactly," he said.

She sighed and placed the call, circling her shoulders and stretching her neck from side to side as prep for the impending legal boxing match with Martell.

"Well, hey there," the other lawyer said, way too cheerfully as, still on camera, he answered his phone. "Let'ssss . . . make a deal."

Clearwater, Florida
Ten years ago

"But you'll lose your scholarship," Sheldon told Aaron as they stood shivering in the night, in the shadows of the wall surrounding their private high school.

Aaron had sneaked out of the Brentwood dorms, and Shelly, a day student, had walked all the way over from his father's house on the other side of town. He hadn't dared drive, for fear someone would recognize his car.

It was late and it was cold—freezing for Florida—but Aaron had been adamant that they have this conversation in person. Tonight. And Shel had never been very good at telling Aaron no.

"Fuck my scholarship." The wind off the Gulf was sharp and damp, and Aaron's shoulders were hunched against it, his hands in the pockets of his jeans as he glared back at Shel. He never had gloves, or if he had them, he never wore them, even on the coldest winter nights. "What about you? What happens when your father finds out?"

This nightmare had started last weekend, when they'd realized that someone had seen them together.

Not *friend* together. *Together* together. *Romantically* together.

And suddenly, what had been one of the loveliest evenings of Shel's short life—a beach blanket, a secluded stretch of dunes, a gorgeously setting sun, his wonderful, beautiful boyfriend Aaron in his arms, whispers of *I love you, too*—became a reason to panic.

It was bound to happen. Sooner or later.

He should've known it wouldn't last—his ridiculous happiness and his sense of finally belonging. In fact, it still seemed surreal.

It had started mere months ago, when Shelly got hired as a math tutor for Aaron Dunn, one of Brentwood's star football players. He'd expected to have to feed stolen test answers to a gorilla, but instead had found a smart, articulate friend.

He and Aaron watched the same movies, the same TV shows. They liked the same books. Aaron may have been math-challenged, but his writing skills were excellent, and he read more than anyone else on campus. Maybe even more than Sheldon.

They'd started hanging out together outside of tutoring time, and they'd talked and talked. And talked.

And then, miraculously, one day, a few months ago, Aaron had leaned in and kissed him.

Turned out Shel wasn't the only kid at Brentwood hiding his sexual orientation from the world.

Turned out Aaron had been crushing back on Shel for months.

It was like *The Wizard of Oz*, where a world that Shel hadn't even realized was in drab black and white suddenly exploded in amazing Technicolor.

But then, last weekend, they'd gotten careless on the beach, and today, the shit had hit the fan.

Today, they'd found that someone hadn't just seen them together, someone had taken video. Of them. Together.

He and Aaron had found this out at the exact same time as the rest of the students at Brentwood—when the video was posted to the school's social message board on the Internet.

True, the video was crudely made. It included about a dozen still photos of Sheldon and Aaron on campus—some quite blurry, and none at all incriminating—simple shots of them hanging out together. Those pictures were edited—badly—into a montage with pirated clips of some poorly produced gay porn from the 1980s. The hairstyles alone were blindingly awful.

It would've been easy to shrug off as a joke, or as an attempt at bullying—Shel had had plenty of experience with that—except for the fact that the actual incriminating footage from their beach blanket encounter was tacked on to the end.

Yes, it was alternately grainy and blurry, with the colors completely washed out. But that was definitely Aaron. Shel was harder to identify. In fact, he could've been anyone in a T-shirt and jeans—male or female, blonde, brunette, or redhead, truth be told. Anyone with short hair, that is, since the camera only caught the back of his badly lit head and the exposed nape of his neck.

But then, whoever had crept up on them and shot that footage had pulled back, right at the end, to include Shel's car in the frame. And there it was. His license plate clear as day as, in the shot's background, he went down on his boyfriend.

Aaron wanted to throw himself on the grenade.

He wanted to step forward and publicly admit that, yes, that was him on tape. His plan was to announce that yes, he was gay, and to say that he'd borrowed Shel's car to have this rendezvous with his boyfriend.

He wanted Shel to pretend he knew nothing, and even to condemn him.

What happens when your father finds out? Aaron was still waiting for Shelly to answer his question.

"I don't know," Shel finally said. And it wasn't just his father's reaction that he was worried about. No one knew his secret. Not even his sister Francine.

But if Aaron took the blame, he'd not only lose his scholarship, he'd be kicked out of school, out of the dorms. He'd have nowhere to go with his mother dead, his father in prison, and his older brother in the Navy, serving overseas.

"I can't let you do it," Shel said. "I can't."

"Yeah, you can," Aaron said softly, almost gently, as he looked at Shel, his heart in his beautiful hazel eyes. "When I said I love you, I meant it."

"I love you, too," Shel whispered now, past his heart in his throat. "Which is why I can't—"

"No one's gonna kill me for this," Aaron interrupted. "Ian knows. Really. I know you don't believe that, but he's always known. I'm me, and he knows me and he loves me. But we both know your father's a fucking lunatic. God knows what he'll do, where he'll send you. No. Shel, you've gotta let me do it." He stepped forward then, his hand warm against the side of Shelly's face, his thumb gentle as he brushed it across Shelly's lips. "It's only a few months before you graduate, a few months after that until you go to MIT. I'll meet you there. We'll make it work. I borrowed your car that night," he repeated. "Say it."

And suddenly Shelly knew. What Aaron could say. How they could fix this—for both of them. "You borrowed my car," he repeated, stepping back, away from Aaron's hypnotizing touch. "To spend the day with your *girl*friend."

Aaron was already shaking his head. "Have you seen that video?"

"It could be a girl."

"With short hair?" Aaron scoffed. "About your height and weight?"

"That's the story we're going with," Shel insisted. *If you don't . . .* He didn't say the words, but they hung in the cold night air, between them. He felt his eyes well with tears. "Please, Air. At least *try* to save yourself."

"Save myself," Aaron repeated, as the moonlight made his eyes glisten, too. "By hiding. By lying. By making it be only about the sex, when the truth is I would die for you."

Sheldon kissed him. He couldn't not. "Please," he whispered.

And Aaron nodded as he wiped his face. God forbid anyone ever see him cry, not even Shel. But he said, "This world? It's fucked up." He gestured with his head, toward town, in a move that was pure Aaron Dunn. "Come on. I'll walk you home."

"You don't have to," Shel said. "I'm perfectly capable of—" *taking care of myself.*

"I know," Aaron cut him off. "It's not about that. It's about me being scared that this bullshit's gonna backfire, that this could be the last time I see you for a while."

It won't be, Shel wanted to say, to reassure him. *And if it is . . . Whatever happens, I'll find you again. Somehow. Some way. Count on that.* But he couldn't speak.

"Come on," Aaron said, and he started down the road toward town, glancing back to make sure Shelly was following.

Shel jogged a little to catch up, to keep up, and when he did, Aaron smiled at him and sang in a purposely funny falsetto, "Ain't no mountain high enough . . ."

To keep me away from you, babe.

Their eyes met and caught, and Sheldon knew they were both thinking the exact same thing.

Always you. Only you. Always and forever.

Aaron's hands were back in his jeans pockets, and Shel had tucked his own into his jacket. He wanted to reach out and hold hands as they took this, their potential final walk together.

But he didn't dare.

Once Ian agreed to sell his soul to Martell's government overlord, things moved quickly.

Mostly because their answer to nearly all of his demands was no.

No, he couldn't have the additional manpower he'd requested.

No, he couldn't have the limitless equipment, vehicles, and weaponry he'd asked for in order to properly surveil the consulate and perform the rescue op. There wasn't enough time to get him sanitized materials—that is, equipment that couldn't be traced back to the U.S. government.

Instead, he was going to get a suitcase—a *small* suitcase—of cash, from which to outfit, arm, and hire his support team. He'd also have access to an FBI undercover operative to assist him in making untraceable cash purchases. But heads up, because that suitcase would not be bottomless. And if he failed to rescue the kids? He'd have to pay the money back.

All of it.

Another *no* came in response to Ian's request for full autonomy. What he *wanted* was to drive off with Aaron and Phoebe in an unmarked car, into the darkness of the night. He'd do what he had to do to rescue the kids and not reappear until he had them safely in hand.

Martell had laughed in his face.

Oh, the FBI got Ian an unmarked car. And it was fine with them if Phoebe drove it. But one of their agents—Deb Erlanger, the hot goth dominatrix—was going to be sitting securely in the back with Aaron, while Martell trailed behind them in a second vehicle.

And Phoebe was going to drive them not to *Ian's*

choice of a securely hidden location from which to prep for his mission-from-hell, but rather to a so-called government safe house that another FBI agent was currently setting up—first here in Sarasota, then down in Miami.

So Martell, Deb, and one of her FBI buddies were going to be Ian's babysitters. Or prison guards. Or personal shoppers. Whatever their official titles were, they'd be on hand to meddle and get in his way but would be completely unavailable to help him out with the actual rescue—when he'd most need their assistance.

Thanks, Uncle Sam.

It was the worst of both worlds. No real support or top-of-the-line equipment, but constant eyes on him, watching and micromanaging his every move.

As if that weren't enough, there was one more, great, big, screaming *no* that won the honor of pissing Ian off the most. It was attached to the only *yes* that he'd gotten—and Ian had to admit that was, really, the only *yes* he'd needed—the *yes* to his request for amnesty and/or immunity for Aaron, Shelly, and Francine. For himself, too.

If Ian could pull this off and successfully rescue these kids from their kidnappers, they were all going to get a fresh start. A clean slate.

It was exactly what his brother needed. It would allow Aaron and Shel and their baby to leave the country, if they wanted to.

Still, of course, this being the FBI with whom Ian was negotiating, there was a catch.

The amnesty and immunity wouldn't be granted until *after* the mission was over and those kids were safe.

So *that* meant Ian would be attempting a very high risk, highly dangerous job with not only the Dellarosas' private army trying to find and kill both him and Aaron, but an entire cadre of law enforcement—local, state, and federal—chasing them down as well.

Hoo-yah.

During part of the conversation, Phoebe had put Martell on speakerphone, because he'd wanted specifics as to how Ian was intending to pull off the children's rescue.

Ian had laughed when Martell asked, but then he realized that the lawyer was dead serious. So Ian had made some noise about having to see the FBI's intelligence as well as their files and reports on the consulate, because he knew that saying *Frankly, bro, I haven't yet given it a single fucking thought* would not be well received.

But the truth was, he *hadn't* given it a single fucking thought since he'd left Northport prison. His complete focus had been to make sure Aaron and his family were safe. Also? He had no intention of taking on a no-win scenario. No, thanks. No way in hell was he going to let himself get pressured or blackmailed into running this mission. He had his own battles to fight. The FBI was going to have to find someone else—someone more capable.

Or so Ian had told himself, even while knowing

that—after he'd gotten Aaron and his family to safety—he was probably going to volunteer to help.

Just help. A little. Because, after all, he *did* know the alleged kidnapper, the douchebag known as the Dutchman.

Thinking about the Dutchman, AKA Georg Vanderzee, always brought back the sudden, sharp, and extremely unwanted memory of the ornate wallpaper in the man's palace dining room, high in the mountains of northern Kazbekistan. That wallpaper had been a mix of textures—some kind of velvet forest green pattern, backed with a metallic, shiny gold. It was far too baroquely self-indulgent for Ian's taste, even to start with. But it became sickening when sprayed with bright red blood . . .

Ian pushed the images away, along with the heaviness of the guilt he carried for not killing the bastard when he'd had the chance.

Away. Away. There'd be plenty of time to think about the Dutchman, and to figure out how best to save those kids, after he got Aaron the hell out of here, and after he then—somehow—figured out a way to extract Shel from whatever Dellarosa dungeon he was currently languishing in.

More info to keep secret from his new FBI bosses.

Of course, right after Ian had agreed to the FBI's deal, the universe gave him one last bitchslap when the local TV station ran footage from a news copter circling this house.

It showed the massive destruction, and all of the police and emergency vehicles in the street.

It looked bad—really bad.

So bad that Ian had had to break radio silence. He'd had to call Francine, who'd gone, with little Rory, to Contact Point Charlie. She was the only one who'd actually followed his protocol and checked into the Ocean Breeze motel, up by the airport, under the alias of Charles.

Ian called the motel and got patched through to Ms. Charles's room. She answered, and yes, she'd seen the news footage and was preparing to return to the neighborhood, to see if she couldn't somehow help. And wouldn't *that* have been grand, if she and the baby got their asses grabbed by Davio Dellarosa's men, who were no doubt still lurking in the area despite the heavy police presence.

Since the negotiating was over and done, Martell won the short-straw assignment of going to meet Francine. His task was to escort her to the FBI safe house where they'd regroup under Uncle Sam's watchful eye.

Yeah, this was going to suck.

Phoebe was looking at Ian as he got off the phone with Francine, so he said, "Yes?" because she clearly had a burning question for him.

"I'm sorry this isn't working out the way we'd hoped it would," she said, as the phone immediately rang again.

Aaron picked it up. It was probably the call

announcing that their car had finally arrived.

"Yeah, well," Ian said to Phoebe, because really, what else could he say? Dressed as she was in too-big borrowed jeans and a T-shirt, with her hair still damp from the pool, makeup rinsed from her face, those clunky glasses on her nose, she looked impossibly young and sweet.

"If you want," she said, "after I drive you to wherever you're going, I could attempt to contact the Dellarosas. I know I said I couldn't, but I've been thinking about it and . . . Jerry Bryant's not really your uncle."

Ian shook his head and answered, even though she'd made it a statement instead of a question. "No."

"It's pretty obvious that Mr. Bryant was hired by Manny Dellarosa, to be your contact while you were . . ." She glanced over at Aaron, who was on the phone, but still, discreetly, didn't say *while you were in jail*. She cleared her throat. "Anyway, *some*one at the law firm might know how to get in touch with him. Manny, that is. If I can reach him—*when* I reach him—I can explain what's going on. With you. Without going into any breach-of-national-security details, of course."

"Yeah, that's not gonna work."

"It might," she countered.

"No," Ian said, "it won't."

"Car's here," Aaron announced, interrupting them. "It's time to go."

Ian's brother's desire to find Shelly trumped his

fear that he was going to be arrested the moment that the panic room door was opened.

"I'm going to have to give you a crash course in mobster ethics—clearly your law school didn't offer Dellarosa Douchebaggery one-oh-one," Ian told Phoebe as he shouldered Shelly's go-bag. "Manny's a bad guy. His brother Davio's worse. He's a freaking crazy bad guy. If Manny's in the hospital, and we know he is, you'll be dealing with Davio, who is—say it with me—a freaking crazy bad guy."

"I'm talking about making a simple phone call," Phoebe said with exasperation as she gathered up her own still-soggy purse and clothes. "At worst, a meeting in the office conference room."

Jesus, she really had no clue. She believed that she lived in a world where lawyers were considered to be a sacrosanct part of the court system, where they were respected as such by all.

Or maybe she was just pretending to believe that—it was a nice embellishment to her role as the wide-eyed, innocent young lawyer—when in fact she was a hardcore Agency operative.

"Let's play out that conference room meeting," Ian said. "Davio will walk in and say, *Where's Dunn?* And you'll say, *I assure you he's no danger to you, Mr. Dellarosa, blah blah blah-blah-blah.*" He made his voice high and squeaky in an intentionally terrible imitation.

Phoebe laughed her disdain. "I don't even remotely sound like that."

"Towel," Aaron said, handing one to Ian as he draped another over his head.

Ian wasn't done with his story. "And then he'll leave, and you'll pin a little star on your shirt for being such a crackerjack negotiator, except his thugs will be in the parking lot, waiting for you to go home. They'll follow you around for a few hours, but if you don't lead them to me or Aaron, they'll get more aggressive—see if maybe you'll divulge my location if they beat the crap out of you." He put the towel over his head, hiding his face, as punctuation.

But Phoebe made another dismissive sound. "I've worked as a criminal defense attorney for quite a few years," she told him. "And one thing I've learned is that even *freaking crazy bad guys*"—she imitated him this time, pitching her voice low and adding a generous helping of stupid to her tone—"need lawyers. In fact, they need lawyers more than the completely sane good guys do. And if they went around *beating the crap* out of their legal team on a regular basis, they would find it impossible to get anyone to represent them."

Jesus. "Great," Ian said. "Fine. You believe whatever myths or fairytales you want to believe, so you can sleep at night. But I'm telling you, no. Thank you, but no. I've changed my mind. I no longer want you attempting to contact any of the Dellarosas. At least not at this time. I'll be sure to let you know if that changes."

"Can we please do this?" Aaron asked.

"Yes," Ian told him, and together they threw back the bolts on the door and stepped back to let it swing open.

At that point, the entire situation could have gone drastically south. A SWAT team could've rushed in, arresting them both and dragging Phoebe to safety.

Instead there was only silence and stillness.

Phoebe led the way out of the closet and into the ruins of Aaron's living room, and no one stopped them. Aaron carried his go-bag, inside of which he'd put his handgun. Pheebs had stashed her Glock in her still-dripping giant-sized lady-purse-thing. Ian carried Shel's bag, which was huge and heavy as hell.

A group of uniformed officers kept their hands securely atop the weapons in their belts, but other than that aggressive posturing . . . Nothing. No one so much as spoke a word to them. It was true, the identity-concealing towels that he and D.A. both wore over their heads weren't a fashion statement that screamed *stop and chat*.

Agent Goth was silently waiting for them inside of Aaron's attached garage where a nondescript, dark-colored sedan had been pulled inside, bay door closed.

It was dim in there, although light filtered in through an array of bullet holes.

"*Son* of a bitch," Aaron muttered, disgusted by the damage as Ian loaded Shelly's heavy luggage into the trunk. Aaron kept his grip on his own bag—good man—as he got into the backseat.

The car was an older model that no one would look at twice.

Ian climbed into the front passenger side as Phoebe arranged herself behind the wheel. The FBI agent got in, too, and with a shudder and a rattle of its chain, the garage door started to go up.

"Towels, gentlemen," Phoebe said as she started the car.

Ian adjusted his towel as the door ended its journey with a *ka-chunk,* and Phoebe backed carefully out of the garage and down the driveway.

She sighed—just the smallest of *oh*s—as she saw the damage done to her car.

"I'll make sure it gets fixed," Ian told her.

Her voice was bemused. "In your copious free time."

He smiled wryly at that. "Good point."

"I've already called to have it towed," she told him briskly. "After we get to the safe house, I'll take *this* car, since you don't want to keep it and—"

"Sorry, no," he said.

"Left on Clark," Goth ordered from the backseat, and Ian heard the signal clicker go on.

Phoebe misunderstood. "So you *do* want to keep this car."

"No, this car's gotta go. We'll get another. One that fifty cops haven't seen." Ian aimed his voice toward the back. "You're making sure we're not being followed, right?"

"I'm on it," Goth said. "So far so good."

Meanwhile, for Phoebe, light dawned. "No, no,"

she said. "Oh, no. Ian. You said you needed me to *drive,* not—"

"Honey, I hate to break it to you, but you can't leave. I know you think otherwise, but it's not safe. Plus, your work here has just begun," he said.

He heard her bristle. "There is *so* much wrong with what you just said."

"Phoebe," he corrected himself. "I hate to break it to you—"

"What, you need me as part of the crack team that's going to rescue Sheldon from the Dellarosas, before going in after those kids?" she asked.

Agent Goth sat forward, her voice suddenly louder. "I'm sorry," she said. "What?"

"Of course not," Ian told Phoebe and ignored Goth. "I *was* however, thinking about what you suggested—that someone at your firm knows how to get in touch with the Dellarosas. And it occurred to me that in the event I can't contact Manny, it might be a good option to have you make that call—but from the safe house—and pretend to negotiate with freaking crazy Davio, distracting him—"

Phoebe was already speaking over him. "Because of my incredible ability to . . . to . . . climb the outside of a twelve-story building or—"

"—while I break Shelly out," Ian finished.

"Rescue *who?*" Goth asked, clearly pained.

"—grapple," Phoebe continued, still just talking right over them both. "Although, really, I'm not all that sure what grappling is, so there's *that.*"

"Jesus," Aaron said from the backseat. "Will you please just pull over and kiss the shit out of each other? Get it over with already. You'll both feel much better."

Phoebe turned to aim some of her outraged disbelief in Ian's brother's direction, even as Ian lifted his towel to shoot D.A. a pointed WTF look in the rearview. Which of course Aaron didn't see, thanks to the towel over his own head.

"I'm sorry," Phoebe said icily, echoing Agent Goth's earlier words. "What?"

"My brother has a thing for you, and obviously it's mutual," Aaron said, slowly and clearly as if he were talking—obnoxiously—to someone who was mentally challenged.

Ian glared at his brother. "Cut it out. Don't take this out on her. I know you're mad at me, and I know you're scared for Shel, but don't be a dick." He didn't dare do more than glance at Phoebe, who was still carefully heading west on Clark, her eyes on the road.

"Rescue," Agent Goth said again, louder this time. *"Who?"*

Aaron pulled back his towel and turned to her. "My husband, Sheldon, has just been kidnapped by a minion of his crazy father, who hates me and wants me dead. Perhaps you've heard of my douchebag father-in-law? His name is Davio Dellarosa."

Agent Goth started to laugh. She tried to stop herself. "Sorry," she said. "That's not funny. It's *really* not funny, but oh my God, you know?"

"Yeah," Ian said. "We know." He pulled the towel off his head because enough was freaking enough.

Phoebe still had her eyes glued to the road, her knuckles almost white as she gripped the steering wheel. "There's no *thing* here," she said, as Ian shot his brother another disgusted look. "There's really not. If I've done anything at all to make *anyone* think—"

Aaron rolled his eyes at Ian in an insincere apology, as if he were fourteen again. "I'm sorry, no, you're fine. You haven't done anything wrong. I'm sure it's just my imagination. But I'm going crazy here. I have no idea where Shel is, or what that son of a bitch Berto is doing to him." His voice broke.

Shit. "He's gonna be okay," Ian told him.

"You keep saying that," Aaron shot back. "If you know something that you haven't told me . . ."

"You're going to have to trust me. I'm going to get him back." Ian didn't know for sure, but he suspected that as long as Sheldon was with Berto, he'd be safe. Safer than he might otherwise be, that is.

"Trust you." Aaron sat back and shook his head in disgust. "Because you know best. You always have. Always will. And if you think I didn't catch that *I* when you were talking about breaking Shelly out —*I,* as in without *me*—your head is so far up your own ass you don't even know what planet you're on anymore."

"Here in Head-Up-My-Ass-Landia," Ian shot

back, "we use common logic to solve problems. We pay attention to details like, oh, look, Rory's already got one parent in danger. Let's not make it two."

"Like you give a shit about Rory," Aaron said hotly. "You've never even met him. I know working for Manny must've been a bitch, but surely you had at least a *few* days off to come and meet my son."

"All right," Phoebe said, lacing her voice with a whole lot of angry librarian, which was disturbingly hot, as she looked at Aaron in the rearview mirror. "Stop." She then aimed her incinerating glare back at Ian. "If you don't tell him, I will."

"Tell me what?" Aaron demanded.

Francine got to the Starbucks first.

She parked Aaron's car as far in the back of the lot as she could, license-plate-free front facing out.

She kept Rory in his car seat, lugging him, along with his diaper bag and her go-bag, into the coffee shop. She ordered a small whatever, paying in cash—rental for a table in the corner.

Rory was doing his best-baby-in-the-world imitation, looking around in wide-eyed wonder and smiling his goofy baby smile at anyone and everyone who caught his eye.

And that was problematic when it came to blending in anonymously. A too-cute baby would be noticed. Remembered.

Francie unfastened him from his parachute-worthy system of halter plus restraints, hoping if she held him on her lap and sang softly to him, he'd close his eyes and be more average.

At the very least, he'd present the far less adorable back of his head to the other people in the shop and . . .

Martell Griffin had come in while she was leaning over.

Ian had sent her a screenshot of the man she was meeting—the man who was going to bring her and the baby to some FBI safe house, where she'd connect with Ian, Aaron, and Shel, and finally get some answers to her current question, *WTF is going on?*

Griffin was tall, dark, and handsome, and at some point between the screenshot and right now, he'd managed to find a shirt with sleeves.

As Francie watched, he edged closer to one of the other women with babies in the place—a woman who tried not to appear frightened by the big black man looming over her.

The woman shook her head emphatically, and Griffin immediately eased back a few steps, his hands up in an *easy there* gesture. Somehow, he kept a smile on his face.

Francie could read his lips. *Sorry to bother you, ma'am. Have a good one.*

Of course, she knew what that was like, to be looked at with mistrust—in her case, by every other woman on the planet. As for the men? They looked at her . . .

Kind of exactly the way Martell was looking at her right now.

He'd turned to find her watching him, and his relief at not having to scare any of the other suburban ladies morphed into a flash of *found Jesus* surprise, and then something contained and careful.

France had seen that expression before, too. It was the classic male *Maybe if I play my cards right I'll get to tap that* face.

She flattened her own eyes into an appropriately bored *Not in this lifetime or the next* as he approached, as she packed Rory back into his seat.

This was why she'd stopped wearing makeup, stopped wearing her hair in anything other than a messy ponytail. And still, the objectification raged on and on.

Her hope at finding someone who would love her for her, and not her pretty face and slamming body, had died years ago.

"Francine? I'm Martell." He held out his hand.

She ignored it. Gestured with her head. "Grab my coffee, will you? I've already been here much too long."

"I got here as quickly as I could." He picked up the diaper bag, too, and would've taken Rory if she'd let him.

But she didn't. "Thank you. I'm sorry. I didn't mean to sound ungrateful."

"We're all under a lot of stress," he said easily as he led the way out to his car.

And wasn't that crafty of him? Use the word *we,* which put them into the same subset in his personal Venn diagram of life. *We who are under stress*. It was the first step toward getting her into a much smaller, more exclusive personal subset: *we who are having sex*.

Francie didn't respond. She just focused on buckling Rory's car seat into the back of his crappy car.

He pretended he hadn't been checking out her ass as she straightened up.

"Mind if I drive?" she asked.

Martell blinked. "No," he said. "You want to drive? You can drive. Sure." He handed her the keys, went around to the passenger side.

Francie got in. Adjusted the seat and mirrors. Glanced at him. "You FBI?"

He laughed. "Nooooo." He said it as if the idea was really funny as she pulled out of the lot. "How about you? I'm not really sure where you fit in. I got the sense that you were watching Dunn's brother's baby." He glanced into the back. "Cute kid." Said with the absolute insincerity of a man with no desire to have children for at least another decade. Back to her. "But other than that . . . it was more important that I get you to the safe house than understand . . . But I'm guessing, from the way Dunn was talking, that you're part of his merry band . . . ?"

France looked at him, but he was serious. This was not bullshit. He wasn't just saying what he thought she'd want to hear. Although even if that *were* the case, that type of perception would already be a huge step above the assumption she usually got. Which was *You must be Dunn's girlfriend*.

Still, as much as Francine would've liked to acknowledge the truth—*I'm his partner in an extremely dangerous long con. It's a job where he's in jail for eighteen months, a job that even his own brother doesn't know about*—she hadn't survived this long by flapping her mouth.

So instead, she said, "I'm Ian's sister-in-law. Sort of. My brother Sheldon is married to his brother Aaron. So Aaron's really my brother-in-law. I'm not sure what that makes me and Ian, officially, anyway."

Martell ingested that info, then said, "So the baby is Aaron and Sheldon's kid?"

It was time for her to start asking the questions. "What, exactly, is going on? Why is Ian out of prison?"

Martell didn't answer for such a long time that she glanced at him again. He was watching her steadily. "I'ma let Dunn answer that for you when we get to the safe house," he replied. "Interesting, though, that you know about him being in prison, because Phoebe texted me to say that Dunn's own brother—Aaron—didn't know he was serving time. I'm supposed to be careful not to spill those beans when we show up, and I'm guessing you should do the same."

Shit.

Francie wasn't the only one who'd just let information slip. She glanced at Griffin again. "Is Phoebe the FBI agent?"

"No, that's Deb," he said. "Phoebe is Dunn's lawyer."

Francie frowned. "No, she's not."

"Yeah, she is."

"His lawyer is some creepy old rich guy who drinks too much and hits on me," she told him, "every two weeks when I do a face-to-face. I've learned to start each meeting with *No, I won't blow you for five thousand dollars*."

Martell shook his head. "Men like that think they own the world. That there's a price tag on everything and everyone. For the record, I'm not for sale, either."

And there he went again, putting them both in the same subset.

"FYI," he added, "the creepy old rich guy is up on manslaughter charges for driving drunk and killing his own daughter in a car accident."

"Oh, shit," Francine said. She wouldn't wish *that* on her worst enemy.

"Yeah," Martell agreed. "Phoebe's filling in for him. Last name Kruger. Dunn's in good hands. She's good at the game."

Francine glanced over at him before returning her attention to the road. She suspected that Martell Griffin, as enlightened as he might seem to be, had no idea that when Ian played games, he never—ever—followed the rules.

CHAPTER SEVEN

"Tell me what?" Aaron leaned forward from the backseat to ask Ian again.

Phoebe was driving the getaway car to the FBI safe house—although she supposed it wasn't *precisely* a getaway car, since no one was chasing them.

Ian sat beside her in the front, and Aaron in the back, next to the FBI agent, who was quietly feeding Phoebe directions. Apparently, making sure they weren't being followed was a lengthy, tedious process of turns and turns and turns again.

"What does Phoebe know that I don't know?" Aaron petulantly asked his brother.

And Phoebe glanced up from the road to shoot another look at Ian, who was as close to unsettled as she'd ever seen him. *Tell him,* she wanted to say. *Tell your brother why you haven't met your nephew yet. Tell him where you've been for all this time. And don't forget to make sure he understands the reason* why *you were in a maximum-security prison—because you were protecting him and his family.*

The look Ian shot back at her was a wry mix of exasperation and amusement, with the briefest glimpse of a flash of something that seemed sweetly vulnerable and . . .

Oh, crap, what was *that?*

Sweetly vulnerable, her well-educated ass. Seriously. If she was going to fantasize about the former SEAL, she should keep it purely physical.

There was plenty of daydream-worthy material in her memory of his pulling her out of the pool. The sensation of his athletic body, solid against her; the way her hands had slipped along the smooth, cool expanse of his broad shoulders; the way he'd unselfconsciously stripped naked afterward—proving that there was a God, because divine intervention *had* to have played a part in the creation of such anatomical perfection.

But no. Instead of fantasizing about the basic facts, Phoebe had added fiction. She'd seen what she'd wanted to see—that allegedly sweet vulnerability—in his eyes, even though it hadn't actually been there.

Ian's brother was at least partly right—she was *way* too attracted to this man. And Ian knew it, too, and was taking advantage. Any flash of anything even remotely sweet or vulnerable was part of his carefully calculated attempt to manipulate her.

She glanced at Ian again, this time forcing herself to be objective about what she saw. An intelligent, dangerously attractive man. "Tell him. Just do it," she said, proud of herself for sounding so matter-of-fact. "Band-Aid pull. Nice and fast."

"Ouch." He smiled at her. Ruefully, with extended eye contact that acknowledged a connection between them.

Phoebe shut down any and all feelings of warmth

or—God help her—tingle while simultaneously forgiving herself for being human as she gave the road her full attention.

"Sorry, little brother," Ian said, managing to sound sincerely apologetic. "You're gonna have to wait. This is not a conversation I'm having with a federal agent in the car."

"You'll have immunity," Phoebe pointed out.

"But I don't have it yet, so I'm not going to risk it," he countered. "Pull over. Up here."

"What?" Deb said from the backseat.

When Phoebe gave him a *Do you think I'm crazy* look, Ian reached over and pulled the steering wheel to the right, so she had to brake to a jerking stop at the side of the road. "Oh my God!"

"Wait, what are you doing?" Deb asked, as Aaron chimed in, "I'm coming, too."

Ian answered his brother. "No, you're not—unless you want to get us both killed. Besides, I need you to be at the safe house when Francine arrives or she's gonna take Rory and bolt." He was already out of the car before he turned back to say to Deb, "I need to make a stop. I'll be two hours, tops."

The FBI agent was adamant. "No way in hell am I—"

He cut her off. "It's nonnegotiable, so save your breath. I'll meet you at the safe house."

"But you don't know where that is," Deb protested.

"Call me," Ian said. "I have the burner phone. You've got the number. Trust me, I'm not leaving town." He leaned in to look at Phoebe. "I know you think your law degree gives you some kind of magic shield or super-power against the Dellarosas, but it doesn't."

She started to argue, but he cut her off.

"I know what I'm asking is a pain in your ass, but if what I'm doing here, right now, doesn't work—and I don't expect it to—I *am* going to need your help. So will you please stick around until I get back?"

"What *are* you doing here, right now?" Deb repeated Ian's words as Phoebe grudgingly nodded. "At least tell me where you're going."

But Ian ignored her. "Thanks," he said, giving Phoebe one last smile before he shut the door. And with that, he was gone.

"Shit," Deb said. "*Trust me, I'm not leaving town*. Great."

"Welcome to the club," Aaron muttered.

Phoebe pulled away from the curb, glancing up into the rearview mirror at Aaron, who also knew exactly where Ian had gone.

They weren't too far from the hospital where Manny Dellarosa was recovering from a heart attack.

No doubt about it, Ian was intending to walk directly into the lion's den.

Looking out for his brother yet again.

Sheldon was dreaming. Had to be.

Rory was tiny—a newborn—and crying, always crying. They couldn't get him to stop crying.

Aaron was calm—calmer than Shel, who wanted to scream, too. He comforted both of them, his voice soothing and low. "It's okay, little man, you're gonna be okay. We'll get through this, together."

And then suddenly, he and Aaron were teenagers again and sitting outside the Brentwood headmaster's office—knowing full well that the shit was about to hit the fan, and they were going to be outed. The school had sent a copy of the sex tape to Aaron's brother and to Shel's father. Jesus, his father was going to kill him. . . .

"You need to get out of here," Aaron was telling him, his voice low so that the headmaster's secretary couldn't hear him. "Pretend to go to the bathroom, and just keep walking. Do it, Shelly, go."

"What about you?" Shel asked.

"I'll be okay," Aaron promised, but the headmaster's door had opened.

And with that, the dream shifted and changed again.

Aaron was right beside him now. He'd put his hand over Shel's mouth, whispering, "Shhhh!"

They weren't at school anymore, they were in their own living room, sitting on their sofa. Rory was finally sleeping.

And Aaron wasn't seventeen anymore. He was older. He was full grown and even more handsome, with that glint that was half possessiveness, half exasperation, and half adoration in his eyes.

And that was too many halves, Shelly knew that, but that was Aaron—larger than life. It was impossible not to smile back at him, but then Aaron's smile turned to a grimace and when he leaned close to whisper, "Don't make any noise," his voice was harsh and weird-sounding.

But Shel couldn't speak, couldn't ask why not, couldn't move with that heavy hand over his mouth and something holding his hands and feet tightly in place—but it wasn't Aaron, it was—

Sheldon awoke with a gasp, with a hand that *definitely* wasn't Aaron's covering his mouth.

"Shhhhh," that same gruff voice hissed again, close to his ear, close enough so that he could feel the warmth of the man's breath and smell the garlic he'd eaten for lunch.

Or maybe dinner. It was pitch-dark in here, wherever here was. And it was hard to tell how much time had passed since Shelly had first awakened, groggy, with his head pounding, to find himself being turned over so that his hands could be tied uncomfortably behind his back. Whoever had flipped him over restrained his feet, too, before the trunk hood slammed shut, plunging him back into darkness.

He'd been imprisoned in the trunk of a car for hours, he knew that much. Sometimes the car had been moving, but most of the time, it had been parked.

When he'd woken up again, less groggy this time, but his head still hammering, he'd been thirsty and hot. Still he knew immediately that this car was parked in a garage, probably underground. If the car had been left in the blistering Florida sun, he'd already be dead.

He'd tried to get out, but this was not your average car trunk. This one was made to contain. He'd been tied—via those plastic restraints on his wrists—to an anchor that was bolted to the body of the car.

He tugged on it now—it was still holding him firmly in place.

He was still a bit foggy on exactly how he'd gotten here. All he knew for sure was that Aaron had been in danger. There'd been gunfire at the house—lots of it. And, God, Berto had been there—Sheldon remembered that, too. It had been ten years since Shel had last seen his half brother—who'd hit him, hard, in the head. Knocking him out. After . . .

This was weird, but Shel distinctly remembered Berto punching him in the stomach, but pulling it at the last minute, so that the blow hadn't hurt.

It was Berto's hand that now covered his mouth, Shelly knew that with certainty, even as disappointment gripped him. Because although he'd been expecting to be awakened by a hand over his mouth, he'd been hoping the surprise would come from Aaron, in the form of a rescue.

Aaron was coming for him—of that Shel had absolutely no doubt.

"Shhhh," Berto said again, and Shelly nodded his head emphatically in the darkness.

Four years older, Berto had spent most of his childhood living with his mother, who had been

Daddy Davio's first wife. Sheldon had been seven years old before he'd realized that the sullen older boy who visited once a year wasn't just another random cousin, but instead his own half brother.

Their family had been the Brady Bunch 2.0—with Berto's divorced father marrying Pauline and Francine's widowed mother. They'd then had Sheldon. He was half brother to all three of them—although Pauline was much older and had been sent away to boarding school before Shelly could even talk. He couldn't remember a time when she, too, lived at home.

But when Shel was twelve, Berto had turned sixteen, and he'd moved in with them, full-time. He'd gotten into trouble for stealing a car and was flunking out of school, so his mother washed her hands of him and passed him over to their father.

Despite their age differences, Berto and Shel and Francine became unlikely allies, in part due to Berto's instantaneous crush on fourteen-year-old Francie, who was blond and ethereal and sweet. It had seemed a little creepy at first—like Greg Brady having a thing for Marcia. But, like Greg and Marcia, Berto and Francie weren't really related, so Sheldon gave Berto a pass.

Who was he to judge, anyway?

They'd stayed close—all three of them—right up until Shelly was a senior in high school. Until the fiasco with the video.

Berto now released his death grip on Shel's mouth. As he did, Shel remembered—all in a rush—that he'd been unarmed and taking cover on a neighbor's lawn when two of the attacking gunmen had spotted him. Instead of killing him, they pulled him to his feet, and he'd realized immediately that they recognized him.

"Where's Ian Dunn?" one had asked. "Is he inside the house?"

It had been easy to answer with complete honesty, because Shel had had no clue if Ian was, in fact, inside of his house. Although it didn't surprise him one tiny bit that this situation had something to do with Aaron's notorious former-SEAL brother.

Back when Shel and Aarie had worked with Ian, as part of the support team for his private-sector information-gathering business, the world had revolved around the man—and rightly so. As smart as Sheldon was, Ian was smarter. And as strong and tenacious as Aaron was, Eee was stronger and even more tenacious. The monsters that drove the man were meaner, with far sharper teeth—mostly because Ian had spent his life shielding Aaron from them.

He'd been a worthy team leader—right up to the day, about a year ago, that he'd disappeared.

"I honestly didn't know Ian was back," Sheldon told Berto now. He spoke quietly, quickly, suddenly scared that Berto was going to use him as bait to ambush Aaron. "And Aaron didn't know either. I'm certain of that. He still might not know." Guilt gripped him, as it always did when he thought about the whole mess with Francine, and Ian being in prison, down in Northport. . . .

His half brother's words surprised him. "Yeah, I know, Shel, just . . . keep your voice down, aight? Dunn was released from prison this afternoon. Davio's shitting bricks that he made some kind of deal with the feds, and with Manny in the hospital—because he had a heart attack . . . A mild one . . ."

Holy God, was Berto actually cutting . . . ?

He *was*. Sheldon's wrists were released from the plastic restraints that held him, and he moved his stiff and aching arms up across his chest, rubbing his shoulders and biceps as Berto used his pocketknife to cut Shel's feet free, too.

"Can you walk?" his brother asked, closing and pocketing his knife, and then helping Sheldon up and out of the trunk.

"I think so," Shel said, but he had to lean heavily against the car.

They were in a garage of an undetermined size, in what had to be some McMansion. He could smell the new construction—the wood, the paint, the sharpness of mulch from a freshly opened bag—even though he couldn't see anything.

Berto was a shadowy shape. "You sure?"

"I could use some water."

Berto opened the front door of the car without a light going on. Shel heard him close it with an almost silent click. And then a bottle was pushed into his hands. It was both already opened and warm, which was better than nothing, but just barely. He took a sip, afraid if he guzzled it the way he wanted to that he'd throw up.

His legs were wobbly, and not just because he'd been locked in a hot trunk for hours. His head still pounded to the point of dizziness.

As if he'd read Shel's mind, Berto explained. "I had to do it. Hit you. Quick and easy. You had to be contained. If you'd fought back, you might've gotten badly hurt. More badly."

"You'll forgive me if I don't thank you."

Berto laughed, a short burst of air. "Believe me, I didn't expect it."

"Where are we? Is this your place?"

"No, it's Davio's."

"Jesus! We're up in Clearwater?"

"Shhh! I had to," Berto said. "Bring you here. I live here, too—part of the time, anyway. When I'm not in Miami. And with Manny in the hospital, I'm not in Miami. He's gotten even more paranoid—Davio. There's GPS tracking on all the cars and . . . I couldn't risk him getting suspicious. I would've been out here sooner to cut you loose, but I had to put out about a hundred fucking fires first."

"So now what?" Sheldon asked. The water, as awful as it was, was actually helping. "Where are we going?"

"I don't know," Berto admitted. "I thought we'd start with the-fuck-outta-here. Get you someplace safe, and then regroup. Figure out our next move. I've got a car—with no GPS signal—waiting out at the edge of the estate."

The rush of gratefulness that Shelly felt was almost instantly replaced by disbelief. "Why would you do this?" he asked, taking a step forward to try to see his brother's face in the shadows. "Davio's going to find out. Those men who grabbed me—"

"Were mine. They'll keep their mouths shut." Berto took a step back, maintaining his distance, and Sheldon stopped. Berto may have been willing to help him, but the man still didn't want him to come too close, maybe get some of Shelly's gay on him.

"So you're going to drive me back to Sarasota and just take me home?" Shelly asked.

"No, you can't go there," Berto told him. "The police are still all over that shit. Plus Davio's got a team watching. I'll take you to wherever your . . . whatever-you-call-him is."

"Husband," Shelly said. "Partner. Lover. Spouse. Love and light of my life. I'll let you pick whatever you're most comfortable with."

Berto smiled at that—Shelly could see his teeth gleaming, straight and white. He'd worn braces at age sixteen, when he'd first arrived. He'd given tips to Shel and Francie on how to handle the discomfort, when they, in turn, had gotten theirs.

"Why *are* you doing this?" Shel asked his former big brother again. And big brother was exactly what Berto had been, to both him and France, too. Mentor. Teacher. Protector. Friend.

But that had changed. Dramatically. Drastically.

Back on the day that the sex tape blew up not just

his world, but Aaron's, Francine's, and Berto's worlds, too.

God, he'd been dreaming about it again, just moments ago. It still haunted him, and probably always would.

"Let's go," Berto said now, instead of answering him. "Be silent when we're outside of the house—you remember how to be silent, right?"

"Just go. I'm right behind you." Berto *had* taught Shelly a lot through the years. But after his time as a Marine, he could probably teach Berto a thing or two about stealth.

Together they moved soundlessly out of the garage, through a door that led into the humidity of the evening. Shel *had* been in that trunk for hours—it was dark outside.

There was plenty of time to think while he followed Berto into the dense brush—wherever it was that Davio was living these days, the property was huge and private. A vague flickering of distant lights marked the house of his closest neighbors—well out of visual range and earshot.

It didn't take much imagination to wonder if his half brother wasn't, in fact, leading him to some deserted part of some swampy land, to kill him and dispose of his body, in a warped retelling of the Snow White fairytale. But if Shel was Snow White, and Berto was the huntsman, well, that would make Davio the crazy Evil Queen, which was pretty damn funny. Or it would've been funny if he wasn't worrying about Aaron and Rory—forget about the potentially impending execution-style double-pop of bullets to his own head.

But they finally reached a clearing where a car was parked, just as Berto had said. His brother got in first, sliding behind the steering wheel. At that point, Shel could've run, and he knew from the way Berto was looking at him through the front windshield that he half-expected him to do just that.

But there were more dangers in a swampy Florida jungle than gangsters with guns. There were alligators. Poison ivy and oak. Rattlesnakes or water moccasins or copperheads or cobras or whatever the hell else lived out here. Brown recluse spiders and black widows. Mosquitoes carrying West Nile virus . . .

Shelly got into the car. And it was only then, as Berto turned the key, as the car lights went on and the dash lit the older man's face, that he turned and looked at Shel. Even though his hairline was receding at warp speed and his face was lined and tired, his brown eyes were the same as ever. Slightly amused, slightly pissed off, slightly kind, slightly crazy.

"I owe your sister," Berto said quietly. "Big time. This is me still desperately trying to make amends. If I can."

He put the car in gear and pulled away, eyes now on the dirt path ahead of them.

Out of all the reasons and all of the excuses Berto could've given, Shelly bought this one. Almost.

"So, where to?" Berto asked. As if Shel would

just take his word for it—that this wasn't a ploy to get him to lead the Dellarosas directly to Aaron and Ian.

Still, Shel played along. "Let's head for Sarasota and get to a Kinko's," he told Berto. "There's a twenty-four-hour branch on Forty-One, near Bahia Vista. Unless you know of a closer one in Tampa or St. Pete?"

Berto nodded. He knew what Shel wanted—access to a computer to get a message to Aaron and Francine. "There's an Internet cafe right in Clearwater—we're about fifteen minutes north of town. We'll drive right past it."

"I'd rather not stop in Clearwater," Sheldon said.

"You know you can use my phone to send an email," Berto said, anticipating Shel's headshake *no*. "Yeah, I wouldn't use it either." He glanced at Shel again. "You don't have to look at me like that. I'm not an idiot. I'm not expecting a miracle—I know there's no happy ending to my story. I don't get the girl. I know that. It's not gonna happen. She's never gonna forgive me. Shit, *I* don't forgive me."

Shelly had a flash then, of a memory from Christmas morning, this past year, when Aaron was on the floor with Rory, helping him tear open presents. He'd been laughing at their antics—it was hard to tell who was more excited, Rory or Aarie. When Shel had caught a glimpse of his own face in the mirror over the sofa, the delight and joy that shone from him had made him pause. Take stock. Be thankful for his life and his beautiful family.

He'd come far since that awful night when his world had exploded.

But he'd also seen Francie in that mirror, on Christmas day. His sister had been sitting beside him, and although she'd been smiling, there had been a sadness on her face—a sorrow that she couldn't disguise.

And Shel realized now, at this moment in this car with Berto, that the last time he'd seen France alight with true happiness . . . had been back before the disaster with that video, before Francine had gotten sucked in, so to speak, before Berto had turned on her, and in one violent and irreversible moment, embraced the life that he, Sheldon, and Francine had all been desperately trying to escape.

Now, the best Shelly could offer was, "I'll tell France you said hi."

"Better not to even mention me at all," Berto said, and with that, they drove in silence through the night.

The FBI safe house was in a trendy part of Sarasota, relatively near the bay. Modest concrete block houses built in the 1960s sat beside enormous, recently built mansions. It was an eclectic neighborhood, for sure. But one thing was uniform: regardless of house size, the yards were all lushly planted and neatly maintained. And nearly every house boasted waterfront property, thanks to the series of canals that snaked through this part of town.

Phoebe knew the neighborhood well. In fact, the house that the FBI had rented was on her jogging route. She lived just a few blocks to the south, in a luxury condo complex that overlooked one of the wider, deep-water canals.

As she got out of the car, which she'd parked out of sight in a driveway that looped back behind the safe house, she had to stop and hike up her too-large borrowed jeans. She longed—desperately—for the chance to run home to shower and change into her own clothes.

Ten minutes was all she'd need, she was that close. Okay. Realistically? It would take more like twenty-five.

Still, it didn't seem too much to ask, considering her day had included very nearly getting killed. More than once.

"I live around the corner," she told Deb, the goth-disguised FBI agent who was wearing Martell's shirt. But Deb held up one ebony-nailed finger, turning purposely to show Phoebe that her phone was to her ear.

There was another FBI agent already at the house, a dark-haired Asian American man with a deadpan yet friendly face, who held open the back door to help hustle them into the house. Aaron had his towel back over his head, and he went in first, clutching his bag.

"Are Francine and Rory here yet?" he asked.

"Not yet," the new FBI guy answered.

"Shel's bag is in the trunk."

"I'll get it," the agent said, nodding a greeting at Phoebe, who let herself get herded inside by Deb, who was all huge gestures and wide eyes, with her phone still to her ear as she indicated Phoebe should go through the door first.

But once inside the kitchen, Deb beelined into the main part of the house, heading for a distant corner or maybe a room with a door as Phoebe heard her say, "Sir. I understand, but . . . No, sir, that's not the case. Sir, this would be *much* easier if I could just speak directly to Mr. Cassidy, the agent-in-charge. . . ."

This house was one of the smaller, nonrenovated ones in the neighborhood. It was a single-story structure, built close to the ground as if to hug the earth in the event of hurricane-force winds. The ceilings were low and claustrophobic. The small rooms jammed with ancient motel-style wicker-and-overstuffed furniture added to the effect. The windows were old-school Florida jalousie-style—and all securely covered by blinds or curtains.

Which was the reason this house had been chosen over the vast number of upscale rentals in this area. Most of the newer places had crescent-shaped windows cut high into the walls and kept uncovered because no one could see in.

Unless they really wanted to.

The male FBI agent lugged Shelly's bag in from the car, closing and locking the kitchen door behind him. His expression—or lack thereof—hadn't changed. But when he spoke, there was a certain quizzical note to his voice. “We’re missing one person,” he said. He was a slow-talker, as if each word was carefully chosen. “There should be three of you, plus Deb.”

Aaron had dropped his own bag on the floor in order to open the refrigerator and the kitchen cabinets. Empty and empty.

“Ian—Mr. Dunn—had an . . . errand to do,” Phoebe answered, since Aaron was silent.

The FBI agent nodded. “Oh, good,” he said. “No wonder Deb’s head is imploding.”

“When my kid arrives,” Aaron announced. “He’s going to be hungry. There’s nothing to eat here.”

“I haven’t had a chance to stock the place with food yet,” the FBI agent said, looking from Aaron to Phoebe. “I’ll do that next. If there’s something you want in particular—”

“Diapers,” Aaron listed. “Baby food and formula, but a very specific kind. Rory has allergies.”

“Write it down, please,” the man said gesturing toward the yellow laminated counter, where there was a long narrow pad and a pen. He’d already started a list that included *toilet paper* and *dishwasher detergent*. He held out his hand to Phoebe as he introduced himself, partly because she was closer and partly because Aaron was now giving his full hostile attention to filling that pad. “I’m Yashi. Joe Hirabayashi.”

Phoebe already liked him. She shook his hand and said, “Phoebe Kruger. I’m Ian Dunn’s lawyer. I’m only here until he gets back, to make sure he has what he needs."

Yashi blinked. Just once. "Is that what Deb told you? Because I'm pretty sure you're here for the duration. That's what makes a safe house safe. Civilians aren't allowed to come and go."

Allowed? That was not a happy word, considering the amount of work on her desk. "I'm used to keeping secrets," Phoebe said. "Lawyer-client privilege?"

"Of course," Yashi said, but then added, "This is different."

"I'll discuss it with Deb," Phoebe said.

He nodded. "Good."

Aaron, meanwhile, had finished his list. "The irony is that I had a car full of groceries when this bullshit started. Can you get this stuff now, please? Before Rory gets here? I've already heard him cry enough for a lifetime."

"I'll do that," Yashi said, reaching for the list. "I'll pick up some pizzas, too."

"Bless you," Phoebe said.

He smiled at that—a microscopic movement of his mouth. He held out the list to her. "Anything to add?"

"No, I'm fine," she said. Like she'd said, she didn't expect to be staying long. But breakfast had been a long, long time ago, so pizza would be a win. "Thanks."

"Tell Deb where I've gone," he ordered. "If someone comes to the door, don't open it—go get her."

"Understood," Phoebe said, glancing at Aaron who was silently moving both his and Shelly's bags into the living room.

"Lock up behind me, please," Yashi said as he went out into the evening.

Phoebe did, locking both the button on the knob of the door and a thumb-turn bolt that was above it. Neither would be particularly effective against someone with a burning desire to kick the door open.

She turned back to find Aaron vanishing into the gloom of a hallway opposite the one Deb had gone down. "I'm going to find a shower," he announced, "and take one, before Rory gets here, while I try not to throw up."

"Ian will get Shelly back," Phoebe said.

Aaron stopped, and slowly turned around to look at her. "You really don't see it, do you? That you're already a high priestess in the church of Ian. Don't worry, you're not the first. He has that effect on almost all women, across all continents."

Phoebe laughed her embarrassment, turning it into a disbelieving scoff. "You're wrong. I'm really not—"

"Yeah whatever," he said. "I've heard that before, too." He vanished down the hall.

Leaving Phoebe standing there, completely alone.

Deb was still on the phone at the other end of the low-ceilinged but sprawling house.

And Phoebe knew in that instant that Deb was not going to let her leave. Not to run home to change or to grab her own—what did Ian call it? A go-bag. She was going to be locked in here despite the fact that she wasn't in danger. Apparently Jerry Bryant had been working for Manny Dellarosa, and regardless of what Ian believed, Phoebe knew—*knew*—that someone in Manny's line of work would not harm one of his legal advisors.

And she also knew, in that instant, what she had to do.

Leave.

Now.

Before Deb got off the phone.

Go home—it would take her five minutes to walk there—take a shower, wash the chlorine out of her hair, put on jeans that actually fit, grab the clothing and work files she needed and . . .

She'd be back before anyone missed her, long before Ian's couple of hours were up. If Yashi could go out into the world and run an errand, surely she could, too.

Phoebe shouldered her still-damp bag, opened the door—checking to make sure that she could trigger the lock in the knob, even though that deadbolt would stay open. She pushed the button in and shut the door behind her and . . .

It worked. It was secure.

She went briskly down the driveway to the sidewalk and headed for home.

CHAPTER EIGHT

They were almost there.

"Which one is it?"

Martell glanced over at Francine, who was driving his car. She'd taken the left turn onto the street where the safe house was supposed to be and had slowed to a crawl. "Five eighty-five."

They both peered through the darkness, searching for a house number.

"It's down a bit more, on the left," Martell said, pointing to the right, where the reflective numbers 240 were on a mailbox in front of what looked like a castle, complete with moat.

She nodded and drove a little faster. And then said, "If I were you, I wouldn't be in such a big hurry to get there."

He looked at her, waiting for further explanation, and she actually laughed as she shot him another glance. Sure, it was a laugh of disdain, but it transformed her, and damn, she was beautiful. Even with no makeup on, dressed in faded jeans and a no-frills tank, she still managed to be prettier than 99.9 percent of the women on the planet. With her long blond hair, blue eyes, and a body that killed . . .

And maybe there was something he was missing here, because he'd gone and gotten himself all distracted, but it sure seemed as if she were implying that . . . "You think Dunn is going to, what? Kick my ass?"

"He's already kicking your ass," Francine said, pointing to another mailbox, this time in front of a house that looked as if it had been built by Frank Lloyd Wright on meth. "Three ninety-seven."

Martell nodded. They were almost there.

"Look at the assignment he gave you," she continued. "Chauffeur-slash-babysitter."

"Maybe he likes me the most," Martell countered, even though he knew she was right. He was definitely on Dunn's shit list. "Putting me in a car with an attractive young woman—"

She blew him a raspberry. "And a baby he expected to cry for the entire ride? No, he hates you. I wonder what he'll have you do next? Surveillance from inside a Dumpster?"

"Please don't suggest that to him," he said as she slowed way down, because there came 585, on the left, as expected.

It did not look like a castle or as if a drug-addled famous architect had been anywhere near the blueprint. It was boxy and built long before Martell had been born. It was both small and unassuming.

"Is this really it?" he said aloud as she pulled up in front. It was quaint and even charming in an old-time Florida way, but he really would have preferred the descriptors that popped to mind be *defensible* and *fortresslike*.

Considering it was supposed to be a *safe* house.

"Maybe you should call your FBI contact,"

Francine said. "Make sure we got the number right."

Martell dug for his phone, but then didn't have to, because there came Deb, still wearing his shirt, barreling down the driveway as if she'd come racing out of a back door. Before she hit the sidewalk, she was already scanning the street, looking both ways.

Martell opened his window, leaned out. "Hey. What's up?"

He'd startled her, so much so that she nearly drew on him. Instead, she came over, leaned down to look in to see Francine and the baby. "Get this car back behind the house," she said, pointing. "Now. But be ready to leave, immediately. We're pulling out."

"What? What happened?" Martell asked again.

"It's Phoebe," Deb told him grimly. "She's gone. She must've just . . . walked away."

"She lives nearby," Aaron said as he helped the FBI agent nicknamed Yashi transfer the bags of groceries into Martell's ancient car. Aaron had used Francie's phone to call Ian on the burner cell, to let him know that Phoebe was gone, but his brother hadn't picked up. Hopefully he'd call back soon. "Phoebe said that when we pulled up. Am I the only one who heard her?"

"I didn't hear it," Yashi said, as deadpan and unexcited as he'd been when they'd first arrived.

"I was on the phone," Deb said. She was pissed.

And not just because Phoebe had disappeared. She was pissed because the big, handsome black guy, Martell, had shown up with Rory and Francine—with his tongue hanging out.

France had that effect on the het male population. Even Yashi's pulse rate seemed to have rocketed up to forty-five upon sight of her. Dude had even blinked. Twice in a row.

"I have three contact numbers for Phoebe," Martell said. Aaron still wasn't sure exactly what his deal was, other than that he was a lawyer who seemed to be working closely with the feds. Also, whatever upper-body workout the man did was highly effective. As Aaron watched, Martell stopped helping with the groceries and got out his phone. "Work, cell, and home phone—"

"Do *not* call her." Aaron said it at the same time as both Yashi and Deb. He was pretty sure Francine would've joined in the chorus, too, if she hadn't ducked inside, upon arrival, to use the bathroom.

"Give me her home number, though," Yashi offered. "I'll do a reverse lookup to get her address." He had his own phone out and working, Internet connected.

Martell was still frowning, so Aaron explained. "If the Dellarosas are watching her place, they've hacked into her phone line. If you call and she picks up, they'll know for sure that she's there. That's if they don't know it already."

There were numerous possibilities to this scenario. One, that Phoebe had walked home, arriving before Davio's men staked out the place.

Two, that they'd been there when she'd arrived and they'd already grabbed her, and . . .

Three, that they'd been there when she'd arrived but she'd walked right past them, unrecognizable due to her funky clothes, thanks to her repeated dunkings in his swimming pool.

Martell was still skeptical. "You really think she's under surveillance? By Manny Dellarosa?"

"Davio, probably," Aaron said. "Manny's in the hospital."

"Phoebe lives, literally, one block south of here, two streets down," Yashi reported.

"And the Dellarosas have already IDed her," Martell pushed, "by . . . osmosis?" He answered his own question as he remembered, "Her car was parked out in front of the crime scene. Of course. Sorry. My bad. It's been a while since I've done police work. But just as an FYI, if I wasn't thinking about that, Phoebe probably wasn't either. Also, as a lawyer, you kinda get used to having meetings with alleged criminals. You expect them to call you, not abduct you."

"At this point, for all we know," Deb said shortly, "she's working for the Dellarosas."

Holy shit. Aaron was stunned. The *FBI* didn't know . . . ?

And now there was a fourth possibility—that Phoebe was working for Davio and had gone home so that she could call him and divulge the current whereabouts of Aaron, Francine, and Rory.

"Forget the rest of the food," Aaron said, looking over at Rory, who was waiting patiently in the back of Martell's car. "We need to leave. Now."

"I'm sorry, *what* did she just say?" Francine was back from the bathroom and focused on Deb. She stood now in the kitchen door, angelically backlit. The look on her face, however, was not beatific. She turned to glare at Martell. "You told me Phoebe's a lawyer."

"She is," he said. "She works for Bryant, Hill, and Stoneham."

"There was a slight SNAFU," Deb admitted. "We didn't get a chance to clear her—"

"*That,* I didn't know," Yashi said, his eyes wider open than Aaron had yet seen them.

"We don't know all that much about her," Deb continued grimly, "other than she has no criminal record, and yes, she passed the bar in Florida, and as of last week has been employed by BH and S."

Francine came down the stairs. "Are you"—she looked at Rory, his car seat still belted into the back of Martell's car—"effing kidding me? And you just let her walk away . . . ?"

"That's my fault," Yashi started, but Deb cut him off.

"No, it's mine," she said. "I should have told you. I just assumed you'd stick around until I got off the phone."

The cell phone that Aaron was holding rang, sparing him from joining in the self-blamefest with his own recrimination of *I shouldn't've taken a shower and left her alone.* It was Ian on the other end, and he'd apparently listened to Aaron's message about Phoebe being gone. Unlike Francine, he didn't bother to curb his language.

"How the fuck did this happen?" Ian asked, plainly pissed.

"Overwhelm," Aaron told his brother. "I'm pretty sure Deb hasn't slept in three days. Plus with you gone, there's no clear chain of command. Typical charlie foxtrot." That was military radio code for the letters *C* and *F,* which was the short form for clusterfuck, synonymous with goatfuck. A *goat* was an ineffective leader whose head was up his or her ass. Sometimes due to lack of sleep.

"I need her home address," Ian said. The *her* he was referring to was, of course, Phoebe.

"Bad idea," Aaron countered. "A waste of time, when we need to find Shel."

Ian sighed. Hard. "I'm not leaving her," he said.

"That's right," Aaron said. "You're not. She walked away."

"She's not working for Davio," Ian said. "I know this."

"Do you know this with your brain or with your dick?" Aaron asked.

"Home. Address."

Aaron rattled off the address and apartment number.

"Now get the fuck out of there. Is Francie with you?" Ian asked. "She must be—you're on her phone."

“Yeah,” Aaron said. “Why?”

“Tell her to get you to Contact Point Zebra. She’ll know where that is, she’ll know what to do. Chain of command? Fuck the FBI. *She’s* now in charge. I’ll meet you there soon.” And with that Ian cut the connection.

Aaron turned to his sister-in-law and repeated Ian’s words. “He said to tell you Contact Point Zebra—and that you’re now in charge.” He got up in Francine’s face. “Why would Eee do that? What the hell do you know, that I don’t?”

Francine didn’t back down. She lifted her chin and said, “I’ve been working with Ian all this time, most of which he’s spent in prison, down in Northport.”

“What?” Aaron felt all of the air leave his lungs—in fact, all of the oxygen in Florida left Sarasota as he struggled to keep breathing and to understand. Prison? Ian had been in *prison?*

“I’ll tell you as much as I can,” Francine said, “which isn’t a lot. But right this second? We’re leaving. So get your ass in the car. *Now*.”

Ian was pissed.

As a Navy SEAL, he’d been trained to expect disaster.

Murphy’s Law was a given—whatever can go wrong, *will* go wrong—and Ian was never surprised when he got bitchslapped by the universe.

But *this* entire day had been clown-car ridiculous. He was trapped in an ugly spinning vortex of *Are you fucking kidding me?*

And that vortex had just been kicked to a higher speed, thanks to Phoebe Kruger.

And this was on top of Ian's arriving at the hospital to discover—of course—that Manny Dellarosa was in prep for an angiogram, which meant he was out of reach until tomorrow. Ian had already reached the acceptance stage of his grief about that, and was out in the hospital's parking garage when he'd gotten Aaron's message about Phoebe going AWOL.

It hadn't taken him long to "borrow" a car to rush to her rescue—although the way this day was going, he'd half-expected the damn thing to be infested with rats or maybe poisonous snakes.

He'd ditched the car without getting bitten—a small victory, but he'd take it—about a block away from "The Dockside," Phoebe's fancy-ass condo complex. Since he had no idea what was coming, he preferred to go in on foot, so he could keep to the shadows.

As he moved through the humid evening, Ian hoped that Phoebe wasn't there, in her condo, but he knew that she probably was.

He also knew that his carelessness was in part, at least, to blame—he should've been more aggressive about the fact that she was in danger from the Dellarosas. Clearly, she hadn't believed him. Lawyers. Jesus. They actually thought they were bulletproof. *We deal with criminals all the time.* Yeah, well, not like the Dellarosas, honey.

Of course, there was also the idea that Ian

couldn't quite shake—that Phoebe's naïveté was just an act, that she herself might work for the Agency. The Glock in her bag, her sharp mind, and her ability to think on her feet, plus her relative coolness under fire . . .

Maybe she hadn't innocently and/or stupidly gone home, but instead had faded back to Agency HQ, wherever that was.

And *that* thought pissed Ian off even more than the sweat that dripped down his back. Oddly enough, he hated the idea that this woman might've vanished, possibly forever, since her mission had been accomplished when Ian had agreed to help rescue those kidnapped kids.

He spotted a Dellarosa-dark car with two occupants, parked across the street from Phoebe's condo building's driveway at the exact moment that the burner phone shook in his pocket. He blended into the foliage as he pulled it out and glanced at the number. It was Martell, so he took the call.

"Yeah."

"Sorry to be the bearer of more bad news," Martell told him. "But Phoebe just called my cell from her condo landline."

"Shit."

"Yeeeeah." The lawyer drew the word out. "She wanted me to tell you that she was running a little late, that she'd be another fifteen minutes before she returned."

And that was that. No experienced Agency operative, she. Although it was interesting that

Phoebe's intention had been to return to the safe house. She was doubly naïve for not realizing that the FBI would've already gone into red alert and bugged out the moment she'd turned up missing.

"I told her to stay put," Martell continued. "That we had a situation that needed my attention, that I'd have to call her back. I didn't let her say anything else, just stressed that she should stay where she was and wait for contact."

And wasn't that unexpected and remarkably astute? "Thanks," Ian said, and he must've sounded surprised.

Because Martell added, "Yeah, I'm not a total idiot, Dunn. Call me if there's anything I can do to help. FYI, we're safely on the move." He hung up.

A helo extraction would've been helpful, but as of yet, Martell and his FBI buddies hadn't even managed to get Ian a sandwich—let alone extra handguns to arm his motley crew. And since no way had Ian been willing to leave Aaron without a weapon, that meant he himself was currently out here carrying only a Bic pen.

Ian moved closer to the complex, mentally working out a Plan B, since his Plan A was no longer feasible. Of course, his Plan A had been super-simple—walk up the driveway, find condo 204, knock on its door. *Hey, Phoebe. C'mon. Get your stuff. Let's go. Move it.*

Now, thanks to that car parked out front, he was going to have to go all covert and shit.

Fricking pain in his ass.

Ian focused on the building, looking past the decorative railings to the layout and architectural structure.

The Dockside was an artfully arranged series of attractively stuccoed buildings. It had a lot of windows and ornate balconies—i.e. hoo-hahs to grab and swing from, should grabbing and swinging become necessary. It also had copious waterfront views, with several of the structures overlooking one of Sarasota's many canals. There was a relatively high wall around the nonwater side of the property, with one driveway leading both in and out, and a pedestrian gate at the north end of the grounds.

He was pretty sure, from the relaxed postures of the two men he could clearly see sitting in the car, that they hadn't recognized Phoebe as she'd walked past them.

While Ian's Plan A had been to grab her and leave, his Plan B was to do the exact same thing, but without the men in the car seeing them.

Except now that he'd found out that Phoebe'd used her landline to call Martell . . . ?

Any minute, whoever was tapping her home phone was going to sound the alarm, and call the thugs in that car. They were about to find out that their target had just made an outgoing call, therefore, she must be home. She was there, and she was abductable.

And Ian knew that the men in the car would abduct her rather than attempt to follow her, because she'd obviously evaded them once already. Rather than risk her getting past them again, they'd play it safe and get Ian's whereabouts from her the good old-fashioned way.

By tying her to a chair and beating her up.

Sure enough, as Ian watched, the two men now got out of the car. The driver was on the phone. And because he didn't know Ian was lurking in the bushes, he didn't bother to keep his voice down.

"Well, what's their facking ETA?" he asked in an accent that screamed Boston Southie, with an attitude that dripped of ripe annoyance. It didn't take a degree in rocket science to theorize that he'd been chastised and told to wait for backup before going in after Phoebe.

And that was both good news and bad. Good, because the waiting-for-backup thing gave Ian a little more time to get into Phoebe's condo, explain what was happening, and get her the hell out of there. Bad, because if something went wrong, he'd have to deal not just with two Dellarosa goons, but instead a larger, undetermined number.

As Ian kept to the shadows, soundlessly moving closer to the Dockside's wall, Southie ended the phone call, his aggravation radiating from him. "Go keep an eye on the other gate," he told his compatriot. "Yeah, the footpath. She must've come in that way. Although, Jesus. Who the fack walks around in this heat?"

The other guy's voice didn't carry, but Southie

responded to whatever he'd said with, "No, watch and wait. Mr. D's on his way."

Ian went up and over the wall, dropping lightly into one of the Dockside's many courtyards. He was well aware that the Mr. D in question was Davio Dellarosa, and that Davio wouldn't show up with anything less than a small army to protect him. Particularly since he knew that Ian was on the loose.

Ian moved swiftly through the courtyard, searching for condo 204 . . . 204 . . . Please let it be in the long, low building—only three stories high—that sat right at the edge of the canal. And yes. It was.

The other buildings, on the noncanal side of the complex, were taller—seven or eight stories—with upper-level condos that offered excellent views despite their distance from the water.

Of course, this meant that the roof of Phoebe's building was probably decorative and sloping, not flat and ugly. Since it could be looked down upon from all of those high-rise balconies, the roof was probably covered with barrel tiles, which could be slippery as all hell.

Going up to the roof to escape Davio's men was Ian's backup Plan C, or maybe he was up to D by now. He bypassed the elevator and took the outside staircase up to the second floor, where he spotted a sign telling him that 204 was down toward the left. But he quickly went up one more flight—to get a partial view of the street where Davio's goons were parked.

He couldn't see their car, but he could see what looked like three, no four, no—*shit*—five additional vehicles pulling up, their headlights blazing.

Apparently, Davio's ETA was *now*.

Ian took the express route back to the second floor, making each half-flight in a single jump, holding on to the banister for support.

He sprinted down the outside hallway to condo 204, skidding to a stop as he hammered on the door with one hand, even as he found and leaned on the doorbell with his other.

"Come on, come on, come on," he muttered, and he finally heard movement from inside, so he stepped back slightly so that Phoebe could see him through the peephole.

As she unfastened the locks, he saw that although she had three on the door, they were nothing special. Davio and his army would blow through them in short order. And that meant that Ian and Phoebe had to leave. Now.

"What are you doing here?" Phoebe asked in amazement as the door finally opened. She'd washed her hair, and it hung around her face in shiny waves.

Ian lost a full two seconds just staring at her before he pushed past her. "Glock," he said, aware as hell that she smelled really good. "I need it. Now."

"My Glock?" she asked. "Why?"

"Yes, your Glock. Hello. Does anyone else here have a Glock?"

She was wearing jeans that fit her far better than the pair he'd given her in Aaron and Shel's panic room. And while the shoes she had on were significantly less stupid than the heels that had come off in the swimming pool, she was going to need something with better traction.

"Sneakers," he told her, snapping his fingers and pointing at her feet. "Get your sneakers."

But she was standing there, staring at him, her brown eyes wide behind her glasses as she waited for an explanation, so he clapped his hands and added, "Move! Now!" even as he realized that this was, absolutely, the proof beyond all proof that she wasn't Agency or even former military. This woman had no clue how to take an order.

Ian had learned through time that when dealing with civilians, concise explanations worked better than *Because I'm in charge and I say so, so do it, God damn it!* So he went with "Davio Dellarosa has tracked you here. Get your sneakers. We've got to leave, now."

But he could tell from the way she was looking at him that she still honestly didn't think she was in danger, so he continued, "He's got six cars out there. At least twice as many men. All armed. These are not people who only want to talk to you. In fact, what Davio wants is for *you* to talk to *him*. To tell him where I am. To reveal the location of the safe house."

"But I'd never do that," she said.

"You might," he countered. "After the second or third beating."

Doubt flickered in her eyes. "You seriously think . . . ?"

"I don't think it, I know it. I know Davio. There's a very good chance that Sheldon's getting the shit kicked out of him right now. And I'm standing here, screwing around with you," Ian told her. "This isn't a game. Glock and sneakers. Now."

Finally, thank God, Phoebe leapt into action, dashing from her foyer and into a condo unit that was virtually empty of furniture, with unpacked boxes lining the wall. She called back to him, "The Glock's in my bag—kitchen counter. I'll get my cross-trainers."

"Yeah, 'cause you wouldn't want badminton shoes at a time like this," he fired back at her. Cross-trainers, Jesus.

The condo's great room—a spacious, high-ceilinged Florida-style combination of living and dining room—was barely separated from the equally enormous kitchen by a granite island counter. The big combined room had one wall that was entirely glass, made up of a series of huge sliding doors that led onto a massive screened lanai-style balcony, complete with three giant ceiling fans overhead.

"I'm assuming you had no luck contacting Manny at the hospital," she called from the other room.

"He was unable to take a meeting," Ian told her as he stepped closer to the balcony to see . . . Yes, it directly overlooked the canal. Which meant he now had a last-ditch Plan Z. "Hurry."

But hopefully, it wouldn't come to that.

Phoebe's kitchen was chef-worthy, with a gas stove and rich wood cabinets, but Ian didn't give it more than a quick glance as he beelined for what had to be her bag on the counter. It was different from the lady-luggage she'd had earlier in the day—a light beige leather, which wasn't good for those hiding-from-the-bad-guys-in-the-night moments that were sure to come. But the darker one was probably still wet. This was equally gigantic though, with a zipper he had to unfasten before diving in.

Sweet Jesus, did she really carry all of this shite around with her, as necessities? Power bars, makeup, tampons, twenty thousand pens of various colors, an assortment of different-sized note-books . . .

But he was not here to judge. Something as heavy as her Glock would've sunk to the bottom, so he searched with his hand, just gingerly reaching in and feeling around, on the assumption that the weapon would be hard to miss. He was right. He found it quickly enough and pulled it and its holster free, only to have a bra come with it. He untangled the two, jammed the bra back into the bag and the handgun into the back waist of his jeans. And look. His disturbance had caused her house keys to float to the top of the debris. He pocketed them, too.

"Any extra ammo?" Ian called out, even as he opened the cabinet under the sink, searching for trash bags. Bingo. A box. Except they were white. "Shit."

"Some. Not a lot. It's in one of these boxes," Phoebe said, emerging from her bedroom with her sneakers—her cross-trainers, forgive him—already on. She'd grabbed a sweatshirt, too, which was provident, since it was dark blue and therefore exactly what he needed. "Sorry, I don't know which one. Although, for the record, I'd prefer it if you didn't kill anyone with my gun, please."

Ian zipped her bag back up as he carried it and met her in the middle of the empty great room. "I'll do my best not to," he told her. She grabbed for her bag, but he held it out of reach as he took her sweatshirt from her instead. He put the light-colored bag inside the torso of the sweatshirt, turning it into an easier-to-carry hobo bundle by tying the two arms together. Only then did he hand it to her. "It's dark out there."

She nodded. "Your shirt?"

Was white. She clearly understood the concept.

"I'll take it off," he said. "If they see us. I can use it to misdirect."

He could tell she didn't quite understand, and Ian didn't want to take the time to explain the vast intricacies of E&E—escape and evasion. One time-honored trick was the art of changing one's appearance midchase. If everyone was looking for a tall man in a white T-shirt, then ditch the T-shirt.

"Just like this afternoon," Ian told her instead as they moved to the door, "in the pool. When I tell you to do something you do it. No questions, no hesitation."

Phoebe nodded, but then said, "I'm not sure why we're not simply calling the police."

"They won't get here in time." Ian opened the door just a crack to look out.

"Before what? Dellarosa's men kick down my door, and drag me out, scratching and screaming? I think my neighbors might notice—"

"No," he told her, pulling her out with him onto the outdoor corridor. "They won't. Dellarosa's men'll do it quickly and quietly. You will not be conscious. They'll make sure of that. Now, *shh.*"

To most people, *shh* meant stop talking. Phoebe chose to interpret it to mean that she shouldn't speak quite as loudly. "So why don't we make it noisy, right now?" she whispered. "Why don't we start shouting and banging on doors—get as many of my neighbors out here as possible, create an anti-abduction flashmob?"

It was, at least in theory, an interesting idea. But it carried a huge amount of risk. "And put them in danger?" Ian asked. "That's if anyone actually bothers to come to our aid. Which is assuming a lot. Most people won't even open their door after dark. They'll pretend they don't hear."

And . . . *fack,* as the driver of the first car would say. Dellarosa's men were already in the courtyard. There was no going down the stairs. Their only options were up to the roof, or back into Phoebe's apartment.

Ian quickly unlocked her door and pulled her inside.

“This can’t be good,” Phoebe correctly surmised.

“It’s not,” he said, as he went into the great room and picked up the nearest box. Jesus, what did she have in here? Although the fact that the boxes were heavy was a good thing. “Help me.”

She caught on fast enough and helped him pile the boxes in front of the door, creating a barricade.

“This is not going to keep anyone out for very long,” she pointed out as he grabbed another and another. She was right behind him. “Not if they’re determined. I mean yes, it’ll slow them down—”

“That’s all we need,” Ian told her. “Just to slow them down.”

“Except I can’t help but notice that we *still* haven’t called the police,” she said.

“They *still* won’t get here in time,” he said again. “And even if they did, the Dellarosas have people working for them everywhere. We wouldn’t be safe.” Ian humped the last few boxes as she stood there, staring at him. “Grab a knife from the kitchen, will you? A paring knife if you have one. Something small and sharp.”

His request snapped Phoebe out of whatever disbelieving reverie she’d fallen into, and she swiftly went behind the island counter to open a drawer.

“Oh my God,” she said. “We’re going off the balcony, aren’t we? I have to warn you, I have terrible upper-body strength. The thought of climbing down . . . I just don’t think I can—”

Ian interrupted her. “Don’t worry about that.”

"Why?" she asked. "Do you really think you can carry me?"

"Don't have to." He smiled because he knew from the look in her eye that she'd already figured out what he was going to say next.

"Oh my God, Ian . . ."

He said it anyway. "We're gonna jump."

Phoebe looked down into the murky depths of the canal, to where the water came up against the wall just outside of the Dockside condos. She'd seen large, deep-keeled sailboats pull right up to that canal wall, so she knew that the water there was plenty deep enough for a two-story plunge.

She also knew that Ian could swim really well, being a former Navy SEAL.

That didn't make it any better.

"Do you have a case or something for your glasses?" Ian asked, because no, they would not stay on her face when she hit that water, way down there. She untied the arms of her sweatshirt so that she could get her glasses case out of her handbag.

Oh my God, they were really going to do this—*she* was really going to do this. Still, she couldn't help but make a small sound of pain and despair as he used one of her new kitchen knives to cut the balcony screen.

"This won't be hard to fix," he said.

"As opposed to the kicked-in door and the damage to the apartment done by looters after the place is left open?" Phoebe asked, taking off her glasses and closing the hard case with a snap. It was better not to watch.

"I'll keep these in my pocket." Ian took the case from her, which was his subtle way of telling her that she was probably going to lose the entire contents of her handbag in the canal.

This was all her fault. She'd naively refused to believe that she was in danger, refused to accept that she'd stepped into a situation that was right out of the pages of some fantastic fictional spy thriller. Although truth be told they hadn't even gotten to the spy part, complete with its *Mission: Impossible* rescue of those poor kidnapped children. They were here, sidetracked—indeed, her fault entirely—by the murderous mob boss and his thugs, who were out for blood, and who *could've* gotten her to reveal the location of the safe house after her second beating, if not her first.

Phoebe had truly believed that her being a lawyer made her untouchable. But no doubt about it, she'd become the woman who idiotically went into the basement to check the circuit breakers when the lights went off, with a serial killer on the loose.

She was, officially, too stupid to live.

And yet Ian had come after her.

"I don't want to do this," Phoebe said.

Ian nodded. "I know. But you don't have a choice."

"God, I hate this. I hate you," she said.

"Yeah, I know that, too. I'm sorry. Give me your

bag, I'll take it. Come on. Climb up here." He patted the balcony railing.

She sat on it, intending to swing her legs over, but he shook his head. "Feet on the rail. We'll need to push off. I know it looks like the canal is right below us, but it's not. There's a few feet of wall. We'll need to get past that. It'll help if you can push, but if you can't, just hold on to me. I'll get us where we need to go."

"Oh my God," Phoebe said, as he helped her up, helped her balance, showed her where to hold on to the frame of the screen while he pulled himself up beside her.

"Do you know how to do a cannonball? That's the best way to hit the water from this height—arms and legs in close, head tucked down."

"I can try," Phoebe told him.

Ian's face was blurry in the dimness of the moonlight, but he came into focus as he leaned in close. "You're gonna be great," he told her with a smile that made his eyes impossibly blue. "After we hit the water, we'll swim beneath the surface, and then we're going to hide under a dock at that marina that's just to the north." He pointed, but without her glasses she couldn't see that far. Still, she knew the marina in question, so she nodded. "We'll need to be as quiet as possible each time we surface for air. No talking. At all. Do the best you can to control the sound of your breathing. You understand?"

She nodded again and whispered, "I'm sorry. I'm

the one who should be sorry, and I am. I truly am. I'm—"

Ian leaned in even farther, and she was so surprised she didn't move back—she just stood there clinging to the edge of her balcony—as he shut her up by brushing his lips against hers.

It was barely a kiss, but it still qualified, and then it definitely qualified as he did it again. Slower, longer, deeper.

Even sweeter.

"And I'm truly sorry that you hate me," Ian whispered, and it would've been insanely romantic had they not been about to jump off her balcony. "On three. One . . . two!"

He jumped on two.

The bastard jumped—and he pulled her with him—on freaking *two*.

Shelly looked over at Berto, who was lost in his own thoughts, driving through the night. The darkness of silent citrus groves and fields for grazing cattle had finally given way to the chain restaurants, motels, strip malls, and gas stations on the outskirts of Sarasota.

Their destination—a copy and shipping store where he could use a computer and send Aaron and Francine an email—wasn't too much farther away.

"Why didn't you trust her?" Shel asked his half brother now.

Berto glanced at him. He knew exactly who Shel was talking about. Francine.

“You should have trusted her,” Shel said.

“Yeah,” Berto said. “I know.”

“She saved my life,” Shel said. “I remember sitting there, outside of the headmaster’s office, with Aaron and just thinking that I was going to die. That Davio was going to kill me.”

The sex tape had made its way into the email of the staff and administration of the private school, and Shel and Aaron had been called in. They’d spoken to the school social worker first—Mrs. Thompson was an older woman who was terrible at her job—and she’d informed them that both Aaron’s brother and Shel’s father had been notified and emailed a copy of the video.

Shelly had gone into shock at that news—and Aaron knew it. After Thompson had delivered them back to the waiting area outside the headmaster’s office, Aaron urged him to leave, to run away.

“But then Francine called my cell,” Shel told Berto. “She said she saw the video when she was at class, over at the community college, and she came home to make sure I was okay, but that Davio had gone ballistic. She was whispering, she must’ve been in the bathroom, and she said—I will remember this for the rest of my life. She said, *I got this. It’s gonna be okay*. And then she told me to tell Aaron to check his text messages.”

“She cut her hair,” Berto said. “I should’ve known, because she cut her hair.”

Francine *had* cut her hair. Really short. As short as Shel’s.

She must've done it herself, because the back was really ragged. Still, on her, the style had looked elegant. It drew attention to the shape of her face, and her astonishingly beautiful eyes. She was beautiful with long hair, but strikingly so with it cut that short.

"She sent Aaron a bunch of texts," Sheldon told Berto. "*LOL, baby, let's do that again soon.* And pictures."

He knew Berto had seen them. Pornographic selfies that, once they were on Aaron's cell phone, confirmed her confession: Francine was the one in that video with Aaron.

"She saved my life," Sheldon said again. "You know that Davio would've killed me."

Berto nodded now, his hands tight on the steering wheel as the muscles jumped in his jaw.

"I didn't hit her," he finally said. "That was Davio. But what I did? It was just as bad. I walked away and I let him do it. Francine needed my protection. My trust. And I abandoned her."

CHAPTER NINE

Phoebe swallowed a scream, turning it into a mere squeak, as she attempted to pull herself into a cannonball as Ian had advised.

She went into the water with a splash at almost the exact moment he did. She could feel him beside her as the water closed over her head as she went down, down, down, down, bubbles surrounding them both.

He'd let go of her hand at some point during their leap from the balcony, probably so as to not wrench her wrist on impact, but now she felt him reach out and securely grab hold of her shirt.

And then she was being pulled up—at least she thought it was up, it was so dark beneath the water. She could feel his legs brushing against her, solid and strong as he kicked and kicked, and then, finally, thank God, they broke the surface.

Phoebe heard herself gasping and gulping and she tried to do it quietly, but the water tasted like gasoline, and it was probably filthy with all the boats that motored out from their docks to the open Gulf; not to mention the fact that there were men with guns after them, probably breaking into her apartment right now, and *God,* her skinned knee was stinging in the saltwater.

And despite all of that—and despite the fact that the shower she'd sneaked home to take was now completely for naught—she found herself a little too focused on that stupid kiss.

Ian must have done it to distract her—he'd jumped on *two* for the same reason.

It had worked. She was here; they were safe.

For now.

"Arms locked around my neck. Big inhale, then under again," Ian now breathed into her ear, and she nodded, turning to face him and loop her arms around him.

He waited for her to suck in another lungful of air, then they went back beneath the surface, and she held on for dear life even as she tried to kick, too, to help propel them forward. And when they surfaced again, she knew it was only for her sake—he surely could have swum much farther without another breath.

"Again," he commanded, and she obediently obliged.

And the next time they surfaced, Phoebe was a little alarmed at the darkness until she realized that they were, absolutely, underneath one of the nearby marina's wooden docks. There was just enough space for them to lurk beneath it, their heads out of the water, their noses up in the stagnant, fishy-smelling air. Ian reached up and grabbed onto one of the barnacle-covered beams as she continued to cling to him.

Dim light slid in between the wooden slats, but it shifted and moved with the swell of the water.

And that was both disconcerting and awkward, since there wasn't much to look at besides Ian's face, which was up-close and in *her* face as she held tightly to him, their bodies pressed together, their legs occasionally accidentally intertwining with the movement of the tide.

At least they had their clothes on, thank God.

A shaft of light lit their faces, illuminating the fact that Ian was looking down into her eyes, and in that moment, Phoebe could've sworn that he knew exactly what she was thinking.

She narrowed her eyes at him, trying despite their forced silence to convey her disapproval about that inappropriate kiss.

Ian, of course, thought that was funny and he smiled. And he shrugged very slightly, as if to respond with *It got the job done, didn't it?*

Phoebe shook her head—just slightly—back at him, which of course made his smile broaden.

The son of a bitch was enjoying himself. They were hiding beneath a foul-smelling dock after leaping from her balcony to avoid being taken captive by mobsters who wanted to kill him.

And he was having fun.

I hate you, she mouthed at him, making a point to overenunciate those unvoiced words so that he would understand.

The smile turned wry as he nodded. *I know. I'm sorry,* he mouthed back as the light made another pass across their faces. *I really am.*

There was a vaguely musical rhythm to the shift of the water—it wasn't always precise, sometimes the pattern repeated in four, sometimes in five or six. But light would shine in for a moment, then disappear. Then shine, then disappear.

And right before the light vanished again, Phoebe looked up into Ian's eyes, and she realized that in order to talk without making any noise, she was forced to stare at his mouth to read his lips. And while staring at his mouth, it was impossible *not* to think about that kiss.

She closed her eyes as they were plunged once

again into darkness, grateful that he couldn't see her and do that mind-reading thing he did so well. She managed to compose herself and was ready when the light came back, at which point she looked at him and said, *How long?*

In other words, how long did they have to hide here? But Phoebe knew he'd understand the short version, and this way she didn't have to endure him gazing intently at *her* mouth for more than just a few seconds.

She raised her eyebrows to emphasize that she'd asked a question, and he nodded. And he leaned toward her. This time, she quickly leaned away from him, shooting him a solid WTF with her face, and he smiled again, right before it went dark.

The truth was, there was no getting away from him in their current predicament. But she was grateful for the darkness as he put his mouth against her ear and said, "Relax."

Right. Relax. She didn't make noise as she rolled her eyes and silently laughed her disdain. He read her mind again, because she felt the warmth from his exhaled answering laughter against her ear, and when the light came back, he was smiling again.

Or maybe he'd never stopped smiling—because this was so damn funny and fun for him.

"If you're okay for me to leave," he breathed into her ear, "I'll recon and figure out our next move."

Phoebe nodded as she looked into his eyes, letting him see that she understood. His escape plan had only brought them this far. They were hidden from Davio Dellarosa's men, but obviously they couldn't stay in the water indefinitely.

And while the thought of Ian leaving her here, alone, was not a happy one, she could see how it was a necessity.

Phoebe tilted her head back to look up at the way Ian was holding on to the dock, and of course, the light immediately vanished. But she loosened her hold on him with her right hand and reached up, encountering first the taut muscles of his forearm and then his hand. She could feel how he was holding on, and she did the same, letting go of him with her other arm so that when the light came back they were still face to face, but she was no longer clinging to him.

She held out her hand, motioning with it—she wanted her bag. He handed it over, but stopped her when she moved to loop the tied arms around her neck.

"Don't," he said it aloud before wincing at his mistake. Leaning forward, he spoke into her ear. "If you have trouble, let it go. It's replaceable. You understand?"

Phoebe nodded. Wearing her bag around her neck could be deadly if she couldn't get it off and it weighed her down, pulling her underwater. Of course, that was assuming that she lost her grip and got dunked. Which was a possibility only if a tsunami suddenly struck, or in the case of an alien attack, or . . .

If a large boat went by, creating a huge wake. Yeah, okay. That was possible. He was right.

"Stay here," Ian continued. "In the unlikely event that I don't come back, don't go to the police. And don't use a credit card to check into a hotel. Get cash from an ATM. There are cheap motels up near the airport where you can give a fake name—"

She pulled back to look at him and for once the light worked for her, so that he got a clear look at her mouthing the words *Are you ditching me?*

Ditching wasn't an easy word to lip read, so she had to lean close to say it again, into his ear. "Ditching." Of course the water pushed her so that her mouth was awkwardly pressed up against his ear. "Sorry."

As she pulled back, he was shaking his head rather vehemently. *Not ditching you,* he mouthed back. *No. Never.* Again, he knew what she was thinking, because he leaned close to say, "Yeah, yeah, I know. That's what I'd say if I was ditching you. But I'm not. I promise. I'll be right back."

And with that he was gone, slipping into the water, leaving her alone in the darkness beneath the marina's dock.

Alone and bemused.

Phoebe had fully expected him to take advantage and kiss her again. And it was only because he hadn't that she believed he'd keep his promise.

Francine's phone buzzed, and she looked to see that she'd gotten an email. From Sheldon. And she knew, even before she opened and read it, that Berto had saved the day again.

She and Aaron were sitting in the back of Martell's car, with Rory's car seat between them. Martell was driving, and the FBI agent named Deb rode shotgun as they headed for the interstate. The baby was sleepily clutching his bottle-with-a-straw, his eyelids heavy as he slipped into formula-induced unconsciousness.

"Shelly's safe, at least temporarily," Francie told Aaron, keeping her voice low for Rory's sake. She reached across the car seat to hand Aaron the phone so he could read the email for himself.

He read it aloud, also at a sleeping-baby volume. "*I'm okay.* Thank God. *With Berto. R U safe? Stay away from house, Davio's men watching it. Awaiting instructions. Shel.*"

In their haste to leave the FBI's no-longer-safe house after Phoebe's vanishing act, they'd piled into Martell's crappy old car. The fed named Yashi had gone in a separate direction. He'd pointed his rental up toward Tampa, where he was going to gain access to both the files and funds that Ian would need to pull off that crazy B&E-of-a-foreign-consulate stunt.

When Martell first told Francie about it—that they'd taken Ian out of Northport to lead a covert rescue op—she'd laughed, because she'd thought he was kidding.

But it was not a joke. The FBI had—with very straight faces—released Ian from prison so that he could break into the Kazbekistani consulate in Miami and rescue the kidnapped children of a nuclear scientist.

And okay, there *was* a joke there, but it was on the FBI, who'd clearly bought into Ian's badass reputation as *the* best-ever B&E man, a jewel thief extraordinaire.

In truth, it had been years since Ian's private-sector spy team had attempted this kind of covert assignment. Francine's own breaking-and-entering skills were seriously rusty. As for Eee's? Pssht. He was capable of getting past any and all kinds of security, sure. But because he was the size of a small mountain, it was hard for him go unnoticed for very long.

As for Shelly and Aaron—neither were particularly skilled when it came to ninja moves. They weren't bad, but it certainly wasn't their forte. Shel's main talents were computer-based. He was the team's hacker, and he worked his plugged-in magic from the surveillance van. Aaron's role—one at which he also excelled—was to keep Shel safe while in said van.

Their only real hope of pulling off this kind of *Mission: Impossible* assignment would've come from Ian's former SEAL chief, John Murray, reupping. And since Johnny wasn't already here, Francie knew that the SEAL's participation was a no-go.

Talk about a truly impossible mission. Ian was going to have to get creative—although that *was* what he did best.

"He said, *awaiting instructions,*" Aaron repeated now, while quickly zapping back a message to Shelly that said, *We R OK, B safe, hang tight, more soon,* before handing the phone back to Francie. "So we know he doesn't trust Berto."

His words caused Little Debbie FBI to turn around. Martell glanced at them, too, via the rearview.

So Francine interpreted. "It's code," she explained. "For precisely this kind of situation. If you use those words, *awaiting instructions,* in an email or a phone call, it's a warning. Proceed with caution. Shel's telling us that he's not convinced Berto's help is coming from a place of brotherly love."

Aaron snorted at that. "You think? Berto's a douche," he told Deb and Martell. "He works for Davio, his double-douche of a father. He's hoping Shelly will lead him—and Davio—directly to me."

"So Berto's your brother," Deb said, looking directly at Francine. "Yours and Sheldon's."

"Berto's not *my* brother, he's Shel's," Francie explained. "And they're only half brothers. They have the same father, different mothers." She could see that Deb was struggling to understand. "Think of our family as a modern version of *Yours, Mine and Ours*. My mother married Berto's father, Davio, because he got her pregnant with Sheldon. And we all lived happily ever after, except, no, wait, we didn't, because Davio thinks stealing cars and selling drugs and women is a reasonable way to earn a living. Shel and I escaped. Berto didn't."

“Because Berto’s a douche,” Aaron said again. “I don’t like that Shel’s with him. I want to get him out of there.”

“We will,” Francie promised him. “But we’re going to do this right. Wait for Ian—”

“Wait for Ian,” Aaron said. “How did I know you were going to say that?”

Francine looked into the eyes of this man who was not only her brother-in-law, but also one of the best friends she’d ever had. And she knew that he was still tremendously angry at her. As he had every right to be. For the past year, she’d kept the truth from him.

And Aaron was going to be even more bitterly wounded when he found out that Sheldon, too, had known that Ian had spent all that time in prison—that Shel had stumbled across that fact, and that Francine had made him promise not to tell.

But she was going to let Ian deal with *that* fallout, since *he* was the one who’d been adamant—month after month—that Aaron never be told where he was.

“Think about this,” Francine told Aaron now. “We want Shelly back, but we don’t want him to get hurt and we don’t want you to get hurt.”

“I’d prefer not to get hurt, too,” Martell chimed in from the front.

“Even though he’s with Berto,” Francie continued, “that doesn’t mean Shel’s not safe. He is, right now—even if Berto’s just pretending to help him. Because Berto’s got to sell it, right? If he wants to convince Shel that he's an ally, he's got to act like an ally. And as long as Berto's acting like an ally, then Shel's safe."

Aaron nodded grudgingly.

"So I'm going to email Shel," Francine continued, "and tell him to go to the safe house that we just vacated. Number five eighty-five. In the event Phoebe already gave that info to the Dellarosas, we're not telling them something they don't already know."

Deb nodded. "That's a good plan. But hold off—I need to clear it with Yashi first."

Aaron wasn't happy. He didn't trust Berto, but he didn't want to *not* trust him, either. "If Phoebe's working for the Dellarosas, then we're potentially putting Shelly back into Davio's hands. What if Berto's really helping him without Davio knowing?"

Francine shook her head. "Lotta *if*s there, Air." She leaned forward to tell Martell, "Go north on Seventy-five. We're going to exit at University and head east.

"Shelly'll be safe enough at five eighty-five," she continued. "It's centrally located, plus we'll be able to keep an eye on him, make sure Berto's behaving himself." She aimed her next words at Deb. "Right? You planted surveillance at the safe house? Full setup of cameras and mics?"

Little Debbie was clearly uncomfortable disclosing that, especially when Martell looked over at her in genuine surprise.

"Seriously?" Martell asked the FBI agent.

"That's how you make friends with Ian Dunn? By watching his every move? Eating a sandwich, taking a dump . . ."

"It's procedure," she answered shortly.

"New theory," Martell said, glancing into his rearview mirror, directly at Francine. He'd clearly believed Ian when he'd left that message saying Francie was now in charge. "What if Phoebe's working with Dunn—more closely than we'd thought? What if her departure from the safe house was part of *his* plan to get us out from under FBI surveillance?" He looked into the mirror again, eyebrows up, as if expecting confirmation from the backseat.

But Francie shrugged. "I don't know Phoebe from Adam. I've never met her. If she's working with Ian, he didn't bother to tell *me*."

"Welcome to *my* world," Aaron said dourly. "Sucks, doesn't it?"

Even without binoculars, Ian could see Dellarosa's men swarming the marina. Despite his wishful thinking, they had not given up and moved on in their search for him.

Davio Dellarosa knew that Ian had once-upon-a-time been a SEAL. He'd correctly deduced that Ian would instinctively head for the water.

And he'd also apparently figured out that having Phoebe in tow would significantly slow Ian down.

That was true. If it wasn't for Phoebe, Ian would've been long gone.

The canal beneath her condo's balcony opened up into the bay just west of this marina. If Ian had been on his own, he would have swum to a part of the bay that was Dellarosa-free and gone ashore. Done and done.

Instead, he swam out here, to the mouth of the bay, where larger boats—yachts and sailing vessels almost big enough to be called ships—were anchored, most of them empty, their cabins securely locked.

He found one, surrounded by others that were dark and deserted, with a built-in cabin door lock that he could easily pick. So easily, in fact, that he opened it in advance. Best not to spend too much time with Phoebe up on the bright white of the deck. Best to get her on board—which was going to be some kind of trick, in and of itself—and then safely down below as quickly as possible.

Because if he were Davio, he'd have most of his men up on the private little marina's commissary roof, scanning the harbor with night-vision glasses. If he had 'em. And if he didn't, he'd get some soon.

One thing Ian had learned from his pre-prison quality time with Manny Dellarosa was that the Dellarosa family operation did not lack for high-tech equipment and weaponry.

Ian now surfaced at the halfway point back to the dock where he'd left Phoebe, his head and shoulders safely concealed behind what had to be a ten-million-dollar yacht. He traced his route back to the sailboat where they were going to take shelter and hide, memorizing each stopping point—he'd need to stop more often when he swam back there with Phoebe.

He could barely see their destination from here —of course *he* wasn't wearing NVGs.

He went back under the water, aware that he was working some seriously underused muscles. It had been close to a year since he'd done any swimming at all, due to the lack of recreational pools in the state prison system.

He broke surface only one more time before coming up for air beneath the dock where Phoebe was hiding. He didn't mean to startle her, but he brushed past her by accident because it was so damn dark.

She was breathing hard as he moved closer to her. She had no doubt imagined sharks or stingrays or maybe even a deadly Portuguese man o' war when he'd bumped her, but she was trying her best not to make any noise.

"Sorry," he breathed, moving close enough so he could speak directly into her ear, reaching up to hold on to the dock above them.

To his surprise, she let go, and wrapped her arms around his neck, pressing herself against him like a long-lost lover. It wasn't until she spoke directly into his ear that he realized she'd grabbed him merely to communicate. "I heard footsteps above me, then shouting and running. I was afraid they'd spotted you."

She pulled back to look at him just as the on-again-off-again light shone in through the slats in the dock, and Ian could see her concern in her eyes. It wasn't so much sharks she'd feared as him not coming back, despite the fact that he'd promised he would.

I'm okay, he mouthed silently as her gaze dropped to his mouth.

He instantly became aware of the intriguing mix of both firmness and softness of her body against him, of his arm around her waist. Because her shirt had floated up a little in the current, his fingers were against the smoothness of her skin.

It was hard not to think about Aaron's snotty comment. *Will you just pull off the road and kiss the shit out of each other? Just get it over with already. You'll both feel much better. . . .*

And yes, okay, in truth Ian *would* like to do way more than kiss the shit out of this woman, because yes again, he could use a good pressure release after nearly being killed, twice in one day. *And* because it had been too damn long since he'd gotten naked with anyone, let alone a woman to whom he was truly attracted.

The way Phoebe's eyes lit up when she laughed was just a bonus, as was the fact that she was fiercely intelligent and had the uncanny ability to read his mind at times.

As Ian stared, hyperaware of every centimeter of her that was touching him and vice versa, she looked back up into his eyes.

And there it was. His brother was right. The attraction Ian felt was absolutely mutual.

The dock shifted with the water, and it was as if a light switch was flipped. Their world went dark.

And something flipped inside of Ian, too, and he closed his eyes—not that it mattered in the darkness—and kissed her.

Her mouth was warm and sweet—and salty, too, from the water splashing in her face. And Ian knew she was going to pull away from him. He expected it. It was coming. Any second now . . .

Except she didn't.

There was a moment of surprise, mixed with the briefest of hesitation, but then she was kissing him back pretty damn enthusiastically, her arms tightening around his neck.

Ian clung to the beam above them, willing his fingers to evolve and quickly develop suction to keep him from slipping. He knew he was destined to get a splinter or twenty, but it didn't matter as he surrendered to this moment. He gave himself fifteen seconds to enjoy it, then gave himself fifteen more when she wrapped her legs around him, too.

Was it really called dry humping, if they did it underwater? Probably not.

It was a crying shame that they both had their jeans on, because this was definitely one of those adrenaline-fueled moments of passion with a total loss of inhibition, where need and desire trumped all reason.

But those moments were nearly always followed

by an awkward aftermath, and that would absolutely be so in this instance, particularly since Ian knew the truth. Most people experienced a strong biological urge to have sex following a near-death experience, or even a semi-near-death experience like jumping off a second-story balcony. Phoebe's kissing him back was just a normal human reaction to danger.

Ian gave himself a third and final fifteen seconds and then waited slightly longer for the light to vanish before he broke their kiss—in hopes that Phoebe would be less embarrassed under cover of darkness.

He knew what to tell her, too, and he put his mouth against her ear. "Breathe. Catch your breath. Don't say anything, we're gonna swim now, you'll have plenty of time to talk when we're safe, okay?" His voice sounded odd to his own ears, and he felt strangely out of breath himself.

He saw her nod as the light came back, but she kept her face turned away from him even as she unlocked her legs from around him.

Ian closed his eyes, suddenly cognizant of the splinters in his hand, and the fact that his right arm and shoulder were screaming from the strain of anchoring them beneath the dock after swimming all that way.

He didn't really expect her to be silent, and she didn't disappoint. She turned her head and put her mouth to his ear. "Sorry."

And there was the problem. She was sorry.

He wasn't.

"Big breath and then under, okay?" Ian breathed back into her ear.

Phoebe nodded again, and he felt her draw air, lots of air, into her lungs.

And together, they went beneath the water, and out from under the dock.

CHAPTER TEN

"Wet clothes off—put everything in here," Ian said, pointing to a plastic trash bag that was on the floor. He held out a beach towel and shook it a tad impatiently until Phoebe took it from him. "Stay on the deck—don't step onto the carpeting until you've dried off. If they come on board looking for us, anything wet will give us away."

Phoebe stood there, dripping and close to exhausted from the long swim and the ridiculously awkward climb up the slippery side of this yacht. She was still more than slightly shell-shocked from that molten lava kiss, too, and she wasn't quite sure what Ian wanted her to do. Take off her clothes and put them where . . . ? Because why . . . ?

As she watched, Ian yanked his soaking wet T-shirt over his head and jammed it into the trash bag. He seemed to know that she needed more information. "If Davio Dellarosa sends a team of men out in a skiff, and I'm pretty sure he will, they're not going to search every boat at anchor in the bay," he said as he unfastened his jeans. "There're too many of 'em. But if they see a sign that we're here—and water or recent watermarks on the deck is the equivalent of flashing neon—they *will* board. In which case we're screwed. Let's do whatever we can to not be screwed, okay?"

Phoebe nodded as she opened the towel and started to blot her dripping hair.

"Good girl," Ian said.

She looked at him sharply. "Excuse me . . . ?"

His laughter was low and warm. "Just making sure you were paying attention. Good to know you are." He swept his jeans down his long legs, getting stopped by his muscular calves, having to push and pull at the wet denim to get it unstuck from his skin.

He still wasn't wearing any underwear, yet he was completely unselfconscious, as if being naked in front of her was no big thing.

It was relatively dark in the yacht's cabin, although nowhere near as dark as it had been beneath the waters of the bay. Moonlight shone in through the windows, but it wasn't very bright. Still, Ian's now-naked butt reflected what little light there was, making it hard not to stare, hypnotized by its splendorous if not somewhat blurry shine, as he bent over to put his jeans plus her entire soaking sweatshirt-wrapped purse into the extra-large black plastic bag he'd grabbed from somewhere aboard this vessel.

"I could only find one towel," he said, standing up

and turning to face her, which meant that now she was staring at . . . The phrase *no big thing* came immediately mind, although it was completely inappropriate. Big thing. *Big* thing. In so many equally inappropriate ways. But he was talking. What was he saying? Towels. Only one. Found. Had he. So far. As in, the towel that was currently wrapped around her as she wrestled her way out of her own wet jeans. "Hopefully there are more below. I'm gonna need you to go down there and search since I'm still too wet."

She nodded, and kept her underpants on. Her bra was padded, each cup acting like a little sponge. Streams of water ran down her ribs every time she moved. It was going to have to go. Damn it.

"If you can't find more towels," Ian continued matter-of-factly, full-on conversationally, as if he weren't buck naked, and also as if the tongue he was using to talk hadn't recently been licking the inside of her mouth, "see if there's anything else to wrap around yourself, because I'm gonna need this towel to dry myself and then mop up this mess." He gestured down to the puddle at their feet, as well as the one out on the actual deck—which was where it mattered the most.

"You really think they're going to come out here looking for us?" she asked, putting her jeans, shirt, and bra into the bag, along with her cross-trainers and socks. She kept the towel, now quite sodden, securely wrapped around her, tight beneath her arms.

"Davio's kinda crazy. I think we need to be ready in case they do."

Phoebe looked down at the half-filled trash bag. "My Glock."

"Yup. Already got it. But unless you discover a cache of ammunition down below, it's not going to do us all that much good if they do figure out we're hiding here."

She saw that he'd taken her weapon out of her bag and had set it on the counter of some kind of wet bar, complete with a sink, here in the foyer—did yachts have foyers?—that connected the open-to-the-air aft deck to the yacht's enclosed multilevel cabin. His cell phone—the one he'd taken from his brother's panic room—was nearby. It was open and apart, its battery out, as if that would somehow bring it back to life—as if it hadn't been permanently ruined by its immersion in the bay.

Her eyeglasses were there, as well. Ian had opened the hard case that she'd put them in, so they could dry off, too—which was thoughtful and kind of him.

"Thanks," Phoebe said as she reached for them, put them on her face. Of course, now Ian and all of his thoughtful kindness was sharply, nakedly in moonlit focus.

"You're welcome."

It was probably true that almost everyone looked good when bathed in moonlight. Still, when Ian Dunn smiled . . .

Phoebe kept her head down as she carefully dried

her feet and then stepped onto the pale-colored Berber carpeting, passing through what looked like a living room, complete with built-in leather sofa, and a flat-screen TV on the wall.

There were carpet-covered stairs going up as well as down, and she hesitated.

"Down," Ian said again, clearly sensing her uncertainty. "Up goes to the bridge. There're at least two bedrooms and a head below. Better chance of finding more towels."

Right. Towels. That was what she was after.

Along with a supply of nine-millimeter ammunition, preferably in ready-to-use clips.

Of course the stairs going up were better lit by the moonlight—more windows up there, apparently—but Phoebe headed downward, feeling her way in the gloom.

"Head's the nautical term for bathroom," Ian added.

"Not an idiot, thanks," Phoebe countered.

"Not implying that you were," he called back, his voice low but still carrying down the stairs. "Most people are unfamiliar with the term. I realized that, when I said it, so . . ."

"I'm not going to sleep with you," Phoebe said, just *bang*—point-blank—because she realized that this was, by far, the best time to have this particular conversation. While Ian was unable to follow her downstairs, thanks to his wet feet and the must-stay-dry carpeting that imprisoned him.

Back where she'd left him, Ian cleared his throat. "Okay."

It was said with agreeable wariness, and she closed her eyes briefly, fully conscious that her back had instantly gone up. Was that relief she heard behind his *okay?* Was she jumping to conclusions? She didn't think so, but . . . Oh, God. There was nothing to do but plunge onward.

"I realize that I may have given you the wrong impression," she said, feeling her way to a closed door that opened into a tiny, dimly lit cabin in which there were built-in bunk beds. But both mattresses were bare, and there was nothing in the minuscule closet or any of the drawers that were beneath the lower bunk. "By essentially jumping you under the dock."

Next to the bunk-bed room was an airplane-sized bathroom. It, too, was towel-free. There was half a roll of toilet paper attached to the wall, though.

"You didn't jump me," he said, and it was clear he was going to elaborate on that theme, so she cut him off because, really, they both knew that she had.

"It was relief, mixed with terror," Phoebe confessed as she went into the next and final room. It was much bigger, with larger windows. Portholes. And it had a private head with a roomy, two-person shower. Surely there'd be towels in here. "A brainstem reaction. Plus you're a very nice-looking man, who also happens to be intelligent and funny and, well . . . sweet."

"Sweet?" Ian echoed with a laugh, just as she'd suspected he would. Want to change the subject fast? Call an alpha male *sweet*. Get him stumbling all over himself about that, then change the subject again. Original topic over and done.

"How could there be no towels in here?" she asked, mostly rhetorically, opening the miniblinds that covered the cabin's portholes in an attempt to let in more light.

He went with the subject change, just as she knew he would. "Grab a blanket or sheet from one of the bunks," Ian called back.

But again, the mattress on this bed—king-sized at the top, but narrowing toward the front of the boat, where one's feet might go—had been stripped down to its ticking-inspired blue-and-white plastic.

"Yeah, sorry, there's nothing here. Not even a mattress pad or a pillow." She opened the closets and all of the drawers. Empty, empty, and empty. "It's like a hotel; as if the maid service took everything but didn't replace it. Maybe because it's so damp?" She went back into the narrow passageway. "Where did you find that trash bag?"

"It was here in the galley, in the cabinet under the sink." Galley was the yo-ho-ho nautical term for kitchen. He didn't bother with the definition this time.

"*That's* the galley?" she asked, heading back up the stairs, where, yes, his butt was still cheerfully reflecting the moonlight.

"Most of the time, if you own a yacht like this, when you're hungry, you pull up to a dock at a fancy restaurant," he pointed out. "Or you have someone come in to cater your sunset cruise."

"Please don't tell me the trash bag was the last one," Phoebe said, even as he leaned over to open the cabinet.

"It wasn't," Ian said, handing her another. "But this one is."

Of course it was. One remaining bag, between the two of them? Tough shit, it was all hers. She took the flimsy plastic and turned her back on Ian, unfastening the towel and holding it out behind her. It was pretty wet, but he took it without complaining and used it to dry himself as best as he could. At least that's what it sounded like he was doing as she staunchly kept her back to him, concentrating on opening the plastic bag and making, yes, a poor man's poncho.

She pulled it over her head and put her arms through the additional holes she'd ripped into it. It came only to the tops of her thighs, plus the plastic stuck to her skin in the steamy Florida heat. But it was better than walking around topless, in her transparent panties.

"Take the bag of wet clothes down below," Ian commanded, and she did, glad to have something to do besides watch him use the towel to mop the floor. Which of course was going to make the thing too wet for him to wrap around his waist. God help her.

Phoebe took advantage of the spacious-for-a-ship master bathroom to wring out their clothes onto the shower floor, and then hang everything on a variety of hooks and towel racks. The contents of her purse were a mess, and the darkness didn't make it easy, but she set anything salvageable out on the floor.

"Hey. You didn't happen to find one of those battery-powered fans, or maybe a hair dryer . . . ?"

She turned toward Ian, who had come to stand, a darker shadow in the narrow doorway, only aware at the very last minute that she should aim her gaze higher, toward his face. Except that thought had come too late, and there she was, her eyeline directed at . . . the brighter white of a discreetly hanging dish towel?

Yes, he must've found a dish towel in the alleged kitchen, and he'd fashioned a ridiculous and somewhat precarious-looking loincloth with a piece of string tied around his hips.

Phoebe laughed her surprise. She couldn't help it.

Ian laughed, too, but he was definitely annoyed. "Hey, babe, this is all for you. I'm fine with walking around naked. You're the one who's—"

"No. I mean, *yes*. I know. Thank you. I'm so sorry." She stood up. Pulled her trash bag dress down as far as she could, which wasn't far at all. "I really am. Sorry. About everything. About getting you into this mess. I've practiced criminal law for years, and I just didn't believe that anyone would go after me, you know, to get to you."

"Davio Dellarosa's not anyone," Ian told her.

"I'm finally getting that, yeah," she said.

"I have to go back up where I can keep an eye on the shore," he said, pointing over his shoulder. "I could really use a fan—maybe one of those little handheld ones?—if you can find one. Or a hair dryer, although most of those are power vampires. It'll kill the boat's battery, and no way are we firing up the generator, so I guess it's really kind of moot."

"You want a fan or a hair dryer," Phoebe repeated, following him back up the stairs and discovering that his loincloth didn't have a back panel. "Because . . . ?"

"Because whoever took most of the towels off this boat also took the two-way radio." His teeth actually glinted in the moonlight as he smiled at her confusion. "If I can dry the cell phone out," he told her, pointing to the pieces out on the counter, "I might be able to get it to work. Then we can call one of your FBI buddies and ask for a ride, instead of having to swim for shore."

"Seriously? Because I'm pretty sure it's dead once it's wet."

"I turned the phone off before we went into the canal," he told her as he took a pair of binoculars from a hook on the wall. "If the battery's not on, there's a chance—if I can get it completely dry before I turn it back on . . . Well, there's no guarantee—saltwater can do some serious corrosion to the wiring—but I rinsed it, back when I first came on board, so . . ." He shrugged, as he looked through the binoculars and scanned the shore. "I figured it was worth a try."

"There's one of those ineffective little wired-into-the-wall hairdryers in the main head," she told him. "I don't know if it works. I didn't try it, since I'm pretty certain my hair already looks fabulous."

Ian laughed at that, glancing over at her, his gaze skimming down her bare legs. "Actually, the bedraggled look suits you."

"Oh," Phoebe said, moving to sit on the bench behind a built-in table. "No. Please. Don't. Really. God. I thought we moved on from all of that. Crossed it off our list. So to speak."

"All of what?" he asked, turning his attention back to the twinkling lights on the distant shore. She had no idea how he could see anything out there in the darkness, even with the binoculars.

"Okay, look. I don't know much about you," Phoebe said, "but I do know you're not stupid."

"I'm also not sweet," Ian countered. "I believe that's where we left *all of that.*"

Okay. "What you were doing for your brother and Sheldon," she pointed out, "is very sweet. Eighteen *months* in prison to keep crazy Davio away from your brother's family?"

Ian shook his head. "We weren't talking about that. We were talking about you—how did you phrase it—*jumping me* under the dock."

Phoebe winced despite herself. "Well, good. At least we agree about who jumped who, which is a good place to segue into my concluding remark on this pathetically awkward topic, which is, I'm sorry. Again. About that. I really am. I shouldn't have kissed you."

He glanced over at her. "Yeah, well, I kissed you first."

His words were spoken with intentionally surly one-upmanship.

"You weren't . . ." she started. "That wasn't . . ."

Ian waited for her to finish, one eyebrow raised.

Phoebe sighed. She knew if she said, *You kissed me—first—on the balcony, as a distraction,* he'd argue that she couldn't possibly know what he'd been thinking, even though she absolutely, positively did.

"You just agreed that I jumped you," she pointed out instead.

"No, I didn't." He was back to scanning with those binoculars. "I said we were talking about the fact that you *thought* you jumped me. I'm pretty sure I was actively and enthusiastically involved. At the very least, I met you wholeheartedly midjump."

Phoebe put her head in her hands and exhaled her frustration. "Okay. Fine. Why don't we just agree that it certainly didn't help that you've been in prison for all those months, and that what I did was completely unprofessional."

"Wow," Ian countered. "So what you're saying is that I'm sex-starved and you're a bad lawyer? That's pretty dark."

"That's not what I said," she argued, even though it was, essentially, what she'd said. She tried again. "It's not what I meant." Although it kind of was.

"For the record," Ian said, lowering the binoculars so he could look directly at her. "It was a really nice kiss. I enjoyed it very much, thank you, and I'm not sorry, so I'm not going to apologize for it, and I don't think you should either. I can't speak to why you kissed me, because I'm not inside your head. But I *can* tell you that I kissed you because I wanted to, because I like you, because I wanted to see what it felt like. For the record, it was about fifty thousand times hotter than I imagined, which means that on the cosmic scale of kisses it clocked in at a solid pretty-fucking-great."

He paused.

She was now speechless, so he continued. "But it was just a kiss. There are millions of people kissing right now, right this very second, somewhere in the world. And you know how many of them are going to have an epic conversation about it afterward? Maybe, I don't know, ten? The rest of them are going to say, *Hey. Nice. Let's do that again, either right now or later.* Which is exactly what I want to say—in conclusion—to you. So, hey. Nice. Let's do it again. But later, okay? When people aren't trying to kill us."

Phoebe found her tongue. "I'm pretty sure *way* more than ten—"

"Ten thousand, then," he said. "Out of millions of kissing people, ten thousand is still a very small number."

Phoebe started again. "As your lawyer—"

"They're definitely all lawyers," Ian said. "All those epic conversationalists. Every single one of 'em. Holy Jesus Christ."

"You're a client," she pointed out. "So I'm sorry, I'm not kissing you later."

"Well, I'm sorry to hear that," he said. "So I guess, in the end, we *are* both sorry."

If ever there was a conclusion to a conversation—awkward or otherwise—that was it. Phoebe stood up. Cleared her throat. "I'll go see if that hair dryer works."

Ian didn't look up. "Good plan. Take the cell phone with you," he said.

She took it off the counter, and headed back down the stairs to the so-called head, feeling her way, and also feeling oddly bereft when she should have been relieved and grateful that her awkward conversation with Ian had finally ended.

She opened the pocket door to the bathroom and pulled the hair dryer from its cradle on the wall. It was attached by a curly cord. She peered at the buttons, but couldn't read the tiny print in the low light, and finally just hit one of them.

Nothing happened.

She hit the other.

Silence.

No power.

Perfect.

Contact Point Zebra was a boarded-up and unlit former gas station, out in the middle of nowhere, well east of the north-south-running interstate.

Martell would have missed it completely if Francine hadn't told him to slow down.

He pulled into the pothole-filled lot carefully, braking to a crawl as his car jostled and bounced. All he needed was to lose a muffler—make his shitty day complete.

"Pull around back and kill your lights," Francine commanded.

Martell could feel more than see Deb nodding a silent *Make it so,* and he glanced at her, even though they both knew that she was no longer the captain of this little away team. Dunn had given that honor to the petite blonde in the backseat.

Deb wasn't the only one pissed off about that. Dunn's brother was less than thrilled, too.

"What the hell is this place?" Aaron put voice to what they were all thinking—everyone but Francine, who'd led them here.

"Home sweet home," Francine said, as she checked a weapon that she must've had stashed in her bag. "For now, anyway."

"Jesus," Aaron said.

"It's in better shape inside than it looks from out here," she told him. "It's intentionally outwardly shitty. We'll be fine."

The building itself was heavily graffitied brick and boarded-up glass—or maybe just brick and plywood, with no real glass left in the window frames. It was two stories high, and as Martell slowly pulled around back, he could see, in the moonlight, a rickety set of wooden stairs leading up to an equally unstable-looking deck that spanned the length of the place. There were windows and a couple of doors up on that second floor—one of them a glass slider covered with old-fashioned hurricane shutters.

If Martell had to guess, he'd bet there was a small apartment—one bedroom, maybe two tops—up above the former convenience store.

"Ian bought this place," Francine continued her narrative, "back around the same time he bought the house in Sarasota. It was a two-birds-with-one-stone deal. He had some money he needed to put into property, plus he wanted to set up a place where we could hide out in the event of the coming zombie apocalypse."

Whoa. Zombie apocalypse. Blondie'd actually made a funny. But Martell was the only one who chuckled. In fact, because he laughed, Deb shot him a look that he couldn't begin to interpret.

As Martell put his car in park, Deb started to reach for the handle to her door, but Francine was already unbuckled and she leaned forward, stop-ping the FBI agent with a hand on her shoulder. "Stay in the car, please, while I do a quick look-see—make sure that the locks all held and we haven't acquired any squatters. It's been a while since I've been out here."

"Be careful," Martell said.

Francine met his eyes as she nodded, then opened the car door and vanished into the night.

Deb didn't like being ordered around, even with that *please*. Aaron, from the back, was even less happy. But he had his husband's safety first and foremost in his mind.

"How do we get access to the surveillance footage from the safe house?" he asked Deb, his voice low so as not to wake the sleeping baby.

"Yashi'll bring computer equipment with him," Deb said. "From Tampa."

Yashi.

Who used the exact same deodorant and hair care products as did Deb. Martell had watched the man as he and Deb had prepared to go in two different directions while back at the safe house, and neither of them let slip even the slightest hint that they were anything other than co-workers. There was no badly disguised touching—in fact, there was no touching whatsoever. There was also no lingering eye contact, and no shared smiles—just a whole lot of impersonal mutual respect.

But they both had recently used the same marketed-to-men brand of personal care products.

And wasn't *that* a conundrum. For two people who were being super, ultra careful about keeping an intimate relationship secret, there were limited choices to be had when it came to postsleepover grooming. You either used your lover's products—and risked someone with a good nose, like Martell, picking up on that. Or you kept a small supply of your own products in your lover's bathroom—and risking a visitor seeing it there and having the eureka lightbulb go on, in all its glory.

Of course, choice C was simply to not shower—instead to just walk-of-shame it on home.

And . . . scene.

Time to stop thinking about this before it classified as full-force obsessively crazy.

All Martell really needed to know was that, despite the warm camaraderie he'd felt while sharing French fries with the quirkily attractive Deb and her frequently escaping but undeniably lovely rebel breasts, she *had* shared her FBI partner's showering supplies.

Ding. Game ended before it began.

Truth be told, that was a good thing. He had no business sniffing around after a little something-something while in the middle of a difficult and serious job. Yes, the woman was hot, and the whole goth thing was intriguing even though he knew it was a disguise.

But there was work to be done. Lives to save.

Diapers to change—yes, that *was* the baby he was smelling. Holy Jesus, lamb of God . . .

Francine opened the car door, and they all jumped—at least Martell did.

"We're good to go inside," she reported. "Whoa."

"What did you feed him?" Aaron asked her, prickly as ever as he worked to free the kid from his car seat.

"The usual," she said. "Nothing new. I swear. Get him inside before he wakes up and starts to cry."

"He did that in his sleep?" Martell asked, but Aaron had already moved on.

"Any word from Ian or Shelly?" Aaron asked Francine, who checked her phone.

"Nothing from Eee." Francine grabbed Rory's

diaper bag. "Shel got my email. He's heading for the safe house, but I don't know if Berto's still with him. I gotta assume he is." She looked at Deb and Martell. "Let's get this stuff inside. Voices down—keep it quiet."

Aaron and Rory had already gone up those stairs, and Francine closed the car door as quietly as he'd ever heard it done.

Martell opened his own door, intending to follow, but Deb caught his arm. Pulled him close.

"I don't trust her," she breathed into Martell's ear. "Francine. But it's kind of obvious that she likes you, and, well, vice versa. So see if you can't get closer. I want to know if she's going to be trouble. Oh, and find out if she was working with Dunn back when he knew the Dutchman—the alleged kidnapper. Maybe she can give us some information."

And with that, she, too, got out of the car.

Oh, good. Just what he needed. A game of spy v. spy to make his shitty day even shittier.

Martell sighed, and grabbed the last bags of groceries out of his trunk, and followed the rest of Team Grumpy up those rickety outside stairs.

CHAPTER ELEVEN

"Here they come."

Phoebe looked up from where she was sitting on the carpeted floor of the largest bedroom cabin, fanning the plastic cover of an uninspired-looking DVD movie called *Jerri on Top* in an attempt to dry off the cell phone thoroughly enough so that it would work when the battery went back in.

In her search for a handheld battery-powered fan, she'd gone through the living room cabinets and had come up with a full collection of DVD porn, two decks of cards, a pack of unused crayons, a well-stocked but unplugged wine fridge filled with a variety of high-priced reds, a bottle of Windex, some Christmas-tree scented candles, a battery-powered lantern that actually worked, a pair of scissors, and—alleluia—an unopened box of Goldfish crackers.

But there was no drinking water on board, and it was only recently that Phoebe had reluctantly opened a rather lovely pinot noir to accompany the crackers and offset the Sahara-desert-mouth she'd acquired during their extensive saltwater swim. There were no glasses, so she was drinking directly from the bottle, but taking tiny little sips.

Trapped, alone, on a luxurious yacht with a nearly naked former Navy SEAL that she'd recently kissed, and a dozen bottles of wine. What could possibly go wrong?

Ian, of course, refrained when she offered him some. He'd stayed up in the main cabin, keeping watch. But now he'd come below with this warning.

"It's a relatively small skiff. Three men aboard. We can assume they're all armed. They've been out there for a while, but now they're heading to our part of the harbor."

She scrambled to her feet. "What do we do?"

"Shhh." He held out both hands, but he had her Glock in one of them, so it really wasn't all that comforting a gesture. "We need to stay quiet and be still. Don't rock the boat—literally. I don't know if anyone on Davio's crew is nautically inclined, but if they are, that's what they'll be looking for. Unusual movement coming from a boat that should be empty. Along with water on the deck. Which I've taken care of, so we're good there." He looked up at one of the window covers she'd opened so that the wan moonlight could come in. "It's too late to close the blinds. We'll need to stay down, out of sight of the portholes, in case they board."

"Do you really think they'll board?" she asked, trying to keep her voice low even as she pointed toward the bathroom—the head. There were no portholes in there. It had a pocket door that they could close most of the way, too. She picked up the wine, the crackers, and the cell phone and led the way inside.

"Murphy's Law says they will," Ian told her as he quietly slid the door halfway closed, making it even darker in there. "So that's what I'm preparing for. With a little luck, though, they'll just cruise on by. We should sit—stay low to the deck—because their wake will toss us a bit. I don't want any thumps or bumps. You want?" He held out her Glock, grip first.

Phoebe was familiar with Murphy's Law. *Whatever can go wrong, will go wrong.* It applied in the courtroom, too. What she *wasn't* familiar with was a person with a Y chromosome voluntarily giving her back her weapon during a time of crisis. Oddly enough, it made her feel okay about him holding on to it. She was a good shot, but she wasn't a former SEAL. Plus, she'd never actually fired it at anything other than a paper target.

"You keep it," she said as she sat down on the floor, but then narrowed her eyes at his shadowy form. "You knew I'd say that, didn't you? If you offered to give it back?"

"You want it, just say the word," he countered as he sat, too—and arranged his makeshift loincloth. "It's yours." He set the handgun down on the floor between them.

She didn't pick it up. "So what's our plan, if they do board?"

"Stay quiet," he said. "Hope they don't have the ability to pick the lock into the cabin."

Out in the bay, the Dellarosa search party had moved close enough for Phoebe to hear the buzz of what had to be a skiff with a small outboard motor. That was a good thing, because it meant they were looking, not listening.

Still, she had to ask, "And if they do? Pick the lock and come into the cabin?"

"How's that phone coming?" Ian answered her question with a question. "Almost dry?"

Oooh-kay. So he *didn't* have a plan, other than to pray the phone was dry enough to work so that they could call for help. Which brought them right back to where they'd been before they'd jumped off the balcony of her condo.

"Do you think they know what I look like?" Phoebe asked as she held out the two pieces of cell phone.

He took them from her as that buzz from the skiff got louder. And louder. "They've probably seen a picture of you, yeah. Probably whatever was on the law firm's website."

Phoebe nodded. Then they had no real idea of what she looked like. "That picture's awful." She'd sat for that photo in her most expensive power suit, blouse buttoned to her neck, glasses on her face, and it had come out horrifically, like a school portrait gone comically bad. Her hair had been up, and in the photo it had looked flat and odd—the perspective making it look as if she wore it short. And the boxy cut of the jacket had instantly added twenty pounds. "It makes me look prim and earnest and weirdly frumpy." It didn't look anything like her. God, at least she hoped not.

Meanwhile, Ian was hefting the heavy cell phone battery in his hand as if considering the option of using it to hurl at the thugs, but now he looked up at her, his eyes gleaming a little in the dimness. "So what are you thinking?" he asked.

"I'm thinking this means that maybe they won't recognize me. So now we have a plan if they board. I'll pretend they've woken me up, that I was sleeping on the boat because . . . I don't know, something classic and pathetic, like—"

He interrupted. "Yeah, no, I don't like that. *Maybe?* Plus, you face-to-face, talking to them? Nuh-uh."

She kept going anyway. "Like, I just found out my husband was cheating. I'm mad and I'm drunk"—she gestured toward the wine bottle—"and now I think the son of a bitch has sent thugs out to try to contain or handle me."

"As soon you interact with them, they'll use the opportunity to come on board and search the boat. At which point they'll find me. Unless . . ." He paused for a moment, peering out of the bathroom at the ceiling of the cabin, where a small square hatch led up to the foredeck.

Phoebe pressed on. "I'll scream and make like I'm calling nine-one-one. They won't know that the phone doesn't work. Strangers on my yacht, yada yada. Eek, eek, help help, noise, noise, noise—they run away."

Ian shook his head. "Yeah, no. I still don't like it." He examined the two parts of the cell phone in the thin stream of moonlight coming in through the cracked open door. "While I appreciate your creativity, and while I'm also *sure* you have top-notch acting skills—"

Phoebe laughed at the condescending disingenuousness of his tone. She raised her voice a little to be heard over the skiff's motor. "I'm a criminal lawyer. Believe me, I can act. Besides, what's *your* plan? Activate the magic and all-powerful cell phone and . . . what? Call for help? Remind me again why we didn't do that *before* we jumped into the canal."

"The cell phone's to call for medical assistance," he said as he snapped the battery into place. "After I overpower whoever's on that boat, while you stay safely hidden." He glanced up at her. "I'm still working out the details of how I get that done, but the ending's a given."

His self-confidence crossed the line into authoritative. In fact, he oozed such command and certainty it teetered on arrogance, which was something that Phoebe usually didn't find very appealing. But combined with those eyes and that physique—and okay, face it, the whole loincloth look helped enormously—he was outstandingly attractive.

But wishing something would happen wouldn't make it so. Even if you were a former Navy SEAL badass.

Three against two were not good odds for anyone, forget about the fact that the pair of them had a single weapon to share. With a limited amount of ammunition.

The outboard motor came closer and closer. Louder and louder. In just a few seconds, whoever was on that skiff would go past. And the sound would fade, and the danger would be over, and she and Ian would both smile and even laugh, and she'd take a larger-than-normal sip from that bottle of wine with a hand that she'd pretend wasn't shaking. . . .

As the buzz became a roar, Ian broke their eye contact, looked down at the phone, pushed the power button and . . .

Nothing happened.

Nothing with the phone, that is.

Outside the yacht, the roar of that motor suddenly sputtered and went out.

Ian carefully put the phone down and reached for the Glock as from out on the water, a voice carried: "Just let it drift for a minute, so we can listen."

Phoebe met Ian's gaze, nodding slightly at his unspoken message. *Be silent.*

Another voice from outside: "This is a waste of time. They're long gone."

"Mr. D said the guy's been in Northport for almost a year. You really think he can swim miles, weighed down by some super-sized bitch?"

She widened her eyes at Ian, hoping he'd read the look as a *See? They don't know what I look like,* rather than a less meaningful and more egotistical *Hey, those mofos just called me fat!*

His response was to again offer her the grip of the Glock, and it was hard to tell if he'd misunderstood her facial expression, or if he was merely making some kind of twisted Navy-SEAL-gone-bad version of a joke. Like, *Yes, you now have my permission to kill them.*

It was then the first voice said, “Okay, let’s go. There’s no one out here.”

Whereupon two things happened near-simultaneously. The cell phone—the miraculous, powerful back-from-the-dead cell phone—started to ring. Shrilly. Loudly.

And the outboard motor started with a sputtering cough.

Phoebe reacted instinctively, slapping her hand down over the phone, and feeling—and finding—the button along the side that would silence it.

Only then did she look up to find Ian vigorously shaking his head. *No!*

She realized why he was sending her that vehement message almost immediately. Because an unanswered phone ringing aboard an anchored yacht was just that—an unanswered phone that someone had left behind on an otherwise empty boat. But a phone whose ring was interrupted meant that the boat was not uninhabited after all.

She had blown it.

The men on the skiff were about to leave, and she’d gone and blown it.

“Oh, God, I’m so sorry,” she said.

Time slowed way down, and fractions of seconds clicked by as Phoebe crouched there in the darkness next to Ian, waiting to see if that snippet of ringtone had been drowned out by the outboard motor that was now at full roar.

Please motor away. Please motor away. Please . . .

The motor coughed, then sputtered, then fizzled out.

"It came from this one," one of those voices said, much closer now.

And Phoebe felt something solid—the skiff—bump the side of their hiding place.

"Looks like we have to use your Plan B," Ian asked, thrusting the Glock into her hands. "Do it, but don't get shot, and for the love of God, don't shoot me. I'll be coming out of the water. And don't call nine-one-one unless you have to. Got it? Good."

He kissed her. It was just a slap of his lips against hers, so quick that it barely counted as a real kiss.

With that, he vanished out into the cabin and up, yes, through that almost impossibly small hatch.

Phoebe set down the handgun, tore off her trash bag shirt-slash-dress, and grabbed Ian's T-shirt from where she'd hung it over the towel rack on the wall. She pulled it over her head—it was cold and still wet, and it clung to her skin, but she forced it down to the tops of her thighs. She stuck the cell phone between her shoulder and ear, and grabbed the Glock with her right hand and the nearly full bottle of wine with her left. She dumped most of it out in the sink, as she said, loudly enough to be heard by the men in the skiff, "*I'm* being unreasonable? *I* am? You were *fucking* my best friend, you arrogant prick—excuse me, no, wait, my *former* best friend! So, no, I'm *not* telling you where I am!"

She took one last fortifying slug from the now nearly empty bottle before she went out of the bathroom, out of the cabin, and up the stairs to the galley, shouting, "Yeah, well, I'm setting my phone on silent, bastard! You'll hear from my lawyer in the morning, and we are going to bleed you dry. Just go to hell—and take that lying bitch Tiffany with you!"

The so-called safe house where the email from Francine had directed them to go was a large step up from the lowlife pay-per-hour motel that Sheldon had been expecting.

Berto had been able to pull his car back beyond the house, out of view of the street, which was useful.

The back door had been locked, but that hadn't slowed them down.

"Have you been here before?" Berto asked as they went through a kitchen and into a living room that was jammed full of slightly musty-smelling furniture.

This house was a vacation rental—had to be. Still, it was nicer than some of Shelly and Aaron's rendezvous locations, back when they were both still in the military.

"No," Shel answered his half brother honestly. "But this is where Francine said to wait for further contact."

That seemed to satisfy Berto—who didn't spot the carefully, professionally hidden ultra-high-tech surveillance cameras and mics that were strategically positioned around the place. There was even a camera in the bathroom where Sheldon took a leak and gingerly washed his grime-streaked face.

He had a lump on his head from the blow Berto had delivered out in the street—the pain from that was down to a dull ache. He also must've landed on his face when he was tossed into the trunk. He had a scrape on his cheek, and his lip was swollen. He'd cut the inside of his mouth with his own teeth—that was going to make eating a bitch for the next week or so.

It could have been far worse.

And it could still *get* worse. He was well aware of that.

It was highly likely that Berto was only playing the part of the hero, only pretending he wasn't a threat.

But Shel knew better. He certainly knew that his half brother was carrying concealed. He could see the bump of a shoulder holster beneath the older man's left arm.

And although it seemed jarringly incongruous with the quiet, seemingly sensitive boy who'd been his and Francie's protector when they were kids, he knew that Berto had—at least once, and probably far more often in the many years since then—killed a man.

It had happened as a result of the sex tape—for a long time, everything messed up in Shel's life could be traced back to that stupid prank or outing attempt or whatever it had been, perpetrated by some of his fellow students at Brentwood Academy.

When the video was sent to Davio, he had a major meltdown.

Which Francine overrode by cutting her hair, by sending incriminating X-rated selfies to Aaron, and by flat-out admitting the "truth" to her wicked stepfather. That it wasn't Sheldon in that video—don't be ridiculous. It was Francie. She'd been seeing hunky Aaron Dunn on the down-low for weeks. . . .

Unfortunately, while her "confession" took the heat off Shelly, it submerged Francine in hot water. Because not only did Davio believe her—and beat the crap out of her for bringing such public shame to their family—but Berto did, too.

Berto—with whom Francie had fallen in love. Berto—who had been planning to run away with her to Europe, as soon as Sheldon graduated from Brentwood. Berto—who loved Francie back, with all his heart and soul . . .

But Berto had believed Francine, and had gotten his gun and gone hunting for Aaron.

He hadn't killed him, but he'd come close. And in the chaos of the anger and the gun-waving, an innocent bystander—a homeless man—*had* been killed.

It was only after that awful, unfixable mistake that Berto had realized the truth—that it was Shelly with Aaron in that video.

And Berto—instead of doing the right thing and turning himself in to the police—went to his father for help in covering up his crime. He'd sold his soul to the devil on that night, and had been paying for it ever since.

Shel dried his face on one of the towels hanging there in the bathroom, then combed his fingers through his disheveled hair. He tried to brush the worst of the dust from his clothes. His shirt and pants were soaked with sweat and dirt from the trunk, and he didn't want to ruin the furniture. He was also stalling, since sitting around, shooting the shit, and catching up with Berto was around number fifty-seven billion on his want-to-do list.

He took a deep breath as he looked at himself in the mirror. He may have been battered and sore, but he was still standing.

And Aaron was out there, somewhere, maybe even watching him right now. Certainly waiting for the right moment to come to his rescue.

Shelly looked up, directly into the camera that was hidden in a deceptively dusty silk fern on an overly decorated bamboo shelf. "Berto picked up some beer and whiskey on the way over here—he still probably drinks too much. So, I'm gonna try to get him drunk and sneak away," he whispered. "I know I look like crap, but I promise, I'm okay. Don't do anything rash. Berto's armed."

He left the bathroom light on as he went back into the living room of this safe house that was, without a doubt, one of the most dangerous places he'd been since his last tour in Afghanistan.

CHAPTER TWELVE

Ian went over the side and into the water without any of Dellarosa's men spotting him.

They were all distracted by Phoebe doing her woman-scorned act at high volume, as she pretended to talk on the phone to her philandering fictional husband. Her hope was that she'd scare the men away, but Ian knew better.

He silently swam toward the stern of the yacht, where one of the three occupants of the skiff was attempting to board the larger vessel.

Judging from their uncertainty and low skill level at what should have been a fairly easy nautical act, Ian was pretty sure at least two of the men—a hulking giant, and a more normal-sized man wearing a backward baseball cap—were land-lubbers. The third, the yacht boarder—wiry, slight of build, and clearly in charge—was an amateur sailor at best.

And none of them had a visible weapon in hand as they vainly fought the contrapuntal motion of the two bobbing boats. But then they stopped trying to board entirely as a light went on in the cabin. All three of them looked up and then stared, transfixed.

Phoebe had turned the battery-powered lantern to high, and she held it up and out with her left hand, as if to try to see who was out there.

It mostly worked to illuminate her.

How had she described that website picture of herself? As frumpy?

Her hair was a riot of curls down around her shoulders, and the T-shirt she'd pulled on, while oversized, was clinging to her body in all the right places. It was white and still wet and very nearly transparent and holy God.

Frumpy was *not* the word that leapt to mind.

"Who's out there?" she called in a British-tinged accent as Ian took advantage of the spell she'd cast by silently swimming to the side of the skiff that was farthest from the yacht. "John? Is that you?"

She'd set a bottle of wine—obviously uncorked—on the counter, as a very effective show-and-tell. *Look, I know it's on the early side to be such a mess, but when I got here I started drinking heavily and passed out from too much wine and anger. My ringing cell phone just woke me.*

Ian hoped the men in the skiff weren't familiar enough with the yachting set to recognize how odd it was that she was there with no obvious means of transportation from the dock, i.e. a dingy tied to the anchor.

Phoebe set the lantern down on the counter to unlock the door to the aft deck, doing it all with her left hand.

Ian hated that she was leaving the safety of the locked cabin, but he couldn't exactly shout cautions or instructions to her at this point. And while it was true that she was putting herself in peril, he had to admit that it *was* what someone might do: see what had bumped into her yacht in the darkness of the night. Because in most cases it would be a *what* and not a *who.*

And because she was using her left hand—to pick the lantern back up after she'd opened the door—and because she was keeping her right concealed behind her, hidden by the fabric of that T-shirt, Ian knew that her finger was on the trigger of the Glock. Where she'd tucked the cell phone, he had no idea.

"Oh my God! Who are *you?*" she called, with just the right amount of drunken indignation and surprise in her voice as the light hit the faces of Dellarosa's men. "What are you doing out here?" She drew in a deep, disapproving gasp of realization that was damn near perfect for someone who was, allegedly, not firing on all cylinders. "Did John send you?"

She didn't let the men in the skiff speak as she stood there, lantern still held high, her chest heaving in righteous anger. The fact that her arm was raised made the T-shirt ride up to expose the edge of her panties, and the full effect made her long, bare, shapely legs look even longer, barer, and more shapely.

She was statuesque. Magnificent. Goddesslike. One hundred percent frump-free.

"I know John sent you, but it's *my* yacht now," she continued her improvised monologue. "Mine! You can tell John that it's *my* yacht, *my* house, *my* Porsche nine fifty-nine, *my* Upper West Side pied-à-terre. You tell John that I am going to make him *bleed*. Go on, get out of here! Get away from my yacht! Right! Now!"

And there it was, the moment of truth.

Giant and Baseball Cap and their leader, Skinny, were either going to make apologetic noises and push off, away from the yacht or . . .

"We're the marina's security patrol, ma'am," Skinny lied as effortlessly as Phoebe had. Maybe he was a lawyer, too. "We've had reports of break-ins on the boats out in this part of the harbor. I realize this is an inconvenient time for you, and I apologize for that, but I'm going to have to ask to see some ID."

Skinny finally managed to push himself up and over the lifeline, landing with an ungraceful thud on the deck.

But Phoebe saw him coming, and backed up, quickly setting the lantern on the hard plastic of one of the built-in seats.

Skinny's hands were both empty, but after he stumbled out of his landing, he moved to reach inside his jacket, which was never a good sign.

Phoebe apparently knew that, too. "Now, Ian!" she shouted, even as Ian yelled a slightly more efficient "Go!"

She had the Glock out and aimed at the center of Skinny's mass, in a very fierce two-handed stance, even as Ian launched himself out of the water, grabbing Giant and hurling him back, over his shoulders, into the water with an appropriately monstrous splash.

"Freeze!" Phoebe shouted at Skinny, as Ian hauled himself up and over the side of the skiff. "Hands where I can see 'em! Now! Higher! Up and over your head! *Now! Do it!*"

He'd expected to have to deal with a somewhat frantic Baseball Cap, but the severe rocking motion caused by Ian's throwing Giant into the water and then clambering up and into the skiff had apparently done the job—the man had already fallen overboard.

On the yacht, Skinny was reaching for the moon as Phoebe maintained her Charlie's Angels pose.

Ian found himself grinning—God, he liked her more and more with each passing moment—but he was well aware that his jubilance was premature. They were not out of danger yet. It wouldn't be more than another few seconds before the displaced men came up wet, angry, and shooting.

"Into the water, Pheebs!" Ian shouted as he grabbed the starter rope of the outboard motor and gave it a solid pull. It roared to life.

"What?" Phoebe shouted back. "Me?"

"Get *him* into the water," Ian shouted back.

"Do it, mofo!" Phoebe ordered Skinny, who immediately joined his buddies in the Gulf, even as Ian brought the skiff around to the thug-free side of the yacht.

Phoebe tossed Ian the Glock, which he caught. But then she hesitated, because it was a daunting prospect, leaping down into a dingy from a much bigger boat.

But Skinny had gone so willingly over the side for one reason and one reason only: It allowed him to go for and draw his handgun without risk of getting a bullet in the chest.

Skinny's first shot was wild—more into the sky than aimed at Phoebe, because he slipped during his attempted clamber up the starboard side of the yacht—but it wouldn't take him long to be more accurate.

Phoebe knew that, too, and she stopped hesitating and jumped. But she went purposely wide, aiming for and hitting the water just in front of the skiff. There wasn't enough time to pull her aboard, so Ian shouted, "Grab this, wrap it around your wrist, and don't let go!" as he threw her the painter that was tied to the bow of the little boat.

She immediately understood. The nylon rope that he'd tossed her was long enough so that it wouldn't put her in danger from the propeller of the outboard motor. She quickly called back, "I've got it! Go!"

So Ian opened up the throttle and the skiff jumped forward.

It took a few seconds for the line to go taut, but then Phoebe was pulled, like a water skier sans skis, bumping and jerking along behind the skiff, no doubt getting a face full of water, spitting and gasping for air.

But the range on most handguns wasn't all that large, so it wasn't long before Ian cut the motor and turned the boat. Her momentum brought her right up to the side, and he reached over and caught her, keeping her from crashing into the skiff. She was gasping and breathless, but she understood that this stop was only temporary—to get her aboard as quickly as possible so that they could flee more thoroughly.

She tossed her glasses into the skiff along with something else that was hard to see in the moonlight—apparently she'd been holding it all with her free hand—before she grabbed on to Ian. Together they got her up and over the side, where she lay like a landed fish in the briny water that sloshed in the bottom of the little boat, catching her breath, as he opened the throttle and took off once again, skimming north along the coastline.

"They might be working with a team on shore, who could have access to another boat, so I want to ditch this thing and go ashore as soon as we can," Ian shouted over the motor as Phoebe coughed and spat and even retched a little.

Still she nodded and found enough of her voice to call back, "Good idea." She pushed her hair from her face, squeegeeing the water out of it, before she started feeling around for her glasses. She found them, and put them on. And then quickly looked away from him.

Ah, yes.

"Sorry I lost the dish towel while I was saving our lives," Ian said. He still had the stupid string tied around his waist—fat lotta good it was doing there now. But untying the knot would require both hands and his full attention. Plus, having a piece of string might come in handy, wherever they ended up.

"Yeah, well, I was saving our lives, too," she said. "But I kept my shirt on."

"It's my shirt," he pointed out.

The look Phoebe gave him was so dark that he couldn't help but laugh.

"But I'll let you keep it as a token of my gratitude," he added as he finally slowed, not wanting to attract attention as a too-loud boat going too fast in the darkness past a well-moneyed neighborhood.

The slower speed made it easier to talk without having to shout. Which maybe wasn't a good thing, as she accused him, "You're having fun again."

What? "Fun? Not really. Not with Shelly grabbed by Berto Dellarosa, and Aaron out there doing God knows what to try to save him. Forget about the fact that after I take care of *that* goatfuck, I'm supposed to engineer some magical rescue of two kidnapped children, in order to save the world."

Phoebe immediately sobered. "You're right. I wasn't thinking about . . . I'm so sorry."

He could tell from the way that her face changed, and from the look in her eyes, that she was going to start up with the whole *Everything you've done is for your brother* conversation again. *Allying yourself with Manny Dellarosa, prison time, risking your life—I know it's all for Aaron and Shelly, which makes you honorable and heroic and worthy and sweet.*

Sweet.

Jesus.

Ian didn't want to go there. Not right now. So he needled her by saying, "It's okay, though, if *you're* having fun."

It worked. She gave him an exasperated gasp. "You seriously think *I'm*—"

Ian didn't let her finish. "To glass-half-full it," he pointed out, "or to make the best of a bad situation, I will absolutely agree that a boat ride in the moonlight is not unpleasant. It's been a long time since I've been out on the open water. I'm definitely enjoying that, too."

Now she was looking at him as if he were crazy.

"Naked," she said. "*Naked* boat ride on the very, *very* open water."

"Some might see that as a negative," he agreed. "Although really, you're the one who should've grabbed more of our clothes, so . . ." He let his voice trail off.

But Phoebe wasn't an idiot. She narrowed her eyes at him. "Wow, you are working hard to piss me off. What? To keep me over here, on this side of the boat? Are you really afraid I'm going to find your naked magnificence irresistible?"

"I am pretty freaking magnificent," he said, well aware that that was the exact word that had come to *his* mind as he'd watched *her* earlier, in the lantern light.

Truth be told, it still pertained.

Phoebe didn't realize it, but the soaking wet T-shirt she was wearing—his T-shirt—was a lost cause. It was glued against her. And in the moonlight . . . ? She might as well have been naked, too.

And that added to the not-unpleasantness of the boat ride, despite his worries about his brother and Shel, and the upcoming rescue op from hell. Although Ian *was* forced to spend a large portion of his attention checking to see that they weren't being followed, either by sea or by land, he still felt it was also his duty to keep glancing at Phoebe, to be absolutely sure that she wasn't about to fall overboard.

She was half laughing, half shaking her head. "I'm sorry, but I'm pretty sure I made it crystal clear, back on the yacht—"

"I'm just being cautious. What's that old saying?" Ian interrupted her. "Jump me once, shame on you; jump me twice, double shame on you . . . ?"

She fully laughed her disdain at that. "That's hilarious, coming from a man who's *completely* shameless."

He surprised her by agreeing. "True."

Still, she wasn't ready to accept her win—there was more she wanted to fight about. "I'm not the one who kissed you in the bathroom. In case you're thinking I forgot about that, or somehow missed it, or . . ."

"Kind of hard to miss," Ian again agreed. "Your lips, mine. A distinct smacking sound. Yup, that was me kissing you. Still, it was short—quickly over and done. A kiss good-bye. The subtext was *I hope we don't die, but if we do, it was nice meeting you.* Not at all like that under-the-dock kiss." He paused. "The one where you jumped me. The first time. So far." He narrowed his eyes at her, much the way she'd done to him. "Naturally I'm suspicious. Did you *intentionally* leave my clothes behind?"

"If I'd known we were leaving the yacht—" Phoebe told him tartly, but then interrupted herself to ask, "And that *was* your intention after the cell phone rang, wasn't it? To leave?"

Ian nodded. "Once they'd found us, taking their skiff was our only real option."

"Thanks *so* much for sharing that with me," she said. "And I'm not just being snarky. I'm serious. You really should have told me. It would've been far more useful than any allegedly subtext-laden good-bye kiss."

"I was thinking on my feet," he admitted. "Plus I thought it was obvious. Even if they bought your whole angry wife act, we couldn't just let them go away—and maybe come back with reinforcements. I mean, we could've, but we'd've ended up swimming again."

"Still, if I'd known, I *could've* taken more of the clothes," she said. "Along with my bag—with my wallet. And all my credit cards. Which are now in the hands of criminals. Oh my God, what a pain in the butt."

"A minor inconvenience," he corrected her.

But she'd picked up whatever it was that she'd tossed into the skiff when he'd first pulled her in, and she held it up. He realized that it was the cell phone. "Instead, I have this—which, congratulations, is finally fried." She laughed. "Nice job, by the way, for failing to set it on silent."

"It was on silent," Ian said. "It probably reset to default when I took out the battery. And better that it's fried than left behind. I'm glad you took it—I was worrying about it."

He could tell she didn't quite believe him.

"I'm serious," he echoed her words. "If you'd left it there, they might've been able to pull up some information from it that could've put Aaron and the others in danger. I'm pretty sure that was him calling—patience is not his strong suit. So, well done. And as far as your credit cards go, you're working with the FBI. I'm sure you can get what's-her-name—Deb—to cancel them for you."

"First, we need to reconnect with Deb," Phoebe pointed out.

"Won't be too much longer now," Ian said.

"What's our plan?" she asked.

"I'm still working on it," he said.

"Oh, good."

They were approaching the lights of Sarasota's main marina. The line of private homes—mansions, really—ended, and a public park claimed the shore, followed by several busy waterside restaurants. Ian could see, even from the distance, that people—many of them—were out in the evening air, strolling through the sculpture gardens, eating dinner on those open decks, sitting on benches, walking dogs . . .

And where there were that many people, there were always large, shadowy parking lots somewhere nearby.

They rode in silence for a few moments before Phoebe spoke again. "Look, I understand that it's no big deal for you. But I know that you must often get mixed signals from women, and I apologize if I've done that, too. Because you *are* magnificent." She quickly added, "I mean in your own arrogant, totalitarian way, of course."

"Of course." Ian aimed the skiff toward the edge of the park lights, and that last private dock, tucking the skiff in toward the seawall. On the far side of the wall, up a rolling lawn, the house was dark.

But the neighbors to the south were home. The neighboring dock was well lit, plus a full set of little sparkly white lights adorned most of the palm trees in that yard. Still, heading for the unlit house was their best option, since he hoped that its neighbor to the north was—bingo!—the parking lot for the park.

"I respect you," Phoebe continued, and it was clear she was choosing her words carefully. "And despite having been unwillingly dragged into a frustrating, inappropriate, and highly dangerous situation, thanks to your less than conventional lifestyle choices, I really do want to be your friend. Without any fear or threat—from either of us—of inadvertent jumping."

Friends.

Huh.

Ian knew damn well that he wasn't the most

handsome man on the planet. But he also knew how to make his eyes twinkle in just the right way as he smiled, and that, combined with the genes that had given him his impressive physique, made him enormously attractive to many women. It had been decades since he'd gotten the *friends* speech, in part due to his appearance, but mostly because he'd gotten really good at recognizing women who were ready, willing, and able to have a fling.

And there was no doubt about it. If he'd walked into a bar and seen Phoebe sitting alone at a table, he would have avoided her at all cost. Not because he didn't find her attractive. And not even because she probably would've had legal files spread out across the table, along with an open laptop. A busy, hardworking woman was often a good target for a one-nighter.

But Phoebe gave off a vibe that screamed *trouble.* She was complex and intriguing, yes, but way too much work, even at very first glance. There was nothing simple about her.

And she'd clearly scared the shit out of herself by kissing him like that, under the dock.

Scared *him* a little, too, truth be told.

Here and now, Ian knew that the right thing to do would be to reassure her. Promise that he would be a gentleman, even though he was nothing of the sort.

Instead he found himself continuing to tease her. "From this point on, then," he told her, "any jumping will be advertent."

"That's not what I meant."

"Yeah, I know. We're friends. I get it. But even friends have the right to change their minds. I'm just promising you that we'll have a forty-five- or fifty-minute conversation before we engage in any incredibly hot, passionate, deliciously creative, triple-orgasm-inducing monkey sex. Which is absolutely what would happen if we ever hooked up. Judging not only from that kiss, but from other circumstantial evidence as well."

Interestingly, Phoebe didn't have anything to say in response to that, although she did look away from him, instead gazing pointedly down at the water moving past the side of the skiff.

Ian cleared his throat. He may have pushed it too far. "I just wanted to be honest."

She looked up, her expression unreadable. "No, you didn't. You wanted exactly what you got, which was to get me all . . ." She stopped.

Please say *hot and bothered* . . .

She didn't. "Flustered. And embarrassed. Why do you do that? I'm making a genuine attempt to be an adult about what happened and—" She threw up her hands. "You know what? Forget it. I made a mistake, and I apologized. It's over and done. If you want to keep teasing me about it, be my guest. You just keep living in your macho, misogynistic, pathetic little world where you can't take an attempt at friendship from a woman at face value. Because if that's who you are, I guess we have no chance of being friends anyway. So there it is."

It was then, as they approached the lights, that Phoebe finally realized that the T-shirt she wore was transparent. She tried to wring it out and pull it away from her body, but that didn't help and she soon gave up with a muttered curse. Instead she attempted to arrange her arms so as to keep her breasts covered. But that wasn't going to work very well, either. Especially since it was nearly time to adios the skiff and climb out onto shore. She'd need to use her hands to steady herself.

Ian pulled them in close to the dock and cut the motor. He quickly tied the painter to a post—even though the dock's owners would immediately realize that that was not their skiff, it was better to tie it than to let it drift free.

Nothing drew attention like a drifting, empty boat.

Except maybe a large naked guy carrying a handgun, and a pissed-off woman who looked like the grand-prize winner from a wet T-shirt contest, sneaking through a potentially busy parking lot and attempting to hotwire a car.

"Look, I'm sorry," Ian started to say as he attempted to give her a hand out of the skiff. But she both cut him off, and refused his help, scrambling onto the dock all by herself.

"Nope. Done talking about this," she said briskly. "So. Where are we going and how are we getting there?"

"On the other side of those shrubs is a fence, on the other side of that is a parking lot," Ian told Phoebe. "We're going to move, quickly, up the ramp, and head straight for that shrubbery. Stay in the shadows, and be aware that your shirt is white."

"I'm *very* aware of that, thanks," she said dryly. "Are you sure you don't want to check the house—maybe someone left towels or even a bathing suit on the deck."

"We don't know that they're not home," he said.

"If they are, even better," she countered. "I can play mortified damsel in distress. I was skinny-dipping with my bullshit ass-hat of a now-ex-boyfriend, and he stole both my clothes and my car. Might I borrow some towels? Please. I'll pay you back. I promise."

God, she was good, standing there gazing up at him, wide-eyed behind those endearing glasses. Ian was suddenly intensely aware that he was naked. And that he'd just succeeded at making her not like him very much.

"I'm just disappointed," he admitted. "That you're so horrified by that kiss. I liked it. I think I've been pretty clear about that. And about the fact that I like you. A lot. More than what's good for you."

He'd surprised her again, that much was clear. "Shouldn't that be my choice?" she asked. "As a grown woman? Deciding what is or isn't good for me?"

"It's not a choice," he said, shaking his head. "It's a fact, Pheebs. And instinctively you know it. It's a very good plan for us to be friends—to just leave it at that. Because, to be honest, keeping this weird thing between us to friendship is better for me, too. The complications and entanglements . . ." He shook his head again.

She nodded as she held out her hand. "Then it's a deal. We're friends."

Ian made himself nod, too. And he took her hand. Shook. Should've let it go right away. But didn't. Couldn't. Damn it.

He also couldn't stop himself from speaking, even though he had to clear his throat before he could get the words out. "Can we just make one conditional rule here? That if we get into a situation where we know—absolutely—that we're going to die, we can have—"

She pulled her hand away. "Don't say it!"

He did. "Sex."

She glared her disbelief. "You are *such* an asshole!"

"I am," Ian agreed. "I'm afraid that accepting me for who I am comes with the territory when talking friendship."

"Stay in the shadows, asshole," she said, then turned to stalk up the lawn toward the deck.

"Thank you," he said as he headed for the shrubs. "I appreciate your open-minded acceptance of my asshole-ishness."

And he wasn't sure, but he could've sworn that he heard Phoebe laugh.

"The stupid thing," Francine said as they all waited for the software to upload on the computer she'd pulled out of a heavy-duty lockup in this crazy, secluded Batcave-type place that she called *Zebra,* "is that Sheldon could get this to work in about four seconds, blindfolded, with his hands tied behind his back." She glanced up at her brother-in-law, who'd changed Rory's diaper of doom and now stood, bouncing and rocking the baby who'd finally decided that it was time to cry. Noisily. "That's not helping."

It truly wasn't.

Martell straightened up, intending to throw himself on the grenade and offer to take the shrieking kid into the other room so that Aaron could stay here and help. But Deb shot him a look that screamed *don't* from beneath her black-dyed bangs.

That's right. She wanted him to grill Blondie. How silly of him to forget.

"I'd offer to, you know," Martell said to Aaron instead, making a loser-appropriate gesture that might have meant *take the baby* on some distant planet where babies were shaped like basketballs, "but I'm not very good with kids that little, and I don't want to scare him—or *you,* by, I don't know, *dropping* him or something, so . . ." He shrugged expansively. "Sorry, man."

"Just tell me when the program's up and running," Aaron said tersely, then took the kid into the larger of the two bedrooms and shut the door.

Deb, too, faded back toward the kitchen area, phone to her ear as she took another call from her man, Yashi, who was still in Tampa.

Turned out they hadn't had to wait for ol' Yash to bring back a computer in order to monitor the surveillance at the safe house—because Zebra here was stocked with a variety of equipment.

If you could call a hefty amount of C4 explosives and the contents of a rather large, holy-shit-worthy gun locker *equipment*.

Yes, there was a shortwave radio among the gear, as well as a generator to power the place in the event of blackout.

Or zombie apocalypse.

There was also this slightly outdated computer, and yes, the hardware needed to create a wireless hotspot.

Which allowed them to upload the software that allegedly would let them sneak a peek at Sheldon and his half-bro captor, Berto. That *allegedly* was because so far they hadn't been able to get the damn thing to work.

Several phone calls to Deb ago, Yashi—whose excitement level was permanently set to comatose—had instructed them to uninstall the software and then reinstall it. And yeah, listening to him do his slow-talk thing over the speaker on Deb's phone nearly made Martell go blind with frustration. Or maybe it was envy that was causing that icepick of pain above his left eye.

Dude got to get some from Deb, as often as he wanted it, and he probably saved all of his whooping and hollering for the nights that she got out her handcuffs and whips and—

Sweet baby Jesus, what was wrong with him?

Thinking about the potentially molten hot, kinky sex life of two people Martell barely knew was not helping in *any* way.

Not when he had a job to do.

"So Shelly's the computer specialist, Ian's the brains, Aaron's the brawn," Martell said to Francine who was glaring at the computer message that announced the program's uploading. "That makes you in charge of . . . B&E?" he guessed. Although a beautiful woman like Francine wouldn't have to break anything to enter, at least not in most instances. There was a wide variety of ways to enter a locked building, and picking a lock, crawling through an air vent, or even breaking a window were usually last on the long list of options that usually started with conning or seducing a guard.

Francine shot him a deadeye look, similar to the ones she'd given him back in the coffee shop, where they'd first met. Other than that, she didn't respond.

"Must be nice to have the trust of a man like Ian Dunn," he tried.

"I'd prefer not to talk while I'm doing this."

"It's still only forty percent uploaded," Martell pointed out. "Not a lot of *doing* right this sec. And I thought as long as we're going to be working together—"

"Fine," she said. "Why don't you tell me more about this bullshit no-win mission you and Little Debbie Cupcake are forcing Ian to pull off?"

"It's not a no-win—"

"Breaking into the K-stani consulate?" she interrupted with a scornful exhale. "With the kind of paranoid security they probably have?"

"That's funny," Martell said, "because I was just thinking about the B of B&E, and how Ian won't have to actually *break*—"

"How do you even know these kids are there?" Francine demanded. "Every hour that passes, it's more and more likely they've been moved to—"

He interrupted her this time. "They haven't been moved. We know this. We know where they are, we're watching the consulate, and we've put safeguards in place to make sure they *can't* be moved until we're ready to send Ian in after them."

"Safeguards," she repeated, heavy on the disbelief.

"You really want to get into weeds on how—"

"Damn right I do, and Ian will, too, so if you don't know—"

He cut her off again. "U.S. intelligence has warned the Kazbekistani government that there's an assassination plot brewing against their prime minister."

Francine snorted. "Prime minister? He's the fucking dictator."

This woman had a problem with almost every word Martell spoke. He stopped trying to hide his impatience, giving some of it back to her. "Yeah, well, *this* dictator wants to be called prime minister," he pointed out. "So that's what we'll call him. Obviously the plot is fabricated, and includes a laundry list of reasons for the K-stani Imperial Guard to search, extensively, all diplomatic pouches and packages going from the U.S. to K-stan. Since only a few people in the K-stani embassy are involved in the kidnapping of these children, blah, blah, blah. You get it? The kidnappers can't move 'em until the searches stop, aight? And TSA and the Coast Guard have bumped their threat level up, so the bad guys won't try to take 'em out via other means, for fear of getting caught. Plus, we've got a BOLO, with a sketch of the perp—unidentified—we don't want him to know that *we* know his name. It's just enough to make him cautious about boarding a plane. Ergo, the kids are still in the Miami consulate. We know this for a fact."

"You've implied that Ian's not going to break in to get them out," she surmised. "That means he's going to walk right in. And since you've just said you've IDed the perp—the kidnapper . . ."

"And now I see why Ian trusts you," Martell said. "You pay attention."

She brushed aside his attempt at a compliment, her eyes intense as she gazed at him. "So who is it?"

"You ever hear of a guy, goes by the nickname the Dutchman?"

"The *Dutchman?*" She repeated it with a touch too much disbelief in her tone. Hells yeah, she'd heard of him, but she was playing it like her answer was a great big no. "Seriously? Does he wear, what? Wooden shoes? And live in a windmill?"

Her skills were gold-medal-worthy, but Martell knew she was lying.

"Georg Vanderzee." He gave her the man's real name. "Rumor has it he's a sociopath. So if you have any information that you can share that will allow me to provide more effective support for Ian while on this mission . . ." He let his voice trail off.

Francine had returned her attention to the computer screen, where the download was closing in on 95 percent complete. She was managing to keep her face devoid of the *oh shit* that Martell knew she was feeling. But then she surprised him by looking up. Meeting his gaze.

"Total sociopath," she admitted. "I've never met him myself, and I'm pretty sure I only heard part of the story from back when Ian had to deal with the son of a bitch. I'm certain there were parts that Ian thought were too terrible for me to hear." She shook her head. "And that's not him being sexist. He told *me* more than he ever told Shelly or Aaron. I know *that* for a fact."

"Can you tell me what Ian said?" Martell asked.

"It's been a while," Francine said, and she wasn't bullshitting him. Her face was somber. "Years. I think it would be better—more accurate—if you got the information directly from Ian."

"Fair enough." He paused. "Thanks for being honest with me."

She looked at him again. "This has nothing to do with you. In fact, fuck you."

Martell had to smile. "Wow, Deb was right. You really do like me."

Francine actually laughed as the computer beeped. But then her face changed—it hardened and her eyes flattened, almost as if she were shutting herself down.

And Martell saw that the surveillance program was running. A variety of boxes were up on the screen, each showing a different viewpoint of the former safe house. Some of the rooms were dark, but lights were on in the kitchen and the living room—which had a TV blaring. A bathroom was lit up, too.

A slender, dark-haired man with scrapes and bruises on his face stood in that little pink room, in front of a sink, while another significantly stockier man with a receding hairline loaded beer into the fridge in the kitchen.

Francine sharply drew in her breath. "Get Aaron," she said, her eyes glued to the screen. "Now."

CHAPTER THIRTEEN

"There're no towels out," Phoebe reported to Ian in a whisper, as she handed him what looked like a cushion from a deck chair. "I figured this was better than nothing."

She held one, too, hugging it against herself like a shield. It was striped—white and red—and made of waterproof material that gave it a plastic shine that caught and reflected the light from the neighbor's dock.

"What, there were no giant flags to wave to make sure people notice us as we attempt to borrow someone's car?" Ian asked.

She got defensive. "Hey, it was the best I could do. And if anyone sees us, they'll think it's some kind of beach chair. If you hold it right, they'll think you're wearing a Speedo, and that we're walking back from the beach—"

"It freaking glows in the dark."

"Your ass glows in the dark," she retorted sharply, her frustration getting the better of her. "Speaking of giant flags."

He wanted to kiss her. Now more than ever. "Magnificent," he reminded her. "Giant and magnificent."

She sighed heavily. She was not amused. "Look, I'll just go next door, where they *are* home, and do the woman-with-the-ass-hat-for-a-boyfriend act—"

Ian caught her arm, keeping her from walking away. "No, you're right. This'll do. We've already been out of contact with Aaron and the feds for too long. We have to connect with them. ASAP."

She leaned in slightly, squinting a bit as she looked at him in the shadows. "Finally. You're serious. Thank you. About damn time. FYI, the house is empty. No one's home. There's an alarm system, but it looks rudimentary. Piece of cake for an international jewel thief."

Ian shook his head, avoiding dangerous territory

by simply saying, “We need to get out of this area. Davio Dellarosa is a persistent SOB. We’ve already been here too long.”

Phoebe solemnly nodded her understanding. “Well, maybe this’ll help. There’s a car parked in the driveway. The very secluded driveway.”

“There we go,” Ian said. “I knew our luck was changing.”

He let her lead the way across the lawn and toward the house, where indeed there was an older-model car in the shadow of the house, hidden from the waterfront, the street, *and* the next-door neighbors. It was, perhaps, the perfect car in the perfect location. He dropped his deck chair cushion and got to work unlocking the driver’s side door, while Phoebe stood guard.

She carefully kept her gaze everywhere and anywhere but on him. Although, considering her earlier reference, she apparently *had* looked, at least long enough to make note of the fact that it had been impossible for him to maintain his all-over tan while in prison.

As Ian popped the lock and opened the car door, he turned to Phoebe. “Can you do me a huge favor?”

She immediately stepped toward him, fully embracing their new mature relationship. “Of course.”

Ian looked pointedly over his own shoulder, and said, “Tell me the truth. Does this car make my glowing ass look fat?”

She'd naturally followed the direction of his gaze, but now she looked up, hard, into his eyes. And she smiled back at him despite herself. She even laughed. "You're an idiot."

"When things get too serious, I get a rash."

She pointedly looked back down at his nether regions, despite the fact that doing so made her blush. Still, she spoke coolly, dryly. "Not on your ass."

If Ian believed in love, that would've been it for him. Instantly. Enthrallingly. Eternally. Instead, he just laughed. "Thank God for that. See if there's anything remotely clothinglike in the backseat or the trunk." He popped it open. "ETD's in about thirty."

"Minutes?" she asked.

"Seconds."

"Seriously?"

He glanced up at her. "Now she's impressed. Note to self: Steal more cars."

"Borrow," she reminded him. "These people are much too tidy. There's nothing in the trunk. At all. Or on the backseat."

Of course there wasn't. It had been that kind of day. As Phoebe closed the trunk—remembering to do it quietly, which now impressed Ian in return—he started the car with a sputter that he nursed into a smooth purr. He climbed in behind the wheel—the seats were vinyl and his still-damp skin stuck, oh joy—as she got in on the passenger side. She was still holding her cushion, and she'd grabbed the one he'd dropped as well.

"In case we need it," she said.

Ian took it from her. Put it on his lap. And pulled out of the driveway.

When Shelly came out of the safe house bathroom, Berto was puttering around in the kitchen, opening cabinets and clinking various dishware, looking for God knows what.

He'd turned the TV on in the living room, and a sports newscast was blaring.

Shel found the remote and hit *mute*—to make things easier for whoever was watching and listening in. He sat down on the ancient La-Z-Boy sofa right in front of the main camera, which was hidden in a dusty fake pony palm tree. Whoever had planted it there without disturbing any of the dust was a true artist. He hoped he'd get a chance to meet him or her. But not even half as much as he hoped he'd soon be back with Aaron and Rory.

Berto came out of the kitchen with a bowl of pretzels tucked into his elbow, and a beer in each hand. In cans. Because in the thuggery business, you never gave a bottle—a potential weapon made from broken glass—to an adversary. Even if that adversary was your half brother.

"Thanks," Shel said as he reached for one of the beers.

Berto put the bowl on the coffee table, and complied by sitting in an easy chair that was safely in the frame of any reputable wide-angle lens.

Shel grabbed some pretzels and pretended to

drink his beer, while Berto didn't. Pretend, that is. To drink.

"They gonna call you soon?" Berto made it half question, half not.

It was safe to assume that Ian or Francine had the number of the landline here. And yes, Sheldon expected them to make contact sooner or later. "If you're expecting Aaron to show up so that you can kill him, you're going to be disappointed," he said.

Berto exhaled, part laughter, part frustration. "I don't want to kill Aaron."

"Could've fooled me," Shel countered.

"That was Davio who sent that guy to kill him," Berto said. "Not me. I was at peace with the whole gay thing by then."

Shel put down his beer. "Wait. Are you saying that *wasn't* about Aaron being a witness—"

"To what?" Berto asked.

"You know exactly *to what,*" Shelly countered. It was actually kind of amazing how quickly they'd slipped back into their teenaged-brother speech patterns. It had been years since they'd seen each other. A full decade.

"Aaron didn't see shit that night," Berto said.

The night that their lives changed. The night that Francine told their father that *she* was in that video, having sex with Aaron. The night that Berto had believed her, and gone after Aaron with a loaded gun—and killed someone else.

Aaron had told Shel that he hadn't seen what happened. He'd been locked in the trunk of Berto's car, parked outside of a supposedly deserted warehouse, when Berto had fired his weapon—twice—and killed a homeless man. Whether the shooting was intentional—in a spasm of murderous rage—or accidental, Sheldon still didn't know.

It didn't really matter, because instead of taking responsibility, Berto had called his father for help. And Davio had made the body and all of the evidence disappear.

"Does Davio know," Shel asked, "that Aaron was in the trunk of your car?"

"The body's long gone," Berto said dismissively, putting his feet up on the coffee table. *Thunk* and *thunk*. "Trust me when I say that Davio hasn't thought about that shit in years."

But Berto clearly had.

Shel didn't want to argue about why his half brother had made the choices that he had, so he changed the subject. "It's kind of weird, isn't it, that we call him Davio. Instead of *Dad*."

"Not really," Berto said. "I mean, biologically, yeah, sure, he's our father but . . . He's my boss. My owner. My lord and master." He laughed, but it was devoid of humor, then took another long slug of his beer, before toasting Shelly with the can. "Worst choice of my life—doing what I did that night. Taking my handgun out of the lockbox before going after Aaron. You know, I've thought about turning myself in. Full confession, guilty plea. If only to get Davio off your back. Because he'd go to jail, too. Aiding and abetting, coverup of a murder, conspiracy . . . I'm sure there's something I'm leaving out." He laughed then. "But sorry, I'm *not* going to jail for the rest of my pathetic life. It'd be different if I knew for a fact that I'd get the death penalty, because the needles would make it all finally fucking end."

Sheldon had to laugh his disbelief. "You don't mean that."

"Not all the time." Berto finished off his beer. "But sometimes . . . I kinda do." He gestured with his chin toward Shel's can. "You ready for another?"

"Yeah, sure. I'm almost done," Shelly lied. "Thanks." He tried to hold the can as if it were lighter instead of still nearly full. "So are you saying that Davio tried to kill Aaron only because of . . . ?"

"The gay thing," Berto confirmed. "After you got out of the Marines, and you didn't have to hide it anymore, he couldn't pretend he didn't know, so . . ." He shrugged.

Shelly realized that the timing was right. He and Aaron *had* just left the military. They'd just gotten back to the States when Francine called to warn them that Davio had put a price on Aaron's head.

Berto got up and went into the kitchen, raising his voice to say, "His latest thing is that you couldn't possibly be his kid. *No son of mine blah blah blah*. Your mother must've screwed around on him."

Shel could barely remember his mother, who'd died when he was little. When he closed his eyes, he got a flash of someone blond and beautiful. Like Francie, only more outwardly feminine, and less emotionally stable. Always wearing dresses and high heels. Always smelling good. Almost always crying. "I wish," he said as he set his can on the back of an end table, behind a framed picture of a palm tree.

"I feel you. You know, you might want to fake a paternity test that proves that, I don't know, Bruce Springsteen is your real father, send a copy to D. Prove his delusions." Berto laughed, coming back with two more cans, and handing one to Shel before flopping back into his seat.

It was crazy. Davio Dellarosa had two sons. One was gay; the other was a murderer. And the gay one was the embarrassment.

Sheldon cleared his throat, and took another pretend sip of his new can of beer.

"So you and Aaron actually got married, huh? What's it been, five years now?"

"Almost six," Shel said, and he couldn't help but smile.

"What'd you do, go up to Massachusetts to do it?" Berto asked.

"Canada," Shel said. "I was in Iraq, Aaron was in Afghanistan. We met in London and flew to Montreal. Ian couldn't make it, but Francine was there. It was nice."

And that was an understatement. Sheldon could still picture Aaron, resplendent in his tux, smiling into Shel's eyes as they held hands and promised to love one another forever. Love, honor, respect, trust, be honest with, always . . .

"You didn't invite me," Berto said.

"Nope." Shel took a larger sip of his beer, wishing he could wash the taste of dread from his mouth, knowing that Aaron was going to be angry and hurt when he found out the truth—that Shelly had known, for months now, that Francine had been in contact with Ian, who was in prison.

Shel had known, but not told Aaron.

"Hurt my feelings when I heard," Berto said.

That was bullshit and they both knew it, so Sheldon didn't respond. He just pretended to drink more, hoping that seeing that beer can at his mouth would prompt Berto to do the same.

But Berto just sat there, looking at Shel.

"I'm glad you're happy," he finally said. "You and Aaron. What you have is really special. I envy you, bro. And now, with the baby? Rory? I meant to say congratulations about that, so . . . congratu-fucking-lations."

Sheldon felt himself go very, very still. "How do you know his name?"

Berto toasted him again with his beer. "Oops. I guess I might as well tell you that I know where you work, too, Junior—*and* that the company just moved. I know they pay you under the table, which is convenient when you're living under an assumed name, isn't it? I know your address, your home phone, and your cell. I haven't managed to hack your current email. I don't think that's gonna happen, your security's too tight. But I *do* know you sometimes go to church at the touchy-feely UCC with that rainbow flag, over by the YMCA; that a guy named Robert, from Hamilton-Ladieu on Main Street, cuts your hair—"

"Enough," Shel said. His head was spinning. "Jesus Christ, B., all this time, Davio's actually been—"

"Not Davio," Berto said. "No, no. Up until today, he thought you and Aaron split up about six months ago. That you're in California. Silicon Valley, working for some dot-com. And that Aaron, at last sighting, was in Manchester, New Hampshire. Working at a Radio Shack. I thought that was a nice embellishment. Radio Shack, right?"

"Why does he think . . ." Shelly couldn't finish his question because he suspected the answer, and it was too unbelievable. But then he remembered the way Berto had punched him in the stomach, pulling the blow so that he wasn't really hurt.

Berto, meanwhile, said it anyway. "Because that's what I told him. I take an extra three thousand dollars from petty cash each month to *pay*"—he made air quotes with his fingers—"some fictional detective agency to track you guys down. But you always fucking elude us, you crazy gay bastards. Turns out you were paying off the detective to give us that cockamamie madeup bullshit while, holy shit, you were in Sarasota the entire time. Good thing the guy's fictional, or I'd have to kill him." Berto leaned forward. "I'm your fucking guardian angel, Sheldon. Who do you think tipped off Francine all those years ago, when Davio set up that hit on Aaron, huh?"

Francine couldn't believe what she was hearing.

Aaron obviously couldn't either. He'd managed to get the baby to fall asleep, and he now stood behind Francie, along with Martell and FBI Deb, watching the conversation between Sheldon and Berto playing out on the computer screen. They'd enlarged the picture from that one camera—the one in the living room—so that it dominated the screen. The quality was unbelievably good. They could see every scrape and bruise on Shel's face.

As for Berto . . .

The past decade hadn't been kind to him. While he was still powerfully built, his bulk wasn't all muscle. He needed to be more careful with his diet. Maybe not drink quite as much.

Maybe not drink, period.

"Is that true?" Aaron asked, lightly touching Francie's shoulder as Berto claimed to be behind the anonymous email that had warned her about the hit.

She shook her head. "I don't know," she admitted. "I never knew who sent it, but . . ."

"But what?"

She said it. "I thought it might've been. Him."

At first, Francine had thought it was an attempt to get her to emerge from the woodwork where she'd been hiding, which was near Chicago at that time. Make her take a trip over to Boston where Shel and Aaron were living after being discharged from the Marines, where Berto would be waiting so that he could . . . what? Apologize? Kill her? Kidnap her and bring her back to his fuckwad of a father . . . ?

Any of it was possible.

But she'd dug deeper, getting in touch with an old family friend, and she'd come up with some very convincing evidence that Davio *had* ordered a hit on Aaron. At which point she'd taken the warning seriously.

"And who do you think," Berto said, after waiting a good long time for Shel to answer his first question, and getting no response, "sent that email to Francie, just last year, letting her know where to find Pauline?" He turned his head then, and looked directly into the hidden camera.

And Francie realized that he'd known, all along, that the surveillance equipment was there, and that she was probably watching.

"Who the *hell* is Pauline?" Martell murmured, and Aaron quickly and quietly gave both him and the FBI girl a bullet-point list of basics:

> 1) Pauline was Francie's much-older sister, also adopted by Davio when he'd married their mother.
>
> 2) Decades earlier, she'd run away from private school, where she'd been sent for

bad behavior, and Francine had been searching for her for years, hoping to reconnect.

3) A year ago, Francine found her sister, eight months pregnant and addicted to heroin. Pauline gave birth to Rory, then died.

Back in the safe house, Berto still looked right at the lens—looked right at Francie, into her eyes, and said, "It was me, France. Pauline came to see Davio, hoping for some get-the-fuck-outta-here money, or maybe some genuine help, I don't really know. But he wasn't home—I was. I got her out of there, fast, because I knew he'd kill her if he could—he hated her that much. And it was me who told you where she was, that she was pregnant, and that she was using again."

"Is that true?" Francine heard Aaron murmur from behind her, as back in the safe house, Berto looked at Sheldon.

She'd never told Shel and Airie exactly how she'd found her long-missing and troubled older sister. "It is," she told Aaron now. "I got an anonymous email, just like he said."

Francine had, at great risk, followed the email's instructions and had finally found her sister. With Shel and Aaron's help, and with Ian's connections, they got her to a facility where she went on methadone for the remainder of her pregnancy. But getting that kind of medical care meant that Pauline's whereabouts were made public. Davio would be able to find her. And, like Francine, he'd been searching for her for years.

Berto was right about that—Davio hated Pauline with a passion. He blamed her for everything that had gone wrong with his life, including—irrationally—the untimely death of Francie, Pauline, and Shelly's mother.

"Rory was born addicted to methadone?" Martell asked Aaron quietly.

"Yeah."

"Shit."

"Yeah."

"You got Rory thanks to me," Berto told Sheldon now. "So yeah, I know his name. You're welcome." He finished off his second beer. "All kidding aside, at the time I didn't know you wanted a kid. All I knew was that France always talked about finding her sister. And here I was with info that could make that happen. So . . ."

He put his feet back on the floor and his beer can down on the coffee table with a *thunk* before pushing himself up and out of his chair. Still, he was careful to stand so that the camera caught most of his face, even as he spoke to Sheldon.

"These are the keys to the car." He tossed a set over, and Shelly fumbled before catching them. "I know you probably think otherwise"—a glance to the camera—"but there's no tracking device, no GPS on the vehicle. It's clean. You are, too. Nothing on your clothes, nothing, well, whatever. I know you're going to take that info with a mountain of salt. So be it. Do whatever you have to do, bro. But here's the truth: I'm walking out of here. I'm not going to follow you, and no one else is gonna, either. There's no one watching this place—no one knows about it. Like I told you before, I didn't say anything to Davio, and the two men who found you were mine. They won't talk.

"I'm gonna walk over to that bar by the harbor—the Pelican Deck—where they have that stupid website 'fun-cam,' and I'm going to sit my ass down in front of it." He looked at the camera again, steadily this time. "So you know where I am. So you know you can meet Shel or pick him up or whatever you want to do without any interference from me."

He stepped closer, looked right into the lens, right into Francine's soul. "I know we're not close to even. I know we'll never be. But maybe this helps. Maybe just a little bit."

And with that, he walked away.

Francine activated the keyboard and the mouse, tripping over herself to bring the other cameras back to the computer screen and, yes, there was Shelly on his feet in the living room as Berto walked through the kitchen and out the back door.

"Lock this bolt behind me," Berto called.

Sheldon followed him into the kitchen to do just that, as a camera outside of the house picked up Berto, now a shadowy shape walking around the side of the house and down the driveway to the street.

Sheldon looked into the camera that was hidden there in the kitchen. "I think he was serious. I think he's really gone," he said.

Aaron looked down at Francine, disbelief on his face. "What the hell just happened?" he asked. "Is this real?"

His questions were echoed in both Martell and FBI-Debbie's eyes.

"I don't know," Francie had to admit. "God, I don't trust him."

Sheldon said it at almost exactly the same time, via the camera and microphone. "I don't trust him. Look, I'm going to take the car, and I'm going to get out of here. I'm going to go and pick up some new clothes, in case the ones I'm wearing are somehow tagged, and then I'm going to shower and change." He paused, then added, "Aaron, I'm so sorry for . . . everything. I love you."

And with that he, too, was out the door.

"What do we do now? Intercept him or . . . ?"

Francine looked up to find that Martell was looking at *her* to answer his question, not Deb.

Of course, Rory chose that exact moment to wake up and start to cry.

Aaron immediately headed toward the bedroom, but was stopped by the sound of a car pulling off the road and into the gravel parking lot. And sure enough, the surveillance cameras here at Zebra—there was one out front, one out back of this building—picked up the blurry image of a car. A four-door sedan. Older model. With what looked like two people in the front seat.

"That's not Yashi," Deb said. She'd already drawn her handgun. "Couldn't be. Not yet."

Francine reached for her weapon, too, checking to make sure she was locked and loaded.

"Ian's still not answering the burner phone," Martell reported. "I'd think he'd call to warn us, if it was him."

"He might've had to ditch the phone." Aaron held out his weapon to the former police detective, before swiftly going to quiet the baby.

Outside, the car stopped directly under the security cam, as if on purpose. And the driver opened the door and . . .

"What the *hell?*" Martell put voice to what they all were thinking.

"It's Ian," Francie called to Aaron. "It's okay. We're good."

Martell didn't sound sure about that. "*What* the hell . . . ?"

Ian was naked, save for some kind of . . . something beachy-looking that he modestly used as a fig-leaf substitute, which was a very non-Ian thing to do.

Still, as Ian looked up at the camera, he signaled that everything was okay—something he'd never have done if he were under duress. Francine knew for a fact that he'd die before putting them in danger.

A woman was with him, and Francie leaned closer to the monitor to get a better look at what had to be Phoebe—who may or may not have been working for Davio Dellarosa.

She was tall, with thick, wavy hair that spilled down around her T-shirt clad shoulders. But that was all she was wearing. Her long legs and her feet were bare. She clutched a similar beachy-something to her generous bosom. Light bounced off the lenses of a pair of intentionally nerdly glasses that kept Francie from clearly seeing her face. Was she pretty? Francie couldn't tell, but the way Ian looked at the woman was certainly interesting.

Martell had moved over to the door, but he hadn't opened it, and Francine realized he was looking at her, waiting for her go-ahead.

So she gave it. "Let them in," she said as she went to the supply lockup to find Ian a pair of pants.

Ian had promised Phoebe that there would be clothing for them to put on at this place he called "Contact Point Zebra," and indeed there was.

Jeans—again too big, but she wasn't complaining—and an overshirt that was too warm but at least helped hide the fact that she was without a bra.

Ian's brother Aaron, along with Martell and the goth-costumed FBI agent named Deb, had been joined by what was possibly *the* cutest baby in the world, and a petite blue-eyed blonde who looked simultaneously kickass and gorgeous, as if she were ready to join the cast of whatever postapocalyptic show was currently popular on TV. She was stunningly beautiful but fiercely makeup-free, and had long, glistening hair that didn't require much besides a rubber band to keep it sleekly controlled. She wore hiphugging jeans and a tank top that showed off the svelte muscles in her arms, and clunky, jungle-worthy boots on her feet.

Upon welcoming them inside a cozy and well-equipped two-bedroom apartment, the blonde had greeted Ian with a kiss on the mouth and a slap on his bare butt, which had made him laugh.

Introductions were quickly made—as she'd guessed, the blonde was Sheldon's sister Francine—but Phoebe focused on pulling on the clothes that Martell handed her, and thus didn't have to directly face the woman's challenging, proprietary, *I'm the only one here who gets to slap Ian's bare butt* glare.

Everyone was talking to Ian at once.

Francine: "So what the hell happened?"

Ian: "Long story. Short version, bottom line: we survived an encounter with Davio's goon squad."

Francine: "Or you brought one of his crack hoes back here, with you." And yes, that was a hostile look she was aiming at Phoebe.

And Phoebe couldn't help herself. She laughed as the conversation swirled around her. She'd been called a lot of things in her life, but *crack ho* was a new one.

Ian (to Francine): "Don't be stupid. Any word from Shel?"

Aaron: "He's safe, no thanks to you. Effin' Berto got him away from Davio."

Francine: "We sent them to the safe house, where Berto just left Shelly. He walked away, leaving Shel his car. We have surveillance tape of their conversation. You'll want to see it."

Ian (to Francine): "You know Berto best. Is this a trap?"

Francine: "I don't think so. No."

Aaron: "I wanna go pick him up. I think he'll be at the Y, showering and changing his clothes." He had to be talking about his husband, Sheldon, not Berto.

Martell: "After you catch your breath, Dunn, I want to talk about your previous contact with the man known as the Dutchman."

Ian (to Aaron, ignoring Martell): "Yeah, no, you're not going anywhere." (to Francine) "You're certain Zebra's secure?"

Francine: "So far."

Aaron: "So, what? I'm supposed to just wait here?"

Ian (to Francine): "No one followed you out here? You're sure about that?"

Francine: "Absolutely."

Aaron: "While you send, who? Deb? Shel's never met her. That's not gonna go well. He'll think she works for Davio."

Deb: "No, I'm not leaving. Not when Dunn just got back here. Nuh-uh. At the very least I need to be part of that conversation about the Dutchman."

Ian (over Deb): "Will someone please get Phoebe some water? And something to eat while you're at it . . . ?"

Martell: "There're cold cuts for sandwiches in the kitchen. And breakfast cereal and milk, some fresh fruit . . ."

Francine (over Martell): "We got one more federal agent, guy named Yashi, had to go up to Tampa. Since we left the safe house, we've been communicating with him through a scrambled connection. He doesn't know where we are."

Martell (over Francine as he handed Phoebe a bottle of water): "And some kind of microwavable meals in the freezer . . ."

Phoebe said, "Thanks."

Deb: "But we're going to have to give Yashi our location. He's part of this op, and you're seriously undermanned. May I remind you that the agreement we made was that the rescue mission would start as soon as Sheldon was free. And he appears to be free."

Francine: "*Appears* isn't good enough."

Aaron: "The deal was that we get him back. He's not back."

Ian was now fully dressed—he'd had boots in his extra-large size waiting for him in this little apartment's copious and well-stocked closets. He held up one hand, even as he took a long drink from a bottle of water that Martell had given to him as well.

It was actually kind of amazing that he'd followed

all of that. He not only had, but was more than ready to take over in his role of commander.

"Aaron's right," Ian told Deb. "The deal was that we get Shel back, and he's *not* back. Not yet." He looked at Aaron. "But you're not going anywhere. Francine'll pick him up." He turned his focus to Francine, ignoring Aaron's outraged sputtering of dissent. "*After* you apologize to Phoebe for calling her a crack whore. I'm gonna need a new phone, so make sure you have that new number, because I want a call as soon as Shel is secured."

Francine rolled her eyes at the idea of an apology to anyone, but grimly nodded.

"Oh, and don't hate me too much, France—I realize that's an impossibility—but I want someone riding shotgun. Eyes open wide, because I don't trust Berto." Ian turned to Martell. "And it looks like France's wingman is going to be you, because here's all you need to know about the Dutchman: He's a douchebag—a very dangerous one—but he likes me. He thinks I saved his life a few years back." Now he ignored Martell and Francine, both bristling for different reasons as he turned back to Deb. "What I need from *you* is the complete intel from the team that's watching the Miami consulate, where these missing kids are allegedly being held."

"Not allegedly," Deb interjected.

"Yeah, well, I'll need proof of that. I also want all the info available on everyone involved—not just the kids and the captors and every staff member working at the consulate, but on the mother and father, too. And when I say complete, I mean *complete*. I want to know everything. No surprises. But first, before you hit me with video footage and e-files, I want a sandwich—and I need to meet my nephew."

There was a moment of stunned silence.

"Do it," Ian ordered. "Now."

Francine was the first to put herself into motion. She stomped past Phoebe, muttering a very insincere "Sorry," as she headed for the closets to grab that new phone Ian had demanded.

Martell followed. "I'ma need firepower if I'm truly riding shotgun," he said to Francine.

Deb, too, faded back toward a simple wooden table, where a computer had been set up, her phone to her ear.

And that left Ian, Aaron, Rory, and Phoebe.

Ian turned to his brother, who was holding that candidate for world's cutest baby, and held out his hands. "May I?"

Phoebe realized that Ian hadn't asked his question of Aaron, but instead had been talking directly to the baby, who gave his answer with a drool-filled smile.

As Phoebe watched she tried to move back and away, suddenly hyperaware that she was witnessing something that should've been private. But this place was so small, there was really nowhere for her to go as Rory went easily into Ian's arms.

"Hey, buddy," he whispered with an expression on his face that, on any other man, she would have described as awe. “Wow, you are a big guy, aren’t you? I’m your Uncle Eee. It’s very nice to finally meet you.”

Ian laughed as the baby reached for him—maybe for his hair or his nose—and ended up smacking him in the face. “Why am I not surprised that he packs a punch,” he told his brother, who had clearly forgotten his own anger for a moment, as he smiled, too.

It was then that Ian glanced over at Phoebe. And the smile he gave her was a mix of amusement and embarrassment, probably because he was unable to hide his absolute, softhearted, fully human pleasure.

And idiot that she was, that shared smile—probably because it was accessorized by that very, very cute baby who looked completely at home in his massive arms—made her stomach go into freefall and her treacherous heart skip a beat.

God help her.

“Maybe you should at least *pretend* that you’re not already madly in love with him.”

Phoebe looked up to find Francine standing beside her, holding out a cell phone with unconcealed hostility.

“Give this to Eee for me,” the blond woman continued. “I’ve got the number and I’ll call him when I connect with Shel.” She started for the door, but then stopped. “It’s locked with his usual code, so you can’t use it to call out,” she added. “So don’t bother trying. And for the love of Christ, don’t sneak away again. You know, you really fucked things up before by leaving the way you did."

The nasty-ass attitude had gone on long enough. Phoebe got up in Francine's face to say, "It was a mistake, and I apologize. I won't make it again, so you can stop with the hating. FYI, I'm not a threat—of any kind."

Francine blinked her surprise, apparently unused to being challenged, but then she laughed. "Is it possible that you're really that stupid?" she asked, leaving Phoebe no chance to retort because she swept out of the apartment.

Martell followed her, shooting Phoebe a *what the hell have we gotten ourselves into* look before he closed the door behind him.

Still on the phone, Deb drifted across the room like a goth-flavored ghost, and locked the many deadbolts on that door.

Meanwhile, Ian remained enthralled by Rory. "I have heard a *lot* about you," he told the little boy, as Phoebe tried her best not to watch.

But it was right then that Aaron's smile vanished. "Have you really?" he asked his older brother, instantly antagonistic again.

Phoebe tried to be as invisible as Deb as she headed for the corner of the room that was set up as the kitchen. She opened the cabinets and found several loaves of bread and a package of deli rolls.

But Aaron didn't lower his voice, so it was impossible not to overhear him as Phoebe found a plate and opened the refrigerator, searching for the cold cuts. "Because none of whatever you heard came from me." He was trying to keep his voice as calm as possible, for Rory's sake.

Still, a quick glance in their direction was all it took to know that the baby was thinking about crying.

"Apparently it was decided that I should be left in the dark, as clueless as Rory, as to what the hell was going on with you," Aaron continued. He took Rory from Ian's arms as Phoebe found the sliced turkey and Swiss cheese. There was mustard in the fridge door. She set it all out on the counter as he took a deep breath. "Apparently I'm—What was the reasoning, Eee? I'm unable to keep a secret, or not worthy of knowing the details or—What? I'm dying to know."

Ian sighed. "Look, Air, I had to keep it from you. It was hard enough to do, without having to face your anger and disappointment." He aimed his next words at Phoebe. "Leave that out for me, okay?"

She looked up at him. "Oh. Sure. You want me to make you one?"

"No. Thank you. I'll do it."

Rory was clearly on the verge of howling, but Aaron held him close. "It's okay, little man," he murmured as he rocked the boy. "Daddy's not mad at you. Daddy's not even really mad. I'm just . . ." His exhale came out sounding a little too much like a sob as he rather obviously did his best not to cry, too. "Really, really upset with Uncle Eee."

"See, I knew you'd be upset," Ian said.

"You should have told me before you made the deal with Manny," Aaron whispered. It was clear that his two choices for volume were whisper or shout. "Because Jesus, eighteen months in prison, Eee? That is not okay. I would've vetoed it. I would've chosen another way entirely."

"What other way?" Ian asked almost gently. "Running and hiding, and running again?" He shook his head. "I want you to have a life."

"And I want you to have one, too," Aaron countered.

Ian didn't back down. He didn't even blink. He just stood there, gazing at his brother. "Do I look like I'm unhappy?"

Aaron didn't hesitate. "Hell yeah."

"Well, look again, little brother, because I'm not."

"Not unhappy," Aaron repeated. "That's great, Eee. That's something to really strive for. To be *not unhappy.* Brav-fucking-o."

He walked away, taking Rory into one of the bedrooms, where he closed the door behind him, almost impossibly quietly.

Ian watched him go, then looked back at Phoebe.

Making choices for others seems to be a chronic problem for you. Things not to say, at least not out loud.

Instead, as he came over and reached into the bread bag to build his own sandwich on the plate she'd gotten out for him, she said, "If you want, I can talk to Deb and set up full immunity for you, so that you can share what you know about the Dutchman with the feds without fear of repercussion."

Ian laughed as he helped himself to the rest of the sliced turkey, piling it onto the bread in a single thick slab. "Thanks, but no thanks."

"I'll make sure you're protected," she said. "We can set the fact-gathering session up like a deposition. Cut and dried. Just you, me, Deb, Martell—"

"Nope." He reached across her for the mustard, forcefully squeezing a small mountain onto the turkey.

"Oooh-kay," she said. "I can make arrangements for Georg Vanderzee to receive immunity as well, if he's a friend of yours—"

Ian put the plastic bottle of mustard onto the counter with a bang as he turned to face her. "What part of *The Dutchman's a dangerous douchebag* implied that he's any kind of friend?"

Phoebe refused to back down even though he was standing much too close. "Important business contact, then."

"Yeah, he's not that, either."

And there they stood, face to face, eye to eye. And there it was again, that shifting-earth-beneath-her-feet sensation.

There hadn't been much conversation in the car on the ride over here. Ian had been deep in thought, and Phoebe had found herself lulled by the sound of the tires on the road, and to her amazement, she'd actually dozed off.

She was still exhausted, and she longed for the comfort of her own bed.

Which was probably being carted out of her condo by looters and thieves, right this very moment. Still, that thought wasn't as awful as the realization that had dawned when Sheldon's perfect blond sister had slapped a very possessive hand against Ian's bare butt.

It was more than obvious that Ian was not romantically involved with Francine. But Francine surely wanted them to be.

And even though, just a few short hours ago, Phoebe had recited the *friends* speech to Ian, the sight of Francine kissing him had sent a roiling wave of emotion coursing through her.

She was jealous.

And stupid.

Because even though she didn't want the complications that came from kissing Ian Dunn, she didn't want anyone else kissing him, either.

And that was not just stupid, but freaking stupid.

That was an irrational, selfish reaction that absolutely, positively didn't belong to a woman thinking about a man who was only a friend.

Add in the elevator-ride-like stomach flips that didn't only happen when the man held a baby in his arms, but instead occurred at nearly all eye contact, and . . .

God *help* her.

"I *am* sorry," Ian said now, quietly. "That you got

dragged into this. I seem to be saying that a lot, don't I?"

His words broke whatever stupid spell it was that he had the power to cast over her, and Phoebe turned back to her sandwich. "Yeah, well, now that I'm stuck here for some undetermined amount of time, it seems beyond foolish not to let me help." She took a bite for emphasis. "You could at least let me make you a sandwich," she added balefully through her mouthful.

"That was me being respectful of your law degree," Ian said.

She gave him a very intentional side-eye and he laughed. God, she liked making him laugh.

"I can definitely use your help," he admitted, "sifting through the dump of information I'm about to receive from the FBI. I want you to start your part of the digging with the details of how the mother originally got out of Kazbekistan and the legal standing of her divorce, as well as her custody of those kids. You know anything about international law?"

"Not much, but I know how to read and research. I'll find what you need to know."

"Good. Because I want to know what the father thinks *his* rights are. I also want to know exactly who he is. How big of an enemy am I going to be making. Because the Dutchman's not the only person I'll be fucking with when I pull off this rescue mission."

When, not if. It was possible this man's

vocabulary didn't include the word *if.* Once again, Phoebe found herself admiring Ian's conviction and resolve.

She took another bite and again spoke through it, pointing with her elbow at the cell phone on the counter. "Francine gave me that to give to you. And she managed to do it without shivving me through the heart, but just barely. You *do* know she's in love with you."

Ian laughed again at that. "Nah, she's just messing with you. Trying to make you think that. You scare her, because she hasn't known you for twenty-five years. She's hypercautious." He sighed. "She's earned the right to be."

"How long has she worked with you?" Phoebe asked.

"A long time," Ian admitted.

It was his first acknowledgment that, yes, he had the crack team that she kept asking about. But Phoebe kept her *Hah! I knew it!* to herself. "It hasn't occurred to you that the reason she's stuck around for *a long time* is that maybe she really *is* in love with you?" she asked instead.

"She's not," Ian said as he carried his now-empty plate to the sink. Somehow he'd eaten his entire giant sandwich before she'd gotten through half of hers. "But I appreciate the fact that you think she might be. Good *friend* that you are." He grabbed his phone off the counter and raised his voice. "I'm ready to see that surveillance video from the safe house."

Deb, still on her own phone, pointed to the computer that was out on the table, and Ian headed toward it, glancing back at Phoebe. "You'll probably want to see this, too."

And there it was again, at even that briefest of eye contact. That whoopsie-daisy feeling that she was trying her best to deny.

Phoebe made her voice businesslike and brisk, as she carried the rest of her sandwich toward the computer. "If Berto really is an ally, he might be a way to get in touch with Manny, and convince Davio to stand down."

"I'm pretty sure Manny's not capable of doing any convincing right now," Ian said. "I think his condition is worse than the Dellarosas are letting on. As for Davio—he's completely incapable of negotiation."

"So, then, what's the plan?" Phoebe asked, her heart sinking as she already knew the answer. A declared, mutual truce with the Dellarosas would allow her to return to her regularly scheduled life and job. By *not* establishing that truce . . .

Ian hit *play* on a video that was on screen and waiting for him. "I'm going to use this feud with the Dellarosas to get me inside the K-stani consulate in Miami," he said, as a very handsome dark-haired man—Sheldon Dellarosa—sat down on a sofa directly in front of the surveillance cameras. Shel picked up a remote and muted the booming male voices of what had to be a TV sportscast.

Not establishing that truce would require Phoebe

to stick around for her own safety. And Ian knew that.

He glanced at her, pretending to be extra apologetic. "It's the quickest way in. Quicker than setting up some bullshit cover story. Vanderzee—the Dutchman—*will* run a check to verify whatever I tell him. And it won't take much for him to confirm that I am, absolutely, on the official Dellarosa shit list. You can't buy that kind of cover." He added a final volley. "This gets those kids rescued days, possibly an entire week, earlier. I know it's inconvenient for you, but there you have it."

"I'll live," Phoebe said shortly as, on the computer screen, another man who was heavier and older but still quite handsome—the family resemblance was obvious—carried a bowl of pretzels and a couple cans of beer into the room.

"Good."

She glanced at Ian, who met her eyes and smiled at her.

And the world shifted, just a little. Just enough to know that she was in big, *big* trouble here.

CHAPTER FOURTEEN

"She has no idea," Francine said, after climbing behind the wheel of Martell's POS.

She hadn't asked. She'd just assumed, correctly, that it was okay with Martell if she drove.

He'd gotten in the passenger side, whereupon she took off west, back toward the city and its harbor. She was heading, he knew, for the Pelican Deck, a tourist bar that was right on the water, where Martell's task was going to be to keep eyes on Berto Dellarosa while she went over to the YMCA and picked up her brother.

"She who?" he asked now. "Has no idea of what?"

"Phoebe," Francine answered. "Has no idea how freaking crazy it was that Ian risked his life, going after her the way he did."

"Was it?" Martell asked. "Really that crazy? Because for all of his reputation as the spawn of Satan, Dunn seems to me to fit more in the tried-and-true former-Navy-SEAL-slash-Boy-Scout mold."

Francine laughed at that, heavy on the scorn, complete with trademark eye roll.

"So what do *you* care what Phoebe thinks?" Martell asked her.

"I don't," she lied. "I'm just commenting on it."

"I don't," he imitated her. "You are so full of crap. FYI, I am watching your tension levels rise exponentially with each fraction of a mile we get closer to your old boyfriend."

Martell knew right away that he'd pushed it too far, because she practically turned to ice. This woman was cold to start, but now . . . ? He could feel his nose hairs start to freeze in the deadly silence.

But then Francine surprised him. "My old boyfriend," she said, in an upbeat, conversational tone that contrasted markedly with her white knuckles on the steering wheel, "let his father rape me."

And okay.

That was so not what Martell had expected her to say, and she laughed—a brittle sound—at his inability to speak. "Nice, right?"

"Let?" he managed to echo.

"He saw Davio hit me," Francie said, "and he just walked away. He knew what would happen. I was being punished, and that's how Davio punishes women. Or girls. Age pretty much doesn't matter to him."

"I don't know what to say in response to that," Martell admitted.

"Good," she said. "So shut the fuck up."

She was the one who'd started the conversation in the first place, but he chose not to remind her of that.

But then she looked at him again and whispered, "Don't tell Shel or Aaron, because they don't know. They think he just beat me up. Don't tell anyone."

"I won't," Martell promised, thinking *Shit*.

They rode the rest of the way in an oddly frigid silence, as he tried to come up with the best way to say *Maybe you should talk to someone about this. Like a licensed therapist or a rape crisis center counselor, if you don't want to tell your family. . . .* But he didn't dare.

And it wasn't until Francine pulled to the side of

the road, to drop him about a quarter mile away from the bar, that he ventured to speak again.

"Are you, um, okay?" he asked.

She looked at him with those weirdly flat blue eyes. "Text me when you have visual confirmation that he's sitting at the bar."

Martell nodded as he climbed out, turned to lean back into the open window. "You know, Berto might not be working this gig alone."

"I'm aware," she told him. "I'll make sure we're not followed."

"Followed back here?" he asked. "Or—"

"No. You're going to have to find your own way to reconnect with Little Debbie and Team Hero."

"That's my car you're driving," he reminded her.

"So what?"

Right.

She pulled away from him, forcing him to jump back to avoid having the rear tire roll over his feet.

Martell watched the glow of his taillights fading into the night as he walked toward the bar. He was well aware that moments after Sheldon's return, the entire group—Team Hero, as Francine had called them—would bug out and leave Zebra.

No doubt they'd head immediately to Miami, where the next phase of this fuck-tastrophe was due to take place. Martell was going to have to get creative in order to find a car in which to make the three-hour-plus drive.

He made peace with that as he finally reached the Pelican Deck's pitted gravel parking lot. He went up the wooden boardwalk and through the bar toward the so-called party deck that overlooked the water.

The party that was happening out there was a sad and lonely one. And it was winding down, despite it still being hours before last call. The *partiers* were a mix of German tourists on beach vacations, elderly yachters, and sleepy drunks.

But sure enough, there was Berto, the man from the surveillance tape, nursing a pint of draft beer as he sat alone at the table that was, yes, directly beneath the self-labeled “fun-cam.”

Whoo-hoo! Whoo! Whoo?

Berto looked tired and sad and as if that wasn’t the first beer he’d ordered from the laid-back, tattooed waitstaff since he’d gotten here.

Martell walked past him to verify, pretending he was looking for the men’s, before he typed the text to Francine. *He’s here, whatever that’s worth.*

As he hit *send,* the table next to Berto cleared, its previous occupants heading back to *das Beach Condo.* Martell perched himself on one of the still-warm stools and settled in, trying not to let his disgust for Berto show as he thumbed through his contact list on his phone to figure out whose car he could beg, borrow, or steal to get his ass to Miami.

“You’ve really never met her?” Francie turned from where she was nestled in the crook of Berto’s arm, her head on his broad shoulder, to look up at his face.

He kissed her instead of answering, his mouth soft and sweet. As always, when he kissed her, she felt something stir, deep inside. Something hot and heavy and powerful and consuming and . . .

She pulled back abruptly, only to find him smiling at her, his brown eyes amused beneath their heavy lids. He murmured, "Would it really be that bad if you just let me—"

"Yes," she said, no hesitation, pulling away from him to sit up on the tattered sofa they'd brought into the empty warehouse where they'd been hanging out since Berto had come to live with his father at age sixteen.

They'd been over and over and over this, countless times. It was the conversation that would not die.

Francie wanted to wait.

She wasn't ready to go all the way.

She wasn't willing to end up like her mother—forced to drop out of school and get married to some loser before she was twenty.

"Hey." Berto now pushed himself up so that he was sitting next to her. He tucked her hair behind her ear. "You know I'd wait for you forever, right?"

She looked into his eyes and saw the truth behind his words. "Yeah," she said on an exhale. "I know." She also knew how lucky she was. And how unlucky Pauline, her older sister, had been.

She'd been thinking about that a lot lately. Somewhere, out there in the huge wide world, her sister was getting ready to celebrate another birthday.

Francine brought the conversation back to the question Berto hadn't answered. "You really never met Pauline? Not even once?"

Berto scratched his head through his thick, dark curls. "I don't think so."

"She was at the wedding." When Davio married Francine and Pauline's mother, and the world went from tenable to terrifying.

"Yeah, but I wasn't. Are you kidding? My mother was bullshit about Davio getting remarried so soon. Your mother was already pregnant with Shelly, which made it even worse. We spent most of that summer in Long Island with my grandparents, getting shitfaced. Well, I didn't. At least not all the time."

He was joking—he'd been a child. Or God, maybe he wasn't joking. . . .

Berto laughed at the expression on her face. "I'm kidding. She was a terrible mother, but she didn't let me drink."

"How about that one Christmas?" Francine asked. "When we went to San Francisco?"

He shook his head. "I've never been to California."

"I know that Pauline was gone before you moved in with us," she said. It was odd that Berto's visits before then had never, not even once, lined up with her older sister's erratic schedule.

Pauline had hated Davio from the start, and she and Francine were frequently sent to visit their mother's parents. The year Francie turned six, Pauline's "bad behavior" got her shipped off to boarding school. And when she finally ran away, the response had been one of weary inevitability.

But Francie had loved her big sister fiercely.

"She was . . . brilliant, and beautiful, and . . . I wanted to be her," she told Berto now.

"You don't need to be her, because you're you, and you're all of those things and more," he said, catching her mouth with his again.

"I want to find her," she said, after he'd kissed her breathless. "I've always wanted to. Make sure she's okay."

"I'm sure she is," Berto reassured her. "Maybe she's in Paris. Maybe we'll be neighbors when we finally go to Europe."

Francine laughed. "That would be perfect. Really unlikely, but . . ."

After Sheldon graduated from high school, their plan was to pack their bags and escape overseas—travel, far from Davio and the Dellarosa family business.

"We'll find her," Berto promised. "Wherever she is. I'll help you. You know that, right?"

"Yeah." Francie smiled into the warmth of his eyes, and lost herself in the sweetness of his kiss.

As Francine now headed toward the YMCA, where she was certain she'd find her little brother, it was hard not to think about that idyllic afternoon nearly ten years ago—one of the last that she'd spent with Berto before he'd turned on her.

Francine had spent much of the past decade searching for her long-lost sister. But then, finally, last year, she'd received an anonymous email that had pointed her toward Pauline.

She'd known it was Berto who'd sent that email—even before today, when he'd confessed as much as she listened in on his conversation with Shel.

It had to have been Berto. There was no one else who'd known about Francie's quest.

And when Francie went into one of the darkest, shadiest parts of Tampa, to some rotting hovel back behind one of the city's strip clubs, she'd had the unnerving sensation that she was being watched.

Not in a creepy stalker way. More in an *If anything bad happens, I'll swoop in and save you,* Batman way.

And although she'd been prepared to kick ass to find her sister and pull her out of there, it was clear when she first went inside, that the regulars at this particular crack house—or opium den or whatever the hell it was—were expecting her.

They were ready for her arrival. Greeting her politely, even calling her *ma'am*. Happy to help her carry her barely conscious sister out to her car. Defanged and, in fact, scared shitless by whoever had given them the heads-up that she was coming.

And that had to have been Berto.

She's in a bad way, he'd written in that email. But

despite that warning, Francie had been unprepared. Pauline was only in her thirties, yet she looked nearly elderly, her hair graying and lifeless, her skin stretched tight across her somehow still-beautiful face. She was bone thin, with a huge bulge of baby in front of her. . . .

The email had said Pauline was pregnant, but Francie also hadn't been prepared for how far along she was.

As she drove away with her sister unconscious in her backseat, Francine had been swept up by the urgent need to find immediate medical help for both mother and unborn child, and she hadn't spent much time thinking about the remarkable ease with which she'd pulled off the rescue.

The next few days had been filled with dealing with the medical emergency—with Shelly, Aaron, and Ian's help.

Pauline was put on methadone, with the understanding that the baby would be born addicted, also in need of detox.

The bad news was that the baby's first months would be miserable, but the good news was that opiates were less destructive developmentally than alcohol or other drugs. And after he detoxed, with plenty of love and care, he'd be okay.

Francine had also discovered that, thankfully, her sister had been clean and sober right up until the very end of her pregnancy, which further increased the baby's chance of survival.

Pauline, however, had lost all desire to live. She

didn't want the baby, and after she signed custody of Rory over to Shelly and Aaron, she essentially quit. No one was surprised when she drew her final breath.

And it was only then, after Pauline's funeral, that Francie finally reached out to the writer of that anonymous email. *Thank you,* she wrote, keeping it simple.

But her email had bounced back. The recipient had closed that account.

You know I'd wait for you forever, right?

Francine didn't have to dig deep to stir up the clear-as-day memory of Berto's youthful promise.

But on its heels came a vivid image from that terrible, horrible day she'd pretended that she was in that sex tape with Aaron—Berto's hatred for her darkening his eyes, and then changing to an even more awful indifference, as he said, "Whatever." As then he turned and walked away, leaving her with Davio, who didn't wait for the door to close before he slapped her again, brain-jarringly hard, across the face.

Now, as always, Francine blinked and boxed it up, and pushed it all aside. She had a job to do. Find Sheldon and bring him home. And then convince Ian that this *Mission: Impossible* bullshit in Miami was not a job worth risking. Yeah, he'd given his word and said that he'd do it, but fuck that. It wouldn't take much for the five of them to vanish, to go fully off the grid, and never be heard from, ever again.

• • •

"This is ridiculously inefficient."

Ian looked up from the computer to find Phoebe gazing at him from across the table. Because there was only one computer at Zebra, he'd dug a printer and a ream of paper out of the main lockup, and had printed out hard copies of several of the many FBI files that had downloaded onto the laptop's hard drive. That way, she could read while he sifted through another of the documents onscreen.

"I'm reading this report," she said, "and I'm finding out all about the father of those kidnapped kids. Guy's name is Sulislaw Taman Hamad, and I see that he attended Yale and spent a great deal of time in the West, going by the name Steve Hamad. He met and married Lusa Vaszko while he was in school. Then, about five years ago, he fully embraced his standing as some kind of prince from something called the Kazak tribe and denounced his ties to America. But without Internet access, I can't Google *Kazak,* so I don't really know what that means."

"It means I'm screwed," Ian said. "It means he's a fundamentalist with access to money, and a knowledge of the West, so I can pretty much guarantee he's going to target me after this is over. It also means we take the concept of U.S. law—or international law, for that matter—and throw it right out the window. The only law this douchebag follows is his own. So that divorce that his ex-wife filed for and received? In his mind, it doesn't exist.

Same thing for her custody of the kids. That's an impossibility in his world. She's his property, and the kids are, too. He's taking back what he believes he owns."

"Hamad may not follow U.S. or international law," Phoebe pointed out, "but the government of Kazbekistan—"

"Has little to no control over the Kazak region of the country," Ian finished for her. "And every interest in the repatriation of a nuclear physicist like the ex-wife."

"Is a draconian husband really going to let his wife work for anyone, let alone a government he probably doesn't recognize?" Phoebe asked.

"Ex-husband," Ian corrected her. "Here, he's her ex-husband."

"But there, he thinks he's not," she countered. "And I was going there. With both feet. Worst-case scenario."

"Worst case, Dr. Vaszko returns to K-stan in pursuit of her children, and he immediately executes her. Just boom. Gun to the head, she's dead as soon as she steps off the plane."

Behind her glasses, Phoebe blinked, but otherwise didn't react. "Worst case on a world-wide level," she pointed out, "is she returns to K-stan, builds them a nuclear weapon, and *then* he kills her." She leaned across the table. "But really, how likely is that to happen over your far-more-personal-to-*her* worst case? Again, since I can't Google Kazak or delve more deeply into our guy's time spent at Yale to find out how open he'd be to letting his wife work . . ."

"Maybe he'd do it in exchange for the K-stani government's help in getting his kids back."

Phoebe shook her head. "We've been told that the ambassador's not involved."

"That doesn't mean the government's not," Ian told her. "And the way that we're tiptoeing into this mission makes me believe that *our* government knows that *their* government is—absolutely—involved on some level."

Ian knew that Phoebe was well aware that *that* meant rescuing these kids and keeping their mother out of K-stan was a mission that could not fail.

"I could really use a computer," she said again.

"In Miami," Ian said, "we'll have access to more than one."

"Good, because I also have some questions specific to the K-stani consulate staff's immunity to U.S. law. As far as I can tell, it's only the ambassador and his or her family who have such protections. The idea that an embassy or consulate is sacrosanct is a Cold War myth. Yes, there are exceptions—and I'm simplifying, of course."

"Of course," Ian murmured.

She narrowed her eyes at him. "This is *well* outside of my area of expertise, so forgive me if I'm missing something obvious, but from what I've read, it seems that if, say, a kidnapped child had access to a cell phone and was able to call for help, saying *I'm here, held against my will in the*

Kazbekistani consulate, the police would be able to go in to investigate."

"From what I know," Ian told her, "that's true."

She leaned toward him. "So why not simply hack into their security system and set off their fire alarm. Go in with the first responders—"

"If the kidnappers suspected that was happening, they might harm the children. Hamad's instructions may well have been *If I can't have them, you can't either.*"

"God," she said, sitting back in her seat.

"You're not going to be happy when you *do* get to Google Kazak," Ian told her.

She leaned in toward him again. "Okay," she said. "So execute a simple middle-of-the-night break-in. You locate the kidnapped children, barricade yourself in with them, and *then* hit the fire alarm. While simultaneously giving them your cell phone so they can call nine-one-one for help."

In theory, it wasn't all that bad an idea. Still . . . "It's not that simple," Ian told her. "That approach would jeopardize our diplomatic relationship with—"

"Kidnappers," she interrupted and finished for him. "Our diplomatic relationship with a country whose consulate staff includes lawless murderers and kidnappers. Whom the K-stani government's leaders would immediately disavow the moment the plot was revealed."

Again, she had a point. But . . . "It's really not that simple," he said.

"Why not? I've been thinking about this for a while, and I keep coming back to the fact that this approach—breaking in versus getting back in touch with the Dutchman, whom you haven't seen in years . . . A break-in could be done immediately."

"That's not true," he said. "It's just not. The prep time would be extensive."

"But with your expertise," Phoebe argued, "and talents, and experience at this exact type of thing . . . international jewel thief that you are. Allegedly. And yes, you protest—rather weakly—that you're nothing of the sort. While at the same time effectively propagating your notoriety. *Very* effectively, I might add. Which is finally starting to make sense, the longer I know you."

With his peripheral vision, Ian could see Deb on the far side of the room. The FBI agent was sitting on the sofa and sifting through another printed file. "Get to the point," he told Phoebe. "This dancing around is not like you."

She glanced at Deb, too, then leaned in even further, and lowered her voice. "The point is that you're a liar, Ian Dunn. A professional one. You're not really a jewel thief, at least certainly not the cat burglar kind. I'm betting it's been years since you've broken past any kind of security system whatsoever. And I think that's because you don't have to, not as long as you can talk your way past the guards. Which is something you're very, *very* good at, because you're a con artist."

He kept his expression bland. "Well, you're

certainly entitled to your uneducated, action-movie-inspired opinion."

"Or my sophisticated, observant, and erudite opinion," Phoebe countered. "It really is making sense now. Your unwillingness to break past the piddling little security system at that house near the harbor, despite being naked and knowing that the place was empty, and that there *had* to be clothes or at least a blanket inside . . . ?"

"There weren't any blankets on the boat," he pointed out.

"You're not stupid," she countered. "What are the odds of that happening to us twice in a row—that a waterfront vacation home would be completely empty?"

"Actually quite high," he said. "In this economy? Lotta property for sale here in Sarasota, much of it unoccupied, I imagine."

"Why would someone take everything out of the house but leave deck furniture? No. You didn't break in because you *couldn't* break in. Some jewel thief."

Deb's head was still down—Ian could see her in his peripheral vision as he made himself smile broadly at Phoebe. "You have a very vivid imagination."

"I do," she agreed, "combined with excellent deductive reasoning. Is that really the best you can come up with? A condescending nonargument?"

"I don't need to prove anything to you, or to anyone," Ian said. "If you want to think I can't break past a basic home security system, well, honey, you go ahead and think that."

"Condescending nonargument complete with belittling term of endearment it is," Phoebe said. "How about your immediate decision to use both your past relationship with the Dutchman and the threat from the Dellarosas to get you inside the consulate—without waiting to see what kind of info the FBI has on the building's security system?"

Ian laughed. "So now my desire to use the easiest, simplest, quickest approach is somehow sinister? Seriously, Pheebs—"

"Seriously, Eee," she mimicked him. "I'm your lawyer. I won't tell."

"Yeah," he said, "because anyone you try to *tell* will be convinced that you're crazy. Which you are."

"Don't forget my vivid imagination," she shot back at him. "Honey."

Ian sighed heavily.

"Before you make some excuse—you need another sandwich, have to take a leak, want to check on your brother—and walk away from me, take a second to listen to this. It's occurred to me, as you're figuring out your big con-game plan, that if you do manage to rescue—" She stopped, corrected herself. "—*when* you rescue those kids, it might be worth thinking ahead. Maybe set something up that makes the Dutchman and his buddy Steve believe that the kids and their mother are dead. Because what little I *do* know about the father? If he's got money—and you seem to think he does—he's going to try again. That means this threat to national security exists as long as he's . . ." She cleared her throat. "Alive. Or as long as she and the kids are. And I'm betting it's easier to fake-kill *them* than it is to fake- or even real-kill him."

Ian gazed across the table at her. Again, she had a very good point.

She didn't wait for him to make any more noise along the *vivid imagination* line. "So that's it," she continued. "Discussion concluded. You now know what I think. You heard my suggestion. If you can use anything I said to protect those kids, then good. If you can't, that's okay, too, because just getting them out of there is . . ." She nodded her head, her eyes behind those glasses so warm and brown. "It's enough. It's plenty. I didn't mean to imply that you needed to do more than that. I just thought—"

"Oh, don't go soft on me now," he said. "It's hot when you get all in my face, order me around, grab me by the junk and squeeze—and suggest *you* know the best way to risk my life, the lives of my team members, and the lives of these kids. *Your* life, too, sweetheart, should our nasty friend Steve find out you helped."

She didn't respond. She just gazed at him with those eyes.

Ian couldn't help himself. He went into total asshole mode. He drew in a deep breath. "Mmmm," he said. "Could you move your hand a little higher and . . . ? Ooh, that's nice."

"Don't do that," she said quietly. "Just . . . don't."

Ian spoke just as softly. "Don't *you* be foolish and naïve and make assumptions about what I am or am not capable of."

Phoebe blinked first. "Fair enough. But I wish you would be honest with me. It must be exhausting to never really be yourself—not even with your own brother. Maybe especially not with your brother . . ."

"You want to know my secrets?" Ian asked her. "You've gotta sleep with me first."

"Wow, I must be hitting very close to home," she countered. "For what it's worth, I respect and admire you enormously. I happen to think you're brave and extremely intelligent and generally just . . . really pretty wonderful. And I know you don't know me and certainly have no reason to trust me, but . . . I'm on your side. And not just because I'm paid to be."

Time hung for a second as he held her gaze, and held it, and held it.

It was then, thank God, that his phone rang. "It's Francine," he said.

As he reached for the phone, Deb approached, which meant his conversation with Phoebe, double thank God, was over, out of necessity. Aaron, too, emerged from the bedroom.

"Seven Charlie," Ian said, after hitting *talk*.

"Oscar five alpha," France said. "I got him."

Ian looked at his brother and said the words, knowing Aaron needed to hear them. "Shel's safe."

"Thank God," Phoebe breathed.

Aaron nodded and disappeared into the bedroom to get Rory ready to travel. "Anyone following?" Ian asked Francine.

"Nope," she told him, and Ian shook his head, so that Phoebe and Deb understood that she and Shelly were free and clear.

"Head for Miami," he ordered. "I'll be in touch." He hung up the phone. "Let's do it. Let's get out of here."

But before he could start organizing which of the supplies and equipment he wanted to take—all of it, because he was on a budget and God knows what they were going to need—Phoebe blocked his path.

"You want me to make you another sandwich," she asked him. "That this time you can actually taste while you eat . . . ?"

And Ian realized that she'd seen through him. She'd known how terribly worried he'd been about his brother-in-law, and what a blessed relief it was to know, for certain, that Sheldon was secure.

But he wasn't willing to admit it. Not any of it. Not yet. He mentally bitchslapped himself. Make that *not ever*. In a matter of days, this assignment would be over, and they'd both return to their previously scheduled lives.

At least Phoebe would.

Ian was going to make sure of that.

"No, thanks," he told her, then got to work.

"There they are." Aaron pointed, leaning into the front, as Ian pulled their borrowed car toward the back of the truck stop's nearly empty parking lot.

And there they were. Francine and Shel, sitting on the hood of Martell Griffin's car. Their body language was not only easy to read but followed their individual, usual pattern to a T. France was leaning back, supporting herself with straight arms, hands braced behind her on the hood, in a position of open strength that Ian knew was deceptive. Not the strong part—she was that and more. The relaxed openness was pure pretense. Francie was more tightly wound and secretive than anyone he knew, save for his own self.

As for Shel . . . His shoulders were hunched and he was curled into himself, as if he were cold—or as if he'd recently been grabbed and knocked unconscious by someone who should have greeted him with a hug.

Shel straightened up, though, as he saw them approaching, and Aaron breathed his relief. "He's okay. He looks okay." He put his hand on Ian's shoulder and squeezed. "Thank you for stopping here. For arranging this."

Deb had wanted to push straight through, meet Francine and Sheldon in Miami. But Ian had insisted they pull into this open-all-night throwback to the 1970s, about ten miles south of Fort Myers. And it wasn't just because he knew Aaron was anxious to get eyes—and hands—on Shel. This was a good place to meet the other federal agent, Yashi, too.

But it wouldn't hurt to let his brother think this

was all for him, so Ian said, “Anything to make it a little easier.”

“Yeah, right,” Aaron scoffed, then slapped Ian upside his head. Not gently.

“Ow!”

“I know that this is more about ditching this car than *making it easier,*” Aaron said, lowering his voice in an imitation of Ian—that is, if Eee sounded like a moron. “I’m still mad at you, fuckface.”

Ian glanced in the rearview mirror to find Phoebe watching him, her eyebrows up. He wasn’t sure what that look meant, but it couldn’t be good.

“Yashi’s ETA is between five and ten minutes,” Deb reported from beside him in the front seat.

That was good, because Aaron was right. Yashi’s arrival meant they could shift over to his vehicle and leave behind this car that Ian and Phoebe had “borrowed.” Not driving a car that could light up the databases of thousands of police officers was always a good thing when one didn’t have time for an arrest booking in one’s busy schedule.

As Ian parked next to Martell’s car, Aaron had the door open and was out before the wheels stopped rolling.

“I’m gonna hit the head,” Ian announced, as outside the car, his brother threw himself into his husband’s arms. He couldn’t watch, because it was too intense. Too sincere. Too raw, too real.

He’d always thought that seeing Aaron with Shel, and witnessing the power and passion of their love for each other, was probably a lot like seeing God.

Particularly at an emotion-filled time like this one. You couldn't look directly or you'd go blind from the sheer perfection.

Ian turned to Deb. "I can trust you not to drive off without me, right?"

"I'd prefer it if you waited in the car until Yashi got here," the federal agent said tightly.

"What, do you think *I'm* going to run away?" he asked.

Deb cleared her throat delicately. "I think anything is possible, now that you've got your brother-in-law back."

"I'll go with him," Phoebe volunteered. "Babysit."

Ian shot her an exasperated look in the rearview mirror, and she smiled.

"Yeah, that doesn't make me happy," Deb said with a frown.

"Too bad." He disconnected the wires and the engine went dead. "I gotta whiz."

"Just stay close to the sleeping baby," Phoebe advised Deb as Ian got out of the car and stretched. "If you've got Rory, you've got Aaron and Shel. And if you've got Aaron and Shel, you've got Ian. And yes. It's adorable."

Shaking his head, Ian didn't wait. He headed for the distant building, scanning the structure and open parking lot around it, making sure they truly were alone. He didn't slow even as he heard Phoebe running with a weird, scraping shuffle to catch up. "Adorable," he repeated.

"Well, it is," she insisted. Everything she was

wearing—not just her footwear—was too big. Still, he couldn't shake that image of her on the boat, in only his T-shirt and her panties, hair loose around her shoulders. *Magnificent.*

She'd found a ponytail holder of some sort at Zebra, which was a shame.

He focused on watching the single 18-wheeler that was idling out in the truck parking area. Otherwise, the place was quiet; the filling pumps, both gas and diesel, were deserted.

"Just a few hours ago, you accused me of having too much fun," he said. "I now think you're enjoying this a little too much."

Phoebe snorted. "Yeah, because back at the Apocalypse Hut, while you and Aaron were packing up your armory, I took a moment to talk to Deb. Who let me know that, no, I will *not* be able to call my mom to tell her I'm okay, nor will I be able to provide my new bosses at BH and S with the reason as to why I'm blowing off my fabulous new job over the next few workdays. So my mother is going to think I've been murdered, *and* I'm going to be fired. On my personal fun index that's a negative five, thanks so much."

Phoebe had a mom. Ian had never actually thought about that. Most of the people he dealt with didn't have moms, or any kind of normal family life. Or if they did, they didn't talk about it.

"I'm sorry about that," he told Phoebe as a somewhat stout middle-aged woman—the truck driver—came out of the building and headed for her rig.

"I know," she said. "After this is over, I'm going to make Deb call the law firm and get me my job back, *and* apologize to my mother, too. She'll do it. She's pretty nice."

He glanced at her, but she said nothing about asking him to make a call—either because she thought Ian's request might hurt more than it would help, or she was convinced that the second this mission was over, Ian would vanish into the night.

"What *are* you going to do with your newfound freedom?" Phoebe asked, as if she'd been thinking the very same thing. "With Aaron's criminal record cleared, you could finally leave the country. Get away from Davio Dellarosa, once and for all. I hear New Zealand's nice. Probably a fair number of jewels to heist there, too. That was a joke," she added as Ian glanced at her again.

"When we get to Miami," he told her, "you can help with the research if you still want to—"

"I do," she said.

"Good," he said, opening the door and going in first. Manners were put on hold when crazy assholes were gunning for him. But the convenience store was empty with the exception of a long-haired, tie-dye-wearing kid working the cash register. "Thanks. But other than that, your primary job is going to be to keep your head down, be quiet, and stay out of the way."

"I'm good at that," she said.

He looked at her.

"I am. Excuse me," she called to the clerk, in a southern accent that was pure coal miner's daughter. "Does your men's room have windows or . . . ?"

"Oh, come on," Ian said. "That's what you call being quiet?"

"You didn't say I was supposed to start now," she countered quietly in her regular voice, putting the sugar back in when she raised it again. "Or any kind of exit, maybe a back door . . . ?"

Doh-ahr. She made the word have two syllables.

"Um, no?" the kid called back. "I mean yeah, there's a window, but it doesn't open."

"Thank you," she called. "It prolly does, so FYI, I'm just going to stand in the doorway, with the door propped open. No worries, nothing funny or freaky going on." She laughed in a southern accent, too. "You know how it is. Just keeping my eye on my man."

"Really?" Ian said as she leaned back against the open men's room doh-ahr, waving cheerfully at the wide-eyed clerk. "You mistrust me that much? What about that whole adorable *If you've got Rory, you've got Aaron and Shel* thing?"

She smiled sweetly up at him. "For all I know, Rory's been trained to crawl out of his car seat after hypnotizing whoever's watching him, and he, Aaron, Sheldon, and Francine are already halfway to Contact Point Aquarius, where you'll meet them after escaping through the bathroom window, riding away on a bicycle that you stashed back behind this facility four years ago, in anticipation of this *exact* scenario."

"Except if your theory's right and I'm just a con man, I wouldn't have to do all that. Instead I'd merely *say* that I did."

"I've been told by a very reliable source," Phoebe said, "not to underestimate you. *Don't assume that you know what I can or cannot do*." She lowered her voice in an imitation of Ian that was significantly better than Aaron's had been. "And I know. I'm paraphrasing. But that *was* the gist of it. So this is me, not assuming." She gestured for him to go in. "If you're afraid I'll peek, feel free to use a stall."

Ian had to laugh at that. "You *are* funny."

"And yet my earlier joke about the bike fell decidedly flat."

"Ah, fuck it," he said. "I know we had a deal and that I'm not supposed to, but—"

He kissed her.

And it wasn't a repeat of the dry little peck that he'd given her back on the yacht, but rather a great, huge, tongue-in-her-mouth, full-body contact, souls-are-probably-about-to-touch event as he wrapped his arms around her and pressed his knee between her legs. At least that's what he hoped it looked like from the cashier's perspective.

Sadly, Phoebe didn't melt against him, which was a shame, since he would've loved a reenactment of that kiss beneath the dock. Instead, she said, "Wait! Don't! Gahhh!"

But he kissed her again and again, and in doing so swallowed her words—at least he thought the last one was *gahhh*—as he lifted her up so that she was straddling him in a most suggestive way, even as he pulled her with him into the men's room. The doh-ahr shut behind them with a solid-sounding *clunk.*

Only then did he put her down, albeit reluctantly, because she was warm and soft in all the right places, and although she was a larger-than-average woman, her butt fit damn near perfectly in his larger-than-average hands.

Plus, she wasn't wearing a bra, and having her pressed up against him was, absolutely, as fantastic as he'd imagined.

"You asshole," she started, but if she'd said anything more, it was drowned out by the sound of the clerk hammering on the door.

"No sex in the bathrooms! No sex in the bathrooms!" the kid was shouting. "You come out here right now, because I will not hesitate to call the police!"

With one last exasperated look at Ian—because she clearly knew right from the start that this was why he'd kissed her and pulled her in here—Phoebe yanked open the door. "No one's having sex in here," she told the boy.

"Damn straight," the kid shouted, "because you are out of here! Both of you! Right now!"

Phoebe held her hands up as she went out of the bathroom. "All right, all right, calm down, it really wasn't what you think," she said, adding, "What? No!" as she turned around.

No doubt she'd expected to see Ian right behind her. But Ian had already moved so that he was standing in front of a urinal, where he was taking that leak. Obviously it was now or never.

"Sorry, can't stop once I start," he said. "And I sure don't want to piss on your floor. All the way from here to the front door? Hate to make you clean *that* up."

"Don't you dare leave without me!" Phoebe said.

And as Ian looked at her over his shoulder, right before the door swung closed, he caught a flash of real fear in her eyes as she added, "Please, Ian . . ."

Shit. He'd pushed it too far. "I'm not going anywhere," he called, even as he heard the clerk berating her out in the hall.

"This is a family-owned establishment," the kid—who was actually older than he'd looked from a distance—was informing her.

"Still not going anywhere," Ian called. As he flushed and zipped and went to wash his hands, he whistled loudly, so that she could hear him.

"You get your skanky ass off this property," the kid said. "I don't want to see you in here again."

"*I'm* the one with the skanky ass?" Phoebe asked, apparently reassured enough by Ian's whistling to take umbrage. "Why am *I* the one with the skanky ass? Are you going to give *him* the same warning?"

"Yes, I am," the kid said.

And sure enough as Ian shook his hands dry—no

paper towels—and pushed the door open with his shoulder, the kid turned his venomous glare onto him. Ian stopped whistling and looked back at him, eyebrows raised.

"Get your skanky ass off this property," the kid said. "Sir."

"Hey," Phoebe said. "Why does he get a *sir?*"

Ian grabbed her arm, and pulled her, with him, out of there. "This is what we, in the *con* business, call *making a spectacle of ourselves*. Let's try to avoid that from now on."

"Except if Davio or his men *do* come here, looking for us, they're going to be looking for a giant, two gay guys, a baby, and a really gorgeous blonde. Mr. No-Sex-in-the-Bathrooms is going to describe two probably drunk people who staggered in. Plus, he thinks I'm a prostitute. We can double down on that by . . ." She stopped him, glancing back into the store through the big plate-glass windows. Ian looked, too, and sure enough, the clerk was still watching them warily.

"Perfect," she said, and then made what was, absolutely, the international two-handed gesture for sexual intercourse. She then added a couple of exaggerated hip thrusts, saying, "I want to make this absolutely clear, because this guy's kind of an idiot." She then rubbed her fingers together, after which she held out her hand, palm up, as if to say *Pay me.*

Ian cracked up. "That's actually kind of scary. Sex with a mime. Do I have to pay extra to make sure you don't do the trapped-in-a-box thing while we're doing it?"

"He's still watching," she said. "Maybe we should shake on the deal."

"Shake? I don't think so." He picked her up in a firefighter's hold, her belly against his shoulder, his hand, again, against her ass.

Phoebe whooped her surprise, but then laughed, as he carried her around the side of the building.

He put her down carefully, which meant that the entire front of her body slid against his chest, which made her T-shirt ride up—and *that* meant his hands were now against the soft, warm smoothness of her waist and back.

Which made his mouth go dry, especially when she locked her arms around his neck instead of stepping back and putting proper distance between them.

"Thanks for not leaving," she said quietly.

"And put you in danger? You didn't ask to be here. Frankly, I didn't either," he said. "But this is what it is, and . . . I'm not going to let anyone hurt you."

Her face was in shadow, but still, somehow, he could see her eyes behind those glasses. He could see that she believed him. Believed, and trusted, and . . .

Maybe even, despite everything she'd said through the course of what had been a very long day and night, maybe she wanted him to kiss her, too.

But Ian couldn't kiss her. He wanted to, but God,

he couldn't. Not after what he'd just told her. Instead, he said, "Also? I figured it was probably best for me to leave that bicycle back there for a real emergency."

She blinked, but then she laughed as she understood, and she finally stepped back. Realizing her shirt was askew, she used both hands to pull it down, making that strip of skin disappear.

But the joke he'd made wasn't enough to soften the impact of his macho promise.

And as they walked back toward the cars—Yashi had arrived, and the team was transferring their supplies out of the stolen vehicle and into his SUV—Phoebe must've sensed his unease. She glanced at Ian and said, "Rash?"

He met her eyes only briefly as he nodded, because yes, things had gotten much too serious. "Little one," he lied.

Phoebe nodded and didn't call him on it. But Ian caught her watching him, oddly subdued, as they organized who was going in what vehicle—Yashi taking the stolen car back to Sarasota to return it, get another, and pick up Martell—and he had a strong suspicion that she knew the truth.

Ian drove on to Miami with Aaron, Shel, and Rory, and put Phoebe in the other car with Deb and Francine.

As if, somehow, that would help.

PART TWO

CHARLIE FOXTROT

CHAPTER FIFTEEN

Thursday (Three days later)

Ian was still sitting in front of his computer when Phoebe went downstairs.

"Morning," she said.

He barely glanced up, his full focus on the screen. "It's afternoon."

He was right. It was.

"Have you slept?" Phoebe asked. "Like, at all, since we got here?"

He was still wearing the clothes he'd had on when she'd finally gone up to bed at dawn.

It was day three of this little locked-in, cabin-fever-inducing safe house adventure. And ever since they'd arrived here in Miami, Ian had been avoiding her. Not only was he taking care to never be alone with her, but he evaded any and all of her attempts to have a real conversation.

At least not one that didn't start with *Will you check out this file for me?* and end with *Thanks.*

Phoebe now knew *way* too much about the Kazak tribe, and how international law dealt—poorly—with outliers who refused to acknowledge the existence of any law other than their own.

She'd also spent a significant amount of her downtime researching the Dellarosa "tribe." She'd discovered that both Manny and Davio seemed to be Teflon when it came to deflecting criminal cases. Prosecutors could never find anyone willing to testify against them. Even convicts facing decades in prison couldn't be flipped. Whatever system the Dellarosas had in place for ensuring that kind of lasting loyalty and silence—it was rock solid.

As Ian now finally looked up, both at her and around the room, Phoebe saw him register the fact that they were alone. The *uh-oh* that flared in his eyes was quickly covered by the detached, too-polite smile that she'd come to despise.

"I'm sorry," he said as he pointed back at the computer. "I'm right in the middle of . . ."

"Of course," she said, going into the kitchen to get some coffee. Time of day didn't matter for that—the pot was always fresh. "Sorry. Carry on."

She couldn't really complain. She was the one who'd pushed to keep their relationship as mere friends. And Ian certainly wasn't being unfriendly.

He was just using his intense focus on the job at hand to keep her at a safe distance.

Safe distance, safe house.

Phoebe was pretty certain, after nearly three days of confinement, that staying in an FBI safe house in Miami was exactly the same as staying in an FBI safe house anywhere else in the world.

The house itself was comfortable enough, with plenty of beds, a kitchen to cook in, and a large combined dining and living room that Ian had turned into his war room.

The place was well stocked with both food and

computers—plus they had access to the full arsenal of weaponry and equipment that Ian had brought with them from Zebra.

The blinds and curtains were all tightly drawn, so the house was lit with electric light rather than sunshine—which gave the place a vaguely Vegas casino feel. Miami's legendary humidity and heat weren't a problem since the house was climate controlled. In fact, the AC was up so high, Phoebe kept a sweatshirt close at hand.

Thankfully, she *had* a sweatshirt. In fact, she had an armload of clothing in her size—jeans, T-shirts, Bermuda shorts, underwear!—plus a pair of flip-flops.

And if she needed anything else, Yashi would get it for her.

The FBI agent was their conduit to the outside world. Yashi, and Yashi alone, went and picked up anything that anyone added to a list that lived on the counter in the kitchen. Not only had he gotten them clothing and food, but he'd also procured two pristine white cargo vans and an array of expensive-looking surveillance equipment.

And even though today Phoebe was tempted to put *diamond bracelet* or perhaps *Ryan Gosling* at the bottom of the list to see what Yashi might bring back, she'd settled for less problematic and easier to obtain items like deodorant, laundry detergent, and last but not least, a bit of makeup.

Because, truth be told, sharing a house with Francine's flawless perfection was daunting. Even

Deb made the effort to put on lipstick whenever the blonde came into the war room.

Which, thankfully, wasn't often. Francie didn't spend much time in the main part of the house. Ever since their late-night arrival, she and her computer-genius brother, Sheldon, spent every waking moment in the huge five-bay garage, transforming those two newly purchased vans into high-tech surveillance vehicles, complete with an array of cameras—some infrared—and supposedly super-accurate long-distance mics.

Shel and Francine were installing those fancy microphones because Ian flatly refused to wear a wire when he contacted the Dutchman. *That* had set off some fireworks as he'd argued with Deb.

"Best way to get killed," Ian said. "Number one, top of the list: Go undercover wearing a wire. Jesus, just shoot me now."

"Technology has advanced considerably," Deb argued, "with the miniaturization of microphones—"

"I'm not worried about Vanderzee *seeing* the fricking mic," Ian shot back. "I'm worried about electronic detection devices. Bug sweepers. He'll use one, and I'm dead."

"And *I'm* worried about being unable to monitor you."

"You'll have to trust me," Ian said.

"I'm worried about not being able to protect you."

"I can protect myself, as long as I'm not wearing a freaking wire." Ian then threw her own words back at her. "Technology has advanced considerably. The microphones we'll use are extremely sensitive. They're directional mics, that means you point them at the subject—me—and pick up my conversation. It works."

Deb was unconvinced. "So the team in the van—from out in the parking lot—they just randomly aim their mics at a noisy bar and magically pick you up?"

Ian's plan, as of right now, was to "bump into" the Dutchman at Henrietta's, a local strip club he was known to frequent. And Deb was right. It would be noisy in there, with music playing and the drooling patrons hooting and howling. Assuming, that is, that a real-life strip club was similar to those Phoebe had seen on TV.

Sheldon spoke up, telling Deb, "It won't be magic. We'll use FLIR thermal imaging technology—special cameras that detect human body heat."

"I know what FLIR is," Deb said, annoyed. "But if the club's busy, there'll be a lot of bodies in there, generating heat."

"I'll carry a hand warmer," Ian explained. "A little chemical device, they sell 'em at camping stores. Yashi's already picked some up for us. When I'm inside, I'll crack open the package, that'll activate it. Stick it in my pocket. The infrared sensors on the cameras'll pick up that pop in temperature. From that, Shelly'll know exactly where to aim the long-distance mics."

At which point, they'd be able to listen to and record his conversations.

It all seemed very sci-fi to Phoebe, but Ian assured Deb that they'd do a test run—be certain that the equipment worked exactly the way it was supposed to work.

If it didn't, Deb warned, then Ian would have to give in and wear a wire.

Phoebe had smiled when Deb had said that. If the FBI agent really thought she'd win *that* fight, she was woefully underinformed. *Give in* was not in Ian's vocabulary.

As she added milk to a bowl of cornflakes, Phoebe heard Martell come downstairs. She could see him through the pass-through that connected the kitchen to the dining part of the main room, leaning to look over Ian's shoulder.

"What are you looking at?" he asked.

"Photos of the K-stani consulate staff," Ian replied.

"Including the janitorial crew?" Martell sounded incredulous. "Seriously?"

Ian gave him his full attention. "Seriously. I've spent some significant time in Kazbekistan. If I'm going to run into someone who recognizes me from a previous mission, I want to know about it in advance."

Aaron had come downstairs, too, and as he headed for the kitchen he chimed in. "Hot tip: The janitors at the consulate aren't really janitors."

"Excuse me, sir," Sheldon said. Phoebe looked up to see that he'd come in from the garage. "We're ready to do that dry run with the surveillance vans."

He took off his work gloves, and mopped his brow with the sleeve of his grimy T-shirt. The garage was not air-conditioned, but neither Francine nor Shel had complained once about the heat.

"Time to test our technology?" Ian asked.

"Yes, sir."

Aaron smiled at Shelly on his way to the coffeepot. "You don't need to call him *sir,*" he teased as he poured himself a mug.

"Did I really?" Shel asked. "Wow. Old habits die hard." He looked back at Ian. "Sorry, sir. *Crap!*" Laughing, he added, "Whenever you're ready. Ian."

"Thanks," Ian said, still distracted by the photos on his computer. "It's going to be just . . . a sec . . ." He interrupted himself to add, "Longer than a second. Look, why don't you get something to eat. And a shower, while you're at it. Let me know when you're ready after that."

"So what's your official plan?" Martell asked Ian, as Shel and Aaron explored the depths of the fridge.

Phoebe took her cereal bowl and coffee out to the table and sat down to eat, even as Deb came downstairs, her hair still wet from a shower.

"Test the equipment this afternoon," Ian said, already refocused on his computer screen. "Try to connect with Vanderzee tonight."

There was a clatter from the kitchen as a frying pan was dug out from a cabinet. "Anyone want in on an omelet?" Aaron called.

"Ooh, me!" Phoebe said.

"And me," Deb called. She met Phoebe's eyes

and widened her own. They were in total agreement. Both Martell and Aaron had a magic touch in the kitchen, and over the past few days, whenever either of them offered food, the default answer was *oh, yes*. And when they cooked *together* . . .

Phoebe turned to look hopefully at Martell at the same time that Deb did, but he was waving Aaron off, focusing on Ian.

"Still nothing figured out for after that?" Martell had been an extra-unhappy camper ever since Ian had made the decision to *not* make a decision about the best way to rescue those kids. Ian wanted to connect with the Dutchman first. He'd told them that his best plans were organic—whatever that meant.

Martell was clearly convinced that Ian was clueless, and wasting their time.

"Yup," Ian said now. "Still in wait-and-see mode."

"You know we all hate that," Martell told him. "Right? Except maybe Yashi, who is too zen to hate anything. But I'm the only one here brave enough to say it aloud. That, and *tick tock, bitch*. I'm starting to wonder why you just don't grab a ski mask and climb in a window at the consulate, get this over with. You've had the FBI's files for days now."

Ian didn't glance at Phoebe, or even anywhere near Phoebe, as he finally looked up at Martell. "Their security is too tight," he said. "And last time

I checked, I don't have a license to kill innocent people, which is what I'd have to do if I went in like that. All of our intel shows that most of the guards don't know those kids are there. Do we really have to rehash this?"

"Can't you use, I don't know, trank darts on 'em or—"

"Trank darts," Ian repeated flatly. He raised his voice. "Will someone please explain the obvious flaws in that plan, so I can finish what I'm doing before we go out to test the equipment?"

Deb pulled Martell away from Ian's part of the table. "The biggest problem is that any guards in the consulate would be firing real bullets at Ian. Trank guns are an option when the target's an unarmed mountain lion."

"Trank guns are also single-shot weapons," Phoebe pointed out. "Reloading is a whole big thing."

"Yeah, yeah, I know," Martell said. "I was just being a dick and—"

"Are you *fucking* kidding me?"

They all turned—Phoebe, Martell, Deb, Ian, and even Yashi, who'd just come back from a shopping run—to see Aaron aiming not just his loudly spoken words, but his full-on incredulity at Shel, who was gazing back at him, stricken, as he clutched a carton of eggs.

Francine had just joined them in the kitchen, coming in from the garage, but she now looked as if she wished she were anywhere else on earth.

"You knew?" Aaron shouted at his husband, only half-asking. He turned to Ian. "You let *Shel* know you were in prison, that whole fucking time, but not *me?*"

"I didn't know the whole time," Shel said. "I found out in June."

"Well, shit," Aaron said. "Since you've only been lying to me for eight months instead of nine—"

"I didn't lie," Sheldon insisted. "I just . . . didn't . . . tell you—I couldn't tell you. Aaron, God, I swear. I promised Francie."

Francine held up both hands and backed away. "Hey, don't lay this on me. I was following Eee's stupid-ass orders."

Aaron was beyond furious. "*What's up, Air, you okay? You seem a little down.* Yeah, Shel, I don't know, I guess I'm just worried about Ian. I wish he would call me. I just can't shake the feeling that he might be dead. I mean, it's been so long since I heard from him. I mean, other than those postcards. Anyone could've sent them. *Well, no, Aaron, I happen to know for a fact that Ian's* not *dead because Francie told me he's in prison.*" He got loud again. "Things you fucking didn't say! It's called lying by omission. How many times did we talk about Ian in the past eight months? Huh? How many?"

"I promised her," Sheldon whispered.

"Yeah, well, you're *married* to me! Jesus! Fuck, Shel!"

Ian turned and aimed his words at the rest of

them. “Let’s give the guys the house. We’ll go out and test that equipment.”

But from the upstairs bedroom, Rory awoke from his nap and let out a thin wail.

Francine ducked around her brother and crossed the room, clearly heading to the stairs, to deal with the crying baby.

Ian stood, intercepting her. “Can you stay here, watch Rory?”

Her answer was to grab one of the laptops and take it with her upstairs, so that she could work while locked in with the baby—while his parents talked out this issue.

“Don’t bother.” Aaron’s voice was harsh. “It’s not going to change a fucking thing.”

Phoebe grabbed her sweatshirt—a white zippered hoodie that spelled out the words *Siesta Key* in pink letters across its chest—and quickly followed Deb, Martell, and Yashi out the door.

Ian needed sleep.

He’d intended to take a combat nap—quick but revitalizing—after he went through the files of the K-stani consulate staff one more time. He’d figured he could get in a solid half hour while Sheldon ate and showered.

Instead, this had happened.

He was in the front passenger seat of surveillance van one, with Joe Hirabayashi driving and Phoebe strapped into the passenger seat in the back. Deb was driving van two, with Martell beside her.

It may have been a mistake to leave the safe house. Ian couldn't stop thinking of Aaron, and how angry he'd been. Jesus, maybe he shouldn't have asked Francine to stay behind. With Air knowing that Francie was watching Rory, he might do something stupid—like storm out of the house—and put his ass in danger. Although without Francie there to watch the kid, there was no way Aaron and Shel would have had a real chance to talk, at least not openly and loudly and . . .

Something icy brushed his arm, and he jumped and turned to find that Phoebe had leaned forward from her seat in the back. Had she really just touched him? Was it possible that her fingers were that cold? He caught her hand, and yes, she was freezing. She was wearing her sweatshirt zipped up to the neck because the air conditioning in the van was blasting, and had been for a while.

"Sorry," he said, and let her go so that he could adjust the dial up from the coldest setting.

But that wasn't why she'd gotten his attention. "Yashi needs you to tell him where you want to go," she said, her dark eyes somber in her pretty face, and he knew that this was not the first time the question had been asked. "We didn't want to guess."

"Shit, right, sorry," he said—it was becoming his new refrain—then turned to address the FBI agent, who'd left their safe house's neighborhood and was driving them north on the main drag. "Let's go to Henrietta's. It's over by the airport."

The FBI had been following the Dutchman, and the intel reports made note of the strip club that the suspect frequented in the evenings. He didn't hang out there every night, but he showed up often enough to make it a good place for Ian to encounter him seemingly by chance.

The full name of the club was Henrietta's Wild West Emporium, and from what Ian had read from the file, the women who waited the tables there wore cowboy hats and boots, and little else.

Yashi nodded and pulled into the left lane to do a youie, get them turned around. He must've been connected to Deb via Bluetooth, because he passed along the info even as he consulted a GPS. He quietly arranged for the two vans to take two different routes so they wouldn't arrive at the club together, in a suspicious-looking convoy. Instead, Yashi would approach from the south, and Deb would approach from the west.

"We might as well do an actual dry run," Ian announced, and the federal agent passed that along, too. "Identify any dead zones or locations that might be too noisy for the directional mics. I'll go in, order a drink, walk around, talk to myself, make sure you can hear me."

"I could go in with you," Phoebe volunteered.

He laughed. Right. He turned to look at her. In her jeans and that touristy sweatshirt, plastic thongs on her feet, with her hair pulled back in a ponytail, she looked like an adorably bespectacled college girl on vacation. In a dive like Henrietta's, she couldn't stand out more, even if she held a flashing neon sign that read *I don't belong here,* with an arrow pointing down at her.

But she was serious, so he responded, "That's not a good idea." And wasn't *that* an understatement.

"So that you have someone to talk to," she persisted. "So no one thinks you're crazy . . . ?"

"No. You're staying in the van. You wouldn't be out of the house if my brother wasn't a spoiled child."

"Oh, I'm really glad he didn't hear you say *that,*" she said.

"Yeah, me, too." Ian sighed, his own anger suddenly deflated. This *was* his fault. He'd had no idea that Sheldon had somehow gotten the truth out of Francine months ago. And maybe what was messing him up the most was that, even in hindsight, he had no idea how he would've or should've handled that if he'd known.

But even as relationship-challenged as Ian was, he recognized that withholding the truth from an intimate life partner for nearly a year could seriously damage even the strongest of unions.

Phoebe touched him again, on the shoulder this time, as if she knew exactly where his thoughts had gone. "They're going to be okay. Aaron is smart enough to recognize that Shelly's not perfect, either. Mistakes get made. Forgiveness is given. It's part of life. You know. Growing and learning and getting stronger?"

"The irony is that I was doing it for him. For

them." The words escaped before Ian could stop them.

"I know," she said quietly. "And I'm pretty sure Aaron knows that, too."

What was he doing? Talking to her like this was *exactly* what he didn't want to do. This feeling of closeness, this spark of connection wasn't anything that could help him. In fact, he knew from past experience that it could only hamper and hinder and slow him down.

Or get him killed.

But the hard truth was that he honestly liked this woman. And as for his physical attraction? It had moved from annoyance to full distraction.

Ian made a mental note to talk to Deb about finding a different safe location for Phoebe to stay for the remainder of the mission. Surely the feds could foot the bill for a resort hotel room and a coupla 24/7 guards for the next few days. A week tops . . .

"They'll be okay," Phoebe said, reaching out again to squeeze his shoulder.

Ian wanted her to keep her hand there. It was all he could do not to reach up and cover it with his own, maybe warm up her fingers a little bit more. But he didn't, so she let him go and sat back in her seat.

Yeah.

If the feds wouldn't cover the expense, he'd pay for it himself.

At this point, God help him, it was a necessity.

• • •

Expulsion from private school just a few months before graduation was significantly better than being shot and killed by his boyfriend's brother.

Aaron had to keep reminding himself of that, especially when his own brother came striding down the hall to the Brentwood headmaster's office. Ian had had to request emergency leave in order to deal with his now homeless little brother.

Wearing BDU pants in a desert camouflage print, he was sporting a decidedly nonmilitary haircut and a full beard—and an expression of tight anger.

Ian didn't try to argue with the headmaster. He simply signed whatever papers he needed to sign, collected Aaron, and left. Of course, Eee thought the "sexual misconduct" that had gotten Aaron booted was due to his little brother's orientation.

Turns out that the conservative school didn't discriminate. A sex tape was a sex tape, and if you were in one, even inadvertently, you got kicked out.

Still, it wasn't until after they'd loaded Aaron's bags into Ian's rental car that Aaron was able to tell his brother what had really happened—including the part where Francine had thrown herself on the gay grenade to save Sheldon from his crazy father's wrath, and also the part where Berto had come damn close to killing Aaron in a jealous rage.

He told Ian that he was worried about Shelly. He

hadn't seen or heard from him in days—of course, during that time Aaron had been confined to his room, without Internet access or phone privileges.

"Berto's as crazy as their father, and now he knows," Aaron said, as he used Eee's BlackBerry, fumbling in his haste to check his email to see if Shelly had sent him anything and . . .

There it was. An email. He opened it. It was brief, just a few lines, with no *Dear Aaron* or *Love, Shel*.

> **We can no longer be in contact. It's not safe for you, or for me.**
>
> **I've been transferred to a new school. I can't tell you where.**
>
> **Don't call, or even email. I'm changing this address right after I send this to you. I won't get your response.**
>
> **I wish to God I never met you.**

Aaron's eyes stung. Shel didn't mean that. He couldn't mean that.

Ian glanced over, and correctly read the agony that was on Aaron's face. "He dump you?"

"No," Aaron said, blinking back his tears. "He's just scared."

Ian reached over and took his phone. Read the email himself. Sighed heavily. "Scared enough to dump you. Douchebag."

"He's not. Don't call him that."

Ian sighed again. "I guess you gotta do denial

before you get to anger. Fair enough. I ran the gamut with Nadia, back when she fucked me over."

"Shel's *nothing* like Nadia—"

"Except for being a human being, and human beings have sucked and done shitty things to one another since the beginning of time. You're not the first, and you sure as hell won't be the last. Look, we'll go get something to eat, then head to Tampa. I know a coupla guys in the recruiting office—"

"No, I'm not going to do that," Aaron said. "Enlist? No way. No, I'm going up to Boston. Cambridge, actually. Next fall, Shel's going to MIT—"

"Aaron," Ian said.

"I'll get a job," he said. "We figured it all out. I'll work while he goes to school, then when he graduates, I'll get my degree. I don't mind waiting, I really don't."

"Aaron."

"I know that apartments in Cambridge are expensive, but we could maybe find a place in Somerville, take the T. Public transportation up in Boston is really good. We did research."

"Aarie. There's no *we.* Your boyfriend bailed." Ian held up his phone. "This kid wishes he never met you."

"Tough shit," Aaron said as he fought another wave of tears. "Because he *did* meet me." He took a deep breath, exhaled hard. "I'm going north anyway."

"And what? Hope to bump into him when school starts? Ten to one, he'll be with his new girlfriend from Harvard. That'll suck."

Jesus, the thought of that made him sick. "I don't have anywhere else to go!"

"Which is why enlisting is the only option. You'll get an education—"

"Newsflash, Eee! I'm gay. They don't want me."

"You're wrong," Ian said. "They do—they just don't know it. You're strong, you're smart, you're a natural leader—"

"So I'm just supposed to lie."

"It's not a real lie if the rules are bullshit. What if someone put a gun to your head and told you they would pull the trigger unless you told them that your favorite color was red? Even if you were into blue, you'd say red. It's the exact same fucking thing." He got quiet. "We don't have a choice. I have less than forty hours left—"

That was more than Aaron had expected. "That's enough time to drive to Boston, find an apartment—"

"And pay for it with what? The cost of gas, alone, for a thousand-mile trip is over a hundred dollars. How much do you have saved, because this rental car is gonna bleed me dry."

Aaron stared at his brother. "They seriously pay you that little . . . ?"

"I was paying for you to go to school."

What? "I had a scholarship."

"For your tuition. It didn't include your room and

board. Or your books. Or athletic fees and equipment. School uniforms. I've been paying for all that shit. It costs nearly everything I earn. I have nothing saved and I won't be paid again for a while."

Aaron was aghast. "I didn't ask you for any of that."

Ian sighed. "I know."

"I'll get a job," Aaron said. "In Tampa, then. I'll earn enough to be able to move north by August."

"And where will you stay between now and then?" Ian asked.

"I don't know. I'll get an apartment."

"With what down payment?" Ian asked. "You think you just walk into an apartment building and they give you a key because you say you scored a job working the night shift at the Seven-Eleven? No. You give them first month's rent, last month's rent, and a security deposit—after you've proven to them that you have a steady job that'll pay you enough to spend a chunk of it on their overpriced bullshit rent."

Jesus. "Okay, so what? I didn't know that. I'll get a job, then, somewhere where I can camp out for a while."

"Gee, Skippy, maybe you could be a cowboy," Ian said. "Better yet, find a time machine so you can be a cowboy in the wild, wild west. *That'll* be fun—"

"I'm doing my best here!" Aaron shouted at his

brother. “I’m trying to find a solution to a fucking no-win scenario!”

Ian jerked the wheel hard and pulled off the road into a gas station, where he slammed them to a stop far from the other parked cars.

“You already lost, D.A.,” he said, his voice both gruff and oddly gentle as a cloud of dust from the gravel rose around the car. “That’s what no-win means. It’s over and done. The only solution is to accept it and move on.”

“I can’t. I love him. And he loves me.”

“Maybe he does,” Ian gave him that. “But he doesn’t love you enough.”

It was then that Aaron felt himself break, and try as he might, he couldn’t keep from crying. And once he started, he couldn’t stop.

Ian pulled him into a rough embrace. “It’s okay, buddy. Let it out. Let it go. One of these days, I promise you, you’re going to find someone who loves you, too.”

Aaron cried and cried and cried, until he had no tears left inside of him.

I wish to God I never met you.

He sat there—exhausted, anguished, heart-broken, and completely and utterly defeated.

But grateful—and he would be, always and forever—for the time, although fleeting, that Sheldon Dellarosa had been part of his life.

He sat up to wipe his face with the bottom of his T-shirt, and Ian finally let him go and sat back, too.

“Marines,” Aaron said, after he cleared his

throat, when he could finally meet his older brother's steady gaze. Ian's eyes were filled with kindness and even sympathy, but not pity, thank God. "Fuck the Navy. Screw the SEALs. I'm going to be a Marine."

"Let me out here," Ian said, and Yashi pulled into the parking lot of a tired-looking strip mall.

They were in the world of cheap motels, pawnshops, palm readers, massage parlors, and storefronts advertising *Cash for Gold!* Phoebe could see the signs stretching down the busy road.

"Henrietta's is down a few blocks," Ian continued, "on this side of the street."

"Deb and Martell hit traffic," the FBI agent reported. "They're still twenty minutes away."

"That's okay. It's going to take some time," Ian pointed out, "for you to find the best vantage point for the van. There's limited parking out front, and a bigger lot in the back—at least according to the bar's website. I'll go in, sit down as centrally as I can, and open the hand warmer"—he held up the little orange packet—"so you can find me. I'll sing 'Row, Row, Row Your Boat,' and you can track me with the mics."

"A classic," Yashi said with approval. "And unlikely to show up on the club's playlist or as someone's cell phone ringtone."

"If, for whatever reason, I can't sing or hum it, I'll tap it," Ian said as he opened the door and got out.

"Merrily, merrily, merrily, merrily," Yashi

responded, even as he nodded to Phoebe's quiet *May I?* "A pattern of four triplets'll stand out in a world filled with shave-and-a-haircuts—intentional or accidental."

But as Phoebe climbed up into the front, Ian said, "Shit," and then opened the door. "Did I leave my . . . ?" He checked the floor and around the seat before tapping the side of her leg with the back of his hand. "Lift up for a sec."

She pressed her shoulders against the seat back and raised her butt, but there was nothing beneath her. "What did you lose?" She checked the floor on the far side of the passenger seat, but it was clear.

"I must've left it at the house," Ian said. "My cell phone." He sighed his exasperation. "While I was in prison, I got a little too used to traveling light."

Phoebe looked at Yashi. "Is there an extra one in here?" She opened the glove box, but the only thing inside was the owner's manual for the van, and a temporary registration card.

"Maybe Shel left an extra phone in the back?" Yashi suggested, and Phoebe went to look.

Shelves of impressive equipment were bolted down along both sides of the windowless van, including two separate wide-screen computer monitors, and the hardware and batteries necessary to run everything.

There was a tool kit that was strapped in, along with a container marked with a red cross that, indeed, held medical supplies. The only other bag held an assortment of wires—USBs, quarter inches,

RCA plugs, and some that Phoebe couldn't identify. She found an unopened packet of thumb drives at the bottom of that bag, but no spare cell phone.

"Nothing here," she announced.

"It's not that big a deal," Ian was saying. "I've been on plenty of assignments without one."

Including, according to Phoebe's theory, his most recent assignment at Northport prison. He'd been up to something in there, besides simply serving out the sentence for a crime he didn't do. He'd been in far more danger there than he'd be in a Western-saloon-themed strip club in Miami, in the middle of a sunny weekday afternoon.

Yashi was not happy. "We should do this another time. Or at least wait until Deb and Martell get here." He touched his earpiece. "Yes, Deb says *wait*. She says you can go in with Martell's phone."

"Tell them when they finally catch up that Martell can bring it inside to me." Ian backed away from the van as Phoebe returned to the front seat.

"Oh, fine," she said. "He can go in, but I can't." As she was speaking, she realized that, of course, Ian's decision had nothing to do with discrimination based on gender. So she added, "Which makes sense, seeing that he's a former police detective, and I was a Girl Scout for about fifteen minutes in sixth grade."

Ian actually smiled at her. "And *that's* how we work in a team," he said.

"We need any cookies sold, I'm on point," she told him.

That one he actually laughed at—before he remembered that he wasn't letting himself laugh at her jokes anymore. At least not with a genuine smile like that one, with his teeth flashing, complete with an almost unbearably attractive crinkling around his too-blue eyes.

He sobered up much too quickly. "Tell Martell no cloak and dagger. I want this to be an overt drop and go. *Hi, how are you,* shake my hand, *You left your phone on my desk* or whatever, and then back out, but not to the van. Have him go get coffee or lunch and plan to pick him up later."

Phoebe nodded, but then realized he was talking to Yashi.

When Ian looked back at her, something shifted in his eyes and she knew that having her there worried him.

"I'll stay in the van," she promised, as Yashi put it in gear and they rolled past him.

Ian didn't respond, and as they pulled out into the traffic, she could see him in the side mirror, watching her, until he vanished from sight.

"Will you let me at least try to explain why I did what I did?"

Aaron opened his eyes to see Shel, fresh from the shower, his hair dripping onto his bare shoulders, towel wrapped around his waist.

"Fuck you," he said. "You're not going to fix this with sex. Not this time."

Shel's smile was wan as he came further into the

room, where his go-bag was on a chair, unzipped. "That's not what I was doing. I'm sorry." He grabbed a clean pair of briefs and did something Aaron had never before seen him do. He pulled them on underneath his towel.

"I owe her, Aarie," Shel said as he put on cargo shorts, too—still doing the summer camp beneath-the-towel thing. "Francine." He yanked a clean T-shirt over his head, and used the towel to mop the rest of the wet from his hair. Only then did he meet Aaron's eyes. "We both owe her. Too much to ever really repay."

"I want to kill him," Aaron said. "Davio. I just want to . . ." He couldn't keep tears from filling his eyes as he thought—again—about that email Sheldon had sent him all those years ago—in an attempt to keep Aaron far away from Shel's father, to keep him alive and safe.

An attempt that had worked a little too well, since it had succeeded at separating them for too many years.

I wish to God I never met you.

"It happened on June eighteenth," Sheldon said. "My finding out that Ian was in prison. It was twelve minutes after eight in the morning—in case you were thinking I didn't mark it as momentous. I went to pick Rory up from Francie's after we took that night off. Remember?"

Aaron did. It was the first night in months that one of them hadn't been on call for Rory 24/7. They were supposed to go out, to the movies, have dinner . . .

But instead, they'd stayed home. Made love. Slept. Together. For the first time in what felt like forever.

Yes, Aaron remembered. And because Aaron had been Rory's primary caregiver throughout the worst of the baby's detox and recovery, Shel had gifted him with those extra few moments of blessed alone time, and had gone to Francie's to pick up the baby and bring him back home.

"So I'm in France's apartment. I let myself in with the key, and she's asleep on the sofa, with the baby on top of her and . . . There's this cell phone on the table, and it's set on silent, but it starts to vibrate and buzz, and I'm afraid it's going to wake them both, so I answer it. But there's this weird silence, and suddenly the connection is cut. And I look at it, and there's a number there, so I hit redial, and I get this odd message. From Northport prison. And everything suddenly jelled. And I just knew. Where Ian had gone. And when Francine woke up, I held up that phone and I said, *Ian called,* and I knew I was right, just from the look on her face.

"When she knew she was busted, she asked me not to tell you. She begged me."

"Francine?" Aaron asked. "Begged you."

"I know. It was intense. She said she didn't know what was going on—only that Eee spoke to her by phone, every other week, to make sure that we were all right. She didn't say it, and I sure as hell didn't ask, but I pretty much assumed that it had something to do with Davio. And after that, I swear to you, we never spoke of it again. It wasn't like, every time we were together we whispered about Ian when you were out of the room," Sheldon said, shaking his head. "I know that's what you think, but it was just that one time. That one conversation."

"Is that supposed to make it better?" Aaron asked. "You shouldn't have lied to me, and Francine sure as hell should *not* have asked you to."

"I know," Shel said, tears in his eyes. "But she did. What was I supposed to do?"

"Tell me anyway," Aaron said. "That's what you were supposed to do."

It was the perfect exit line, but Sheldon blocked the door. "It's always so black and white for you, isn't it?" he said, his voice shaking; he was that upset. "Francine died for us, Aaron. Maybe you can't possibly understand this, because you never knew her before. You don't know what she was like, who she was. She was happy. She was . . . *goofy*. She was nothing like she is now, so hard and cold and angry."

Shel had told him all of that many times before—that his beloved older sister had changed on that terrible day when Berto believed she'd betrayed him. But he'd never used those words: *She died for us*.

"I'm so sorry," Sheldon said now, "that I lied to you. And you're right. Omission *is* still lying, and I remember each awful time I did it, and I hated myself. But Francie saved my life that day. And your life. Davio would've killed you, too. Or maybe he would've only killed you. Maybe he would've spared me. But a world without you in it is not a world I could live in."

Sheldon left the room with that, closing the door behind him.

As far as exit lines went, he won.

But then he blew it, by coming right back in. Except he now had Rory in his arms, and Francine was with him.

"I just got another email from Berto," she said. "I was online, thank God, and it popped up onscreen. Apparently, Davio's put a million-dollar bounty out on Ian, so everyone and their stripper girlfriend is looking for him, all across the state. And someone just saw him walking into Henrietta's, out by the airport. Berto said Davio's called in a team of shooters from Oakland Park—they're heading over there to take him out."

"Where the hell's Oakland Park?" Aaron asked.

"Just north of Fort Lauderdale," Francie said. "About twenty minutes from Henrietta's. Depending on traffic."

Please God, let there be traffic.

"I just tried calling Eee, and then Deb, and then Yashi," Francie continued. "No one's picking up."

CHAPTER SIXTEEN

Ian had never particularly liked strip clubs. There was something inherently unpleasant about watching desperate women take off their clothes for money. And even if they weren't desperate, even in the unlikely scenario that they wanted to be there, it still seemed distasteful to watch.

Like paying for sex.

Or agreeing with someone's bullshit opinions about politics or crappy movies or badly written books only to get laid.

It was really not Ian's style.

Henrietta's was doubly unpleasant—a vast, cavernous room decorated as if the management couldn't decide whether they wanted to own a strip club version of a Cracker Barrel or an 1880s wild west whorehouse. There were lots of red and black velvet curtains with gold braided trim combined with quirky period signs and pictures and antique farm implements hanging on the walls.

The bar was rustic with a brass kickbar. Ian approached and ordered an Arnold Palmer from a tired-looking woman wearing bikini bottoms and blue-sequined, star-shaped pasties.

He'd opened the hand warmer out in the parking lot and had slipped the packet into the pocket of his T-shirt, where it was acting like a beacon. It was also making him wish that the club had a more powerful air-conditioning system.

He swiveled in his seat, elbows back on the bar, to give the place a more detailed look-see as he hummed his first verse and chorus. *Row, row, row your boat* . . . The big room had a main stage, which was currently dark. But there were a half a dozen smaller stages off to the sides, where pole dancers were unenthusiastically phoning it in.

Tables dotted the carpeted main floor, and there was a balcony level, with box seats like that of an old-timey theatre. Hanging signs pointed the way upstairs, where there were also, apparently, private party rooms and—*merrily, merrily, merrily, merrily*—a VIP lounge.

His drink finally came. The exhausted bartender apparently had had to look it up in a book to figure out it was half lemonade and half iced tea, no alcohol, and it must've been hard to read in the dim light. Ian paid for it, leaving a hefty tip for her future-eyeglasses fund or maybe her buy-a-shirt campaign, then wandered toward those stairs. "Ground floor is mostly one main room—bathrooms behind the bar, and of course, there's gotta be an extensive backstage area, but that's probably moot," he said into his drink, hoping those expensive mics were picking him up. "I'll walk the perimeter in a sec, but I'm going upstairs while I have the chance."

His route up was blocked by a dark red velvet rope with dull brass ends that hooked it to the wall on both sides of the staircase. Apparently, the upper section wasn't open to the public at this time of day.

But the bartender was settling in for a siesta, and the bouncer by the front door was still checking his Twitter feed, head down as he peered at his phone. So Ian and his high-heat-radiating chest quickly went past the rope. The packet was on the verge of burning him, and he pulled the fabric of his shirt slightly away from his chest. "Row, row, row your boat, gently up the stairs . . ."

Black-framed daguerreotype reproductions of stony-faced cowboys, outlaws, and tight-lipped pioneer women covered the red-painted walls. Their grim scowls and accusatory eyes seemed an odd choice for the route to the "private party rooms"—unless the thrill of getting a lap dance or maybe even a hand job in an Americana-themed museum was on more men's bucket lists than Ian had previously imagined.

Cast-iron handrails stretched up, on both sides, and even though the red-and-gold-patterned carpeting was showing its age, the management had installed rubber guards on the edge of each step—to make it slightly harder for drunk clientele to fall and destroy what few shreds remained of their dignity.

There were a lot of steps. What should have been two complete flights led to a half turn. Whatever was beyond that Ian couldn't see. But before he got to that turn, he stopped—and stopped singing—because someone was coming. There must've been a door at the very top of the stairs, because he heard it open, heard someone grunting as he or she—he, had to be—came through. Whoever he was, he was either grossly overweight, or maybe he was carrying something heavy.

There was a murmur as he spoke.

It was possible he was carrying some*one*.

He spoke again—in that same deep voice, his words indiscernible. Even the language being spoken was questionable—Ian didn't think it was English, but the coaxing tone was unmistakably clear. *Just a little bit farther, almost there. Please don't puke on my shoes. . . .*

But then there was a stumbling sound, and Ian quickly transferred the hand warmer from his shirt to the back pocket of his jeans, and put his drink on the back edge of the nearest step, since a collision with whoever was coming down the stairs seemed imminent. He went up, ready to help catch whoever was falling.

But the man who was conscious—capable of walking and talking—didn't need help as he used the triangular landing at the turn in the stairs to anchor the man he was supporting against the wall. His back was to Ian as he staggered slightly beneath his drunk companion's weight.

At least one of the two was definitely skunked. His eyes were closed and his balding head lolled on a thick neck as his buddy kept him from tumbling down the stairs. He was short but stout and clearly heavy—with a dark mustache and almost comically bushy eyebrows.

The other man—the conscious one—was taller, with sun-streaked brown hair and broad shoulders beneath a dark, well-cut business suit.

There was something familiar about him—about the way he was standing or moving or . . .

That taller man lifted his head as he turned, suddenly aware that he and his barrel-shaped friend were not alone in the stairwell.

And because Ian had moved closer to assist, he and the tall man were face to face. He. Was now. Face to face.

With Georg Vanderzee.

AKA the Dutchman.

Ian froze, and Vanderzee did, too. And Ian knew that, like the Dutchman, he, too, failed to hide the spark of surprised recognition in his eyes.

In truth, Ian was more than surprised—he was shocked. Last thing he'd expected was to run into this man, here and now. But he was good enough at thinking on his feet to recognize that surprise—and even shock—was absolutely the correct expression for this situation, so he didn't make the mistake of trying to hide it. He let it all hang out.

He even hammered it home, simultaneously letting Yashi know what had happened. Provided he and the others had the surveillance mics up and running—and working correctly. Although, shit. Martell was supposed to come inside to bring Ian a phone. Hopefully this information would stop him. "My old friend from Holland." He didn't want to use Vanderzee's name, and potentially blow the man's cover. "No freaking way," he added.

But then Ian went on the offense, hard, and looked at the man sideways, letting suspicion and accusation into his voice. "Who the fuck told you I was in Miami?"

"Holy shit," Martell said, as the van he was riding in with Deb moved another four feet forward before coming to a complete stop in the bumper-to-bumper traffic.

Yashi and Phoebe were parked behind a Dunkin' Donuts—it abutted the strip club's back lot. They were successfully using their high-tech super-spy microphones to follow Ian as he moved about the club. Yashi had set up some kind of scrambled radio signal so that Deb and Martell could listen, too.

And they'd all just heard Ian make contact with the Dutchman.

"No one told me you were in Miami," said the voice that had to be Vanderzee's. "I had absolutely no idea you were even in the States."

"You expect me to believe that?" Ian came at him. "You and whoever the fuck *this* is, showing up here on the exact same day I'm supposed to be meeting . . . Well, you probably know who I'm meeting, right, because I sure as shit don't believe in coincidences."

"Okay," Deb said, as she inched the van another few feet forward. She'd washed the deep-space black from her hair and now it was just a non-descript light brown. She couldn't do anything about those ultra short bangs, though, and they gave her a quirky European look that Martell found appealing. "So now we know the Dutchman is with another person."

Martell's phone rang, and he quickly silenced the ring, even as he looked down to see . . . "Francine," he said, " 'Sup, baby?" and Deb shot him a look, one eyebrow raised.

"Is Ian with you?" Francine demanded, without verbally slapping him upside his head for that unauthorized *baby,* which should have been his first clue that something major was wrong. "Tell me Ian's with you, back from scoping out the club, and then get out of there—fast."

"No, I'm in van two with Deb," he said, lowering his voice and turning away because now Deb was giving him an *I can't hear Ian* look. "We're stopped on the expressway. There's been some big-ass accident up ahead—must've just happened. We're in the breakdown lane, but that's not moving either. Ian's inside Henrietta's, where he just made unplanned contact with our man."

"Are you kidding me?" she asked. "*Shit*. That must be why he's not answering his phone."

"No, he's not answering because he left his phone back at the house," Martell said. From what he could tell, Ian was continuing on upstairs while the Dutchman and the other guy staggered down to the main floor, where Dutch was going to put his mysterious friend into a cab. At which point Vanderzee would join Ian back upstairs. Or so he'd promised. That was either a really good thing or a really bad thing. "I was supposed to go in there and bring him mine when we arrived, but we've been twenty minutes away for the past half hour now. What's going on?"

"Where's van one?" she demanded. "With, what? Yashi and what's-her-name? Phoebe? Are *they* near the club?"

"Did you hear me when I said he's made contact?"

"Yes," she said. "Fuck. Martell, put me on speaker, so that both Deb and Yashi can hear me."

"Yeah, I don't think—"

"PUT. ME. ON. SPEAKER!"

Ow. It was possible he was now deaf in his right ear. Martell cleared his throat. "I'm sorry to have to interrupt this incredibly important life-risking mission. But here's Francine. On speaker. Go ahead."

"I got an email from Berto," she said, speaking loudly and clearly. "And I just called him back to verify the following: Davio Dellarosa knows that Ian's in Henrietta's, and he's just sent a four-man kill squad out to delete him, ETA ten minutes."

Beep. Beep. Beep-a-beep! Bee-bee-beep, bee-bee-beep, bee-bee-beep, bee-bee-beep . . .

"It's brilliant," Phoebe told Yashi, who was hitting the van's horn to the pattern of the lyrics in "Row Your Boat." "*You're* brilliant. You really are. But Ian can't hear you from where he is, inside the club. You have to let me go in there to warn him."

"I can't," Yashi said.

"And I can't let you *not* let me do it," she countered. "Someone's got to go. If it's you, the mission's scrubbed." He'd just told her that if an FBI agent, i.e. himself, got *that* close to the Dutchman, they'd have to assume Ian's cover was blown. "I, however, am not an FBI agent," she reminded him.

He held out his left hand. "Mission scrubbed," he said, counterweighing it with his right hand. "Dunn kills me for putting you in danger. . . ."

"I won't be in danger," she told him. "Ian'll be right there. He'll keep me safe."

"From the Dutchman?" Yashi asked. "Or from Dellarosa's four-man kill squad?"

"Just fucking let her go." Francine sounded distorted. Her voice was coming through the speaker of Martell's phone, and then through the scrambled connection between the two vans. "Shelly called Henrietta's but went straight to a recorded message. There's no reaching Eee that way."

"Van two is too far away," Deb's voice announced. "Even if Martell could run five-minute miles he wouldn't get to the club in time."

"If I could run five-minute miles, I wouldn't be here," Martell pointed out. "I'd be practicing for the Olympics."

"If this mission is scrubbed," Phoebe asked, "what happens to those kidnapped kids?"

A whole lot of silence answered her—both from

the van she was sitting in, and the one stuck in traffic.

"Yeah, that's what I thought," Phoebe said, and got out of van one.

"ETA seven and a half minutes," Yashi shouted after her as she ran. Across the parking lot to the back door of the club. Seven and a half minutes before four men with guns came looking for Ian, to kill him.

She yanked open the door and stepped from the brightness of the afternoon into dim, musty darkness.

A gigantic man was standing there—all big biceps and shiny shaved head. Little goatee. Tats escaping out the collar of his shirt and up his no-neck. Phoebe blinked at him—he must've been a bouncer—as she tried to get her bearing. Ian had reported that he'd gone upstairs.

The man blinked back at her but thankfully didn't ask to see her ID—she'd left it on that yacht, back on Monday night, which was the *last* time men with guns had tried to kill Ian.

"You one of the new girls?" the bouncer said instead.

So she said, "Yes. Why, yes, I am," as she looked around the room. When she'd left the van, the Dutchman hadn't yet joined Ian upstairs. But she didn't see anyone even remotely Dutch-looking over by the front doors. Which, of course, didn't mean anything. He might've been outside. He might've run away. He might've returned and gone upstairs while she was running through the parking lot. He might not even look Dutch—which meant what, anyway? He was carrying tulips?

"You're supposed to come in the stage door," the bouncer chastised her. "Every time. No exceptions. Not even for picking up a paycheck."

"Will you let it slide, this time?" she said in her best Marilyn Monroe, adding breathy exclamation points to her words. "I was called in for an emergency private party! I'm supposed to go right upstairs! Don't want to get Mr. Mrrph-Rff mad at me! Please!"

And there it was—an arrow pointing to the stairs that Phoebe then pointed to with both hands, like a stripper version of a car-show model. The bouncer hesitated and that was all she needed.

"Thank you!" She bolted, crossing the lobby and ducking under the decorative barricade that was intended to deny access to the second level. She took the stairs two at a time, pulling herself up by the banister, turning a corner, and bursting out the door into a long, narrow hallway that had three separate closed doors leading off of it. What had once been an upper lobby had been cheaply renovated into the club's so-called private party rooms. And Ian was in one of them.

Phoebe had no idea what exactly went on in the private party room of a strip club, although she could certainly guess. That rope at the bottom of the stairs gave her hope that two out of three rooms were empty. Although logic dictated that if one room was being used, all three could just as well be occupied.

But the clock was ticking as she went to the first door and leaned close to listen.

She heard nothing.

The second door, too, revealed only silence, and she realized that the rooms might have been intentionally soundproofed. But then she looked at the construction—shoddily slapped-up drywall and door frames that were not quite square—and she rejected that theory, moving toward the third door.

Which was where she heard him. ". . . gently down the stream . . ."

Phoebe grabbed and turned the doorknob, opening it even as she knocked lightly on the hollow door.

And there was Ian, alone in a room that defied the western theme by being filled with a 1990s man-cave-appropriate dark fake-leather sectional sofa that made up three sides of a square. A wet bar was along one wall, and next to it, the far corner of the room had been claimed for a half bath, with a toilet and sink. Phoebe double-checked, but the door was open and the little room was empty. The Dutchman hadn't yet made it back upstairs.

Ian was standing near a window that was glazed over, not just for privacy, but because it faced the extremely unglamorous back parking lot. The look of shock on his face would've been funny had the message she'd come to deliver not include the words *kill squad.*

"Bad timing," he said. "Bad, *bad*—"

She spoke over him, realizing that for all he knew, the equipment had malfunctioned, and she had no idea that he'd made contact with Vanderzee. "We know," she said. "We all know. We've been listening. They're listening still."

"Shh!" he said, and she realized that her instincts had been right—these rooms weren't soundproofed. And the Dutchman could well be on his way back up.

"But here's the SNAFU," she continued, closing the door, lowering her voice and moving closer to him. "A four-man kill squad's ETA is five minutes. Four. Better bank on four. Three to be safe."

Ian was just standing there, as dumbstruck as she'd ever seen him. It was a lot to process, so she elaborated, giving him as much information as she knew. "Berto emailed Francine with the warning that someone recognized you when you walked into this place, and whoever they were, they called Davio. Francine called Berto to confirm, and he told her Davio hired four men to come here and kill you, from someplace called Oakland Park—"

Oakland Park was apparently the right amount of detail to convince him, because he finally moved. Toward her, saying, "Shit. *Shit!* You promised you'd stay in the van."

That was what he was upset about . . . ?

"We didn't have a lot of options, considering you forgot your phone, and Martell and Deb are still stuck in traffic. It was me or Yashi, and it couldn't be Yashi."

He grabbed her by the arm. “You need to go back downstairs, get back into the van, and get the *hell* out of here—”

“Drive away and leave you?” she asked as he pulled her toward the door. “Did you not hear what I just—”

“I’ll use this,” Ian countered. “I will. It’s actually perfect. But I can’t have you here.” He opened the door and peered out, looking both ways down the corridor before he pulled her out of the room with him. “There’s gotta be a back stairway. And you’re going to take it and go.”

“And leave you on foot, unarmed, against four killers in a car? Ian—”

“Phoebe. Think. If I don’t connect with Vanderzee here and now, it’s not going to happen. Because from here on out, Davio’s going to be watching for me. Not just in Henrietta’s, but every-fricking-where in Miami.”

“He already is,” she told him as he dragged her with him, toward a left turn at the end of the hall. But that led to the dead end of a balcony, and to what looked like a series of boxes with special seating.

“*Jesus*. This place is a freaking fire hazard. How can there not be a second set of stairs?” Ian pulled her back the way they’d come. “Okay, look. I’m going to go wait in that room, but you just keep on walking. Down the same stairs that you came up, and right out the door. Do you understand? Don’t stop to talk to anyone. In fact, burst into tears and run if anyone says anything to you.”

Burst into . . . ? "You must think I'm a really good actor."

"I know you are. Don't argue with me. Just do it. Go." They'd reached the open door to the party room in which she'd found him, and he let go of her arm, but she stopped, too.

"Please," Phoebe begged. And it wasn't all that hard to imagine being able to conjure up a full-scale, noisy tear-burst if she needed it. In fact, she could feel her eyes already starting to fill.

"Shit," Ian swore again. And then he kissed her.

He put his hands on either side of her face, not roughly, but not quite gently, either, as he covered her mouth with his. Perfectly. Tenderly.

"I can take care of myself," he said, looking into her eyes before he kissed her again, and then one final time. It was over too fast, before she even got a chance to kiss him back. And now he was backing away. "Go," he said again.

And great. Now she *was* crying, a tear slipping down her cheek that she impatiently brushed away. "Ian, God help me, if you get yourself killed—"

"Hello. Who's this?"

Phoebe closed her eyes, because she knew even without turning around, just from the look on Ian's face, that Georg Vanderzee, AKA the Dutchman, had returned. She also knew that he'd heard her calling Ian by name. She could see the reality and implications of that in Ian's eyes—since she'd just spoken to him in a very familiar way, there was no way they could pretend she was just some woman who worked here, and besides, who in their right mind, in broad daylight, would mistake her for a stripper, anyway?

So she did the only thing she could think to do that would get Ian out of there in advance of the coming kill squad—the only thing she could think to do that would also maintain his current connection to the Dutchman.

She turned toward Vanderzee, wiping her face, and said, "I'm Phoebe. I'm Ian's wife." She reached over and took Ian's hand, even though the look in his eyes was not a happy one. "And I'm not supposed to be here, so he's *very* mad at me, but he lost his stupid cell phone so I couldn't call him and warn him that Davio Dellarosa, a man who hates him very much, knows that he's here. Davio has sent a team of gunmen to kill him. Ian told me that you're an old friend, a good friend, and I'm hoping that's true, and that you'll please, *please* help us. We need to get out of here. Now."

Phoebe couldn't have timed it better if her words had been a dialogue cue in an action movie.

She said *now,* and the next thing Ian heard was the sound of squealing tires from a car skidding to a stop in Henrietta's parking lot.

He went back into the private room and over to the window, which was covered with a sheet of stick-on plastic that made it translucent. He peeled back a corner and revealed—yes. A dark midsized sedan with all four doors open was sitting right by the club's back exit. And four men—all wearing ski masks and long coats despite the heat of the afternoon—were already pushing their way inside.

Vanderzee was right beside him, looking at them, too. "*Merde*, what are you into?" he asked.

"Oh, this and that," Ian said. And look. Here was how the club had passed its safety inspection—there was a metal fire escape right outside. He opened the window, kicked out the screen. "Phoebe. Come on. *Move*."

She took the hand he held out for her, and together they clattered down the metal stairs, with Vanderzee right behind them, cursing a blue streak in a mix of French, Dutch, German, and English.

"My car's over here," the man said, and he led the way, at a sprint, across the lot.

Ian knew Vanderzee wasn't helping them out of friendship or the kindness of his generous heart. He was helping them because if he didn't, they were going to be gunned down, right there, in broad daylight. And because it was broad daylight, and because people in this neighborhood were out and about, someone, or maybe some surveillance camera, would catch sight of his car speeding away from the scene, and suddenly Vanderzee would be up to his balls in a murder investigation. And since he was currently involved in a kidnapping and murder of his own, he couldn't risk that.

Phoebe's cheap plastic sandals were slowing her down, so Ian put his arm around her waist and half-carried her with him as he chased after the

Dutchman, past the car that Davio's hired guns had left by the door. If it hadn't been a necessity to stay close to Vanderzee, Ian would've jumped in and driven away in it, because the last thing he needed was a car chase through Miami. Stealing the killers' car was one surefire way to prevent that.

Instead, he dragged Phoebe toward Vanderzee's embassy-staid town car.

"Let me drive, let me drive, let me drive," Ian said, but the man ignored him, climbing in behind the wheel and ducking down, because—shit—a shooter had opened fire.

Everything went into slow-mo.

The world was already in high-def, and had been ever since Phoebe'd introduced herself to the Dutchman as Ian's *wife*. The color of the sky was an unnatural shade of blue, and the sunlight skipped and danced off the few cars sitting there in the lot. He could see the white cargo van in a neighboring lot, parked in the shifting shade of a palm tree, the barely visible shape of Yashi behind the wheel. He could see power lines overhead and potholes in the asphalt and Phoebe's face in between the two as she heard the gunshots—her wide eyes, her nostrils flaring as she tried to move faster, that beautiful mouth he'd just kissed . . .

What the hell was wrong with him? He shouldn't have kissed her again. What was he thinking?

Ian yanked open the back door and pushed Phoebe inside as a bullet plowed into the shiny black finish of the Dutchman's car.

He spun to look back at the club. And yes, the first of the gunmen had emerged through the window that Vanderzee, the freaking amateur, had carelessly left open. The man had come onto the fire escape, where he'd spotted them. But he was armed only with a handgun. At this distance, with that weapon, even a sharpshooter's aim would've been erratic. Still, Phoebe was shouting something, and her head was still up, so Ian dove into the car, pushing her down beneath him onto the floor, shouting, "Go, go, go!" as the Dutchman did just that, peeling out and heading away from the club, toward the exit at the back of the parking lot.

Phoebe was shouting something else, something urgent that included Ian's name, and he tried to lift at least some of his weight off of her. But Vanderzee took a hard left and then a hard right as he maneuvered his way around the few parked cars, and as the movement tossed them, Ian struggled to regain his balance.

If he were driving, he would've taken a different approach, heading instead for the front exit. Even though doing so would've brought them temporarily under fire, he would've rammed the shooters' vehicle with this boat of a car, ensuring that they wouldn't be followed.

Now, as he poked his head up to peer out the back window, he saw the gunmen running down the fire escape to their car, so they could do just that. One, two, three of them . . .

The fourth man wasn't moving, and Ian registered

the fact that he was standing there—at an elevated level, aiming what must've been a rifle—a split second before a hole was punched into the back windshield. He was already reacting and ducking—just barely. He felt the bullet whiz past his head even as he heard the sharp retort of the gunshot, even as the bullet crunched, simultaneously, into the door's padded armrest, as beneath him Phoebe shouted her alarm.

"They're following," Ian grimly announced to the Dutchman, who responded with more of that multilingual cursing as the car pulled out onto the back road. "Don't let them follow us!"

That last was aimed at Yashi—hopefully the fed had turned his roving microphones in the town car's direction. Ian needed interference, and he needed it now, even if it meant sacrificing one of the vans. Because this mission would not happen, and Ian wouldn't win Aaron's immunity, if one of these hired goons got a clear look at the town car's plates, and camped outside of the K-stani consulate, day and night, looking for the bounty he'd receive by delivering Ian's dead body to Davio Dellarosa.

And that was far from the worst-case scenario.

The worst case, if the kill squad was allowed to follow, involved imminent death, not just for Ian, but for Phoebe, too.

Another bullet hit the car, somewhere on the side, in the back—which was good, because it meant they weren't yet following. Either that, or they'd left their sniper behind on the fire escape.

"Try to get some buildings—something with some height—between the shooter and us," Ian ordered Vanderzee as he pushed himself up and found himself nose to nose with Phoebe.

"You think I don't know that? There's nothing here but rows of shitty little houses. There's nowhere to turn!"

Perfect.

Ian pulled himself up on the seat to risk another look out the back.

"Oh my God, Ian," Phoebe said, and started to sit up.

"Stay down." He reached out with his left hand—and realized that his fingers were dripping with blood. He wouldn't have thought the world could get any sharper and brighter, but just like that, it did. "Are you hit?" he asked her, seeing that yes, there was blood on her sweatshirt, garish and red against the crisp white. He felt himself going into full mental overdrive as he tried to figure out the fastest way to get her to the closest hospital. To hell with this mission, to hell with the Dutchman, to hell with everything but making sure that this woman didn't die . . .

But she was speaking over him. "Ian, *you* were shot! *You!*"

He was the one who was bleeding, thank you sweet Jesus. Phoebe was trying to sit up again, reaching toward his T-shirt sleeve. It was soaked with blood that was dripping down his arm.

He pushed her back down. "I'm okay," he told

her, although there was too much adrenaline in his system to know that for a fact. Still, he wasn't gushing blood—this was not bad for a bullet wound. Plus, he'd been using his arm to support himself, so he knew it wasn't broken. "Stay down!"

He again used his injured arm to brace himself so that he could poke his head up above the seat—up and back—to get a quick look out the back window. And sure enough, the kill squad's sedan was behind them, shooters leaning out the windows, waiting to fire until they got closer. And closer . . .

"They're behind us," Ian reported. "Shit, they're close enough to get your plate number!"

"No, they're not," the Dutchman said. "I'm not a fool—it's smeared with mud. I made sure of it before I came here."

Well, *that* was a break, at least. Now all they had to do was keep Davio's men from shooting out their tires and killing them. "Do you have a weapon?" Ian asked.

Phoebe thought he was talking to her. "It's in the lockup, remember?"

"Vanderzee," Ian said. "Are you armed?"

The other man didn't answer right away.

"Are you carrying?" Ian asked again.

The Dutchman swore again, this time in Farsi. But he handed Ian his weapon, a compact SIG Sauer that wouldn't ruin the lines of his jacket.

And thus trust was established. "Thanks, bro," Ian said. Or it would be, if they survived this goatfuck.

If this were a Hollywood buddy movie, this was where Ian would deftly shoot out the pursuing car's front tires and save the day, after which he'd hand the SIG back, butt first, to Vanderzee. And then they'd both smile, and the audience would nod because it would be clear that the two main characters were on the path to true friendship.

Except Vanderzee was an asshole sociopath that Ian would never, ever, *ever* call *friend*.

He lay back on the seat as he checked the weapon, making sure there was a round chambered and ready to go. As soon as he raised his head to aim that weapon, he'd shout for Vanderzee to hit the brakes to put him into range. But the shooters would then be in range, too, and there were going to be two, maybe three men firing back at Vanderzee's car.

"Are there two of them now?" Vanderzee asked. "White van—behind the sedan?"

What? Ian peeked up again, and—glory, hallelujah—there was Yashi, in the white van, behind the bad guys, gunning the powerful engine that Ian had paid extra for, and—bang! He slammed the van, full force, into the back of the sedan.

"Who the fuck *is* that?" Vanderzee asked, even as he raced the town car faster down the seemingly endless narrow residential street.

As they both watched, Yashi did it again, this time hitting the sedan at a slight angle, from the back and to the side, pushing it, hard, toward a line of parked cars.

"That's my guardian angel," Ian told Vanderzee, using the same words that Berto had with Shelly just a few nights ago. And just like that, the entire plan for this rescue mission became clear to him, in a flash—the way his best plans always did. Just *bang,* and it was all right there, like a delivery via Dropbox into his brain. In that instant, he knew what he had to do to rescue those kids, and exactly how to pull it off.

He was not only going to use Davio's unbridled hatred of him and his family, but he would also use Davio's son Berto, who was proving to be Ian's newest bestest friend, thanks no doubt to Francine. It was risky, sure, but he knew instinctively that it would work.

"His name is Berto Dellarosa—the guy in the van," Ian told Vanderzee, as the shooters' sedan sideswiped the row of cars parked on the street. "He's the guy who called Phoebe to warn her about this hit. He didn't think he would get here in time to pull me out, but I guess he did. I'll tell you all about it—about the deal I've got going with him, a deal that double-crosses his father. There's a potential to make a lot of cash—just, please, get us out of here first."

The kill squad's sedan was going so fast that when it sideswiped the cars its front wheel got snagged. It went into a spin that caused an oncoming truck—the only other traffic on this road—to jam on its brakes and skid to a shrieking stop in someone's dusty yard.

Yashi, meanwhile, was driving like a demolition derby pro. He'd braked, but now he accelerated again, hitting the sedan one final time to send it rocketing into a telephone pole, where the front hood crumpled and the airbags exploded.

The last thing Ian saw was Yashi doing a hard youie and driving—fast—back the way he'd come, as the Dutchman finally found a cross street and turned.

Hold on. It was what Vanderzee should have said before he took the sudden sharp right. Instead he just blasted into it and Ian tumbled on top of Phoebe again.

"Slow down, slow down, slow down," Ian told the Dutchman, even though he was nose to nose with Phoebe again, and was looking directly into her eyes. "And weave, man. Let's not stay on this same street for long."

Ian could see Phoebe's questions—*Berto Dellarosa? In a white van?*

"We're safe," he told her, nodding and mouthing *Yashi*. "Berto must've found a way around the traffic. He knocked Davio's kill squad into a telephone pole, at the very least popped their airbags, which neutralizes their car." He pushed himself off Phoebe and up onto the seat as he raised his voice slightly to address Vanderzee. "That was fucking great driving, man. Don't stop, though—we need to keep going, but we also don't want to get pulled over for going too fast. I don't know about you, but I could really use not having to explain the bullet holes to the police." Ian made himself laugh, as if that was a good joke.

From the front, Vanderzee laughed, too. "That was . . . Shit, Dunn. You're one crazy bastard."

"Yes, I am," Ian agreed, as he helped Phoebe up so that she was sitting beside him on the seat.

"How about the bullet hole in your arm," she said tartly. "Can we maybe take care of that before we have to explain it to the police?"

"I'm fine." He shot her a warning glance. Let him spin this fiction. She'd done quite enough already, thanks.

She ignored him. "He's bleeding all over your nice car," she leaned forward to tell Vanderzee. "Are you okay? Were you hit, too?"

It was actually a nice touch—the realistic reaction of his "wife" to his getting grazed. And Ian *had* only been grazed, he saw as he pushed back his sleeve. There was a strip of skin missing from his arm, true, but it was a relatively small strip. In a perfect world, he'd go to the ER for stitches. In his current world, he'd patch it himself and end up with a souvenir scar.

Assuming he was going to live long enough for the wound to heal.

"I'm unhurt," Vanderzee told Phoebe.

"Thank God," she said. "And thank *you*. You saved our lives. I don't know how we can ever, *ever* repay you."

Ian poked her leg. That second *ever* was a little heavy on the drama.

"Your husband saved my life once," the Dutchman told Phoebe. "I think this makes us even." He glanced up into the rearview mirror to meet Ian's eyes. "I can't believe you got married."

"At times, I honestly can't believe it either," Ian said dryly. "It happened so fast. Here. Thanks. I'm glad I didn't need it." He used the opportunity to lean forward and return the SIG. As much as he hated to let it go, it was better to do that sooner than to wait until the man asked for it back. "Safety's back on."

"Thank you, my friend."

And weren't they all just the perfect picture of geniality? But now that not getting killed was off his to-do list, Ian's most-pressing need was to get Phoebe back to the FBI safe house.

"Seriously, man, I made a mess of your car," Ian said. "Why don't we stick this puppy in one of the long-term parking garages at the airport. Back it in, so the damage to the rear windshield doesn't show. As soon as I can get to a phone, I got people who'll come out, replace the glass, patch the hole, clean it up good as new—no questions asked."

"You want us to walk through the airport looking like this?" Phoebe asked.

Was she trying to make this harder for him? Or was she just getting into playing the part? Well, Ian could do that, too. If she really was his wife, he'd be pretty freaking bullshit angry about her being in a place where bullets had been flying. "I need to get you someplace safe," he said, not bothering to hide the tightness in his voice. “So no, we *won't* walk through the airport. We’ll stay in the garage. Find a car that we can borrow. Get you out of there.”

Phoebe looked back at him, blinking rapidly, which appeared to be her version of SOS or maybe WTF. “But you were going to talk to, um, your friend Vanderzee? Mr. Vanderzee? About the you-know-what. Deal. With Berto?”

Ian widened his eyes at her, and she quickly added, “Or maybe not with Berto. Maybe I got that wrong and . . . I’m so sorry.” She was aiming her words now at Vanderzee. “This is really awkward because we haven’t been properly introduced on account of the fleeing-for-our-lives thing. I mean, you know I’m Phoebe. Dunn. And I’ve heard Eee call you Vanderzee, but is that your first name or your last? All I know for sure is that you knew Ian before I did, that you used to be friends, and that you’re amazing. A real hero.”

The Dutchman laughed, smiling back at Ian in the rearview mirror.

And Ian saw exactly where this was going. He knew exactly what was happening—and he couldn’t do a damn thing to stop it. Georg Vanderzee was falling in love with his wife.

“I love her,” the Dutchman proclaimed, just as Ian knew he would. “Please call me Georg. And to be honest, we’re not that far from my rental. I’ll put the car in my garage—I have people who will take care of it, too. It’s not a problem. In fact, I’d prefer if my people handled it. You and Phoebe—a very pretty name for a lovely lady—can get cleaned up. We can all have a drink to celebrate our adventure and our newfound friendship. And we can talk about this lucrative opportunity you mentioned. I happen to have a project of my own that's going to pay out quite nicely, but it's temporarily on hold, so funds are tight. Depending on your time frame, this could well work out perfectly for all of us."

Perfectly was not the word Ian had in mind. He must not have been able to hide the muscles jumping in his jaw, because Vanderzee glanced at him in the mirror again, and said, "My house has top-of-the-line security. Your bride will be safe."

"Well, that sounds great," Phoebe said.

And Ian had to nod, forcing a smile as he attempted to incinerate her with his eyes. "Oh, yeah. It sounds *great*."

CHAPTER SEVENTEEN

It was late December, and the abundance of Christmas lights and decorations added an unnecessary garishness to Vienna's elegant beauty. The sparkle and natural glitter of the freshly fallen snow on the rooftops should've been enough.

Aaron had met his brother here once before, during the summer, and although he now missed being able to stroll through the cobblestone streets in the warmth of the evening, the city was still pedestrian-friendly. With his collar up and his scarf around his neck, he was ready for anything.

Well, almost anything.

"Aaron. Hi. Yeah. It's me. Shel?" The strapping young man said his own name as if he were the one who was uncertain about it as Aaron stood, frozen in place, and stared.

It had been nearly four years since he'd last seen Sheldon Dellarosa. Three years, ten months, and twenty-nine days, to be precise.

This version of Shelly was taller, broader—nearly four years older. The boy had become a man.

He was wearing a military uniform beneath his overcoat. Like Aaron, Shelly was now a Marine. Unlike Aaron, Shel was an officer. A first lieutenant.

Aaron didn't know whether to salute—or to shit or maybe even go blind.

"Crap, I knew this was a mistake," Sheldon said. "But when I saw you leaving your hotel, I thought . . . why wait. Except I should have, because here we are now, standing in the street, in the snow, and it's awkward, and you're probably going somewhere. . . ."

"To get dinner," Aaron said. "Sir. I'm going to get dinner. Ian—he's my brother. I was supposed to meet him, but he's been delayed."

"I know Ian's your brother," Shel said. "Did you really think I would forget that?"

"I really have no idea, sir," Aaron said.

“Stop calling me that.”

“You’re supposed to say *At ease, Sergeant,* and even then, I’m supposed to call you *sir.*”

“You’re still mad at me,” Sheldon realized. “*Really* mad. About that email. Oh my God.” He started to laugh.

“You think it’s *funny?* Fuck you, *sir!*” Aaron turned and walked away, heading back to the hotel because his appetite had just vanished.

But Shelly followed him. “No, wait, I don’t think it’s funny. I think it’s . . . Ah, God, Aaron, the worst thing would’ve been if I’d spent all this time searching for you, and you didn’t even remember me. And if you’re still this mad, then maybe you’re also not over me, maybe . . .”

Aaron stopped and spun back around, and Sheldon nearly crashed into him. “I’m over you, douchebag,” he said, his voice low. “I was over you in a heartbeat when I found out just what a coward you are—”

“It was good, wasn’t it,” Shel said, standing his ground, chin up in that manner that was still so familiar, “what I wrote in that email? It had to be good. It had to be convincing. If you tried to get in touch with me—at all—you were dead. Berto told me if I talked to you again, if you so much as called or tried to come see me—he’d tell my father, who would kill you. And he meant it. If my wanting to keep you from dying makes me a coward? I’m a coward. You’re right.”

Aaron couldn’t listen to this. Sheldon’s words

were everything he'd hoped and prayed that he would hear throughout that first year of boot camp, of training, of going to war. He'd even left his high school email account active—it was still there, hanging in cyberspace. The same one that Sheldon had used, time and again. He'd checked it just yesterday, but it still held only spam in its in-box. If Sheldon truly had searched for him? He hadn't tried very hard.

Aaron now did the only thing he could do. He turned and walked away.

But Sheldon followed, again hustling to keep up. "Can you please at least give me three minutes. Just three minutes—"

"I thought we both just agreed that you're a coward," Aaron said. "I'm not sure what else you can say—or do—in three minutes—"

"I didn't email you," Sheldon spoke over him, "because Berto hacked your account—doubleadoublen@zoomail.net. I knew if I tried to contact you there, he'd know. And I couldn't risk him coming after you, just to spite me."

Aaron blew past the entrance to the hotel. He didn't turn in, he just kept going, waiting until they were past the uniformed doormen to turn to Shel to say, "So I'm just supposed to believe that one of the smartest people I know took *four fucking years*—"

"Yes!" Sheldon shouted over him. *"It took me four fucking years!"*

Sheldon, who rarely raised his voice, and who

had, in all the time Aaron had known him, never dropped the f-bomb, was shaking with anger. Or maybe it wasn't anger. Maybe it was the agony that remained in the aftermath of a shattered heart. Despite years of hiding from it, of pretending that the wounds had finally healed, Aaron still felt it, too.

"You let me down, too, you know," Sheldon said, his voice a whisper now, as his eyes filled with tears. Still, he held Aaron's gaze as he kept going. "I went up to Cambridge even though my father wouldn't let me accept that scholarship to MIT. He wanted me to go to school in Tampa, and Berto turned the screws, so that's where I went. On paper, anyway. They dropped me off at my dorm and I pretended to unpack, but as soon as they left, I took the bus to Boston." He exhaled hard. "Because I hoped you'd be there, waiting for me. I hoped you'd realized that I sent that email under duress. You know, I hung out on campus for a month, Air. I slept in shelters when I could, and on the street when I couldn't. Even though I knew you weren't there when I didn't find you that first day. I gave you a month, in case I was wrong."

Dear God. After getting that email, Aaron had given Shel all of ten minutes.

"I knew you'd join the Marines," Shel said. "So I joined, too. By then, my father and Berto were actively looking for me. But once I signed up, there was nothing they could do about it. They couldn't touch me. From that aspect, it was great. I was finally safe. And I thought once I was in, it would be easy to hack into the computers and find you and . . . Well, I was wrong about that. But once I did finally find you, I kept getting screwed because our leave didn't line up. Until now. So, yeah, it took me this long. But I never gave up."

And there they stood, just looking at each other.

"I'm not sure what you want," Aaron finally said. "An apology, or am I supposed to just, I don't know, fall into your arms?"

"I guess I was hoping we could start with dinner," Sheldon said. "Although your falling into my arms was always part of the fantasy. Unless you're seeing someone—"

"I'm not," Aaron said. "I was. For a while, but I broke it off. Because he wasn't you."

Shelly didn't try to hide his hope from his eyes. He just let it show, let it shine out from inside of him, the same way he'd done all those years ago, when they were both still kids.

And then there wasn't anything left to do but fall into his arms. Except they were standing there, on the sidewalk of a busy city street. Still, Aaron reached for Shel, and Shel all but leapt at him, and God, it was better than any fantasy he could have imagined.

Aaron tried to make their embrace as manly as possible, aware of the passersby eyeing them curiously, even as he felt the glacier inside of him begin to melt as Shelly breathed his name. "Aaron, I'm so sorry."

Aaron lifted his head to look into Shel's eyes. "I'm sorry, too."

This entire surreal experience had been one surprise coming on top of another, and Aaron could barely catch his breath. Especially when Shelly smiled. It was that same mix of hot and sweet that Aaron had adored. "I forgive you," Shel whispered, and then iced the WTF-cake by kissing Aaron. Right there. On the mouth. In the middle of freaking Vienna.

When Shel pulled back, he was out of breath but he was grinning. He didn't look around; he clearly didn't give a shit if anyone had seen them. "It's been a long time, and I know we've both changed—how could we not've," he said as he straightened his coat and cover, as if kissing a fellow Marine were something he did every day. "I mean, yeah, it's freezing, and you still aren't wearing gloves, but . . . You're different, I know it, and I am, too. But I think you're going to like me. I like me—much better now. And I want to get to know you. So come on, Sergeant Dunn, let's go have dinner, and do this right."

"Sir, yes, sir," Aaron said as he followed Sheldon.

Who looked at him out of the corner of his eye. "Well, okay," Shel said. "So *that's* gonna be hot."

Aaron laughed as he tucked his hands into his coat pockets. He would've liked to hold Shelly's hand, but really, just walking beside him was more than he'd thought he'd ever have again. "Yes, it is," he agreed.

And after three years, ten months, and twenty-nine days of being frozen and barely breathing, Aaron's heart started beating and his life began again.

The Dutchman lived in a spacious rental house on a large, flat, fenced-in plot of land in a development that had been built on the site of a former grapefruit grove. Most of the trees were still in rows, which shouldn't have been visually appealing, yet somehow oddly was. Or maybe anything would have looked outrageously beautiful to Phoebe, after surviving both an attack by a kill squad and a high-speed car chase.

The fear that she'd felt when realizing that Ian had been shot had been replaced by relief that was nearly as immobilizing. When she'd finally gotten a look at his wound and saw that he wasn't going to bleed to death, the wave of thankfulness that swept over her had been extreme.

But now they were met in the Dutchman's garage by a small army of bodyguards who were not happy at all about the bullet holes in Vanderzee's car—or the fact that their employer had been in danger. Still, he waved them off and led the way inside.

Phoebe followed on shaky legs as the Dutchman took them into the enormous, pristine house. As they trooped into the kitchen, he spoke in another language—Farsi?—to a pair of female housekeepers who worked it, hard, to avoid eye contact even as they leapt into action. One of the women raced ahead, through the house and up a flight of stairs to what their host called his guest suite.

As Phoebe followed, Vanderzee led her and Ian into a private sitting room with a bedroom beyond it.

Like the open and airy first floor, the rooms were decorated in 1990s groovy-Florida-grandma. Heavy on the aquas and pinks, with an over-abundance of whimsical dolphin statues. Phoebe let herself love them all, completely, with just the faintest dash of irony. And why shouldn't there be space in her new-and-improved not-dead life for an albino dolphin who winked while tail-walking on an end table?

The silent housekeeper carried a pile of fluffy white towels in with her, slipping through the door into the bedroom, heading for the attached bathroom.

"There's a first-aid kit under the sink," the Dutchman told them, "and robes in the closet."

Phoebe turned to look at him, realizing that although they'd just survived a life-threatening situation together, everything had happened so quickly that she would not have been able to pick him out of a police lineup.

"How about some rags or older towels?" Ian asked, smiling his thanks at the woman as he went through the bedroom so he could look into the bathroom. Phoebe heard the familiar screech of metal on metal as he pushed back a shower curtain. "I'm afraid I'm going to make a mess."

"Don't worry about that," the Dutchman said, dismissing the housekeeper with a nod.

Georg Vanderzee was not quite as tall as Ian, and far less broad. In fact, his build was very similar to Ian's brother Aaron's. Without Ian standing immediately nearby to compare, Phoebe would've thought of them both as muscular—and they were. Just not as. This man's hair followed the not-as rule, too. Like Ian's, it was thick and wavy—just not as. The Dutchman had glimmers of red in his brown, and it looked as if he'd added highlights, to make him appear even more fair. He might've been handsome, with his straight nose, strong chin, beautiful olive-toned skin, and exotically colored green-brown-gold eyes. But there was something about the set of his mouth or maybe it was the oddly chilly distance or flat disconnect in those eyes that made him look . . . off.

"Your making a mess is the least of my concern," he continued.

Or maybe the man was fine—just *not as* fine as Ian—and Phoebe's imagination was running rampant since she knew Ian not only didn't like Vanderzee, but hadn't wanted to give the FBI any details of their previous encounter. And that made her suspect that Ian hadn't wanted to recall awful memories of how he'd been forced to watch as the Dutchman tortured puppies.

Or worse.

Vanderzee now turned to Phoebe and smiled. Nope, he was not fine. He was definitely creepy.

"I'm counting on you to let me know if your husband needs additional medical care."

Her husband. Ian had returned from the bathroom, and she glanced over to meet his gaze just long enough to confirm that, yes, he was still pissed about that little detail. "I trust him when he says he's all right," she said.

"I'm glad to hear that, since trust is paramount in any lasting relationship." She'd heard the Dutchman speaking a variety of languages while driving their getaway car. But his English was close to perfect, with just a hint of northern Europe—Germany or perhaps Holland—in his faintly British vowels. That should have been sexy, but instead, coming from him it was, again, creepy. "I'll let you get cleaned up," he said. "Make yourself at home."

Still, when Phoebe said, "Thank you so much, for everything," she was sincere. Whoever this man was, whatever he'd done in the past, however oily his smile and odd his eyes, today he'd helped her get Ian away from four men who'd wanted, badly, to kill him. And for that she *was* grateful.

He smiled again as he bowed, very slightly—yikes—and closed the door behind him.

Phoebe turned to find that Ian had moved. He was now standing right beside her. "If I hadn't seen him in direct sunlight, I might be thinking *vampire,*" she said.

Ian spoke over her, completely ignoring her attempt to break the awkwardness with a Buffy joke. "Why don't you get into the shower first?" He pulled her with him into the bedroom, where the decor was less dolphins and more palm trees and—double yikes—decidedly sinister monkeys.

"I'm not sure I need a shower," she said. The dolphins returned in the bathroom, which was surprisingly small and old-fashioned, considering the rest of the house. A single sink with a small beadboard cabinet, full mirror covering the wall above it, a medicine cabinet sticking awkwardly out above a toilet with a fuzzy cover on the lid, a tub with a bedolphined shower curtain, more dolphins on the walls. "I think the blood is only on my sweatshirt—"

He cut her off again. "It's also in your hair."

"Really?" Phoebe leaned forward to look at herself in the mirror, but of course she couldn't see the back of her head. What she *could* see was Ian using the very same mirror to get a look at the wound on his shoulder. "I'm not much of a paramedic," she said, and he met her eyes. The look he gave her was so intense, her voice trailed off. "But if you tell me what to do, I can try to bandage . . ."

Phoebe knew, just from the way he was looking at her, that he was trying to communicate telepathically. But what was he telling her? That Vanderzee *was* a vampire? No, that was almost as absurd as the idea that this generically decorated rental house was somehow bugged or—

Really?

She looked at Ian harder, narrowing her eyes in a silent question.

"Why don't you take a shower," he said again, quietly, his eyes never leaving hers. "Mrs. Dunn."

That *was* what he was telling her, wasn't it? By calling her *that* while the Dutchman wasn't around to overhear them . . . ?

Of course, maybe she was now completely paranoid, and there was no hidden message in the way Ian was looking at her. Maybe she smelled bad, and that was sheer annoyance on his face and nothing more—Phoebe knew that she'd royally pissed him off by promising to stay in the van and then showing up inside Henrietta's. And then she'd put the cherry on top of the bullshit pie that she'd baked, by telling the Dutchman that she was Ian's wife. . . .

But in case there *were* cameras and microphones or whatever, she chose her words carefully. "I know you're mad at me, but there really was no other option—"

Ian kissed her.

Phoebe didn't see it coming. It must've happened when she blinked, because one second he was staring at her in the mirror, and the very next, his mouth was covering hers, keeping her from saying anything more. He pulled her tightly against him, his arms around her so that she couldn't get away. Not that she was fighting him. On the contrary.

This had to be proof that Ian thought there were cameras and mics in here.

And she wanted to make it look good.

Yeah, *that* was why she'd wrapped her arms

around his neck and was kissing him back as if her very life depended on it. That was why she angled her head to let him kiss her more deeply, why she moaned when his hand slid down her back to her butt so he could press her body against the very solid length of him.

And . . . okay. Who, really, was she fooling here? Herself? Ian knew damn well that she was hot for him. She'd given him all the proof he'd needed when she'd kissed him the way she'd kissed him, beneath that dock.

As Phoebe kept kissing him now, she heard the door close and she felt him gently maneuver her toward it—it was cool and hard against her back. Only then did he stop. He lifted his head to say, "Don't talk, don't move." His mouth was still so close to hers she could feel his breath, feel his lips against hers.

He raised an eyebrow, just a fraction of an inch, and Phoebe realized he was waiting for some kind of acknowledgment, so she nodded.

Only then did he push himself away from her, but he watched her closely—as if he didn't quite believe she wasn't going to blurt something out and give them away. Eyes still on her, he leaned past the shower curtain and turned on the water into the tub, then adjusted the dial so the shower sputtered to life.

The sound of rushing water filled the room as Ian came back to her. "We'll let it heat up," he said, and then he kissed her again. Lightly this time, his hands in her hair, on either side of her head as he kissed not just her mouth but her face, her chin, her cheeks, her neck . . .

He'd kissed her that same way back in the hall outside of Henrietta's private party room, she realized. His hands warm against her face, almost chastely, with space between their bodies. And there'd been no cameras there, no reason to playact. So maybe this *wasn't* a game . . .

"Oh, God, Ian," Phoebe heard herself say, as he kissed her throat, her jawline, her ear . . .

"Camera and mic in the frame of the picture across from the sink," he breathed, and that was that. No more *maybe*s.

He kissed her on the mouth again as she mentally kicked herself and called herself names. Fool. Loser. Even as she kissed him back.

For the sake of the camera.

Although, really? Had she *really* thought, at any point, that there was anything even remotely real about anything this man did or said to her?

Yes.

But that was on her, for being naïve and pathetic.

Ian kissed his way around to her other ear so that he could say, "But that's the only one in here, so we can talk in the shower."

Her eyes opened at that.

Of course they could talk in the shower, with the water running to obscure their words, and the curtain hiding them from the camera.

But . . .

Ian straightened up, and in doing so, unzipped her sweatshirt. He looked at her body, at her breasts beneath her T-shirt, and the heat in his eyes was enough to boil the next two weeks of her very hot and sweaty dreams.

Phoebe looked from the picture in question—a frame of orange, pink, and aqua shells surrounding a frolicking dolphin, captured midleap—to the mirror over the sink, to the tub, with the shower running and the curtain that would provide privacy.

Privacy, that is, from the cameras, but not from Ian.

He was already taking off his T-shirt and kicking off his boots. His back was to her—although that was just an illusion. All he had to do to see every inch of that little bathroom was to lift his head and look into the mirror.

Still, she stepped out of her flip-flops and let her sweatshirt drop onto the floor. She pushed off her jeans, yanked her T-shirt over her head, and she hightailed it up and over the edge of the tub and into the shower, pulling that curtain closed behind her with a screech.

It was probably a mistake to get her underwear wet—she'd recently gone too many consecutive hours without any at all—but no way was she going to have a naked conversation with Ian Dunn, so she just stepped under the showerhead and let herself get soaked. She'd kept her glasses on, too, so she carefully kept the water from running down her face as she rinsed the back of her head—but there wasn't even the faintest hint of blood as it washed down the drain. Obviously there had been none in her hair to start with. Which, okay, bright-siding it, was actually a good thing, because *ew*.

The water got too hot, so she turned to adjust the temperature as she stepped back out of the spray—and bumped into Ian, who had joined her behind the curtain while her back was turned.

He was solid and . . . solid. Very, very solid. She'd felt his erection during their embrace, and okay, since he was human and subject to the laws of biology, it was probably not a reasonable belief that he could have somehow made it vanish, but, whoa.

He'd also brought a wrapped condom in with him. He must've found it in the medicine cabinet, and he dropped it, a little red square, into the soap dish that was built into the tile wall.

"Whoa," she said, aloud this time, turning to face him, determined to keep her eyes aimed above his neck. Of course she couldn't. There was no woman alive who could have, and *whoa.*

"Sorry," he said, his voice a whisper, but he didn't sound very sorry at all. "You seriously keep your glasses on in the shower?"

"Not usually, no," she whispered back. They were starting to steam up, so she took them off and put them up on the windowsill, next to a row of shampoos and body washes. He got blurrier, but not blurry enough. "And *I'm* sorry, but I'm *not* having sex with you."

"No," Ian said. "*I'm* not having sex with *you*."

"I get that I'm supposed to be insulted when you say that," she said, "that there's an implication there that you don't *want* to have sex with me, and that's fine—"

"That's not even close to what I said."

"—And yet, you come in here, spouting Mount Kilimanjaro, tossing condoms around like Mardi Gras beads—"

"One condom," he said, laughing his disbelief. "And while I appreciate the compliment, this"—he motioned to his package—"is adrenaline. That, plus the way you were kissing me—"

"Excuse me. You were kissing me."

"Jesus," he said. "Yes. That, plus the way *I* was kissing *you*—because *you* told Georg fucking Vanderzee that you're my wife, and now we're stuck with that cover, so what the hell am I supposed to do? Not kiss my smoking hot wife after I nearly get her killed?"

"Ding, ding, ding, ding, ding," Phoebe said. "Sorry, you had me up to *smoking hot wife,* but then you pinned the bullshit meter."

"Are you really going to stand there, pretending that you're not completely aware that Vanderzee is into you?" Ian countered. "A little *too* into you. I was staking my claim. And, FYI? If we're going to start keeping track of pinned meters, you *broke* the one for hyperbole, with *Mount Kilimanjaro* and the *Mardi Gras beads*."

"Yes," Phoebe said tartly. "Let's get back to talking about the size of your penis. It's not like we don't have anything else to discuss. Like, maybe the best way for me to distract Vanderzee, while you wander through the house—making sure there are no clues or to-do lists saying things like *Transport kidnapped children to Wichita for safety*."

Ian shook his head. "Even if that wasn't ridiculous, I'm not leaving you alone with him."

"You say that like you'd be locking me into a cage with a ravenous lion," she countered. "I'm talking about me going down into the kitchen a few minutes before you do. About taking advantage of our being here to—"

"No."

And there they stood, with water pounding down on her shoulders and steam filling the air between them.

"Look," she said. "I know you're angry that I got out of the van when I promised I wouldn't. You're angry that I'm here. I get it. And I'm sorry, but there really was no other option. Davio Dellarosa sent those men to that club to kill you, and I was not going to let that happen. And I also was not going to let Yashi go in there and force us to scrub this mission. So long, kidnapped kids? Good luck to you and your rocket-scientist mother? Nuh-uh. And yes, it was unfortunate that Vanderzee saw us in the hallway—"

"No, it was actually good that that happened. If you'd gone down those stairs, you would've bumped into the gunmen going out the back door. And if they'd recognized you, which they would've . . . I'm sure Davio gave them your picture. It would've been bad. Way worse than this." He exhaled hard. "I've been flashing hot and cold, just thinking about that . . . I really need to get you out of here. As quickly as possible."

"Well, telling him that I'm newly pregnant won't fly," Phoebe said. "Too bad, it's a classic excuse. *Oh, I'm so tired, what with all the morning sickness. . . .*"

Ian looked down at the condom he'd brought into the shower. "Shit."

"I'm right about that being a visual aid," Phoebe sought to clarify, "to explain why we're in here for so long . . . ?"

"Yup," Ian said. "And you're right, too, that it kills pregnancy as an excuse for me to wrap you in gauze and stash you someplace safe."

"Unless you were running on automatic pilot and forgot?"

Ian shook his head. "Wouldn't happen."

"But not impossible."

"Yes," he said. "Impossible."

"Maybe I just told you. Surprise! It's a girl!"

"That's pretty half-assed," he said, "considering you were just running down fire escapes and through parking lots."

"Pregnant women still have legs and feet," Phoebe argued, but he was shaking his head.

"It's too much of a stretch, especially considering cultural differences. In K-stan, women don't run, even when they're not pregnant. I don't want him forced to think too much, because we've already got this weirdness to explain." And yes, he'd gestured toward her, when he'd said *this weirdness*.

She must've looked outraged, because he added, "Who wears their underwear into the shower?"

"I do, obviously," she said. "Because . . . it's sexy and it turns you on?"

"You ever hear that expression, the devil's in the details?" Ian asked her. "Well, it applies, in a different way when you're undercover. We have to make this look real, down to the tiniest details, or the Dutchman is going to do the math and either throw us out or kill us. The devil cannot be in our details. So, no. You were right. We can't tell him you're pregnant, and need to rush you home to spend the next six months on bedrest. Not after I bring a condom with me—into a shower into which you've worn your underwear. It's too much."

"Maybe it's edible underwear," Phoebe suggested.

Ian just looked at her.

"Okay, then . . . Maybe I'm *not* an idiot," she tried, "and I'm well aware of the kind of man I'm married to—danger being your middle name and all that. And therefore I'm cognizant of the company you keep. Maybe—no, *definitely*. I *know* that the Dutchman has surveillance cameras all over this place, and I'm unwilling to parade around naked in front of him for the duration. In fact, I'll say as much after we turn off the water."

Ian was nodding now. "That actually works."

"And why, really, do we have to have something

like bedrest as a reason to want to leave?" she asked. "This is his house, we're guests. After we use his laundry room to wash and dry our clothes—maybe you could borrow a T-shirt because that blood's gonna stain. . . . Anyway, as soon as we're no longer wandering around looking like you've just been shot, we *can* leave. And then it's just *So long, thanks again for not leaving us to die*. You can make plans to meet him later." She lowered her voice in a bad imitation of him. *"Don't want to talk business in front of the little woman."*

"I've never used the phrase *the little woman* in my entire life," Ian told her.

"Well, thank God for that, at least," Phoebe said. "So is that our plan? May I please get out of here?" The close quarters, full frontal nudity, and steam were making her light-headed. "Unless you want me to help you wash your shoulder?"

"Nah, I got it," he said. "But we're not done. I need you to understand that Vanderzee is a sociopath whose only allegiance is to himself. He cares nothing for other people, and even less for women and children." The intensity with which he was looking at her was similar to that look he'd shot her, in the mirror. And again, she knew he wanted her to read his mind.

"What did he do to you?" she asked, and he shook his head.

"Not to me," he said. "To one of his wives. He's got dozens. And this one, he . . . he shot her in the head. It was . . . I was standing right there and . . ."

I couldn't stop him. Or maybe *I didn't stop him.* Ian didn't say the words, but Phoebe didn't have to be telepathic to know what he was thinking. If they'd had their clothes on, she would've reached for him. Instead, she stood there, awkwardly, with the water pounding down on her back, not sure what to say.

"Lookit, I don't want to give you too many details, because I need you to be able to smile at this douchebag," Ian continued. "But you need to know he's unforgiving and cruel. Jesus, what else can I tell you? He's socially conservative, so don't bring up Aaron, okay? He's not religious, but he follows K-stan's strict religious laws—if those laws serve him. He's superstitious—possibly even slightly OCD about it and . . . I don't want you alone with him."

Phoebe nodded. "Understood."

"Just a few more things," Ian told her. "First, I know from intel that the feds've already tapped into Vanderzee's surveillance system here."

"Oh, good," she said. "That means they got to see me in my underwear, too."

"That means we can communicate with them," he corrected her. "Two, let *me* do most of the talking. With Vanderzee. Follow my lead. We're still newlyweds and you're really into me, okay?"

Phoebe nodded again, not daring to speak.

"Last thing. You can't go out there with your underwear still on. You can grab a towel, wrap it around yourself in here, but . . ."

He was right. Keeping her wet underwear on after having shower sex with her new husband was beyond quirky and camera-shy and well into *Something weird is going on here*. "Will you at least turn around?"

"I'll close my eyes. Here, trade places with me," Ian said, and they maneuvered around so that he was under the water's stream, his hands on her waist to keep her steady. He flinched as the water hit his wound. "Ow. Actually, there *is* one more thing."

Phoebe turned back toward him, ready to help if he needed it.

"Don't look so serious when you go out there. Try to look like a woman who's orgasmed three or four times."

She laughed her surprise. "Three or *four* . . . ?"

"We've been in here for a really long time," Ian pointed out. "Don't explode the myth that I've worked so hard to build. No, no, no—what you're doing there is a little too incredulous. Think dreamier. Like you've just found God."

"This is me, being incredulous about what you're telling me," Phoebe said, pointing to her face. "Do I really need to audition my dreamy, just-had-three-orgasms-and-found-God smile for you?"

"Four," he said. "I'm pretty sure it was four. Because I'm that good. And yeah. I'd like to see it."

"Tough luck," she said. "Close your eyes." She didn't wait to see if he complied, she just turned her back on him, slipped out of her soaking underwear, then grabbed a towel from a rack on the wall, and wrapped it around herself as she stepped out of the tub.

The devil was in the details.

Yeah, that was why Ian had put the condom on as he stood there in the shower, letting the warm water cascade down on his head and his back. He'd put it on so that he'd have something to wrap in toilet paper and leave in the bathroom waste can. And since it had to be used . . .

Details.

He was also doing this so that he'd leave the shower sporting the equivalent of that dreamy look he'd recommended Phoebe wear upon exiting.

Just thinking about her made him smile, but then he started thinking about the way she'd melted against him when he'd kissed her. About that sound she'd made, low in her throat as he'd—

"Ian?"

He opened his eyes and froze, because shit, he was close, but she'd pushed open the bathroom door.

"Yeah?" he managed, and his voice was only marginally higher than normal. "I'm still, um, washing out this wound?"

"Oh," she said. "Okay. But I left my glasses in there."

She had. They were on the tile-covered sill of a translucent glass-brick window. There they sat, with the earpieces extended, drops of water dotting both the lenses and the thick, dark, quirky frames.

"I'll bring 'em out when I'm done," he told her.

"Okay," Phoebe said. "Thanks." But she didn't leave and close the door behind her, so he waited, just listening . . . "Are you sure you're . . . okay? You don't need help?"

She had no idea.

Or . . . maybe she did. She was, after all, a very smart woman.

"Nope," he said, which wasn't quite a lie. He would've loved her help. He desperately wanted her help. But he didn't need it. Not here or now. Realistically, not ever—an oddly depressing thought. "I got this."

"All right." The door finally closed with a click, and he was alone.

And acutely aware of it.

It was doubly weird, since being alone was something he should have cherished and enjoyed—particularly after all those months in prison. But right now it seemed to sit on him with a heaviness that had to be connected to his fatigue.

He was tired. Maybe that was it. Tiredness often felt a lot like sadness and longing and . . . Ian pushed it all away. Boxed it up. Proceeded with this step of this part of *this,* his current plan.

And the words to that famous old poem by Lord Tennyson popped into his head, paraphrased and altered. *His not to wonder why . . . His but to do, or die . . .*

He had to laugh. If Phoebe knew he was thinking

that, while he was doing *this,* she would think it was pretty funny, too.

Ian found himself looking at her glasses again. They were so uniquely Phoebe—it was almost as if she'd left a vital part of herself behind. It was almost as if she were watching him.

God, he wished she was watching him, wished she was touching him, stroking, kissing, and then, yes, opening herself to him, welcoming him, clinging to him. . . .

He could imagine her eyes behind those lenses, lit up with humor, her lips quirking upward, too. He could imagine her sighing and breathing his name as she moved with him. . . .

He came in a hot rush that left him breathing hard, weak-kneed, and a little light-headed. *Shit.*

He took off the condom and tossed it onto the far edge of the back of the tub—exactly as he would've done, if he'd used the damn thing with Phoebe. He washed himself, and finally turned off the water.

He pulled back the shower curtain, dried off, cleaned up—got everything organized that needed to go into the wastebasket. He wrapped his towel around his hips, then took Phoebe's glasses down from the windowsill and wiped them clean for her.

He opened the bathroom door to find her sitting on the edge of the bed, wearing a white bathrobe, her towel wrapped like a turban around her long hair.

She stood up, came toward him. "Thanks," she said as she took her glasses, put them on. "It was probably best that the evil monkey decor was out of focus or I might've had to huddle in the corner in a fetal position. Can you imagine trying to sleep in here?"

Evil monkeys? Ian looked around a room that was decorated in rich shades of green and gold. He saw too many palm trees, and then monkeys. Whoa. He had to laugh. There *were* a lot of them. "I think they're probably mischievous and not necessarily evil."

"One man's mischief is another man's evil," Phoebe told him solemnly. "I'm going to put the clothes that need washing into the laundry, then I'll help you bandage that."

"It's not bad," he said, craning his neck to attempt to see the back of his shoulder. It was still oozing, but just a little.

"Only because you moved the way you did, when you did," she came back. "If it had hit you straight on . . ."

Ian kissed her, because—cameras. It was, without a doubt what he would have done if she'd looked at him like that, with those eyes and that impossibly kissable mouth, had they really been married.

He meant to make it light. Patronizing. *There, there, dear.* Instead, he found himself lingering over her lips, kissing her again and again, longer, deeper, sweeter. He made himself stop and step back from her. "Don't go there," he said, although he wasn't quite sure exactly who he was talking to—Phoebe, or himself.

"Where I really want to go," she told him, "is home."

It was the perfect thing for her to say with Vanderzee or his minions listening in. She had the exact right amount of emotion trembling in her voice. It would fit their story, perfectly, when they declined their host's kind offer to let them spend the night so that they'd be extra safe from the men who'd tried to kill Ian. *Sorry, man, but my wife really wants to go home. . . .*

It was more than enough.

But then Phoebe stepped toward Ian, put her arms around his neck and her mouth up to his ear. She spoke in a stage whisper, but without the shower running, it was loud enough to be picked up by the listening mics—she knew that as well as he did: "So I can screw you sideways, without worrying about all these cameras and microphones."

And thus she'd also explained the underwear-into-the-shower detail.

Of course, at the same time, she'd managed to blow his mind—she was *that* convincing. As no doubt was his own disbelieving laughter, and the way he shook his head as he watched her go into the bathroom to gather up the clothing that needed to be washed.

It was right then, in that instant, that Ian knew the truth.

He was already screwed.

Completely and utterly and upside down *and* sideways.

He didn't just *want* her words to be reality rather than cover. He didn't just *wish* that she'd meant what she'd just said.

He needed for it to be so.

And the devil was, indeed, in that particular detail.

Yashi had hidden the damaged van back behind a shopping center in an upscale part of town. The stores and restaurants out here were all those of national chains, and the place had a flavorless, *Stepford Wives* vibe to it that Martell found unsettling.

They could've been in Ohio.

No, strike that. The rats by the Dumpster were Florida rats—big and ugly and defiant—and out for a stroll, just before dusk.

Deb slowly rolled van two past both Dumpsters and rats. "Where are you? I'm back behind the steak house, but . . ."

"Keep coming." Yashi's voice was being broadcast over their sound system. "I'm way in the back."

Martell saw the other van at the same moment that Deb did. It was closer to what looked like a long-abandoned construction site than the steak house's Dumpster.

"Wow," Deb said.

Martell worded it differently: "Holy *shit*."

While they'd been stuck in traffic, they'd heard Davio Dellarosa's hitmen arrive at Henrietta's.

They'd listened as Dunn and Phoebe survived the attack by escaping in the Dutchman's car. They'd sat, stone still, seething with frustration and impatience, impotent to help in any way as they'd witnessed, via audio, Yashi's efforts to keep the gunmen from following. They'd heard the sound of metal on metal as he pushed the shooters' car off the road, even as he narrated in his usual deadpan: "Hit 'em. Hit 'em again. They're out of commission. I'm out of here."

He'd gone on to report that the van he was driving was, in his words, "limping," and that he was going to go to ground, i.e., hide somewhere safe. He'd told Deb to give him a ring when they were moving again.

But they'd gotten back in touch to pass along info when Francine reported the news that Dunn and Phoebe had arrived safely at the Dutchman's rental house. And because Vanderzee had outfitted the place with high-tech surveillance, *and* because the FBI had already tapped into that plethora of cameras and microphones, Francie and da boise back at the safe house were monitoring them successfully.

So far, so good, Francine had reported. Apparently Mr. and Mrs. Dunn—an obvious cover—were getting along swimmingly well with the alleged kidnapper. So, high-fives all around for putting that part of Dunn's plan in motion.

Assuming, of course, that Dunn finally had a plan and wasn't still just freestyling it. *That* Martell would believe only when Dunn told him the details.

After the news sharing, Deb and Martell had gone back to residing in their pathetic level of traffic hell. Martell had tried to lighten Deb's dark mood with a little flirtation, but when she'd shut him down for the sixth or seventh time, he'd given up.

But things had finally started moving, at which point Deb called Yashi back and . . . here they now were.

Rolling up on a van that looked like it'd been in a head-on with an 18-wheeler.

"Airbags should've gone off," Martell mused. "With little bursts of confetti and horns and signs saying *Congratulations, you've totaled your vehicle.* He must've disabled them."

Deb nodded. "It would've been a bummer to paralyze a car carrying four gunmen, and then not be able to drive away."

Yashi stuck his head out of the cargo area of the near-demolished van. "Hey."

"Seriously?" Martell asked Deb. "We pull up to see this . . . this . . . deathtrap, and he says *Hey?*"

She backed up alongside of the other van and parked. "We need to move quickly. We have to transfer any equipment or parts that we can. Everything else gets sanitized." She jumped out, walked past Yashi, and got to work.

And okay. If they were sleeping together—and Martell was 99.999 percent certain that they *were* sleeping together—they deserved to win some kind of co-worker Emmy or Oscar for successfully hiding that fact.

In fact, Martell was the one who had to ask, "Dude. Are you really okay?"

"Seat belts," Yashi told him. "They work. Plus I was driving, so I knew when to hold on. Help me with this, will you?"

Martell climbed up into the back of what had been van one and helped move the main computer screen. While Yashi was waiting for them to break free of that traffic, he'd apparently used the time to unfasten all of the bolts that held the surveillance equipment in place.

Working together, the three of them quickly got everything moved into the other van—including a few chunks of the engine, the license plates, and even a little piece of the windshield that had held the tag info.

Through it all, Deb and Yashi exchanged maybe five sentences, total. Including, "Jules call?" "No, he call you?" "Nope."

That might've been their code for *"You really scared me back there." "Yeah, it was intense. I can't wait to have hot screaming beast-sex with you." "Me too, baby, me too."*

But probably not.

It was finally time to wipe that sucker down. Martell tried to help, but he was getting in the way, so he eventually just stood back and watched. It was obvious that Yashi and Deb had done this type of extensive fingerprint removal before. No point in slowing down their dance.

But he was curious. "Why not just burn it?" he asked.

"Bad for the environment," Yashi said as they climbed back into surviving van number two—which they probably should now call van one. Or maybe just *van*.

"Plus, fires don't always do what you want them to," Deb pointed out, as she started the engine, and began the journey back past the Dumpsters. Her annoyance was heavy in her voice. "A lot like assignments. And people."

"And the weather," Martell added. "And life in general. You know, I have a nephew. Ten years old. In chemo for cancer. It's not going well."

Deb looked at him, and her heart was in her eyes. "I didn't know," she said softly. "I'm so sorry."

And now he felt like a dick. "I didn't say that to make you feel less-than. Like, my bad shit's worse than yours, so whatever it is that you're feeling isn't valid or important. It's just that we're all just kind of here, spinning madly in this chaos. And I see you trying really hard to be puppetmaster, but there are just too many variables that you cannot control. I mean, Ian Dunn? Come on."

"Work the serenity prayer," Yashi said from the back. "Getting mad never helps."

"He never gets mad," Deb told Martell. "Makes me batshit crazy."

"That's not true," Yashi said. "I get mad. I just don't let it interfere."

"You want me to drive?" Martell asked Deb. "Because you definitely don't want to get pulled over for driving while batshit crazy."

She laughed at that. But then she surprised him. "Yeah," she said as she pulled to the side of the parking lot. "Why don't you drive? It's been a long few months and . . . I'd appreciate it."

CHAPTER EIGHTEEN

At first, Phoebe let Ian talk.

But then her silence started to feel weird and unnatural, so when he told a very convincing story of how they'd met, involving a dog, a storm, and a downed power line, she spoke up to add some colorful details.

"It was a Boston terrrier!"

"The hail was *the* biggest I've ever seen!"

"But then a rainbow appeared—right over Ian's head—like a sign from above!"

Somewhere in the telling, he'd pulled her down so she was sitting on his lap, which was much too comfortable.

And then, because she didn't want to look too stiff and unnatural sitting there, Phoebe started playing with Ian's hair, which was deliciously soft and thick. And the way he sighed and leaned into her touch was really quite perfect, too.

Ian went from how they'd met to where they'd married—Vegas.

"Oh, don't tell the story about the soft-boiled egg." She widened her eyes at him, actually starting to enjoy herself a little, because he was very, very good at this game.

He smiled back at her. "I wouldn't dare," he said. "I promise to leave out all of the unfortunate and embarrassing room-service incidents."

"The whipped cream fiasco, though, was pretty funny," she said, wiggling her eyebrows at him.

Ian laughed at that. "It was," he agreed, following the primary rule of improv. Agree with everything.

"We ordered berries and cream," Phoebe explained to Vanderzee, "and the room service waiter came up and wanted to do the whole thing with setting up the table in the room, but we were . . . in something of a hurry, so Ian just signed for it all, right at the door, and took the tray. It wasn't until much later, when we left for dinner, that we saw this neatly covered bowl of strawberries outside of our door. And we realized that neither of us noticed that there hadn't been any berries on our tray—we were a little, um, *involved* with the whipped cream. The poor man must've come back and knocked and knocked—"

"I didn't hear anyone knock," Ian contributed as he smiled up at her.

Laughter lines, sparkling eyes, beaming smile—if this man ever really looked at her like this, she herself would probably never hear another door knock again. Phoebe leaned down to kiss him, but then had to clear her throat before she could tell the Dutchman, “He finally must’ve just given up and left that bowl at the door.”

It didn’t take much to imagine being locked in a hotel room with Ian Dunn and a bowl of whipped cream—full hours spent licking it from various outrageously attractive body parts.

Ian, too, had to clear his throat.

“So you were married in Las Vegas,” the Dutchman said, clearly wanting more details, and when Ian looked at Phoebe, she knew he was a little lost.

This was not a man who’d spent much time—okay, *any* time—dreaming of his wedding day.

Phoebe, however, could picture the perfect scenario for a ruggedly handsome con artist and the woman who’d captured his heart.

“The wedding itself was a total surprise. Ian planned everything,” she told the Dutchman, who smiled back at her as he sipped his wine. He’d opened a very nice Merlot from a boutique winery in Napa, and had poured a glass for Phoebe, too. Ian was having club soda, which shouldn’t have been a surprise, and yet somehow still was. There was something slightly off in his reaction to her having a glass of wine, too, so she only took pretend sips. “He made all the reservations—hotel, restaurants, the most romantic wedding chapel. I mean, you tend to think Vegas weddings are tacky. Like, an Elvis impersonator officiates. *Ah now pronounce you husband and wife. Thank you. Thank you very much.*"

She realized with a flash of both hot and cold, even as she did her best Elvis and everyone laughed, that neither she nor Ian were wearing wedding rings, and her left hand suddenly felt suspiciously naked. Her lack of a ring was one of those details that the devil was in, as Ian had mentioned in the shower. Had he thought of that? He probably hadn't. And maybe the Dutchman wouldn't either, but maybe he would. Of course, some men just didn't wear a wedding ring. But why wouldn't a woman wear a ring—especially one who was as clearly in love with her husband as Phoebe was pretending to be?

She heard herself talking, still telling this story as her mind raced. "Or you dress up like, like . . . Sonny and Cher, or Spock and Uhura . . ." She was just babbling now as she glanced at Ian. "But, seriously, it was lovely. And of course, because I was not expecting it *at all,* when he said, *Hey, we're going to Vegas, pack light, but bring something nice,* I brought a bathing suit, a pair of shorts, and some sexy lingerie."

"Which was *very* nice," Ian said, right on cue, as if they'd rehearsed it.

"But not for what he had in mind," Phoebe finished the story. "He ended up buying me the most beautiful dress. And oh, my God! The ring? It's gorgeous—a *huge* diamond in a beautifully simple setting. It's in our safe deposit box. That's where we keep it when we're working undercover like this."

She heard herself say the words, and yes, it was an answer to the question *Why aren't you wearing a ring?* But it was not the only answer. It couldn't be. Still, she couldn't think of another reason, other than *I'm painting my house,* but even then, she would've put her ring back on after she'd washed her hands.

Still, maybe her words would go right past the Dutchman. Maybe he didn't hear. Maybe . . .

"You work with Ian?" the man asked, pouncing directly upon it. He looked from Phoebe to Ian and back. "That's . . . not really that much of a surprise, as I think of it."

Ian's smile had tightened. "Oh, it was for me," he said. "I was very, *very* surprised."

"It really is the perfect match," Phoebe said, even though she knew she'd already said too much. But maybe she could fix this—make the fact that they worked together somehow more believable. "There are things a woman can do that a man can't. That's just a fact. Places I can access, because I'm not perceived to be a threat." Inspiration struck. "Plus, Ian always says when I'm around, I bring him luck. I'm his good luck charm. Can't beat that, right?"

"Oh, yeah," Ian said, gazing up at her, now with murder in his eyes. "I am so lucky." He took her wineglass from her hand—yes, there was definitely something wrong with her drinking wine—and he set it on the table beside them, before hoisting her to her feet. “Why don’t you go check with the housekeeper and see if our laundry is dry?”

“Ooh, getting rid of me to talk business,” she said, narrowing her eyes at him while simultaneously trying to send him an apology.

“Please go,” Ian said.

So she went.

Up the stairs. Figuring she could check the clothes herself, rather than searching for one of the women who drifted like ghosts around the big house.

She could hear the murmur of Ian’s voice as she turned on the laundry room light and opened the still-spinning dryer.

There were, in fact, dozens of reasons why a woman wouldn’t wear her wedding ring, other than *I’m working some kind of illegal job, undercover, with my husband* or *I’m painting my house.* She could well have taken off her ring for safety’s sake before going into a dive like Henrietta’s. That would’ve explained it quite neatly. Or maybe the ring was so gargantuous that she only wore it out, or in the evenings. Maybe she was a potter, and worked all day throwing clay. Or she was a painter—but not the house kind. Or a dental hygienist, who had to wear latex gloves.

Except why, then, wouldn’t she at least wear a simple gold band? Unless she was pretending that she wasn’t married, while working some kind of con with her devious husband. . . .

Maybe Phoebe had said the right thing, after all.

Inside the dryer, their clothes were mostly done. Ian's jeans were still a little damp, so she left them in as she took her underwear back into the guest suite's bathroom to pull it on beneath her robe. Her jeans and T-shirt hadn't been bloody, and she'd hung them on the back of the door. She put them on, too—Ian really *had* bled far less than she'd thought in those first terrifying moments in the car.

God, she'd been scared.

At the time, Phoebe had been certain Ian simply hadn't realized how badly he'd been injured. She'd imagined him dying in her arms, while she was completely unable to help him.

It made her uneasy—knowing that Davio Dellarosa's men were actively looking for Ian.

And maybe, the next time they found him, whoever was aiming the rifle wouldn't just graze him.

Phoebe suddenly needed to sit and put her head between her legs—she was dizzy, just thinking about it.

But she couldn't show any sign of weakness. She'd just been downstairs talking and laughing and pretending she was Ian's wife.

Ian's wife wouldn't go all girly and light-headed.

Ian's wife, married in Vegas to the man of her dreams, was made of sterner stuff.

But Phoebe was not Ian's wife.

In fact, Phoebe had to pee rather badly.

She looked at the garishly colored frame where Ian had said the bathroom camera was hidden, and channeling Ian's wife one more time, she flipped it the bird and blew it a kiss.

Then she put the bathrobe up and over her head, covering herself in a terrycloth tent as she pulled down her jeans and panties and sat, completely hidden from the camera's view, on the commode.

"I'm going with you," Aaron announced.

Francine looked up from her replay of the FBI surveillance video, streaming in from the Dutchman's house, in which Ian told their suspect that he had a standing order for his second-in-command to pick him up between eight and midnight at a bowling alley in Miami Gardens, should he ever go missing like this. Since Vanderzee had access to a second embassy car, he was going to drive them over and drop them there. Although, this time, his bald-headed bodyguard was going to ride along.

Francine now looked at Shel and he met her eyes, before they both looked back at Aaron.

Francie spoke first. "Ian implied that *I* should pick them up—"

"He didn't say I *shouldn't* go," Aaron pointed out.

"How was he supposed to say that you shouldn't go," Shelly asked as he kept Rory quiet by rocking him back and forth, shifting from one foot to the other, "while he's having a conversation with the Dutchman? I think we can take it as a given that he doesn't want either one of us leaving this house while Davio's still actively hunting both you and Ian."

"Well, what about what *I* don't want?" Aaron asked. "I don't want Francine going anywhere near Ro-freaking-berto—and I'm a little taken aback by the fact that you actually seem to consider it an option."

"What?" Shel said. "You want me to pull an Ian and tell her what she can and cannot do? She's a big girl, and if she wants to do this—"

"No way does she want to do this," Aaron countered. "But do you honestly think she's going to admit that?"

"Hello, she's standing right here," Francine said, but neither looked up because they were both so intent on widening this terrible rift between them—a rift that she had, in part, helped to create.

They'd been monitoring the conversation between Ian and Georg Vanderzee, and Francine knew—from the skeletal description of the alleged "job" that Ian had described, that he was intending to take heavy advantage of the latest olive branch that Berto had extended to her.

I'm working a deal with Berto Dellarosa. I can't go into details until I clear it with him, but our buyer has just backed out. So we've got product that we need to move, fast. With your contacts, I'm certain you can connect us with someone who wants what we've got—at a deeply discounted price. And, of course, you'll collect a finder's fee.

After hearing that, Francine knew that after they got Ian safely back here, he was going to ask her to contact Berto and arrange a face-to-face—get him to be a major player in this con.

And Berto was going to say yes.

She wasn't quite sure how she felt about that, but right now she didn't have the time or energy to sit and explore her vast array of emotions. She was going to have to settle with *Seeing Berto again was going to suck.* But then again, nearly everything in her life sucked, so how could it be all that much worse?

"Look, I'm going to go pick up Eee," she told her brother and Aaron, taking Martell's car keys out of the bowl on the counter and going to the equipment closet to grab the bug sweeper. Knowing Ian, he wouldn't be willing to say more than *Hey, how's it going* until he and the lawyerette had been swept clean—and until he was certain they weren't being tailed. That should make for a really shitty, tension-filled ride. Whee. "I'm just going to the contact point—the bowling alley—and back. If you really want to come along, knock yourself out."

"Well, *I'm* not going to go, because *someone's* got to keep Rory safe," Sheldon said, heavy with the snit.

Aaron was already heading for the door to the garage, where Martell's car was parked, and he didn't look back.

"Please say good-bye to me," Shel called after him. "Aaron!"

But Aaron didn't stop and the door closed behind him.

"I'm so sorry," Francine told her brother. "For what it's worth, I'll keep him safe. I'll bring him back in one piece."

"Don't bother," Shelly said as he started to stomp away. But then he stopped and turned back, holding tightly to Rory. He kissed the top of the baby's head. "I don't mean that."

"I know," she said quietly.

"And you don't have to have any contact with Berto," he said. "Not if you don't want to. I wouldn't want to, and I'm related to him."

"I think I might," Francie said. "Want to. Is that weird?" She didn't wait for her half brother to answer. She just went out the door. "I'll call when we're on our way back. Lock this behind me."

"Tell Aaron I love him."

Francie looked back at her baby brother. "He doesn't deserve you."

"You're right, he doesn't. He doesn't deserve any of this crap," Shel said, then closed and locked the door behind her with a *click*.

CHAPTER NINETEEN

Ian was *bullshit*.

Bull.

Shit.

"You know the drill," he told Phoebe as Vanderzee and his thug dropped them in the shadows at the edge of the Bowl-a-Rama's parking lot and then drove away. "No talking—at all—until I give you the all-clear."

She nodded, and actually obeyed him for once. She was aware that she'd messed up. She just had no idea how badly.

After the Dutchman had pulled out of the bowling alley lot and back onto the main drag, a set of headlights went on from over where most of the cars were parked. And sure enough, Martell's POS pulled toward them. Francine was driving, with freaking Aaron riding shotgun.

Ian opened the back door and Phoebe scrambled quickly into the car, without his help, before he climbed in behind her.

Francine started driving away before he got the door closed. She glanced into the rearview mirror to briefly meet his eyes, and Ian shook his head—taking her silent what-the-fuck and raising it a million.

Aaron activated the sweeper, handing it back to Ian so he could do a more thorough check. It was highly unlikely that the Dutchman had tagged them with a ride-along surveillance device. Still, Ian was nothing if not cautious.

"Clean," he announced, and as soon as he said it he realized he had to clarify, adding, "but not yet clear," because, sure enough, Phoebe had drawn in a deep breath, in preparation for the dozens or maybe hundreds of sentences that he knew she was dying—*dying*—to say to him.

But they wouldn't be clear until they were

certain—without a doubt—that they weren't being followed by the Dutchman's men, or by anyone else for that matter.

Francine was well prepared, as usual. She'd used whatever wait time she'd had to map out a route, and she now took them swiftly and surely through a series of right and left turns, taking back roads that only longtime Miami residents used.

And she said it first. "We're clear."

Phoebe looked at Ian. She finally seemed to understand that the words had to come from him. So he said what he always said. "Take it one more time around the block."

They did.

He caught a flash of Francie's eyes in the mirror as she nodded to him again.

"We're clear, but don't speak," he told Phoebe. "Just sit there, silently, while I ask my brother what the *fuck* he's doing in this car."

"He's not mad at you," Phoebe leaned slightly forward to tell Aaron. "He's mad at me."

"Oh, no," Ian said. "I'm pretty fucking mad at *both* of you right now. And I'm pretty sure I'm capable of being mad at Francine simultaneously, too. So come on, France. Hit me. What's the latest thing *you've* done either to put yourself in deadly peril or to jeopardize the mission, or hell, why not make like Phoebe and do both at the same time!"

Phoebe drew in a very loud, very outraged breath. "I was saving the mission," she told him, and he knew that she believed what she was saying. This wasn't just an attempt to deflect the blame or to otherwise cover her ass. "I was protecting our cover story. Badly, okay, but I'm new at this. And all I could think was: *I've gotta give him a reason for why I'm not wearing a ring*. At least I caught the mistake—you didn't even realize it was a problem."

"It wasn't a problem," he said. "Some people don't wear rings. I don't. I've never worn a ring, and I never will."

"Well, my character—happy-flirty-sexy Ian's wife—*she* wears a ring," she told him. "And I'm sorry, but your character does, too."

"My *character?*" Ian repeated. "I don't have a *character*. I'm me. I'm always just *me*."

Phoebe spoke right over him. "A man who goes to all that trouble to surprise the woman he loves with a wedding in Vegas . . . ? Guy's gonna wear a ring. So where *is* yours, Ian? Oh, it's in the safe deposit box with mine. Of course. Detail handled. You're welcome."

"You're *welcome?*"

"The detail wasn't handled *perfectly,*" she continued. "I know that. And I'll fully take responsibility. But at least Vanderzee's not going to sit up in the middle of the night going, *She wasn't wearing a wedding ring; they're not really married—it was just a con, I better kill Ian the next time I see him!*"

Aaron spoke up from the front seat. "She's got a point."

"Sage words, douchebag," Ian shot back at his

brother. "What's your excuse for putting Francine in danger like this? You wanted to punish Shelly? Nice work."

Aaron definitely wanted to join this fight. "You put France in danger all the time."

"Not for bullshit reasons," Ian said.

"But don't you see?" Phoebe interjected. "When I did what I did, it was precisely *not* for bullshit reasons! It was to make sure that you're safe and—"

"When you did what you did," Ian repeated, turning back to her. "What did you do, Pheebs? Do you really understand the enormity of what you've done here? The massiveness of how *thoroughly* you screwed up?" Even as he asked that, Ian knew that she didn't know. She honestly thought that she'd saved the day more than once in the past few hours. And Jesus, maybe Aaron was right and she had. A ring was a detail that he hadn't considered, because until that afternoon he'd never had anyone, not even Francine, pretend to be his wife. Wedding rings. Shit. "Why don't you tell me? Start back at the beginning, when you got *out* of the fucking *van*."

Phoebe was undaunted. "I got out of the van, when, yes, I know, I promised that I wouldn't," she said. "But I had to. It was me or Yashi, so it had to be me. And then, okay. I said that we were married, which complicates things. . . ."

"Oh, keep going," he prompted her.

"And then, because of my lack of a ring, I said that I was working with you—"

"Oh, ding!" Ian said, ringing the same imaginary bell that she'd rung in the shower. "Dingity ding! Georg Vanderzee now believes that you work with me—because you told him that you work with me. With. Me. So now you're gonna *have to work with me*—and with this asshole psychopath that I didn't want you anywhere near—because not only did you tell him that you *work with me,* you told him that you're my lucky fucking charm—after I told you, I *told you,* that he was superstitious!"

"I know," Phoebe said. "That's why I said it. I thought it was perfect. I thought, otherwise he won't believe that someone like me could possibly be working with you—"

"Oh, he believes it," Ian shouted at her. "Now, he *really* believes it. So now you can't suddenly go visit your mother, or stay home to house-train our adorable new puppy, or whoops, hey, looks like I *did* get you unexpectedly pregnant so now you've *got* to stay home and sleep all day—*no!* We can't use those convenient excuses to keep you safely out of danger, *because if my fucking lucky charm's not along for this job, this asshole's gonna get spooked and bail!*"

Phoebe was wide-eyed behind those glasses, and for once she was speechless. Or so Ian thought. Wrongly.

Her silence was only temporary. And when she spoke, she actually had the audacity to sound testy. "Well, maybe if you'd been clear that he was *that* superstitious . . . I mean, dangerously, pathologically, *insanely* superstitious. You made it seem like a quirk. Like, he collects four-leaf clovers, and hangs horseshoes—"

"You weren't supposed to get anywhere near him!" Ian shouted. "You were supposed to stay in the van! God *damn* it! I was hours—*hours*—from moving you to a safer location, to a different safe house in a different fucking state! I wanted you *farther* away from me, not in the up-close-and-personal danger zone of this motherfucking, nut-crushing, bullshit, gun-to-the-head con job from goddamned hell! Jesus Christ! *You've been driving me goddamn crazy!*"

And . . . okay. *Now* Phoebe was speechless. Up front Francine and Aaron were barely breathing, too.

Probably because Ian was huffing and puffing and sucking all of the oxygen in the car into his angry lungs. In the sudden silence, he sounded like a raging bull.

Jesus, he had never lost it like this before. Never.

And yeah, he may have gone too far, said too much, been too brutal.

But *Christ.* If something happened to Phoebe, if he couldn't keep her safe . . . The mere thought of that made his stomach churn.

Phoebe had turned away from him and was looking out the window at a passing car, and the oncoming headlights made her eyes glisten with her unshed tears.

As Ian finally got his breathing back to near

normal, the silence in the car was deafening.

But then Phoebe surprised him by speaking. "I'd say that I'm sorry, but I'm not. Well, I'm sorry that I've been driving you crazy. That having me around was so . . . unpleasant and difficult for you. I didn't . . . realize that." She cleared her throat. "But I'm certainly not sorry that I got out of the van. And I'm not sorry that you're not dead because I *did* get out of the van. I'm just not." She turned and looked at him, and with her chin slightly raised, she was a picture of defiance. But she was unable to hold his surely still-crazed gaze for very long and soon turned away, again, to study the darkness on the other side of the car window.

From the front, Francine delicately cleared her throat. "Well, since *that's* handled," she said, "why don't you fill me in, in terms of what you want me to say to Berto."

Martell was ready to go.

He stood in the garage as the door went up. Ever since he was a kid, automatic garage doors made him think of *Star Trek* and the shuttlecraft landing bay. As he watched, Francine pulled his car inside, the door went back down—*The* Galileo *is secure, Captain*—and Ian, Phoebe, and Aaron disembarked.

Phoebe made a beeline past him for the door to the house, not even nodding hello as she pushed her way inside.

"You're going with Francine?" Ian asked Martell,

adding "Good," at his affirmative. The former SEAL looked exhausted. "I'll be riding along in the van, with Yashi and Deb."

"I still think Francie shouldn't do this," Aaron said with a boatload of challenge in his voice.

"And I think Berto's proven himself an ally," Ian countered.

But Aaron hadn't waited for his brother's response. He was already heading inside the house, tossing a "Whatever" over his shoulder.

"With all due respect," Martell said to Ian. "If the plan really is just for Francine and me to meet Berto Dellarosa, make sure he's not wearing any kind of wire, and then bring him back here, maybe it'd be best for you to let us do that. Stay behind and take one of those crazy Navy SEAL combat naps, instead of doing something that Yashi and Deb can do well enough on their lonesome."

"I'll be in the van," Dunn repeated. "After I get my phone and a weapon."

"Knock yourself out, Mr. Crazy Man," Martell muttered as he went to the car and got in next to Francine.

She was her usual bubbly self. She greeted him with, "So you're my new boyfriend."

"Ooh-kay."

She gave him an eye roll that was so massive it damn near created a sonic boom. "Not literally. But as far as Berto's concerned, you and I are soulmates."

That was a game that Martell understood. "Okay.

Are we . . . touchy-feely, PDA-creating soulmates, or . . . ?"

"Knock *yourself* out," she said. "Cop all the feels you want. The idea is to make him uncomfortable. And he'll definitely be uncomfortable that we're together. He's a racist prick."

"Ah," Martell said. Now he *really* understood. "Is he gonna, like, try to kill me?"

"If he does," Francine told him, "that'll be a clue that his intentions are corrupt."

"That's . . . good to know?"

"Don't worry, even if he tries, I'm not going to let him kill you," she informed him. "We're meeting him at the Pelican Deck. I told him to come unarmed, and to leave his wallet and phone at home while he's at it."

"You spoke to him?" Martell asked. "Already? On the phone?"

"Yup."

"That must've been strange," he said.

"Yup."

Francine looked past Martell, and he turned to see Ian approaching the car. He rolled down the window so that Ian could speak to them.

"You were right," the man said, and Martell realized he was talking to him. "I'm going to stay back—let Deb and Yashi take the van. Unless you need me there." Now he was talking to Francine.

Something subtle had changed in her eyes or on her face—she was very hard to read, but Martell picked that up. For a microsecond, she'd looked like a little girl—lost, alone, and trying to be brave. And he wanted to tell Ian, *Whoa, no, sorry, I was* not *right. Francine needs you. You totally have to come with, bro.*

But she'd already said, "I'll be fine."

Ian believed her. "If I'm asleep, wake me when you get back," he ordered.

She nodded, and he went back into the house.

And there Martell and Francine sat, in silence, for several long, weird moments, waiting for Yashi and Deb to get ready to roll.

"So I used to be a cop," Martell finally said. "Plainclothes detective. I went to night school, got my JD, passed the bar. Favorite color is blue. Favorite food is Cajun anything. Blacken it and I'm in heaven. Things a soulmate would know about me."

Francine looked at him with those flat blue eyes, made colorless in the dim light from the dashboard of his car. "Berto's biological father, Davio, legally adopted me and my older sister, Pauline, when he married our mother," she told him, starting the car as the garage door finally went up. "I don't know for a fact that he abused Pauline, but I'm pretty certain he did. She went away to boarding school, on account of her *acting out*"—she made air quotes—"when I was six. Before she left, she installed a deadbolt on my door and made me promise to lock it every night, without fail. Which I did. What I do know for certain is that Davio hated her, and he hated me, and he really hated Shel after he found out that he was gay. He tried to kill Aaron right after they got out of the Marines. He sent a hit man after him, and Aaron killed the son of a bitch in self-defense, and we all went into hiding, where we stayed until Pauline resurfaced about a year ago. She was pregnant—obviously—and addicted to heroin, and in order to save her baby, we had to take her to a hospital, which meant Davio would be able to find us. At which point, Ian stepped in to save the day by making that deal with Manny—until *you* fucked it all up by pulling him out of Northport. Things a soulmate would know about *me*."

She backed out of the garage and into the street, where she pulled away from the house. Behind them, the remaining surveillance van followed, several car lengths behind.

Martell cleared his throat. "No, um, favorite color? Favorite song . . . ?"

Francine glanced at him. "My favorite everything is Rory. My favorite everything else is Shelly and Aaron. FYI, don't call me *honey* or *baby,*" she warned him. "I hate terms of endearment. If you use one, Berto will know he's being conned. Oh, and since the plan is to bring him back to the safe house, you and I are going to share a room tonight and have really noisy sex."

Martell looked at her.

She gave him another sound-barrier-breaking eye roll. "Faux sex. Come on."

"Right," he said, inwardly thinking a solid mix of *too bad* and *thank God*. "You know, to be honest, that just seems kinda mean. Rubbing his face in it."

"Yup," she said.

They rode in silence for several miles, and Martell thought the conversation was over, but then she spoke.

"I thought *he* was my soulmate. Berto. He knew about Pauline. He knew the kind of man his father was. He knew and . . . Now I just want him to see me being happy."

"Fair enough," Martell said. To suggest that Berto would probably know it was all a bunch of make-believe crap seemed about as productive as pointing out that no man alive would look at Francine and think, *Look at the happy young woman, tra la*. She was a lot of things, but happy wasn't one of them. She was grimly determined, chronically intense, fierce and strong and unstoppable and driven in her quest to protect her family.

But she'd said as much herself—her favorite everything was her nephew, her brother, and his semi-annoying husband. Without the danger and the intrigue and the countless risks and peril she went through to protect them, without the constantly simmering anger that she wore like a badge, she'd have nothing. She'd *be* nothing.

Except perhaps deeply empty and clinically depressed.

Shelly looked up from his book as Aaron came into the master bedroom, but Aaron made it more than clear he was only there to say good night to Rory.

He didn't even say hello, he just walked past Shel, through the splendorous master bath to the huge walk-in closet on the other side, where they'd set up the crib that Yashi had provided. The room-sized closet was lined with wire shelves and hanger bars, but it also had a window and an air-conditioning vent, so since they had exactly four extra T-shirts and five pairs of socks and briefs between them, they'd designated it as the nursery.

Shelly leaned forward to watch as Aaron looked down at their peaceful son.

"It took a while to get him to sleep," Shel said quietly, so as not to wake the little boy. "Without you here. He wanted you to read to him. He was pretty annoyed with me." He forced himself to smile as Aaron came back out through the bathroom, leaving the door only open a few inches. "I told him that he and you could start a club."

Aaron went over to his go-bag and rummaged through, pulling out his iPod and his noise-canceling headphones. The headphones being, of course, the internationally known symbol for *Don't talk to me.*

But then Aaron took it one step further by not coming over to the other side of the bed—instead he headed for the door.

And wasn't *that* the supreme opposite of helpful and productive? Still, Shel managed to keep his voice even. "Please don't go," he said.

Aaron stopped. But he didn't turn around.

"Francine and Martell are going to bring Berto back here. I thought I'd do one of the mindfulness meditations before they arrive."

That was probably a very good idea. "You can do it in here."

"No I can't."

"Yes, you can," Sheldon countered as he felt his patience slipping. "God, Air—"

Aaron finally faced him. "Look, I'm sorry I can't just let this go. I'm not just *annoyed*. I'm angry and hurt and . . . You need to give me at least a *little* fucking time."

"What if we don't have it?" Shel asked. "Time. What if you go out there—and let's set aside all discussion about your sudden, childish need to take unnecessary risks—"

Aaron physically recoiled. "Oh, that's nice. Let's not talk about it, let's *set it aside*—instead you can just call me names."

Shel put his book down more forcefully than he needed to. "I'm trying my best here, but I'm angry, too! You walked out of here before, like you were ready to never come back. And guess what, Aaron? You might not've come back! My father has a freaking army out there, looking to kill you. At least have the courtesy, the *decency* to say good-bye to me the next time you unnecessarily risk your life, in case it *is* the last time I see you alive!"

For one awful second, Aaron looked like he was ready to tell Sheldon that he didn't give a crap if he never saw him again, that he already *had* said everything he'd ever wanted and needed to say—that it was all right there in that giant load of empty and broken silence he'd handed Shel before he'd stomped out of the house.

But then the fight seemed to go out of him, and he sat down in the overstuffed chair in the corner of the room as if his legs couldn't hold him up any longer. He shook his head, and didn't lift his eyes from the ornately tiled floor as he said, "You should've told me that you knew Ian was in prison."

"I'm so sorry that I didn't. That I couldn't."

Aaron looked up at that, and Shel knew he'd caught the difference—Aaron understood that Shelly hadn't said, *You're right, I should have, and I'm so sorry that I didn't.*

"I can't lie to you again," Shel told this man whom he loved more than life itself. "I just can't. I did what I had to do. I did what was right, yes, even knowing it would hurt you. And I can't pretend that I wouldn't do the exact same thing, if I had to do it over again—with the limited choices that I had."

"And so I'm, what? Childish for not understanding? Childish because I disagree with your priorities—which are good to know. Thanks. Up to this point, I was under the misguided impression that Rory and I were first in your life."

"You *are* first in my life," Shel said.

"Why, because you say so? Saying doesn't make it true." Aaron suddenly stood up. "I gotta not do this right now."

"I love you," Shel told him. "And Rory. I love you

both so much. I would do anything for you." His voice broke despite his efforts to keep it steady. "Please always remember that."

But Aaron didn't look at him again. "Right," he said, and closed the door behind him.

Over the past few nights, Phoebe had been sleeping in the room with the two sets of bunkbeds, trying to take up the least amount of space as possible. But now she grabbed her Yashi-procured clothes and pharmacy bag of toiletries, and claimed occupancy of the little room that had what she thought of as a grandma bed.

It was a standard double, and it was covered with a white cotton spread that in turn was covered with thousands of little white pom-poms, evenly spaced about an inch from one another, in a grandmother-pleasing design.

The bedside tables and dressers all had doilies, and there was a rocking chair in the corner, which helped with the whole elderly-interior-decorator effect.

The room didn't have an attached bath, so Phoebe used the common one on the second floor to brush her teeth and wash her face. She changed into the clothes that she'd been using to wear to bed—a pair of flannel pants and an extra-large T-shirt over which she wore her sweatshirt, necessary since the air-conditioning was perpetually set at arctic tundra.

Her white sweatshirt was clean but trashed—

permanently stained with Ian's blood. It somehow seemed appropriate to wear it, though. She stood there for several long moments, just looking at herself in the bathroom mirror with that big rusty stain in the center of her chest.

When Phoebe finally moved, she took a stack of tissues from the box on the sink counter because she suspected, even as exhausted as she was, that she was not going to fall asleep right away. And while she hated it when she broke down and cried over truly stupid things, she hated it even more when she broke down and cried but was unable to blow her nose afterward.

Phoebe carried the tissues and her clothes back into her new room, her fatigue making her move as if she were wading through molasses. The switch for the overhead light did nothing when she flipped it—tomorrow she would add *lightbulbs* to Yashi's current kitchen list—and since there was no other lamp in the room, she simply closed the door.

The blinds were not room-darkening, and a light outside shone in and made a striped pattern on the ceiling. It was just bright enough to be able to see to put her glasses on the bedside doily, to pull back the covers, to crawl into the bed and—

"Oh my *God!*"

Someone big and hulking was sitting in the rocking chair in the corner, and as she shouted, he jumped to his feet and launched himself on top of her.

It was Ian.

"What the—*oof!*" Phoebe gasped as he pushed her down onto the bed, covering her with the full weight of his body.

"Stay down, keep your head down!" he said, his voice low and urgent, and she knew in a flash that he'd fallen asleep in that uncomfortable chair, and that she'd startled him awake—or maybe not quite awake—with her shout of surprise.

"It's okay, we're okay, we're safe, Eee, we're safe," she told him, her mouth near his ear. Her right arm was pinned, but her left was free, and she put it around him. He was pressed so tightly against her, she could feel his heart hammering in his chest. She stroked the back of his head, her fingers in his hair.

Ian pulled back then, just slightly, just enough to look down into her eyes. "Oh, fuck," he breathed as awareness dawned. "I didn't hurt you, did I?"

Phoebe was already shaking her head. "No. I think you were trying to protect me and—"

Ian kissed her.

He just lowered his head and took full possession of her mouth in a move as surprising and breathtaking as his across-the-room leap had been.

More so.

He was already nestled between her legs, and he pushed himself against her, and in that moment of time-stopping total surprise, Phoebe felt herself responding. Her body arching up, her mouth opening wider, her fingers tightening in his ridiculously, deliciously soft hair . . .

Ah, God, she wanted this, wanted him so badly, except—

"Asshole!" She yanked her mouth free. *"Asshole!"* She squirmed, trying to get out from underneath him, smacking him with her free hand to push him away. "What is *wrong* with you?"

"Ow!" Ian managed to catch and pin her hand even as he rolled off of her and over to the other side of the bed.

She jerked herself free from his grasp as she sat up, grabbed her glasses and put them on so she could properly glare at him. "What the hell was *that?*"

"I don't know," he said, flopping onto his back. "I just wanted . . . Jesus, I don't know."

"Rubbing your randy man-parts against me and putting your tongue in my mouth is the *opposite* of sending me to *another fucking state,* as you so eloquently put it. Unless you were talking nirvana and not Georgia, and I'm *certain* that's *not* what you meant!"

He turned his head to look at her. "Randy man-parts?"

"I drive you crazy," Phoebe reminded him, but as the words left her mouth, she realized there was more than one definition of crazy. And everything he'd said, and how he'd said it—how completely and uncharacteristically angry he'd been at her—flashed through her head, along with the very clear memory of the way he'd looked at her and kissed her at the Dutchman's house.

The way he'd kissed her *all* those times, starting back on her balcony . . .

"Oh my God," Phoebe said. "I drive you *crazy*."

Ian was looking up at her in that dim light and his eyes held a mix of wry amusement, chagrin, and . . .

Heat.

"You do," he whispered. "I'm afraid I let that slip. And now I'm so fucked, aren't I?"

"Yeah, well, I kinda am, too," Phoebe whispered back, and then she slowly leaned over and kissed him.

She knew he saw it coming, his gaze slipping from her eyes to her mouth and back as she got closer, but he didn't move. He didn't run away. He didn't stop her.

He just closed his eyes, and she did, too, as she brushed her lips against his—his mouth was so soft. She both felt and heard him sigh—a sound that she echoed, even as she gently deepened their kiss.

His nose bumped her glasses and she reached up and took them off, folding them up and stashing them under the far pillow as she kissed him again and again, as she threw her leg across him, to straddle him.

It was a bold move on her part, but she wasn't thinking about that—she wasn't thinking at all. She just wanted better access to his delicious mouth. It wasn't until she was atop him that she realized she was essentially humping him—his randy man-parts fit against her equally randy woman-parts like a human jigsaw puzzle, but one where the pieces were frustratingly shrink-wrapped. He reached up, his hands on her butt to pull her even closer, as he licked the inside of her mouth with his tongue.

Her hair was coming loose from her ponytail holder—in her upset, she hadn't bothered pulling it into her nightly braid—and she stopped kissing him and sat back, just for a moment, just to gather and collect the wayward strands, to keep it out of their way. And to unzip and shrug out of her sweatshirt.

Ian was watching her, and his gaze kept slipping down to her mouth as if he couldn't wait for her to kiss him again. "I came in to apologize," he said. "I shouldn't have lost it like that—not in front of France and Aaron. That was . . . not okay."

"Were you really planning to send me away?" she asked him.

"Yeah," he said. The truth in his eyes and on his face was raw. Honest. "We shouldn't do this."

"This?" she asked, leaning forward to kiss him.

Ian sighed again, and even laughed a little, which made her smile, too.

"You want to kiss me, all night? That's okay," he said. "But maybe we should leave it at that."

"Who says you get to make the rules?" she asked, and for emphasis, she pulled her T-shirt up and over her head.

Until that moment, she hadn't come to any conclusions about what they were actually doing there, in that grandma bedroom, in the dark. Kissing—yes. Acknowledging a sexual attraction—absolutely. Making out—most definitely.

Making love?

As of right now, if she had anything to say about it, another resounding *yes*.

But as soon as she took off her shirt, as the cool air hit her bare breasts, she was instantly self-conscious, because Ian froze. He'd been moving, subtly and persistently beneath her, but now he went completely still.

But then he spoke. "We shouldn't do this," he said again as he looked up into her eyes. "But, God, I want to. I just . . ." He closed his eyes, exhaled hard. "Pheeb. I'm a bad bet. There's no future here. I know this feels big, this thing between us, right now it feels *huge*—and shh, don't make a dick joke, I'm serious. But it's not going to feel as big or special tomorrow, or, shit, even later tonight. I mean, yeah, I can make you feel good. I know it. And God knows you can make me . . . Jesus, you're so beautiful, I just—"

She stopped him there, again, with a kiss, and just like that, it was as if something snapped. Not just for her, but for Ian, too. She heard herself moan as he ran his hands up and then down her back, pushing his way past the loose waist band of her pajama pants.

And then, God, he was suddenly, frantically pushing them off her, and she fell back onto the bed to better help him, pulling her legs free, even as she grabbed his shirt and helped him pull it over his head as he unfastened his jeans, all the while muttering, "Shit, shit, shit, shit . . ."

"*That's* not getting annoying," Phoebe said as she helped him take off his boots and socks. "I heard what you said, by the way, so I have exactly zero expectations. You don't have to worry."

She grabbed the legs of his jeans and pulled as he covered himself with a condom that he'd somehow conjured out of thin air. But then she saw that it had the same red wrapper as the one he'd brought into the shower at the Dutchman's. He must've slipped at least one extra into his pocket as he was dressing.

"I don't secretly want you to marry me," she continued, as his jeans hit the floor, "or even be my boyfriend—okay, maybe boyfriend—but *temporary* boyfriend."

Ian reached down and caught her arm and hauled her back up toward him, and kissed her. The shock of all that skin against skin made her gasp. He was as lovely to touch as she'd imagined, and she wanted to take her time, maybe lick him all over, slowly and thoroughly, but she'd just said the word *boyfriend,* and she didn't want him to start muttering *shit* again, so she lifted her head to explain.

"But that's only because I can imagine wanting to do this more than once," she told him, as he shifted her so that she was once again straddling him. "Five times, maybe. Okay, realistically, more like fifteen . . ."

He was touching her breasts, which was lovely—and even more lovely when he sat up to kiss and to lick and suckle. It felt unbelievably good, but she wanted . . .

What she wanted was right there, between them, pressed against her stomach—so big and accessible and user-friendly—neatly covered and ready to go. As ready as she was.

So she grabbed hold of him to guide her as she lifted herself up and pushed herself down so that he filled her—completely, utterly, absolutely. And then she pushed his shoulders down, back against the bed, so that he filled her even more.

"Gah," he said, which would've made her laugh if she weren't trying so desperately hard not to make too much noise.

Ian did laugh up at her as she moved against him, as she rode him with long, slow, delicious strokes, as she gazed down at his face while he looked from her eyes to the sway of her body and breasts and then back, as he smiled and she let herself thoroughly love the heat in his eyes, without any hesitation.

"You're killing me," he said. "Come here and kiss me."

She leaned down to do just that, and he put his arms around her and rolled them over, so that he now was on top.

Phoebe laughed up at him. "You know, you could've just said, *I don't like it like that.*"

"Problem was," Ian said, kissing her mouth, her cheeks, her nose, her throat, but otherwise not moving at all, "I liked it a little too much. I didn't want to end the party before it started."

"How do you know that I wasn't right there, on

the verge, too?" she asked. "You know, if you'd *asked*—"

"Why does it not surprise me that you talk during sex?" Finally, he started moving, even more slowly and more deliciously than when she'd had control.

"Is that bad?" she asked, but then answered her own question. "How could that be bad? Don't you want me to tell you things like—that! That! Oh, God, do that again. Do . . . that . . ."

"Okay, see, I *want* to keep doing that, but if I do . . . Ah, shit . . ."

"Again, with the *shit*. How could *this* deserve a *shit?*" Phoebe asked, but this time he didn't stop with the almost unbearably exquisite, mind-blowingly deep thrusts, countered with almost, but not quite, full withdrawals. "Oh, keep doing that." She could hear him breathing, and the sound was almost as ragged as her own. "That. *That!* Yes!"

Ian laughed but then said, "Ah, sweet Jesus, please be close—"

"I'm sorry, but how could you not know that I'm . . ." Phoebe opened her eyes to look up at him, and found herself gazing directly into his incredible blue eyes as he smiled at her and . . . "Oh, *God, yes!*"

Ian came, too. She saw it and felt it and heard it as he drove himself into her, deep and then even deeper as she clung to him and damn near shook apart.

Phoebe heard herself laughing, but she also wanted to cry because it was so overwhelming. Sex shouldn't be that perfect, especially not the first time with a new partner, and yet . . .

He collapsed on her, and again, she could feel his heart pounding.

"Ah, Jesus," he breathed. "That was . . . fucking amazing."

It was. He was right, but all she could manage was a faint "Yeah." And a "Wow."

She felt him laugh. He was still inside of her—he hadn't yet shifted to pull himself out. He seemed content where he was—more than content, actually, as he propped himself up on one elbow to look down at her, to smile into her eyes.

"Ah, Phoebe," Ian whispered. He kissed her then. Slowly, gently, sweetly.

She would've been okay. She'd convinced herself that she *was* okay—right up to that point. Their lovemaking was what he'd said—and what she'd agreed it would be. A temporary connection. A fleeting pleasure. No strings attached. Two ships that passed in the night.

Simple.

Until he breathed her name and kissed her like that.

And now she was thinking the exact same thing that he'd said as she'd hurriedly helped him out of his clothes.

Shit, shit, shit, *shit.*

CHAPTER TWENTY

Even crappy pizza tasted great, if you were hungry enough. Or if you hadn't eaten any pizza in nearly a year.

Ian knew this to be a fact.

The human brain was a funny thing, and it distorted and warped perceptions all the time. He knew *that,* too.

And yet he couldn't shake the sense that, with Phoebe, he'd just had the absolute best sex of his entire life, despite the fact that from beginning to end the time span spent actually engaging in the act was embarrassingly short.

Although it was possible that the foreplay had started back when she'd found him in Henrietta's. And wouldn't *that* be hard to replicate in the future? An attack by a team of professional thugs, a car chase, the heightened sense of danger that came from running a con against a dangerous mark . . . ? If Ian ever wanted to make love to her again—and he already knew that he did—a candlelight dinner might not be enough.

Because she'd liked it. Playing the game.

And despite her mistakes—for which he could take part of the blame for his failure to communicate—Phoebe had been breathtakingly great at it. Including this last bit, where she'd completely rocked his world.

She was still breathless and clinging to him and looking up at him with those bottomless-pit eyes. He waited, giving her plenty of eye contact, but she didn't say a word, so he finally pulled out and away from her softness and heat. He'd been half-expecting a lecture on the proper use of condoms—immediate withdrawal was mandatory, don't let that thing leak, et cetera. But she stayed uncharacteristically quiet even as he sat on the edge of the bed and cleaned himself up—she'd conveniently brought a stack of tissues into the room with her.

As if she'd somehow known.

No, she couldn't have known. Her surprise had been genuine.

Shit. He himself hadn't known. He'd come into the room to apologize for his outburst and try to explain that he'd wanted to send her away because his worry for her safety was taking up too much space in his head. He'd have tactfully left out the part where another huge amount of his mental real estate was being used by his near-constant desire to do what they'd just done.

And yeah. Part of him must've known. He hadn't snagged that condom from the Dutchman's guest bathroom in case of an emergency need to make balloon animals.

Phoebe finally spoke. "When do you expect Francine to get back with Berto?"

Ian turned to see that she'd pulled the covers up to her chin, which was a crying shame.

"I don't know," he said as he put his trash into a

white container with sides reminiscent of a flower's petals. "Soon. She'll text when they're on their way."

"And you're sure he's not dangerous?"

"Oh, Berto's dangerous." Ian found his phone in the pocket of his jeans as he pulled them back on. There was nothing from Francie yet. "I just don't think he's dangerous to us."

"Even though his father wants to kill your brother and what, send Sheldon to conversion therapy?"

"Probably, yeah. Or worse. But Berto's different from his father. That whole *like father, like son* myth is the biggest crock of bullshit." He heard his voice getting louder and he laughed at himself as he sat down again on the end of the bed. "Sorry. Apparently that's still a hot button issue for me—being myself the progeny of a miscreant scumbag."

"Although it really must help with the ongoing development of the bad-guy myth," she pointed out.

He looked over at her, intentionally choosing to misunderstand. "For Berto? I'm sure it does."

"And for you," she said, but he spoke over her and pretended not to hear. No way were they going there.

"I've been hearing stories about Berto for years," Ian told her. "What he did. Who he was, and who he became. How he changed—this sudden Jekyll-and-Hyde type transformation, like he finally showed his true shit-ugly colors. Like he'd been hiding himself from Francine and Shelly, the whole time they were kids—and I just don't buy it. Francie's condemnation of him was the harshest, and again, I think she got it at least partly wrong. Just to be clear, I don't blame her at all for thinking what she thinks—feeling what she feels. What that douche-bag did to her was awful. Unforgivable, even. But I think he was just a stupid kid who fucked up—in a very huge way that he couldn't take back. Some mistakes can't be fixed."

Phoebe sat up at that, but kept the covers still demurely tucked beneath her arms as she found her glasses and put them on. Her hair had mostly come loose from its ponytail, and she let the rest of it down so that it tumbled around her shoulders.

As Ian looked at her, he felt something in his chest slip and shift. The pressure came with a blood-tingling rush of triumph and satisfaction, pride and a deeply burning sense of possessiveness. His inner caveman warrior had been awakened and wanted to rush around the room, peeing into the corners, marking it—and her—as his own, while shouting *Mine!* and randomly smashing things for emphasis.

But he knew that what he was feeling was the equivalent of emotional and hormonal indigestion. He hadn't done this in a long time. And he particularly hadn't done it with a woman he liked as much as this one. In fact, he'd never had sex with anyone that he genuinely liked as much as he liked Phoebe.

And God damn, but he wanted to crawl back into

that bed with her and dive down beneath the covers and—

"Are you allowed to tell me?" she asked him as if she were repeating herself. "What exactly Berto did?"

Ian cleared his throat. "Yeah," he said. "Sorry. I was just, um, making a mental to-do list." He cleared his throat again. "Talking about Berto should probably be on there, too, but . . . If we're going to do this thing right, you really need to know everything that I know about the Dutchman and . . . That's gonna suck. I've gotta share that story with the rest of the team, too, so I want to tell it only once, if that's okay."

"Of course," she murmured.

"Meanwhile, part of my brain is still trying to figure how to do this job without you. And if I can't do *that,* how do I keep you safe? Or turn you into a field operative with a Navy SEAL skill level, with only twelve hours of training?"

She smiled. "I think you can stop expending any mental energy on that one."

"Yeah, I know." He ran his hands through his hair. "I gotta go talk to Aaron, too. He's a freaking mess. I need to apologize, try to fix things."

"Maybe you should close your eyes for a little while," Phoebe said. "But maybe not here—not that I don't want you to stay. I do. But . . . I'm afraid I'll distract you."

Jesus. Please stop being perfect.

"When we're with the Dutchman," Ian told her,

"when we're running the con, you are so fucking in love with me that you don't leave my side. Do you understand?"

Phoebe nodded, her face solemn, her eyes serious. "I can play it that way."

"He's gonna want you," Ian told her. "Because he thinks you're mine, and he's a twisted son of a bitch. So he's gonna try to get you alone. That is *not* gonna happen."

She nodded again. "So I *was* right. About the whole con-artist thing." At his blank look, she added, "You just said *when we're running the con.*"

Ah. "Yeah, well, you're not entirely right," Ian said as he found his shirt and yanked it over his head. "My team and I can get past nearly any security system if we need to. Or at least we could a year ago, when we were up and running. But why go to the trouble, if I can talk my way inside?"

"Still," she said.

Ian gave it to her. "Yes. You were right."

She didn't whoop, hands above her head as she ran a victory lap around the room. She didn't say, *I knew it!,* or even so much as smile.

She simply sat there as she nodded again, graciously accepting her win like a mature adult. "Go talk to your brother," she said. "And then try to get some sleep."

Ian kissed her—how could he not?

He must've been looking at her oddly then, because she laughed a little and asked him, "What?"

So he told her. "I wouldn't've been able to not gloat."

"I bet you'd refrain if you knew *I* was facing an ass-kicking from *my* brother. If I had one. Go," Phoebe said. "Just do it. Get it over with."

So Ian grabbed his socks and boots and went, looking back at her one last time before quietly closing the door behind him.

It was only then, when he was out in the hall, that he heard her say, "Yes! I *knew* I was right."

And Ian had to smile, because *he* knew that she'd said it for him to overhear.

Berto was in the Pelican Deck, sitting at the same table, drinking what looked like the same brand of beer, and quite possibly wearing the same clothes he'd had on last time Martell had been in here.

Francine hesitated when she spotted him, and Martell briefly touched her on the arm. "If you want to wait in the car, I can make first contact," he murmured, but she shook her head and kept going.

Possibly because Berto had already turned to see her coming.

Martell was the only one in the bar who seemed to notice their time-slipping, thunderclap-worthy first moment of eye contact after a decade of separation. For a moment, as Berto gazed at Francine, he lost his dead-eye look. He actually lifted his heavy lids and tightened the slack and underused muscles in his usually expressionless face.

The man still loved her—of that Martell had absolutely no doubt.

But oh, the humanity vanished as Berto's eyes flickered in recognition as he looked from Francine to Martell and back.

"Silly me. I should've known your boy here was a member of Team Dunn," he said, and then he started to sing that old *Sesame Street* song. "One of these things is not like the others . . ."

Martell glanced at Francine. "Wow, you were right about that whole racist dickhead thing. So much for my hopes and dreams of being besties with your ex."

"He's not Team Dunn," she told Berto flatly. "He's Team Francine."

As Berto glanced at him again, Martell presented him with his best Mona Lisa smile—assuming Mona Lisa's knowing expression was the result of happy memories of being hoovered by a beautiful hot blonde.

"Don't call him *boy* again," Francie added.

"Lotta *don'ts*," Berto said. "Don't come carrying, don't bring ID. Especially considering Dunn's the one wants *my* help."

"Let's cut the bullshit," Martell said. "We all know you're the one who's been reaching out to Francine, trying to earn, what? Redemption? You want this more than we do—that's a fact. So let's take a walk out into the back parking lot, where we'll make sure you followed all those *don'ts*. 'Kay?"

Berto picked up his glass of beer. Finished it. Set it back down. Climbed down off of his stool. "Lead on."

"No fast moves," Francine warned. "Hands where I can see them at all times." She nodded at Martell who led the way to the back door.

He held it open for Berto and then Francine. It was dark out there, but he could see the white van, with Yashi and Deb inside, parked out on the street. They'd surveilled this place thoroughly upon arrival—taking nearly two hours to conclude that Berto had, indeed, come here alone.

Francine had left his car at the shadowy edge of the half-filled parking lot, and Martell now led the way there as she drew her weapon, keeping it trained on Berto. She kept the handgun in close to her body, though, so that it wouldn't catch the light or otherwise draw attention.

She'd already given Martell back his keys after making sure that his trunk was completely clear. He unlocked and opened it now as Berto sighed heavily.

"Are you fucking kidding me?" he asked.

"Nope." Francine smiled tightly at him. "It was either this or bag over the head, and darn it, I couldn't find any bags."

Another big sigh. "Great." He turned to climb in, but she stopped him.

"Yeah, not so fast," she said. "Take your clothes off, first."

The heavy eyelids did their vanishing thing again,

and Berto glanced very briefly at Martell before he refocused on Francine.

"Yeah, that's not what this is about," Martell interjected. "*This* is neither one of us wanting to get close enough to do a pat-down. So strip it to your briefs, Holmes, and if you're not wearing briefs, sorry, the boxers gotta go, too."

"Jesus effin' Christ." Berto shrugged out of his jacket and held it out as if he were the lord of Downton Abbey and Martell were his valet. Martell took it—and dropped it on the driveway. Berto was not happy. "Hey. That's an expensive sports coat."

"And I'm sure some grateful, homeless drunk will enjoy it very much before he pukes down the front of it," Martell told him.

Shaking his head, Berto didn't bother trying to hand him his shirt. He dropped it onto his jacket with a dark look in Martell's direction. His shoes followed, along with his socks.

The man could've stood to say *no* five or six dozen of the times in the recent past that he'd been asked if he wanted to super-size his fries. He had maybe thirty extra pounds on him and was understandably self-conscious about it. He was not at all happy about having to take off his T-shirt or his pants. His pants went first—he was wearing silk boxers—and like a lot of too-heavy men, he had strong, muscular legs. No shame there.

"Look, you can see I'm not carrying or concealing anything," Berto said, running his hands across his chest and then down the front of his shorts.

"Sorry, bro," Martell said, "but the mere fact that you want to keep it on means you gotta take it off."

"No, it's okay," Francine suddenly said, handing her weapon over to Martell. "I'll . . . just . . . Turn around. Assume the position."

Berto turned and gave her the classic perp stance, bracing his hands against the side of the car as he spread his legs.

Watching Francine pat him down was a little weird. But Martell held that weapon at ready as she ran her hands across the man's chest, under his man-boobs and his arms, and then down and around the elastic waistband of his shorts, and . . . ooohkay. She gave him a swift but thorough package and butt-crack check—all the while gritting her teeth so hard that Martell could almost hear them breaking.

"Hands behind your back," she ordered Berto, who glanced back at her as he complied.

She had a pair of handcuffs that she pulled out of her jeans pocket, and she clipped them around his wrists in a way that was pure *Top Cops*. Or maybe Aardvark the Bounty Hunter or whatever mammal was currently bounty hunting on reality TV. She'd clearly done it before.

"Get in," she said, and Berto rolled himself into the trunk with one last baleful glance at Martell.

Francine didn't check to make sure all of his fingers and toes were accounted for. She just slammed the trunk closed and took back her handgun from Martell, stashing it wherever she usually kept it. "I still want to sweep him, but I'm pretty sure he's clear," she said briskly as Martell gathered up the man's clothes. Despite what he'd said about the homeless man, that jacket was nice and those Italian leather shoes were expensive. And from what little he knew of Ian Dunn's plan, Berto was going to have to look like Berto. Provided the clothes weren't bugged, they would give it all back. "We can do it on the road. Let's go."

She climbed into the car, but she got into the passenger seat, which was weird, but okay. He'd drive. Maybe like Deb, she was tired. That entire encounter couldn't've been easy.

As Martell slid behind the wheel, she said, still in that clear, crisp voice: "Unless you want to fuck me first, here in the parking lot."

Martell glanced over his shoulder, into the back, where the seat cushions were the only thing separating them from the trunk. No doubt old Berto could hear every word they spoke. Particularly when she enunciated that clearly.

"As tempting as that sounds," he said. "Dunn's waiting on us."

But when Martell looked back at Francie, he saw that she'd covered her face with hands that were shaking.

Crap. "But if you insist," he said. He started the car with a roar and kept his foot slightly on the gas so that his POS was even noisier than normal. Just to be safe, he turned on the radio, too. It was set to a local AM station, and happy, joyful salsa music pounded out of the ancient speakers.

But that was good. It was probably deafening in the back. And those lyrics sung in Spanish would be perceived as an extra *fuck you* to old Berto. That felt pretty right, too.

"I'm sorry," Francie whispered as her eyes brimmed with tears.

"For what? Being human? It happens to the best of us," Martell whispered back as he put his arms around her, held her close, and just let her cry.

Aaron didn't want to talk to anyone.

But when Ian found him, sitting in the living room with the lights off, headphones on, he sat down, too.

So Aaron embraced the military acronym KISS—*keep it simple, stupid*—and used language that he knew his brother would understand: "Leave me the fuck alone."

There had been times, in the past, when Aaron had said that without meaning it, but this was not one of them.

Ian, being Ian, pushed. "I know you're mad at me, but I'm not sorry for doing everything in my power to make sure that you, and Shel, and Rory are safe."

Aaron took off his headphones then and looked at him. "You don't give a damn about Shel and Rory. You do whatever the fuck you think you need to do to take care of *me*. Shel and Rory are just appendages that you now have to deal with. Attachments that I drag around—that's how you think of them, that's how you treat them. You have no idea what it means to be in a relationship, to be part of a real family—so you have no idea of what's best for me. In fact, you still think of me as *your* appendage—a responsibility *you're* forced to drag around."

"That's not true—" Ian started.

"The fuck it is," Aaron shot back at him. "Look at you, sitting there. What, you came to talk to me, to counsel me, impart your *wisdom*—to tell me that life's too short not to accept Shel's apology? What the fuck do you know about the kind of relationship I have with my husband? It's a partnership, douchebag—and you've never, not once in your life, had that. It's not king and subject, or father-figure and child, or owner and encumbrance, or however you think of it. It's fifty-fifty—no, it's a-hundred-a-hundred, because you give everything, and you get everything in return. And you don't keep the kind of secrets that you made Sheldon keep from me. You fucking *don't*."

"I'm sorry," Ian whispered. "The choices that I had—"

"The choices *you* had," Aaron cut him off. "Listen to you. *I* not *we*. *We* had choices, Eee, last year, when Francine found her sister. *We* made the choice to put Pauline into a hospital, even though we knew that her medical records would lead Davio back to me. *We* chose to try to save her life—to save Rory's life, even though we knew that Davio was going to come after me again. *Me*. I'm the one he wants to end. But you shut me out. You took control. You decided that you knew best, so you made the rest of the choices all by yourself, because you knew damn well that I wouldn't have let you go to fucking *prison*—"

"There was no time—"

"Is that what you tell yourself? You know what I think?" Aaron told his brother. "I think you liked being there, in prison—running that kind of a long con. And I gotta assume that's what you were doing there, that you weren't really only working for Manny—that your plan was to bring the Dellarosas down from the inside out, because you're Ian fucking Dunn, and that's what you do."

Ian didn't say anything, which was the closest Aaron was going to get to an affirmative.

"*And* I think that *you* think being in prison is also a fitting punishment for all of your various sins," Aaron continued. "It's a grand, beautiful, selfless sacrifice, so win/win, right? Plus, you're safe when you're in there—same way you're safe when you're on a mission—because you're not yourself. It's not real, even if you let people get close. Kinda like what you're doing right now with Phoebe."

Ian looked up at that, and Aaron laughed.

"Yeah, you really think I didn't know?" Aaron asked. "And the stupid thing is that you have no clue, no idea just how much you honestly care about this woman. Or maybe you do, and that terrifies you. So you're just going to run your same old pattern with her. Use her, then push her away. You fucking coward."

Ian finally spoke. "You done?"

"Yeah, I'm done," Aaron said, putting his headphones back on as he got up and walked out of the room. "Now leave me the fuck alone."

After the scathing dressing-down from Aaron, Ian went back into the kitchen. Or at least that's where he'd intended to go. Grab some quick protein from the cold cut drawer to keep his stomach from rumbling as he closed his eyes and shut down his brain for a few minutes, because Jesus, after that verbal battering, he needed it.

Instead he blinked and found himself upstairs, standing outside of Phoebe's bedroom door. Knocking. Softly. In case she was asleep.

"It's unlocked," he heard her say, so he opened it. Peered in.

She'd sat up and was peering back at him.

"Everything okay?" she asked, her voice rich and warm with her concern. He had a flash of a very vivid, very recent memory, of kissing her as she wrapped herself around him, her body soft and warm and welcoming.

No, it's not okay, actually, because my brother just ground my face in a truth that I've known for years—that I'm irreparably broken. Everything I do, I do for him, in part because I feel as if I let him down—badly—back when he was a kid, and in part because, with his love for Shel and Rory, he has something beautiful and precious that I know I'll never be able to have—because I'm irreparably broken.

“Yeah,” Ian said. “Still no word from Francie. Shel’s gone to bed, and Aaron’s still really angry and upset . . . and I’m . . .”

A fucking coward.

“Come in,” she said.

So he did, leaning against the door to close it behind him.

“This isn’t a booty call,” he told her, and as soon as the words left his lips, he realized how stupid he sounded.

Phoebe laughed. “I’d be impressed if it was. You haven’t been gone all that long.”

He moved closer, needing contact. “Do you mind if I . . . ?”

She answered by shifting over and flipping back the edge of the covers.

He’d carried his socks and boots with him when he’d gone looking for Aaron, but he hadn’t put them on—which made taking off his jeans that much easier. He now shucked off his T-shirt, too and slid back under the covers.

And there Phoebe was—warm and smooth and soft—exactly what he wanted and needed. He wrapped his arms around her and pulled her against him so that they were spooning, their legs entwined. He had one hand against the fullness of her stomach, the other filled with as much as he could hold of her generous breasts. Her ass was tight against him, and she glanced over her shoulder and up into his face, her eyes filled with amusement.

“How youthful of you,” she said.

"It's part of that whole *crazy* thing," he admitted. "I've had a major hard-on for you since, well, you want me to be honest?"

That got the rise out of her that he expected. "No, because women love it when men lie."

Ian kissed her neck, not only because he wanted to, but because it was the next step in this dance they were engaged in—a dance that, according to his brother, was going to end with him pushing her away. But, God, right now he wanted her closer—as close as humanly possible. She was a perfect mix of solid and soft, and she smelled unbelievably good. "Since I walked into the prison interview room and caught you checking me out. That was pretty hot, you know."

"But then you got to know me and grew to want me for my brilliant mind and snappy sense of humor," she said. "Which was even hotter."

She was smiling, and Ian knew that she was expecting a lighthearted, flirty response—for him to say, *Oh, much,* much *hotter,* and then kiss her as he ran his hands across the silk of her skin.

It was what he should've done, but Aaron's words were still bouncing around in his head, so he went with the truth instead. "I could've resisted you, if you were just a beautiful woman with, you know, a killer body. Not that I don't appreciate it, but I've always been able to walk away from that. Apparently, though, I have no defenses against the way you make me feel."

Phoebe didn't seem to know what to do with his

honesty. She was disarmed to the point of silence, which was good because he'd freaked himself out with that one, too. Feel? *Feel?* What the fuck? And really, what was the point? Aaron was right. Ian knew exactly how this was going to end.

But Phoebe turned toward him and kissed him, thoroughly, and as Ian kissed her back, he tried to drown out his brother's accusations. He thought about Berto. About Francine, who was talking to Berto probably right now. About Phoebe having both saved his life and fucked up his plan by telling the Dutchman that they were married. Married, Jesus. *You fucking coward.* About where to charter a luxury speedboat—a big one, with room for cargo—for the least amount of cash. About whether the Dutchman would take the bait and call him in the morning. About the best way for Ian to guarantee Phoebe's safety when he did—

Phoebe stopped kissing him. "I can hear you thinking."

Ian sighed and forced a smile. "Yeah. Sorry."

Phoebe shifted over, further onto her side so that she could see him better. "You want to talk?"

Ian laughed.

She laughed, too, before she kissed him again, but sadly, then, she stopped kissing him.

"Okay," she said. "I get that you have way too much testosterone to *want* to talk, but we could either both lie here, awake, or . . ." She pushed his hair back from his face, running her fingers through it. "Tell me about Berto. And Francine? What happened between them? I mean, don't feel you *have* to share anything with me that isn't important, but . . ."

"No," Ian said again. "You should know. You're involved with this mission now, like it or not, and he's going to be a part of it—so the whole messed-up dynamic's going to be in your face for the duration." He took a deep breath. "Let's see if I can't explain this in as few words as possible. Ready?"

"I am," she said, now playing with the hair on his chest, which felt unbelievably good.

He gave her what he thought of as the *Dragnet* version. *Just the facts, ma'am.*

Aaron and Shel's secret relationship, started in high school.

The sex tape that threatened to out them both.

Francine's sacrifice.

Berto's rage and jealousy as he accepted, without question, her obvious lie—that she was the one in that tape, having sex with Aaron.

"Berto took a loaded weapon with him," Ian told Phoebe, "when he went to confront Aaron—who ended up locked in the trunk of Berto's car, outside of one of the Dellarosa family warehouses. He's not really sure what happened. He was pretty certain that Berto brought him there to kill him, but before he escaped from the trunk, he heard shouting and gunshots. We still don't know what happened, whether it was an accident or intentional or what, but it was Berto's gun that was fired. When Shel and Francine showed up—they were searching for Berto so they could tell him the truth before he did something stupid; too late—they found him trying to keep a homeless man from bleeding out."

"Oh my God," Phoebe murmured.

"The man died from his bullet wounds," Ian told her. "It was then that Berto even more fully embraced the dark side. He called his father instead of the police. And Davio came and got rid of the body—covered the whole thing up. In return, Berto went to work for his family."

They were both silent then.

And Ian could have let it go at that—he'd told her what Berto had done, and how, try as he might, the man couldn't take any of it back. He couldn't fix the mess he'd made.

But Ian found himself opening his mouth and saying, "The bitch of it is, that what Berto did, by not trusting Francine . . . ? I made Aaron do the same thing to Shel."

Phoebe looked searchingly up at him. "Is this what they're fighting about?"

"No," Ian said. "That's . . . me continuing to screw things up for them." Jesus. He rolled onto his back again, so that he wouldn't have to meet her gaze. "What happened back then was, well, after the sex tape went viral—at least at Brentwood—Aarie got kicked out of the school for sexual misconduct. It wasn't an issue of gay or straight; the rule was no sex. At all. Turns out his scholarship had a morality clause—which should've tipped me off at the start. Aaron didn't belong there, and I don't know what I was thinking when I made him accept that scholarship."

Phoebe propped her head up on her elbow, which put her back into eye contact range. "You were probably thinking, *Yay, a scholarship to a good prep school*. This *was* the award that made it possible for you to stay in the Navy, right? After your elderly aunt died? The one that Aaron was living with . . . ?"

That's right. He'd almost forgotten. Phoebe had read his file. "Susan Bergeron wasn't related. Not by blood," Ian said, pulling Phoebe close so that she was nestled in the crook of his arm, her head against his shoulder. He could now see the top of her head, and feel her breasts against his side and chest. God, he didn't want to stop touching her. Not ever. "She was a friend." He laughed. "A savior, actually. She let Aaron live with her so I could be a selfish prick and run away and join the Navy."

For a few years, the arrangement had worked happily. Ian had just gone through BUD/S, the rigorous SEAL training, when he got the call about Susan's fatal stroke. He took extended leave, both for the funeral and to spend time with Aaron, who'd just lost the closest thing to a mother that either of them had ever known.

"That must've been hard, when she died," Phoebe murmured.

"It was," Ian said. "Aaron was devastated."

"I meant, hard for you," she said, pulling back

and pushing herself up so that she could look into his eyes again. "*You* must've been devastated. I mean, to lose someone you thought of as a *savior?*"

And yes, he *had* used that word, hadn't he? "I couldn't be," Ian admitted. "Devastated. I had to take care of Aaron."

"Yeah, but that's not how it works," Phoebe told him. "You feel what you feel, whether you want to feel it or not, whether you show it or talk about it or not."

"Yeah, well, when you don't show it or talk about it, it's easier to set aside," he admitted. "That was a hard year. Maybe the hardest ever."

"Harder than being in jail?"

Ian laughed. "Oh, yeah. Compared to that, Northport was a cakewalk. This situation was extra bad, because on top of Susan's dying, which was awful, it also looked like I was going to have to leave the Teams to take care of Aaron," he told her, then explained, "The SEAL Teams. I'd made it in by then, and it was . . . an honor that I wanted to keep. It was proof that I was worthy." Jesus, what was he telling her? He swiftly went on. "*Anyway,* I was sure I'd have to take at least some kind of temporary leave, but then my CO found this scholarship program. To Brentwood. Aaron said he wanted to go, but I knew he didn't. It was not the right school for a kid like him."

"If he hadn't gone, he wouldn't have met Sheldon," Phoebe pointed out.

That was true. But it was long past time to end this conversation.

Except she moved closer, shifting her leg up and across him, all that smooth skin sliding up his thighs and then even higher as she said, "Rewind a sec, back to Berto." She'd also started tracing the muscles in his chest and abs, and it all felt too freaking great to make her stop. Not yet anyway. "I'm still not sure why he was at fault for believing Francine when she said she'd hooked up with Aaron. I mean, she *said* it, right? Was he supposed to read her mind and know that she was lying?"

"No," Ian said. "Yes. Maybe. Okay, I know it sounds crazy, but I'm gonna go with *yes*. Berto abandoned Francine because he didn't have faith. She'd told him, repeatedly, that she loved him. Told him and showed him, too. I mean, that's how it's supposed to work, right? You let down your guard, you let this one person see you without all the bullshit and the walls and the pretense and . . ."

He was suddenly hyperaware of the way Phoebe was watching him—the quiet somberness in her eyes, the empathy and understanding on her face. But she didn't say anything this time—no comments, no questions, no quips. She just watched and waited.

So he kept going, because there was a point here to be made. "Berto knew her. She risked a lot to *let* him really know her. She's sweet, she's funny, she's smart, and she's lived most of her life in danger of some kind, so she's cautious and wary. And it's insane that she would just suddenly, randomly hook up with some high school kid—some friend of Sheldon's? Come on. It doesn't take much imagination to figure *that* out. But when push came to shove, when it mattered the most, Berto chose to believe this one, single, completely *fucking* insane thing." He searched for the exact words to explain this to her. "Look, I know it seems crazy when you define it as his ability to read her mind, and that's not what I'm saying. I'm saying that this kid had a *ton* of data to use when he hit this particular what-the-fuck scenario. And he chose to accept this one jarringly dissonant statement that Francine told his father, even though it clashed with everything else—*everything else*—he knew about her.

"He didn't have faith in her," he said again. "And because of that he lost it all."

Phoebe nodded. "I get it," she said softly. "But I also get that it's really hard not to be stupid when love's involved."

"No kidding."

They lay there in silence for several long moments.

"So what awful thing did Aaron do to Shel?" Phoebe asked. "You said . . . ?"

"Yeah. Okay. Part two of this amazing fuckup," Ian told her on an exhale. "Aaron got expelled while I was prepping to go to Afghanistan with my team, and suddenly I had forty-eight hours to get to Florida, collect him from school, and figure out what the hell I was gonna do with him. Shelly, meanwhile, was dealing with the aftermath of Berto's meltdown. See, when Berto finally realized that Francie lied to protect her gay brother—when he realized that he'd majorly fucked things up, his head exploded and he took it out on Shel. So Shel wrote Aarie an email, telling him it was over, breaking things off—in an attempt to keep him safe."

"Which . . . you think was somehow, in some way, the equivalent of the lie that Francine told?"

"That email was just as bullshit insane," Ian told her. "*Stay away from me. I wish I'd never met you.* It was just as dissonant. So yes. After getting that email, Aaron abandoned Shelly for the exact same reasons that Berto abandoned Francine. Because he didn't have faith. Well, he did, but I talked him out of it, freaking genius that I am."

He stopped, suddenly aware that his voice had broken, and that his eyes had filled with tears. *You have no idea what it means to be in a relationship, to be part of a real family. . . .* Aaron was right about that. Ian didn't know—he hadn't known—and he'd fucked it up for his little brother, big-time.

Here and now, though, he could feel Phoebe listening. Just waiting for him to explain.

Ian swallowed. Cleared his throat. Kept his eyes closed as he tried to push away all of the bullshit emotion that blurred his vision. "They had this plan for their future. Go north together. To Boston. They'd get an apartment, and Aaron would work while Shel went to school. MIT. Shel got a scholarship."

"That's kind of amazing," Phoebe said softly. "That they recognized how well they fit together, that they wanted *forever,* starting all the way back when they were teenagers."

"Yup, it was amazing—until I dropped in and saved the day," Ian said. "Aaron knew that the breakup email Shel sent him was crap. He wanted to go to Massachusetts and wait for Shel to show and . . . I stopped him. I made him enlist. I made him accept the lie, to admit defeat. I made him join the Marines—because anything else was fucking inconvenient. For me."

"To be fair to you, he was just a kid, and you *were* responsible for his safety."

"He was days from turning eighteen," Ian countered. "Did you know, Shelly loved Aaron so much, he spent four *years* searching for him? If I hadn't butted in and convinced Air that having his heart broken was just another normal part of life, Aaron would've been waiting and Sheldon would've found him, that very first August. But no, I was an impatient douchebag with places to go."

She laughed. "I'm sorry, but Afghanistan isn't exactly high on most people's list of fascinating travel destinations. And I think the phrase you originally used was *selfish prick.*"

Uh-oh. He had said that, hadn't he?

"Although, I'm not sure how accurate that is, considering how many years you'd spent raising your brother—back when you were supposed to be a kid yourself."

Jesus, he didn't want to talk about this. Ian closed his eyes, and they both lay there for several long moments, just breathing.

Phoebe finally laughed—just a little. It was more of a voiced smile than an actual chuckle. "I can tell from your terrified silence," she said, "that you've started praying to whatever God you believe in that I don't say something like *Wow, Eee, with those feelings of intense responsibility, it's really not that surprising that you would sacrifice your own life and go to jail as part of some Quixotic quest to protect Aaron and Sheldon.*"

Ian didn't open his eyes, because she was right. He really didn't want to go there.

"*There are some mistakes you can't fix*. I think I'm paraphrasing, but that's the gist of what you said, isn't it? About Berto. But it applies to you, too. Right? And since you can't fix four lost years, you, what? Try, instead, to get redemption some other, only *nearly* impossible way?" She shifted then, and kissed him. "Don't panic. I know this thing we're doing here is temporary, and that your craziness about me is going to pass. Maybe it already has." She laughed lightly. "I suspect I'm helping it along. But you're a smart guy with a really big brain, and it seems silly to take me as a temporary girlfriend, and then only use me for sex."

As Phoebe spoke, her hand—the one she'd been using to trace circles on his chest and stomach—moved lower. She shifted her leg, too, found his semi-erection, and stroked him, her fingers soft and warm.

"It's nice to have someone to talk to," she murmured. "Every now and then. You know, you asked me, a couple days ago, about why I carry a gun."

Ian opened his eyes at that. "You don't have to—"

"I know," she interrupted, smiling at him. "But at this point, I'm pretty sure you won't judge me—certainly not as much as I judge myself. See, I had a roommate in college—a really good friend—Emma. Junior year, she was sexually assaulted. Without going into much detail: it was bad, and it really changed her. She became so fearful—I'm not blaming her, of course, but her fear ruled her. It overwhelmed her. I went with her to all these support groups, hoping she'd find some relief, but . . ." She shook her head. "Nothing helped. I finally signed us up for a class at a firing range. I thought maybe that would empower her, but it didn't help, either. She dropped out of the class after the second week. She ended up leaving college—she just went home and hid. I think she's still hiding. I don't know—we lost touch."

"And I would judge you because . . . you knew when it was time to let her go?" Ian asked.

"Being her friend got really hard," Phoebe admitted. "And yes, I let her go, but I stayed with the class at the firing range. I was good at it—I'm not a great marksperson, but I'm pretty good, and . . . I liked it. I took more classes, learned all about gun safety, got licensed. . . . I did it to help her, but I benefited."

"That's not a bad thing," Ian told her.

"I feel as if I should've done more," she said.

"I know that feeling well," he said, but of course she already knew that—as perceptive as she was.

"Thank you for letting me talk," she said with a smile that was pure innocence.

Ian smiled back at her, because they both knew damn well that he would be willing to "talk" to her for hours, provided she kept touching him like that.

"Of course, if you don't want to have a conversation," Phoebe added, "you know how to shut me up."

Ian laughed and shifted slightly in an attempt to see her face. "Tragically, I'm out of condoms," he said, losing himself a little in her eyes and her touch.

"Do you think Yashi would say anything if we put them on the list? Or would they just appear?"

"I'm betting they'll just appear," Ian said.

"Hmm," she said. "Future tense. I approve that message. Present tense—we're both extremely creative. Of course, we *could* always talk more—"

Ian felt her smile as he kissed her and swept his hands down her incredible body. And then, as he waited for Francine to call and Berto to arrive, he did his best to limit Phoebe's talking to exclamations of the affirmative, and whispers of his name, while he ignored the echo of Aaron's voice that resounded over and over in his head.

You fucking coward.

He didn't have to worry about pushing Phoebe away.

Life was going to do that for him.

CHAPTER TWENTY-ONE

"Wait until I give the signal that we're clear before you let anyone take Berto out of the trunk," Francine told Martell as he pulled his car into the FBI safe house garage.

He nodded, his eyes kind as he glanced over at her. "I got it. Take your time."

Fahking great. Confirmation of her worst fears—that she still looked like shit on a stick. Francine did not cry beautifully. She knew that. Her nose got red and her eyes got puffy. And the whole mess took way too long to fade.

And Martell understood that Francine did *not* want Berto seeing her like this.

The surveillance van pulled in alongside them, and the nanosecond that the garage doors closed behind both vehicles, Francine got out of the car and headed quickly for the door into the house, hoping to make it into the privacy of the bathroom before having to talk to anyone.

She'd purposely waited to send Ian a text saying *10* until they were only two minutes away so that she'd have the chance to splash cool water on her face before seeing him.

But he'd apparently heard the mechanism for the automatic doors going up and then down, and had leapt into action. He was waiting just inside the door.

He'd obviously been resting while they were out. His feet were bare and his hair was messy, but his gaze was sharp, and he was immediately alert to the fact that she'd been crying.

"Fuck you," she told him—a preemptive strike, when he started to open his mouth to comment as she pushed past him.

Martell was right behind her, and she heard him tell Ian in a low voice, "She needs a couple minutes. That was harder for all of us than we thought it would be."

And great, the door to the first floor half bath was closed. Francine headed for it anyway, even as she sharply told Martell, "Why don't you do something useful instead of speaking for me? Like move our stuff into that empty bedroom."

"It's not empty anymore," Ian said. "Phoebe's in there."

Of *course* she was. "Well, she'll have to get her big ass out." As Francie tried the knob anyway, it turned beneath her hand and the door opened to reveal who else but the owner of the big ass of which Francine had just loudly spoken. Loudly enough for Phoebe to have heard her through the door.

But the look of annoyance that the taller woman wore morphed into one of sisterhood and sympathy as she saw Francie's mottled face.

But Francine had time for neither, even as Phoebe quickly surrendered the bathroom.

"You're going to have to move your things out of that bedroom," she told Phoebe as she went inside and started to close the door.

"No," Ian said from across the room. "She won't."

"Berto's really not going to believe—" Francine started to argue, but then she stopped as she looked from Ian to Phoebe and back. Ian's T-shirt was on inside out, and Phoebe was also barefoot and disheveled, as if she'd dressed hurriedly, too. She was also actually blushing, a faint line of pink beneath those smart-girl glasses. It wasn't hard to do the math. Especially since anyone with eyes had seen it coming from miles away. "Oh, how cute. An op romance. *That'll* last."

"It's not . . ." Phoebe trailed off, probably because she wasn't quite sure yet what it was, let alone what it was not. Ian had that kind of power over women. All that charm, focused in a deadly beam, could leave a path of pure and total destruction. She cleared her throat as she lowered her voice and told Francine, "If we're going to make the Dutchman believe we're together, we need to, um . . ."

Now it was Francine shooting a look of pity at Phoebe. "Is that what Ian said? Oh, honey. And you fell for his bullshit?"

"No," she said. "That's not what he . . . He didn't—" But she cut herself off, because across the room, Ian was talking to Yashi, who'd come in from the surveillance van.

"No, you know, I think I'm going to talk to him out in the garage first," Ian was saying, about Berto. "Just the two of us."

"That's not okay," Francine said, even as Phoebe asked, "Is that really a good idea?" Phoebe headed for Ian's side—caught once again in his charismatic tractor beam.

"Yeah, I'm not comfortable with that either," Martell chimed in, even as he came toward Francie, clearly wondering why she was still standing there, letting everyone see her shame. "You okay?"

He was serious. His concern was sincere.

It was possible she'd misjudged him on her first impression, and he really was that rare breed of men—a truly nice guy. Yes, he had a certain arrogance and male-know-it-all-ness that came, in part, from being good-looking and having access to a mirror. But maybe what she'd seen as him working hard to get into her pants had merely been an attempt to be a team player. He used *we* and *us* all the time, when he was talking to Ian and Yashi, too. He'd used it again when he'd first come into the house tonight—*That was harder for all of us than we thought it would be*—sharing in the distress instead of throwing it all on her.

Even though it was hers to own.

Ever since Martell had picked Francine up at the coffee shop, he'd been nothing but respectful and kind.

He could've taken advantage in the car, when she'd started to cry.

She'd expected him to.

But he hadn't.

Across the room, Francine could see that Little Debbie FBI had come into the kitchen and was watching them. But she quickly looked away when she caught Francine's eye.

"You have enough towels in there?" Martell asked.

She glanced in and saw that there were plenty, in a pile on the back of the toilet. "I'm good," she told him. "I'm okay."

The way he was looking at her, she knew that he didn't believe her. And the truth was, she didn't quite believe herself. But he nodded and accepted her version of reality. "You need anything, just let me know."

Again, those weren't just words. He meant what he said.

"Make Berto believe it," Francine said. "You and me? I need him to believe it."

Martell nodded, as serious and determined as if she'd asked him to find and bring her the Holy Grail. "Consider it done."

"You can start by adding condoms to Yashi's list," she said.

"Good idea," he said. "Hashtag extra large." He smiled back at her. "Trust me, I got this."

"Thank you," Francine said, and finally closed the door. When she looked into the mirror, she was still smiling—and even though her eyes were still red, she didn't look half as awful as she'd imagined.

• • •

Ian opened the trunk carefully. For all he knew, Francine and Martell had missed a weapon, but the man in there was cuffed and had been stripped down to his underwear. The only thing he threw at Ian was a baleful look.

"I feel like I should say something pithy here," Ian said. "Like, *Monsieur Dellarosa, so we meet at last.*"

"Are you fucking kidding me?" Berto said.

"*Are you fucking kidding me* works," Ian told him, reaching in to unlock the cuffs. "It sums it up just about perfectly, from my end, too. The FBI and their crazy brothers and sisters who are closer to A on the alphabet agency scale pulled me out of jail in a Hail Mary move, to help them find some very important missing kids. I didn't want it, I didn't ask for it, and I certainly didn't make a deal for it, but there it is. My unexpected freedom has nothing to do with you or your family. How's Manny, by the way?"

Berto blinked at his sudden change of subject. "He's fine."

"Is he? Because if he's on life support, with a priest standing by, that would be good to know. My deal was with Manny, not Davio."

"No, he's really okay," Berto said, rubbing his wrists. "He's in the hospital for tests."

"That sounds like bullshit," Ian said. "I'll ask you about him again, after we agree to a detente."

"My agreement—to anything—depends on your terms," Berto said.

Ian gave him a hand, helping him out of the trunk. "My terms are pretty simple. You help me with this job, earn some cash, and gain a few good karma points in the process. When it's over, we push the reset button, and I go back to prison and finish serving my time, according to my deal with Manny."

He had yet to arrange that detail with the FBI, but he was certain that that esteemed organization would have no trouble coming up with a feasible reason for him to go back to Northport, when everything was said and done.

It had come to him, a few hours ago. Manny and Berto had no idea why Ian was out of prison. And since they didn't know that his release was permanent, it didn't have to be.

If the FBI could pull him out of jail, they could certainly put him back inside. Doing so would reactivate his deal with the Dellarosas. Manny and Berto would keep Davio in line.

He hoped.

"I know you've been working closely with Manny," Ian told Berto, "and that you and your uncle have both been juggling furiously, to counter-balance your father's . . . bad choices, shall we say."

Berto didn't respond, but Ian knew he was listening.

He handed Berto his shoes and clothes as he quickly outlined the FBI's assignment to steal back the kidnapped children from the Dutchman.

"I know you have both a fleet of trucks and a series of warehouses across the state," Ian told

Berto as the man got dressed. “I want to pay you, for use of both. Plus, your presence adds a certain authenticity. The Dutchman already knows Davio’s after me.”

“And how do you know I’m not just going to kill your brother?” Berto asked. “When I have the chance?”

“I don’t,” Ian admitted. “But I suspect you’re not a threat since you’ve risked your father’s wrath many times these past years, to save Aaron and Sheldon—although really, it’s always been about Francine, hasn’t it?”

Berto didn’t so much as blink. But then he asked the question Ian was hoping he’d ask. “How much are you going to pay me?”

“Enough to make you shake my hand,” Ian said, and indeed, when he told Berto the dollar amount, they then shook. With their hands still clasped, he asked again, “How’s Manny?”

“He’s fine,” Berto said again. “I went into the hospital see him just this morning. He’s up and around. He’s old, but he’s tough.”

“Good,” Ian said.

And with that done, the rest was easy.

At least it should have been. It would’ve been.

Before funny, quirky, perfect Phoebe Kruger had walked into Ian’s life, and made him long for the impossible.

“I need a high-speed luxury yacht,” Ian said, “with at least three private bedrooms, and enough space down below to hold cargo. It's gotta have a cruising speed of at least 35 knots. I need a secluded, private dock, south of Miami, with access for an eighteen-wheeler. Oh, and I'm gonna need both the TSA and the Coast Guard to make themselves scarce for around twelve hours."

Yashi actually laughed out loud.

Phoebe was in the living room in the Miami safe house, one of a diverse group that included an ex-con Navy SEAL, two FBI agents, two lawyers, and a mobster. It almost felt like the setup to some terrible joke. *Walked into a bar . . .* Except these eclectic nine individuals were working together, as Ian put it, on a "short-term, relatively low-risk, high-yield con" that would result in the return of the two kidnapped children. No joke. No breaking in, no clandestine rescue, no violence, no gunfire, either.

At least none that was real. Or so Ian promised.

His plan was to convince Georg Vanderzee, AKA the Dutchman, that Ian had a quick, easy, foolproof way to smuggle contraband—of any type, human included—out of the country. At which point, at least according to theory, the Dutchman would enlist Ian's aid in moving those children. He would, quite literally, hand them over.

But the con wouldn't work unless they made it look real. All of it. Down to the minute details.

Because of that need for accuracy and precision, they were all present at this meeting, despite the late hour.

Even Sheldon had been woken up and dragged from his bed. He sat on the sofa wearing only a pair of blue plaid pajama pants. His hair was standing straight up, and his arms were folded across his movie-star-worthy pecs.

Francine was next to him, sitting so close to Martell that she was almost on the man's lap, his arm around her shoulders, their legs intertwined. Apparently, they'd made a connection. Or maybe it was for show, for Berto's sake. Phoebe wasn't sure. But the softness in Martell's eyes as he smiled at Francine didn't seem make-believe.

She herself sat on Martell's other side, with Aaron sprawled in the easy chair next to her, intentionally and grimly not looking at his half-naked husband. And *that* was a clue that, despite their private time together, nothing had been resolved.

Yashi and Deb were sharing the love seat—ever the consummate professionals.

Berto—who'd been given back his clothes after he'd done his little one-on-one with Ian and apparently struck a deal to help them with this mission—was across from them and on edge, because of his proximity to the FBI.

Ian was next to Berto, but he'd pulled over one of the stools from the kitchen counter, which, as he sat on it, put him up on a higher level than the rest of them.

Phoebe was certain that that was not by mistake.

Ian was undaunted by Yashi's laughter. "I know you can do it, so don't pretend that you can't." He looked at Sheldon. "It takes approximately four hours, by boat, to get from south Florida to certain parts of Cuba. But of course we're not going to go there, we're only going to make Vanderzee *think* that we did. So, we'll need a mapped-out nautical route, heading south, but then turning back toward a second, even more secluded dock, somewhere else in Florida—within easy driving range of Miami for those in the surveillance van. But we'll want to be on the open sea for nearly four full hours."

Sheldon sat up, engaged. "We'll need the yacht's computer compass to say we're heading south for the entire trip. I can definitely do that. And north for the return. I'm assuming there'll be a return . . . ?"

"There will be," Ian confirmed. "We're going to fool Vanderzee into believing that we took him to Cuba, and then back to the original dock south of Miami."

"We'll need smartphones with doctored GPS, too," Sheldon said.

Yashi was making a procurement list, and he looked to Ian for confirmation.

Ian nodded. "You can get that info from Shel—what he wants to work with," he told the FBI agent.

"If we're just going to be out on the ocean for four hours," Yashi pointed out, "twice, neither the Coast Guard or TSA's gonna care." He made a note on his pad. "But I'll make sure we're left alone."

"But when we're at the second dock," Ian said. "The one that's going to be our fake Cuba . . ."

"We won't want any U.S. agencies nearby," Yashi said. "Got it. No signage, nothing that says we're still in the States, either. I'll also clear the airspace, so we don't have some Cessna pulling a sign advertising Miami Jack's Shrimp Shack flying overhead."

"Hopefully, we'll have this timed so we're only there at oh dark hundred," Ian said. "Both when we arrive and depart. But yes. It's good to be prepared." He kept going. "We'll need a cargo van or truck, possibly two, beat-up, with Cuban plates." He looked around at them, as if counting heads. "I need black clothes for everyone on Team Ian, which is going to be me, Phoebe, Aaron."

Aaron sat up. "Holy shit. I get to play?"

"Yeah," Ian told his brother. "I hate it, but since Pheeb's playing, too . . ." He glanced at her. "With Berto's help, this mission is going to be as low-risk as possible. No one is going to be alone with the Dutchman—not even for a second. We'll be working in groups. And you'll stay with your group, you'll stay on script, no improvising, no coloring outside of the lines." He looked at Phoebe again. "Since you're the least experienced person here, you and I will go over your role, extensively, later tonight."

Francine noisily cleared her throat, and Phoebe shot her a look, feeling heat rising in her face. Ian's eyes narrowed—he didn't know that Francine had done the Ian-plus-Phoebe-equals-hot-hookup math. Or . . . maybe he did. It was hard to imagine anything getting past him. But he'd already turned back to Yashi and continued with his list.

"Black clothes for me, Phoebe, Aaron," Ian said again. "They've gotta be lightweight, including masks. I don't want anyone overheating—we're going to be moving boxes and it's going to get hot. Phoebe and I will also need a variety of other clothing, including yachting wear, whatever that is—head to toe, nothing too fancy, but do make us shine—and a nice overnight bag to put it in. Leather. Remember, my character"—another glance at Phoebe—"has money."

"Check," Yashi said.

"I need rent-a-cop security guard uniforms for Martell and for you, Yash. And a coupla burlap sacks to put over your heads."

"Oh, that's gonna be fun," Martell murmured. "I can't wait to find out why."

"We're going to need ammo—and blanks," Ian continued. "Along with special-effect blood packs, and the blood to go in 'em."

Francine perked up at that. "Please tell me we're killing Phoebe."

"What?" Phoebe asked, half laughing, half perplexed.

"Not for real," Francine explained with her usual disdain. "But we can use plastic bags of fake blood to make it look—realistically—as if someone's been killed. And since Ian doesn't want you participating in this job, and I agree—your lack of experience could get us all *really* killed—I thought . . ."

But Ian was shaking his head. "I thought about that, too, but no. If Phoebe were dead, my character would have no reason not to stay in Cuba. We have to maintain a balance. Create urgency, but not cross into tragedy.

"So here's what's going to happen: Berto's going to be already badly injured when Phoebe, Aaron, and I arrive at the warehouse with the Dutchman. We'll be coming to pick up the contraband, but we'll discover that Berto interrupted a robbery attempt—which emphasizes the fact that this shipment is hot, that we need to get it out of Miami, now, or it'll be taken from us. Two of Berto's guards will be tied up—one will already be dead, killed by the robbers who've made their escape, but they might be coming back with reinforcements, so *go, go, go,* load those boxes into the truck. It's the reason we need to move fast. I'll kill the surviving guard over his failure to protect Berto—proof that I'm both serious and deadly, plus this makes Vanderzee an accomplice to murder, simply by being in the room. For someone with his psychological makeup, the fact that blood's been spilled makes him less likely to bail. So. We leave with the goods—drugs or guns—head for the dock and the yacht and our trip to Cuba, while Berto stays behind to get medical aid. After we return to the States, I'll receive the terrible news that he died of his injuries. Which now means that Davio's going to come after me even harder. And *that* provides the urgency we'll need to convince Vanderzee that if he wants to move those kids, he'll have to do it right away—now or never—because Phoebe and I have decided it's time to flee the country, that we're taking our yacht, and this time we'll stay in Cuba."

"So we're essentially putting on a show, a play, for Georg Vanderzee," Phoebe realized.

"You could say that," Ian told her, turning back to Yashi. "Martell will need tropical wear," he continued. "Casual clothes, but don't make it cheap—Hawaiian shirt, linen pants. And military garb for the rest of Team Martell."

"Ooh, I get a team, too," Martell said. "And *that's* why I wear a bag on my head as the security guard—so Vanderzee doesn't recognize me when we get to Faux Cuba."

"Yes. You're my Cuban partner," Ian told him. "American expat, so don't try to fake an accent—that never works. Like me, you're richer than God. You've got an infallible connection to your new country's government, and everyone looks the other way when American yachts—and their cargos—arrive and depart from your private dock. Your minions are Francine, Sheldon, Yashi." He pointed at them. "France, you're his kickass security chief"—he turned back to Yashi—"so extra heavy with the weaponry for her, although I do want everyone armed."

Ian smiled at the other FBI agent. "Deb, sorry, but I want you with us on the yacht, in case there's trouble with the Coast Guard. You're our stewardess."

"Of course I am," she said with a sigh. "I can't be the captain?"

"Sorry, no. When you're getting her clothes, think high-class hooker," Ian told Yashi, and when Deb made an exasperated sound, he added, "Vanderzee won't expect you to be a black belt if you're wearing heels."

"I know, I know." Deb looked over at Yashi's extensive notes and made a disbelieving face at him. "Did you really just write *sideboob?*"

"I did," he admitted, looking back at Ian. "What else?"

"Cash," Ian said. "A twenty-K packet, a ten-K packet, and a briefcase with five million—obviously that can be mostly newspaper. But I want it to weigh what it needs to weigh, so don't take shortcuts. Dollars or Euros, doesn't matter which. I'll let that be your choice. And drugs or guns for our contraband. I'd prefer drugs—specifically meth—it's hot, and there's a market for U.S. product in Eastern Europe. Plus, it doesn't weigh as much as AKs or ARs. Remember, we're going to have to lift this shit—*and* it'll slow our speedboat down. Also, if it's guns, I'm going to need them crated and moved into Berto's warehouse before tomorrow night, which could be problematic."

"You think?" Berto said.

"If it's drugs," Ian continued, "we'll be hiding them inside of electronics—desktop computer towers—which are already in the Dellarosa warehouse. So all I'll need is a big enough bag of meth for show-and-tell with the Dutchman. But again, your choice. Oxycontin works, too. However, I *will* need to know in advance—by tomorrow morning—exactly what our contraband is going to be."

"Yeah," Yashi said. "And I kinda caught that *tomorrow night* that you mentioned, too?"

"This *has* to go down tomorrow night," Ian told them. "Davio—Berto's father—is gonna be up in Sarasota, at the hospital, at a meeting with Manny that he is not going to miss. I don't want him anywhere near this, so we're doing it then. Plus, I want this job over and done ASAP—and I'm sure those kids want to be back with their mother sooner rather than later, too."

"We can do this," Deb said confidently. "And I'm sure we can get you the drugs—so let's make it drugs, not guns." She frowned down at Yashi's notepad. "How about a truck or some kind of vehicle on this end? To get the illegal goods from Berto's warehouse to the departing airfield?"

"The electronics are *not* illegal," Berto was quick to say. "I purchased, legally, an overstock from a regional chain of stores being downsized—"

"But the Dutchman's not going to know that," Francie said. "Will you just relax? We're all on the same side here. No one's going to arrest you."

"I'm renting a truck from Berto," Ian told them. "He's got a fleet of semis—"

"All legal," Berto pointed out, and Francine rolled her eyes.

"I want the truck for the Miami warehouse pickup to be big—an eighteen-wheeler," Ian told them. "I want it to be more than just a van or a rinky-dink U-Haul. This truck is part of what we're selling to the Dutchman."

What they were "selling" to the Dutchman was a sure thing. A foolproof way to transport those kidnapped kids out of the Miami consulate, and out of the U.S.

If they did this right, Phoebe realized, Georg Vanderzee was actually going to *pay* Ian to take those kids, to put them into one of Berto's very big, very safe-looking trucks, believing that the truck would carry the children to a boat, which would then transport them to Cuba. At that point, Vanderzee or his agents would pick them up and charter a flight to Kazbekistan, where they'd be delivered to their father, in exchange for some millions of dollars in payment.

In truth, the truck would drive those children safely to their mother's waiting arms, while Vanderzee's men searched Cuba for them, in vain.

It was brilliant.

But it started tomorrow night, with the Dutchman seeing—up close and personal—exactly how Ian's smuggling operation worked.

"And that," Ian said, "brings us to the Dutchman."

He glanced at Phoebe, and her stomach clenched. She knew he was going to tell them, now, about his past experience with Georg Vanderzee. She also knew that this was going to be bad.

"Our mark," Ian told them, his eyes deadly serious, "is a sociopath."

Ian felt Phoebe watching him, her eyes somber behind those glasses that he'd come to love.

"Georg Vanderzee. His father was a tulip farmer from Holland, his mother was a woman's rights activist and the only daughter of a wealthy Kazbekistani man, who was and still is the right hand of a powerful warlord. She somehow escaped and fled to Paris, where she met his dad, who was much older, and was on some kind of midlife-crisis walkabout. Georg was their only child.

"When he was six years old, armed militants attacked a crowded marketplace in Yemen, and his parents were killed. He was with them at the time, but his life was spared."

"Oh, God," Phoebe breathed.

"He went to live with his maternal grandfather in Kazbekistan, which would not have been his parents' wish. In fact, prior to that, he'd never so much as met his K-stani relatives—his mother had been hiding from them, all that time. He's now convinced the attack in Yemen was carried out by men in the employ of his grandfather—and he seems to view the brutal murder of his parents as an acceptable expression of familial love."

Francine spoke. "Seriously?"

"Yep," Ian said. "He's not a religious man, but he's

almost ridiculously superstitious. I never did figure out the cause of that, but there it is. I've used it in the past to my advantage. He walks the line between his country and the West—he looks European, but he's fully embraced his grandfather's tribal customs. By age fifteen, he was already married with two wives—and apparently, in his part of K-stan, teen grooms acquire preteen brides. However, this is something he's continued to do, well into his forties. His most recent wife just turned twelve."

"So in other words," Francine said, "if something goes wrong, and we find ourselves in a firefight with this piece of shit, we're cleared to shoot-to-kill?"

"Nothing's going to go wrong," Ian said.

"How many wives does he have?" Shelly asked. "If he started getting married back in his teens? Where does he keep them all?"

"He doesn't keep them all," Ian told them. "By the time he was in his mid-twenties, his wives started dying mysteriously. These days it's not so mysterious. While I was at his home, having dinner, his favorite wife—alleged favorite—knocked over a glass of wine. It didn't touch me, I moved away, I didn't get hit—but she did."

Ian had to stop for a moment. God, he hated having to tell them this, but he had to. They had to know. He couldn't look at Phoebe as he tried to focus on the facts. Just the facts.

"He backhands her, and she goes flying—she's sixteen years old, maybe ninety pounds. Maybe.

I'm trying to be a diplomat, to calm him down. My goal is to stop him from hurting her. I get him to back away and I'm pretty sure it's going to be okay, because he finally seems calm. But it's a little weird, because now *she's* crying and cowering and I realize that she's begging me to let him hit her and . . ."

"Oh, God," Phoebe said and Ian made the mistake of looking at her.

She obviously knew where his story was going, and he had to look away.

He cleared his throat. "But he goes back to the table and sits down, and now I'm looking at her, and talking to her, like, *Hey, it's okay,* when he shoots her. Just *pop*. Bullet in the head. It took me a second to realize what had happened—all of her noise stopped, and she hit the floor—of course, because she was dead. I was close enough so that her blood sprayed my pants. It hit the wall behind her, and . . . somehow it got on me. And he sees that and goes, *Oops*.

"I didn't even know he was armed," Ian continued. "And he just puts the weapon down and goes back to eating his meal. Servants come in and quickly and quietly clean up the mess. They remove the body, as if a murder in the dining room is an everyday occurrence." He had to stop and clear his throat, before he added, "I found out later that if I'd let him beat her up, he probably wouldn't've killed her. Apparently, that was his pattern. A beating or a bullet."

"You couldn't possibly have known that at the time," Phoebe said, quick to defend him.

"I know it now," Ian told her. "The bitch of it is, the day before, I'd saved his life. For real. I'd fake-saved his life, about a week before that, to get him to trust me, and he did. I got the info I needed, I'd even passed it along to the international taskforce that was . . . Anyway, whatever. The mission was over, and I was in that place where I was making the choice either to end or maintain the relationship. And I went for maintain and I stuck around for a few days. And I ended up killing that girl."

Phoebe was just sitting there, looking at him with her heart in her eyes, as if they were the only ones in the room.

"So he just gets away with it?" Martell asked. "Just regularly killing his wives?"

"It's not illegal," Francine answered for Ian. "Not according to local law. He owns them. He can do whatever he wants with them."

"Yeah, but you'd think he'd at least run out of girls who were willing to marry him," Martell argued.

"The girls don't have anything to say about it," Francine told him. "Their fathers pick their husbands, and I'm sure Vanderzee pays well."

"So, essentially," Martell concluded, "we're dealing with a pedophile serial killer. And we're all going to play kissy face with him, and smile at him. High-five him. Shake his hand."

"Yes," Ian said, "we are."

• • •

Aaron was in the kitchen, making himself a sandwich, when Shelly came in from the garage.

"What were you doing out there?" Aaron asked, his curiosity overcoming his ongoing frustration and anger at his husband.

Shel stopped. His hope was suddenly palpable—simply because Aaron had asked him a faintly hostile question. "I was putting Rory's car seat into the surveillance van," he said. "Making sure it was safe. If you're going out there, I want to be in the van—not back here at the house. I figured you'd want to do the same."

Aaron nodded. He'd figured right, angry or not. "So it's safe?"

"It is," Sheldon said. "As long as everything goes according to plan."

They both just stood there, then, looking at each other, letting that statement echo in the otherwise empty room.

And then they both spoke at once. "Did you see the pictures of what Yashi did to van one?" Shel asked, as Aaron said, "When, with Ian, does anything ever go according to plan? I mean, he always gets it done, brilliantly, but this Dutchman guy sounds dangerous. . . ."

And then, also at the same time, Shel said, "I wonder if Yashi can find us a babysitter . . ." as Aaron said, "I'll talk to Eee, tell him we need to get someone in here to watch Roar. . . ."

"So we can both be out there."

They said it in perfect unison.

Shelly smiled, with more of that hope brimming in his eyes, mixing with his unspoken plea for forgiveness. “Good to know we haven’t lost our ability to do that,” he said.

He was so beautiful—both inside and out. But Aaron’s love for this man, which always rang inside of him like a clean, clear bell now felt heavy and murky and burdensome, weighed down by his anger and hurt.

“I wish you’d put on a shirt,” Aaron said, turning back to his sandwich.

“I wish you’d take yours off and come to bed.”

“I’m taking the second shift,” Aaron informed him. “Guarding Berto.”

Ian’s policy was trust, but verify. And they were currently in the verify stage with Sheldon’s half brother. Berto had been assigned to the pullout couch in the den—a room right off the main living room that had French doors with glass panes. They were all taking turns watching him—making sure he wasn’t working some kind of secret agenda for Davio, with a plan to murder Aaron in his sleep.

“You shouldn’t be guarding him at all,” Shel said.

“Believe me, while I’m on guard, I’m not going to blink—let alone fall asleep.”

“Yeah, I was more concerned about B.’s safety.”

“Ha,” Aaron said, “ha. *You’re* the one who shouldn’t guard him.” Shel’s ongoing mistrust of his half brother was more than evident.

Mistrust and loathing.

"Yeah, well, I'm *not* guarding him, am I?" Shel said.

Aaron looked up from putting the mustard back on the door of the fridge. People didn't normally look at Sheldon and think *badass,* but there was something about the way he was now standing, or maybe it was the shadows being thrown across his face, which whispered of danger. Of course it was easy to forget sometimes, that his computer-nerd high school sweetheart had also been a decorated officer in the Marines.

"I volunteered," Shel continued, "but Ian said no. He sometimes says no to me, too, you know."

Aaron had to give him that one, and he nodded. Grudgingly. "But he's not your brother. You have no idea what it's like living in the constant fucking shadow of his almighty perfection. It's even harder when—"

"No," Shel said, interrupting him, stepping forward into Aaron's personal space. "I'm sorry, but you wouldn't know *hard* if it kicked you in the face. There's nothing hard about having a brother like Ian—everything he does for you, he does out of unconditional love. *Hard* is having a brother who's so fucking disgusted by you, he beats the *hell* out of you for months to try to turn you into something that you're not—that you can't be. Hard is living in fear, from his constant threats. His manipulation. His revulsion. Hard is wondering when my dear brother is going to help my fucking crazy father kill *you,* Aaron, because if you're dead, I'll look less gay, and they'll look less related to someone gay—forget about the fact that you are everything to me. You're the love of my life, and I'd die to protect you."

Sheldon so rarely lost his cool, Aaron had forgotten what it was like when he did.

Shelly wasn't done. "So tell your brother—who loves you, and who would also die to protect you—that you're not going to guard Berto, that you're going to keep a safe distance between him and you throughout this job. And then come the fuck to bed, so that if something goes wrong during this allegedly low-risk assignment, we don't regret it for the rest of our pathetic lives."

As much as Aaron complained when Ian ordered him around, he'd always really loved it when Sheldon did so.

A lot.

"This doesn't mean I've forgiven you," Aaron said, even though from the sudden shine of tears in Shelly's eyes, it was clear that he absolutely thought it did.

And truth be told, Shel was probably right.

"God, I'm so sorry that I—"

"Just stop there," Aaron said. "Can you please just say *I'm sorry,* and let me pretend that you're sorry for what I want you to be sorry for?"

"I'm sorry," Sheldon whispered. "I love you."

"Yeah," Aaron said, offering Shel half of his sandwich. "I love you, too."

• • •

Francine came into the bathroom while Martell was brushing his teeth.

Because this bathroom was family-style, with double sinks, a toilet that was in its own little closet, and an opaque curtain across the roomy shower stall, the safe house rule was to keep the door ajar so that their fellow campers could use it simultaneously. So he wasn't surprised when she came in.

" 'Sup?" he asked, and rinsed and spat, stashing his toothbrush in the mug he'd snagged from the kitchen. He then splashed water up and onto his face, drying off with the towel he'd looped around his neck.

He realized then that she'd closed the door behind her. She was still leaning back against it, her hand on the knob, where she'd pushed in the little button to lock it.

"Berto saw you come in here," she told him, her voice low. "I thought I'd let him see me come in, too. And it's occurred to me . . . Well, I was thinking . . ."

Uh-oh.

Crazy woman alert.

Without a doubt, Martell was a bona fide crazy-woman magnet. Somehow, they identified him as an easy target—or what was that word that Dunn had been throwing around earlier? Mark. He was, indeed, an easy mark.

And what did that say about him—that he was

likewise drawn to crazy? And truth be told, crazy-woman sex was beyond hot, and it was going to be hard to turn *this* down, because it had been a long, cold while since he'd used his penis for its primary and yet most rewarding task.

And Francine was a beautiful, healthy young woman, with a neat little body, that beautiful, silky long hair, and that perfectly shaped angel-princess face—with those pale, crazy eyes.

Her eyes weren't crazy right now, but probably only because she was gazing down at her boots, and at the floor—anywhere but up and into his face. She actually seemed a little embarrassed by what she was about to say. It was possible she was blushing a little, which was weirdly endearing—and *that* was not a good thing for him to be thinking.

Martell needed to focus on the fact that if he didn't stay strong, if he *did* give in and have sex with her—right up against this wall, no, *that* wall would be better, or hell, maybe she could perch up on the sink counter, it *was* the perfect height—it would be great while it was happening, but not so great after, when she, oh, say, tried to decapitate him and eat his brains.

And even if, like most of the crazy women he'd bumped into in the past, her brand of crazy didn't include psycho-killer violence, there was still plenty to avoid when it came to figurative brain-eating.

"I was wondering," Francine started again, chewing her lower lip a little this time. "God, I'm bad at this."

The lip chewing made Martell want to weep because what he wanted and what he *wanted* were two entirely different things. And the devil on his shoulder—or maybe it was the angel, he never could quite tell them apart. But whatever it was that whispered stupid things to him was whispering *If it was Deb who'd come in and locked the door, you'd've already said yes.* But that wasn't going to happen. Deb wasn't crazy enough.

So he cleared his throat, and attempted to save Francine from more embarrassment, not just by stopping her before she got any further, but by letting her save face.

"I really like you," he said—which was not untrue. "And I'm happy to help you with Berto, but, see, it just wouldn't feel right to do more than pretend, because I'd feel like I was taking advantage. And I . . . I would be." He shook his head. "So I can't."

She was looking at him now, and her face was completely blank. He couldn't read her at all.

"As much as I might want to," he added, because someone had to say something. "But . . . thank you?"

Francine laughed at that, and her sudden smile transformed her, eradicating the crazy. Her eyes danced and sparkled with what looked like genuine amusement. "Did you think I . . . ?" She laughed again. "You thought I was going to ask you to have sex with me?"

"Um," Martell said.

"And you were saying *no*." She seemed really

happy about that. "God, you are ridiculously nice, aren't you?"

"*Nice* isn't really the word I'd—"

"Believe me, it's not hard to ask for sex," she interrupted him. "I know how to do that. It doesn't involve much talking. I take off my shirt. I take off my bra. I take off my boots and my pants. . . ."

"Ah," he said. "Yeah, I could see how that would work really well."

"What I was wondering," she said, back into serious mode, "is if, maybe, after this is over, you might want to, I don't know, have dinner? Or maybe see a movie?"

"You want to go on a date?" Martell realized.

Francine nodded.

He looked at her, standing there, so sweetly uncertain, her crazy no longer her defining feature, but more of a distant vibe or a light sprinkling.

"There's a really good Cajun restaurant on Hillside," she said, and he realized that unlike the other crazy women he'd known, she'd listened when he spoke. Listened and remembered. He knew dozens of non-crazies, both male and female, who never did that. "Their jerk chicken is . . . Well, it's really good, so I thought . . ."

Martell nodded. "Yeah."

"Yeah?" She didn't seem to believe him. It was possible he'd been a little tentative.

So he put more into it. "Yes," he said. "I'd love to. Have dinner. With you. That . . . sounds kind of great."

Her smile was a mix of relief and pleasure, and again he was struck by the way it transformed her.

"Good, then," she said, unlocking the door. "We'll do that, and . . . Thanks."

As she slipped out of the bathroom, Martell said, "Well, all right," and to his surprise, it actually was.

Phoebe found Ian in the living room as everyone else in the house—except Yashi and Deb, who were already hard at work procuring everything on Ian's list—was getting ready to go to bed.

Ian was taking the first shift guarding Berto, who had agreed to stay in the safe house overnight. Whatever Ian had said to the man when he'd first arrived, it was clear that the two now considered themselves to be at least temporary allies. Whether it was money that was behind this alliance, or Berto's desire for redemption, or something else entirely, Phoebe didn't know.

The lights were off in the den where Berto had been assigned to sleep, but Ian had parked himself on the sofa, a good distance away from the glass-paneled doors. It was far enough away so that they could talk without disturbing Berto, and without fear of being overheard.

Ian had pulled the coffee table close to him, and was cleaning his guns, one at a time. He was methodical and meticulous, and he seemed to welcome the familiar task.

He didn't say *What's up?* or *Why are you here when you should be upstairs, sleeping?* in words, but a question was clear on his face as he glanced over at her.

Phoebe sat down next to him. "Francine knows," she told him, figuring she'd start with the easiest and work her way up to the more difficult topics of conversation. "That we've hooked up."

Ian winced. "If she was rude to you, I apologize—"

"She wasn't," Phoebe said. "I mean, not more than usual."

He smiled briefly at that. "Aaron figured it out, too. He says it's just a matter of time now, before I push you away."

His candor surprised her, but she tried to be matter-of-fact as she nodded and asked, "Is that your usual MO?"

"Pretty much."

"Huh," she said. "Well, since everyone knows, you shouldn't be shy about just coming up to my room—our room—when your shift is through."

That got her a laugh, although she could tell from his expression that she'd puzzled him a little by not jumping all over that *push you away* statement. "I don't think I've ever been accused of being shy."

"Reticent, then," Phoebe said.

"A much manlier word," Ian agreed, then said, "Don't wait up for me."

"Would you mind very much if I did?"

He glanced at her again before returning his full attention to his weapon. "It's late," he finally said. "And I know you're tired."

"It *is* late, and I *am* tired, but I'd like to wait up.

Do you know you have this slightly annoying, although incredibly selfless habit of defining a given situation by what everyone else is feeling? Aaron's devastated. Francine's angry. I'm tired. How do *you* feel, Ian? Would *you* mind if I wait up for you?" She didn't give him a chance to answer. "Would it help if I told you that some generous soul must've seen the addition to the list in the kitchen, because a small pile of condoms appeared, like magic, in the medicine cabinet in the upstairs bathroom? And that I snagged us a few?"

That got her another flash of blue from his eyes. "Then yes, wait up," he told her. "If that's why you're waiting. But if you're looking to talk, please don't. You heard the story, you now know the facts. There's nothing more to say."

"Okay," she said, and stood up.

She'd surprised him again, but then she blew it by adding, "It wasn't your fault. When Vanderzee killed that girl in front of you. You couldn't have known he was going to do that. And besides, if you hadn't saved his life, we wouldn't be this much closer to finding and rescuing those kidnapped children."

"If I hadn't saved his life, he wouldn't have kidnapped them," Ian said, but then closed his eyes, shook his head. "How hard is *I don't want to talk about it* to understand?"

"If you hadn't saved his life, someone else would've grabbed those kids," Phoebe countered. "And I'm not talking about it—I'm just stating a few more facts. When you come up . . ." She made a classic zipping and locking motion near her mouth, tossing the imaginary key over her shoulder.

Ian laughed. "Yeah, I'll believe that when I see it," he said.

"Well, then I'll see you upstairs, believing me completely, in just a little bit," she told him.

He sighed. "I don't know, Pheeb . . . I just don't see how this ends happily and, um . . ."

"Uh-oh," she said sitting back down. "Is this how it begins? The pushing away?"

He sighed again. But then nodded. "Yeah. I guess so."

"How about we break the pattern," she suggested, "and agree right now that when it's over, it's over. We get the kids back, when? Day after tomorrow, if everything goes according to plan. That's kind of soon. I mean, what? We get to spend tonight and then maybe tomorrow night together? I'm not sure that's enough."

He laughed at that. "It's definitely not for me."

"What if we hop a plane afterward," Phoebe said. "Go to Vegas. Or anywhere, really. Just get a room and a lot of room service for three or maybe four days. *Then* we shake hands, say good-bye, and return to our regularly scheduled lives."

It was a terrible idea. Even as she was suggesting it, she knew that. But it was significantly better than pretending whatever this was between them was real—while watching him start to push her away. God.

And now he was looking at her with something else entirely in his eyes. "To avoid disappointment, you may want to rework your expectations about what happens when this job ends. Usually there's about four days, possibly a week, of debriefings with the feds. We'll continue to be in a safe location for that, although sadly, we'll all be separated and isolated—it's standard procedure. But then, there's Davio. You can't go out into the world with him still looking to find me through you. It might take more than a week to get him to calm down."

Phoebe absolutely hadn't thought about that. "How is *that* going to happen?" she asked.

"I'll be able to reach Manny through Berto," Ian said. "Manny'll keep Davio in line." It wasn't so much the way he looked at her when he said that, as it was the way he *didn't* look at her.

And Phoebe suddenly understood, at least basically, what Ian had promised Berto, while they were talking in the garage.

"Oh my God," she said. "You're going back to jail, aren't you? Even though you don't have to . . . ?"

He was. She knew from the way he glanced over toward the den where Berto was sleeping, and from the tight expression on his face, that Ian had already reactivated the deal he'd originally made with Manny Dellarosa. After this rescue was over, he was going to go back into the state prison system to take up where he'd left off. Somehow or another, he'd get back in there. If the FBI didn't help him, he'd probably hold up a liquor store and let himself get caught.

"What exactly did you promise him you'd do in there?" she asked, lowering her voice. "Manny? I mean, in addition to serving what's-his-name—Vincent's—time."

She watched as Ian decided whether to tell her everything, or nothing, or something in between the two. She knew him well enough to know that he was going to go with nothing, so she pushed.

"Who does he want you to kill for him?" she asked.

That got her a solid shake of his head. "No," Ian said. "That's not . . . I wouldn't."

Well, that was good at least. "Then why does he need you inside?" Phoebe asked.

Ian didn't say a word, but the way he shook his head again made her realize—with a sudden flash of understanding—that she was asking the wrong question.

"Why do *you* need to be in there?" she whispered as she tried to further read his mind by searching his eyes. *To protect Aaron and his family*. She knew that. It was Ian's mission statement, his raison d'être. But how could he protect them from inside of a prison?

By bringing down the Dellarosas, for once and for all. "Oh my God . . ."

He must've realized that she'd figured it out and that she was not going to stop pushing, because he leaned close to explain, "There's a sentencing hearing coming up for a man who's believed to have worked for Manny and Davio Dellarosa. It's a money-laundering case."

"I read about that," she said. "The accountant."

Ian nodded.

She'd read and learned a lot about the Dellarosas over the past few days, but this ongoing case had stood out. She couldn't remember the man's name, but according to the record, there had been much excitement in the Tampa DA's office when he was found to be laundering money. Huge amounts of money. There was believed to be a connection to the Dellarosa family, and there was a statewide *Now we've got them* sense of elation. But evidence tying the Dellarosas to the crime had never surfaced, and the accountant refused to turn against his alleged former bosses.

The accountant's case had been lost and an appeal filed—but recently denied by a higher court. The guilty verdict would stand. The defendant had been out on bail all this time, but his sentencing was impending—after which time he would go directly to jail.

"I've already spoken to Deb," Ian told Phoebe now. "She'll make sure he's sent to Northport, where I'll eventually flip him."

"Even though no one's ever turned against the Dellarosas before this?" she asked.

"This is different," he said, his attention back on the maintenance work in front of him. "This guy's never been to jail before. He's an accountant. I'm going to scare the shit out of him—tell him that Manny told me to kill him—and *that's* going to flip him. It might take me a year—I might have to break someone's arm to stay in longer—but I know that I can get him to testify, and that'll put both Manny and Davio away for good. Now, do me a favor and pretend you never asked me about this."

But Phoebe wasn't done asking questions. "How long have you been planning this?" The trial had happened well over a year ago. The appeal had been in motion as soon as the guilty verdict came down.

"I'm done talking about it," Ian said.

He may have been, but she wasn't. She had to assume—since he wouldn't admit it—that when Ian had first gone to prison, he'd known that this man, the accountant, would end up with him, behind bars, at some point during his eighteen-month sentence.

Talk about a long, *long* con.

"But we ruined it for you," Phoebe said. "By pulling you out of Northport. You can't just go back in."

"Yeah, I can," he said.

"It's too dangerous," she argued. "How are you going to explain why you were released, and why you're suddenly back?"

"I'll think of something."

"Ian . . ."

"Pheeb, I gotta. I know it'll work. I need to do this. I'm sorry."

Phoebe laughed her disbelief, because the alternative was to cry. And she realized in that moment that all of her tough talk was just that—tough talk. Sure, she'd said they'd say good-bye after three or four days, but she hadn't really believed it. She'd expected, instead, some kind of Hollywood rom-com happy ending. With Ian, as the hero, realizing that he was wrong, and running through the airport to stop her from boarding a plane to Tibet, or pulling up in a stretch limo outside of her apartment to proclaim his love and whisk her away to his billionaire lair, where they'd live happily ever after.

"Well, damn," she said. "I guess we don't need to fabricate an end date."

Ian nodded. "I am sorry. If it's any consolation, I mean that. Very much. I don't think I've ever been this sorry about anything." He looked at her directly now, as if he wanted her to see the truth of his words in his eyes. And the stupid thing was that she *did* believe him—even though she knew he was a con artist, a bullshitter, a professional liar.

"I want, more than anything, to spend this time—these next few days—with you," he admitted. "But I don't want to make this worse, or harder for you, or, Jesus, you really want to know how I feel? Like I need to protect you *from* me."

"No, you don't," Phoebe whispered. "I'm a grown woman, and I know what I'm doing."

He finally looked away. "Look, I'm just gonna just sleep down here."

"Hey," Phoebe said, and when he turned to look at her, she kissed him. And the way he kissed her back convinced her that this was not a mistake. When she pulled back to look into his eyes, she managed, somehow to smile. “Don’t you dare. It is what it is. And I’ll take it. From now, right to the moment it ends. Don’t make choices for me.”

She left him with that, and made it all the way upstairs and into her room—their room—before she let herself start to cry.

But when Ian finally came up—and he did, closing the door behind him with such heat in his eyes—she was able to smile before she kissed him. And, as he took her to heaven, she even managed not to talk.

At least not too much.

CHAPTER TWENTY-TWO

The morning was gorgeous. The air wasn’t quite crisp—Miami didn’t do crisp, not at this time of year. Still, the sky was blue and the humidity was bearable. And the weather forecast—sunny all day—was perfect for an evening cruise.

Of course this was Florida, where the sky could go from clear to towering cumulonimbus in the blink of an eye. Still, Ian took the sparkling sunlight as a good sign.

He was fed, he’d slept well, he was wearing dry clothes, and he’d just gotten laid. Again.

He’d woken up to find Phoebe, soft and naked in his arms. They’d slept that way all night—spooned together with her back to his front—and despite that, he was loath to let her go.

His breathing must've changed, or maybe she just sensed that he was awake, because she woke up, too, with a sigh and a smile, pushing her hair back out of both of their faces, even as she reached between her legs to find him in his full boy-howdy morning state.

The temptation to just shift a little and enter her was powerful. Ian didn't want to move away from her, not even long enough to reach for one of their few remaining condoms.

There was one under his pillow. When he'd put it there last night, Phoebe had teased him about expecting a visit from the sex fairy, and he'd laughed and kissed her. And kissed her. And kissed her . . .

It was right there. He could grab it, open it, and put it on. It would take less than a minute, even if he only used one hand.

But God *damn,* he didn't want to. For the first time in his entire life he wanted . . . more. And it wasn't him wanting the pleasure of sex with nothing between them—he respected them both too much to risk everything for that. No, it was the idea of sharing himself with this woman, and of having her share herself so completely in return.

Herself and her life.

It wasn't fifty-fifty, Aaron had told him. *It's a-hundred-a-hundred, because you give everything, and you get everything in return.*

Ian wanted *that*. And he knew that he had it—right there, in his arms.

Phoebe, meanwhile, was playing with fire. She was touching him, stroking him, using him to stroke herself, daring to push him—just a little bit—inside of her.

"Ian," she breathed. "I want you."

He wanted her, too. But she wasn't his to have, to hold, to keep.

So he dug for the condom, and gently pulled himself away from the silken touch of her hands, and made damn sure that she was safe.

She breathed his name as he came back to her, as he pushed himself home. And he took his sweet time, touching her in all of the places, in all of the ways that he knew gave her pleasure, until she came in slow motion around him, and he let himself go, too, still wishing for the impossible. . . .

He'd gotten out of bed almost immediately after, unable or maybe just unwilling to talk, murmuring, "I need to get moving," and she'd let him go.

He'd showered, gotten dressed, and gone downstairs, where Francine was watching Rory, and Martell was making breakfast and watching Francine. Hard to tell if that was for Berto's sake, or if Martell had become genuinely enamored. And that—the idea of Francine finding happiness—was probably just more wishful thinking on Ian's part.

He took his coffee out onto the back lanai, where the morning was beautiful, even with the privacy shades pulled down. But it wasn't as beautiful as it had been just minutes ago, with Phoebe in his arms. And then he gently pushed her from the forefront of his thoughts and took out his phone and dialed the number that the Dutchman had given him.

The man picked up on the first ring. "Vanderzee."

Ian had expected to leave a message, and he had to work to sound pleased that he'd made human contact. When in need, channel Captain Kirk. In other words, go big. "Georg. It's Ian. Good morning."

"It is a good morning, my friend. I was hoping to hear from you."

Words to warm the cockles of his heart, assuming both that his heart had cockles and that he was as big of a douchebag as the Dutchman. "About that business situation we spoke of yesterday—I'm afraid my time line has moved to *now,*" Ian told the man. "I'm experiencing a clusterfuck and . . . I'm calling on a scrambled line—is yours secure?"

"It is."

"Okay." Ian exhaled hard. "That's good. And, look, I'll understand completely if you're unable to help. I realize I'm asking a lot, but it's also a financial opportunity, so." Another deep breath. "I've got six point five mill of product—good-quality crystal meth. It's not top tier, but it's very good—except my buyer just bailed. I've got to move this shit fast, it's on fire, *and* I'm in a cash hole, which, as you know, is not a good combination. I've got an asshole breathing down my neck, looking to seize the entire shipment in lieu of the million-one that I owe him, and while I'm willing to take a loss, one that big would . . ." He laughed. "Jesus, it would cripple me."

Vanderzee murmured words of consolation.

Ian continued. "I've got to get this out of the country tonight, I've got a safe way to do it, but I don't have warehousing overseas, so it needs a destination. It doesn't matter where, I can get it there, as long as it's OCONUS. If you've got a connection to *any*one who might be in the market for it outside the U.S., I'll take a deep cut. I'll let it go for four mill, maybe even three point five, plus you'll get a finder's fee, but only if and when the deal goes down. And I apologize if that last part sounded hostile, that was *not* my intention at all. After yesterday, I owe you my life."

The Dutchman chuckled. "You owe me nothing. After all these years, we're finally even."

"Still," Ian said. "I know I'm asking too much. You don't know my operation. I thought we'd have more time for me to show you how it works. And I'm sorry about—"

"I'll see what I can do," the Dutchman jumped in, exactly as Ian had expected him to.

He could tell from the man's voice that he'd swallowed the bait.

"Thank you," Ian said, and actually meant it.

"I'll be in touch," and with that the call was ended.

Ian looked up to see Francine standing in the doorway with Rory.

“So that was a thing of beauty,” Francie said as she bounced the little boy on her hip.

Ian nodded. “He’ll call back, within the hour. He’ll offer three point six, with apologies. He’ll sweeten the deal by telling me that his finder’s fee will come from the buyer.”

“Putty in your capable hands,” she said. “You want pancakes?”

“No, thanks,” Ian said. “I’m good.”

“Hmm,” she said as she walked away, and maybe she didn’t mean anything, but he took it to mean *Then why are you down here when Phoebe’s upstairs, and what’s up with that anyway?*

Or maybe she meant, *Why don’t you predict an accurate future for Phoebe as long as you’re being clairvoyant? You know you can do it. . . .*

Francine was right. Ian could do it.

Over the next few days, Phoebe would help him with this job, save those kids, feel great. And then, she’d try to save him. Try, and fail, and probably cry, get angry, rail, grieve, and finally accept. And eventually, as he sank back into the bowels of the state prison system, as days, then weeks, then months slipped past, she’d go about living her life. She’d remember Ian fondly as a moment of madness, a crazy encounter, a temporary boyfriend—as she herself had called him. Eventually though, she’d find a man who recognized how special she was, and *he’d* wake up beside her every morning, well aware of how infinitely lucky he was.

And Ian could sit here pretending that he would be glad for her when that happened—that what he truly wanted more than anything was her happiness.

But all he could think was: *shit.*

Aaron woke up to find Sheldon, with his clothes and his shoes in his arms, heading for the door, on the verge of sneaking out of their room as what looked like midmorning light leaked in around the window shades.

"Hey," Aaron said.

Shel turned to face him, guilt flashing briefly in his eyes. "Crap! I'm sorry I woke you. I wanted to let you sleep."

Aaron sat up, reaching for his phone to see . . . It was well after nine. "I should've been up by now."

"It's okay. Most of us are on hold. Ian's still waiting for Vanderzee to call him back," Shel reported. "They spoke earlier, and Ian dropped the bait. Nothing for us to do until the mark bites."

This was the time, during a job like this, where you prepped on sheer faith that the mark would go all in. And while Yashi and Deb were probably scrambling to procure everything that was on Ian's wish list, the rest of the team had already memorized the various maps and floor plans of both the warehouse and the consulate, and they were now mostly holding.

"For what it's worth," Shel continued, "Ian's confident he's gonna call. He's certain that Vanderzee's low on funds, due to being unable to move those children. The kind of security needed for that, both active and passive, can't be cheap."

Active security included payroll for guards, who knew damn well what they were guarding. *Passive* was paying people to look the other way or to stick their fingers in their ears and go *la la la*. Ian was right about that—hiding two kids for this many days was a hardcore cash suck.

Aaron agreed with his brother in that it was just a matter of time before the Dutchman called them back.

He stretched. He'd slept better than he had in days—thanks to Shel's demand for forgiveness. "What time did Roar get up?"

"The usual."

"I can't believe I didn't hear him."

"I was already awake," Shel said. "I got to him pretty quickly."

"Thanks."

"He's in the kitchen with Francie," Shel told him. "Martell's making pancakes. With blueberries and real maple syrup."

"Ugh," Aaron made a sound of despair as he suddenly remembered. "I should've reminded Eee about the babysitter."

"Already done," Shelly said. "Due to arrive in a few hours. Alex Murray."

Aaron laughed. "Seriously? Johnny Murray's kid." Murray'd served in the SEALs with Ian, and had worked with them all on a number of jobs.

"Johnny's coming, too," Shel said. "He could do

this for Eee without risking jail time, so it's all working out."

"Well, we now know Rory's going to be super-safe. That's good." As Aaron pushed back the covers and got out of bed, Sheldon slightly shifted his armload of clothing, as if to hide what he was carrying, which was kind of weird, since it wasn't Aaron's birthday.

He was holding a yellow legal pad right on the top of his shoes and clothes, and Aaron could see that the front page was completely covered with Shel's messy handwriting. Except, as he got closer, he saw that—whatever it was on that pad—it wasn't messy. Shel had taken extra time to be legible. Damn, he'd actually printed in careful block letters.

"What's that?" Aaron asked, pointing as he shuffled past, on his way into the bathroom.

"Oh. Just notes," Shel said, following him to the door. "I couldn't sleep, so I outlined the changes that need to be made to the computer program for the ship's compass. You know, in case Vanderzee goes onto the bridge and we want him to believe we're heading south. Or north. Depending. I didn't have my laptop, and I didn't want to wake you, so I just wrote it out longhand and, um . . ."

"And here I'd thought you'd started writing me poetry," Aaron teased as he flushed and went to the sink to wash his hands and then brush his teeth.

Shelly smiled at that. "Yeah, you definitely don't want that."

"I might." Aaron turned on the shower, to let the

water warm up. He spat and rinsed and put his toothbrush back, then took Shel's armload of stuff from him on his way past, carrying it over to the bed. Now that Aaron was up, there was no longer any need for him to leave the room to shower. "I'll join you in there, in a sec. I just want to stretch out my leg." An old injury, a twisted knee, acted up in the rain. It helped if he kept limber and . . . Whoa, wait. "This is *notes?*"

The legal pad was covered in clearly written, clearly worded instructions that bore little to no resemblance to Shel's usual scribbled notes. Aaron flipped through the pages—and there were pages. And pages. No way was this notes. It was, instead, a carefully penned recipe.

So that someone besides Sheldon could program the yacht's computer, as well as the GPS on whatever phones Ian brought on board.

Aaron turned back to see Shel still standing in the bathroom door, that guilty look back in his eyes.

And in a dizzying rush, Aaron understood what this was. What all of it was. Why it had been so important to Shel that Aaron forgive him, that they make up, make love. His words, from earlier yesterday: *I love you. And Rory. I would do anything for you. Please always remember that.* He'd repeated the sentiment, in a similar message, last night.

Sheldon was saying good-bye.

"If you aren't going to be here, to program the computer and the phones," Aaron asked, even though he already knew the answer, "where *are* you going to be?"

Shel didn't try to bullshit him. He told the truth. "I thought I'd . . . try to talk to him."

"Davio." Aaron laughed even though he could feel his head imploding.

Shel nodded. "Ian said he'd be at that meeting tonight, at the hospital. In Sarasota. I thought maybe, since Manny'd be there—"

"No." Aaron crossed the room to him in several large strides. "Nuh-uh. Nope. You are *not* doing this." He put his arms around Shelly, as if that would somehow keep him from leaving. Jesus, he'd tie him up if necessary, but he'd start here.

"It's been ten years," Shel said as he clung to Aaron, too—as if he likewise didn't want to let him go. "I just keep thinking, maybe if I go and try to talk to him—"

"Talk?" Aaron repeated. "To the crazy man?"

"I have to try," Shel whispered. "All this bullshit—it's all my fault. Right from the start. God, you deserve more. You deserve better."

So said the man who'd spent four years searching for him. Aaron had had other boyfriends in that rough and rocky time after high school, while they were apart, but Sheldon hadn't. Shel had loved him, and he'd stayed true.

"What I deserve," Aaron said now, working it hard to keep his voice from shaking, "is a chance to argue more about what you should or shouldn't have told me when you found out that Ian was in

Northport. What I deserve is a chance to watch our son grow up with you beside me. *God, grant me the serenity to accept the things I cannot change*." Aaron pulled back to look into Shelly's eyes. "Baby, you *know* that your father is one of those things that will never, *ever* change."

Shel was silent.

"I love you," Aaron continued. "You—with your miserable family and bullshit emotional luggage that doesn't quite match mine, but comes pretty damn close. I even love you when I'm hurt and angry and when I stomp around and pretend that I might leave."

"That was pretend?" Shel asked. "Because it felt kind of . . . not."

"I promise you, I *swear* to you, that I won't ever leave," Aaron told him, "if you promise and swear that you won't either. Although I think we already agreed to this, years ago, in Canada."

Shel smiled at that. It was shaky, but it was definitely a smile. "I'm so sorry," he said.

"I forgive you," Aaron said, and this time, he honestly meant it.

He was leaning in to kiss Shelly, and then move this conversation into the steam-creating shower, when someone with fists of stone hammered on the bedroom door.

Boom boom boom!

It had to be Francine. She could pack one hell of a punch. "Shel! Aaron!" It was. "Get your asses out here! Vanderzee just called Ian. We're *go*. I repeat, this mission is *go!*"

• • •

Phoebe held the world's most adorable baby while the team leapt into action around her. She wasn't particularly good with children, but this one was a living advertisement for procreation, with his long eyelashes, cherub's cheeks, bright eyes, and joyful if drool-soggy smile.

As she and Rory watched, Martell and Yashi tried on their security guard uniforms—Martell fiercely fashion-walked in his—while Francine pretended not to be amused. Phoebe hung close, fascinated, as the blonde instructed Yashi as to how the fake-blood pack worked.

Across the room, Berto had drawn a floor plan of his warehouse, and he and Ian were discussing exactly where, inside, the coming meeting with the Dutchman should take place, where the tied up and head-bagged guards—AKA Martell and Yashi—should be positioned, and where Francine could be hidden with a sniper rifle, watching and ready, in case something went wrong.

Ian made Phoebe look at the drawing, too. In case of that dreaded something-goes-wrong scenario, she was supposed to stay close to him, but if something—again with the impending doom of that dire-sounding *something*—happened to him, she was to head for the office in the back. And if she couldn't get there, she should take cover behind a hill of crates.

Phoebe discovered that she really didn't like thinking about what she would do if *something* happened to Ian.

God help her, she was in trouble, because something *was* going to happen to him. After this was over, he was going back to prison, where, if Manny or Davio or even Berto found out that he was really there trying to bring them down, he would immediately be killed. She couldn't stop thinking that. Surely there had to be a better way. . . .

But there was no time to talk to Ian about any of it. In fact, they hadn't had a real conversation since last night. Between then and now, the talking they'd done hadn't gone much beyond *Oh, God,* and *Yes, please, more, yes!*

Phoebe'd woken up to find Ian watching her, and they'd made love again—exquisitely, beautifully, tenderly—in the pale morning light.

Afterward, he got up almost immediately, and she let him leave the room, even though she wanted to sit up and say, *Wait. Let me help you negotiate a new agreement with Manny and Berto—one that doesn't involve prison time.*

But she didn't dare.

And by the time she'd showered and followed him downstairs, Ian had already spoken to Vanderzee—twice—and was hard at work, prepping for this dangerous game of make-believe. It was a game that Ian seemed confident they'd win.

In fact, his confidence was contagious. His charisma was irresistible. And as leader of this insane mission, he knew exactly where each of his team members would be, and exactly what they would be doing, at any given moment, over the course of what he called the “sting.” He was, without a doubt, the king of all details.

And when Ian asked her to, Phoebe dutifully studied a map of the area—filled with warehouses and other industrial buildings, and a labyrinth of roads and driveways and canals—so she would be familiar with the lay of the land.

“Here’s where Aaron’ll pull up the truck, to load the computers,” Ian said, enlarging the map on the computer screen so that Berto’s warehouse and its loading area was enormous. He hovered the cursor on a point next to the big building.

“Aaron knows how to drive an eighteen-wheeler?” Phoebe asked as Shel took a now-squirming and fragrant Rory from her arms. She immediately answered her own question. “Of course he does.” That was not something Ian would’ve overlooked.

Next to them, on the table, was one of Berto’s desktop computer towers, out of its factory packing and open to reveal a huge amount of empty space inside the metal frame. The hardware used in this type of computer didn’t take up much room, so the outer shell was a perfect vessel for contraband. Nearby was an extra-large plastic bag with a zipper closure, filled with the actual illegal drugs, procured from some FBI evidence locker. They didn’t need enough to fill all of the computers—just one. That would be enough to fool the Dutchman.

Although, “What if we lose that?” Phoebe asked

Ian, pointing to the bag. "What if it falls overboard, or the boat sinks, or—"

"I try to take life one goatfuck at a time," he said, tapping on the computer screen to return her attention to the map. "Here's where we'll park when we arrive"—he hovered the arrow over a spot near where the truck was to go—"and here's where the surveillance van'll be hidden."

Sheldon would be inside of the van, monitoring the situation, and keeping an eye on the feed from a series of video cameras placed around the perimeter to make sure that there were, as Ian put it, "no uninvited guests to the party."

But that was unlikely, given the geography.

Berto owned a number of warehouses in Miami, but the one he and Ian had chosen was the last building on a dead-end street, which meant they wouldn't have to deal with a stream of traffic driving past. It had a long driveway and the delivery bay was around the back of the structure, facing the windowless wall of a neighboring warehouse—providing them with even more isolation.

Francine was going over to the site early, and with Martell's and Yashi's help, she would set up the cameras—as well as help Berto prep. He needed to look as if he'd been shot, and it not only had to appear real, but as if he'd already given himself first aid. They didn't want the Dutchman playing the medic-hero and ripping open Berto's bloody shirt to find no bullet wound beneath.

Deb, meanwhile, was already over at the dock,

awaiting the arrival of the luxury speedboat that would take them—and their "illegal" cargo—to Fake-Cuba and back. She had *not* done a fashion-walk in the clothing she was going to wear, but she had grimaced when looking into the shopping bag that held her sideboob-baring outfit.

If the yacht arrived promptly, Deb would come to the warehouse and join Shelly in the surveillance van.

"We'll be meeting Vanderzee at sixteen hundred—four o'clock." Ian translated the time into nonmilitary-speak for Phoebe. "With a goal of departing from the dock by seventeen thirty."

Phoebe did the math: If they left at 5:30 P.M., they would arrive in Pretend-Cuba just before ten o'clock, long after the sun set. That would give them plenty of hours of darkness to unload the cargo and make the four-hour journey back. And it would have to be dark when they left in order for the charade to succeed, since Florida was decidedly more built up than the part of Cuba to which they were allegedly going. And of course, there was the matter of the sun, rising in the east, and hanging there in the sky, making it very clear as to whether they were traveling north or south . . .

"I'm going to try to talk him into going to Berto's warehouse in our car," Ian continued, *him* being the Dutchman, "but I'm not sure that'll happen. He might want to take his own vehicle. He'll also be accompanied by some of his men. I'm going to try to pare that down to the smallest possible number. I doubt we'll get him to come alone, in fact we probably don't want that, because we're going to go straight from the warehouse to the dock, and I *know* he's not going on a four-hour boat ride without at least one bodyguard."

"A four-hour tour," Sheldon sang to the tune of the *Gilligan's Island* theme song, as he danced past them with Rory. "A four-hour tour!"

The baby's laughter made Ian smile, and there it was again, that terrible earth-shifting feeling inside of her, but this time it was accompanied by a powerful layer of warmth.

"You should probably talk to Francine and Martell and Yashi before they leave for the warehouse," she told Ian, as he said, "I really need to touch base with Berto."

"Him, too," Phoebe added, nodding as she stood up, needing to put some distance between them before she did something stupid, like throw herself onto the floor while sobbing *But I don't want this to end!* "And I should try on the clothes that Yashi got for me, and figure out what I'm going to do with my hair. If we're supposed to be dressed up, I should probably look less like a refugee."

"I love your hair." Ian looked a little surprised by what he'd just said.

And okay. She, too, was also a little flustered, both by the way he was looking at her, and the fact that he'd used the word *love* in a sentence that started with *I*. True, it was only her hair that he loved. Still . . .

He added, “And however you want to wear it, I’m sure it’ll be . . . beautiful.”

“You were going to say *fine,*” Phoebe realized, “but you recognized that no one, male or female, ever wants to be told that they look merely *fine,* so you did a quick substitution. That is truly remarkable.” She started to slow-clap, mostly because it kept her from grabbing him and kissing him. “You are, indeed, a highly evolved *Homo sapiens*.”

But as Ian laughed, he pushed his chair away from the table, pulled her down onto his lap, and kissed her. Thoroughly. In front of everyone.

When he finally stopped, her fingers were in his hair—his beautiful, thick, wavy hair—and as she held his gaze, as he smiled at her, Phoebe dared to say it back. “I really love your hair, too.”

Berto’s Miami warehouse was mostly empty, and Francine’s footsteps echoed as she went inside.

It was cooler in there than it was out in the blazing heat of the parking lot, but not by much, which meant this whole stage of the job was going to be a sweaty, stinking ordeal. But that somehow seemed appropriate, considering she was back in a warehouse with the man whom she’d once believed was the love of her life.

The boxes of computer towers were stacked close to the loading dock, but other than that, there were only a few other small hills of crates in the entire huge space.

There was, however, a line of forklifts at the ready, should the need arise.

There was a small office in the back corner—a bathroom, too, which was good. That meant she wouldn't have to pee in the parking lot, since she was here for the next few hours—until Ian and the Dutchman came and went.

Martell had driven over here with her and Berto —*that* had been a fun half hour ride. Francine had closed her eyes and pretended to sleep in the back, while Martell rode an uneasy shotgun. He'd started a short discussion about music. Stevie Wonder. Al Green. Motown. Nobody hated Motown, so it was a good try. But Berto clearly hadn't wanted to chat, so they soon fell into an uncomfortable silence.

While he drove, Berto had made a phone call to the security team that checked in on his property as part of their local rounds—letting them know that they should scratch his address off their list for today and tonight. He was, ahem, holding a private party in his building, and didn't want to be interrupted.

Apparently, it was not uncommon for him to make that request.

Berto had opened up the huge bay doors to the loading dock when they arrived, and now, with Martell close at hand, he followed Francine as she looked around.

She squinted upward, where there was a metal catwalk. As the daylight continued to fade, it would disappear into the darkness of the high ceiling and become invisible. It wasn't her first choice for a sniper position—she would be vulnerable to counterattack—but it was probably the only real option.

The benefit would be a bird's-eye view of the action. If she positioned herself right, she'd have a clear shot of the driveway and the well-lit loading dock, too.

Martell knew what she was planning and was concerned. "We've got time—we can move some of those other crates closer," he said. "Give you some cover."

"Said the man who's going to be lying out on the floor in a puddle of fake blood, with his hands cuffed and a bag over his head," she countered.

"Yeah, that's going to be harder to do than I thought," he agreed. "Let's make sure Dunn has blanks in his weapon, aight? Or maybe we could stuff those rent-a-cop unies with straw instead?"

Francine smiled. "Yeah, because the Dutchman won't notice *that*. No, the catwalk'll do fine. Even if I'm needed for a demonstration of force, I'll be far enough away that he won't see my face."

Berto spoke up. "When I bought the place, I had a five-year contract with a regional pharmacy chain," he said, apparently feeling that he had to explain the lack of ware in the house. "Four months in, they went bankrupt. We've been limping along, month to month, ever since."

Francine nodded as she again looked around. "You could subdivide this space. Bring in some mattresses. Turn it into a whorehouse. Warehouse, whorehouse—I'm surprised you didn't think of that sooner."

"Easy there," Martell murmured.

"I'm not a pimp," Berto said on a tired exhale.

"Oh, so it's your *father* who handles that part of the family business?" she asked. "While you just, what? Look the other way? I guess that's not as bad. Oh, wait. No. It is."

"Let's get this makeup and costume thing happening," Martell interjected. "Review the scenario." He clapped his hands, in Tony Robbins–like fake excitement. "So, the story is that Berto drives up, and finds two men and a truck parked here at the loading bay, getting ready to steal his extra-special, mind-altering, super-valuable shipment of computers. His guards are tied up, bags on their heads, one of them's dead—that would be me—the other's unconscious."

But Berto had turned to face Francine. "You have the right to hate me for a lot of things, but not that," he said.

"I have the right to hate you for whatever the fuck I want!" she shot back, and she heard Martell sigh.

"Look," Martell said. "Kids. This isn't the time or place—"

"I didn't mean to kill that man," Berto told Francine, surprising her by just saying it, outright. "That night."

"Or maybe it is," she heard Martell say, as he

gave them both some space. "I'll be over here, if you need me."

"He broke into the warehouse—our warehouse—and he came screaming out the door like a bat out of hell," Berto told her. "Scared the shit out of me. He came right at me. He was out-of-his-mind high."

The man who was talking, the man Francine was looking at, was tired and aging ungracefully. He was overweight and balding and the lines on his face were markers of sorrow, not laughter. And yet, in his eyes, she could see a ghost of the boy he'd once been. And she couldn't look away.

"He was fried," Berto told her. "He was fucked up, and he came right at me, with his crazy hair and his psycho eyes and . . . He jumped me, he tried to knock me over, he tried to take the gun, and it went off. And then he was dead."

"You fired twice," she whispered. "Aaron heard the gunshots."

He shook his head. "I don't remember that. I guess I must've, if that's what he heard. But it's really a blur. Although the trigger was always . . . sensitive, so . . ."

She believed him. Still . . . "Why did you take your gun?" she asked. "Why did you even have it with you?"

"I wanted to scare him," Berto said. "Aaron."

That she *didn't* believe.

He corrected himself before she could call *bullshit*. "I wanted to kill him, but I wouldn't have."

"I think you would've," she countered. "I think

you were going to. Because I know you knew what your father was doing to me—probably right when you were loading that fucking gun." She could tell from his eyes that she was right. He *had* known. "And I think you brought Aaron there—to our place, our special place—to punish me even more."

"Maybe," he admitted.

"I consider myself lucky," she said, "that I saw the real you, the ugly you, before I did something stupid, like marry you."

Except even as she said those bitter, angry words, she had the sense that the boy she could still glimpse in this man's eyes was, in truth, the real Berto Dellarosa. Even after all this time.

"Yeah, well, then, lucky you, right?" he said as he blinked, as he turned away from her, as the boy disappeared. But then he turned back, this man, this stranger, and said, "You know, I forgive you, Francine."

She laughed her surprise, but he was serious.

"For not telling me, in advance, what you were doing," he continued. "For not trusting me, long before that, with the news—and it *was* a knock-me-over news flash when I found out that Shel was gay. For assuming—ridiculously—that I really believed that you loved me, that I didn't wake up every fucking day and wonder what someone like you was doing with a piece of crap like me."

His words made her want to throw up, filling her with a mix of anger and frustration and sorrow and despair. She honed in on the anger, using it to banish the less-useful emotions. “Do you forgive Davio, too?” she asked, her voice harsh. “When you’re busy being so generous?”

“Do you forgive a rabid dog for acting like a rabid dog?” he countered.

“Fuck you, Confucius,” Francine said. “You don’t forgive a rabid dog, you fucking put it down.”

“Yeah, but Uncle Manny wouldn’t like that,” Berto said. “He feels responsible for Davio. The rabid dog is still Manny’s brother. You of all people should understand that, all those years you spent searching for Pauline.”

“Whatever,” Francine said as she led the way across the scarred and pitted concrete floor to the air-conditioned office where they’d get Berto into his blood-soaked bandages. “You want to think there’s a comparison between a child and her abuser, you go on and think that. But you’re full of shit.” She raised her voice. “Martell!”

“Yes, ma’am!” He was, as he’d promised, nearby, and as she looked into his eyes, she knew he’d heard everything. “Whatever you need. I stand ready to help.”

Francine had to look away. “Let’s do this thing,” she said.

CHAPTER TWENTY-THREE

Everyone was wearing radio headsets for this phase of the job. Martell and Yashi would wear a security guardlike version beneath their burlap sacks. Even Phoebe wore one. Hers and Ian's both looked like Bluetooths, and since she'd never used one before, it felt cumbersome and cyborgish attached to her ear.

According to Ian, Sheldon was already in place. He would be monitoring the entire meeting from the safety of the surveillance van. He'd have access to the feed from a collection of strategically placed security cameras, and if something went wrong, he'd be their eyes and ears.

Aaron, too, had already reported in from the warehouse. The 18-wheeler was in position. In fact, he and the others—Shel, Francie, and Yashi—had already moved half of the boxes into the trailer. Berto and Martell were sidelined from that task, due to not wanting to mess up their realistically bloody stage makeup.

At least Phoebe hoped it looked realistic.

She tried not to be nervous as she and Ian headed for Georg Vanderzee's house.

"I may need some help," she told Ian. "Some coaching, in how to hide my revulsion."

He smiled briefly as he glanced at her. "I focus on the outcome," he said. "Saving those kids.

Getting Aaron's record wiped clean. And if that doesn't work, I think happy thoughts. You and me. I'll replay this morning. That'll make me smile."

"I could imagine learning to love my alarm clock," Phoebe agreed, even as she blushed a little, "if *that* always happened, immediately after it rang."

"Alarm cock," he said, glancing at her again. "Sorry, I had to say it. You know you were thinking it."

"Sorry," she said, laughing. "But I wasn't. Because I'm not a fourteen-year-old boy disguised as a thirty-something anti-hero."

"I think I might be on to something that could sell *really* well," Ian said, full on ignoring her anti-hero comment.

"Yeah, if *you're* what you're selling," Phoebe countered. "The alarm part kind of doesn't work without the . . . you know."

He glanced at her again. "Say it, say it, say it. I bet that you won't say it," he said beneath his breath, but of course, intentionally loud enough for her to hear.

"You'd win that bet, man-child," Phoebe told him as she laughed.

"Will you promise that you'll whisper it in my ear, if something happens," Ian said, "and it looks like I might die?"

He realized, maybe because she'd stopped smiling, how *completely* unfunny she found his request. Joke. It was supposed to be a joke, but God.

"That's not going to happen," he said quickly. "Shit, I'm sorry."

"Cock," she said. "Okay? Now you can . . . die happy, or whatever."

"Okay," he said. "Whoa. Wait. I wasn't ready for that. Totally unexpected. Would you mind very much saying it again?"

Phoebe laughed again, despite herself. "Yes," she said. "I would mind."

They were approaching a red light, but instead of stopping, Ian pulled into the parking lot of a convenience store. He jammed the car into park, grabbed her, and kissed her.

And when he was done, he held her face between his hands and looked into her eyes and told her, "Nothing bad is going to happen to me, and I'm going to make damn sure that nothing bad happens to you. We're going to smile at this asshole, we're going to do this job, we're going to save those kids, and then I'm going to kiss you, just like that, for about four hours. Okay?"

Phoebe nodded, looking into his eyes, unable to speak. But then she found her voice. "Ian, we really need to talk about—"

"Shhh." He kissed her again. "One goatfuck at a time, okay?"

She nodded.

"Tell me again," Ian said, "what you're going to say, when we get to the warehouse."

Phoebe widened her eyes, and gasped in appropriate horror as she said, "Berto, my God! What happened? Were you *shot?*"

"I'm okay." Berto's response came through the radio headsets that Sheldon and all of the other team members were wearing.

As Shel watched on the surveillance van's main monitor, Berto limped toward Phoebe. Ian, the Dutchman, *and* the Dutchman's bald-headed, bulgy-eyed, little bodyguard were right behind her.

The limp was maybe a little much, but Francine had done such a first-rate job with Berto's bandaged wound—it was leaking just a bit of "blood"—he could get away with the extra drama.

Deb was in the van, monitoring along with Shel.

Just moments ago, as Ian's car had turned onto the road leading to the warehouse's driveway, he'd announced to the team, "Here comes Eee and Phoebe. They've got Vanderzee with them in their car—he's got one, repeat *uno*, guard with him. Everyone, final check in."

"Deb, in the van. I'm here, too, gang. I didn't think I'd make it back in time, but I did. FYI, the yacht's perfect."

"Aaron, out by the truck." Shel's husband waved to the camera that was out on the loading dock.

"Martell. I'm dead. So I'm not moving."

"Yashi. Unconscious. Also not moving."

"The camera on you guys is working fine," Shel reported. "You look great."

"Berto." Shel's half brother sounded and looked tense as he gazed up into camera seven.

"Annette, overhead." Trust Francine to make the smartass Mouseketeers reference in a deadpan from her perch up in the catwalk.

"Ian and Phoebe, I know you're close enough now to be listening in. Do not acknowledge this, but—all of you—know and believe that I am the Lord your God for this phase of the mission," Sheldon reminded them. "If you hear my voice in your ear, you do it, you don't ask. So here they come—Ian is parking, Phoebe's getting out. Here comes Berto to greet them. . . ."

"Berto, my God! What happened? Were you shot?" Phoebe could've worked in film—she was that realistically shocked as she caught sight of Berto's bandages.

And now, over Shel's headset, Berto gave an account of the story: "I pulled up and there was a truck in the bay, and I walked in on a fucking robbery. I started shooting, they shot back, and I got hit. One of my guards is dead, the other is unconscious—I find it fucking hard to believe this wasn't some kind of inside job, because who else knew this shit was stored here?"

"Your father knew." That was Ian.

Phoebe: "Berto, you should sit down."

Berto: "We need to move this stuff now—get it the fuck out of Dodge." They moved into range of the loading dock camera, and he looked at Vanderzee as if he'd just realized the other man was there. "Are you the new buyer?"

Ian answered for him. "He was."

"*Was?* What the fuck, Dunn?" Berto was doing great. Shel wouldn't have thought he'd be much of an actor, but he was convincing in his own thuggish way.

Beside him in the van, Deb switched off her lip microphone and pointed to the part of the screen that showed the feed from the surveillance cam that was out on the main road. "Vehicle approaching. Looks like an SUV."

It was still some distance away—lot of turnoffs between where it was and the street leading to this warehouse's drive. Still, there wasn't much traffic in this recession-hit part of town at this time of late afternoon, so it was certainly worth the mention. Shel covered his mic. "Let's keep an eye on it."

Deb nodded as the show at the warehouse rolled on, and Ian and Phoebe helped Aaron lug the rest of the boxes into the truck.

Ian was explaining to Berto what he'd obviously explained to Vanderzee in the car. "My friend Georg found us an interested buyer, but at a dismal three point six. Not that I didn't appreciate it, since it was significantly better than the nothing we were looking at. Still, this morning when we spoke, I told him it was contingent not only on his testing the quality of the product, but also on our not finding another buyer between then and the time we hit Cuba. And while we were on the way over here, hallelujah, I got a call. Martell's backup guy came through, and we're going to get a full five mill."

"Jesus, that's great news," Berto said.

Ian continued: "I told Georg that I'd give him a finder's fee, out of respect for his time spent. He's also coming along to see how the operation works—which is good, since you're not going anywhere but to the doctor. You have a medic on staff?"

"Yeah, I'm gonna fucking need more than stitches for this one," Berto said, wincing.

Deb cut in, still off-mic. "Shel. They're still coming."

Sheldon looked up at the monitor. That SUV was big and black, with heavily darkened windows. . . .

Kind of like the SUVs that Davio and his men drove.

Shel found the video controls for the camera positioned right at the end of the road leading down to their turnoff. He zoomed in on the windshield of the approaching SUV, praying that it would just go past.

"Holy shit," he said, as instead the vehicle made the turn.

It was Davio. It was *Davio.* How the hell could it be Davio, who was supposed to be in a meeting with Manny, up in Sarasota . . . ?

There was no time to think, only to act, because Shel could *not* let Davio drive around to the loading dock, where Aaron was freaking standing next to the truck, like a giant target.

In a flash, he was out of the van, and running toward the car that Ian had arrived in—it was closer than Martell's, and hopefully had more power under the hood.

"Deb is now God," Shelly announced into his headset as he stopped at the edge of the building and drew his weapon from his holster. He was close enough to be able to dive for cover, but out far enough so that the men in that vehicle would be able to see him. He hoped. "We have an approaching SUV. Big enough to hold at least six men, and one of them is Davio."

Ian heard Shel's words, and his initial reaction was to kill Berto. Right then, right there, because he must've been behind this.

But Berto was looking at him, eyelids all the way up in genuine surprise, shaking his head as the first sound of gunfire echoed outside of the warehouse.

"What the hell, what the *hell!*" Aaron started shouting, his voice coming in both via headset and live, from just outside by the truck. "Sheldon, God *damn* it! What are you doing?"

Phoebe was already moving, taking Vanderzee firmly by the arm, and leading him toward the back, toward the office. "Our surveillance team just told us that we have an unannounced visitor," she told the Dutchman. She was remarkably calm, waving for the bodyguard to follow them, too.

But the man didn't do it, instead nodding at some unspoken command from his boss. He drew his own weapon, and was watching Ian, ready to back him up. If that hadn't been Davio out there, Ian would've been glad for this proof that the Dutchman considered himself part of this "team."

"Eyes, I need eyes," Ian said into his headset, even as he pushed Berto after Phoebe and Vanderzee. "Go with her. *Stay* with them," he ordered him. If he was going to war with Davio, no way did he want to be distracted by thoughts of Phoebe, alone with the Dutchman. But, fuck, his weapon was filled with blanks, while Baldy, his new sidekick, was packing serious heat. He heard the sound of gunfire again as he ran toward the loading bay, Vanderzee's man on his heels. "Deb! *Shit!* Where are you? What the fuck is happening?"

"Ack, sorry, sir, my mic was off," Deb's voice came into his ear as even more shots were fired. She brought him up to speed with a staccato narrative. "Shel just fired at the SUV. They stopped, backed up—I think the driver was hit. Now they're coming again—someone else is behind the wheel—but Shel's got your car. He's driving toward the SUV. I think he's going to try to lead them away from here—to get them to chase him."

"That's exactly what I'm doing." Sheldon, sounding stressed, his voice pitched high. "He's gonna follow, too, because he hates me, but first I've got to make sure that he saw that it was me."

"God damn it, Shel, don't! You promised! You *promised!*" Aaron was running toward the side of the building, but Ian put on a burst of speed to catch up with him.

"Shots are being fired," Deb narrated the obvious. "Sheldon is driving toward them. He's got his window down. . . ."

Ian hit his brother like a linebacker and wrestled him down to the pavement, holding him back as what sounded like a small army opened up and emptied their magazines into metal. Vanderzee's man peered around the corner of the building, looking quickly but then pulling his head back.

"Shit!" Ian heard Shelly say. "Oh, shit!" But then there was static and his voice cut out.

Tires were squealing and engines were revving, and Aaron was fighting him, and Ian could hear Phoebe, Francine, Martell, and Deb all talking at once.

Phoebe, telling Vanderzee: "It's okay. It's going to be okay. Ian will take care of it."

Martell, sounding extremely spooked: "What the *hell* is happening . . . ? I do not like this."

Francine, to Martell, her voice low: "If you move, Martell, I will make you deader than you're pretending to be."

Deb's voice was really the only one that mattered, as she alone had a visual of what was going on. "I think Shel's okay. I lost radio contact, but his car's still moving. He's heading away from the warehouse and the SUV . . . yes, is following.

Repeat, the SUV is following Sheldon's car."

"Call him," Yashi's voice came in, low and clear and calm from his place on the warehouse floor next to Martell. "Deb. Reestablish contact with Shel via cell phone."

"I'm trying," Deb said, strain in her voice. "I'm working now to get cell phone contact! But I wish you were in here! I need hands, now, to help me—Aaron, are you open?"

Ian had his arm pressed up against his brother's throat, and he gave it a shove to make sure Aaron could hear him. "If I let you go, you go *only* to the surveillance van."

The look on Aaron's face was one of sheer pain—they both knew that even if Shelly wasn't already badly wounded, it wouldn't be long, with that much firepower after him, before Davio killed him. But he nodded, and Ian released him.

Aaron scrambled away as over their headsets, Francine said, in a voice that matched Yashi's calm, "As soon you get phone contact, connect me to Shelly. I know the best route out of here. I'll get him away from Davio."

Phoebe spoke, again to Vanderzee, from where she and Berto had contained him in the back office: "We need to be ready to leave immediately when Ian gives the word. I know that one of our men took the car we arrived in, but that's okay. I'll go in the truck with Aaron. You, Hamori, and Ian can go with Berto, in *his* car."

It was a good plan, but it wasn't going to work.

Aaron wasn't going to be able to drive the truck if Shel was dead, or even just badly injured.

But what had Ian told Phoebe earlier? One disaster at a time.

And *Hamori*. That was the name of Vanderzee's bald bodyguard. The guy was looking right at Ian, as if awaiting instructions.

Meanwhile, Deb's voice was coming in through Ian's headset. She spoke over Phoebe. "Francine. How well do you know this area?"

"Map in my head's pretty complete," Francie said.

"So if I can put out an APB," Deb said, "get the police to go after the SUV and all of its passengers, Davio Dellarosa included, you could have Shel lead them to an intercept point that's—"

"Do it!" Ian said it at the same time as Francine.

Maybe, just maybe, if the police in the area were on the ball, if they stopped the SUV, if Sheldon wasn't already too badly injured . . .

Maybe Aaron's world wasn't about to end.

Shel was bleeding.

He didn't know exactly where he'd been hit, he didn't know how bad it was. It didn't hurt, but he knew from past experience that it wouldn't. Not at first. Not while his adrenaline was spiking. Of course, in Iraq, he'd been hit not by bullets, but by shrapnel from an IED.

There'd been a lot of blood that time, too. And now, as he'd done then, he tried his best to wipe his hands clean on his pants legs. Last thing he needed was a slippery steering wheel.

The back windshield shattered and he tried to make his head a smaller target, while the men in his father's SUV continued to shoot at him as he gunned it much too fast down a pitted and potholed road.

Something was ringing, and ringing and ringing, and by the time he remembered that his headset included a cell phone, the ringing had stopped. He couldn't spare the time or effort to look down to find and hit the button that would allow him to return the call, but he didn't have to wait long before the caller—Deb—called back.

"Sorry," he said, "I'm a little distracted."

"Are you hit?" It was Aaron on the other end, trying his best to be crisp and professional, and failing—his anguish evident in every syllable.

"I love you, and I'm so sorry," Shel said as his answer. He didn't think he was badly hurt, at least not yet. But he'd just tried to kill his father, and that was not going to go unpunished. If he wasn't already dead when they caught him, he'd immediately be executed. Davio would have no choice. And, God, Shelly wanted his sacrifice to be worth it. "Get out of there while you can. Do it, Aarie, *now,* for Rory's sake!"

"Please, baby, just tell me if it's bad," Aaron said.

"Deb, cut Aaron's mic, he's not helping. Shel, it's France. Where the fuck are you?" his sister asked, with her usual charm.

"I think I'm on the main road," he said as a bullet hit the headrest on the passenger side, "but I'm not sure. Aaron, God, I'm sorry. I swear, I didn't plan this."

"Focus," Francine said. "Tell me the turns you've made, and I *will* get you out of there."

"Right at the end of the driveway, then another right. I've been going straight ever since."

"Have you gone over the railroad tracks?" she asked.

"No, I'm approaching that now. Shit!" His side mirror exploded.

"First right after the tracks," she said. "Take it. If they manage to make the turn behind you, keep going straight, but if they miss it and you lose them—even just temporarily—take the first right after that. There's a parking garage there, on the corner. Do *not* go in it—instead take your first left and then your first right. That's going to send you back in our direction. Meanwhile, when they trace your route and try to catch up to you, they're going to see that garage and think you've gone to ground there."

All four tires left the ground as he went over the tracks, and when he landed, he was jarred and . . . Yeah. *Now* it hurt. "Tell Aaron—" he started, but his sister cut him off.

"Fo. Cus," Francine said again, "and you can tell him yourself. Now, tell me when you turn."

"I'm turning," Shel said as he took the corner and fishtailed wildly—Jesus! The back of his car hit a parked truck, but he wrestled with the wheel and it didn't stop him. It only slowed him a little.

"Are they behind you?"

"No!" But there, on his right, was the parking garage she'd described.

"Good. Turn right, go *past* the garage, don't go in there," she warned as if she knew how dark and inviting it looked—like the perfect place to hide when being chased by lunatic madmen. "Now take the next left," she told him again, talking him through it. "Slow it down. Way down. Full stop before you take the next right. When you do, move at normal speeds. Deb, can you send the police directly to that parking garage? Davio's gonna think Shel's gone in there. They're going to drive through it, search it. Let's have the police waiting when that SUV comes out."

"I'm already on it," Deb said. "Police are on their way." She repeated the vehicle description and plate number—obtained through the video—to whatever dispatcher she had on the other line.

"Shel, stay alert," Ian's voice popped in. "Don't be careless, it's not over yet. Eyes on the rearview."

As Shel pulled up to the stop sign, he saw that a police car had just gone past. Emergency lights turning, it was moving fast and heading in the direction of the garage.

And Deb's voice again came through. "I'm getting a report of police activity, an SUV with a shattered windshield and bullet holes stopped, on the corner of . . ." She kept talking but her words faded out as Aaron came back onto the conference call.

"Shel, are you—"

"I'm okay," Shelly said as he started to shake. He must've gotten hit by a spray of breaking glass, because he had a piece embedded in his forearm, and the side of his face was cut—that was where most of the blood was coming from—but it was mostly superficial. He'd torn the crap out of his elbow as he'd skidded on the pavement, running to the car. But other than that . . .

"Go to ground," Francine's voice cut back in. "There's a strip mall on your left that's mostly boarded up. Pull behind it. We'll come and get you."

Martell continued to lie on the cold-ass warehouse floor even after Deb called, "Clear."

He'd heard the truck pull away with its faux-illegal cargo. Ian, Phoebe, Dutchie, and Hamori left, too, in Martell's car. It was kind of amazing, really, that as car after van after car got trashed, his stalwart POS remained up and running.

Martell pulled the canvas bag off of his head and sat up to find Yashi carefully detaching the FX blood pack from his chest.

"Guess Ian didn't feel the need to kill me," Yashi said with his usual blasé matter-of-factness before he headed outside. "What with everything else going down."

"Let's go," Francine said, and Martell looked up

to find her aiming her ire at him. "We need to move fast. We'll change in the van. For all we know Davio's already sicced a kill squad on us."

Yeah, plus, Deb and the surveillance van needed to get into place at the dock before Ian and the semi arrived. They were purposely taking the Dutchman to the yacht via a longer and less direct route, but that didn't mean the van could dally.

As Martell peeled off his fake-blood-soaked shirt, he followed Francine as she headed for the loading bay. "So that was pretty amazing. What you did. Saving Shelly's life?"

She glanced at him. "I'm good with maps."

"Yeah, like eidetic good."

"I always plot six different escape routes, in the event of emergency," she told him flatly as he followed her out into the late afternoon. "Which is what you're supposed to do when you're prepping for a situation in which people will be in danger. It's really not that big a deal. I did my job."

"Yeah, well, you're really good at it is all I'm saying and . . . What the *what?*" Martell did everything but roll. He stopped and dropped open his mouth as he stared at the surveillance van, which had transformed from white to a pearly blue. It was the fastest, cleanest paint job he had ever seen, but then he realized that the white had been courtesy of a shrink-wrap, which had covered the shiny blue paint. Deb and Berto had merely peeled it off.

"We're not sure if Vanderzee or Hamori got a look

at the van," Deb explained, stopping to wipe sweat from her brow as she used a wire brush to take some of the shiny newness off the thing. "But we have to assume one of them did."

Bam!

Martell looked around the side to see that Berto, meanwhile, was applying dents with a crowbar. "Baldy certainly saw Shel," he pointed out with a certain Eeyore-worthy mix of grim and glee.

"Yeah, we won't be able to use Shelly as a member of Martell's army," Francine said. "But that's okay. He can man the surveillance van."

"I continue to love that I have an army," Martell said. "Although I'll love it a lot less if Davio drops in on us in Faux-Cuba, too."

"He won't," Deb said. "He and his men are being held. But probably not for more than twenty-four hours."

"Will Sheldon actually stay inside the van this time?" Berto asked Francine.

She got in his face. "He not only saved our asses, he saved the entire sting. So what the fuck happened with the all-day meeting with Manny at the hospital?"

"I honestly don't know," Berto said.

"Where does Davio think you've been all this time?" she asked with her usual point-blank charm.

"He thinks I have a girlfriend here in Miami," Berto said. "I spend a lot of time down here, away from him, and I use that as an excuse."

Yashi came out of the van, holding a new license

plate, and Martell saw that Deb had already taken off the old one. While Yashi held the thing in place, she used a power screwdriver to attach it. Damn, these people were organized and ready. This was like a master class in working undercover.

Except for the part where Davio had shown up.

"It's not a quick and easy drive from Sarasota to Miami," Martell pointed out. "Even if Davio flew, it'd be two or three hours, what with going through security. So it took some effort for him to get here. And then, to find out where you were? At that particular warehouse, at *that* particular time?"

"And I'll say it again: I don't know why he wasn't at the meeting with Manny." Berto didn't back down.

"I do."

They all turned to see Deb, looking unhappy. "Yashi did some digging, and he just told me that the news was just released. Manny Dellarosa died this morning from a massive heart attack."

"No fucking way," Berto said. He was either the best actor in the world, or he was stunned. "I just saw him. He was *fine*."

"These things can happen," Yashi pointed out. "He may have hidden his real condition from you."

"No," Berto said grimly, shaking his head. "Davio fucking killed him in a power grab. I don't know how he did it, but he did. And that's why he was coming here. To make sure he had my allegiance. And if not, he was probably going to kill me, too."

"You might want to rally your troops while you

can," Francine advised him. "You've got twenty-four hours before he'll be released."

Berto nodded.

"We've got to move," Deb reminded them. They were all going to pile into the van, leaving Berto behind since his part of this job was over. "Be careful," she added.

Berto smiled in what looked like genuine amusement. "Words I'd never thought I'd hear from the FBI. Maybe those fucking idiots on TV are right, and it's end times."

"Not a chance," Francine said as Martell shook Berto's hand, then followed her into the van.

Yashi drove while Deb changed her clothes, right there in the back of the van, and Martell did his best to try not to watch.

CHAPTER TWENTY-FOUR

"Wow, I have really good taste," Phoebe said, as Ian locked the door of their cabin behind them.

They'd come below to shower and change before dinner, which they were having with the Dutchman up in the dining room in an hour. This yacht was big enough to have a dining room. And a living room. And a den.

The master bedroom cabin was huge, too. It was decorated in blues and turquoises and sea greens, with shiny white-painted wood. It really did have a delightful, airy, oceany feel. A bathroom was attached and it, too, was huge, with a big, glass-enclosed shower, and with racks on the walls that were overflowing with towels in those same tropical-water colors.

If this was their yacht—and they were pretending that was so—then it stood to reason that Phoebe had had at least a small amount of input into the furnishings and colors used in the decor. Of course, she'd said it completely as a joke, an attempt to lighten Ian's very dark mood—because after a day like today, the color of the curtains was the last thing that mattered.

Ian had been shaken—they both had—by Davio's unexpected attack, and by Sheldon's unbelievably risky near-sacrifice. The grim reality of what could have happened had Shel *not* led the SUV filled with heavily armed thugs away from their game of make-believe still lingered.

The entire job could have exploded, and not only would Davio and his men have been trying to kill Ian and his team, but the Dutchman and Hamori suddenly would've been gunning for all of them, too, once they'd realized they were being conned. And they would have realized it when the "dead" and "unconscious" security guards leapt to their feet to help fight off Davio.

There were also a variety of smaller catastrophes that could have happened—including Vanderzee bailing, instead of taking this nighttime cruise to "Cuba" in a boat carrying drugs.

But the man hadn't bailed.

"Are you all right?" Phoebe asked Ian, following him into the bathroom and watching as he turned on the shower.

Ian shook his head *no.*

And okay, the fact that he hadn't said *yes* or *I'm fine* stunned her. That was why she was frozen with shock when he reached out, took her by the hand, and pulled her in, hard, to his chest. It was like hitting a wall, he was that solid, and if that wasn't enough to take her breath away, he said, "But I will be, soon," before he kissed her.

It was an echo of the searing kiss they'd shared beneath the dock—hungry and desperate and filled with blessed relief while still laced with remnants of pure fear.

He'd been as scared out there as she had, Phoebe realized with another jolt of shock—maybe even more scared. It was his brother's husband who'd nearly been killed, and that loss would've been unmanageable.

For someone who managed everything for everyone, for someone who seemingly effortlessly kept dozens of balls in the air at all times, facing the very real possibility of Shelly's impending, unfixable death must've been terrifying.

But right now Ian tugged at her clothes, unfastening her pants even as he shucked off his own, and Phoebe helped him. She put her glasses on the bathroom counter, pushing them down into the sink for safekeeping, and then pulled her shirt over her head and kicked off her boots.

Ian nearly fell over in his haste, tripped by pants that were down around his ankles. He sat on the floor to untie his boots, leaving Phoebe free to lose her underwear as she ransacked the cabinets and drawers, searching for . . .

Found 'em.

Phoebe tore a condom free from the accordion-pleated strip, and turned to find Ian back on his feet. He pushed between her legs as he lifted her up onto the counter of the sink—good thing she'd moved her glasses or she'd be sitting on them—and simultaneously took the little square package from her, opened it, covered himself, and slammed himself inside her with lightning speed.

"This," he said, as she wrapped her legs and her arms around him, trying to move him even closer, because as good as that felt, it wasn't enough. "Oh, God, Phoebe, this. This is what I wanted, what I *needed*. Right here. I just fucking wanted to jump ahead to now, to skip all that bullshit with the cargo, and the Dutchman, and Aarie and Shel. . . ."

"I know," she told him. "Me, too. I know."

After the cargo had been moved from the truck to the yacht, Vanderzee had pulled Ian aside to let him know that he would not be *comfortable* if Aaron and Shel joined them on their ocean journey.

A bit earlier, he'd asked Phoebe if the two men were brothers, and she'd told him that they were Ian's brother and brother-in-law—which could have been interpreted in a number of ways. But no doubt he'd figured it all out when he saw Aaron and Shel sharing a very nonbrotherly kiss.

She knew that Ian had had to tread very lightly in the face of the Dutchman's prejudice. They'd come too far to blow up this mission at this late stage—and Ian had said very little in response. He'd simply left Aaron back on shore with Shelly.

Which was probably exactly where Aaron wanted to be.

Still, Phoebe knew Ian was not pleased by having one fewer teammate aboard the yacht. And when Ian had glanced at her while discussing this with Vanderzee, she knew *exactly* what he was thinking—about the man's child brides, and the way he disposed of them. And *he* was *uncomfortable?*

But Phoebe also knew that Ian was thinking, too, about those kidnapped children, and the mother who was probably going mad with worry. . . .

So he'd done what he'd had to do. He'd kept Aaron on shore, but he wasn't happy about that.

Ian was, however, much happier now.

Phoebe kissed him as she moved both with him and against him. God, this felt so unbelievably good.

But then Ian picked her up—effortlessly. When was the last time *that* had happened? But he was stupid strong. And even though the muscles in his shoulders and arms stood out, and even though the effort of lifting her expanded them from huge to gigantic, he didn't seem strained or winded or uncomfortable in any way as he carried her into the shower, and stepped under the spray.

It was a little too cold, and she gasped and then laughed, because it felt so good after the heat in the warehouse, after the fear-induced sweat that had dripped down her back while she'd smiled reassuringly at the Dutchman while praying that Ian didn't get himself killed.

He lifted his chin and let the water stream onto his head and face, opening his eyes—still so startlingly blue—to look at her, water beading on his ridiculously long eyelashes.

He breathed, "Jesus, I've been wanting to do this since . . ."

Phoebe nodded, breathless, too—barely able to speak. "Me, too." Ever since they'd shared the shower more platonically at the Dutchman's house.

She was trying to create more of that mind-blowing friction, but he held her so tightly. Without proper traction, her movement was restricted and minuscule. Just enough to tantalize and torment.

Ian smiled at her efforts through half-closed eyes.

"I need to start doing more sit-ups," she said.

"No," he told her, "you don't. You're perfect."

This moment. *This* moment. *This* was the one that she wanted to slow down, so she could remember it, always.

The water, warmer now, streaming down her breasts.

The slickness of his skin, the delicious feel of him heavy and hot inside of her.

His eyes, his smile fading as he tried to show her he was serious. *You're perfect. . . .*

"You are, too," she whispered back. And he was—not that he was perfect for everyone. Not even close. His language was atrocious. His sense of humor was a mix of sophisticated and purely juvenile. He was, admittedly, a thief and a liar—a con artist, no matter how extraordinary and artistic his skill.

But tomorrow, when he brought those two children home to their mother—that would not be the first time he'd used his talents and notoriety to make the world a better, safer place. And she also knew that it wouldn't be the last.

He was far from perfect. But for Phoebe . . . ?

She'd never before met a man more fascinating, intriguing, and infuriatingly perfect for her.

Ian was standing there, holding her, looking into her eyes as if trying to see inside of her, but then he shook his head and said, "I don't really know what to do with you."

Keep me around, she wanted to tell him. *Don't push me away. Write to me from prison. Let me visit. And please, please, come find me when you're out and finally free.* But she was afraid—not just of scaring him, but of scaring herself with the weight of those words.

Instead, she leaned in close and whispered in his ear just what she wished he would do to her, right here, at this moment, using words she knew he'd enjoy but that she rarely, if ever, said aloud.

"Well now," Ian said, laughing. The expression on

his face was one of pure delight. It was good to know he was that easy to please. "*And* you're blushing. That's just too fucking great."

And with that, Ian backed her up against the shower wall, providing her with the traction that she needed. And with his mouth, hands, and the exceptionally large part of his body that had an equally large variety of rather rude and silly nick-names, all of which made him laugh when they tumbled from her apparently pristine lips, he made her wishes come true.

Even a root canal eventually ended.

Everything awful always did.

So Ian knew that this dinner with the Dutchman, too, would end.

It helped if the time spent was subdivided into more easily manageable segments. He'd already survived drinks, appetizers, and the main course, all served by Deb, as their stewardess.

All that was left now was dessert. After that, the remainder of this four-hour segment of this job would be easy, as they all went into their private cabins for a rest. The excuse—and it was a good one that would also act in Ian's favor on the return trip—was that while this yacht could travel at an impressive thirty-seven knots, holding on was involved while at high speeds, as was shouting over the engine and the wind.

The ride, as on any boat, was always less rocky down below.

And even if this super-luxury yacht had an impressively even keel, their pilot—a former U.S. Navy Special Boat Squadron guy and current alphabet agent going by the bland name "Captain Bob"—could make it as bumpy as Ian needed it to be.

As Vanderzee drank his wine, he told a long and self-indulgent story of his last visit to Paris. And Ian watched Phoebe pretend to be fascinated.

She sat with her chin in her hand, wearing a dressy black top complete with plunging neckline with her jeans and flip-flops, hair down around her shoulders. She was beautiful, and it wasn't hard to follow the very same advice he himself had given her, just a few short hours ago, while they were in the car that Shel later destroyed.

Don't think about the fact that Shel had nearly died, or that look on Aaron's face when he thought he'd lost him. Think about Phoebe. In the shower. Think about doing, about feeling. Think about pleasure—not pain and fear and loss.

Think about the way Ian had made them so late to dinner that she'd had to rush to dry her hair and get dressed, about the way he'd grabbed her and kissed her before they'd gone out that door together, about how oddly right it had felt when she'd slipped her hand into his as they'd walked into the dining room.

Mr. and Mrs. Dunn.

Phoebe turned, right at the moment he was thinking that, to look at Ian with an expectant smile, and he realized with a start that their guest had finished his story and asked them a question.

How long had they owned this yacht?

Um . . .

In prep, Ian had been given a massive amount of information, including the make, model and year of the *Lady Mysterious*, as well as floor plans and photos of the contents of her storage lockers. He remembered that there was a travel Yahtzee and a backgammon board in the living room lockup—bottom shelf on the left—but when it came to the year this yacht had been built, his mind was blank.

Phoebe saved his pathetic ass, laughing as she said, "He's zoning out, he's so tired, poor Ian. The *Lady*'s relatively new for us, but Eee's had similar boats for quite a few years, right, baby?" She didn't wait for him to answer. "When we're in Florida, we make this trip south pretty regularly. It's our little home away from home."

Deb came in then, carrying a tray with tea and coffee, and Ian was again struck by how young the FBI agent had made herself look. Her clothes were pure Vegas hooker, but she'd purposely done her makeup and hair in such a way as to make herself appear to be in her teens. No doubt she'd paid attention to the story Ian had told about Vanderzee's preference for underage girls.

And sure enough, the man was watching her now.

"I'm sorry, where are the facilities?" the Dutchman stood up as he asked Deb.

She smiled as she made sure the tray was secure. "Right this way, sir."

Hamori, Vanderzee's man, stood, too—he'd been sitting by the door throughout the meal. But now he followed Deb and Vanderzee out of the dining room. He stood in the passageway, waiting, as his boss took a leak in the nearest head.

Deb came back in to finish removing the mugs from the tray, and in a low voice she told Ian, "We've got weather coming in. A pretty big squall. Small-craft warnings, the whole thing."

Ian's first reaction was *Jesus, we can't catch a break*. But then he realized that they had, in fact, caught a Christload of breaks to date, even despite the multitude of screw-ups. The fact that they'd gotten this far was pretty damned miraculous.

"It's not going to disrupt this leg of the trip," Deb informed them quietly. "But it's definitely going to delay our departure."

And *that* was not okay. They had to leave Faux-Cuba, as Martell called it, around two hours before sunrise or the charade wouldn't work.

"Delay it for how long?" Ian asked, bracing himself.

"Right now?" Deb said. "Too long. But it's weather. With luck it'll change."

"Can we go around it?" he asked. "Even if we take a little longer to get back. If we approach Miami from the east . . . ?"

"We're working on it," she told them, even as she shook her head *no*. "In a few minutes, I'm going to come back in, and suggest you move below as we increase our speed. After you're settled, I'll bring fresh towels to your cabin. We'll talk contingency then."

Ian nodded. "Okay."

At the sound of Vanderzee opening the bathroom door, Deb went back to the galley, and Ian realized that, at some point during their conversation, Phoebe had reached over and taken his hand.

She gave his fingers a squeeze, but then let him go as Vanderzee sat back down and started fussing with his coffee. Hamori, meanwhile, reclaimed his seat just inside the dining room.

Both these men were armed and dangerous. That was too easy to forget. No more zoning out.

"I've been meaning to ask you," the Dutchman said as he stirred milk and sugar into his coffee, "if you insist on working, always, with your brother."

And here it was. A question Ian was hoping this man wouldn't ask. He looked over to find Phoebe watching him, and he knew she was going to say something—it would be hard for her to stay silent—so he shook his head, just slightly, and she closed her mouth and waited.

Vanderzee took a sip of his coffee, and as he put his mug down, he looked over at Ian, his eyes cool. "You know, if he were my brother, living in my country, he would have already been put to death."

"I did know that," Ian admitted. It was the moment of truth. He knew it was entirely possible that what he said in response would mean life or death for those two kidnapped children and their mother. And he would have told any lie, said anything to ensure their safety, but his instincts were screaming for him to be bluntly honest here. In fact, he was certain that this was a test, and that for him to lie and bow to Vanderzee's archaic ideology would actually prevent them from moving further along in this game they were playing.

So Ian took a deep breath but waited until Vanderzee looked up at him again before he said, "My brother and his husband, both, are two of the bravest, most honorable men I've ever worked with. I trust them not just with my life, but with the life of my wife, who is the most important person in the world to me."

He glanced over at Phoebe, who had no idea what he was doing, but was clearly ready to cheer him on. *When we're with the Dutchman, you are so fucking in love with me,* he'd told her. She was doing a damn fine job of it, right down to the pure adoration he could see brimming in her eyes.

"Aaron and Sheldon are, *both,* valuable members of my team," Ian continued. "You know, Georg, I raised my brother."

"I did not know," the man murmured.

"I took care of him. Our mother died, and our father . . . had many problems. I was in charge of Aaron, pretty much from the moment he was born. Making sure he had food to eat, and a place to sleep. And I knew, early on, that he was special. I didn't know he was gay until . . . Well, it was after I was twelve, at least. Because when I was twelve—he was five—he got sick. He had such a high fever he started having seizures, which scared the hell out of me. I knew I had to get him to the hospital, but my dad was so drunk he was nearly unconscious. Somehow I woke him up, and when the ambulance came, I got him in there with us, and we all made it to the ER. Aaron was put on intravenous antibiotics, which saved his life, and all night long, I just kept nudging my father awake to talk to the doctors and nurses. And then I pretended that he didn't speak English, so he didn't have to, you know, put words together in an intelligible sentence."

Ian was aware that Phoebe was listening to him, too, quite possibly with even more intensity than the Dutchman.

"That night, there was one nurse in the ER who saw through my charade," he continued. "She was the only person who cared enough to sit down and really talk to me. I remember she brought in sandwiches and cookies, and when she saw me starting to wrap them up, so that I'd have something to give Aaron later, she brought me more, and made me eat some of it myself. She told me that there was a rule when you're flying on a plane, that if something bad happens and you need oxygen, and the masks drop down from the bulkhead, you're supposed to put the mask on yourself first, and only then tend to the other people around you. Because if you don't take care of yourself, then you can't take care of anyone else.

I don't know—that doesn't really have anything to do with this story, but I've just always remembered that. It made sense to me, and I remember because of that, I liked her. I didn't like a lot of people when I was a kid, but I liked her. A lot. Her name was Susan"—he glanced at Phoebe, and he knew she recognized the name as belonging to the woman Aaron had lived with when Ian first joined the Navy—"and she tried to talk me into meeting with someone from child services, but I wouldn't. I was afraid they'd split me and Aaron up, and I wasn't going to let that happen. I pretended that my father's condition was a fluke, a rare occurrence, and I'm sure she didn't believe me, but . . . she let me have that. She told me her work schedule—she mostly worked nights—and she said if I ever needed someone to talk to, or something to eat, that I should come by, because the sandwiches were free. She was lying, but I was twelve. What did I know? I took her up on it, a lot, over the next few years. And sometimes when I went over to the hospital, I brought Aaron with me.

"And one day we were in the cafeteria with Susan, and Aaron went back up to the line to get an apple, and she looks at me and goes, *Did you know that sometimes boys fall in love with other boys, and that that's okay?* And I didn't know it at the time, I didn't put it together, but she was talking about Aaron. She knew, even back then. She saw him. And one day, maybe a few years later, when I looked at him, *I* saw him that clearly, too. And I knew she was right. Aaron was who Aaron was—and how could that be wrong?"

Vanderzee opened his mouth to tell him, no doubt in detail, but Ian stopped him by raising his hand.

"It doesn't matter," he told the man. "You believe what you believe, and your idea of truth is not going to change my mind. But here's something that might help you understand where I'm coming from: He's my brother. I have always protected him, and I always will. Likewise, as I said before, I would trust him with my life. And with Phoebe's life. And you probably know me well enough to recognize that I do not say or take that lightly."

Vanderzee looked from Ian to Phoebe and back, and he said, "You're a man of strong convictions."

"He is," Phoebe said, reaching over again to take Ian's hand.

And then Vandezee said what Ian hoped he would say. "I like that about you."

The second dock could've been Cuba.

Especially in the dark.

Nestled in a remote cove, way south of Miami, it was a little worn out, a little run down, and a whole lotta overgrown.

Martell had changed into his richie-rich expat partner clothes—a very nice green-and-yellow Hawaiian shirt worn open over a snug-fitting beater and a leather-holstered Browning. He wore another nine millimeter, a Colt—more ornate—at the waist of his cargo shorts, which he was grateful to be wearing with action-treaded sandals after the long-pants sweat-fest in the warehouse.

Especially considering that the humidity was now hovering at about a billion percent.

Francine and Yashi were dressed as his minions, and okay. Color him a graphic-novel-reading, sci-fi/fantasy-loving geek, but he was enjoying having minions. Especially one wearing what Francine had on, which was kind of a cross between Lt. Starbuck and Buffy from season eight, when what was left of the Scooby Gang went paramilitary high-tech.

She was a walking armory with handguns holstered everywhere—not to mention her sharply muscular arms, which looked like they should've been registered as weapons, too. She wore jungle-print cammie cargo pants stacked over masculine boots, and the mix of that with her blond cheerleader's ponytail, her womanly bosom accentuated by her no-frills olive tank, and a mouth that looked soft and inviting, regardless of how tightly she clenched her teeth . . .

Yeah, it pushed all the right buttons for Martell, and he found himself revisiting last night's bathroom encounter and imagining a different scenario and outcome.

And then, because there was not much else for him to do while in wait mode, he imagined Francine on one side of him, and Deb, in her full goth ensemble on the other, each more capable and kickass than the other . . .

"Help me make one more check of the truck."

Martell looked up to find Francine standing over him, hands on her hips. "Yes, ma'am."

She offered him a hand up, and he took it, not surprised to find that she was strong enough to haul him to his feet with very little help on his end.

"I thought Yashi was in charge of that," he added as he followed her back down the dock to the clearing that was barely big enough to hold the beat-up and ancient cargo truck, to which the FBI agent had affixed a Cuban license plate.

"He is, but you have eyes, too, so let's use them," she said.

"I'm not sure what I'm looking for," Martell said, as they walked around the truck.

"Anything thing that says *You are not in Cuba*."

"Yeah," Martell said, "but if my buddy and his boat drop in regularly from Florida, it stands to reason that the Starbucks cup on the floor came from a care package." But the truck was clean, at least of trash, both inside and out. The only things on the bench front seat were an unopened box of Cuban cigars and a pile of audiobooks on cassette tape—a nice touch that said, *Yes, you're in the middle of nowhere*.

"The cigars are your gift to Vanderzee," Francine told him. "Should you choose to give it. Have you come up with a reason for why you're understaffed?"

Sheldon was supposed to have been one of Martell's minions, but thanks to the SNAFU at the warehouse, the Dutchman had already met him.

That was one of the limiting parts of running this kind of an operation. When things went south, people got used up at a crazy-fast pace.

It was why Francine had been so adamant about Martell not pulling that bag off his head at the warehouse. If he had and Dutch had seen him, suddenly Yashi would be playing the part of Dunn's expat partner, with Francine as his army of one. Unless Martell slapped on a Rastafarian wig and some sunglasses—but that would've been risky.

"Yashi recommended I go simple," Martell told her now, "and say the bulk of my army's out protecting the perimeter, making sure none of my neighbors stumble onto us. Plus, I figure I could add that it's best if the fewest possible of my peeps get a glimpse of Ian and his yacht. This op is trusted eyes only."

She was nodding. "That's good."

"This whole thing is kinda like adult cosplay," he said, and then quickly word-stumbled all over himself to add, "And as that came out of my mouth and I heard it, I realized that there probably *is* something called adult cosplay, which no doubt means something else entirely, something *adult* as in triple X, which is not at all what I meant and—"

"I knew what you meant," she said with a smile. "It's okay. You've already established yourself as not-a-dick."

"Yeah, but I'm fully capable," Martell confessed. "Of being a dick. I've been a dick. And it's actually kind of weird for me, that you seem convinced that

I'm not, so . . ." He was babbling again, so he changed the subject. "What does it mean for you, that Manny's dead?"

Her smile was gone. "It means Davio's unleashed."

"Do you think Berto's right, that Davio somehow killed Manny in, what did he say? A power grab?"

Francie sighed. "If Davio found out that Manny and Berto had some kind of alliance going—an agreement that didn't include him—which they did, because he's a fucking nutjob . . . Yeah. It's possible. And it affects Ian most of all. He may resort to . . . other means of taking down Davio, like . . ."

"Killing him?" Martell suggested.

She didn't confirm, but she also didn't deny. She just kept going. "Like things he couldn't do before, because Manny would've then come after him—after all of us."

"Things like . . . sending Davio to jail for rape?" Martell asked.

Francine didn't understand, so he clarified.

"I've been wondering why Davio is still walking around after what he did to you," he said. "The statute of limitations on sexual assault takes a very long time to run out—"

Francine cut him off. "You really think I didn't try to press charges after it happened?" she asked. "I did. But my mistake was that I didn't go the police or to the hospital the very same night. I showered, and I waited because I wasn't thinking—I just wanted to stop hurting, and when I finally went, there was no DNA evidence. There were only my cuts and bruises—and my word. Which wasn't enough, because Davio got to the police ahead of me. He claimed I'd fallen in with the wrong people, that I'd gotten involved with drugs, that I'd started stealing from him—money and jewelry and alcohol. The necklace I always wore, it was my mother's . . . The police detective, she actually took it from me, to return to him. Then she told me to walk out of there, because Davio apparently wasn't willing to press charges, but if I persisted with *this nonsense,* he probably would."

Dear God. Martell did the only thing he could do. He put his arms around her. "I'm so sorry that happened to you," he told her. She was stiff and unyielding, until he dropped a kiss on the top of her head and said, "It's unjust and unfair and . . . You deserved better." That seemed to wake her up, and she hugged him back, almost fiercely, as if no one had put their arms around her like that in a good long time.

"Hey, guys?"

They both looked up to see Yashi, heading toward them from the surveillance van—now blue—that was down at the end of the driveway, parked so that the dirt and pebble path was blocked off from any traffic.

"Sorry, but I need you in the van," Yashi said. "The storm that's coming in is bigger than we thought. There's going to be a delay before the yacht can make its return trip, which could be trouble. We've got Ian on a scrambled signal—he wants to brainstorm possible Plan Bs."

"There are plenty of very good reasons why an American couple and their guests should not go wandering about Cuba in the middle of a stormy night," Aaron pointed out testily from the surveillance van back on shore. "Arrest by the government for illegal entry into the country being a biggie."

Phoebe was on board the yacht, sitting on the bed in the cabin she shared with Ian. He was pacing as they spoke to the other team-members via secure connection. Deb was in there with them, sitting in the room's only chair.

Instead of putting the call on speaker, they were all tied in via their headsets and mics—so that they could hear over the sound of the yacht's engine, and speak relatively quietly.

Vanderzee's cabin was not that far away. And Hamori was even closer, sitting in the passageway outside his boss's closed door, constantly on guard.

"But when night turns into daylight?" Deb asked. She looked tired. "It's going to get harder to keep Vanderzee confined to the yacht. He's not exactly a rule-follower."

"Nuh-nuh-no," Ian said. "No way can we delay our return trip for nearly twenty-four hours, until tomorrow night. That's not an option. If we're that late, he'd need to call to let his people know, and how do we do that? No. We have to leave as soon as we can."

And yet, at the same time, they couldn't depart from Faux-Cuba after daylight, since it would be obvious that they weren't heading north, simply from the position of the sun.

And if you didn't set a northern course to the open sea when departing from the north coast of Cuba, well, then you were obviously not in Cuba. It wouldn't take the Dutchman long to figure that out.

Shelly was crunching the numbers to figure out the dead-last split-second they could leave—not just by sunrise, but before that ghostly predawn twilight time when the soon-to-be-rising sun first lit the horizon. It was like one of those horrid math equations that Phoebe remembered from school. If a yacht sailed at its top speed of thirty-seven knots, and the total travel time of its journey was to be no less than four hours . . .

"So we'll have to distract him," Francine's voice cut through, clear and calm. "Keep him in his cabin."

"Make sure he's sleeping," Phoebe suggested, because it stood to reason that if Vanderzee's eyes were closed, he wouldn't be able to see the sun. And if he were in his cabin, Hamori would be planted, absolutely, outside it in the porthole-free passageway, too. "Is there something we can give him? Slip an Ambien, or shoot, even just a heavy antihistamine in his drink? We can open a bottle of wine to celebrate our departure . . . ?"

"He'll know it," Ian said. "If not in the moment, then the next morning. I'd know it, if I'd been drugged."

"Me, too." Deb and Francine both said it at once.

"He'll wake up and wonder what we're hiding," Ian told her. "We don't want that."

"So maybe we don't slip it, then." Phoebe was unwilling to give up on her idea. "Maybe, because of the waves from the storm, it's going to be rough passage. So we give him something like Dramamine, to keep him from getting seasick. Only we tell him that he's gotta take it *before* he gets sick—we tell him it won't work after he's nauseous, so he *has* to take it before we depart? And P.S. it'll make him feel drowsy?" She looked from Ian to Deb and back, but neither seemed impressed.

"What if he refuses?" Deb asked. "Besides, do we even have anything to give him?"

"I can send Aaron and Shelly to the drugstore," Yashi's voice came through clearly.

Ian vetoed that. "No."

"Davio's not a threat if he's being held—" Aaron started to say, also from the van.

"Assuming he's still being held," Ian pointed out as he continued to pace. "And even if he *is* in temporary custody, that doesn't mean he hasn't got his men on full alert, sweeping Miami for the two of you."

"And you," Aaron countered.

"But I'm not in Miami, am I?" Ian said, his hand

up on the back of his neck as if he had a headache. "And *you're* not going to the drugstore."

"Then I'll go," Yashi volunteered.

Martell spoke up, his *no way* heavy in his tone. "And suddenly, if you don't get back in time, I'm down to Francine as my security force? She's kickass, but that's stretching belief."

"There might be something like Dramamine already on board," Deb said. "I can check, but again . . ." She shook her head. "That's a pretty risky Plan B. Will Vanderzee take it? Will it affect him? You know, it doesn't make everyone fall asleep."

"Give him three," Yashi intoned. "It will."

"But what if, instead, he's extremely susceptible?" Deb countered. "And he's still unconscious when we pull into port? That could be awkward, too."

"So we go with distract," Francine said from the van, in a voice that implied she, for one, had made up her mind. "I'll come back with you, on the return trip. When we reach the point of no return—right before the sun's about to rise—I'll bring a tray with a nightcap to Vanderzee's room, and I'll make it clear that I'm a part of the special delivery."

"No freaking way." Martell's voice was up a full octave in his outrage, expressing exactly what Phoebe was thinking.

Francine, however, sounded impervious to his disbelief. "I'll make sure the shades are down and that he doesn't come out of the room until we're safely heading back north. We can set up some kind of signal so I don't have to stay in there longer than I have to."

Phoebe looked at Ian, who was silent, but was shaking his head no. Thank God.

But Deb was watching Ian, too, and she said, "She's right. That would handle the problem. Easily. But it should be me. I mean, I'm already on board, and . . . it's pretty much what I'm dressed for—"

Yashi cut her off, sounding as if he'd finally gotten his heart rate up. "That was *not* my intention."

"Nor mine," Ian said.

"I'm sorry," Martell said from the van. "But are we actually *discussing*—"

"Yeah, well, Vanderzee's already let me know that he's a big tipper," Deb told them, cutting Martell off, "should I care to, how did he put it? Provide service for his personal needs."

"Oh, ew, really?" Phoebe said, and as Deb nodded, she added, "This is *not* okay."

"But it might be the only way," Deb countered. "And *I* should be the one to do it. I'm who he'd expect to knock on his door. Plus unlike Francine, I'm not in a relationship."

"Whoa, wait, *what?*" Martell's voice came back as Yashi made noise, too.

"I still don't like it," Ian said, rolling right over all of them. "Phoebe's right, it's not okay."

"Yeah, like you've never used sex to distract," Francine's voice was tinged with disgust. "If the weather doesn't clear, it's our only viable option, and you know it. Deb offered. She's a grown-up and she's willing to do it. I'm pretty sure this is not her first time at the rodeo."

Dear God. Phoebe looked at Deb, who was studying the toes of her shoes as she nodded her agreement. This may *not* have been her first time *at the rodeo,* but that didn't mean she wasn't going to hate it. Every awful, hideous second.

"Shelly, what's our dead-last possible time of departure?" Ian asked.

"I'm . . . still double-checking," Shel said, sounding vague and distracted. "But it's sometime around . . . four seventeen A.M."

"Then let's hope," Ian said, "that the weather clears well before oh-four-seventeen."

The rain had just started when the *Lady Mysterious* pulled up to the dock.

Martell went on board, where there was a flurry of greetings and introductions, even as the cargo began to be off-loaded into the beat-up and ancient truck.

"I feel bad we can't help," Shel said.

"I don't," Aaron said. He and Shelly were stuck in the surveillance van, watching and listening as the rain drummed on the roof and soaked both Yashi and Francine, who were out in it, in Faux-Cuba.

After the yacht had left the first dock, Aaron had helped Shelly clean his massive collection of cuts and scrapes—the worst being a gash above his eyebrow that probably should've had stitches. Instead, in lieu of surgical thread, he'd done the best he could with a butterfly bandage, all the while fervently thankful that Shel had been struck only by pieces of rock and brick and glass, instead of actual bullets.

Still, going out into the rain would've stung like hell, bringing a new level to the grim misery that Francine and Yashi were enduring with the help of the yacht's "crew."

Martell, meanwhile, was being his usual charming self as he shook off the wet and greeted the Dutchman, box of cigars in hand.

The surveillance van had both video and audio up and running, so Aaron and Shel could watch as well as listen as Martell expounded on the magnificence of his invisible personal army, lurking out in the dark jungle. They would, he said, "protect the cargo ferociously on the next phase of its journey."

Vanderzee was interested in learning more. Aaron could see the man's curiosity on his face.

Shel saw it, too. "Come on, baby, bite . . . ," he murmured.

Vanderzee did, asking, "And where, exactly, will it go from here?"

"*Exactly* is a trade secret," Martell told him with a warm smile. "More generally, it will travel via one of my trucks to one of my airfields, where a jet is currently waiting. It flies from here to . . . let's say, North Africa, where the buyer will collect it, and pay the remainder of his bill. Half up front, half on receipt."

"And do you ever move cargo out of the U.S.," Vanderzee asked, "from an interested party who will send their own jet to your airfield, and pay upon receipt at that point?"

Martell's smile broadened. "Making it easier for us? That would be a hell-yeah, with a big high five." He turned to Ian at that point, and Aaron winced because now he sounded as if he were delivering lines. "I assume your crew has told you about the bad weather moving in? It's going to hover offshore and force you to delay your departure by a few hours. I am sorry about that."

Ian's smile was expansive and hid his horror at the fact that Martell suddenly sounded like an actor in really terrible porn. Of course, he was also hiding the trepidation Aaron knew he felt about Deb whoring herself out for the sake of the mission. "The day you can control the weather," Ian said easily, "is the day we no longer have to work for a living."

"Since we have this extra time, I would love to see your airfield," the Dutchman told Martell. "And perhaps your home."

And Martell froze.

"Come on, come on," Aaron muttered. "Lotta reasons why that's a no-go. This shouldn't be that hard."

It was Phoebe who saved him, stepping forward from where she was standing behind Ian. "Oh, please, no," she said. "Martell lives up near his field. It's lovely but . . ." She turned to Martell. "You know I love you madly, darling, but making that drive—four hours," she turned back to tell Vanderzee, "in good weather. It'll take us six in the rain. All the way up into the hills, on treacherous roads, no thank you. Ian and I are staying here."

"Jesus, she's good," Shel murmured.

"Yup," Aaron said, as Ian jumped in.

"The weather'll clear long before we could get there and back," he told the Dutchman with just the right amount of apology in his voice. "Maybe some other time."

"I'd like that," Vanderzee said, even as he turned and obviously tracked Deb, who entered, carrying a tray with coffee mugs and glasses of whiskey.

"*That's* not at all creepy," Sheldon said.

"Imagine being Deb," Aaron countered, and when Shel met his eyes, he felt a rush of gratitude. "I'm very glad you're not dead, by the way."

Shelly smiled back at him, before returning his attention to the computer monitor and the video feed. "I'm feeling pretty glad, too."

Phoebe was playing the hostess, herding them into the yacht's living room, encouraging them to "Sit down, please, sit down."

Ian did sit, pulling her onto his lap, where she pushed his hair back from his face before she sweetly kissed him.

"Eee's in love with her," Aaron told Shel, who nodded his agreement. "And just watch. Ten to one, he's gonna fuck it up."

• • •

As Deb served coffee, Martell tried to catch her eye. He was sitting in the living room of the luxury yacht with Ian, Phoebe, and the pedophile serial killer that Deb was maybe going to sleep with, for the sake of the mission.

His disapproval and disbelief must've been coming off of him in waves—how could she even *think* about bumping the extra-uglies with that nasty turdnozzle—because she refused to meet Martell's gaze as she held the tray in front of him, even when he took his sweet time, deliberately shoveling spoonful after spoonful of sugar into his mug. In fact, she finally just picked up and moved on with that spoon still in his hand—she simply jammed a clean one into the sugar bowl.

Apparently the not-looking-at-him thing *was* intentional.

And when Francine came into the room, dripping wet and carrying that briefcase filled with money, Ian signaled for Deb to leave, so she did. Again, looking past Martell, her eyes aimed at a distant point on the wall.

Ian, meanwhile, was looking pointedly over at Dutchie as if expecting him to adios his man Gollum, too. The message being, *Shit's about to get real, Georg.* Or secret. Or private. Or whatever.

And sure enough, Golly shuffled on out of the room, as did Francine, who went back outside to help finish humping the boxes off the boat in the rain.

Unlike Deb, Francine *did* meet Martell's gaze with her spooky, pale-colored eyes, nodding very slightly as she went past him, and closing the door tightly behind her. And he had the very non-Christian thought that if anyone could survive close-your-eyes-and-think-of-England-style sex with a psychopath, *she* could. In fact, Dutch himself might not live through the punishment Francine could surely deliver.

But hey, now everyone was looking at him expectantly since he was in possession of the briefcase. So Martell cleared his throat and forced a tight smile before presenting the damn thing—ta da!—to Ian.

Ian met him halfway, shifting Phoebe off of his lap. He took the briefcase—motherfucker was heavy, and it showed—over to a table where he clicked open the two latches, and yes, there it all was. Rows and rows of neatly stacked bills, filling the case. Ian made sure to give Dutch an enticing flash as he pulled out the packet that contained the 20K he'd requested separately. None of the bills in that bundle were newspaper. Martell had double-checked and even smelled it to be extra sure.

"I appreciate the work you did, the effort you went to," Ian told the D-man as he handed him that 20K with a flourish. "I know we didn't use your contact, but really it was just luck that Martell's guy came through."

"It *was* unexpected," Martell agreed as D-bag tried not to make it obvious that he wanted to rub the cash all over his body as he counted it. "I thought we were screwed. It's good to know we had access to an alternative solution. And it's always good to make new friends." He turned and lifted his eyebrows at Ian. "You gonna get those crazies back in line, up in Miami? End the drama for once and for all?"

"Yes, I am," Ian said, adding, "and I apologize again for that . . . *drama*."

"It was handled swiftly and courageously," Vanderzee said with what he probably believed was a gracious nod, even as he pocketed his packet of cash.

There was silence for a moment then, and Martell looked over at Ian. It was highly unlikely that the Dutchman was going to approach them here and now about his need to move those kidnapped kids out of Miami, so when Ian nodded, he stood up. "Well, I'd better get on the road," he said. "Six hours home."

"Maybe the rain'll let up, and you'll make it in four," Phoebe said, rising to her feet so she could kiss him good-bye, her lips cool against his cheek.

Martell didn't envy her—having to spend another unknown amount of time with Mr. Creepy and his boy.

"Before you go," the Dutchman said, and they all turned to look at him.

Phoebe, who had a mad sense of how to do this kind of playacting turned her pivot toward Vanderzee into intention and movement. She glided across the floor toward Ian, and took the briefcase gently from him, murmuring, "I'll put this in our room, in the safe," before adding, "I'll give you gentlemen privacy to talk business."

And with that she swept out the door, closing it tightly behind her.

Dutch cleared his evil throat and said, "I have a friend who has a very important package that he needs to move from Miami. However, the cargo is special, with very special needs."

A friend. Dude had *a friend.* Was that really how they were gonna do this? Martell couldn't speak for fear of laughing or maybe throwing up as a picture of this creature with Deb again flashed through his head—but then he didn't have to speak, because Ian played it like the total pro that he was.

"You've seen the yacht," Ian told him. "Do you feel we could handle the cargo's needs?"

"I do," he said.

"May I ask the value?" Ian said. "Because it may not be worthwhile for . . . your friend. With the payments we need to make for the authorities to look the other way . . . We'd have to receive at least a million. More if the cargo . . . shall we say *breathes?* That makes it more dangerous to transport."

The Dutchman didn't blink, so Martell tried not to either. "The cargo will be crated appropriately. Labeled as antique furniture."

"Label or not, if there are extensive delays—and

there sometimes are—it could get complicated," Ian pointed out.

"The condition in which this package arrives at its destination is allowed to vary," the man told them, and weren't those words to make their blood run cold. Dude was essentially telling them that his client—the children's father—didn't particularly care either way if the kids were dead or alive when they showed up on his palace doorstep. In other words, what he really wanted was to take them away from his ex. He'd kidnapped them to deliver punishment to their mother, not for reasons—misguided ones—of fatherly love. "Of course, the condition affects my friend's payment, but only by a million dollars. Perhaps if you agree to split that, in order to guarantee the cargo's safe arrival . . . ?"

"So a million five," Ian clarified, looking to Martell as if for his agreement. "Assuming, of course, the cargo arrives alive. A flat million if it doesn't."

Martell chose his Buddha face as his response, which Ian, of course, took as a yes.

"I think we could agree to that," Ian said, ending the conversation by standing up. "Check with your friend, and let us know. Take your time—no rush. I'm not going anywhere." He reached out and shook Martell's hand. "You, my friend, better get our current cargo safely home."

D-bag stood up.

Don't make him shake his hand, don't make him shake his hand . . . ugh.

Vanderzee shook Martell's hand.

But then, unlike Ian and Pheobe and Deb, Martell was free to leave. In fact, he *had* to leave. He lingered as long as he could, looking for Deb, but she was nowhere to be found. Francine, however, was waiting for him, and there was nothing left to do but follow her out into the rain, and dash down the dock toward the truck. He let her take the wheel, climbing into the passenger side as he shook the water off his shirt and tried to wipe his hand clean on his shorts.

"There is not enough Purell in all the world," he told her.

She shot him an amused look. "Trust me, I know the feeling."

And now the ugly picture that flashed through his head was of Francine. Younger. Vulnerable. First with Davio. Then, assaulted a second time as she faced the police detective's flat disbelief.

As she pulled away from the dock, heading down the dirt drive toward the surveillance van—which would remain on site until the yacht departed—she said, "I hope the weather clears."

Martell nodded. "I do, too."

The weather cleared.

Well, it didn't so much clear as it shifted—far enough to the west so that they were able to leave the dock at a little before four A.M.

Phoebe was still awake when Ian came into the cabin to give her the news. He'd been up on the bridge, obviously trying to mind-control the weather, but now he could finally get some desperately needed sleep.

He yanked off his clothes and crawled into bed, pulling her close and exhaling the awful worry she knew he'd been carrying.

Phoebe hadn't helped him at all. After Martell left the yacht, Vanderzee had vanished into his cabin to try to get some sleep. Ian had gone to their cabin to tell Phoebe that she should do the same.

She hadn't been able to keep herself from pulling him inside to offer potential solutions. "If he's in his cabin, sleeping, then he won't know exactly when we started for home. We can tell him we've been traveling for hours."

Ian had sighed as he'd sat down on the bed. "Hamori will know. Unless you think he'll believe we set the engine on the stealth glide setting."

Okay, so that wouldn't work. Still . . .

"Hamori can't see out a window," Phoebe had pointed out. "So why don't we shove off, and just motor back and forth across this cove?"

"And if Vanderzee wakes up and looks out the porthole . . . ?" Ian flopped onto his back on the bed, feet still on the floor. "And if he does, we won't know it. He'll just vanish with our twenty thousand dollars—and those kids. He'll cut his losses and kill them. Easier to ship them that way. He only loses a million bucks."

That was an awful thought, but still, Phoebe had to say, "I don't want Deb to . . . do that."

He turned to look at her. "Bad enough so you'd sacrifice the lives of those children?"

"That's not fair."

Ian sighed again. "I know. It's not."

"Would you let *me* do it?" Phoebe asked.

His answer was immediate. "No."

"Then—"

"She's a trained operative," he said, sitting back up. "You're not. She's willing, for the sake of the mission—"

"But you're in charge," Phoebe countered.

"Yes, I am," Ian agreed. "And I wouldn't make her do it, if she didn't want to."

"She doesn't *want* to," she countered.

"Yes, Phoebe," Ian said as he stood up. "She does. She *wants* to, more than she wants to tell Dr. Vaszko, sorry, we lost her kids. Jesus Christ! You think I don't fucking *hate* this?"

He'd stood there, with his heart and soul in his eyes, before making her promise to lock the door behind him, while he went up to the bridge to watch the radar.

"You were right," Phoebe whispered to him now. "About letting Deb make her own choices, about what's more important. I just found it impossible not to think maybe there was a solution that we'd overlooked."

"I know," Ian said, kissing the side of her head.

"I was lying here thinking I'm guilty of being sexist," she whispered. "That it's somehow okay when James Bond does it—sleeps with someone in order to learn the secret code, but then I realized that I kind of hate James Bond. Probably because he sleeps with people to learn the secret code."

Ian sighed, and his breath moved her hair and was warm against her face in the darkness of the cabin. "Just ask me."

She wasn't sure she wanted to know. Had he ever . . . ? Would he ever . . . ? Was he currently making the best of a bad situation; was he using sex to handle or control *her?*

But in the space of her hesitation, his breathing had steadied and slowed—he was already asleep.

So Phoebe closed her eyes, too, well aware that with every passing hour, her time left with this man was ticking down to zero.

After the yacht finally left Faux-Cuba, the surveillance van headed back to the other dock.

They had four hours to kill.

Francine had already staked out the space beneath the console in the back. She'd curled up under there and had been asleep for a while.

Martell was in the front seat beside Yashi, who was driving. Shel was still working on the computer, and Aaron was in the back passenger seat.

Martell could tell that Yashi was exhausted. He was working it, hard, to stay awake.

So Martell said, "Thank God, right?" To keep Yashi awake through conversation.

"I'm glad to be moving on to the next phase," Yashi said.

"No," Martell said. "I mean, Deb. Does she really do that shit?"

Yashi glanced at him. "She's dedicated."

"That's not dedicated," Martell said. "That's fucked up."

Yashi was silent.

"I thought you and Deb were. You know."

Yashi *did* know and he answered succinctly. "Nope."

"And you never wanted to . . . ?"

Yashi's eyebrow went up as he waited for Martell to end his question with a verb.

Hit that. He didn't say it, instinctively knowing that that kind of disrespect would get *him* hit. Damn, if someone else said that to him about Deb, he'd hit *them*.

Instead, he tried: "Wrap her in a cuddly fleece blankie and keep her safe? Make sure she never had to do stupid shit like have sex with psycho turdnozzles?"

Yashi shrugged. "And then what?" he asked. "She's tougher and smarter than both of us, and she's very good at her job. Most of the time she keeps me safe."

Martell persisted. "And you've never slept with her, not even accidentally?"

That got him another eyebrow. "How exactly would that happen *accidentally?*"

"I don't know," Martell said. "I've had some pretty strange accidents happen. You're with her, twenty-four/seven."

Yashi just shook his head.

It was clear he wasn't going to say more, so Martell asked, "So what's the next phase of this thing? The yacht returns to the dock, Dutch and Hamori get their cell phones back, take that twenty grand, and go home."

He'd overheard arrangements being made, so he knew that there would be a hired car waiting at the dock, to drive Vanderzee back to his house. Ian didn't want to drive him—he wanted a little separation. Not just for a chance to breathe air that had no trace of the man's noxious evil, but because the guy needed to walk away with all that money. It was part of the psychological game of building and reinforcing trust.

It reminded Martell of that stupid saying: *If you love something, set it free* . . . Except this had nothing to do with love, and everything to do with greed.

"When Vanderzee gets home, he's going to check his messages," Yashi told him, "and find out that Dr. Lusa Vaszko's name is on the manifest of a flight leaving Miami for Rome."

"She's not really," Martell started.

"Nope. Ian wanted Vanderzee to think that both Dr. Vaszko and the U.S. authorities believe that the kids have already left the country—that they're already in K-stan," Yashi said. "The idea is to make Vanderzee believe that he's under less scrutiny—make him feel like now's the right time to try to move those kids."

Which was when Ian—with his hair on fire—would call Vanderzee and announce that he'd just found out that Berto had died from his wounds, and that now Davio would be gunning for him harder than ever. The threat was dire enough for Ian and Phoebe to make immediate plans to leave the country—via their tried-and-true route to Cuba.

So, hey there, Georg-y boy. If you want to ship your *friend's* "special cargo" via the Ian Dunn luxury yacht express, it's now or never, baby.

At that point Ian would take Berto's giant and safe-seeming truck, and pick up the Dutchman's crated package from its point of origin, which was probably going to be the K-stani consulate. Ian and his brother would load it into the back of the truck, lock the doors, wave good-bye, and drive it not to the yacht, but to FBI headquarters, where Dr. Mommy was waiting.

Check and mate, motherfucker.

"Dutch is gonna be pretty pissed when the dust settles," Martell said.

"After we have the proof that he's involved with this crime," Yashi said, "i.e., the missing children in his crate, he'll be deported. Permanently."

"Not thrown in jail?"

"Can't have everything," Yashi said, as they drove into the night.

CHAPTER TWENTY-FIVE

Phoebe slept through it.

The arrival back at the dock.

Vanderzee's departure in a car that was waiting to take him home.

The high fives Ian gave to the men in the surveillance van, to Team Martell, to Deb, and to the yacht's captain for a job well done.

Phoebe had slept through Ian's shower, too, not even waking up when he brought her breakfast in bed.

It wasn't until later in the morning—not much later, because it apparently all happened very fast—that Ian woke her with a gentle shake to her shoulder.

She opened her eyes, and there he was, already dressed, her first clue that he'd been up for hours.

"Hey," he said, from his seat beside her. He was smiling with all of his being, not just his face, his mouth, his eyes.

Phoebe smiled back at him—it was impossible not to. "Hey." But then she sat up fast. "Oh, no! Vanderzee!" She threw back the sheets, ready to leap into the shower.

"It's okay," Ian said, catching her arm. "You're good. He already left. He sends his thanks for a lovely blah blah blah"—he pitched his voice slightly higher, and more nasal, adding the trace of a northern European accent—"bullshit, bullshit, bullshit."

She laughed, pulling the covers up and around her as a shield, because he not only made himself sound like the Dutchman, he also somehow made his eyes look like the other man's. "That was a very good impression of him."

"I know." His smile of delight banished all remnants of evil as he graciously nodded his thanks. "I'm glad you noticed. So many of my talents are overlooked."

She seriously doubted that, and she laughed again even as she verified, "He's *really* gone?" She pulled back the covers again, this time slipping out of bed and heading into the bathroom.

"Yep." He raised his voice a bit so she could hear him in there. "Drove away. In a car we arranged for, so we've also been tracking it. He didn't stop, didn't double back. In fact, he's almost home."

"Oh, thank God. I was dreading having to be all *air kiss, air kiss,* except he wouldn't air kiss, and then I'd have to go take another shower and scour my face with bleach." She flushed and washed her hands, grabbing her toothbrush as she glanced out at Ian.

He was leaning back on the bed, and she realized that he was relaxed. Not pretend relaxed. Really relaxed. And she realized why, with an equal rush of relief.

"Deb must be in a rockin' good mood, too," she continued, moving to stand in the doorway as she brushed her teeth, stopping to add, “Walking around like, *Yes, I totally did not have to screw the child molester!* FYI, that’s going to continue to freak me out for a while. For years. Probably somewhere between three and five.”

“Me, too.” Ian smiled back at her, his appreciation for her naked rant brimming in his eyes as she went back to the sink to spit and rinse. “But, shh. Don’t tell anyone else. I don’t want to ruin my reputation as a heartless asshole.”

Phoebe put her toothbrush not back on the wall hanger, but into her très chic carrying case—a tired plastic Publix grocery bag. At some point today, they’d have to pack up and leave—so the feds could return the *Lady Mysterious* to its marine-rental owners.

“So are we in wait mode?” she asked, coming back to join Ian. Now that she was morning-breath-free, she had no qualms about getting in his face. She did just that, straddling his lap and pushing his head and shoulders back onto the bed to kiss him.

His hands slid up her bare back, and he sighed his pleasure as she deepened the kiss, licking her way into his mouth. “Mmm,” she lifted her head to say. “Coffee.”

“I brought you some,” he told her. “It’s on the desk. Because no, sadly, we’re not in wait mode. Vanderzee already called back. We’re go.”

Phoebe sat up. “Seriously?” But she could see from Ian’s eyes that he was dead serious. And relaxed. And relieved. “So this ends today?”

She realized as she said those words that she wasn't just talking about the impending rescue of those surely traumatized children, for whom this probably wouldn't ever end. They'd carry the memories of their fear and suffering with them forever.

Likewise, Phoebe would forever carry her memories of this time with Ian.

Which—he was nodding *yes*—was going to end today.

"I'm going to leave you here," Ian told her, "with Captain Bob. When you're ready to go, he'll get you back to the safe house, where he'll stay with you for the duration. You know, along with Rory, and Johnny Murray and his kid. Plus, there'll be FBI outside. Now that we know for sure that we're not illegally entering the consulate, we've got access to even more manpower. You'll be safe."

"Oh my God," she realized, "you're leaving *now*." This was good-bye.

As he nodded, Phoebe was acutely aware that she was completely naked and he was not. And yet she couldn't seem to move.

"I wish I didn't have to," he told her. "But everything's moving fast. I have to go pick up the truck and organize the rest of the team—get everyone into place."

"I want to go in the surveillance van," she said.

Ian was already shaking his head as he gently extracted himself from beneath her and stood up.

"There's no point," he said, not unkindly. "There's nothing for you to do. You'll only take up space."

"Vanderzee will expect me to be with you," Phoebe countered, even as she put back on the clothes she'd been wearing the night before—anything not to have to stand there naked. Vulnerable.

"I'll tell him you're still here," Ian said. "On the yacht. Getting ready to head for Cuba."

"If I were getting ready to leave on a major trip," she countered, "I'd be packing our things from wherever it was we were staying. In Miami. Where Davio's allegedly looking for us. And FYI, if Davio really *was* looking for us, you would *not* leave me alone. Not in the house, not on the yacht, not with a fox, not in a box. I'd be in the van, Sam-I-am—he *knows* we have a surveillance van. And *that's* where I'd be—where he'd expect me to be. Close enough for you to reach me, if you needed to protect me. If you really loved me." Her voice broke on that last part, and she knew she was screwed. While he'd been running a con, she'd gone and stupidly fallen in love.

She could see in his eyes that he knew damn well she was right about the van, and she turned away to gather up the rest of their things, just scooping and stuffing into the leather bag that was monogrammed with his initials: IJD.

As she saw that, it occurred to her, inanely, that Ian's middle name was John. She'd seen it in his file, and only now realized that his name was, essentially, John John Dunn, since *Ian* was the Scottish version of *John*.

"Look, I just want you to be safe," he told her as she went into the bathroom to sweep their toiletries into her grocery bag and then stuff it into the leather case. "And I know you *will* be safe with—"

"If I'm in the van," Phoebe told him, dropping the leather case onto the floor at her feet, as she brushed her hair back into a ponytail, "I can wave to him from the window. Give him a thumbs-up. If he asks where I am. If he doesn't, great, but if he does . . . we're ready to give him a visual."

"A visual," he said. "You don't, under *any* circumstances, get out of the van." He laughed as he said it. His relaxed and relieved demeanor was gone, replaced by frustration, vexation, and ire. "Who the fuck am I kidding?"

"I promise I'll stay in the van," Phoebe said. "I did the right thing at the warehouse, didn't I? I'm not an idiot. I've learned. A lot. From you. And I'm good at this. I am, and you know it. There's *not* nothing for me to do. I can help Shel on the computers. I want to be on the headset, listening in, in case there's a detail that we've overlooked. I want to see this through."

Aaron had to go in the truck with Ian, to collect the Dutchman's cargo.

He knew that his brother didn't like that—that he'd prefer Aaron stay safely in the surveillance van with Deb and Yashi and Phoebe.

But there was really no one else who could help Ian move the heavy crate.

They were close to certain that they were picking the thing up from the K-stani consulate, and neither of the FBI agents could be seen near the place. They had to stay well outside the grounds due to fear of a dreaded *international incident,* which was limiting.

And since Ian had supposedly left Francine, his usual second-in-command, back in Faux-Cuba with Martell, neither of *them* could suddenly appear here with Ian in Miami. Even with a heavy disguise, that would've been too risky.

So that left Aaron.

Who was actually glad for some alone time with his big brother.

The plan was to go to Vanderzee's residence and connect with his bodyguard Hamori, who would lead them to the cargo's location—which had yet to be disclosed. Vanderzee was keeping that info close to his vest—although, again, they all believed the pickup point was the K-stani consulate.

After the cargo was in the truck, Hamori would then follow them to the yacht—see that it got loaded safely on board. Vanderzee would meet them there, at the dock, and they'd all set sail for Cuba.

Except for the part where Hamori would be overpowered and arrested as teams of FBI agents took possession of the truck and its cargo, freeing those children and reuniting them with their mother. *And* the part where Vanderzee showed up at the deserted, yachtless dock, getting the ugly-ass surprise that he'd been stung before he, too, was descended upon and taken into custody by another team of FBI agents.

Aaron hoped someone would be wearing a helmet-cam, so that he could see the stunned expression on the Dutchman's face.

But that was yet to come.

Ian was tightly wound as he climbed into the truck next to Aaron and he put the thing into gear.

"You sure I don't need a disguise?" Aaron asked as the big rig groaned and moved forward. "A baseball cap with a sewn-in mullet, and an *I love pussy* T-shirt?"

Ian didn't crack a smile. "No," he said shortly. "He knows you work for me, and that I trust you, and because of that, he trusts you, too."

"How progressive of him," Aaron said. "Speaking of progress, I couldn't help but notice how both you and Pheebs decided to wear your matching sets of grim today. It's adorable."

Again, nothing.

They drove in silence for a while before Aaron said, "What'd ya do, freak yourself out because now that Manny's dead, there's really no good reason to go back to jail, so suddenly you've got to find another excuse to break up with her?"

The look Ian shot him was practically audible and just short of a physical skull duster. A brain-rattling one. But Aaron kept going, because it had to be said.

"Shel and I figured out why you were in jail," he told his brother. "You made a deal with Manny to serve time for some bullshit crime that Vince committed—getting into a bar fight and trashing most of the cars in some roadhouse parking lot. Yeah, I really believe you were out getting 'faced that night with your buddy Vincent Dellarosa. Hmmm. What's wrong with that picture? Let's start with the fact that you don't drink."

"It was a simple deal," Ian admitted. One thing about Ian was that once he was busted, he copped to the truth. "If I pled guilty to the charges against Vince, Manny would keep Davio away from you."

"But you only did it because you knew the Dellarosas had a solid-gold reputation of protecting the people who went to jail for them. Families are taken care of. Money's paid. And mouths stay shut," Aaron said. "So there *you* were, working for Manny, knowing that we were safe, because if we weren't, word would get out that they'd reneged on their deal, and their whole system would crumble. And *that's* how you were going to take them down. You were going to, what? Find someone else inside the prison, and flip them? Get them to turn state's evidence against Manny and Davio?"

Ian glanced at him, and this time Aaron knew that it was only because Manny had died, that he admitted it. "Yes."

Aaron nodded. "I wish you'd told me," he said.

"Yeah," Ian said on a sigh. "I know. I gotta work on that. On treating you like an adult."

And *there* was an admission he'd never thought he'd hear.

"So what now?" Aaron asked. "With Manny dead?"

"I don't know," Ian said, and Aaron called him on his bullshit.

"The answer to *What now, with Manny dead,* is easy: Find Davio, and kill him." Aaron looked at his brother. "Of course, you do that, you risk going back to jail, this time forever, and this time for something you really *did* do. And that is definitely not something you want to tie Phoebe to." And there it was. One of the reasons for Ian's case of grim. "You break up with her yet? For her own good, of course. Jesus, you're an idiot."

"Just . . . stop," Ian said, pulling the truck into a still-attractive but aging residential development that had been built on a former citrus grove.

Aaron didn't know what he'd been expecting, but it wasn't this Brady Bunch ideal of *normal.*

"Turn on your headset," Ian ordered as he did the same. "Ian here, testing."

"I'm here, too," Aaron chimed in.

"Read you both loud and clear from the surveillance van," Yashi's voice came back as Ian pulled the truck up in front of one of the houses.

"Same from car one." Shel's voice came through clearly, too. He and Francine and Martell were following them in Martell's car, which Shel and Francine had jerry-rigged with some of the equipment from poor deceased van number one.

Since there was only one way into this upscaleish neighborhood, they were hanging back, out by the main road.

"I'm going up to the house," Ian said, telling Aaron, "Keep the truck running. This shouldn't take long."

The place certainly didn't look like an evil overlord's dominion. It was large, but not ostentatious, with a circular driveway that branched off to lead around behind the house to what looked like an additional detached garage. There were two cars parked in front of the house. Both large and dark.

Phoebe's voice came through their headsets, saying what they were all thinking: "Ian, be careful."

"Always am," Ian said, telling what Aaron knew to be another in his vast collection of bald-faced lies.

It started out innocuously enough.

The Dutchman greeted Ian expansively, graciously, gracefully even. Niceties and pleasantries and condolences were exchanged—all of which Phoebe heard loudly and clearly in the surveillance van, courtesy of Ian's headset microphone.

"So sorry to hear about Berto," Vanderzee said, seemingly sincerely. "If there's anything you need done locally while you're away . . ."

Ian cut to the chase. "No, we just need to get out of town. So if your guy is ready, I'd really like to get moving—pick up that package."

“There’s been a slight change of plans,” the Dutchman said.

“Here we go,” muttered Deb, who was behind the wheel.

“Give him a chance,” Yashi said from the back, then covered his microphone to reassure Phoebe. “Ian’s very good at thinking on his feet. He’s adaptable—fully capable of a midsprint pivot. If he needs to change the plan, he’ll do it, and whatever he comes up with will be just as good.”

Phoebe knew that. Quite well. In fact, she’d come face to face with a variation on that theme when she’d first gotten into the surveillance van and heard Deb and Yashi discussing the fact that Manny Dellarosa had died.

She’d been stunned, not just by that information—when? how?—but by the fact that Ian hadn’t bothered to tell her. Not even in passing.

And then her head started spinning. How did this news affect Ian’s plan to return to prison? What did it mean for his future? Apparently, whatever the answers to those questions were, Ian didn’t think they had anything whatsoever to do with Phoebe.

And that had stung. Rather sharply.

Phoebe tried to tell herself that it was an oversight. What was it that Ian had said? *One goatfuck at a time.*

Still . . . *Hey, guess what? With Manny dead, I’m going to have to deal with Davio in some other way, so maybe we could plan to hang out together for a little bit longer than anticipated.* Ian surely could’ve found fifteen seconds—possibly in the shower, while they were having sex—to tell her that.

If he'd really wanted to.

Out on the driveway, Vanderzee was now telling Ian, "I'm uncomfortable putting such a high-value item into your care without collateral."

"Hamori's going to be with me," Ian pointed out. "Right behind me, in your car, every step of the way. If you think I can outrun his car with my rig . . ." He laughed his warm, familiar laugh, and Phoebe became acutely aware of how easy it was for Ian to sound both warm and familiar.

"That's not the issue," Vanderzee said.

Ian continued, "Hell, he can ride along in the trailer, sitting on top of the cargo, if he wants."

"That's not good enough," Vanderzee said.

Ian slipped a little testy into his tone. "I'm doing this as a favor. I should be well out at sea by now."

"You're doing this for the one point five million dollars," Vanderzee corrected him. "I'm not asking a lot. Just some insurance, until we meet at the dock. I promise I'll drive very safely. Phoebe will be well taken of."

"Oh my God." Phoebe realized then what it was that the Dutchman wanted to keep as collateral while Ian went to the consulate and picked up the crate that held those two kidnapped children.

He wanted *her*.

Ian was absolute. "I'm sorry, that's not going to work."

"It'll be for an hour, at most," Vanderzee cajoled.

Around Phoebe, in the van, Yashi and Deb had already leapt into action. Both were working the computers and making frantic phone calls. Over her headset, she could hear Shel, who was in Martell's car, too.

Deb: "Do we still have the dock?"

Yashi: "Can we get the yacht back—fast? Has it even left yet?"

Deb: "Is there a place where snipers can hide, in position, at the dock?"

Shel: "I'm pretty sure there is—Aaron, what do you think?"

Aaron, who was waiting in the truck: "I think it's possible, sure, but it's for shit. No way is Ian going to agree to this."

Yashi: "Could this conceivably work?"

Deb: "Absolutely." She was certain.

Ian spoke—both to Vanderzee and Deb. "Not a chance."

Phoebe said, "Talk him through it. Ian, maybe this will work. Just listen. Deb, go."

"Once we get the crate safely into the truck, taking out Hamori will be easy—we can do that almost anywhere," Deb said, walking through the potential scenario. "Dunn can demand that Vanderzee take Phoebe *immediately* to the dock. We'll put snipers in place there, and as soon as they arrive and Phoebe gets out of his car, we can take down Vanderzee and however many men he's got with him. They won't know what hit them."

Ian spoke clearly and distinctly. "No deal."

"That's a shame," Vanderzee said, "because this is the only way. This cargo is far too valuable . . ." He kept going. *Yada yada yada, bullshit, bullshit, bullshit*. He sounded so much like the imitation that Ian had done earlier, droning on in the background, that Phoebe nearly laughed.

"We've still got both the yacht and the dock," Yashi reported. "That's confirmed. The entire crew can be FBI."

"They can be Navy SEALs," Deb chimed in. "As long as we're nowhere near the consulate, we can bring in the whole freaking Marines as part of the task force, if we need to. This *can* work, Ian."

Phoebe knew what Ian was thinking. What if on arrival, Vanderzee didn't let her out of the car? "I'll pretend I need to use the bathroom. We're friendly. He'll let me go."

"Nuh-uh," Ian said.

"We can truck the crate all the way to the dock, if we have to," Yashi continued, theorizing other scenarios. "We can even put it onto the boat—wait to do the takedown until we're out on the water—seriously, we *could* bring in a SEAL team for that. Assuming we don't have a clear and safe opportunity before then."

"Lookit," Ian told Vanderzee. "I don't have to do this. I don't need the money. I thought I could help you out of a tight spot before I left town. But no way am I going to give you my *wife* as collateral."

"Well, I'm sorry we can't do business, then," the Dutchman said, and their chance of rescuing those two children slipped from a sure thing to a wipeout.

And Phoebe couldn't let that happen. She just couldn't.

She knew Ian was going to be furious. He was going to be livid. And he'd have every reason to feel that way. Worst of all, he would probably never, ever trust her in the future.

Because she had to break her promise to him for the second time in just a few short days.

But, really, losing Ian's trust didn't matter, considering they *had* no future. They'd agreed as much.

And fifty years from now, when she looked back on this day, what would matter more? The fact that she'd helped save those children? Or the fact that she'd pissed off some man with whom she'd had an extremely passionate but short-term fling?

Saving the children won that one by a mile.

So Phoebe did it.

She got out of the van.

CHAPTER TWENTY-SIX

Phoebe. Fucking. Got out. Of the fucking. Van.

And there she came, running up the driveway toward Ian and the Dutchman, waving and smiling a sunshiny greeting, as if they were neighbors in some zany sitcom and she'd popped over to borrow some sugar.

"I was in the van," she explained, "and since your

headset's on, I kind of heard what you were saying, and Ian, baby, I really don't mind—"

"Yeah, but I do, *baby,*" Ian said, hoping that she could tell from the crazed look in his eyes that there was no fucking way in fucking hell that he was going to leave her with the fucking Dutchman as fucking collateral. He turned to Vanderzee. "*I'll* be your collateral. Aaron will drive the truck. He and Sheldon will—"

Vanderzee cut him off. "The men in possession of the cargo have been told to expect *you*. It's too late, at this point in time, to change that, not without my going with you to its location. And as we discussed over the phone, I can't do that. Just as there are those who are looking for you, there are those who are looking for me."

"And they haven't found you here?" Ian asked, gesturing around them, because that's what he would have said, were this real. "Are you telling me that I'm gonna be followed, all the way to the dock, because that's not—"

"Of course not," the Dutchman said soothingly. "This is a safe location, unknown to my enemies." The man honestly believed that—it was said with complete conviction.

Ian gave a silent, inward salute to the FBI, even as he worked to fix this goatfuck. Step one. Get Phoebe's ass back in the van. "Get your ass back in the van," he said to her. "Honey."

She smiled sweetly up at him. "I don't want to. Sweetie."

Ian turned to Vanderzee. "Well, that's good to know, about this location being safe. But you can't just call your people and say there's been a change of plans?"

"If I do, they'll believe I've been compromised, and they'll take measures against your . . . people, when they arrive. I assure you, you don't want that."

"It's really okay," Phoebe told him. "We'll drive right to the *Lady*." There were two cars parked out in Vanderzee's circular driveway, and she motioned to them. "We'll go to the dock right now, right, Georg?" She didn't wait for him to respond. "I'll just get in, no big deal. We'll drive over and we'll wait for you there, along with Captain Bob and the rest of the crew."

All of whom would be FBI agents, already there and in place. Along with a team of snipers, who were currently moving into position. Phoebe's subtext was clear. Ian knew that. He got it. It was the drive from here to there that was the problem.

Meanwhile, Phoebe was looking at him like *no* was no longer in her vocabulary. She wanted to rescue those kids, he knew that, and she was willing to risk everything to do so. Ian admired that. He truly did. But there was no *fucking* way . . .

Still, there weren't many options. If *he* couldn't be the collateral . . . Francine, Martell, and Yashi were all out, because they were supposedly in Cuba. There was Deb, who worked as a stewardess on his boat. If she suddenly showed up here, Vanderzee might get suspicious.

Might? Try *would,* as in *definitely*.

That left Aaron and Shel.

Aarie was obviously thinking the same thing, because he got out of the truck and came partway up the driveway to suggest, "I could go with Phoebe. You know, head over to the boat with her and . . . Mr. Vanderzee."

Ian hated that idea. But he hated it less than letting Phoebe spend any time alone with this douchebag.

Unfortunately, the douchebag wasn't down with that. "I find that unacceptable," he murmured.

Of course. He didn't want Aaron—or Shelly, either, no doubt—to get any of their gay on him.

"Stay with the truck," Ian called to his brother, who did just that, muttering about wigs and T-shirts and stupid brothers.

Phoebe, meanwhile, was unrelenting and serene. "Ian, I'll be okay. I'll be fine."

"Excuse us for a minute," Ian told the Dutchman, and pulled her back, well out of earshot. "The plan—remember the plan? Was for you to never, ever, *ever* be alone with him."

"Hamori will be with us."

He was already shaking his head. "Hamori's taking us to the cargo. You'll be with Vanderzee and Mr. Tall and Ugly."

She looked at the two men standing on the

Dutchman's front steps. "With the vaguely Hitler moustache . . . ?"

"Yes," Ian said. "And I'm sorry, but Hitler Junior does not count as an acceptable chaperone. Neither does Hamori, for that matter."

Phoebe looked at him somberly from behind those glasses. "Ian, if we just give up now . . ."

"Phoebe, I swear, I'll get those kids out another way," he promised her.

She lifted her chin. "Yeah? How?"

"I don't know," Ian admitted, "but we are *not* doing this. We're going to bail. We walk away. Both of us. Together. Right now."

"I'm sorry," she said, and she clearly was. "I can't. If I do, I'll never forgive myself. To be this *close*—"

Ian shook his head. "That was not a request," he informed her. "I wasn't asking. I was telling." He drew himself up to his full commanding height. "That was a direct order."

And Phoebe laughed in his face.

"So, what?" Phoebe asked Ian, who'd made himself all large and imposing. Like he thought he could intimidate her? "Now I work for you again? That's convenient."

He didn't back down. "You're a member of this team, of which I am the leader." He spit the words out like bullets.

"Yes," she said. "I'm a member of this team! I agree. And sitting like a lump in the back of a car, for a forty-minute ride to a place where I'll be very, *very* safe sounds as if it's *exactly* in my particular limited skill set. No grappling, no need to speak Farsi, no bomb defusing or scuba diving. I can do this. And I want to. I'm volunteering. And frankly, team leader or not, it's not up to you to decide. I've already cleared it with Deb. So let's stop wasting time, and do this thing."

The SEAL commander standing in front of her morphed suddenly into Ian-the-lover. *Her* lover. She didn't know how he did it, but suddenly he was warmer and more familiar, and the heat in his eyes spoke of shared intimacies.

"Phoebe," Ian whispered as he took her face in his hands, pushing back the stray strands that were moving in the morning breeze, his thumbs gentle against her cheeks as he looked searchingly into her eyes. "Please. I'm begging you." His gaze dropped to her mouth, and he kissed her.

It was beyond romantic and heartfelt. It was sweet and tender and damn near perfect, and she felt herself melting.

As he pulled back, though, he could clearly see her remaining resolve, because he went even further.

"I can't let you do this because . . . I love you," he said, blurting it out so realistically—complete with a slightly surprised look in his eyes. "Phoebe, Jesus, I really do."

She felt her eyes fill with tears, but there was no time for that.

Ian had made his declaration loudly enough for Vanderzee to have overheard him, and Phoebe now glanced at the Dutchman, forcing a smile. "You know I love you, too, baby," she told Ian, also loud enough to be heard as she extracted herself from his grasp. "I'll be fine. Go pick up the cargo, and I'll see you soon."

As she walked toward Vanderzee, she smiled and even rolled her eyes as if to imply that Ian was an idiot. "We really do need the money," she told the man. "We're leaving behind an awful lot, and who knows when we'll be back. Is it okay if I wait for you in your car?"

She felt Ian watching as the Dutchman unlocked the doors of one of the parked cars and she climbed in.

"Be at the dock in forty minutes," he ordered Vanderzee in a voice that she barely recognized, it was so hard and cold. "You disrespect her in *any* way, and I will hunt you down, rip the lungs from your chest, and stuff them down your throat."

Ian felt sick.

As he jogged back to the truck, his brain came up with dozens of SNAFUs and worst-case scenarios in which Phoebe ended up missing or dead.

This was not okay, this was not okay, this was *not* okay.

And yet, he knew she was right. If they walked away now, those kids would be dead before the day was out.

Ian tried to convince himself that this would work. Georg Vanderzee trusted him. He also knew from the conversation on his headset that Martell's car was going to follow Phoebe every inch of the way. With Francine driving, and Shelly and Martell as additional backup, there was no way they'd lose her.

Aaron was silent as Ian got into the truck. But he didn't have to say anything—Ian knew that everything he'd just said to Phoebe had been broadcast to his entire team.

And they believed him, even if Phoebe didn't.

You know I love you, too, baby.

Jesus H. Christ.

"She'll be okay," Aaron dared to say.

Phoebe's voice came over his headset. "It looks like it's going to be about ten minutes before we leave. Georg's in the bathroom."

Deb spoke up. "Phoebe, we're going to have to cut our connection to you."

"Absolutely not," Ian said.

"Sorry, sir, but you need to reconsider that," Deb countered. "We don't want Vanderzee accidentally listening in on our chatter."

"Shit," Ian said.

"I'm going to take that as an affirmative," Deb continued. "In fact, take the device off and put it in your pocket, Phoebe. You can use it as a phone, to contact us if you need to, plus we can track you via GPS, if we have to. But we won't have to. Martell, Francine, and Sheldon will be right behind you."

"I know that," Phoebe said. "Okay, I'm turning this off. See you at the dock."

Click.

Ian exhaled hard.

Meanwhile, Hamori pulled the other dark car out in front of the truck, ready to lead the way to the cargo's location—which they already knew was the K-stani consulate building.

"Keep breathing, Eee," Aaron covered his microphone and reminded him. "I'd tell you it gets better, that you get used to it, but I sure as hell never have. Not when Shel's in danger—even if that danger's completely in my own head. And since I can't lie the way you can . . ."

"Not helping," Ian said as he jammed the truck in gear and followed Vanderzee's man.

Francine was driving Martell's car, and she had just taken the exit ramp onto the highway, staying close to the vehicle that held Phoebe, when Ian let loose with, "What the fuck, Deb?"

He didn't wait for a response as he continued, just as heatedly: "We're in the same general area as the consulate, but we're pulling up to what looks like a private home."

"Team Martell is heading south on the highway," Francine announced and Ian responded with a tight "Stay close to her, France," even as he continued his conversation with Deb and Yashi, who were trailing behind his truck in the surveillance van.

"We've got a crate in the structure's garage,"

Aaron said from his seat next to Ian in the truck. "Repeat, large crate visible, garage door going up. Two, repeat, two heavily armed adult males nearby."

"You *said* the kids were in the consulate." Ian had about fifty pounds of not-happy in his tone as he spoke to Deb. "You *confirmed* that they were there."

"A confirmation is rarely a hundred percent," Shel said from the backseat, behind Francine. "More like ninety-two point five."

"That's helpful to clarify right now," Martell said, from beside her in the passenger seat.

"I thought it was a definite, too," Francie said.

"So where the fuck are we?" Ian asked. "Because if we can now confirm that these kids are *not* in the consulate, which it sure as shit looks as if they aren't, we can completely revamp our plan—except, *fuck!* Phoebe is now in a car with two men who are armed and dangerous."

"You're on Thompson Avenue," Deb said. Her voice changed, and Francine knew she was asking Yashi, "Why is that familiar?"

Yashi's voice answered. "Thompson Ave's in the database. They're at the K-stani ambassador's girlfriend's house."

"So now we find out that the Kazbekistani ambassador's girlfriend's house," Ian repeated, and Francine knew from his tone that his head was about to explode, "is where these kids have been held for all this time. Not the don't-touch consulate.

Instead, they've been in a civilian's private home. Which, with a warrant that would not have been hard to obtain, could have been raided by the FBI and local police, without *any* threat of international incident."

Deb sounded stressed. "Ian, I'm so sorry, I can only tell you what I was told," she said. "The intelligence was—"

"Save it," Ian said shortly, "for later. Okay. We're here. I am going to walk very slowly to that garage, while Aaron backs the truck down the driveway. Can someone please verify, with one hundred percent certainty this time, that the crate contains, at the very least, something that's alive?"

"Already verified through FLIR-cameras," Yashi's voice came through. "Two human-child-equivalent heat sources are inside, two adults are outside—in addition to Ian, Aaron, and Hamori, who's getting out of his car."

"All right." From the sound of Ian's voice, Francine knew that he'd made his decision. "Let's move forward—but new plan, kids. I'm taking the cargo all the way to the yacht."

Ian's original plan had been to drive the truck straight to the FBI headquarters.

"I am not going to take chances with Phoebe's life," Ian continued, "so Deb, make sure the FBI is ready for our arrival there. Francie, keep me updated. I want reports with your location every thirty seconds, understand?"

"Read you loud and clear," Francine responded.

• • •

Ian was pissed.

He'd believed the intel that he'd been given, and that was his mistake. This entire sting was based on the information that those children were in the consulate, which could not be easily accessed.

Unlike the ambassador's girlfriend's house, which he could have entered with an entire SEAL team backing him up, weapons blazing, as they kicked down the freaking door.

Ian now approached the crate and its two stone-faced guards as Aaron—using his superior driving skills—backed the truck down the driveway, *beep, beep, beep.*

As Ian got closer to the garage, he stopped and just stood there, because *Jesus*. The crate was rigged with what looked like a complex, high-tech booby trap.

That was not good. That was extremely not good.

Aaron, meanwhile, stopped the truck with a squeal and gasp of the air brakes, and jumped down from the cab, coming around to open the back with a rattle of metal. He pulled out the tailgate ramp with another metallic groan and a crash.

"I'm Ian Dunn," Ian said, but the guards didn't seem to care—maybe they'd already IDed him from his picture. Or maybe it was because Hamori was now there, nodding his approval.

Nodding, and making sure that Ian saw what he was carrying—a handheld trigger mechanism, or maybe it was a dead-man switch. Either way it was obviously connected to the small mountain of C4 that was artistically arranged on that booby-trapped crate.

"Make sure you don't lose me during the trip to the dock," Hamori said in his K-stani accent.

Together, the two other men, Ian, and Aaron loaded the crate into the truck, careful to keep it upright and steady.

Ian pushed it to the side and strapped it in as Aaron shoved the ramp back and closed one of the doors, slamming the other and locking it after Ian jumped out.

The guards were already gone, the garage door descending, and Hamori was heading back to his car after his little show-and-tell. This time he waited for the truck to go first—he was going to follow them south to the dock.

As Ian got in behind the wheel and started the truck with a roar, Aaron was wide-eyed. "Holy fuck. Can I say *holy fuck?*"

"Houston," Ian said, "we have a problem."

"It's not technically a dead-man switch," Yashi announced from the surveillance van that was following Hamori, who was following Ian and Aaron in the truck as they all drove merrily through the outskirts of Miami. "There's some sort of electronic signal being sent from this mechanism to the bomb that's attached to the crate—I think it's some kind of verification code that prevents the bomb's timer from automatically activating. The signal is being sent every . . . Yup, it's every sixty seconds."

"That's not good," Martell said.

There was a bomb. Attached to the crate. That held those kidnapped kids. That was in the back of the truck that Ian was driving.

And according to Yashi, Vanderzee's dude Hamori had to input a code into some little handheld device, once every minute, to keep said bomb from starting its countdown sequence and exploding. Like Yashi said, it wasn't a dead-man switch, per se, but it was certainly related, in that should Hamori choke to death on his BBQ hot wings, or have an unexpected aneurism, or get struck by lightning in a freak storm and therefore fail to enter the code . . . *Boom*.

Big *boom,* apparently. At least according to Ian's description of the bomb, which included the word *massive*.

And since Dunn was a former SEAL and therefore an expert in blowing shit up, Martell was inclined to believe him.

He listened to the now-extra-frantic chatter over the radio as he hung on with both hands while Francine pushed his little POS as fast as it could go. They were shaking and rattling and wheezing, all in order to keep up with Phoebe and Vanderzee and the man Ian had aptly nicknamed Hitler Junior.

Both cars—if you could call Martell's a car—were in the left lane of the highway, heading south. It was particularly harrowing since the road was under construction and there was no shoulder. Instead, scarred concrete barriers loomed to their left, separating them from the traffic that rushed past, heading back to Miami.

They were still about fifteen miles from the exit for the dock—info Francine religiously passed along to Ian.

"We're going to need a bomb squad at the dock," Ian was saying, his voice crisp, cool, and in command. "But I think our best bet is to continue the charade. Let's load this damn thing onto the yacht, welcome Vanderzee on board, buy ourselves at least a little time. Maybe once we're at sea, he'll disengage the booby trap to—I don't know—feed the kids?"

From the van, Deb must've said something then, but the signal gave a burp of static and Martell couldn't quite make out what she said.

But he *did* hear Ian's response: "Are you *fucking* kidding me?"

Francine said, "Repeat please. We missed that."

Yashi spoke up. "Deb just got a call from up the FBI chain of command. Way up. This mission is being commandeered by what we believe is another agency entirely. Maybe CIA, maybe Agency, we don't know for sure. But Ian's been given an order to slow the truck down."

"This is *not* the deal I made," Ian said as instead of slowing down, he sped up. "This is my op. I'm in command."

But even as he said those words, he knew they were meaningless if one of the more covert and secretive agencies was reaching in, past both Ian and the FBI, to take over the mission.

Jesus, they were on a long, flat, empty stretch of road surrounded by orange groves on one side and jungle on the other. It was textbook perfect for an ambush.

Back in the surveillance van, Deb was on the phone with whoever'd ordered her to tell Ian to slow the truck down.

"Hell, yes, I'm concerned," she was saying. "I want to know *exactly* what you're planning. I've got a civilian member of this team who is currently in a position of grave danger. I insist that you back the hell off and let this mission continue according to our plan!"

"Eee." Francine's voice came into Ian's ear. "Shel switched me over to a private signal. You're the only one who can hear me. He thinks you should ask Yashi directly to tell you the next time he picks up Hamori's access code transmission to that bomb. He thinks if the Agency's taking over, they're monitoring that signal, too. He thinks they're going to take Hamori out, via sniper, immediately after he sends the next signal. Shel also thinks you should slow down, or else they just might shoot you, too."

Yashi was speaking almost simultaneously, saying the exact same thing. "Ian, I think you need to take this order to slow down very seriously. The next access code transmission will be coming in, in three, two, one . . ."

Ian hit the brakes.

Aaron heard the gunshots from a sniper rifle at the same time that the truck's air brakes noisily kicked in.

He could see the dark car behind them suddenly swerve, driverless, plowing down into the swampy ditch that ran parallel to the road, and flipping and tumbling out of control.

Ian meanwhile was wrestling the truck to a full stop—as from around them black SUVs pulled onto the road. There was even a chopper, big and dangerous-looking, appearing suddenly overhead, coming out from hiding behind the brush.

Ian was shouting, "Go, go, go," as he hauled Aaron with him out of the rig's cab.

Commandos had already blown open the truck's back lock, swarming into the trailer—Aaron saw only glimpses as Ian pulled him away. They ran, full out, back toward the surveillance van, which was backing up, engine whining as it worked to put distance between itself and the truck.

And the bomb.

The team of commandos had shields that were already up and in place to protect them from the blast.

As Aaron looked back, he caught a glimpse of heavily armored men in black carrying a child—limply dangling little legs—and all he could think was *Holy fuck*. The sheer cojones that it had to take, to run *toward* a bomb that was set to blow in sixty seconds or less . . .

He knew he should have been counting seconds, but he wasn't. He relied on Ian to know exactly when to dive for cover in that ditch.

And Ian did.

Ian tackled him, covering him, protecting him as he always did, as the bomb went off with a roar.

Phoebe and Georg Vanderzee were talking movies as Hitler Junior drove them south on the highway, toward the dock.

Phoebe had discovered, back during a college trip to Europe, that most people, regardless of where they came from, had watched at least a few Hollywood films. She'd also learned that there were few males over the age of eleven, who'd spent even just a short amount of time in the West, who hadn't seen *Star Wars*.

And nearly every one of them had an opinion both about the ewoks and Jar Jar Binks.

Georg Vanderzee, in fact, had quite a bit to say. But he broke off midsentence, looking at his phone.

Phoebe couldn't see his face—he was looking down—but when he spoke to the driver, it was in another language, and his voice sounded guttural.

The driver responded, and Vanderzee answered sharply.

Phoebe sat forward. "Is everything all right?"

But the driver turned suddenly—hard—to the left,

with a squeal of tires, and Phoebe was thrown back into her seat, as the car slipped—barely—through an almost nonexistent opening in the concrete construction dividers.

She let out a squeak as the tail of the car noisily scraped the concrete, and then gave a full inadvertent scream as they blasted across two lanes of oncoming traffic, horns blaring. The driver somehow kept them from flipping, using the far shoulder of the highway to regain their equilibrium before merging into the lanes of cars heading north. Back into the city.

Something was wrong. Something was terribly, horribly wrong.

Phoebe resisted the urge to dig into her pocket for her headset cell phone, because there was really no one to call. Who could get here, to help her, in a moving car on the highway?

Not even Ian could do that.

And maybe if the Dutchman forgot that she was carrying a phone, Sheldon or Yashi could use it to trace her.

Or her body.

She played it as innocent. "Did you forget something back at the house, Georg?" She intentionally used his given name. "I do that all the time. . . ."

But Vanderzee unfastened his seat belt, and when turned toward her, his face was hard and his eyes were lit with anger.

And he was holding a gun.

He raised it, but instead of aiming and firing, he used it as a cudgel. Phoebe held up her arm to try to protect her head, but she couldn't.

And when he hit her again, the world went black.

Ian rolled off his brother to watch the flames and smoke roiling up into the brilliant blue of the sky.

Phoebe was dead. Or if she wasn't yet, she would be soon. Vanderzee would make sure of that.

He could see Aaron from the corner of his eye—his brother was shouting something. The blast had temporarily taken out Ian's hearing, and sure enough, when he put his hand to the side of his face, there was blood dripping out of his ear.

Aaron was trying to get him to stand—as if there was a reason to hurry now. He pointed and gestured and soundlessly talked, and Ian obediently turned and looked. And there was the van.

Deb and Yashi had gotten out. Deb was talking—her body language that of pure fury—to one of the men in the black body armor. Yashi was coming toward them at a run, and he helped Aaron with Ian—as if he'd merely been injured instead of killed.

If Phoebe was dead, then Ian was dead, too. God, he didn't want to live without her. . . .

As his ears buzzed and roared, as his hearing began to return, he heard snippets.

Yashi: ". . . get him into the van."

Aaron: "I think he . . . hit his head. Or . . . impact of the blast. Either way . . . out of it."

Slowly, he was improving, and when Deb came over, grimly earnest, to tell Ian, "This wasn't me. This wasn't the FBI. This was Covert Ops, taking things into their own hands," he heard it all.

Aaron: "They couldn't wait? Forty fucking minutes for us to get to the dock?"

Deb: "I tried. I did. I'm so sorry."

Yashi: "The kids are safe. Both of 'em. Although I suspect that's just a bonus outcome for these guys."

As Ian looked up, he realized they'd gotten him into the van. And somehow Deb had been given permission for them to leave the scene. She was already behind the wheel, pulling away—back toward . . .

Miami.

Ian knew what that meant. Vanderzee surely had some sort of alert system in place. He had to know already that the bomb had been detonated. And so he was no longer heading for the dock.

Phoebe was dead. Or she would be soon.

No way was the Dutchman going to let her live.

The only question that remained was, Would he kill her fast or slow?

And just like that, Ian sat up. The fog and the buzzing and the blur shifted and the world came back into pure, sharp focus.

Motherfucker was going to kill her slowly. He knew it. He *knew* it.

And that meant Phoebe wasn't dead. Not yet.

Ian popped his ears—Jesus, he could hear his eardrum buzzing and flapping—as he asked, "Francine?" He couldn't get his headset to work—or maybe it was just that one particular ear that was problematic, so he took it off and turned it around. Tried it with his other ear.

Still, while he did that, he could see from Yashi's eyes that he was going to hate whatever it was that Francine was going to tell him.

Aaron summed it up. "They lost 'em."

Ian clarified. "The car with Phoebe." The news just kept getting worse.

"Yeah, the Dutchman pulled a youie, in one of those breaks between concrete dividers. You know, those places they set up when there's construction on the highway, so that police cars and emergency vehicles can turn around?"

Ian knew.

"France," he said.

"I am so fucking sorry," she told him over the headset. "He made the turn so fast, we couldn't follow, and then we were stuck on the highway until the next exit—"

"Apologize later," Ian said. "Have you turned around yet?"

"Yes," she said. "We're now heading north. And I hope you don't hate this, but I called Berto. For backup. He lives relatively close to the K-stani consulate—"

"Which is where Vanderzee would take her," Ian finished for her. Of course. That would put them back into the dreaded FBI-can't-kick-down-the-doors scenario.

"That's where we're heading now," Deb chimed in.

Yashi added, "We've tracked the GPS signal from Phoebe's headset. It cut out several miles after Vanderzee's car pulled the youie—as if he suddenly realized she had it on her, found it, and killed it. Threw it out the window or whatever. As far as we can theorize, the consulate appears to be where they're heading."

"Deb's been calling in favors," Aaron told him, "making sure that the FBI surveillance positioned around the K-stani consulate stays live and operational."

Ian's team had done everything he would've done.

"Okay," he told them. It was too early for him to say *good job*. "We're going to have to stop Vanderzee before he gets into the consulate. Once he's inside . . ."

They were back to toothless and helpless.

Francine's voice came over Ian's headset. "Berto just called Martell. Besides himself, he's got six men in four cars searching for Vanderzee's vehicle. They have a description of the make and model, plus the plates, and we got a ding. Not far from the consulate. Berto's heading over there now himself."

Ian could see and feel the anticipation, not just from Deb, Yashi, and Aaron, who were in the van, but from Francine, and everyone in Martell's car, too.

They expected him to give the order—to stop

Vanderzee from entering the consulate by any means necessary. Ram his car, shoot the motherfucker, do whatever it took to stop him.

But Ian suddenly realized that, if trapped, the Dutchman would kill Phoebe on the spot.

If Berto's men or the FBI or anyone else tried to stop him, she was dead.

"Let's let him get inside," Ian said, as a plan appeared, fully formed in his head—as all of his best plans did. "Let him go. But let's make sure he doesn't leave."

He could see Deb and Aaron's confusion. Yashi was too zen to react in any obvious way, but he was clearly curious, too.

Deb said what they all were thinking. "Once the Dutchman goes inside the consulate, we can't go in after him. Even going into the parking lot next to the building is too much."

"*You* can't go inside," Ian pointed out. "But I can. And you can go in, to assist, if the consulate comes under attack. Francine!"

"I'm here."

"If you get there before me—"

"I'm pretty sure we will."

"—cowboy up and wait in the lobby. Shel!"

"Yes, sir!"

"Use whatever equipment you've got to scan the building. Let's try to figure out exactly where Phoebe's being held. Once we're inside, we'll need to get to her, fast." Ian then turned to Deb. "Okay. Here's what we're going to do. . . ."

CHAPTER TWENTY-SEVEN

Phoebe woke up alone in a darkened room, with a pounding headache that made her want to throw up.

She was on the floor, in a very uncomfortable position, and it didn't make sense—God, she felt awful, did she have the flu?—until she remembered.

Insisting that she go with the Dutchman in his car. Ian, upset with her, but finally realizing that it wasn't his choice. *I love you.* The car on the highway, sliding across all those lanes of oncoming traffic. Vanderzee holding his gun. Despite the crash of pain, her relief that he'd hit her instead of firing a bullet into her head.

She would not have woken up from that.

Phoebe shifted, trying to move her aching head into a position that was more comfortable, and she realized that her hands were tied behind her back—but the restraint around her wrists was just loose enough so that she could imagine getting free. Her feet were tied at the ankles, but if she could get her hands free, she could probably get her feet free, too.

Assuming the urge to vomit again went away and the room stopped spinning long enough for her to see her feet.

She'd lost her glasses when they'd moved her from the car to wherever she now was—that was why the world was extra blurry.

At that same moment, Phoebe realized that she was gagged. She was *gagged,* and her stomach was churning from the blow to her head, and God, if she threw up, she'd choke to death.

The realization made her even more nauseous, and as she pulled at the rope restraining her wrists, it felt tighter not looser.

Panicking wouldn't help, she knew that, so she closed her eyes and concentrated on breathing through her nose, shallowly and slowly. Air in. Air out.

Ian was coming for her. She knew he was coming.

Unless he was already dead, and okay, thinking that was as bad as thinking about throwing up. Neither negative thought would help her. She would *not* throw up, and Ian was *not* dead.

Which meant he was coming for her. But first he had to find her.

Phoebe pictured the surveillance van, and the equipment inside that Ian and his teammates would use to help them search for her.

And while she had no idea where she was, maybe Ian did.

And if he was out there, somewhere, she was going to help him.

So Phoebe started to hum. With the gag in her mouth, she could only make a relatively soft sound in the back of her throat, but as she gained confidence in the fact that doing this wasn't going to make her throw up, she pushed it louder.

Row, row, row your boat . . .

She closed her eyes and tried to make her hands as narrow as possible, so she could slip free.

The van was still about ten minutes from the consulate when Ian's phone rang.

After the truck had gone up in a blaze of flames and smoke, he'd called Vanderzee's cell phone, repeatedly. He'd even left messages, but only now did the Dutchman call him back.

Ian answered it by playing heavy defense, on the off chance that Vanderzee would buy it. "What the fuck, Georg? I was descended upon by black helicopters—there was nothing I could do to stop them—I barely made it out alive. Your cargo was completely blown to hell—"

"You can stop with the act," the Dutchman said. "I already know, through my sources, that my *cargo* was returned to their mother. And since you're not in custody, you've obviously been working with the authorities—don't deny it."

There were times when denial could work. This was not one of them, so Ian tried pathos with complaint, if only to keep this conversation going. "I didn't have a choice. They had me by the balls—"

Vanderzee cut him off, "I suspect that I have something you want, and I thought, at first, that we might be able to strike a bargain—"

"We absolutely can," Ian said.

"No," the other man said, "we can't. The children and their mother are being spirited away as we speak into your government's witness protection program. Not even someone like you will be able to find them, so my hopes—that you might locate them, and kill them for me—are dashed. Although, even if you'd been able to oblige, you still would've owed me. Their father was willing to pay only three million for them, dead. Ten for them brought home alive."

And there it was. Far more realistic numbers, compared to that *one million extra* that the Dutchman had previously told him he'd get if he delivered the kids alive.

"If it's money that you want," Ian started.

Vanderzee cut him off. "The money's only part of it. I'll be badly disappointing a longtime friend."

"You don't have to disappoint him," Ian said, talking fast. "I can help you convince him that the children were killed in that blast. The group that attacked my truck didn't particularly care if they lived or died—just as long as Dr. Vaszko was kept from returning to Kazbekistan. It's a miracle they survived, and we can certainly spin it that they didn't. I can get you indisputable proof of their death, and reimburse you for the difference in payment—"

"Well, she *does* mean a lot to you, doesn't she?" the Dutchman said, and Ian realized he was doing this wrong.

He made himself laugh. "You're kidding right? Phoebe—if that's even her real name—works for the government. She was holding my leash and driving me fucking crazy, the whole goddamn time. I was conning her, too. You know, I tapped that, and believe me, it's not worth your effort. But hey, do whatever you gotta do. Beat the shit out of her, whatever. Just don't kill her without knowing, clearly, what our government does to people who kill fed agents. You'll be hunted, by drones, to the ends of the earth. You'll live in a fucking cave in northern K-stan until you kill yourself to escape the boredom." He made himself laugh as if he thought he was the funniest man alive. "You want to get away with killing her? Take her back to your country and marry her first. Although good luck with *that*. She's a bitch and a half. But she's worth something to my bosses, so if you change your mind and you want to trade her for those death certificates so your longtime friend can find closure and you can recoup at least some of your losses? Let me know. You've got thirty minutes to call me back before this deal's off the table."

With a click, Ian cut the connection.

Jesus, he was dripping with sweat. "Drive faster," he ordered Deb.

Ian was alive!

Phoebe looked up at Georg Vanderzee, who was standing just inside the locked door.

He'd come into the room while on the phone with Ian.

He'd had the call on speaker, so that she'd heard it all.

I was conning her, too. . . . Bitch and a half. . . . Not worth your effort.

Okay, so *that* was uncomfortable to hear, but what else was Ian going to say? He was clearly trying to convince the Dutchman that he had absolutely no emotional connection to Phoebe. Vanderzee's killing or hurting her would not influence him in any way.

Do whatever you gotta do. Beat the shit out of her, whatever.

Was it possible that Ian knew she might be listening? Was he trying to remind her of the story he'd told, about how he believed that if he hadn't stopped the Dutchman from beating his teenaged wife, the man might've let her live?

Just before Vanderzee had come into the room, Phoebe'd managed to work her hands free. She'd pushed herself up so that she was sitting in a chair—the better to work on the rope that bound her ankles. It was much tighter than the rope around her wrists had been, and she hadn't gotten it off. She *had* removed the gag, though, but she'd put it loosely back into her mouth when she'd heard him at the door.

She'd also quickly tucked her hands back behind her, rubbing them together, trying to create friction, so that she would stand out from all of the other blobs of human body heat in this building.

Phoebe knew if she moved, she'd give away the fact that her hands were no longer tied, but in reality, it was likely that he already knew, since he'd left her in a pile on the floor.

Unless Hitler Junior had brought her inside, and Vanderzee thought he'd set her there . . . ?

She wavered at that thought, her uncertainty flip-flopping with the pounding in her head. Move, stay still, move, stay still . . .

Through it all, as she rubbed her hands to make heat, she kept the song going, tapping her foot on the floor: *Gently down the stream* . . . hoping that someone was out there, listening.

When Francine pulled up to the consulate, the van carrying Ian was still at least several minutes away.

Sheldon was out of the car before she'd even parked, running across the street toward a pizza van that *had* to be an FBI surveillance vehicle. She could hear him over her headset, rattling off the plate number to Deb, who gave the order to let him in.

Sure enough, the back door of the Pizza Express opened, and Shel was quickly pulled inside.

His job right now was to provide Ian with as much information as possible, which meant he needed access to equipment that he didn't have with him in the car.

Francie's job, however . . .

Martell turned off his headset microphone. "I want to go in with you," he said.

"You can't," she said as she looked at the consulate, even as she checked her gun. She was locked and loaded. "You have to wait for Deb."

The consulate was even less assuming than it had

been in the photos she'd seen—a typical Floridian post-WWII era building—a sprawling single-story structure made of concrete block, with a white cast-iron fence enclosing the yard, and a matching white tin roof. It had once been a residence, but it had been renovated and added onto significantly in the back. The former yard had been transformed into a graveled parking area, complete with a covered carport at the edge of the large lot.

It had only cursory protection in place—no giant concrete blocks to prevent car bombs, because really, it existed almost solely to provide the ambassador with the perks of a Miami vacation.

Francine guessed that security at the front door would be fairly limited, too. But there were surely guards, and they were definitely armed. And she knew both Vanderzee and his man Hitler Junior were armed and inside, too.

"If the Dutchman sees you, he'll recognize you." Martell reached out and grabbed her arm, his deep concern for her shining from his pretty brown eyes.

"Found her!" Shel's voice came through Francie's headset, even as she jumped because—holy Christ—Berto knocked on the outside of the car window. He was standing on the sidewalk, looking in at them. "Back wing, room at the very end. She's humming the song Ian uses for microphone tests."

"She's alive," Francine said it with a rush of relief at the same time that Ian did, but she punctuated her statement by leaning forward and kissing Martell—and not just because she wanted to piss off Berto.

"Wait for Deb," she told him again. "I'm going in with Berto."

Move, or stay still, or move, or stay still . . .

Vanderzee was frowning angrily down at his phone, maybe checking his email, maybe waiting for a message from Hitler Junior, or maybe actually considering taking Ian's crazy deal.

Row, row, row, your boat . . .

It really wasn't that crazy—she'd suggested it herself, days ago. Make the children's psycho father believe that they were dead, or else he'd come after them again and again and again. End this, once and for all.

Move, or stay still . . .

While witness protection would be a good way to protect the children and their mother, it might be a challenge to hide a nuclear physicist who wanted to put her hard-earned degree to good use. . . .

Gently down the stream . . .

When Vanderzee finally turned, putting his phone back into his pocket, Phoebe saw a flash of the gun he was wearing holstered under his arm, and she knew with certainty that he was so angry that the very next thing he was going to do was draw that weapon and kill her.

So she took her chances and picked *move,* hoping for the beating over the bullet in the head. She launched herself up and at him, attacking him by hopping toward him even though her feet were still bound, roaring as loudly as she could beneath her gag.

She hit him with her shoulder, aiming low for his center of gravity and he went down—to both of their surprise.

He scrambled back away from her, as his anger bloomed into something awful—something that was mixed with delight—on his almost-handsome face.

And here it came. The beating she'd requested.

Phoebe braced herself for it, even as she continued to hum Ian's tune.

Merrily, merrily, merrily, merrily . . .

He hit her, hard, and she landed on the floor, also hard. He was on top of her, then, punching and pummeling, his body pinning her down as he unleashed a flurry of punishing blows.

But it wasn't until his hands went up, around her throat, that Phoebe stopped singing.

"Jesus, Eee, I think he's killing her!" Shel's voice came through Ian's headset as Deb hit the brakes hard, skidding to a stop just down the street from the consulate.

"Get out of the van," Ian shouted, brandishing his handgun so that Deb and Yashi could say that he had.

"Shirt off," Deb shouted as she scrambled to vacate the driver's seat. "I should've thought of that before!"

Ian knew why she was telling him that, and he yanked his T-shirt over his head even as he slid behind the wheel.

When attacking a foreign consulate, it was best to be absolutely clear about the fact that one wasn't wearing a suicide bomber vest. Going in shirtless would help.

Also, the surgeons wouldn't have to pick pieces of fabric from his bullet wounds.

Should he survive.

"Ready or not," Ian said to whichever of his team members were still able to hear him. "Here I come."

Ian Dunn was freaking crazy.

Martell saw the van—formerly white, now a battered blue—rocketing toward the consulate, picking up speed. He saw Ian behind the wheel, looking like he was posing for a picture that would appear in the dictionary, next to *determination*.

Or maybe the phrase he best represented was *true love*.

Dude looked relatively and remarkably serene, considering he was probably going to die violently in a matter of seconds.

But his plan was now clear to Martell.

Once Ian committed the crime of punching a van-sized hole through the consulate wall, the FBI could rush inside to arrest his ass—and to otherwise assist in evacuating the building.

All of the rooms would have to be searched and cleared, including those holding kidnapping victims.

As Martell watched, the van bounced up as it hit the curb, and was more of a missile than a torpedo as it hit the front left window of the building with a crash and a smash.

Deb went running past him, with Yashi and Aaron on her heels, and Martell followed, praying that they weren't too late.

Francine stood in the lobby of the consulate with Berto. She knew what was coming. She thought she was ready.

But as Ian drove the van through the window, she realized that it wasn't possible to be *completely* ready for an event of that magnitude.

Glass exploded—it was like a bomb went off. Dust and debris—shards of concrete blocks—went in all directions. A curtain rod narrowly missed her head, and the rings that had held the curtains in place bounced and rolled across the now-cracked tile floor.

The guards—two, in matching uniforms with Makarov sidearms—scrambled out of the way, diving for cover behind the podium of a security checkpoint.

Berto grabbed Francie's arm, trying to pull her out of the way of a still-bouncing shard of metal—part of the van's grill? But she jerked herself free because what she had to do here was get *in* the way.

"Help my husband, help my husband," she screamed as she put herself and Berto, both, between the guards with the weapons and the smoking wreckage of the van.

Berto shot her a weary look that said *Really?* But then sank to the floor, nearly on top of the guards, covering his face and screaming, "My eyes, my eyes!"

It was then that Deb burst through the door—"FBI! On the ground!"—as Ian crawled out of the passenger side of the van. Shirtless and bloody—cut by the broken windshield—he kept his hands high in the air, even as he sank to his knees on the debris-covered floor.

Yashi, Aaron, and Martell were right behind Deb.

"I think there was someone else in the van," Francine shouted. "He went *that* way." She pointed to the hall that led to the back wing.

"Stay with him," Deb ordered Martell, who aimed his weapon at Ian, as she ran toward the back of the consulate, shouting, "FBI! We have a possible intruder! I need everyone hands out, down on the floor, for your own safety!"

Yashi followed Deb, and Francine was ready to go, right behind him, when she heard it.

They all heard it.

Sharp. Loud. Unmistakable. Coming from the back of the consulate.

A single gunshot.

Francine looked over at Ian, and the look on his face was terrible.

Berto came up behind her. "Jesus," he said. "Was that . . . ?"

"I think so," Francine said.

• • •

Ian lost it.

Or maybe he found it.

All he knew, when he heard that gunshot, was that enough was enough. He needed to know if Phoebe was dead.

No way was he going to lie on the floor and wait for Deb to return and give him the news that he was a single fucking minute too late.

But Martell was not the only one who was standing there with his weapon trained on him. Other FBI agents—women and men who didn't know Ian from Adam—had come in and were trying to figure out what-the-fuck.

So when Ian pushed himself up off the floor, there was a lot of yelling and posturing. "Get down, get back down! Right now, right fucking now!"

Ian kept his hands up, but really, the only reason that he wasn't instantly shot was due to the fact that Martell and Francine and Aaron and Sheldon, and even Berto—where had he come from?—were there, surrounding him. Protecting him.

But even that didn't really matter. Let them fucking shoot him.

Ian moved, down the hall, faster and faster, still surrounded by his team, which was surrounded by the FBI and the K-stani guards. Everyone was shouting—everyone but Ian.

The hallway turned to the left, and he remembered Shel telling him that Phoebe was in the room at the very end.

There was a man on the floor—it was Vanderzee's guard Hitler Junior. He was on his stomach and his hands were on his head. Yashi was kneeling on his back, cuffing him, and saying something, but Ian couldn't hear him over the yelling that surrounded him.

"If you're going to shoot me, then just fucking shoot me and get it over with!" Ian roared, louder than all of them, and it stunned them into silence as he pushed open the door, where, Jesus, Deb was kneeling next to a bloody body. God, she was covering the face with a jacket or a sweater, but it wasn't a woman, it wasn't . . .

Phoebe . . . ?

Phoebe was sitting up a few yards away, eyes open, alive.

Ian ran to her, which started the yelling all over again, but this time, he let Deb shout over it. "It's all right! It's all right! He's my prisoner, he's in *my* custody, will everyone just step back, into the hall! Move it, now, move!"

As Ian hit the floor, Phoebe reached for him, and then, God, she was in his arms.

"I got here as fast as I could," he told her, even as she said, "I kind of killed Georg, but that's okay, right, because he was going to kill me? He was choking me, and his gun was right there, and I guess he didn't realize that I'd gotten my hands free."

"You did great," he told her, as he held her face between his hands, as he realized what that gunshot had been. *She'd* killed the Dutchman.

And she was really all right. Her voice was raspy and her throat sounded sore. Her lip was bleeding and swollen, and God, her neck was abraded, as if she'd been throttled—which she had. She had a scratch—a deep one—on the part of her chest exposed by the plunging neckline of her shirt, and he could tell from the way she winced that the son of a bitch had bruised if not broken at least one of her ribs.

But she was alive.

"Deb said we saved the kids," she said as her eyes brimmed with tears.

"We did," he told her as he felt his do the same.

"Ian, I'm so sorry," she said. "I shouldn't've gone with him, in his car, but . . . I had to."

"I know," he said. "It's okay."

"Was anyone hurt?" she asked.

Ian shook his head. "Just you."

"I'm all right," she said. "Although that motherfucker lost my glasses."

Ian laughed. And he probably shouldn't have kissed her, but he did. He hated the idea of hurting her poor battered mouth, but he couldn't not do it, and she didn't seem to mind as she passionately kissed him back.

And the emotion that filled him was soul-shaking. Ian felt his chest tighten and he struggled to breathe. And when he pulled back to look at her, he couldn't speak. Instead he just rested his forehead against hers as this time she held his face, her fingers cool against him, soothing in his hair.

But he had to tell her, and in a voice that was embarrassingly shaky, Ian said, “You didn’t believe me when I said it, but it’s true.” He lifted his head to look into her eyes. “I love you. Madly. Passionately. Deeply. Honestly—”

Phoebe smiled then, cutting him off with “I know.”

Ian laughed again, but before he could get in her face about her Han Solo imitation, Deb was back, contrite and overwhelmed.

“Ian, I’m sorry. If we’re going to get away with this whole charade, I really do need to get you cuffed, and bring you in.”

Ian nodded and looked back at Phoebe. “I think I’m gonna need a good lawyer,” he said.

Phoebe nodded. “And a shirt,” she said. “Not that I’m complaining, but I’m thinking you might also want a shirt.”

As Ian put his hands behind his back so Deb could do the honors and perp-walk him out of there, Phoebe made him smile.

“I’ll bring you one,” she said. “When I come to bail you out.”

“Thanks,” he said.

She smiled tremulously back at him, and said what he really wanted to hear: “Ian, I love you, too.”

CHAPTER TWENTY-EIGHT

Aaron and Shel were sitting on the trunk of Martell's car, parked in by the emergency vehicles that surrounded the consulate, when Berto found them.

"Hey," he said.

Aaron looked at Shelly for direction. Did he or didn't he want to talk to his half brother?

But Shel said, "Hey," back, and then, "Thanks for helping. That was above and beyond."

"Yeah, well." Berto shrugged. "Francine called, so . . ."

"We owe you a truck," Shel said.

Yes. Right. The truck that they'd blown sky high had been Berto's. Both cab and trailer. "That might take us a little bit of time to pay back," Aaron said.

"Forget about it," Berto said. "It was insured. What?" he added, no doubt because Aaron had looked surprised. "You didn't think I had insurance? Most of the business I do is legitimate. I'm not my fucking father." He sighed. "Which brings us to . . . our fucking father. I spoke to Davio last night. He definitely killed Manny, but we're both playing it like he didn't. Long story short, we came to an agreement. I got him to promise to leave you the fuck alone. Zero contact. From henceforth. He did it in front of his lieutenants, so I think we can trust he'll keep his word." Berto laughed. "If he doesn't, it'll get out that his word is for shit, and believe it or not, that means something to him. So you can tell Ian that our deal's off. There's no need for it. He's all paid up. You're safe. The two of you and Rory. Ian. Francine."

Aaron glanced at Shelly, who couldn't quite believe it.

"Jesus," Shel breathed. "What did you have to promise him?"

Berto laughed, but it wasn't a laugh of amusement. "That doesn't matter."

"The hell it doesn't!"

"Look," Berto said. "It was eye-opening. The past few days. Seeing you with your kid. Seeing Francine with . . . I fucking hate Martell, but he's a good guy. He's good to her and . . . That makes me . . . glad. All of it does. You've made a family, Shel, a good one—much better than the one you were born into."

"What did you promise him?" Shel asked again.

"I pledged him my allegiance." Berto shrugged, like it was no big deal.

"Oh, God, no," Shel said.

"It's okay, little brother," Berto said, and it was clear that he meant it. "I lost everything I loved a long time ago, because I fucked things up. It was my mistake, my fault. You reap what you sow. And I really love that you're reaping some really good shit. Just keep doing that, okay? And I'll be fine."

He held out his hand to Aaron, and Aaron took it and shook. He did the same with Shel, but then pulled him down off the car and into a rough embrace.

"Take care of yourselves," Berto said, and walked away.

Sheldon looked stunned, and Aaron grabbed his hand, pulled him back up onto Martell's car. He kept their fingers interwoven—which was not something they usually did in this part of Miami. But it had been one hell of a day.

"Am I wrong to just let him go?" Shel asked when he finally spoke.

"No," Aaron said.

"Do you know what this means? With your name cleared and Davio no longer hunting us?" Shelly answered for him. "We get to be normal."

Aaron smiled at that. "As normal as we can be, considering. I'm pretty sure, knowing Ian, that he's going to want to get the business up and running again. I mean, now that he doesn't have to go back to jail."

Shel nodded, so seriously. "We'll need a nanny. And the company HQ is our house, so Rory can be around—to make up for when we're out of town."

"We'll need a general contractor to fix the house."

"And a dog," Shel said, and when Aaron looked into his eyes, he could see their entire beautiful future stretching out in front of them.

"Two dogs," Aaron said.

Shelly smiled and kissed him. "Works for me."

• • •

Martell lingered outside of the FBI's temporary command post, just down the street from the K-stani consulate.

Deb had been talking to the locals, who'd been staking out the consulate ever since those kids had gone missing. But she'd just gotten a phone call from someone very high up the ladder, possibly even the head of DHS, and she was being all *Yes, sir,* and *Thank you, sir,* and *Just doing my job, sir*.

Martell was tempted to snatch the phone from her fingers and say, "Give this woman a promotion, bitches!" But he suspected she wouldn't appreciate that.

Ian had been taken downtown—Yashi had been assigned to babysit him, making sure he didn't accidentally get shipped to non-Faux-Cuba.

Martell had overheard that Deb was getting ready to escort Phoebe first to the hospital for a quick nearly-got-your-ass-killed medical check, and then to her condo to find her spare glasses before they joined Ian at FBI HQ.

As Deb finally got off the phone, Martell caught her eye, and she came toward him with a smile.

"Good job today," she said, even as he said, "You did a really great job today."

Then they both said, "Thanks," like a pair of fools in seventh grade.

Martell added, "I just wanted to make sure I got a chance to say that, before I headed back to Sarasota, and you went . . . wherever you're going next."

"Oh," she said. "Yeah. I don't know. Probably back to Boston. Or D.C. I guess it depends on where they need me."

"Well," Martell said. "If you ever need cheap backup, or, you know, someone to wear a kilt who doesn't look like a Catholic school–girl—" Ah, Christ, had he really just said that? Could he sound any more stupid? "—you know where to find me."

She laughed, because what else was she going to do? Shout *Wow, you're a loser,* and then run away, screaming?

And then, probably because he figured he couldn't embarrass himself any further, Martell said, "I can't stop wondering. About that situation. The other night. On the yacht. To keep the Dutchman from seeing the sunrise. Would you have really dot dot dot?"

And now she was looking at him as if he was a maroon. An offensive one, to boot.

When she spoke it was with some serious indignation. "*You* did. You're seriously going to judge me for the same exact thing that—"

"Whoa," Martell said over her, as soon as he realized where she was going. Holy shit. "Wait. No! You seriously think—"

They did the saying-the-same-thing-at-the-exact-same-time thing again, with Deb saying, "—you did with Francine?" as Martell said, "that Francine and I—"

He soloed on the ending: "—hooked up? Because we didn't. That was just, you know. An act. Pretend.

To fool Berto. That's all it was. Really. And apparently you got fooled, too. But we didn't, you know. Hook up. I mean, even if she wanted to, I wouldn't have. Because. She's seriously damaged. And that's just not okay to take advantage of."

Deb chewed her lip as she gazed back at him, and then said, "Well, I guess you're better than me."

"Okay, whoa," Martell said. "That was *not* what I was implying—"

But now someone was calling her from the command post, which she pointed to with her thumb over her shoulder. "It's really all right," she said. "And I gotta . . ." She turned to leave, but then she turned back. "In case I don't get to see you before you go . . ." She held out her hand to him.

He took it. Was she really saying good-bye with a handshake?

Yes, she was.

And just like that, she was gone.

"Fuck," Martell said, and turned around to find who else standing just outside of his peripheral vision but Francine. Who'd kissed him like she'd meant it, just a short time ago. "Shit. Hi. Hey."

"Yeah," she said, and he instantly knew that she'd heard what he'd said to Deb. *Damaged.* "Look, I was thinking about . . . the whole dinner thing, and . . . it's probably not a good idea."

"Oh," he said, and now, stupid him, he was disappointed. "What?"

"Yeah," Francine said again. "Bad . . . timing. For me. And . . . I'm heading out. Aarie and Shel and I are going downtown, to make sure Eee's okay, but, um, I just wanted to say . . . Thanks again for being so great."

And then she, too, turned and walked away, leaving him close to where he'd started. A guy with a piece of shit for a car. Wondering what the fuck had just happened.

Martell got in, started the engine, and took out his phone and gave his friend Ric a call. It went to voice mail, so he left a message: "Hey, I got your message. I'm glad you're feeling better. I'm heading for home—I'll stop by the hospital to see you tomorrow, and tell you the whole crazy story."

As he pulled away from the curb, he adjusted his sun visor, and a manila envelope fell into his lap, so he braked to a stop.

Holy shit.

It was the twenty K that Ian had given to Vanderzee as a fake finder's fee. Someone had found it, either on his person or in his car or somewhere in the consulate. They'd written on the outside, *For your POS replacement fund and/or your nephew.* And they'd drawn a smiley face.

Martell didn't know it for sure, but he suspected that handwriting was Francine's.

And as he drove away, he smiled, because he knew he couldn't keep it.

Ian was sitting in the interview room at Miami's FBI headquarters when Phoebe arrived.

He did a double take when he saw her, because

she'd decided that as long as she was going home, she'd take a shower. And as long as she was clean, she'd change her clothes. And as long as she was coming here in her official status as his lawyer, she'd put on a suit and wear heels.

Ever since she'd passed the bar, Phoebe had learned that lawyers who dressed down didn't get the same respect as those who dressed up. It shouldn't've been that way, but there it was.

Truth be told, she'd considered wearing what she thought of as her sexy lawyer outfit, which had a skirt that ended well above her knees. One of which was still skinned and raw. The other sported a bruise that *might've* passed for a tattoo of an oddly shaped turtle, but probably not.

So she'd covered her legs with pants, and settled for higher than usual heels.

As she went into the room, she handed Ian the T-shirt that she'd promised to bring—Aaron had gotten it from the safe house when he'd gone to check on Rory.

Someone had found Ian a shirt in the meantime, but it was a little small. Still, he kept it on, putting down the shirt she'd brought him as she headed for the chair that was on the opposite side of the table.

"Yashi's arranging for your release," she told him as she sat. "He's also making sure that the government fulfills its end of the deal that you made with them. When you walk out of here, you're free and clear. And Aaron and the others are, too."

Ian nodded. "Good."

"It seems they won't require four days of high-intensity debriefs," she said. "Particularly since that's really *not* standard operating procedure."

"Apparently not for this branch of the FBI." He smiled at her. "Nice glasses."

They were frameless and barely there—a contrast to her favorites with their clunky frame.

"I assume the looters left them behind," he continued, "along with the hot lawyer outfit?"

"My apartment was in good shape," she told him. "Someone already replaced the door and it was locked. I don't think anything was stolen."

"As soon as I have some time, I'll fix your screen, too."

When he said that, Phoebe felt a rush of relief. Part of her still didn't quite believe he wasn't going to simply vanish into the night after she got him released. Part of the reason she'd dressed up was because she thought it possible that his words of love had been uttered in the heat of the moment. Now that time had passed, reality would kick back in.

She'd been prepared to offer him an out. *I know you really didn't mean* love-*love when you said what you said. . . .*

But now, with the way that he was smiling at her. "I gotta confess," he said, "These are nice, but I like the other ones better. Your glasses," he added at her blank look.

"Yes," she said as her eyes suddenly welled with tears. "Me, too."

"You okay?" he asked, holding out his hand to her, interlacing their fingers when she took it. "You know, I've been doing it, too. Wrestling with the waves of emotion. It happens, after. Particularly when you go to extremes to defend yourself." He met her gaze squarely. "I wish I got there sooner. I would've been okay with killing him."

Phoebe nodded. "I'm kind of okay with killing him, too."

"It helps to talk about it," Ian said. "And I'll be here, whenever you want to. Talk."

He meant it, and the tears welled again. Damnit. She laughed as she wiped them away.

"Shit," Ian said. "Come here. I'd come to you, but I'm cuffed to this chair."

"What?" Phoebe stood up. "Are you seriously . . . ?"

He was. His left hand was attached, via plastic restraint, to the base of the chair, which was, in turn, attached to the floor. No wonder he hadn't changed his shirt.

"I'll get someone to unlock you, immediately," she said, heading for the door.

Ian caught her by the hand. Pulled her down onto his lap. "This is what I want. Problem solved far more quickly."

Phoebe laughed as he kissed her, but then she stopped laughing and just kissed him back.

"Crap, I keep forgetting . . . Is your mouth okay?" he asked, pulling back to look at her, grimacing slightly as he gently touched her lips. "You covered it up well, but . . ."

"I'm great," she told him and it was true. "Although, I may not be taken too seriously as your lawyer while sitting on your lap."

"I take you very seriously," Ian said.

From her perch, she was finally taller than he was. As she looked down into his eyes, she said, "Just so you know, I didn't believe it for a second —the lies you told Vanderzee. It made me think of Berto and Francine. And your brother."

"I thought he might've put that call on speaker," Ian said. He closed his eyes and rested his head against her chest as he held her close. "Jesus, that was awful."

"But in the driveway," Phoebe said. "When you told me you loved me . . ."

He looked up at her at that, but then waited, as if he knew she had more to say.

So she kept going. "I was pretty sure the only reason you said it was to keep me from going with him, almost like . . . a bribe. *I love you, now do what I want.*"

He laughed at that, but she suspected she was not far from the truth.

"Then I realized," Phoebe continued, "that you said it as a bribe, but you also really meant it."

Ian was nodding. "I was desperate," he admitted. "I would have told you anything. But I did mean it—I do. Very much. Although I don't know if I would've had the guts to say it, if I didn't think it was gonna get me something tangible." He winced. "That sounded better in my head. I'm not a total dick. I *do* know what I get, just from saying it."

"Sex," Phoebe said. "And probably a lot of it."

He laughed at that. "I hope so. We'll have to see. Won't we?"

Phoebe didn't try to hide her surprise as she looked at him, as he looked evenly back at her.

And yes, that *had* been his way of telling her that he'd never said *I love you* before, not to any other woman.

Phoebe kissed him again. She had to.

"I came here, half-expecting, I don't know," she admitted. "That maybe this was where the pushing-me-away part would really start. I mean, I was all inside of my head about you not telling me that Manny had died. I thought . . ."

"I didn't tell you," Ian said, "because I didn't want to get my own hopes up. I was hoping that Berto would man up, and take the opportunity to do exactly what he did—which is reach a detente with Davio. Or kill him. Either way would've been okay with me, because it finally sets me free." He smiled at her. "As far as pushing you away? I think we might be past that part. To be honest, what I really want is for you to be closer."

"I'm on your lap," she pointed out.

He nodded. "Yeah, I mean . . . not just here and now physically, but . . . Jesus, I just really . . . want you to stick around."

Phoebe kissed him.

"Hmm," he said. "I'm starting to see a pattern here. Let's experiment. I love you."

She kissed him again.

"Yup," Ian said, "a definite pattern." He cleared his throat. "Look, there's a lot to talk about, and figure out. But just so you know what I'm thinking, I'm considering resurrecting my intel-gathering business, get the old team back, maybe do a little PI work to keep me more local, maybe contract out some assignments from that personal security firm that Martell's connected to. . . . Bottom line, I'd love to stick around and see where this thing between us goes."

"I would love that, too," Phoebe said.

The door opened, and Yashi stuck his head in. "Everything's good. You're cleared to go. Whoops, sorry about that, you should've told me . . ." He came the rest of the way into the room, and unlocked Ian's hand as Phoebe stood up.

"I was very comfortable," Ian said as he quickly changed his shirt, leaving the borrowed one on the table.

"You need me to walk you out?" Yashi asked, holding open the door for them.

"Nah, that's okay," Ian said, as he took Phoebe's hand and smiled into her eyes. "We'll find our way."

ABOUT THE AUTHOR

After childhood plans to become the captain of a starship didn't pan out, SUZANNE BROCKMANN took her fascination with military history, her respect for the men and women who serve, her reverence for diversity, and her love of storytelling, and explored brave new worlds as a *New York Times* bestselling romance author. Over the past twenty years, she has written more than fifty novels, including her award-winning Troubleshooters series about Navy SEAL heroes and the women—and sometimes men—who win their hearts. In addition to writing books, Suzanne Brockmann has co-produced a feature-length movie—the award-winning romantic comedy *The Perfect Wedding*, which she co-wrote with her husband, Ed Gaffney, and their son, Jason. She has also co-written a YA novel—set in the world of her paranormal Fighting Destiny series—with her daughter, Melanie. Find Suz (or Suzanne Brockmann) at www.Facebook.com/SuzanneBrockmannBooks, follow her on Twitter @SuzBrockmann, and visit her website at www.SuzanneBrockmann.com to find out more about upcoming releases and appearances.

Center Point Large Print
600 Brooks Road / PO Box 1
Thorndike ME 04986-0001 USA

(207) 568-3717

US & Canada:
1 800 929-9108
www.centerpointlargeprint.com